FULL SCORE

TWENTY TALES

by

D. H. LAWRENCE

THE REPRINT SOCIETY
LONDON

PUBLISHED BY THE REPRINT SOCIETY LTD.
BY ARRANGEMENT WITH WILLIAM HEINEMANN LTD.
1943

PRINTED IN GREAT BRITAIN AT THE WINDMILL PRESS
KINGSWOOD, SURREY

CONTENTS

CONTENTS

THE PRUSSIAN OFFICER

I

THEY had marched more than thirty kilometres since dawn, along the white, hot road where occasional thickets of trees threw a moment of shade, then out into the glare again. On either hand, the valley, wide and shallow, glittered with heat; dark green patches of rye, pale young corn, fallow and meadow and black pine woods spread in a dull, hot diagram under a glistening sky. But right in front the mountains ranged across, pale blue and very still, snow gleaming gently out of the deep atmosphere. And towards the mountains, on and on, the regiment marched between the rye fields and the meadows, between the scraggy fruit trees set regularly on either side the high road. The burnished, dark green rye threw off a suffocating heat, the mountains drew gradually nearer and more distinct. While the feet of the soldiers grew hotter, sweat ran through their hair under their helmets, and their knapsacks could burn no more in contact with their shoulders, but seemed instead to give off a cold, prickly sensation.

He walked on and on in silence, staring at the mountains ahead, that rose sheer out of the land, and stood fold behind fold, half earth, half heaven, the heaven, the barrier with slits of soft snow, in the pale, bluish peaks.

He could now walk almost without pain. At the start, he had determined not to limp. It had made him sick to take the first steps, and during the first mile or so, he had compressed his breath, and the cold drops of sweat had stood on his forehead. But he had walked it off. What were they after all but bruises! He had looked at them, as he was getting up: deep bruises on the backs of his thighs. And since he had made his first step in the morning, he had been conscious of them, till now he had a tight, hot place in his chest, with suppressing the pain, and holding himself in. There seemed no air when he breathed. But he walked almost lightly.

The Captain's hand had trembled at taking his coffee at dawn: his orderly saw it again. And he saw the fine figure of the Captain wheeling on horseback at the farm-house ahead, a handsome figure in pale blue uniform with facings of scarlet, and the metal gleaming on the black helmet and the sword-scabbard, and dark streaks of sweat coming on the silky bay horse. The orderly felt he was connected with that figure moving so suddenly on horseback: he followed it like a shadow, mute and inevitable and damned by it. And the officer was always aware of the tramp of the company behind, the march of his orderly among the men.

The Captain was a tall man of about forty, grey at the temples. He had a handsome, finely knit figure, and was one of the best horsemen in the West. His orderly, having to rub him down, admired the amazing riding-muscles of his loins.

For the rest, the orderly scarcely noticed the officer any more than he noticed himself. It was rarely he saw his master's face: he did not look at it. The Captain had reddish brown, stiff hair, that he wore short upon his skull. His moustache was also cut short and bristly over a full, brutal mouth. His face was rather rugged, the cheeks thin. Perhaps the man was the more handsome for the deep lines in his face, the irritable tension of his brow, which gave him the look of a man who fights with life. His fair eyebrows stood bushy over light blue eyes that were always flashing with cold fire.

He was a Prussian aristocrat, haughty and overbearing. But his mother had been a Polish Countess. Having made too many gambling debts when he was young, he had ruined his prospects in the Army, and remained an infantry captain. He had never married: his position did not allow of it, and no woman had ever moved him to it. His time he spent riding—occasionally he rode one of his own horses at the races—and at the officers' club. Now and then he took himself a mistress. But after such an event, he returned to duty with his brow still more tense, his eyes still more hostile and irritable. With the men, however, he was merely impersonal, though a devil when roused; so that, on the whole, they feared him, but had no great aversion from him. They accepted him as the inevitable.

To his orderly he was at first cold and just and indifferent: he did not fuss over trifles. So that his servant knew practically nothing about him, except just what orders he would give, and how he wanted them obeyed. That was quite simple. Then the change gradually came.

The orderly was a youth of about twenty-two, of medium height, and well built. He had strong, heavy limbs, was swarthy, with a soft, black, young moustache. There was something altogether warm and young about him. He had firmly marked eyebrows over dark, expressionless eyes, that seemed never to have thought, only to have received life direct through his senses, and acted straight from instinct.

Gradually the officer had become aware of his servant's young, vigorous, unconscious presence about him. He could not get away from the sense of the youth's person, while he was in attendance. It was like a warm flame upon the older man's tense, rigid body, that had become almost unliving, fixed. There was something so free and self-contained about him, and something in the young fellow's movement, that made the officer aware of him. And this irritated the Prussian. He did not choose to be touched into life by his servant. He might easily have changed his man, but he did not. He now very rarely looked direct at his orderly, but kept his face averted, as if to avoid seeing him. And yet as the young soldier moved unthinking about the apartment, the elder watched him, and would notice the movement of his strong young shoulders under the blue cloth, the bend of his neck. And it irritated him. To see the soldier's young, brown, shapely peasant's hand grasp the loaf or the wine-bottle sent a flash of hate or of anger through the elder man's blood. It was not that the youth was clumsy: it was rather the blind, instinctive sureness of movement of an unhampered young animal that irritated the officer to such a degree.

Once, when a bottle of wine had gone over, and the red

gushed out on to the tablecloth, the officer had started up with an oath, and his eyes, bluey like fire, had held those of the confused youth for a moment. It was a shock for the young soldier. He felt something sink deeper, deeper into his soul; where nothing had ever gone before. It left him rather blank and wondering. Some of his natural completeness in himself was gone, a little uneasiness took its place. And from that time an undiscovered feeling had held between the two men.

Henceforward the orderly was afraid of really meeting his master. His subconsciousness remembered those steely blue eyes and the harsh brows, and did not intend to meet them again. So he always stared past his master, and avoided him. Also, in a little anxiety, he waited for the three months to have gone, when his time would be up. He began to feel a constraint in the Captain's presence, and the soldier even more than the officer wanted to be left alone, in his neutrality as servant.

He had served the Captain for more than a year, and knew his duty. This he performed easily, as if it were natural to him. The officer and his commands he took for granted, as he took the sun and the rain, and he served as a matter of course. It did not implicate him personally.

But now if he were going to be forced into a personal interchange with his master he would be like a wild thing caught, he felt he must get away.

But the influence of the young soldier's being had penetrated through the officer's stiffened discipline, and perturbed the man in him. He, however, was a gentleman, with long, fine hands and cultivated movements, and was not going to allow such a thing as the stirring of his innate self. He was a man of passionate temper, who had always kept himself suppressed. Occasionally there had been a duel, an outburst before the soldiers. He knew himself to be always on the point of breaking out. But he kept himself hard to the idea of the Service. Whereas the young soldier seemed to live out his warm, full nature, to give it off in his very movements, which had a certain zest, such as wild animals have in free movement. And this irritated the officer more and more.

In spite of himself, the Captain could not regain his neutrality of feeling towards his orderly. Nor could he leave the man alone. In spite of himself, he watched him, gave him sharp orders, tried to take up as much of his time as possible. Sometimes he flew into a rage with the young soldier, and bullied him. Then the orderly shut himself off, as it were out of earshot, and waited, with sullen, flushed face, for the end of the noise. The words never pierced to his intelligence, he made himself, protectively, impervious to the feelings of his master.

He had a scar on his left thumb, a deep seam going across the knuckle. The officer had long suffered from it, and wanted to do something to it. Still it was there, ugly and brutal on the young, brown hand. At last the Captain's reserve gave way. One day, as the orderly was smoothing out the table-cloth, the officer pinned down his thumb with a pencil, asking

"How did you come by that?"

The young man winced and drew back at attention.

"A wood axe, Herr Hauptmann," he answered.

The officer waited for further explanation. None came. The orderly went about his duties. The elder man was sullenly angry. His servant avoided him. And the next day he had to use all his will-power to avoid seeing the scarred thumb. He wanted to get hold of it and—— A hot flame ran in his blood.

He knew his servant would soon be free, and would be glad. As yet, the soldier had held himself off from the elder man. The Captain grew madly irritable. He could not rest when the soldier was away, and when he was present, he glared at him with tormented eyes. He hated those fine, black brows over the unmeaning, dark eyes, he was infuriated by the free movement of the handsome limbs, which no military discipline could make stiff. And he became harsh and cruelly bullying, using contempt and satire. The young soldier only grew more mute and expressionless.

"What cattle were you bred by, that you can't keep straight eyes? Look me in the eyes when I speak to you."

And the soldier turned his dark eyes to the other's face, but there was no sight in them: he stared with the slightest possible cast, holding back his sight, perceiving the blue of his master's eyes, but receiving no look from them. And the elder man went pale, and his reddish eyebrows twitched. He gave his order, barrenly.

Once he flung a heavy military glove into the young soldier's face. Then he had the satisfaction of seeing the black eyes flare up into his own, like a blaze when straw is thrown on a fire. And he had laughed with a little tremor and a sneer.

But there were only two months more. The youth instinctively tried to keep himself intact: he had tried to serve the officer as if the latter were an abstract authority and not a man. All his instinct was to avoid personal contact, even definite hate. But in spite of himself the hate grew, responsive to the officer's passion. However, he put it in the background. When he had left the Army he could dare acknowledge it. By nature he was active, and had many friends. He thought what amazing good fellows they were. But, without knowing it, he was alone. Now this solitariness was intensified. It would carry him through his term. But the officer seemed to be going irritably insane, and the youth was deeply frightened.

The soldier had a sweetheart, a girl from the mountains, independent and primitive. The two walked together, rather silently. He went with her, not to talk, but to have his arm round her, and for the physical contact. This eased him, made it easier for him to ignore the Captain; for he could rest with her held fast against his chest. And she, in some unspoken fashion, was there for him. They loved each other.

The Captain perceived it, and was mad with irritation. He kept the young man engaged all the evenings long, and took pleasure in the dark look that came on his face. Occasionally, the eyes of the two men met, those of the younger sullen and dark, doggedly unalterable, those of the elder sneering with restless contempt.

The officer tried hard not to admit the passion that had got hold of him. He would not know that his feeling for his orderly was anything but that of a man incensed by his stupid, perverse servant. So, keeping quite justified and conventional, in his consciousness, he let the other thing run on. His nerves however, were suffering. At last he slung the end of a belt in his servant's face. When he saw the youth start back, the pain-tears in his eyes and the blood on his mouth, he had felt at once a thrill of deep pleasure and of shame.

But this, he acknowledged to himself, was a thing he had never done before. The fellow was too exasperating. His own nerves must be going to pieces. He went away for some days with a woman.

It was a mockery of pleasure. He simply did not want the woman. But he stayed on for his time. At the end of it, he came back in an agony of irritation, torment, and misery. He rode all the evening, then came straight in to supper. His orderly was out. The officer sat with his long, fine hands lying on the table, perfectly still, and all his blood seemed to be corroding.

At last his servant entered. He watched the strong, easy young figure, the fine eyebrows, the thick black hair. In a week's time the youth had got back his old well-being. The hands of the officer twitched and seemed to be full of mad flame. The young man stood at attention, unmoving, shut off.

The meal went in silence. But the orderly seemed eager. He made a clatter with the dishes.

"Are you in a hurry?" asked the officer, watching the intent, warm face of his servant. The other did not reply.

"Will you answer my question?" said the Captain.

"Yes, sir," replied the orderly, standing with his pile of deep Army plates. The Captain waited, looked at him, then asked again:

"Are you in a hurry?"

"Yes, sir," came the answer, that sent a flash through the listener.

"For what?"

"I was going out, sir."

"I want you this evening."

There was a moment's hesitation. The officer had a curious stiffness of countenance.

"Yes, sir," replied the servant, in his throat.

"I want you to-morrow evening also—in fact, you may consider your evenings occupied, unless I give you leave."

The mouth with the young moustache set close.

"Yes, sir," answered the orderly, loosening his lips for a moment.

He again turned to the door.

"And why have you a piece of pencil in your ear?"

The orderly hesitated, then continued on his way without answering. He set the plates in a pile outside the door, took the stump of pencil from his ear, and put it in his pocket. He had been copying a verse for his sweetheart's birthday card. He returned to finish clearing the table. The officer's eyes were dancing, he had a little, eager smile.

"Why have you a piece of pencil in your ear?" he asked.

The orderly took his hands full of dishes. His master was standing near the great green stove, a little smile on his face, his chin thrust forward. When the young soldier saw him his heart suddenly ran hot. He felt blind. Instead of answering, he turned dazedly to the door. As he was crouching to set down the dishes, he was pitched forward by a kick from behind. The pots went in a stream down the stairs, he clung to the pillar of the banisters. And as he was rising he was kicked heavily again and again, so that he clung sickly to the post for some moments. His master had gone swiftly into the room and closed the door. The maid-servant downstairs looked up the staircase and made a mocking face at the crockery disaster.

The officer's heart was plunging. He poured himself a glass of wine, part of which he spilled on the floor, and gulped the remainder, leaning against the cool, green stove. He heard his man collecting the dishes from the stairs. Pale, as if intoxicated, he waited. The servant entered again. The Captain's heart gave a pang, as of pleasure, seeing the young fellow bewildered and uncertain on his feet, with pain.

"Schöner!" he said.

The soldier was a little slower in coming to attention.

"Yes, sir!"

The youth stood before him, with pathetic young moustache, and fine eyebrows very distinct on his forehead of dark marble.

"I asked you a question."

"Yes, sir."

The officer's tone bit like acid.

"Why had you a pencil in your ear?"

Again the servant's heart ran hot, and he could not breathe. With dark, strained eyes, he looked at the officer, as if fascinated. And he stood there sturdily planted, unconscious. The withering smile came into the Captain's eyes, and he lifted his foot.

"I—I forgot it—sir," panted the soldier, his dark eyes fixed on the other man's dancing blue ones.

"What was it doing there?"

He saw the young man's breast heaving as he made an effort for words.

"I had been writing."

"Writing what?"

Again the soldier looked him up and down. The officer could hear him panting. The smile came into the blue eyes. The soldier worked his dry throat, but could not speak. Suddenly the smile lit like a flame on the officer's face, and a kick came heavily against the orderly's thigh. The youth moved a pace sideways. His face went dead, with two black, staring eyes.

"Well?" said the officer.

The orderly's mouth had gone dry, and his tongue rubbed in it as on dry brown-paper. He worked his throat. The officer raised his foot. The servant went stiff.

"Some poetry, sir," came the crackling, unrecognizable sound of his voice.

"Poetry, what poetry?" asked the Captain, with a sickly smile.

Again there was the working in the throat. The Captain's

heart had suddenly gone down heavily, and he stood sick and tired.

"For my girl, sir," he heard the dry, inhuman sound.

"Oh!" he said, turning away. "Clear the table."

"Click!" went the soldier's throat; then again, "click!" and then the half-articulate:

"Yes, sir."

The young soldier was gone, looking old, and walking heavily.

The officer, left alone, held himself rigid, to prevent himself from thinking. His instinct warned him that he must not think. Deep inside him was the intense gratification of his passion, still working powerfully. Then there was a counter-action, a horrible breaking down of something inside him, a whole agony of reaction. He stood there for an hour motion-less, a chaos of sensations, but rigid with a will to keep blank his consciousness, to prevent his mind grasping. And he held himself so until the worst of the stress had passed, when he began to drink, drank himself to an intoxication, till he slept obliterated. When he woke in the morning he was shaken to the base of his nature. But he had fought off the realization of what he had done. He had prevented his mind from taking it in, had suppressed it along with his instincts, and the conscious man had nothing to do with it. He felt only as after a bout of intoxication, weak, but the affair itself all dim and not to be recovered. Of the drunkenness of his passion he successfully refused remembrance. And when his orderly appeared with coffee, the officer assumed the same self he had had the morning before. He refused the event of the past night—denied it had ever been—and was successful in his denial. He had not done any such thing—not he himself. Whatever there might be lay at the door of a stupid, insubor-dinate servant.

The orderly had gone about in a stupor all the evening. He drank some beer because he was parched, but not much, the alcohol made his feeling come back, and he could not bear it. He was dulled, as if nine-tenths of the ordinary man in him

were inert. He crawled about disfigured. Still, when he thought
of the kicks, he went sick, and when he thought of the threat
of more kicking, in the room afterwards, his heart went hot
and faint, and he panted, remembering the one that had come.
He had been forced to say, "For my girl." He was much too
done even to want to cry. His mouth hung slightly open, like
an idiot's. He felt vacant, and wasted. So, he wandered at
his work, painfully, and very slowly, and clumsily, fumbling
blindly with the brushes, and finding it difficult, when he sat
down, to summon the energy to move again. His limbs, his
jaw, were slack and nerveless. But he was very tired. He got
to bed at last, and slept inert, relaxed, in a sleep that was
rather stupor than slumber, a dead night of stupefaction shot
through with gleams of anguish.

In the morning were the manœuvres. But he woke even
before the bugle sounded. The painful ache in his chest, the
dryness of his throat, the awful steady feeling of misery made
his eyes come awake and dreary at once. He knew, without
thinking, what had happened. And he knew that the day had
come again, when he must go on with his round. The last bit
of darkness was being pushed out of the room. He would have
to move his inert body and go on. He was so young, and had
known so little trouble, that he was bewildered. He only
wished it would stay night, so that he could lie still, covered
up by the darkness. And yet nothing would prevent the day
from coming, nothing would save him from having to get up
and saddle the Captain's horse, and make the Captain's coffee.
It was there, inevitable. And then, he thought, it was impossible. Yet they would not leave him free. He must go and
take the coffee to the Captain. He was too stunned to understand it. He only knew it was inevitable—inevitable, however
long he lay inert.

At last, after heaving at himself, for he seemed to be a mass
of inertia, he got up. But he had to force every one of his
movements from behind, with his will. He felt lost, and dazed,
and helpless. Then he clutched hold of the bed, the pain was
so keen. And looking at his thighs he saw the darker bruises

on his swarthy flesh, and he knew that if he pressed one of
his fingers on one of the bruises, he should faint. But he did
not want to faint—he did not want anybody to know. No one
should ever know. It was between him and the Captain. They
were only the two people in the world now—himself and the
Captain.

Slowly, economically, he got dressed and forced himself to
walk. Everything was obscure, except just what he had his
hands on. But he managed to get through his work. The very
pain revived his dull senses. The worst remained yet. He took
the tray and went up to the Captain's room. The officer, pale
and heavy, sat at the table. The orderly, as he saluted, felt
himself put out of existence. He stood still for a moment sub-
mitting to his own nullification—then he gathered himself,
seemed to regain himself, and then the Captain began to grow
vague, unreal, and the younger soldier's heart beat up. He
clung to this situation—that the Captain did not exist—so that
he himself might live. But when he saw his officer's hand
tremble as he took the coffee, he felt everything falling shattered. And he went away, feeling as if he himself were coming
to pieces, disintegrated. And when the Captain was there on
horseback, giving orders, while he himself stood, with rifle and
knapsack, sick with pain, he felt as if he must shut his eyes—as
if he must shut his eyes on everything. It was only the long
agony of marching with a parched throat that filled him with
one single, sleep-heavy intention: to save himself.

II

He was getting used even to his parched throat. That the
snowy peaks were radiant among the sky, that the whity-green
glacier-river twisted through its pale shoals, in the valley
below, seemed almost supernatural. But he was going mad
with fever and thirst. He plodded on uncomplaining. He did
not want to speak, not to anybody. There were two gulls, like
flakes of water and snow, over the river. The scent of green

rye soaked in sunshine came like a sickness. And the march continued, monotonously, almost like a bad sleep.

At the next farm-house, which stood low and broad near the high road, tubs of water had been put out. The soldiers clustered round to drink. They took off their helmets, and the steam mounted from their wet hair. The Captain sat on horse-back, watching. He needed to see his orderly. His helmet threw a dark shadow over his light, fierce eyes, but his mous-tache and mouth and chin were distinct in the sunshine. The orderly must move under the presence of the figure of the horseman. It was not that he was afraid, or cowed. It was as if he was disembowelled, made empty, like an empty shell. He felt himself as nothing, a shadow creeping under the sun-shine. And, thirsty as he was, he could scarcely drink, feeling the Captain near him. He would not take off his helmet to wipe his wet hair. He wanted to stay in shadow, not to be forced into consciousness. Starting, he saw the light heel of the officer prick the belly of the horse; the Captain cantered away, and he himself could relapse into vacancy.

Nothing, however, could give him back his living place in the hot, bright morning. He felt like a gap among it all. Whereas the Captain was prouder, overriding. A hot flash went through the young servant's body. The Captain was firmer and prouder with life, he himself was empty as a shadow. Again the flash went through him, dazing him out. But his heart ran a little firmer.

The company turned up the hill, to make a loop for the return. Below, from among the trees, the farm-bell clanged. He saw the labourers, mowing bare-foot at the thick grass, leave off their work and go downhill, their scythes hanging over their shoulders, like long, bright claws curving down behind them. They seemed like dream-people, as if they had no relation to himself. He felt as in a blackish dream: as if all the other things were there and had form, but he himself was only a consciousness, a gap that could think and perceive.

The soldiers were tramping silently up the glaring hill-side. Gradually his head began to revolve, slowly, rhythmically.

Sometimes it was dark before his eyes, as if he saw this world through a smoked glass, frail shadows and unreal. It gave him a pain in his head to walk.

The air was too scented, it gave no breath. All the lush green-stuff seemed to be issuing its sap, till the air was deathly, sickly with the smell of greenness. There was the perfume of clover, like pure honey and bees. Then there grew a faint acrid tang—they were near the beeches; and then a queer clattering noise, and a suffocating, hideous smell; they were passing a flock of sheep, a shepherd in a black smock, holding his crook. Why should the sheep huddle together under this fierce sun? He felt that the shepherd would not see him, though he could see the shepherd.

At last there was the halt. They stacked rifles in a conical stack, put down their kit in a scattered circle around it, and dispersed a little, sitting on a small knoll high on the hill-side. The chatter began. The soldiers were steaming with heat, but were lively. He sat still, seeing the blue mountains rising upon the land, twenty kilometres away. There was a blue fold in the ranges, then out of that, at the foot, the broad, pale bed of the river, stretches of whity-green water between pinkish-grey shoals among the dark pine woods. There it was, spread out a long way off. And it seemed to come downhill, the river. There was a raft being steered, a mile away. It was a strange country. Nearer, a red-roofed, broad farm with white base and square dots of windows crouched beside the wall of beech foliage on the wood's edge. There were long strips of rye and clover and pale green corn. And just at his feet, below the knoll, was a darkish bog, where globe flowers stood breathless still on their slim stalks. And some of the pale gold bubbles were burst, and a broken fragment hung in the air. He thought he was going to sleep.

Suddenly something moved into this coloured mirage before his eyes. The Captain, a small, light-blue and scarlet figure, was trotting evenly between the strips of corn, along the level brow of the hill. And the man making flag-signals was coming on. Proud and sure moved the horseman's figure, the quick,

bright thing, in which was concentrated all the light of this
morning, which for the rest lay a fragile, shining shadow. Submissive, apathetic, the young soldier sat and stared. But as
the horse slowed to a walk, coming up the last steep path, the
great flash flared over the body and soul of the orderly. He
sat waiting. The back of his head felt as if it were weighted
with a heavy piece of fire. He did not want to eat. His hands
trembled slightly as he moved them. Meanwhile the officer on
horseback was approaching slowly and proudly. The tension
grew in the orderly's soul. Then again, seeing the Captain ease
himself on the saddle, the flash blazed through him.

The Captain looked at the patch of light blue and scarlet,
and dark heads, scattered closely on the hill-side. It pleased
him. The command pleased him. And he was feeling proud.
His orderly was among them in common subjection. The
officer rose a little on his stirrups to look. The young soldier
sat with averted, dumb face. The Captain relaxed on his seat.
His slim-legged, beautiful horse, brown as a beech nut, walked
proudly uphill. The Captain passed into the zone of the
company's atmosphere: a hot smell of men, of sweat, of leather.
He knew it very well. After a word with the lieutenant, he
went a few paces higher, and sat there, a dominant figure, his
sweat-marked horse swishing its tail, while he looked down on
his men, on his orderly, a nonentity among the crowd.

The young soldier's heart was like fire in his chest, and he
breathed with difficulty. The officer, looking downhill, saw
three of the young soldiers, two pails of water between them,
staggering across a sunny green field. A table had been set
up under a tree, and there the slim lieutenant stood, importantly busy. Then the Captain summoned himself to an
act of courage. He called his orderly.

The flame leapt into the young soldier's throat as he heard
the command, and he rose blindly, stifled. He saluted, standing
below the officer. He did not look up. But there was the flicker
in the Captain's voice.

"Go to the inn and fetch me . . ." the officer gave his
commands. "Quick!" he added.

At the last word, the heart of the servant leapt with a flash, and he felt the strength come over his body. But he turned in mechanical obedience, and set off at a heavy run downhill, looking almost like a bear, his trousers bagging over his military boots. And the officer watched this blind, plunging run all the way.

But it was only the outside of the orderly's body that was obeying so humbly and mechanically. Inside had gradually accumulated a core into which all the energy of that young life was compact and concentrated. He executed his commission, and plodded quickly back uphill. There was a pain in his head as he walked that made him twist his features unknowingly. But hard there in the centre of his chest was himself, himself, firm, and not to be plucked to pieces.

The Captain had gone up into the wood. The orderly plodded through the hot, powerfully smelling zone of the company's atmosphere. He had a curious mass of energy inside him now. The Captain was less real than himself. He approached the green entrance to the wood. There, in the half-shade, he saw the horse standing, the sunshine and the flickering shadow of leaves dancing over his brown body. There was a clearing where timber had lately been felled. Here, in the gold-green shade beside the brilliant cup of sunshine, stood two figures, blue and pink, the bits of pink showing out plainly. The Captain was talking to his lieutenant.

The orderly stood on the edge of the bright clearing, where great trunks of trees, stripped and glistening, lay stretched like naked, brown-skinned bodies. Chips of wood littered the trampled floor, like splashed light, and the bases of the felled trees stood here and there, with their raw, level tops. Beyond was the brilliant, sunlit green of a beech.

"Then I will ride forward," the orderly heard his Captain say. The lieutenant saluted and strode away. He himself went forward. A hot flash passed through his belly, as he tramped towards his officer.

The Captain watched the rather heavy figure of the young soldier stumble forward, and his veins, too, ran hot. This was to be man to man between them. He yielded before the solid, stumbling figure with bent head. The orderly stooped and put the food on a level-sawn tree-base. The Captain watched the glistening, sun-inflamed, naked hands. He wanted to speak to the young soldier, but could not. The servant propped a bottle against his thigh, pressed open the cork, and poured out the beer into the mug. He kept his head bent. The Captain accepted the mug.

"Hot!" he said, as if amiably.

The flame sprang out of the orderly's heart, nearly suffocating him.

"Yes, sir," he replied, between shut teeth.

And he heard the sound of the Captain's drinking, and he clenched his fists, such a strong torment came into his wrists. Then came the faint clang of the closing of the pot-lid. He looked up. The Captain was watching him. He glanced swiftly away. Then he saw the officer stoop and take a piece of bread from the tree-base. Again the flash of flame went through the young soldier, seeing the stiff body stoop beneath him, and his hands jerked. He looked away. He could feel the officer was nervous. The bread fell as it was being broken. The officer ate the other piece. The two men stood tense and still, the master laboriously chewing his bread, the servant staring with averted face, his fist clenched.

Then the young soldier started. The officer had pressed open the lid of the mug again. The orderly watched the lid of the mug, and the white hand that clenched the handle, as if he were fascinated. It was raised. The youth followed it with his eyes. And then he saw the thin, strong throat of the elder man moving up and down as he drank, the strong jaw working. And the instinct which had been jerking at the young man's wrists suddenly jerked free. He jumped, feeling as if it were rent in two by a strong flame.

The spur of the officer caught in a tree-root, he went down backwards with a crash, the middle of his back thudding sickeningly against a sharp-edged tree-base, the pot flying away. And in a second the orderly, with serious, earnest young

face, and under-lip between his teeth, had got his knee in the
officer's chest and was pressing the chin backward over the
farther edge of the tree-stump, pressing, with all his heart
behind in a passion of relief, the tension of his wrists exquisite
with relief. And with the base of his palms he shoved at the
chin, with all his might. And it was pleasant, too, to have that
chin, that hard jaw already slightly rough with beard, in his
hands. He did not relax one hair's breadth, but, all the force
of all his blood exulting in his thrust, he shoved back the head
of the other man, till there was a little "cluck" and a crunching
sensation. Then he felt as if his head went to vapour. Heavy
convulsions shook the body of the officer, frightening and
horrifying the young soldier. Yet it pleased him, too, to
repress them. It pleased him to keep his hands pressing back
the chin, to feel the chest of the other man yield in expiration
to the weight of his strong, young knees, to feel the hard
twitchings of the prostrate body jerking his own whole frame,
which was pressed down on it.

But it went still. He could look into the nostrils of the other
man, the eyes he could scarcely see. How curiously the mouth
was pushed out, exaggerating the full lips, and the moustache
bristling up from them. Then, with a start, he noticed the
nostrils gradually filled with blood. The red brimmed, hesitated, ran over, and went in a thin trickle down the face to the
eyes.

It shocked and distressed him. Slowly, he got up. The body
twitched and sprawled there, inert. He stood and looked at it
in silence. It was a pity *it* was broken. It represented more
than the thing which had kicked and bullied him. He was
afraid to look at the eyes. They were hideous now, only the
whites showing, and the blood running to them. The face of the
orderly was drawn with horror at the sight. Well, it was so.
In his heart he was satisfied. He had hated the face of the
Captain. It was extinguished now. There was a heavy relief
in the orderly's soul. That was as it should be. But he could
not bear to see the long, military body lying broken over the
tree-base, the fine fingers crisped. He wanted to hide it away.

Quickly, busily, he gathered it up and pushed it under the felled tree-trunks, which rested their beautiful, smooth length either end on logs. The face was horrible with blood. He covered it with the helmet. Then he pushed the limbs straight and decent, and brushed the dead leaves off the fine cloth of the uniform. So, it lay quite still in the shadow under there. A little strip of sunshine ran along the breast, from a chink between the logs. The orderly sat by it for a few moments. Here his own life also ended.

Then, through his daze, he heard the lieutenant, in a loud voice, explaining to the men outside the wood, that they were to suppose the bridge on the river below was held by the enemy. Now they were to march to the attack in such and such a manner. The lieutenant had no gift of expression. The orderly, listening from habit, got muddled. And when the lieutenant began it all again he ceased to hear.

He knew he must go. He stood up. It surprised him that the leaves were glittering in the sun, and the chips of wood reflecting white from the ground. For him a change had come over the world. But for the rest it had not—all seemed the same. Only he had left it. And he could not go back. It was his duty to return with the beer-pot and the bottle. He could not. He had left all that. The lieutenant was still hoarsely explaining. He must go, or they would overtake him. And he could not bear contact with any one now.

He drew his fingers over his eyes, trying to find out where he was. Then he turned away. He saw the horse standing in the path. He went up to it and mounted. It hurt him to sit in the saddle. The pain of keeping his seat occupied him as they cantered through the wood. He would not have minded anything, but he could not get away from the sense of being divided from the others. The path led out of the trees. On the edge of the wood he pulled up and stood watching. There in the spacious sunshine of the valley soldiers were moving in a little swarm. Every now and then, a man harrowing on a strip of fallow shouted to his oxen, at the turn. The village and the white-towered church was small in the sunshine. And he no longer belonged to it—he sat there, beyond, like a man outside in the dark. He had gone out from everyday life into the unknown and he could not, he even did not want to go back.

Turning from the sun-blazing valley, he rode deep into the wood. Tree-trunks, like people standing grey and still, took no notice as he went. A doe, herself a moving bit of sunshine and shadow, went running through the flecked shade. There were bright green rents in the foliage. Then it was all pine wood, dark and cool. And he was sick with pain, he had an intolerable great pulse in his head, and he was sick. He had never been ill in his life. He felt lost, quite dazed with all this.

Trying to get down from the horse, he fell, astonished at the pain and his lack of balance. The horse shifted uneasily. He jerked its bridle and sent it cantering jerkily away. It was his last connection with the rest of things.

But he only wanted to lie down and not be disturbed. Stumbling through the trees, he came on a quiet place where beeches and pine trees grew on a slope. Immediately he had lain down and closed his eyes, his consciousness went racing on without him. A big pulse of sickness beat in him as if it throbbed through the whole earth. He was burning with dry heat. But he was too busy, too tearingly active in the incoherent race of delirium to observe.

III

He came to with a start. His mouth was dry and hard, but he had not the energy to get up. His heart beat heavily. Where was he?—the barracks—at home? There was something knocking. And, making an effort, he looked round—trees, and litter of greenery, and reddish, bright, still pieces of sunshine on the floor. He did not believe he was himself, he did not believe what he saw. Something was knocking. He made a struggle towards consciousness, but relapsed. Then he struggled again. And gradually his surroundings fell into relationship with himself. He knew, and a great pang of fear went through his heart. Somebody was knocking. He could see the heavy, black rags of a fir tree overhead. Then everything went blank. Yet he did not believe he had closed his eyes. He had not. Out of the blackness sight slowly emerged again. And someone was knocking. Quickly, he saw the blood-disfigured face of his Captain, which he hated. And he held himself still with horror. Yet, deep inside him, he knew that it was so, the Captain should be dead. But the physical delirium got hold of him. Someone was knocking. He lay perfectly still, as if dead, with fear. And he went unconscious.

When he opened his eyes again he started, seeing something creeping swiftly up a tree-trunk. It was a little bird. And the bird was whistling overhead. Tap-tap-tap—it was the small, quick bird rapping the tree-trunk with its beak, as if its head were a little round hammer. He watched it curiously. It shifted sharply, in its creeping fashion. Then, like a mouse, it slid down the bare trunk. Its swift creeping sent a flash of revulsion through him. He raised his head. It felt a great weight. Then, the little bird ran out of the shadow across a still patch of sunshine, its little head bobbing swiftly, its white legs twinkling brightly for a moment. How neat it was in its build, so compact, with pieces of white on its wings. There were several of them. They were so pretty—but they crept like swift, erratic mice, running here and there among the beech-mast.

He lay down again exhausted, and his consciousness lapsed. He had a horror of the little creeping birds. All his blood seemed to be darting and creeping in his head. And yet he could not move.

He came to with a further ache of exhaustion. There was the pain in his head, and the horrible sickness, and his inability to move. He had never been ill in his life. He did not know where he was or what he was. Probably he had got sunstroke. Or what else?—he had silenced the Captain for ever—some time ago—oh, a long time ago. There had been blood on his face, and his eyes had turned upwards. It was all right, somehow. It was peace. But now he had got beyond himself. He had never been here before. Was it life, or not life? He was by himself. They were in a big, bright place, those others, and he was outside. The town, all the country, a big bright place of light: and he was outside, here, in the darkened open beyond, where each thing existed alone. But they would all have to come out there sometime, those others. Little, and left behind him, they all were. There had been father and mother and sweetheart. What did they all matter? This was the open land.

He sat up. Something scuffled. It was a little brown squirrel running in lovely undulating bounds over the floor, its red tail completing the undulation of its body—and then, as it sat up, furling and unfurling. He watched it, pleased. It ran on again, friskily, enjoying itself. It flew wildly at another squirrel, and they were chasing each other, and making little scolding, chattering noises. The soldier wanted to speak to them. But only a hoarse sound came out of his throat. The squirrels burst away—they flew up the trees. And then he saw the one peeping round at him, half-way up a tree-trunk. A start of fear went through him, though in so far as he was conscious, he was amused. It still stayed, its little keen face staring at him half way up the tree-trunk, its little ears pricked up, its clawey little hands clinging to the bark, its white breast reared. He started from it in panic.

Struggling to his feet, he lurched away. He went on walking, walking, looking for something—for a drink. His brain felt hot and inflamed for want of water. He stumbled on. Then he did not know anything. He went unconscious as he walked. Yet he stumbled on, his mouth open.

When, to his dumb wonder, he opened his eyes on the world again, he no longer tried to remember what it was. There was thick, golden light behind golden-green glitterings, and tall, grey-purple shafts, and darknesses further off, surrounding him, growing deeper. He was conscious of a sense of arrival. He was amid the reality, on the real, dark bottom. But there was the thirst burning in his brain. He felt lighter, not so heavy. He supposed it was newness. The air was muttering with thunder. He thought he was walking wonderfully swiftly and was coming straight to relief—or was it to water?

Suddenly he stood still with fear. There was a tremendous flare of gold, immense—just a few dark trunks like bars between him and it. All the young level wheat was burnished gold glaring on its silky green. A woman, full-skirted, a black cloth on her head for head-dress, was passing like a block of shadow through the glistening, green corn, into the full glare. There was a farm, too, pale blue in shadow, and the timber black. And there was a church spire, nearly fused away in the gold. The woman moved on, away from him. He had no language with which to speak to her. She was the bright, solid unreality. She would make a noise of words that would confuse him, and her eyes would look at him without seeing him. She was crossing there to the other side. He stood against a tree.

When at last he turned, looking down the long, bare grove whose flat bed was already filling dark, he saw the mountains in a wonder-light, not far away, and radiant. Behind the soft, grey ridge of the nearest range the further mountains stood golden and pale grey, the snow all radiant like pure, soft gold. So still, gleaming in the sky, fashioned pure out of the ore of the sky, they shone in their silence. He stood and looked at them, his face illuminated. And like the golden, lustrous gleaming of the snow he felt his own thirst bright in him. He stood and gazed, leaning against a tree. And then everything slid away into space.

During the night the lightning fluttered perpetually, making the whole sky white. He must have walked again. The world hung livid round him for moments, fields a level sheen of grey-green light, trees in dark bulk, and the range of clouds black across a white sky. Then the darkness fell like a shutter, and the night was whole. A faint flutter of a half-revealed world, that could not quite leap out of the darkness!—Then there again stood a sweep of pallor for the land, dark shapes looming, a range of clouds hanging overhead. The world was a ghostly

shadow, thrown for a moment upon the pure darkness, which
returned ever whole and complete.

And the mere delirium of sickness and fever went on inside
him—his brain opening and shutting like the night—then
sometimes convulsions of terror from something with great
eyes that stared round a tree—then the long agony of the
march, and the sun decomposing his blood—then the pang
of hate for the Captain, followed by a pang of tenderness and
ease. But everything was distorted, born of an ache and
resolving into an ache.

In the morning he came definitely awake. Then his brain
flamed with the sole horror of thirstiness! The sun was on his
face, the dew was steaming from his wet clothes. Like one
possessed, he got up. There, straight in front of him, blue and
cool and tender, the mountains ranged across the pale edge
of the morning sky. He wanted them—he wanted them alone
—he wanted to leave himself and be identified with them. They
did not move, they were still and soft, with white, gentle
markings of snow. He stood still, mad with suffering, his hands
crisping and clutching. Then he was twisting in a paroxysm
on the grass.

He lay still, in a kind of dream of anguish. His thirst seemed
to have separated itself from him, and to stand apart, a single
demand. Then the pain he felt was another single self.
Then there was the clog of his body, another separate thing.
He was divided among all kinds of separate beings. There
was some strange, agonized connection between them, but
they were drawing further apart. Then they would all split.
The sun, drilling down on him, was drilling through the
bond. Then they would all fall, fall through the everlasting
lapse of space. Then again, his consciousness reasserted
itself. He roused on to his elbow and stared at the gleaming
mountains. There they ranked, all still and wonderful
between earth and heaven. He stared till his eyes went
black, and the mountains, as they stood in their beauty,
so clean and cool, seemed to have it, that which was lost
in him.

IV

When the soldiers found him, three hours later, he was lying with his face over his arm, his black hair giving off heat under the sun. But he was still alive. Seeing the open, black mouth the young soldiers dropped him in horror.

He died in the hospital at night, without having seen again. The doctors saw the bruises on his legs, behind, and were silent.

The bodies of the two men lay together, side by side, in the mortuary, the one white and slender, but laid rigidly at rest, the other looking as if every moment it must rouse into life again, so young and unused, from a slumber.

SECOND BEST

"Oh, I'm tired!" Frances exclaimed petulantly, and in the same instant she dropped down on the turf, near the hedge-bottom. Anne stood a moment surprised, then, accustomed to the vagaries of her beloved Frances, said:

"Well, and aren't you always likely to be tired, after travelling that blessed long way from Liverpool yesterday?" and she plumped down beside her sister. Anne was a wise young body of fourteen, very buxom, brimming with common sense. Frances was much older, about twenty-three, and whimsical, spasmodic. She was the beauty and the clever child of the family. She plucked the goose-grass buttons from her dress in a nervous, desperate fashion. Her beautiful profile, looped above the black hair, warm with the dusky-and-scarlet complexion of a pear, was calm as a mask, her thin brown hand plucked nervously.

"It's not the journey," she said, objecting to Anne's obtuseness. Anne looked inquiringly at her darling. The young girl, in her self-confident, practical way, proceeded to reckon up this whimsical creature. But suddenly she found herself full in the eyes of Frances; felt two dark, hectic eyes flaring challenge to her, and she shrank away. Frances was peculiar for these great, exposed looks, which disconcerted people by their violence and their suddenness.

"What's a matter, poor old duck?" asked Anne, as she folded the slight, wilful form of her sister in her arms. Frances laughed shakily, and nestled down for comfort on the budding breasts of the strong girl.

"Oh, I'm only a bit tired," she murmured, on the point of tears.

"Well, of course you are, what do you expect?" soothed Anne. It was a joke to Frances that Anne should play elder,

26

almost mother to her. But then, Anne was in her unvexed teens; men were like big dogs to her: while Frances, at twenty-three, suffered a good deal.

The country was intensely morning-still. On the common everything shone beside its shadow, and the hill-side gave off heat in silence. The brown turf seemed in a low state of combustion, the leaves of the oaks were scorched brown. Among the blackish foliage in the distance shone the small red and orange of the village.

The willows in the brook-course at the foot of the common suddenly shook with a dazzling effect like diamonds. It was a puff of wind. Anne resumed her normal position. She spread her knees, and put in her lap a handful of hazel nuts, whity-green leafy things, whose one cheek was tanned between brown and pink. These she began to crack and eat. Frances, with bowed head, mused bitterly.

"Eh, you know Tom Smedley?" began the young girl, as she pulled a tight kernel out of its shell.

"I suppose so," replied Frances sarcastically.

"Well, he gave me a wild rabbit what he'd caught, to keep with my tame one—and it's living."

"That's a good thing," said Frances, very detached and ironic.

"Well, it *is!* He reckoned he'd take me to Ollerton Feast, but he never did. Look here, he took a servant from the rectory; I saw him."

"So he ought," said Frances.

"No, he oughtn't! And I told him so. And I told him I should tell you—an' I have done."

Click and snap went a nut between her teeth. She sorted out the kernel, and chewed complacently.

"It doesn't make much difference," said Frances.

"Well, 'appen it doesn't; but I was mad with him all the same."

"Why?"

"Because I was; he's no right to go with a servant."

"He's a perfect right," persisted Frances, very just and cold.

"No, he hasn't, when he'd said he'd take me."

Frances burst into a laugh of amusement and relief.

"Oh, no; I'd forgot that," she said, adding, "and what did he say when you promised to tell me?"

"He laughed and said, 'She won't fret her fat over that.'"

"And she won't," sniffed Frances.

There was silence. The common, with its sere, blonde-headed thistles, its heaps of silent bramble, its brown-husked gorse in the glare of sunshine, seemed visionary. Across the brook began the immense pattern of agriculture, white checkering of barley stubble, brown squares of wheat, khaki patches of pasture, red stripes of fallow, with the woodland and the tiny village dark like ornaments, leading away to the distance, right to the hills, where the check-pattern grew smaller and smaller, till, in the blackish haze of heat, far off, only the tiny white squares of barley stubble showed distinct.

"Eh, I say, here's a rabbit hole!" cried Anne suddenly. "Should we watch if one comes out? You won't have to fidget, you know."

The two girls sat perfectly still. Frances watched certain objects in her surroundings; they had a peculiar, unfriendly look about them: the weight of greenish elderberries on their purpling stalks; the twinkling of the yellowing crab-apples that clustered high up in the hedge, against the sky: the exhausted, limp leaves of the primroses lying flat in the hedge-bottom: all looked strange to her. Then her eyes caught a movement. A mole was moving silently over the warm, red soil, nosing, shuffling hither and thither, flat, and dark as a shadow, shifting about, and as suddenly brisk, and as silent, like a very ghost of *joie de vivre*. Frances started, from habit was about to call on Anne to kill the little pest. But, to-day her lethargy of unhappiness was too much for her. She watched the little brute paddling, snuffing, touching things to discover them, running in blindness, delighted to ecstasy by the sunlight and the hot, strange things that caressed its belly and its nose. She felt a keen pity for the little creature.

"Eh, our Fran, look there! It's a mole."

Anne was on her feet, standing watching the dark, unconscious beast. Frances frowned with anxiety.

"It doesn't run off, does it?" said the young girl softly. Then she stealthily approached the creature. The mole paddled fumblingly away. In an instant Anne put her foot upon it, not too heavily. Frances could see the struggling, swimming movement of the little pink hands of the brute, the twisting and twitching of its pointed nose, as it wrestled under the sole of the boot.

"It *does* wriggle!" said the bonny girl, knitting her brows in a frown at the eerie sensation. Then she bent down to look at her trap. Frances could now see, beyond the edge of the boot-sole, the heaving of the velvet shoulders, the pitiful turning of the sightless face, the frantic rowing of the flat, pink hands.

"Kill the thing," she said, turning away her face.

"Oh—I'm not," laughed Anne, shrinking. "You can, if you like."

"I *don't* like," said Frances, with quiet intensity.

After several dabbing attempts, Anne succeeded in picking up the little animal by the scruff of its neck. It threw back its head, flung its long blind snout from side to side, the mouth open in a peculiar oblong, with tiny pinkish teeth at the edge. The blind, frantic mouth gaped and writhed. The body, heavy and clumsy, hung scarcely moving.

"Isn't it a snappy little thing," observed Anne, twisting to avoid the teeth.

"What are you going to do with it?" asked Frances sharply.

"It's got to be killed—look at the damage they do. I s'll take it home and let dadda or somebody kill it. I'm not going to let it go."

She swaddled the creature clumsily in her pocket-handkerchief and sat down beside her sister. There was an interval of silence, during which Anne combated the efforts of the mole.

"You've not had much to say about Jimmy this time. Did you see him often in Liverpool?" Anne asked suddenly.

"Once or twice," replied Frances, giving no sign of how the question troubled her.

"And aren't you sweet on him any more, then?"

"I should think I'm not, seeing that he's engaged."

"Engaged? Jimmy Barrass! Well, of all things! I never thought *he'd* get engaged."

"Why not, he's as much right as anybody else?" snapped Frances.

Anne was fumbling with the mole.

"'Appen so," she said at length; "but I never thought Jimmy would, though."

"Why not?" snapped Frances.

"*I* don't know—this blessed mole, it'll not keep still!—who's he got engaged to?"

"How should I know?"

"I thought you'd ask him; you've known him long enough. I s'd think he thought he'd get engaged now he's a Doctor of Chemistry."

Frances laughed in spite of herself.

"What's that got to do with it?" she asked.

"I'm sure it's got a lot. He'll want to feel *somebody* now, so he's got engaged. Hey, stop it; go in!"

But at this juncture the mole almost succeeded in wriggling clear. It wrestled and twisted frantically, waved its pointed blind head, its mouth standing open like a little shaft, its big, wrinkled hands spread out.

"Go in with you!" urged Anne, poking the little creature with her forefinger, trying to get it back into the handkerchief. Suddenly the mouth turned like a spark on her finger.

"Oh!" she cried, "he's bit me."

She dropped him to the floor. Dazed, the blind creature fumbled round. Frances felt like shrieking. She expected him to dart away in a flash, like a mouse, and there he remained groping; she wanted to cry to him to be gone. Anne, in a sudden decision of wrath, caught up her sister's walking-cane. With one blow the mole was dead. Frances was startled and shocked. One moment the little wretch was fussing in the heat, and the next it lay like a little bag, inert and black—not a struggle, scarce a quiver.

"It is dead!" Frances said breathlessly. Anne took her finger from her mouth, looked at the tiny pinpricks, and said:

"Yes, he is, and I'm glad. They're vicious little nuisances, moles are."

With which her wrath vanished. She picked up the dead animal.

"Hasn't it got a beautiful skin," she mused, stroking the fur with her forefinger, then with her cheek.

"Mind," said Frances sharply. "You'll have the blood on your skirt!"

One ruby drop of blood hung on the small snout, ready to fall. Anne shook it off on to some harebells. Frances suddenly became calm; in that moment, grown-up.

"I suppose they have to be killed," she said, and a certain rather dreary indifference succeeded to her grief. The twinkling crab-apples, the glitter of brilliant willows now seemed to her trifling, scarcely worth the notice. Something had died in her, so that things lost their poignancy. She was calm, indifference overlying her quiet sadness. Rising, she walked down to the brook course.

"Here, wait for me," cried Anne, coming tumbling after.

Frances stood on the bridge, looking at the red mud trodden into pockets by the feet of cattle. There was not a drain of water left, but everything smelled green, succulent. Why did she care so little for Anne, who was so fond of her? she asked herself. Why did she care so little for any one? She did not know, but she felt a rather stubborn pride in her isolation and indifference.

They entered a field where stooks of barley stood in rows, the straight, blonde tresses of the corn streaming on to the ground. The stubble was bleached by the intense summer, so that the expanse glared white. The next field was sweet and soft with a second crop of seeds; thin, straggling clover whose little pink knobs rested prettily in the dark green. The scent was faint and sickly. The girls came up in single file, Frances leading.

Near the gate a young man was mowing with the scythe some fodder for the afternoon feed of the cattle. As he saw the girls he left off working and waited in an aimless kind of way. Frances was dressed in white muslin, and she walked with dignity, detached and forgetful. Her lack of agitation, her simple, unheeding advance made him nervous. She had loved the far-off Jimmy for five years, having had in return his half-measures. This man only affected her slightly.

Tom was of medium stature, energetic in build. His smooth, fair-skinned face was burned red, not brown, by the sun, and this ruddiness enhanced his appearance of good humour and easiness. Being a year older than Frances, he would have courted her long ago had she been so inclined. As it was, he had gone his uneventful way amiably, chatting with many a girl, but remaining unattached, free of trouble for the most part. Only he knew he wanted a woman. He hitched his trousers just a trifle self-consciously as the girls approached. Frances was a rare, delicate kind of being, whom he realized with a queer and delicious stimulation in his veins. She gave him a slight sense of suffocation. Somehow, this morning, she affected him more than usual. She was dressed in white. He, however, being matter-of-fact in his mind, did not realize. His feeling had never become conscious, purposive.

Frances knew what she was about. Tom was ready to love her as soon as she would show him. Now that she could not have Jimmy, she did not poignantly care. Still, she would have something. If she could not have the best—Jimmy, whom she knew to be something of a snob—she would have the second best, Tom. She advanced rather indifferently.

"You are back, then!" said Tom. She marked the touch of uncertainty in his voice.

"No," she laughed, "I'm still in Liverpool," and the undertone of intimacy made him burn.

"This isn't you then?" he asked.

Her heart leapt up in approval. She looked in his eyes, and for a second was with him.

"Why, what do you think?" she laughed.

He lifted his hat from his head with a distracted little gesture. She liked him, his quaint ways, his humour, his ignorance, and his slow masculinity.

"Here, look here, Tom Smedley," broke in Anne.

"A moudiwarp! Did you find it dead?" he asked.

"No, it bit me," said Anne.

"Oh, aye! An' that got your rag out, did it?"

"No, it didn't!" Anne scolded sharply. "Such language!"

"Oh, what's up wi' it?"

"I can't bear you to talk broad."

"Can't you?"

He glanced at Frances.

"It isn't nice," Frances said. She did not care, really. The vulgar speech jarred on her as a rule; Jimmy was a gentleman. But Tom's manner of speech did not matter to her.

"I like you to talk *nicely*," she added.

"Do you," he replied, tilting his hat, stirred.

"And generally you *do*, you know," she smiled.

"I s'll have to have a try," he said, rather tensely gallant.

"What?" she asked brightly.

"To talk nice to you," he said. Frances coloured furiously, bent her head for a moment, then laughed gaily, as if she liked this clumsy hint.

"Eh now, you mind what you're saying," cried Anne, giving the young man an admonitory pat.

"You wouldn't. have to give yon mole many knocks like that," he teased, relieved to get on safe ground, rubbing his arm.

"No indeed, it died in one blow," said Frances, with a flippancy that was hateful to her.

"You're not so good at knockin' 'em?" he said, turning to her.

"I don't know, if I'm cross," she said decisively.

"No?" he replied, with alert attentiveness.

"I could," she added, harder, "if it was necessary."

He was slow to feel her difference.

"And don't you consider it *is* necessary?" he asked, with misgiving.

"W—ell—is it?" she said, looking at him steadily, coldly.

"I reckon it is," he replied, looking away, but standing stubborn.

She laughed quickly.

"But it isn't necessary for *me*," she said, with slight contempt.

"Yes, that's quite true," he answered.

She laughed in a shaky fashion.

"*I know it is*," she said; and there was an awkward pause.

"Why, would you *like* me to kill moles then?" she asked tentatively, after a while.

"They do us a lot of damage," he said, standing firm on his own ground, angered.

"Well, I'll see the next time I come across one," she promised, defiantly. Their eyes met, and she sank before him, her pride troubled. He felt uneasy and triumphant and baffled, as if fate had gripped him. She smiled as she departed.

"Well," said Anne, as the sisters went through the wheat stubble; "I don't know what you two's been jawing about, I'm sure."

"Don't you?" laughed Frances significantly.

"No, I don't. But, at any rate, Tom Smedley's a good deal better to my thinking than Jimmy, so there—and nicer."

"Perhaps he is," said Frances coldly.

And the next day, after a secret, persistent hunt, she found another mole playing in the heat. She killed it, and in the evening, when Tom came to the gate to smoke his pipe after supper, she took him the dead creature.

"Here you are then!" she said.

"Did you catch it?" he replied, taking the velvet corpse into his fingers and examining it minutely. This was to hide his trepidation.

"Did you think I couldn't?" she asked, her face very near his.

"Nay, I didn't know."

She laughed in his face, a strange little laugh that caught her breath, all agitation, and tears, and recklessness of desire. He looked frightened and upset. She put her hand to his arm.

"Shall you go out wi' me?" he asked, in a difficult, troubled tone.

She turned her face away, with a shaky laugh. The blood came up in him, strong, overmastering. He resisted it. But it drove him down, and he was carried away. Seeing the winsome, frail nape of her neck, fierce love came upon him for her, and tenderness.

"We s'll 'ave to tell your mother," he said. And he stood, suffering, resisting his passion for her.

"Yes," she replied, in a dead voice. But there was a thrill of pleasure in this death.

THE WHITE STOCKING

I

"I'm getting up, Teddilinks," said Mrs. Whiston, and she sprang out of bed briskly.

"What the Hanover's got you?" asked Whiston.

"Nothing. Can't I get up?" she replied animatedly.

It was about seven o'clock, scarcely light yet in the cold bedroom. Whiston lay still and looked at his wife. She was a pretty little thing, with her fleecy, short black hair all tousled. He watched her as she dressed quickly, flicking her small, delightful limbs, throwing her clothes about her. Her slovenliness and untidiness did not trouble him. When she picked up the edge of her petticoat, ripped off a torn string of white lace, and flung it on the dressing-table, her careless abandon made his spirit glow. She stood before the mirror and roughly scrambled together her profuse little mane of hair. He watched the quickness and softness of her young shoulders, calmly, like a husband, and appreciatively.

"Rise up," she cried, turning to him with a quick wave of her arm—"and shine forth."

They had been married two years. But still, when she had gone out of the room, he felt as if all his light and warmth were taken away, he became aware of the raw, cold morning. So he rose himself, wondering casually what had roused her so early. Usually she lay in bed as late as she could.

Whiston fastened a belt round his loins and went downstairs in shirt and trousers. He heard her singing in her snatchy fashion. The stairs creaked under his weight. He passed down the narrow little passage, which she called a hall, of the seven and sixpenny house which was his first home.

He was a shapely young fellow of about twenty-eight,

sleepy now and easy with well-being. He heard the water drumming into the kettle, and she began to whistle. He loved the quick way she dodged the supper cups under the tap to wash them for breakfast. She looked an untidy minx, but she was quick and handy enough.

"Teddilinks," she cried.

"What?"

"Light a fire, quick."

She wore an old, sack-like dressing-jacket of black silk pinned across her breast. But one of the sleeves, coming unfastened, showed some delightful pink upper-arm.

"Why don't you sew your sleeve up?" he said, suffering from the sight of the exposed soft flesh.

"Where?" she cried, peering round. "Nuisance," she said, seeing the gap, then with light fingers went on drying the cups.

The kitchen was of fair size, but gloomy. Whiston poked out the dead ashes.

Suddenly a thud was heard at the door down the passage.

"I'll go," cried Mrs. Whiston, and she was gone down the hall.

The postman was a ruddy-faced man who had been a soldier. He smiled broadly, handing her some packages.

"They've not forgot you," he said impudently.

"No—lucky for them," she said, with a toss of the head. But she was interested only in her envelopes this morning. The postman waited inquisitively, smiling in an ingratiating fashion. She slowly, abstractedly, as if she did not know any one was there, closed the door in his face, continuing to look at the addresses on her letters.

She tore open the thin envelope. There was a long, hideous, cartoon valentine. She smiled briefly and dropped it on the floor. Struggling with the string of a packet, she opened a white cardboard box, and there lay a white silk handkerchief packed neatly under the paper lace of the box, and her initial, worked in heliotrope, fully displayed. She smiled pleasantly, and gently put the box aside. The third envelope contained another white packet—apparently a cotton handkerchief neatly folded. She shook it out. It was a long white stocking, but there was a little weight in the toe. Quickly, she thrust down her arm, wriggling her fingers into the toe of the stocking, and brought out a small box. She peeped inside the box, then hastily opened a door on her left hand, and went into the little, cold sitting-room. She had her lower lip caught earnestly between her teeth.

With a little flash of triumph, she lifted a pair of pearl-ear-rings from the small box, and she went to the mirror. There, earnestly, she began to hook them through her ears, looking at herself sideways in the glass. Curiously concentrated and intent she seemed as she fingered the lobes of her ears, her head bent on one side.

Then the pearl ear-rings dangled under her rosy, small ears. She shook her head sharply, to see the swing of the drops. They went chill against her neck, in little, sharp touches. Then she stood still to look at herself, bridling her head in the dignified fashion. Then she simpered at herself. Catching her own eye, she could not help winking at herself and laughing.

She turned to look at the box. There was a scrap of paper with this posy:

> "Pearls may be fair, but thou are fairer.
> Wear these for me, and I'll love the wearer."

She made a grimace and a grin. But she was drawn to the mirror again, to look at her ear-rings.

Whiston had made the fire burn, so he came to look for her. When she heard him, she started round quickly, guiltily. She was watching him with intent blue eyes when he appeared.

He did not see much, in his morning-drowsy warmth. He gave her, as ever, a feeling of warmth and slowness. His eyes were very blue, very kind, his manner simple.

"What ha' you got?" he asked.

"Valentines," she said briskly, ostentatiously turning to show him the silk handkerchief. She thrust it under his nose. "Smell how good," she said.

"Who's that from?" he replied, without smelling.

"It's a valentine," she cried. "How do I know who it's from?"

"I'll bet you know," he said.

"Ted!—I don't!" she cried, beginning to shake her head, then stopping because of the ear-rings.

He stood still a moment, displeased.

"They've no right to send you valentines, now," he said.

"Ted!—Why not? You're not jealous, are you? I haven't the least idea who it's from. Look—there's my initial"—she pointed with an emphatic finger at the heliotrope embroidery:

> "E for Elsie,
> Nice little gelsie,"

she sang.

"Get out," he said. "You know who it's from."

"Truth, I don't," she cried.

He looked round, and saw the white stocking lying on a chair.

"Is this another?" he said.

"No, that's a sample," she said. "There's only a comic." And she fetched in the long cartoon.

He stretched it out and looked at it solemnly.

"Fools!" he said, and went out of the room.

She flew upstairs and took off the ear-rings. When she returned, he was crouched before the fire blowing the coals. The skin of his face was flushed, and slightly pitted, as if he had had small-pox. But his neck was white and smooth and goodly. She hung her arms round his neck as he crouched there, and clung to him. He balanced on his toes.

"This fire's a slow-coach," he said.

"And who else is a slow-coach?" she said.

"One of us two, I know," he said, and he rose carefully. She remained clinging round his neck, so that she was lifted off her feet.

"Ha!—swing me," she cried.

He lowered his head, and she hung in the air, swinging from his neck, laughing. Then she slipped off.

"The kettle is singing," she sang, flying for the teapot. He bent down again to blow the fire. The veins in his neck stood out, his shirt collar seemed too tight.

> "Doctor Wyer,
> Blow the fire,
> Puff! puff! puff!"

she sang, laughing.

He smiled at her.

She was so glad because of her pearl ear-rings.

Over the breakfast she grew serious. He did not notice. She became portentous in her gravity. Almost it penetrated through his steady good-humour to irritate him.

"Teddy!" she said at last.

"What?" he asked.

"I told you a lie," she said, humbly tragic.

His soul stirred uneasily.

"Oh aye?" he said casually.

She was not satisfied. He ought to be more moved.

"Yes," she said.

He cut a piece of bread.

"Was it a good one?" he asked.

She was piqued. Then she considered—*was* it a good one? Then she laughed.

"No," she said, "it wasn't up to much."

"Ah!" he said easily, but with a steady strength of fondness for her in his tone. "Get it out then."

It became a little more difficult.

"You know that white stocking," she said earnestly. "I told you a lie. It wasn't a sample. It was a valentine."

A little frown came on his brow.

"Then what did you invent it as a sample for?" he said. But he knew this weakness of hers. The touch of anger in his voice frightened her.

"I was afraid you'd be cross," she said pathetically.

"I'll bet you were vastly afraid," he said.

"I *was*, Teddy."

There was a pause. He was resolving one or two things in his mind.

'And who sent it?" he asked.

"I can guess," she said, "though there wasn't a word with it—except——"

She ran to the sitting-room and returned with a slip of paper.

"Pearls may be fair, but thou art fairer
Wear these for me, and I'll love the wearer."

He read it twice, then a dull red flush came on his face.

"And *who* do you guess it is?" he asked, with a ringing of anger in his voice.

"I suspect it's Sam Adams," she said, with a little virtuous indignation.

Whiston was silent for a moment.

"Fool!" he said. "An' what's it got to do with pearls?—and how can he say 'wear these for me' when there's only one? He hasn't got the brain to invent a proper verse."

He screwed the slip of paper into a ball and flung it into the fire.

"I suppose he thinks it'll make a pair with the one last year," she said.

"Why, did he send one then?"

"Yes. I thought you'd be wild if you knew."

His jaw set rather sullenly.

Presently he rose, and went to wash himself, rolling back his sleeves and pulling open his shirt at the breast. It was as if his fine, clear-cut temples and steady eyes were degraded by the lower, rather brutal part of his face. But she loved it. As she whisked about, clearing the table, she loved the way in which he stood washing himself. He was such a man. She liked to see his neck glistening with water as he swilled it. It amused her and pleased her and thrilled her. He was so sure, so permanent, he had her so utterly in his power. It gave her a delightful, mischievous sense of liberty. Within his grasp, she could dart about excitingly.

He turned round to her, his face red from the cold water, his eyes fresh and very blue.

"You haven't been seeing anything of him, have you?" he asked roughly.

"Yes," she answered, after a moment, as if caught guilty. "He got into the train with me, and he asked me to drink a coffee and a Benedictine in the Royal."

"You've got it off fine and glib," he said sullenly. "And did you?"

"Yes," she replied, with the air of a traitor before the rack.

The blood came up into his neck and face, he stood motionless, dangerous.

"It was cold, and it was such fun to go into the Royal," she said.

"You'd go off with a nigger for a packet of chocolate," he said, in anger and contempt, and some bitterness. Queer how he drew away from her, cut her off from him.

"Ted—how beastly!" she cried. "You know quite well——" She caught her lip, flushed, and the tears came to her eyes.

He turned away, to put on his necktie. She went about her work, making a queer pathetic little mouth, down which occasionally dripped a tear.

He was ready to go. With his hat jammed down on his head, and his overcoat buttoned up to his chin, he came to kiss her. He would be miserable all the day if he went without. She allowed herself to be kissed. Her cheek was wet under his lips, and his heart burned. She hurt him so deeply. And she felt aggrieved, and did not quite forgive him.

In a moment she went upstairs to her ear-rings. Sweet they looked nestling in the little drawer—sweet! She examined them with voluptuous pleasure, she threaded them in her ears, she looked at herself, she posed and postured and smiled and looked sad and tragic and winning, and appealing, all in turn before the mirror. And she was happy, and very pretty.

She wore her ear-rings all morning, in the house. She was self-conscious, and quite brilliantly winsome, when the baker came, wondering if he would notice. All the tradesmen left her door with a glow in them, feeling elated, and unconsciously favouring the delightful little creature, though there had been nothing to notice in her behaviour.

She was stimulated all the day. She did not think about her husband. He was the permanent basis from which she took these giddy little flights into nowhere. At night, like chickens and curses, she would come home to him, to roost.

Meanwhile Whiston, a traveller and confidential support of a small firm, hastened about his work, his heart all the while anxious for her, yearning for surety, and kept tense by not getting it.

II

She had been a warehouse girl in Adams's lace factory before she was married. Sam Adams was her employer. He was a bachelor of forty, growing stout, a man well dressed and florid, with a large brown moustache and thin hair. From the rest of his well-groomed, showy appearance, it was evident his baldness was a chagrin to him. He had a good presence, and some Irish blood in his veins.

His fondness for the girls, or the fondness of the girls for him, was notorious. And Elsie, quick, pretty, almost witty little thing—she *seemed* witty, although, when her sayings were repeated, they were entirely trivial—she had a great attraction for him. He would come into the warehouse dressed in a rather sporting reefer coat, of fawn colour, and trousers of fine black-and-white check, a cap with a big peak and scarlet carnation in his button-hole, to impress her. She was only half impressed. He was too loud for her good taste. Instinctively perceiving this, he sobered down to navy blue. Then a well-built man, florid, with large brown whiskers, smart navy blue suit, fashionable boots, and manly hat, he was the irreproachable. Elsie was impressed.

But meanwhile Whiston was courting her, and she made splendid little gestures, before her bedroom mirror, of the constant-and-true sort.

"True, true till death——"

That was her song. Whiston was made that way, so there was
no need to take thought for him.

Every Christmas Sam Adams gave a party at his house, to
which he invited his superior work-people—not factory hands
and labourers but those above. He was a generous man in his
way, with a real warm feeling for giving pleasure.

Two years ago Elsie had attended this Christmas-party for
the last time. Whiston had accompanied her. At that time he
worked for Sam Adams.

She had been very proud of herself, in her close-fitting, full-
skirted dress of blue silk. Whiston called for her. Then she
tripped beside him, holding her large cashmere shawl across her
breast. He strode with long strides, his trousers handsomely
strapped under his boots, and her silk shoes bulging the
pockets of his full-skirted overcoat.

They passed through the park gates, and her spirits rose.
Above them the Castle Rock loomed grandly in the night, the
naked trees stood still and dark in the frost, along the boulevard.

They were rather late. Agitated with anticipation, in the
cloak-room she gave up her shawl, donned her silk shoes, and
looked at herself in the mirror. The loose bunches of curls on
either side her face danced prettily, her mouth smiled.

She hung a moment in the door of the brilliantly lighted
room. Many people were moving within the blaze of lamps,
under the crystal chandeliers, the full skirts of the women
balancing and floating, the side-whiskers and white cravats of
the men bowing above. Then she entered the light.

In an instant Sam Adams was coming forward, lifting both
his arms in boisterous welcome. There was a constant red
laugh on his face.

"Come late, would you," he shouted, "like royalty."

He seized her hands and led her forward. He opened his
mouth wide when he spoke, and the effect of the warm, dark
opening behind the brown whiskers was disturbing. But she

was floating into the throng on his arm. He was very gallant.

"Now then," he said, taking her card to write down the dances, "I've got *carte blanche*, haven't I?"

"Mr. Whiston doesn't dance," she said.

"I am a lucky man!" he said, scribbling his initials. "I was born with an *amourette* in my mouth."

He wrote on, quietly. She blushed and laughed, not knowing what it meant.

"Why, what is that?" she said.

"It's you, even littler than you are, dressed in little wings," he said.

"I should have to be pretty small to get in your mouth," she said.

"You think you're too big, do you!" he said easily.

He handed her her card, with a bow.

"Now I'm set up, my darling, for this evening," he said.

Then, quick, always at his ease, he looked over the room. She waited in front of him. He was ready. Catching the eye of the band, he nodded. In a moment, the music began. He seemed to relax, giving himself up.

"Now then, Elsie," he said, with a curious caress in his voice that seemed to lap the outside of her body in a warm glow, delicious. She gave herself to it. She liked it.

He was an excellent dancer. He seemed to draw her close in to him by some male warmth of attraction, so that she became all soft and pliant to him, flowing to his form, whilst he united her with him and they lapsed along in one movement. She was just carried in a kind of strong, warm flood, her feet moved of themselves, and only the music threw her away from him, threw her back to him, to his clasp, in his strong form moving against her, rhythmically, deliciously.

When it was over, he was pleased and his eyes had a curious gleam which thrilled her and yet had nothing to do with her. Yet it held her. He did not speak to her. He only looked straight into her eyes with a curious, gleaming look that disturbed her fearfully and deliciously. But also there was in his look some of the automatic irony of the *roué*.

It left her partly cold. She was not carried away.

She went, driven by an opposite, heavier impulse, to Whiston. He stood looking gloomy, trying to admit that she had a perfect right to enjoy herself apart from him. He received her with rather grudging kindliness.

"Aren't you going to play whist?" she asked.

"Aye," he said. "Directly."

"I do wish you could dance."

"Well, I can't," he said. "So you enjoy yourself."

"But I should enjoy it better if I could dance with you."

"Nay, you're all right," he said. "I'm not made that way."

"Then you ought to be!" she cried.

"Well, it's my fault, not yours. You enjoy yourself," he bade her. Which she proceeded to do, a little bit irked.

She went with anticipation to the arms of Sam Adams, when the time came to dance with him. It *was* so gratifying, irrespective of the man. And she felt a little grudge against Whiston, soon forgotten when her host was holding her near to him, in a delicious embrace. And she watched his eyes, to meet the gleam in them, which gratified her.

She was getting warmed right through, the glow was penetrating into her, driving away everything else. Only in her heart was a little tightness, like conscience.

When she got a chance, she escaped from the dancing-room to the card-room. There, in a cloud of smoke, she found Whiston playing cribbage. Radiant, roused, animated, she came up to him and greeted him. She was too strong, too vibrant a note in the quiet room. He lifted his head, and a frown knitted his gloomy forehead.

"Are you playing cribbage? Is it exciting? How are you getting on?" she chattered.

He looked at her. None of these questions needed answering, and he did not feel in touch with her. She turned to the cribbage-board.

"Are you white or red?" she asked.

"He's red," replied the partner.

"Then you're losing," she said, still to Whiston. And she

lifted the red peg from the board. "One—two—three—four—
five—six—seven—eight—— Right up there you ought to
jump——"

"Now put it back in its right place," said Whiston.

"Where was it?" she asked gaily, knowing her transgression.
He took the little red peg away from her and stuck it in its
hole.

The cards were shuffled.

"What a shame you're losing!" said Elsie.

"You'd better cut for him," said the partner.

She did so, hastily. The cards were dealt. She put her hand
on his shoulder, looking at his cards.

"It's good," she cried, "isn't it?"

He did not answer, but threw down two cards. It moved
him more strongly than was comfortable, to have her hand on
his shoulder, her curls dangling and touching his ears, whilst
she was roused to another man. It made the blood flame over
him.

At that moment Sam Adams appeared, florid and boisterous,
intoxicated more with himself, with the dancing, than with
wine. In his eye the curious, impersonal light gleamed.

"I thought I should find you here, Elsie," he cried boisterously, a disturbing, high note in his voice.

"What made you think so?" she replied, the mischief
rousing in her.

The florid, well-built man narrowed his eyes to a smile.

"I should never look for you among the ladies," he said,
with a kind of intimate, animal call to her. He laughed, bowed,
and offered her his arm.

"Madam, the music waits."

She went almost helplessly, carried along with him, unwilling, yet delighted.

That dance was an intoxication to her. After the first few
steps, she felt herself slipping away from herself. She almost
knew she was going, she did not even want to go. Yet she must
have chosen to go. She lay in the arm of the steady, close man
with whom she was dancing, and she seemed to swim away out

of contact with the room, into him. She had passed into another, denser element of him, an essential privacy. The room was all vague around her, like an atmosphere, like under sea, with a flow of ghostly, dumb movements. But she herself was held real against her partner, and it seemed she was connected with him, as if the movements of his body and limbs were her own movements, yet not her own movements— and oh, delicious! He also was given up, oblivious, concentrated, into the dance. His eye was unseeing. Only his large, voluptuous body gave off a subtle activity. His fingers seemed to search into her flesh. Every moment, and every moment, she felt she would give way utterly, and sink molten: the fusion point was coming when she would fuse down into perfect unconsciousness at his feet and knees. But he bore her round the room in the dance, and he seemed to sustain all her body with his limbs, his body, and his warmth seemed to come closer into her, nearer, till it would fuse right through her, and she would be as liquid to him, as an intoxication only.

It was exquisite. When it was over, she was dazed, and was scarcely breathing. She stood with him in the middle of the room as if she were alone in a remote place. He bent over her. She expected his lips on her bare shoulder, and waited. Yet they were not alone, they were not alone. It was cruel.

" 'Twas good, wasn't it, my darling?" he said to her, low and delighted. There was a strange impersonality about his low, exultant call that appealed to her irresistibly. Yet why was she aware of some part shut off in her? She pressed his arm, and he led her towards the door.

She was not aware of what she was doing, only a little grain of resistant trouble was in her. The man, possessed, yet with a superficial presence of mind, made way to the dining-room, as if to give her refreshment, cunningly working to his own escape with her. He was molten hot, filmed over with presence of mind, and bottomed with cold disbelief. In the dining-room was Whiston, carrying coffee to the plain, neglected ladies. Elsie saw him, but felt as if he could not see her. She was beyond his reach and ken. A sort of fusion existed between her and the large man at her side. She ate her custard, but an incomplete fusion all the while sustained and contained within the being of her employer.

But she was growing cooler. Whiston came up. She looked at him, and saw him with different eyes. She saw his slim, young man's figure real and enduring before her. That was he. But she was in the spell with the other man, fused with him, and she could not be taken away.

"Have you finished your cribbage?" she asked, with hasty evasion of him.

"Yes," he replied. "Aren't you getting tired of dancing?"

"Not a bit," she said.

"Not she," said Adams heartily. "No girl with any spirit gets tired of dancing. Have something else, Elsie. Come— sherry. Have a glass of sherry with us, Whiston."

Whilst they sipped the wine, Adams watched Whiston almost cunningly, to find his advantage.

"We'd better be getting back—there's the music," he said. "See the women get something to eat, Whiston, will you, there's a good chap."

And he began to draw away. Elsie was drifting helplessly with him. But Whiston put himself beside them, and went along with them. In silence they passed through to the dancing-room. There Adams hesitated, and looked round the room. It was as if he could not see.

A man came hurrying forward, claiming Elsie, and Adams went to his other partner. Whiston stood watching during the dance. She was conscious of him standing there observant of her, like a ghost, or a judgment or a guardian angel. She was also conscious, much more intimately and impersonally, of the body of the other man moving somewhere in the room. She still belonged to him, but a feeling of distraction possessed her, and helplessness. Adams danced on, adhering to Elsie, waiting his time, with the persistence of cynicism.

The dance was over. Adams was detained. Elsie found herself beside Whiston. There was something shapely about him as he sat, about his knees and his distinct figure, that she clung to. It was as if he had enduring form. She put her hand on his knee.

"Are you enjoying yourself?" he asked.

"*Ever* so," she replied, with a fervent, yet detached tone.

"It's going on for one o'clock," he said.

"Is it?" she answered. It meant nothing to her.

"Should we be going?" he said.

She was silent. For the first time for an hour or more an inkling of her normal consciousness returned. She resented it.

"What for?" she said.

"I thought you might have had enough," he said.

A slight soberness came over her, an irritation at being frustrated of her illusion.

"Why?" she said.

"We've been here since nine," he said.

That was no answer, no reason. It conveyed nothing to her. She sat detached from him. Across the room Sam Adams glanced at her. She sat there exposed for him.

"You don't want to be too free with Sam Adams," said Whiston cautiously, suffering. "You know what he is."

"How, free?" she asked.

"Why—you don't want to have too much to do with him."

She sat silent. He was forcing her into consciousness of her position. But he could not get hold of her feelings, to change them. She had a curious, perverse desire that he should not.

"I like him," she said.

"What do you find to like in him?" he said, with a hot heart.

"I don't know—but I like him," she said.

She was immutable. He sat feeling heavy and dulled with rage. He was not clear as to what he felt. He sat there unliving whilst she danced. And she, distracted, lost to herself between the opposing forces of the two men, drifted. Between the dances, Whiston kept near to her. She was scarcely conscious. She glanced repeatedly at her card, to see when she would dance again with Adams, half in desire, half in dread. Sometimes she met his steady, glaucous eye as she passed him in the dance. Sometimes she saw the steadiness of his flank as he danced. And it was always as if she rested on his arm, were borne along, upborne by him, away from herself. And always there was present the other's antagonism. She was divided.

The time came for her to dance with Adams. Oh, the delicious closing of contact with him, of his limbs touching her limbs, his arm supporting her. She seemed to resolve. Whiston had not made himself real to her. He was only a heavy place in her consciousness.

But she breathed heavily, beginning to suffer from the closeness of strain. She was nervous. Adams also was constrained. A tightness, a tension was coming over them all. And he was exasperated, feeling something counteracting physical magnetism, feeling a will stronger with her than his own, intervening in what was becoming a vital necessity to him.

Elsie was almost lost to her own control. As she went forward with him to take her place at the dance, she stooped for her pocket-handkerchief. The music sounded for quadrilles. Everybody was ready. Adams stood with his body near her, exerting his attraction over her. He was tense and fighting. She stooped for her pocket-handkerchief, and shook it as she rose. It shook out and fell from her hand. With agony, she saw she had taken a white stocking instead of a handkerchief. For a second it lay on the floor, a twist of white stocking. Then, in an instant, Adams picked it up, with a little, surprised laugh of triumph.

"That'll do for me," he whispered—seeming to take possession of her. And he stuffed the stocking in his trousers pocket, and quickly offered her his handkerchief.

The dance began. She felt weak and faint, as if her will were turned to water. A heavy sense of loss came over her. She could not help herself any more. But it was peace.

When the dance was over, Adams yielded her up. Whiston came to her.

"What was it as you dropped?" Whiston asked.

"I thought it was my handkerchief—I'd taken a stocking by mistake," she said, detached and muted.

"And he's got it?"

"Yes."

"What does he mean by that?"

She lifted her shoulders.

"Are you going to let him keep it?" he asked.

"I don't let him."

There was a long pause.

"Am I to go and have it out with him?" he asked, his face flushed, his blue eyes going hard with opposition.

"No," she said, pale.

"Why?"

"No—I don't want you to say anything about it."

He sat exasperated and nonplussed.

"You'll let him keep it then?" he asked.

She sat silent and made no form of answer.

"What do you mean by it?" he said, dark with fury. And he started up.

"No!" she cried. "Ted!" And she caught hold of him, sharply detaining him.

It made him black with rage.

"Why?" he said.

The something about her mouth was pitiful to him. He did not understand, but he felt she must have her reasons.

"Then I'm not stopping here," he said. "Are you coming with me?"

She rose mutely, and they went out of the room. Adams had not noticed.

In a few moments they were in the street.

"What the hell do you mean?" he said, in a black fury.

She went at his side, in silence, neutral.

"That great hog, an' all," he added.

Then they went a long time in silence through the frozen, deserted darkness of the town. She felt she could not go indoors. They were drawing near her house.

"I don't want to go home," she suddenly cried in distress and anguish. "I don't want to go home."

He looked at her.

"Why don't you?" he said.

"I don't want to go home," was all she could sob.

He heard somebody coming.

"Well, we can walk a bit farther," he said.

She was silent again. They passed out of the town into the fields. He held her by the arm—they could not speak.

"What's a-matter?" he asked at length, puzzled.

She began to cry again.

At last he took her in his arms, to soothe her. She sobbed by herself, almost unaware of him.

"Tell me what's a-matter, Elsie," he said. "Tell me what's a-matter—my dear—tell me, then——"

He kissed her wet face, and caressed her. She made no response. He was puzzled and tender and miserable.

At length she became quiet. Then he kissed her, and she put her arms round him, and clung to him very tight, as if for fear and anguish. He held her in his arms, wondering.

"Ted!" she whispered, frantic. "Ted!"

"What, my love?" he answered, becoming also afraid.

"Be good to me," she cried. "Don't be cruel to me."

"No, my pet," he said, amazed and grieved. "Why?"

"Oh, be good to me," she sobbed.

And he held her very safe, and his heart was white-hot with love for her. His mind was amazed. He could only hold her against his chest that was white-hot with love and belief in her. So she was restored at last.

III

She refused to go to her work at Adams's any more. Her father had to submit and she sent in her notice—she was not well. Sam Adams was ironical. But he had a curious patience. He did not fight.

In a few weeks, she and Whiston were married. She loved him with passion and worship, a fierce little abandon of love that moved him to the depths of his being, and gave him a permanent surety and sense of realness in himself. He did not trouble about himself any more: he felt he was fulfilled and now he had only the many things in the world to busy himself about. Whatever troubled him, at the bottom was surety. He had found himself in this love.

They spoke once or twice of the white stocking.

"Ah!" Whiston exclaimed. "What does it matter?"

He was impatient and angry, and could not bear to consider the matter. So it was left unresolved.

She was quite happy at first, carried away by her adoration of her husband. Then gradually she got used to him. He always was the ground of her happiness, but she got used to him, as to the air she breathed. He never got used to her in the same way.

Inside of marriage she found her liberty. She was rid of the responsibility of herself. Her husband must look after that. She was free to get what she could out of her time.

So that, when, after some months, she met Sam Adams, she was not quite as unkind to him as she might have been. With a young wife's new and exciting knowledge of men, she perceived he was in love with her, she knew he had always kept an unsatisfied desire for her. And, sportive, she could not help playing a little with this, though she cared not one jot for the man himself.

When Valentine's day came, which was near the first anniversary of her wedding day, there arrived a white stocking with a little amethyst brooch. Luckily Whiston did not see it, so she said nothing of it to him. She had not the faintest intention of having anything to do with Sam Adams, but once a little brooch was in her possession, it was hers, and she did not trouble her head for a moment how she had come by it. She kept it.

Now she had the pearl ear-rings. They were a more valuable and a more conspicuous present. She would have to ask her mother to give them to her, to explain their presence. She made a little plan in her head. And she was extraordinarily pleased. As for Sam Adams, even if he saw her wearing them, he would not give her away. What fun, if he saw her wearing his ear-rings! She would pretend she had inherited them from her grandmother, her mother's mother. She laughed to herself as she went downtown in the afternoon, the pretty drops dangling in front of her curls. But she saw no one of importance.

Whiston came home tired and depressed. All day the male in him had been uneasy, and this had fatigued him. She was curiously against him, inclined, as she sometimes was nowadays, to make mock of him and jeer at him and cut him off. He did not understand this, and it angered him deeply. She was uneasy before him.

She knew he was in a state of suppressed irritation. The veins stood out on the backs of his hands, his brow was drawn stiffly. Yet she could not help goading him.

"What did you do wi' that white stocking?" he asked, out of a gloomy silence, his voice strong and brutal.

"I put it in a drawer—why?" she replied flippantly.

"Why didn't you put it on the fire-back?" he said harshly. "What are you hoarding it up for?"

"I'm not hoarding it up," she said. "I've got a pair."

He relapsed into gloomy silence. She, unable to move him, ran away upstairs, leaving him smoking by the fire. Again she tried on the ear-rings. Then another little inspiration came to her. She drew on the white stockings both of them.

Presently she came down in them. Her husband still sat immovable and glowering by the fire.

"Look!" she said. "They'll do beautifully."

And she picked up her skirts to her knees, and twisted round, looking at her pretty legs in the neat stockings.

He filled with unreasonable rage, and took the pipe from his mouth.

"Don't they look nice?" she said. "One from last year and one from this, they just do. Save you buying a pair."

And she looked over her shoulders at her pretty calves, and at the dangling frills of her knickers.

"Put your skirts down and don't make a fool of yourself," he said.

"Why a fool of myself?" she asked.

And she began to dance slowly round the room, kicking up her feet half reckless, half jeering, in a ballet-dancer's fashion. Almost fearfully, yet in defiance, she kicked up her legs at him, singing as she did so. She resented him.

"You little fool, ha' done with it," he said. "And you'll back-fire them stockings, I'm telling you." He was angry. His face flushed dark, he kept his head bent. She ceased to dance.

"I shan't," she said. "They'll come in very useful."

He lifted his head and watched her, with lighted, dangerous eyes.

"You'll put 'em on the fire-back, I tell you," he said.

It was a war now. She bent forward, in a ballet-dancer's fashion, and put her tongue between her teeth.

"I shan't backfire them stockings," she sang, repeating his words, "I shan't, I shan't, I shan't."

And she danced round the room doing a high kick to the tune of her words. There was a real biting indifference in her behaviour.

"We'll see whether you will or not," he said, "trollops! You'd like Sam Adams to know you was wearing 'em, wouldn't you? That's what would please you."

"Yes, I'd like him to see how nicely they fit me, he might give me some more then."

And she looked down at her pretty legs.

He knew somehow that she *would* like Sam Adams to see how pretty her legs looked in the white stockings. It made his anger go deep, almost to hatred.

"Yer nasty trolley," he cried. "Put yer petticoats down, and stop being so foul-minded."

"I'm not foul-minded," she said. "My legs are my own. And why shouldn't Sam Adams think they're nice?"

There was a pause. He watched her with eyes glittering to a point.

"Have you been havin' owt to do with him?" he asked.

"I've just spoken to him when I've seen him," she said. "He's not as bad as you would make out."

"Isn't he?" he cried, a certain wakefulness in his voice. "Them who has anything to do wi' him is too bad for me, I tell you."

"Why, what are you frightened of him for?" she mocked.

She was rousing all his uncontrollable anger. He sat glowering. Every one of her sentences stirred him up like a red-hot iron. Soon it would be too much. And she was afraid herself; but she was neither conquered nor convinced.

A curious little grin of hate came on his face. He had a long score against her.

"What am I frightened of him for?" he repeated automatically. "What am I frightened of him for? Why, for you, you stray-running little bitch."

She flushed. The insult went deep into her, right home.

"Well, if you're so dull——" she said, lowering her eyelids, and speaking coldly, haughtily.

"If I'm so dull I'll break your neck the first word you speak to him," he said, tense.

"Pf!" she sneered. "Do you think I'm frightened of you?" She spoke coldly, detached.

She was frightened, for all that, white round the mouth.

His heart was getting hotter.

"You *will* be frightened of me, the next time you have anything to do with him," he said.

"Do you think *you'd* ever be told—ha!"

Her jeering scorn made him go white-hot, molten. He knew he was incoherent, scarcely responsible for what he might do. Slowly, unseeing, he rose and went out of doors, stifled, moved to kill her.

He stood leaning against the garden fence, unable either to see or hear. Below him, far off, fumed the lights of the town. He stood still, unconscious with a black storm of rage, his face lifted to the night.

Presently, still unconscious of what he was doing, he went indoors again. She stood, a small, stubborn figure with tight-pressed lips and big, sullen, childish eyes, watching him, white with fear. He went heavily across the floor and dropped into his chair.

There was a silence.

"*You're* not going to tell me everything I shall do, and everything I shan't," she broke out at last.

He lifted his head.

"I tell you *this*," he said, low and intense. "Have anything to do with Sam Adams, and I'll break your neck."

She laughed, shrill and false.

"How I hate your word 'break your neck,' " she said, with a grimace of the mouth. "It sounds so common and beastly. Can't you say something else——"

There was a dead silence.

"And besides," she said, with a queer chirrup of mocking laughter, "what do you know about anything? He sent me an amethyst brooch and a pair of pearl ear-rings."

"He what?" said Whiston, in a suddenly normal voice. His eyes were fixed on her.

"Sent me a pair of pearl ear-rings, and an amethyst brooch," she repeated, mechanically, pale to the lips.

And her big, black, childish eyes watched him, fascinated, held in her spell.

He seemed to thrust his face and his eyes forward at her, as he rose slowly and came to her. She watched transfixed in terror. Her throat made a small sound, as she tried to scream.

Then, quick as lightning, the back of his hand struck her with a crash across the mouth, and she was flung black blinded against the wall. The shock shook a queer sound out of her. And then she saw him still coming on, his eyes holding her his fist drawn back, advancing slowly. At any instant the blow might crash into her.

Mad with terror, she raised her hands with a queer clawing movement to cover her eyes and her temples, opening her mouth in a dumb shriek. There was no sound. But the sight of her slowly arrested him. He hung before her, looking at her fixedly, as she stood crouched against the wall with open, bleeding mouth, and wide-staring eyes, and two hands clawing over her temples. And his lust to see her bleed, to break her and destroy her, rose from an old source against her. It carried him. He wanted satisfaction.

But he had seen her standing there, a piteous, horrified thing, and he turned his face aside in shame and nausea. He went and sat heavily in his chair, and a curious ease, almost like sleep, came over his brain.

She walked away from the wall towards the fire, dizzy, white to the lips, mechanically wiping her small, bleeding mouth. He sat motionless. Then, gradually, her breath began to hiss, she shook, and was sobbing silently, in grief for herself. Without looking, he saw. It made his mad desire to destroy her come back.

At length he lifted his head. His eyes were glowing again, fixed on her.

"And what did he give them you for?" he asked, in a steady, unyielding voice.

Her crying dried up in a second. She also was tense.

"They came as valentines," she replied, still not subjugated, even if beaten.

"When, to-day?"

"The pearl ear-rings to-day—the amethyst brooch last year."

"You've had it a year?"

"Yes."

She felt that now nothing would prevent him if he rose to kill her. She could not prevent him any more. She was yielded up to him. They both trembled in the balance, unconscious.

"What have you had to do with him?" he asked, in a barren voice.

"I've not had anything to do with him," she quavered.

"You just kept 'em because they were jewellery?" he said.

A weariness came over him. What was the worth of speaking any more of it? He did not care any more. He was dreary and sick.

She began to cry again, but he took no notice. She kept wiping her mouth on her handkerchief. He could see it, the blood-mark. It made him only more sick and tired of the responsibility of it, the violence, the shame.

When she began to move about again, he raised his head once more from his dead, motionless position.

"Where are the things?" he said.

"They are upstairs," she quavered. She knew the passion had gone down in him.

"Bring them down," he said.

"I won't," she wept, with rage. "You're not going to bully me and hit me like that on the mouth."

And she sobbed again. He looked at her in contempt and compassion and in rising anger.

"Where are they?" he said.

"They're in the little drawer under the looking-glass," she sobbed.

He went slowly upstairs, struck a match, and found the trinkets. He brought them downstairs in his hand.

"These?" he said, looking at them as they lay in his palm.

She looked at them without answering. She was not interested in them any more.

He looked at the little jewels. They were pretty.

"It's none of their fault," he said to himself.

And he searched round slowly, persistently, for a box. He tied the things up and addressed them to Sam Adams. Then he went out in his slippers to post the little package.

When he came back she was still sitting crying.

"You'd better go to bed," he said.

She paid no attention. He sat by the fire. She still cried.

"I'm sleeping down here," he said. "Go you to bed."

In a few moments she lifted her tear-stained, swollen face and looked at him with eyes all forlorn and pathetic. A great flash of anguish went over his body. He went over, slowly, and very gently took her in his hands. She let herself be taken. Then as she lay against his shoulder, she sobbed aloud:

"I never meant——"

"My love—my little love——" he cried, in anguish of spirit, holding her in his arms.

SAMSON AND DELILAH

A MAN got down from the motor-omnibus that runs from Penzance to St. Just-in-Penwith, and turned northwards, uphill towards the Polestar. It was only half-past six, but already the stars were out, a cold little wind was blowing from the sea, and the crystalline, three-pulse flash of the lighthouse below the cliffs beat rhythmically in the first darkness.

The man was alone. He went his way unhesitating, but looked from side to side with cautious curiosity. Tall, ruined power-houses of tin-mines loomed in the darkness from time to time, like remnants of some by-gone civilization. The lights of many miners' cottages scattered on the hilly darkness twinkled desolate in their disorder, yet twinkled with the lonely home-liness of the Celtic night.

He tramped steadily on, always watchful with curiosity. He was a tall, well-built man, apparently in the prime of life. His shoulders were square and rather stiff, he leaned forwards a little as he went, from the hips, like a man who must stoop to lower his height. But he did not stoop his shoulders: he bent his straight back from the hips.

Now and again short, stump, thick-legged figures of Cornish miners passed him, and he invariably gave them good night, as if to insist that he was on his own ground. He spoke with the West Cornish intonation. And as he went along the dreary road, looking now at the lights of the dwellings on land, now at the lights away to sea, vessels veering round in sight of the Longships Lighthouse, the whole of the Atlantic Ocean in darkness and space between him and America, he seemed a little excited and pleased with himself, watchful, thrilled, veering along in a sense of mastery and of power in conflict.

The houses began to close on the road, he was entering the straggling, formless, desolate mining village, that he knew of old. On the left was a little space set back from the road, and

cosy lights of an inn. There it was. He peered up at the sign:
"The Tinners' Rest." But he could not make out the name of
the proprietor. He listened. There was excited talking and
laughing, a woman's voice laughing shrilly among the men's.

Stooping a little, he entered the warmly-lit bar. The lamp
was burning, a buxom woman rose from the white-scrubbed
deal table where the black and white and red cards were
scattered, and several men, miners, lifted their faces from the
game.

The stranger went to the counter, averting his face. His cap
was pulled down over his brow.

"Good evening!" said the landlady, in her rather ingratiating
voice.

"Good evening. A glass of ale."

"A glass of ale," repeated the landlady suavely. "Cold
night—but bright."

"Yes," the man assented, laconically. Then he added, when
nobody expected him to say any more: "Seasonable weather."

"Quite seasonable, quite," said the landlady. "Thank you."

The man lifted his glass straight to his lips, and emptied it.
He put it down again on the zinc counter with a click.

"Let's have another," he said.

The woman drew the beer, and the man went away with his
glass to the second table, near the fire. The woman, after a
moment's hesitation, took her seat again at the table with the
card-players. She had noticed the man: a big fine fellow, well
dressed, a stranger.

But he spoke with that Cornish-Yankee accent she accepted
as the natural twang among the miners.

The stranger put his foot on the fender and looked into the
fire. He was handsome, well coloured, with well-drawn Cornish
eyebrows, and the usual dark, bright, mindless Cornish eyes.
He seemed abstracted in thought. Then he watched the card-
party.

The woman was buxom and healthy, with dark hair and
small, quick brown eyes. She was bursting with life and
vigour, the energy she threw into the game of cards excited all

the men, they shouted, and laughed, and the woman held her breast, shrieking with laughter.

"Oh, my, it'll be the death o' me," she panted. "Now, come on, Mr. Trevorrow, play fair. Play fair, I say, or I s'll put the cards down."

"Play fair! Why, who's played unfair?" ejaculated Mr. Trevorrow. "Do you mean t'accuse me, as I haven't played fair, Mrs. Nankervis?"

"I do. I say it, and I mean it. Haven't you got the Queen of Spades? Now, come on, no dodging round me. *I* know you've got that Queen, as well as I know my name's Alice."

"Well—if your name's Alice, you'll have to have it——"

"Ay, now—what did I say? Did ever you see such a man? My word, but your missus must be easy took in, by the looks of things."

And off she went into peals of laughter. She was interrupted by the entrance of four men in khaki, a short, stumpy sergeant of middle age, a young corporal, and two young privates. The woman leaned back in her chair.

"Oh, my!" she cried. "If there isn't the boys back: looking perished, I believe——"

"Perished, Ma!" exclaimed the sergeant. "Not yet."

"Near enough," said a young private, uncouthly.

The woman got up.

"I'm sure you are, my dears. You'll be wanting your suppers, I'll be bound."

"We could do with 'em."

"Let's have a wet first," said the sergeant.

The woman bustled about getting the drinks. The soldiers moved to the fire, spreading out their hands.

"Have your suppers in here, will you?" she said. "Or in the kitchen?"

"Let's have it here," said the sergeant. "More cosier—*if* you don't mind."

"You shall have it where you like, boys, where you like."

She disappeared. In a minute a girl of about sixteen came in. She was tall and fresh, with dark, young, expressionless eyes, and well-drawn brows, and the immature softness and mindlessness of the sensuous Celtic type.

"Ho, Maryann! Evenin', Maryann! How's Maryann, now?" came the multiple greeting.

She replied to everybody in a soft voice, a strange, soft aplomb that was very attractive. And she moved round with rather mechanical, attractive movements, as if her thoughts were elsewhere. But she had always this dim far-awayness in her bearing: a sort of modesty. The strange man by the fire watched her curiously. There was an alert, inquisitive, mindless curiosity on his well-coloured face.

"I'll have a bit of supper with you, if I might," he said.

She looked at him, with her clear, unreasoning eyes, just like the eyes of some non-human creature.

"I'll ask mother," she said. Her voice was soft-breathing, gently singsong.

When she came in again:

"Yes," she said, almost whispering. "What will you have?"

"What have you got?" he said, looking up into her face.

"There's cold meat——"

"That's for me, then."

The stranger sat at the end of the table, and ate with the tired, quiet soldiers. Now, the landlady was interested in him. Her brow was knit rather tense, there was a look of panic in her large, healthy face, but her small brown eyes were fixed most dangerously. She was a big woman, but her eyes were small and tense. She drew near the stranger. She wore a rather loud-patterned flannelette blouse, and a dark skirt.

"What will you have to drink with your supper?" she asked, and there was a new, dangerous note in her voice.

He moved uneasily.

"Oh, I'll go on with ale."

She drew him another glass. Then she sat down on the bench at the table with him and the soldiers, and fixed him with her attention.

"You've come from St. Just, have you?" she said.

He looked at her with those clear, dark, inscrutable Cornish eyes, and answered at length:

"No, from Penzance."

"Penzance!—but you're not thinking of going back there to-night?"

"No—no."

He still looked at her with those wide, clear eyes that seemed like very bright agate. Her anger began to rise. It was seen on her brow. Yet her voice was still suave and deprecating.

"I *thought* not—but you're not living in these parts, are you?"

"No—no, I'm not living here." He was always slow in answering, as if something intervened between him and any outside question.

"Oh, I see," she said. "You've got relations down here."

Again he looked straight into her eyes, as if looking her into silence.

"Yes," he said.

He did not say any more. She rose with a flounce. The anger was tight on her brow. There was no more laughing and card-playing that evening, though she kept up her motherly, suave, good-humoured way with the men. But they knew her, they were all afraid of her.

The supper was finished, the table cleared, the stranger did not go. Two of the young soldiers went off to bed, with their cheery:

"Good night, Ma. Good night, Maryann."

The stranger talked a little to the sergeant about the war, which was in its first year, about the new army, a fragment of which was quartered in this district, about America.

The landlady darted looks at him from her small eyes, minute by minute the electric storm welled in her bosom, as still he did not go. She was quivering with suppressed, violent passion, something frightening and abnormal. She could not sit still for a moment. Her heavy form seemed to flash with sudden, involuntary movements as the minutes passed by, and still he sat there, and the tension on her heart grew unbearable. She watched the hands of the clock move on. Three of the soldiers had gone to bed, only the crop-headed, terrier-like old sergeant remained.

The landlady sat behind the bar fidgeting spasmodically with the newspaper. She looked again at the clock. At last it was five minutes to ten.

"Gentlemen—the enemy!" she said, in her diminished, furious voice. "Time, please. Time, my dears. And good night all!"

The men began to drop out, with a brief good night. It was a minute to ten. The landlady rose.

"Come," she said. "I'm shutting the door."

The last of the miners passed out. She stood, stout and menacing, holding the door. Still the stranger sat on by the fire, his black overcoat opened, smoking.

"We're closed now, sir," came the perilous, narrowed voice of the landlady.

The little, dog-like, hard-headed sergeant touched the arm of the stranger.

"Closing time," he said.

The stranger turned round in his seat, and his quick-moving, dark, jewel-like eyes went from the sergeant to the landlady.

"I'm stopping here to-night," he said, in his laconic Cornish-Yankee accent.

The landlady seemed to tower. Her eyes lifted strangely, frightening.

"Oh, indeed!" she cried. "Oh, indeed! And whose orders are those, may I ask?"

He looked at her again.

"My orders," he said.

Involuntarily she shut the door, and advanced like a great, dangerous bird. Her voice rose, there was a touch of hoarseness in it.

"And what might *your* orders be, if you please?" she cried. "Who might *you* be, to give orders, in the house?"

He sat still, watching her.

"You know who I am," he said. "At least, I know who you are."

"Oh, do you? Oh, do you? And who am *I* then, if you'll be so good as to tell me?"

He stared at her with his bright, dark eyes.

"You're my Missis, you are," he said. "And you know it, as well as I do."

She started as if something had exploded in her.

Her eyes lifted and flared madly.

"*Do* I know it, indeed!" she cried. "I know no such thing! I know no such thing! Do you think a man's going to walk into this bar, and tell me off-hand I'm his Missis, and I'm going to believe him? I say to you, whoever you may be, you're mistaken. I know myself for no Missis of yours, and I'll thank you to go out of this house, this minute, before I get those that will put you out."

The man rose to his feet, stretching his head towards her a little. He was a handsomely built Cornishman in the prime of life.

"What you say, eh? You don't know me?" he said, in his sing-song voice, emotionless, but rather smothered and pressing: it reminded one of the girl's. "I should know you anywhere, you see. I should! I shouldn't have to look twice to know you, you see. You see, now, don't you?"

The wonan was baffled.

"So you may say," she replied, staccato. "So you may say. That's easy enough. My name's known, and respected, by most people for ten miles around. But I don't know *you*."

Her voice ran to sarcasm. "I can't say I know *you*. You're a *perfect* stranger to me, and I don't believe I've ever set eyes on you before to-night."

Her voice was very flexible and sarcastic.

"Yes, you have," replied the man, in his reasonable way. "Yes, you have. Your name's my name, and that girl Maryann is my girl; she's my daughter. You're my Missis right enough. As sure as I'm Willie Nankervis.

He spoke as if it were an accepted fact. His face was

handsome, with a strange, watchful alertness and a fundamental fixity of intention that maddened her.

"You villain!" she cried. "You villain, to come to this house and dare to speak to me. You villain, you downright rascal!"

He looked at her.

"Ay," he said, unmoved. "All that." He was uneasy before her. Only he was not afraid of her. There was something impenetrable about him, like his eyes, which were as bright as agate.

She towered, and drew near to him menacingly.

"You're going out of this house, aren't you?" She stamped her foot in sudden madness. "*This minute!*"

He watched her. He knew she wanted to strike him.

"No," he said, with suppressed emphasis. "I've told you, I'm stopping here."

He was afraid of her personality, but it did not alter him. She wavered. Her small, tawny-brown eyes concentrated in a point of vivid, sightless fury, like a tiger's. The man was wincing, but he stood his ground. Then she bethought herself. She would gather her forces.

"We'll see whether you're stopping here," she said. And she turned, with a curious, frightening lifting of her eyes, and surged out of the room. The man, listening, heard her go upstairs, heard her tapping at a bedroom door, heard her saying: "Do you mind coming down a minute, boys? I want you. I'm in trouble."

The man in the bar took off his cap and his black overcoat, and threw them on the seat behind him. His black hair was short and touched with grey at the temples. He wore a well-cut, well-fitting suit of dark grey, American in style, and a turn-down collar. He looked well-to-do, a fine, solid figure of a man. The rather rigid look of the shoulders came from his having had his collar-bone twice broken in the mines.

The little terrier of a sergeant, in dirty khaki, looked at him furtively.

"She's your Missis?" he asked, jerking his head in the direction of the departed woman.

"Yes, she is," barked the man. "She's that, sure enough."

"Not seen her for a long time, haven't ye?"

"Sixteen years come March month."

"Hm!"

And the sergeant laconically resumed his smoking.

The landlady was coming back, followed by the three young soldiers, who entered rather sheepishly, in trousers and shirt and stocking-feet. The woman stood histrionically at the end of the bar, and exclaimed:

"That man refuses to leave the house, claims he's stopping the night here. You know very well I have no bed, don't you? And this house doesn't accommodate travellers. Yet he's going to stop in spite of all! But not while I've a drop of blood in my body, that I declare with my dying breath. And not if you men are worth the name of men, and will help a woman as has no one to help her."

Her eyes sparkled, her face was flushed pink. She was drawn up like an Amazon.

The young soldiers did not quite know what to do. They looked at the man, they looked at the sergeant, one of them looked down and fastened his braces on the second button.

"What say, sergeant?" asked one whose face twinkled for a little devilment.

"Man says he's husband to Mrs. Nankervis," said the sergeant.

"He's no husband of mine. I declare I never set eyes on him before this night. It's a dirty trick, nothing else, it's a dirty trick."

"Why, you're a liar, saying you never set eyes on me before," barked the man near the hearth. "You're married to me, and that girl Maryann you had by me—well enough you know it."

The young soldier looked on in delight, the sergeant smoked imperturbed.

"Yes," sang the landlady, slowly shaking her head in supreme sarcasm, "it sounds very pretty, doesn't it? But you see we don't believe a word of it, and *how* are you going to prove it?" She smiled nastily.

The man watched in silence for a moment, then he said: "It wants no proof."

"Oh, yes, but it does! Oh, yes, but it does, sir, it wants a lot of proving!" sang the lady's sarcasm. "We're not such gulls as all that, to swallow your words whole."

But he stood unmoved near the fire. She stood with one hand resting on the zinc-covered bar, the sergeant sat with legs crossed, smoking, on the seat half-way between them, the three young soldiers in their shirts and braces stood wavering in the gloom behind the bar. There was silence.

"Do you know anything of the whereabouts of your husband, Mrs. Nankervis? Is he still living?" asked the sergeant, in his judicious fashion.

Suddenly the landlady began to cry, great scalding tears, that left the young men aghast.

"I know nothing of him," she sobbed, feeling for her pocket handkerchief. "He left me when Maryann was a baby, went mining to America, and after about six months never wrote a line nor sent me a penny bit. I can't say whether he's alive or dead, the villain. All I've heard of him's to the bad—and I've heard nothing for years an' all, now." She sobbed violently.

The black-haired, handsome man near the fire watched her as she wept. He was frightened, he was troubled, he was bewildered, but none of his emotions altered him underneath.

There was no sound in the room but the violent sobbing of the landlady. The men, one and all, were overcome.

"Don't you think as you'd better go, for to-night?" said the sergeant to the man, with sweet reasonableness. "You'd better leave it a bit, and arrange something between you. You can't have much claim on a woman, I should imagine, if it's how she says. And you've come down on her a bit too sudden-like."

The landlady sobbed heart-brokenly. The man watched her large breasts shaken. They seemed to cast a spell over his mind.

"How I've treated her, that's no matter," he replied. "I've come back, and I'm going to stop in my own home—for a bit, anyhow. There you've got it."

"A dirty action," said the sergeant, his face flushing dark. "A dirty action, to come, after deserting a woman for that number of years, and want to force yourself on her! A dirty action—as isn't allowed by the law."

The landlady wiped her eyes.

"Never you mind about law nor nothing," cried the man, in a strange, strong voice. "I'm not moving out of this public to-night."

The woman turned to the soldiers behind her, and said in a wheedling, sarcastic tone:

"Are we going to stand it, boys? Are we going to be done like this, Sergeant Thomas, by a scoundrel and a bully as has led a life beyond *mention* in those American mining-camps, and then wants to come back and make havoc of a poor woman's life and savings, after having left her with a baby in arms to struggle as best she might? It's a crying shame if nobody will stand up for me—a crying shame——!"

The soldiers and the little sergeant were bristling. The woman stooped and rummaged under the counter for a minute. Then, unseen to the man away near the fire, she threw out a plaited grass rope, such as is used for binding bales, and left it lying near the feet of the young soldiers, in the gloom at the back of the bar.

Then she rose and fronted the situation.

"Come now," she said to the man, in a reasonable, coldly-coaxing tone, "put your coat on and leave us alone. Be a man, and not worse than a brute of a German. You can get a bed easy enough in St. Just, and if you've nothing to pay for it sergeant would lend you a couple of shillings, I'm sure he would."

All eyes were fixed on the man. He was looking down at the woman like a creature spell-bound or possessed by some devil's own intention.

"I've got money of my own," he said. "Don't you be frightened for your money, I've plenty of that, for the time."

"Well, then," she coaxed, in a cold, almost sneering

propitiation, "put your coat on and go where you're wanted—
be a *man*, not a brute of a German."

She had drawn quite near to him, in her challenging coaxing
intentness. He looked down at her with his bewitched face.

"No, I shan't," he said. "I shan't do no such thing. *You'll*
put me up for to-night."

"Shall I?" she cried. And suddenly she flung her arms round
him, hung on to him with all her powerful weight, calling to
the soldiers: "Get the rope, boys, and fasten him up. Alfred—
John, quick now——"

The man reared, looked round with maddened eyes, and
heaved his powerful body. But the woman was powerful also,
and very heavy, and was clenched with the determination of
death. Her face, with its exulting, horribly vindictive look,
was turned up to him from his own breast; he reached back his
head frantically, to get away from it. Meanwhile the young
soldiers, after having watched this frightful Laocoon swaying
for a moment, stirred, and the malicious one darted swiftly
with the rope. It was tangled a little.

"Give me the end here," cried the sergeant.

Meanwhile the big man heaved and struggled, swung the
woman round against the seat and the table, in his convulsive
effort to get free. But she pinned down his arms like a cuttle-
fish wreathed heavily upon him. And he heaved and swayed,
and they crashed about the room, the soldiers hopping, the
furniture bumping.

The young soldier had got the rope once round, the brisk
sergeant helping him. The woman sank heavily lower, they
got the rope round several times. In the struggle the victim
fell over against the table. The ropes tightened till they cut
his arms. The woman clung to his knees. Another soldier ran
in a flash of genius, and fastened the strange man's feet with
the pair of braces. Seats had crashed over, the table was
thrown against the wall, but the man was bound, his arms
pinned against his sides, his feet tied. He lay half-fallen, sunk
against the table, still for a moment.

The woman rose, and sank, faint, on to the seat against the

wall. Her breast heaved, she could not speak, she thought she
was going to die. The bound man lay against the overturned
table, his coat all twisted and pulled up beneath the ropes,
leaving the loins exposed. The soldiers stood around, a little
dazed, but excited with the row.

The man began to struggle again, heaving instinctively
against the ropes, taking great, deep breaths. His face, with
its golden skin, flushed dark and surcharged, he heaved again.
The great veins in his neck stood out. But it was no good,
he went relaxed. Then again, suddenly, he jerked his
feet.

"Another pair of braces, William," cried the excited soldier.
He threw himself on the legs of the bound man, and managed
to fasten the knees. Then again there was stillness. They
could hear the clock tick.

The woman looked at the prostrate figure, the strong,
straight limbs, the strong back bound in subjection, the wide-
eyed face that reminded her of a calf tied in a sack in a cart,
only its head stretched dumbly backwards. And she
triumphed.

The bound-up body began to struggle again. She watched
fascinated the muscles working, the shoulders, the hips, the
large, clean thighs. Even now he might break the ropes. She
was afraid. But the lively young soldier sat on the shoulders
of the bound man, and after a few perilous moments, there was
stillness again.

"Now," said the judicious sergeant to the bound man, "if
we untie you, will you promise to go off and make no more
trouble?"

"You'll not untie him in here," cried the woman. "I
wouldn't trust him as far as I could blow him."

There was silence.

"We might carry him outside, and undo him there," said
the soldier. "Then we could get the policeman, if he made
any more bother."

"Yes," said the sergeant. "We could do that." Then again,
in an altered, almost severe tone, to the prisoner: "If we undo

you outside, will you take your coat and go without creating any more disturbance?"

But the prisoner would not answer, he only lay with wide, dark, bright eyes, like a bound animal. There was a space of perplexed silence.

"Well, then, do as you say," said the woman irritably. "Carry him out amongst you, and let us shut up the house."

They did so. Picking up the bound man, the four soldiers staggered clumsily into the silent square in front of the inn, the woman following with the cap and the overcoat. The young soldiers quickly unfastened the braces from the prisoner's legs, and they hopped indoors. They were in their stocking-feet, and outside the stars flashed cold. They stood in the doorway watching. The man lay quite still on the cold ground.

"Now," said the sergeant, in a subdued voice, "I'll loosen the knot, and he can work himself free, if you go in, Missis."

She gave a last look at the dishevelled, bound man, as he sat on the ground. Then she went indoors, followed quickly by the sergeant. Then they were heard locking and barring the door.

The man seated on the ground outside worked and strained at the rope. But it was not so easy to undo himself even now. So, with hands bound, making an effort, he got to his feet, and went and worked the cord against the rough edge of an old wall. The rope, being of a kind of plaited grass, soon frayed and broke, and he freed himself. He had various contusions. His arms were hurt and bruised from the bonds. He rubbed them slowly. Then he pulled his clothes straight, stooped, put on his cap, struggled into his overcoat, and walked away.

The stars were very brilliant. Clear as crystal, the beam from the lighthouse under the cliffs struck rhythmically on the night. Dazed, the man walked along the road past the church-yard. Then he stood leaning up against a wall, for a long time.

He was roused because his feet were so cold. So he pulled himself together, and turned again in the silent night, back towards the inn.

The bar was in darkness. But there was a light in the kitchen. He hesitated. Then very quietly he tried the door.

He was surprised to find it open. He entered, and quietly closed it behind him. Then he went down the step past the bar-counter, and through to the lighted doorway of the kitchen. There sat his wife, planted in front of the range, where a furze fire was burning. She sat in a chair full in front of the range, her knees wide apart on the fender. She looked over her shoulder at him as he entered, but she did not speak. Then she stared in the fire again.

It was a small, narrow kitchen. He dropped his cap on the table that was covered with yellowish American cloth, and took a seat with his back to the wall, near the oven. His wife still sat with her knees apart, her feet on the steel fender and stared into the fire, motionless. Her skin was smooth and rosy in the firelight. Everything in the house was very clean and bright. The man sat silent, too, his head dropped. And thus they remained.

It was a question who would speak first. The woman leaned forward and poked the ends of the sticks in between the bars of the range. He lifted his head and looked at her.

"Others gone to bed, have they?" he asked.

But she remained closed in silence.

" 'S a cold night, out," he said, as if to himself.

And he laid his large, yet well-shapen workman's hand on the top of the stove, that was polished black and smooth as velvet. She would not look at him, yet she glanced out of the corners of her eyes.

His eyes were fixed brightly on her, the pupils large and electric like those of a cat.

"I should have picked you out among thousands," he said. "Though you're bigger than I'd have believed. Fine flesh you've made."

She was silent for some time. Then she turned in her chair upon him.

"What do you think of yourself," she said, "coming back on me like this after over fifteen year? You don't think

I've not heard of you, neither, in Butte City and elsewhere?"

He was watching her with his clear, translucent unchallenged eyes.

"Yes," he said. "Chaps comes an' goes—I've heard tell of you from time to time.

She drew herself up.

"And what lies have you heard about *me?*" she demanded superbly.

"I dunno as I've heard any lies at all—'cept as you was getting on very well, like."

His voice ran warily and detached. Her anger stirred again in her violently. But she subdued it, because of the danger there was in him, and more, perhaps, because of the beauty of his head and his level drawn brows, which she could not bear to forfeit.

"That's more than I can say of *you,*" she said. "I've heard more harm than good about *you.*"

"Ay, I dessay," he said, looking in the fire. It was a long time since he had seen the furze burning, he said to himself. There was a silence, during which she watched his face.

"Do you call yourself a *man?*" she said, more in contemptuous reproach than in anger. "Leave a woman as you've left me, you don't care to what!—and then to turn up in *this* fashion, without a word to say for yourself."

He stirred in his chair, planted his feet apart, and resting his arms on his knees, looked steadily into the fire, without answering. So near to her was his head, and the close black hair, she could scarcely refrain from starting away, as if it would bite her.

"Do you call that the action of a *man?*" she repeated.

"No," he said, reaching and poking the bits of wood into the fire with his fingers. "I didn't call it anything, as I know of. It's no good calling things by any names whatsoever, as I know of."

She watched him in his actions. There was a longer and longer pause between each speech, though neither knew it.

"I *wonder* what you think of yourself!" she exclaimed, with vexed emphasis. "I *wonder* what sort of a fellow you take yourself to be!" She was really perplexed as well as angry.

"Well," he said, lifting his head to look at her, "I guess I'll answer for my own faults, if everybody else'll answer for theirs."

Her heart beat fiery hot as he lifted his face to her. She breathed heavily, averting her face, almost losing her self-control.

"And what do you take *me* to be?" she cried, in real helplessness.

His face was lifted watching her, watching her soft, averted face, and the softly heaving mass of her breasts.

"I take you," he said, with that laconic truthfulness which exercised such power over her, "to be the deuce of a fine woman —darn me if you're not as fine a built woman as I've seen, handsome with it as well. I shouldn't have expected you to put on such handsome flesh: 'struth I shouldn't."

Her heart beat fiery hot, as he watched her with those bright agate eyes, fixedly.

"Been very handsome to *you*, for fifteen years, my sakes!" she replied.

He made no answer to this, but sat with his bright, quick eyes upon her.

Then he rose. She started involuntarily. But he only said, in his laconic, measured way:

"It's warm in here now."

And he pulled off his overcoat, throwing it on the table. She sat as if slightly cowed, whilst he did so.

"Them ropes has given my arms something, by Ga-ard," he drawled, feeling his arms with his hands.

Still she sat in her chair before him, slightly cowed.

"You was sharp, wasn't you, to catch me like that, eh?" he smiled slowly. "By Ga-ard, you had me fixed proper, proper you had. Darn me, you fixed me up proper—proper, you did."

He leaned forwards in his chair towards her.

"I don't think no worse of you for it, no, darned if I do. Fine pluck in a woman's what I admire. That I do, indeed."

She only gazed into the fire.

"We fet from the start, we did. And, my word, you begin again quick the minute you see me, you did. Darn me, you was too sharp for me. A darn fine woman, puts up a darn good fight. Darn me if I could find a woman in all the darn States as could get me down like that. Wonderful fine woman you be, truth to say, at this minute."

She only sat glowering into the fire.

"As grand a pluck as a man could wish to find in a woman, true as I'm here," he said, reaching forward his hand and tentatively touching her between her full, warm breasts, quietly.

She started, and seemed to shudder. But his hand insinuated itself between her breasts, as she continued to gaze in the fire.

"And don't you think I've come back here a-begging," he said. "I've more than *one* thousand pounds to my name, I have. And a bit of a fight for a how-de-do pleases me, that it do. But that doesn't mean as you're going to deny as you're my Missis . . ."

THE HORSE DEALER'S DAUGHTER

"WELL, Mabel, and what are you going to do with yourself?" asked Joe, with foolish flippancy. He felt quite safe himself. Without listening for an answer, he turned aside, worked a grain of tobacco to the tip of his tongue, and spat it out. He did not care about anything, since he felt safe himself.

The three brothers and the sister sat round the desolate breakfast table, attempting some sort of desultory consultation. The morning's post had given the final tap to the family fortunes, and all was over. The dreary dining-room itself, with its heavy mahogany furniture, looked as if it were waiting to be done away with.

But the consultation amounted to nothing. There was a strange air of ineffectuality about the three men, as they sprawled at table, smoking and reflecting vaguely on their own condition. The girl was alone, a rather short, sullen-looking young woman of twenty-seven. She did not share the same life as her brothers. She would have been good-looking, save for the impassive fixity of her face, "bull-dog," as her brothers called it.

There was a confused tramping of horses' feet outside. The three men all sprawled round in their chairs to watch. Beyond the dark holly-bushes that separated the strip of lawn from the highroad, they could see a cavalcade of shire horses swinging out of their own yard, being taken for exercise. This was the last time. These were the last horses that would go through their hands. The young men watched with critical, callous look. They were all frightened at the collapse of their lives, and the sense of disaster in which they were involved left them no inner freedom.

Yet they were three fine, well-set fellows enough. Joe, the eldest, was a man of thirty-three, broad and handsome in a hot, flushed way. His face was red, he twisted his black

moustache over a thick finger, his eyes were shallow and
restless. He had a sensual way of uncovering his teeth when
he laughed, and his bearing was stupid. Now he watched the
horses with a glazed look of helplessness in his eyes, a certain
stupor of downfall.

The great draught-horses swung past. They were tied head
to tail, four of them, and they heaved along to where a lane
branched off from the highroad, planting their great hoofs
floutingly in the fine black mud, swinging their great rounded
haunches sumptuously, and trotting a few sudden steps as they
were led into the lane, round the corner. Every movement
showed a massive, slumbrous strength, and a stupidity which
held them in subjection. The groom at the head looked back,
jerking the leading rope. And the cavalcade moved out of
sight up the lane, the tail of the last horse, bobbed up tight
and stiff, held out taut from the swinging great haunches as
they rocked behind the hedges in a motion-like sleep.

Joe watched with glazed hopeless eyes. The horses were
almost like his own body to him. He felt he was done for now.
Luckily he was engaged to a woman as old as himself, and
therefore her father, who was steward of a neighbouring
estate, would provide him with a job. He would marry and
go into harness. His life was over, he would be a subject
animal now.

He turned uneasily aside, the retreating steps of the horses
echoing in his ears. Then, with foolish restlessness, he reached
for the scraps of bacon-rind from the plates, and making a
faint whistling sound, flung them to the terrier that lay against
the fender. He watched the dog swallow them, and waited till
the creature looked into his eyes. Then a faint grin came on
his face, and in a high, foolish voice he said:

"You won't get much more bacon, shall you, you little
b——?"

The dog faintly and dismally wagged its tail, then lowered
its haunches, circled round, and lay down again.

There was another helpless silence at the table. Joe sprawled
uneasily in his seat, not willing to go till the family conclave was

dissolved. Fred Henry, the second brother, was erect, clean-limbed, alert. He had watched the passing of the horses with more sang-froid. If he was an animal, like Joe, he was an animal which controls, not one which is controlled. He was master of any horse, and he carried himself with a well-tempered air of mastery. But he was not master of the situations of life. He pushed his coarse brown moustache upwards, off his lip, and glanced irritably at his sister, who sat impassive and inscrutable.

"You'll go and stop with Lucy for a bit, shan't you?" he asked. The girl did not answer.

"I don't see what else you can do," persisted Fred Henry.

"Go as a skivvy," Joe interpolated laconically.

The girl did not move a muscle.

"If I was her, I should go in for training for a nurse," said Malcolm, the youngest of them all. He was the baby of the family, a young man of twenty-two, with a fresh, jaunty *museau*.

But Mabel did not take any notice of him. They had talked at her and round her for so many years, that she hardly heard them at all.

The marble clock on the mantelpiece softly chimed the half-hour, the dog rose uneasily from the hearthrug and looked at the party at the breakfast table. But still they sat on in ineffectual conclave.

"Oh, all right," said Joe suddenly, apropos of nothing. "I'll get a move on."

He pushed back his chair, straddled his knees with a downward jerk, to get them free, in horsey fashion, and went to the fire. Still he did not go out of the room; he was curious to know what the others would do or say. He began to charge his pipe, looking down at the dog and saying, in a high, affected voice:

"Going wi' me? Going wi' me are ter? Tha'rt goin' further than tha counts on just now, dost hear?"

The dog faintly wagged its tail, the man stuck out his jaw and covered his pipe with his hands, and puffed intently, losing

himself in the tobacco, looking down all the while at the dog
with an absent brown eye. The dog looked up at him in
mournful distrust. Joe stood with his knees stuck out, in real
horsey fashion.

"Have you had a letter from Lucy?" Fred Henry asked of
his sister.

"Last week," came the neutral reply.

"And what does she say?"

There was no answer.

"Does she *ask* you to go and stop there?" persisted Fred
Henry.

"She says I can if I like."

"Well, then, you'd better. Tell her you'll come on Monday."

This was received in silence.

"That's what you'll do then, is it?" said Fred Henry, in
some exasperation.

But she made no answer. There was a silence of futility and
irritation in the room. Malcolm grinned fatuously.

"You'll have to make up your mind between now and next
Wednesday," said Joe loudly, "or else find yourself lodgings
on the kerbstone."

The face of the young woman darkened, but she sat on
immutable.

"Here's Jack Fergusson!" exclaimed Malcolm, who was
looking aimlessly out of the window.

"Where?" exclaimed Joe, loudly.

"Just gone past."

"Coming in?"

Malcolm craned his neck to see the gate.

"Yes," he said.

There was a silence. Mabel sat on like one condemned, at
the head of the table. Then a whistle was heard from the
kitchen. The dog got up and barked sharply. Joe opened the
door and shouted:

"Come on."

After a moment a young man entered. He was muffled up
in overcoat and a purple woollen scarf, and his tweed cap,

which he did not remove, was pulled down on his head. He was of medium height, his face was rather long and pale, his eyes looked tired.

"Hello, Jack! Well, Jack!" exclaimed Malcolm and Joe. Fred Henry merely said, "Jack."

"What's doing?" asked the newcomer, evidently addressing Fred Henry.

"Same. We've got to be out by Wednesday. Got a cold?"

"I have—got it bad, too."

"Why don't you stop in?"

"*Me* stop in? When I can't stand on my legs, perhaps I shall have a chance." The young man spoke huskily. He had a slight Scotch accent.

"It's a knock-out, isn't it," said Joe, boisterously, "if a doctor goes round croaking with a cold. Looks bad for the patients, doesn't it?"

The young doctor looked at him slowly.

"Anything the matter with *you*, then?" he asked sarcastically.

"Not as I know of. Damn your eyes, I hope not. Why?"

"I thought you were very concerned about the patients, wondered if you might be one yourself."

"Damn it, no, I've never been patient to no flaming doctor, and hope I never shall be," returned Joe.

At this point Mabel rose from the table, and they all seemed to become aware of her existence. She began putting the dishes together. The young doctor looked at her, but did not address her. He had not greeted her. She went out of the room with the tray, her face impassive and unchanged.

"When are you off then, all of you?" asked the doctor.

"I'm catching the eleven-forty," replied Malcolm. "Are you goin' down wi' th' trap, Joe?"

"Yes, I've told you I'm going down wi' th' trap, haven't I?"

"We'd better be getting her in then. So long, Jack, if I don't see you before I go," said Malcolm, shaking hands.

He went out, followed by Joe, who seemed to have his tail between his legs.

"Well, this is the devil's own," exclaimed the doctor, when he was left alone with Fred Henry. "Going before Wednesday, are you?"

"That's the orders," replied the other.

"Where, to Northampton?"

"That's it."

"The devil!" exclaimed Fergusson, with quiet chagrin.

And there was silence between the two.

"All settled up, are you?" asked Fergusson.

"About."

There was another pause.

"Well, I shall miss yer, Freddy, boy," said the young doctor.

"And I shall miss thee, Jack," returned the other.

"Miss you like hell," mused the doctor.

Fred Henry turned aside. There was nothing to say. Mabel came in again, to finish clearing the table.

"What are *you* going to do, then, Miss Pervin?" asked Fergusson. "Going to your sister's, are you?"

Mabel looked at him with her steady, dangerous eyes, that always made him uncomfortable, unsettling his superficial ease.

"No," she said.

"Well, what in the name of fortune *are* you going to do? Say what you mean to do," cried Fred Henry, with futile intensity.

But she only averted her head, and continued her work. She folded the white table-cloth, and put on the chenille cloth.

"The sulkiest bitch that ever trod!" muttered her brother.

But she finished her task with perfectly impassive face, the young doctor watching her interestedly all the while. Then she went out.

Fred Henry stared after her, clenching his lips, his blue eyes fixing in sharp antagonism, as he made a grimace of sour exasperation.

"You could bray her into bits, and that's all you'd get out of her," he said, in a small, narrowed tone.

The doctor smiled faintly.

"What's she *going* to do, then?" he asked.

"Strike me if *I* know!" returned the other.

There was a pause. Then the doctor stirred.

"I'll be seeing you to-night, shall I?" he said to his friend.

"Ay—where's it to be? Are we going over to Jessdale?"

"I don't know. I've got such a cold on me. I'll come round to the Moon and Stars, anyway."

"Let Lizzie and May miss their night for once, eh?"

"That's it—if I feel as I do now."

"All's one——"

The two young men went through the passage and down to the back door together. The house was large, but it was servantless now, and desolate. At the back was a small bricked house-yard, and beyond that a big square, gravelled fine and red, and having stables on two sides. Sloping, dank, winter-dark fields stretched away on the open sides.

But the stables were empty. Joseph Pervin, the father of the family, had been a man of no education, who had become a fairly large horse dealer. The stables had been full of horses, there was a great turmoil and come-and-go of horses and of dealers and grooms. Then the kitchen was full of servants. But of late things had declined. The old man had married a second time, to retrieve his fortunes. Now he was dead and everything was gone to the dogs, there was nothing but debt and threatening.

For months, Mabel had been servantless in the big house, keeping the home together in penury for her ineffectual brothers. She had kept house for ten years. But previously it was with unstinted means. Then, however brutal and coarse everything was, the sense of money had kept her proud, confident. The men might be foul-mouthed, the women in the kitchen might have bad reputations, her brothers might have illegitimate children. But so long as there was money, the girl felt herself established, and brutally proud, reserved.

No company came to the house, save dealers and coarse men. Mabel had no associates of her own sex, after her sister went away. But she did not mind. She went regularly to church, she attended to her father. And she lived in the memory of her mother, who had died when she was fourteen, and whom she had loved. She had loved her father, too, in a different way, depending upon him, and feeling secure in him, until at the age of fifty-four he married again. And then she had set hard against him. Now he had died and left them all hopelessly in debt.

She had suffered badly during the period of poverty. Nothing, however, could shake the curious sullen, animal pride that dominated each member of the family. Now, for Mabel, the end had come. Still she would not cast about her. She would follow her own way just the same. She would always hold the keys of her own situation. Mindless and persistent, she endured from day to day. Why should she think? Why should she answer anybody? It was enough that this was the end, and there was no way out. She need not pass any more darkly along the main street of the small town, avoiding every eye. She need not demean herself any more, going into the shops and buying the cheapest food. This was at an end. She thought of nobody, not even of herself. Mindless and persistent, she seemed in a sort of ecstasy to be coming nearer to her fulfilment, her own glorification, approaching her dead mother, who was glorified.

In the afternoon she took a little bag, with shears and sponge and a small scrubbing brush, and went out. It was a grey, wintry day, with saddened, dark green fields and an atmosphere blackened by the smoke of foundries not far off. She went quickly, darkly along the causeway, heeding nobody, through the town to the churchyard.

There she always felt secure, as if no one could see her, although as a matter of fact she was exposed to the stare of every one who passed along under the churchyard wall. Nevertheless, once under the shadow of the great looming church, among the graves, she felt immune from the world, reserved within the thick churchyard wall as in another country.

Carefully she clipped the grass from the grave, and arranged the pinky white, small chrysanthemums in the tin cross. When this was done, she took an empty jar from a neighbouring grave, brought water, and carefully, most scrupulously sponged the marble headstone and the coping-stone.

It gave her sincere satisfaction to do this. She felt in immediate contact with the world of her mother. She took minute pains, went through the park in a state bordering on pure happiness, as if in performing this task she came into a subtle, intimate connection with her mother. For the life she followed here in the world was far less real than the world of death she inherited from her mother.

The doctor's house was just by the church. Fergusson, being a mere hired assistant, was slave to the country-side. As he hurried now to attend to the outpatients in the surgery, glancing across the graveyard with his quick eye, he saw the girl at her task at the grave. She seemed so intent and remote, it was like looking into another world. Some mystical element was touched in him. He slowed down as he walked, watching her as if spell-bound.

She lifted her eyes, feeling him looking. Their eyes met. And each looked again at once, each feeling, in some way, found out by the other. He lifted his cap and passed on down the road. There remained distinct in his consciousness, like a vision, the memory of her face, lifted from the tombstone in the churchyard, and looking at him with slow, large, portentous eyes. It *was* portentous, her face. It seemed to mesmerize him. There was a heavy power in her eyes which laid hold of his whole being, as if he had drunk some powerful drug. He had been feeling weak and done before. Now the life came back into him, he felt delivered from his own fretted, daily self.

He finished his duties at the surgery as quickly as might be, hastily filling up the bottles of the waiting people with cheap drugs. Then, in perpetual haste, he set off again to visit several cases in another part of his round, before teatime. At all times he preferred to walk if he could, but particularly when he was not well. He fancied the motion restored him.

The afternoon was falling. It was grey, deadened, and wintry, with a slow, moist, heavy coldness sinking in and deadening all the faculties. But why should he think or notice?

He hastily climbed the hill and turned across the dark green fields, following the black cinder-track. In the distance, across a shallow dip in the country, the small town was clustered like smouldering ash, a tower, a spire, a heap of low, raw, extinct houses. And on the nearest fringe of the town, sloping into the dip, was Oldmeadow, the Pervins' house. He could see the stables and the outbuildings distinctly, as they lay towards him on the slope. Well, he would not go there many more times! Another resource would be lost to him, another place gone: the only company he cared for in the alien, ugly little town he was losing. Nothing but work, drudgery, constant hastening from dwelling to dwelling among the colliers and the iron-workers. It wore him out, but at the same time he had a craving for it. It was a stimulant to him to be in the homes of the working people, moving as it were through the innermost body of their life. His nerves were excited and gratified. He could come so near, into the very lives of the rough, inarticulate, powerfully emotional men and women. He grumbled, he said he hated the hellish hole. But as a matter of fact it excited him, the contact with the rough, strongly-feeling people was a stimulant applied direct to his nerves.

Below Oldmeadow, in the green, shallow, soddened hollow of fields, lay a square, deep pond. Roving across the landscape, the doctor's quick eye detected a figure in black passing through the gate of the field, down towards the pond He looked again. It would be Mabel Pervin. His mind suddenly became alive and attentive.

Why was she going down there? He pulled up on the path on the slope above, and stood staring. He could just make sure of the small black figure moving in the hollow of the failing day. He seemed to see her in the midst of such obscurity, that he was like a clairvoyant, seeing rather with the mind's eye than with ordinary sight. Yet he could see her positively enough, whilst he kept his eye attentive. He felt, if he looked away from her, in the thick, ugly, falling dusk, he would lose her altogether.

He followed her minutely as she moved, direct and intent,

like something transmitted rather than stirring in voluntary activity, straight down the field towards the pond. There she stood on the bank for a moment. She never raised her head. Then she waded slowly into the water.

He stood motionless as the small black figure walked slowly and deliberately towards the centre of the pond, very slowly, gradually moving deeper into the motionless water, and still moving forward as the water got up to her breast. Then he could see her no more in the dusk of the dead afternoon.

"There!" he exclaimed. "Would you believe it?"

And he hastened straight down, running over the wet, soddened fields, pushing through the hedges, down into the depression of callous wintry obscurity. It took him several minutes to come to the pond. He stood on the bank, breathing heavily. He could see nothing. His eyes seemed to penetrate the dead water. Yes, perhaps that was the dark shadow of her black clothing beneath the surface of the water.

He slowly ventured into the pond. The bottom was deep, soft clay, he sank in, and the water clasped dead cold round his legs. As he stirred he could smell the cold, rotten clay that fouled up into the water. It was objectionable in his lungs. Still, repelled and yet not heeding, he moved deeper into the pond. The cold water rose over his thighs, over his loins, upon his abdomen. The lower part of his body was all sunk in the hideous cold element. And the bottom was so deeply soft and uncertain, he was afraid of pitching with his mouth underneath. He could not swim, and was afraid.

He crouched a little, spreading his hands under the water and moving them round, trying to feel for her. The dead cold pond swayed upon his chest. He moved again, a little deeper, and again, with his hands underneath, he felt all around under the water. And he touched her clothing. But it evaded his fingers. He made a desperate effort to grasp it.

And so doing he lost his balance and went under, horribly, suffocating in the foul earthy water, struggling madly for a few moments. At last, after what seemed an eternity, he got his footing, rose again into the air and looked around. He gasped, and knew he was in the world. Then he looked at the water. She had risen near him. He grasped her clothing, and drawing her nearer, turned to take his way to land again.

He went very slowly, carefully, absorbed in the slow progress. He rose higher, climbing out of the pond. The water was now only about his legs; he was thankful, full of relief to be out of the clutches of the pond. He lifted her and staggered on to the bank, out of the horror of wet, grey clay.

He laid her down on the bank. She was quite unconscious and running with water. He made the water come from her mouth, he worked to restore her. He did not have to work very long before he could feel the breathing again begin in her; she was breathing naturally. He worked a little longer. He could feel her live beneath his hands; she was coming back. He wiped her face, wrapped her in his overcoat, looked round into the dim, dark grey world, then lifted her and staggered down the bank and across the fields.

It seemed an unthinkably long way, and his burden so heavy he felt he would never get to the house. But at last he was in the stable-yard, and then in the house-yard. He opened the door and went into the house. In the kitchen he laid her down on the hearthrug, and called. The house was empty. But the fire was burning in the grate.

Then again he kneeled to attend to her. She was breathing regularly, her eyes were wide open and as if conscious, but there seemed something missing in her look. She was conscious in herself, but unconscious of her surroundings.

He ran upstairs, took blankets from a bed, and put them before the fire to warm. Then he removed her saturated, earthy-smelling clothing, rubbed her dry with a towel, and wrapped her naked in the blankets. Then he went into the dining-room, to look for spirits. There was a little whisky. He drank a gulp himself, and put some into her mouth.

The effect was instantaneous. She looked full into his face, as if she had been seeing him for some time, and yet had only just become conscious of him.

"Dr. Fergusson?" she said.

"What?" he answered.

He was divesting himself of his coat, intending to find some dry clothing upstairs. He could not bear the smell of the dead, clayey water, and he was mortally afraid for his own health

"What did I do?" she asked.

"Walked into the pond," he replied. He had begun to shudder like one sick, and could hardly attend to her. Her eyes remained full on him, he seemed to be going dark in his mind, looking back at her helplessly. The shuddering became quieter in him, his life came back in him, dark and unknowing, but strong again.

"Was I out of my mind?" she asked, while her eyes were fixed on him all the time.

"Maybe, for the moment," he replied. He felt quiet, because his strength had come back. The strange fretful strain had left him.

"Am I out of my mind now?" she asked.

"Are you?" he reflected a moment. "No," he answered truthfully, "I don't see that you are." He turned his face aside. He was afraid now, because he felt dazed, and felt dimly that her power was stronger than his, in this issue. And she continued to look at him fixedly all the time. "Can you tell me where I shall find some dry things to put on?" he asked.

"Did you dive into the pond for me?" she asked.

"No," he answered. "I walked in. But I went in overhead as well."

There was silence for a moment. He hesitated. He very much wanted to go upstairs to get into dry clothing. But there was another desire in him. And she seemed to hold him. His will seemed to have gone to sleep, and left him, standing there slack before her. But he felt warm inside himself. He did not shudder at all, though his clothes were sodden on him.

"Why did you?" she asked.

"Because I didn't want you to do such a foolish thing," he said.

"It wasn't foolish," she said, still gazing at him as she lay on the floor, with a sofa cushion under her head. "It was the right thing to do. *I* knew best, then."

"I'll go and shift these wet things," he said. But still he had not the power to move out of her presence, until she sent him. It was as if she had the life of his body in her hands, and he could not extricate himself. Or perhaps he did not want to.

Suddenly she sat up. Then she became aware of her own immediate condition. She felt the blankets about her, she knew her own limbs. For a moment it seemed as if her reason were going. She looked round, with wild eye, as if seeking something. He stood still with fear. She saw her clothing lying scattered.

"Who undressed me?" she asked, her eyes resting full and inevitable on his face.

"I did," he replied, "to bring you round."

For some moments she sat and gazed at him awfully, her lips parted.

"Do you love me, then?" she asked.

He only stood and stared at her, fascinated. His soul seemed to melt.

She shuffled forward on her knees, and put her arms round him, round his legs, as he stood there, pressing her breasts against his knees and thighs, clutching him with strange, convulsive certainty, pressing his thighs against her, drawing him to her face, her throat, as she looked up at him with flaring, humble eyes of transfiguration, triumphant in first possession.

"You love me," she murmured, in strange transport, yearning and triumphant and confident. "You love me. I know you love me, I know."

And she was passionately kissing his knees, through the wet clothing, passionately and indiscriminately kissing his knees, his legs, as if unaware of everything.

He looked down at the tangled wet hair, the wild, bare, animal shoulders. He was amazed, bewildered, and afraid. He had never thought of loving her. He had never wanted to love her. When he rescued her and restored her, he was a doctor, and she was a patient. He had had no single personal thought of her. Nay, this introduction of the personal element was very distasteful to him, a violation of his professional honour. It was horrible to have her there embracing his knees. It was horrible. He revolted from it, violently. And yet—and yet—he had not the power to break away.

She looked at him again, with the same supplication of powerful love, and that same transcendent, frightening light of triumph. In view of the delicate flame which seemed to come from her face like a light, he was powerless. And yet he had never intended to love her. He had never intended. And something stubborn in him could not give way.

"You love me," she repeated, in a murmur of deep, rhapsodic assurance. "You love me."

Her hands were drawing him, drawing him down to her. He was afraid, even a little horrified. For he had, really, no intention of loving her. Yet her hands were drawing him towards her. He put out his hand quickly to steady himself, and grasped her bare shoulder. A flame seemed to burn the hand that grasped her soft shoulder. He had no intention of loving her: his whole will was against his yielding. It was horrible. And yet wonderful was the touch of her shoulders, beautiful the shining of her face. Was she perhaps mad? He had a horror of yielding to her. Yet something in him ached also.

He had been staring away at the door, away from her. But his hand remained on her shoulder. She had gone suddenly very still. He looked down at her. Her eyes were now wide with fear, with doubt, the light was dying from her face, a shadow of terrible greyness was returning. He could not bear the touch of her eyes' question upon him, and the look of death behind the question.

With an inward groan he gave way, and let his heart yield towards her. A sudden gentle smile came on his face. And her eyes, which never left his face, slowly, slowly filled with tears. He watched the strange water rise in her eyes, like some slow fountain coming up. And his heart seemed to burn and melt away in his breast.

He could not bear to look at her any more. He dropped on his knees and caught her head with his arms and pressed her face against his throat. She was very still. His heart, which seemed to have broken, was burning with a kind of agony in his breast. And he felt her slow, hot tears wetting his throat. But he could not move.

He felt the hot tears wet his neck and the hollows of his neck, and he remained motionless, suspended through one of man's eternities. Only now it had become indispensable to him to have her face pressed close to him; he could never let her go again. He could never let her head go away from the close clutch of his arm. He wanted to remain like that for ever, with his heart hurting him in a pain that was also life to him. Without knowing, he was looking down on her damp, soft brown hair.

Then, as it were suddenly, he smelt the horrid stagnant smell of that water. And at the same moment she drew away from him and looked at him. Her eyes were wistful and unfathomable. He was afraid of them, and he fell to kissing her, not knowing what he was doing. He wanted her eyes not to have that terrible, wistful, unfathomable look.

When she turned her face to him again, a faint delicate flush was glowing, and there was again dawning that terrible shining of joy in her eyes, which really terrified him, and yet which he now wanted to see, because he feared the look of doubt still more.

"You love me?" she said, rather faltering.

"Yes." The word cost him a painful effort. Not because it wasn't true. But because it was too newly true, the *saying* seemed to tear open again his newly-torn heart. And he hardly wanted it to be true, even now.

She lifted her face to him, and he bent forward and kissed her on the mouth, gently, with the one kiss that is an eternal pledge. And as he kissed her his heart strained again in his breast. He never intended to love her. But now it was over. He had crossed over the gulf to her, and all that he had left behind had shrivelled and become void.

After the kiss, her eyes again slowly filled with tears. She sat still, away from him, with her face drooped aside, and her hands folded in her lap. The tears fell very slowly. There was complete silence. He too sat there motionless and silent on the hearthrug. The strange pain of his heart that was broken seemed to consume him. That he should love her? That this was love! That he should be ripped open in this way! Him, a doctor! How they would all jeer if they knew! It was agony to him to think they might know.

In the curious naked pain of the thought he looked again to her. She was sitting there drooped into a muse. He saw a tear fall, and his heart flared hot. He saw for the first time that one of her shoulders was quite uncovered, one arm bare, he could see one of her small breasts; dimly, because it had become almost dark in the room.

"Why are you crying?" he asked, in an altered voice.

She looked up at him, and behind her tears the consciousness of her situation for the first time brought a dark look of shame to her eyes.

"I'm not crying, really," she said, watching him half frightened.

He reached his hand, and softly closed it on her bare arm.

"I love you! I love you!" he said in a soft, low vibrating voice, unlike himself.

She shrank, and dropped her head. The soft, penetrating grip of his hand on her arm distressed her. She looked up at him.

"I want to go," she said. "I want to go and get you some dry things."

"Why?" he said. "I'm all right."

"But I want to go," she said. "And I want you to change your things."

He released her arm, and she wrapped herself in the blanket, looking at him rather frightened. And still she did not rise.

"Kiss me," she said wistfully.

He kissed her, but briefly, half in anger.

Then, after a second, she rose nervously, all mixed up in the blanket. He watched her in her confusion, as she tried to extricate herself and wrap herself up so that she could walk. He watched her relentlessly, as she knew. And as she went, the blanket trailing, and as he saw a glimpse of her feet and her white leg, he tried to remember her as she was when he had wrapped her in the blanket. But then he didn't want to remember, because she had been nothing to him then, and his nature revolted from remembering her as she was when she was nothing to him.

A tumbling, muffled noise from within the dark house startled him. Then he heard her voice: "There are clothes." He rose and went to the foot of the stairs, and gathered up the garments she had thrown down. Then he came back to the fire, to rub himself down and dress. He grinned at his own appearance when he had finished.

The fire was sinking, so he put on coal. The house was now quite dark, save for the light of a street-lamp that shone in faintly from beyond the holly trees. He lit the gas with matches he found on the mantelpiece. Then he emptied the pockets of his own clothes, and threw all his wet things in a heap into the scullery. After which he gathered up her sodden clothes, gently, and put them in a separate heap on the copper-top in the scullery.

It was six o'clock on the clock. His own watch had stopped. He ought to go back to the surgery. He waited, and still she did not come down. So he went to the foot of the stairs and called:

"I shall have to go."

Almost immediately he heard her coming down. She had on her best dress of black voile, and her hair was tidy, but still damp. She looked at him—and in spite of herself, smiled.

"I don't like you in those clothes," she said.

"Do I look a sight?" he answered.

They were shy of one another.

"I'll make you some tea," she said.

"No, I must go."

"Must you?" And she looked at him again with the wide,

strained, doubtful eyes. And again, from the pain of his breast, he knew how he loved her. He went and bent to kiss her, gently, passionately, with his heart's painful kiss.

"And my hair smells so horrible," she murmured in distraction. "And I'm so awful, I'm so awful! Oh, no, I'm too awful." And she broke into bitter, heart-broken sobbing. "You can't want to love me, I'm horrible."

"Don't be silly, don't be silly," he said, trying to comfort her, kissing her, holding her in his arms. "I want you, I want to marry you, we're going to be married, quickly, quickly—to-morrow if I can."

But she only sobbed terribly, and cried:

"I feel awful. I feel awful. I feel I'm horrible to you."

"No, I want you, I want you," was all he answered, blindly, with that terrible intonation which frightened her almost more than her horror lest he should *not* want her.

FLAME-LURID his face as he turned among the throng of flame-lit and dark faces upon the platform. In the light of the furnace she caught sight of his drifting countenance, like a piece of floating fire. And the nostalgia, the doom of home-coming went through her veins like a drug. His eternal face, flame-lit now! The pulse and darkness of red fire from the furnace towers in the sky, lighting the desultory, industrial crowd on the wayside station, lit him and went out.

Of course he did not see her. Flame-lit and unseeing! Always the same, with his meeting eyebrows, his common cap, and his red-and-black scarf knotted round his throat. Not even a collar to meet her! The flames had sunk, there was shadow.

She opened the door of her grimy, branch-line carriage, and began to get down her bags. The porter was nowhere, of course, but there was Harry, obscure, on the outer edge of the little crowd, missing her, of course.

"Here! Harry!" she called, waving her umbrella in the twilight. He hurried forward.

"Tha's come, has ter?" he said, in a sort of cheerful welcome. She got down, rather flustered, and gave him a peck of a kiss.

"Two suit-cases!" she said.

Her soul groaned within her, as he clambered into the carriage after her bags. Up shot the fire in the twilight sky, from the great furnace behind the station. She felt the red flame go across her face. She had come back, she had come back for good. And her spirit groaned dismally. She doubted if she could bear it.

There, on the sordid little station under the furnaces, she stood, tall and distinguished, in her well-made coat and skirt and her broad grey velour hat. She held her umbrella, her bead chatelaine, and a little leather case in her grey-gloved hands, while Harry staggered out of the ugly little train with her bags.

"There's a trunk at the back," she said in her bright voice. But she was not feeling bright. The twin black cones of the iron foundry blasted their sky-high fires into the night. The whole scene was lurid. The train waited cheerfully. It would wait another ten minutes. She knew it. It was all so deadly familiar.

Let us confess it at once. She was a lady's maid, thirty years old, come back to marry her first-love, a foundry worker: after having kept him dangling, off and on, for a dozen years. Why had she come back? Did she love him? No. She didn't pretend to. She had loved her brilliant and ambitious cousin, who had jilted her, and who had died. She had had other affairs which had come to nothing. So here she was, come back suddenly to marry her first-love, who had waited—or remained single—all these years.

"Won't a porter carry those?" she said, as Harry strode with his workman's stride down the platform towards the guard's van.

"I can manage," he said.

And with her umbrella, her chatelaine, and her little leather case, she followed him.

The trunk was there.

"We'll get Heather's green-grocer's cart to fetch it up," he said.

"Isn't there a cab?" said Fanny, knowing dismally enough that there wasn't.

"I'll just put it aside o' the penny-in-the-slot, and Heather's green-grocers'll fetch it about half-past eight," he said.

He seized the box by its two handles and staggered with it across the level-crossing, bumping his legs against it as he waddled. Then he dropped it by the red sweetmeats machine.

"Will it be safe there?" she said.

"Ay—safe as houses," he answered. He returned for the two bags. Thus laden, they started to plod up the hill, under the great long black building of the foundry. She walked beside him—workman of workmen he was, trudging with that luggage. The red lights flared over the deepening darkness.

From the foundry came the horrible, slow clang, clang, clang of iron, a great noise, with an interval just long enough to make it unendurable.

Compare this with the arrival at Gloucester: the carriage for her mistress, the dog-cart for herself with the luggage; the drive out past the river, the pleasant trees of the carriage-approach; and herself sitting beside Arthur, everybody so polite to her.

She had come home—for good! Her heart nearly stopped beating as she trudged up that hideous and interminable hill, beside the laden figure. What a come-down! What a come-down! She could not take it with her usual bright cheerfulness. She knew it all too well. It is easy to bear up against the unusual, but the deadly familiarity of an old stale past!

He dumped the bags down under a lamp-post, for a rest. There they stood, the two of them, in the lamp-light. Passers-by stared at her, and gave good night to Harry. Her they hardly knew, she had become a stranger.

"They're too heavy for you, let me carry one," she said.

"They begin to weigh a bit by the time you've gone a mile," he answered.

"Let me carry the little one," she insisted.

"Tha can ha'e it for a minute, if ter's a mind," he said, handing over the valise.

And thus they arrived in the streets of shops of the little ugly town on top of the hill. How everybody stared at her; my word, how they stared! And the cinema was just going in, and the queues were tailing down the road to the corner. And everybody took full stock of her. "Night, Harry!" shouted the fellows, in an interested voice.

However, they arrived at her aunt's—a little sweet-shop in a side street. They "pinged" the door-bell, and her aunt came running forward out of the kitchen.

"There you are, child! Dying for a cup of tea, I'm sure. How are you?"

Fanny's aunt kissed her, and it was all Fanny could do to refrain from bursting into tears, she felt so low. Perhaps it was her tea she wanted.

"You've had a drag with that luggage," said Fanny's aunt to Harry.

"Ay—I'm not sorry to put it down," he said, looking at his hand which was crushed and cramped by the bag handle.

Then he departed to see about Heather's green-grocery cart.

When Fanny sat at tea, her aunt, a grey-haired, fair-faced little woman, looked at her with an admiring heart, feeling bitterly sore for her. For Fanny was beautiful: tall, erect, finely coloured, with her delicately arched nose, her rich brown hair, her large lustrous grey eyes. A passionate woman—a woman to be afraid of. So proud, so inwardly violent! She came of a violent race.

It needed a woman to sympathize with her. Men had not the courage. Poor Fanny! She was such a lady, and so straight and magnificent. And yet everything seemed to do her down. Every time she seemed to be doomed to humiliation and disappointment, this handsome, brilliantly sensitive woman, with her nervous, overwrought laugh.

"So you've really come back, child?" said her aunt.

"I really have, Aunt," said Fanny.

"Poor Harry! I'm not sure, you know, Fanny, that you're not taking a bit of an advantage of him."

"Oh, Aunt, he's waited so long, he may as well have what he's waited for." Fanny laughed grimly.

"Yes, child, he's waited so long, that I'm not sure it isn't a bit hard on him. You know, I *like* him, Fanny—though as you know quite well, I don't think he's good enough for you. And I think he thinks so himself, poor fellow."

"Don't you be so sure of that, Aunt. Harry is common, but he's not humble. He wouldn't think the Queen was any too good for him, if he'd a mind to her."

"Well—it's as well if he has a proper opinion of himself."

"It depends what you call proper," said Fanny. "But he's got his good points——"

"Oh, he's a nice fellow, and I like him, I do like him. Only, as I tell you, he's not good enough for you."

"I've made up my mind, Aunt," said Fanny, grimly.

"Yes," mused the aunt. "They say all things come to him who waits——"

"More than he's bargained for, eh, Aunt?" laughed Fanny rather bitterly.

The poor aunt, this bitterness grieved her for her niece.

They were interrupted by the ping of the shop-bell, and Harry's call of "Right!" But as he did not come in at once, Fanny, feeling solicitous for him presumably at the moment, rose and went into the shop. She saw a cart outside and went to the door.

And the moment she stood in the doorway, she heard a woman's common vituperative voice crying from the darkness of the opposite side of the road:

"Tha'rt theer, are ter? I'll shame thee, Mester. I'll shame thee, see if I dunna."

Startled, Fanny stared across the darkness, and saw a woman in a black bonnet go under one of the lamps up the side street.

Harry and Bill Heather had dragged the trunk off the little dray, and she retreated before them as they came up the shop step with it.

"Wheer shalt ha'e it?" asked Harry.

"Best take it upstairs," said Fanny.

She went up first to light the gas.

When Heather had gone, and Harry was sitting down having tea and pork pie, Fanny asked:

"Who was that woman shouting?"

"Nay, I canna tell thee. To somebody, I s'd think," replied Harry. Fanny looked at him, but asked no more.

He was a fair haired fellow of thirty-two, with a fair moustache. He was broad in his speech, and looked like a foundry-hand, which he was. But women always liked him. There was something of a mother's lad about him——something warm and playful and really sensitive.

He had his attractions even for Fanny. What she rebelled against so bitterly was that he had no sort of ambition. He was a moulder, but of very commonplace skill. He was

thirty-two years old, and hadn't saved twenty pounds. She
would have to provide the money for the home. He didn't care.
He just didn't care. He had no initiative at all. He had no
vices—no obvious ones. But he was just indifferent, spending
as he went, and not caring. Yet he did not look happy. She
remembered his face in the fire-glow: something haunted,
abstracted about it. As he sat there eating his pork pie,
bulging his cheek out, she felt he was like a doom to her. And
she raged against the doom of him. It wasn't that he was gross.
His *way* was common almost on purpose. But he himself
wasn't really common. For instance, his food was not particularly important to him, he was not greedy. He had a charm,
too, particularly for women, with his blondness and his
sensitiveness and his way of making a woman feel that she was
a higher being. But Fanny knew him, knew the peculiar
obstinate limitedness of him, that would nearly send her mad.

He stayed till about half-past nine. She went to the door
with him.

"When are you coming up?" he said, jerking his head in the
direction, presumably, of his own home.

"I'll come to-morrow afternoon," she said brightly. Between
Fanny and Mrs. Goodall, his mother, there was naturally no
love lost.

Again she gave him an awkward little kiss, and said good night.

"You can't wonder, you know, child, if he doesn't seem so
very keen," said her aunt. "It's your own fault."

"Oh, Aunt, I couldn't stand him when he was keen. I can do
with him a lot better as he is."

The two women sat and talked far into the night. They
understood each other. The aunt, too, had married as Fanny
was marrying: a man who was no companion to her, a violent
man, brother of Fanny's father. He was dead, Fanny's father
was dead.

Poor Aunt Lizzie, she cried, woefully over her bright niece,
when she had gone to bed.

Fanny paid the promised visit to his people the next
afternoon. Mrs. Goodall was a large woman with smooth-

parted hair, a common, obstinate woman, who had spoiled her
four lads and her one vixen of a married daughter. She was one
of those old-fashioned powerful natures that couldn't do with
looks or education or any form of showing off. She fairly hated
the sound of correct English. She *thee'd* and *tha'd* her prospective daughter-in-law, and said:

"I'm none as ormin' as I look, seest ta."

Fanny did not think her prospective mother-in-law looked at
all orming, so the speech was unnecessary.

"I towed him mysen," said Mrs. Goodall, " 'Er's held back
all this long, let 'er stop as 'er is. 'E'd none ha' had thee for *my*
tellin'—tha hears. No, 'e's a fool, an' I know it. I says to him,
'Tha looks a man, doesn't ter, at thy age, goin' an' openin' to
her when ter hears her scrat' at th' gate, after she's done
gallivantin' round wherever she'd a mind. Tha looks rare an'
soft.' But it's no use o' any talking: he answered that letter o'
thine and made his own bad bargain."

But in spite of the old woman's anger, she was also flattered
at Fanny's coming back to Harry. For Mrs. Goodall was
impressed by Fanny—a woman of her own match. And more
than this, everybody knew that Fanny's Aunt Kate had left
her two hundred pounds: this apart from the girl's savings.

So there was high tea in Princes Street when Harry came
home black from work, and a rather acrid odour of cordiality,
the vixen Jinny darting in to say vulgar things. Of course
Jinny lived in a house whose garden end joined the paternal
garden. They were a clan who stuck together, these Goodalls.

It was arranged that Fanny should come to tea again on the
Sunday, and the wedding was discussed. It should take place
in a fortnight's time at Morley Chapel. Morley was a hamlet on
the edge of the real country, and in its little Congregational
Chapel Fanny and Harry had first met.

What a creature of habit he was! He was still in the choir of
Morley Chapel—not very regular. He belonged just because he
had a tenor voice, and enjoyed singing. Indeed, his solos were
only spoilt to local fame because when he sang he handled his
aitches so hopelessly.

"And I saw 'eaven hopened
      And be'old, a wite 'orse——"

This was one of Harry's classics, only surpassed by the fine outburst of his heaving:

"Hangels—hever bright an' fair——"

It was a pity, but it was unalterable. He had a good voice, and he sang with a certain lacerating fire, but his pronunciation made it all funny. And *nothing* could alter him.

So he was never heard save at cheap concerts and in the little, poorer chapels. The others scoffed.

Now the month was September, and Sunday was Harvest Festival at Morley Chapel, and Harry was singing solos. So that Fanny was to go to afternoon service, and come home to a grand spread of Sunday tea with him. Poor Fanny! One of the most wonderful afternoons had been a Sunday afternoon service, with her cousin Luther at her side, Harvest Festival in Morley Chapel. Harry had sung solos then—ten years ago. She remembered his pale blue tie, and the purple asters and the great vegetable marrows in which he was framed, and her cousin Luther at her side, young, clever, come down from London, where he was getting on well, learning his Latin and his French and German so brilliantly.

However, once again it was Harvest Festival at Morley Chapel, and once again, as ten years before, a soft, exquisite September day, with the last roses pink in the cottage gardens, the last dahlias crimson, the last sunflowers yellow. And again the little old chapel was a bower, with its famous sheaves of corn and corn-plaited pillars, its great bunches of grapes, dangling like tassels from the pulpit corners, its marrows and potatoes and pears and apples and damsons, its purple asters and yellow Japanese sunflowers. Just as before, the red dahlias round the pillars were dropping, weak-headed among the oats. The place was crowded and hot, the plates of tomatoes seemed balanced perilous on the gallery front, the Rev. Enderby was weirder than ever to look at, so long and emaciated and hairless.

The Rev. Enderby probably forewarned, came and shook hands with her and welcomed her, in his broad northern, melancholy sing-song before he mounted the pulpit. Fanny was handsome in a gauzy dress and a beautiful lace hat. Being a little late, she sat in a chair in the side-aisle wedged in, right in the front of the chapel. Harry was in the gallery above, and she could only see him from the eyes upwards. She noticed again how his eyebrows met, blond and not very marked, over his nose. He was attractive, too: physically lovable, very. If only—if only her *pride* had not suffered! She felt he dragged her down.

> "Come, ye thankful people, come,
> Raise the song of harvest-home.
> All is safely gathered in
> Ere the winter storms begin——"

Even the hymn was a falsehood, as the season had been wet, and half the crops were still out, and in a poor way.

Poor Fanny! She sang little, and looked beautiful through that inappropriate hymn. Above her stood Harry—mercifully in a dark suit and a dark tie, looking almost handsome. And his lacerating, pure tenor sounded well, when the words were drowned in the general commotion. Brilliant she looked, and brilliant she felt, for she was hot and angrily miserable and inflamed with a sort of fatal despair. Because there was about him a physical attraction which she really hated, but which she could not escape from. He was the first man who had ever kissed her. And his kisses, even while she rebelled from them, had lived in her blood and sent roots down into her soul. After all this time she had come back to them. And her soul groaned, for she felt dragged down, dragged down to earth, as a bird which some dog has got down in the dust. She knew her life would be unhappy. She knew that what she was doing was fatal. Yet it was her doom. She had to come back to him.

He had to sing two solos this afternoon: one before the "address" from the pulpit and one after. Fanny looked at him, and wondered he was not too shy to stand up there in front of all the people. But no, he was not shy. He had even a kind of assurance on his face as he looked down from the choir gallery at her: the assurance of a common man deliberately entrenched in his commonness. Oh, such a rage went through her veins as she saw the air of triumph, laconic, indifferent triumph which sat so obstinately and recklessly on his eyelids as he looked down at her. Ah, she despised him! But there he stood up in that choir gallery like Balaam's ass in front of her, and she could not get beyond him. A certain winsomeness also about him. A certain physical winsomeness, and as if his flesh were new and lovely to touch. The thorn of desire rankled bitterly in her heart.

He, it goes without saying, sang like a canary this particular afternoon, with a certain defiant passion which pleasantly crisped the blood of the congregation. Fanny felt the crisp flames go through her veins as she listened. Even the curious loud-mouthed vernacular had a certain fascination. But, oh, also, it was so repugnant. He would triumph over her, obstinately he would drag her right back into the common people: a doom, a vulgar doom.

The second performance was an anthem, in which Harry sang the solo parts. It was clumsy, but beautiful, with lovely words.

"They that sow in tears shall reap in joy,
    He that goeth forth and weepeth, bearing precious seed
    Shall doubtless come again with rejoicing, bringing his
        sheaves with him——"

"Shall doubtless come, Shall doubtless come——" softly intoned the altos—"Bringing his she-e-eaves with him," the trebles flourished brightly, and then again began the half-wistful solo:

"They that sow in tears shall reap in joy——"

Yes, it was effective and moving.

But at the moment when Harry's voice sank carelessly down to his close, and the choir, standing behind him, were opening their mouths for the final triumphant outburst, a shouting female voice rose up from the body of the congregation. The organ gave one startled trump, and went silent; the choir stood transfixed.

"You look well standing there, singing in God's holy house," came the loud, angry female shout. Everybody turned electrified. A stoutish, red-faced woman in a black bonnet was standing up denouncing the soloist. Almost fainting with shock, the congregation realized it. "You look well, don't you, standing there singing solos in God's holy house, you, Goodall. But I said I'd shame you. You look well, bringing your young woman here with you, don't you? I'll let her know who she's dealing with. A scamp as won't take the consequences of what he's done." The hard-faced, frenzied woman turned in the direction of Fanny. "*That's* what Harry Goodall is, if you want to know."

And she sat down again in her seat. Fanny, startled like all the rest, had turned to look. She had gone white, and then a burning red, under the attack. She knew the woman: a Mrs. Nixon, a devil of a woman, who beat her pathetic, drunken, red-nosed second husband, Bob, and her two lanky daughters, grown-up as they were. A notorious character. Fanny turned round again, and sat motionless as eternity in her seat.

There was a minute of perfect silence and suspense. The audience was open-mouthed and dumb; the choir stood like Lot's wife; and Harry, with his music-sheet, stood there uplifted, looking down with a dumb sort of indifference on Mrs. Nixon, his face naïve and faintly mocking. Mrs. Nixon sat defiant in her seat, braving them all.

Then a rustle, like a wood when the wind suddenly catches the leaves. And then the tall, weird minister got to his feet, and in his strong, bell-like, beautiful voice—the only beautiful thing about him—he said with infinite mournful pathos:

"Let us unite in singing the last hymn on the hymn-sheet; the last hymn on the hymn-sheet, number eleven.

'Fair waved the golden corn,
In Canaan's pleasant land.' "

The organ tuned up promptly. During the hymn the offertory was taken. And after the hymn, the prayer.

Mr. Enderby came from Northumberland. Like Harry, he had never been able to conquer his accent, which was very broad. He was a little simple, one of God's fools, perhaps, an odd bachelor soul, emotional, ugly, but very gentle.

"And if, O our dear Lord, beloved Jesus, there should fall a shadow of sin upon our harvest, we leave it to Thee to judge, for Thou art judge. We lift our spirits and our sorrow, Jesus, to Thee, and our mouths are dumb. O Lord, keep us from froward speech, restrain us from foolish words and thoughts, we pray Thee, Lord Jesus, who knowest all and judgest all."

Thus the minister said in his sad, resonant voice, washed his hands before the Lord. Fanny bent forward open-eyed during the prayer. She could see the roundish head of Harry, also bent forward. His face was inscrutable and expressionless. The shock left her bewildered. Anger perhaps was her dominating emotion.

The audience began to rustle to its feet, to ooze slowly and excitedly out of the chapel, looking with wildly interested eyes at Fanny, at Mrs. Nixon, and at Harry. Mrs. Nixon, shortish, stood defiant in her pew, facing the aisle, as if announcing that, without rolling her sleeves up, she was ready for anybody. Fanny sat quite still. Luckily the people did not have to pass her. And Harry, with red ears, was making his way sheepishly out of the gallery. The loud noise of the organ covered all the downstairs commotion of exit.

The minister sat silent and inscrutable in his pulpit, rather like a death's-head, while the congregation filed out. When the last lingerers had unwillingly departed, craning their necks to stare at the still seated Fanny, he rose, stalked in his hooked fashion down the little country chapel and fastened the door. Then he returned and sat down by the silent young woman.

"This is most unfortunate, most unfortunate!" he moaned. "I am so sorry, I am so sorry, indeed, indeed, ah, indeed!" he sighed himself to a close.

"It's a sudden surprise, that's one thing," said Fanny brightly.

"Yes—yes—indeed. Yes, a surprise, yes. I don't know the woman, I don't know her."

"I know her," said Fanny. "She's a bad one."

"Well! Well!" said the minister. "I don't know her. I don't understand. I don't understand at all. But it is to be regretted, it is very much to be regretted. I am very sorry."

Fanny was watching the vestry door. The gallery stairs communicated with the vestry, not with the body of the chapel. She knew the choir members had been peeping for information.

At last Harry came—rather sheepishly—with his hat in his hand.

"Well!" said Fanny rising to her feet.

"We've had a bit of an extra," said Harry.

"I should think so," said Fanny.

"A most unfortunate circumstance—a most *unfortunate* circumstance. Do you understand it, Harry? I don't understand it at all."

"Ay, I understand it. The daughter's goin' to have a childt, an' 'er lays it on to me."

"And has she no occasion to?" asked Fanny, rather censorious.

"It's no more mine than it is some other chap's," said Harry, looking aside.

There was a moment of pause.

"Which girl is it?" asked Fanny.

"Annie—the young one——"

There followed another silence.

"I don't think I know them, do I?" asked the minister.

"I shouldn't think so. Their name's Nixon—mother married old Bob for her second husband. She's a tanger, she's driven the gel to what she is. They live in Manners Road."

"Why, what's amiss with the girl?" asked Fanny sharply. "She was all right when I knew her."

"Ay—she's all right. But she's always in an' out o' th' pubs, wi' th' fellows," said Harry.

"A nice thing!" said Fanny.

Harry glanced towards the door. He wanted to get out.

"Most distressing, indeed!" The minister slowly shook his head.

"What about to-night, Mr. Enderby?" asked Harry, in rather a small voice. "Shall you want me?"

Mr. Enderby looked up painedly, and put his hand to his brow. He studied Harry for some time, vacantly. There was the faintest sort of a resemblance between the two men.

"Yes," he said. "Yes, I think. I think we must take no notice and cause as little remark as possible."

Fanny hesitated. Then she said to Harry:

"But *will* you come?"

He looked at her.

"Ay, I s'll come," he said.

Then he turned to Mr. Enderby.

"Well, good afternoon, Mr. Enderby," he said.

"Good afternoon, Harry, good afternoon," replied the mournful minister. Fanny followed Harry to the door, and for some time they walked in silence through the late afternoon.

"And it's yours as much as anybody else's?" she said.

"Ay," he answered shortly.

And they went without another word, for the long mile or so, till they came to the corner of the street where Harry lived. Fanny hesitated. Should she go on to her aunt's? Should she? It would mean leaving all this, for ever. Harry stood silent.

Some obstinacy made her turn with him along the road to his own home. When they entered the house-place, the whole family was there, mother and father and Jinny, with Jinny's husband and children and Harry's two brothers.

"You've been having your ears warmed, they tell me," said Mrs. Goodall grimly.

"Who told thee?" asked Harry shortly.

"Maggie and Luke's both been in."

"You look well, don't you!" said interfering Jinny.

Harry went and hung his hat up, without replying.

"Come upstairs and take your hat off," said Mrs. Goodall to Fanny, almost kindly. It would have annoyed her very much if Fanny had dropped her son at this moment.

"What's 'er say, then?" asked the father secretly of Harry, jerking his head in the direction of the stairs whence Fanny had disappeared.

"Nowt yet," said Harry.

"Serve you right if she chucks you now," said Jinny. "I'll bet it's right about Annie Nixon an' you."

"Tha bets so much," said Harry.

"Yi—but you can't deny it," said Jinny.

"I can if I've a mind."

His father looked at him enquiringly.

"It's no more mine than it is Bill Bower's, or Ted Slaney's, or six or seven on 'em," said Harry to his father.

And the father nodded silently.

"That'll not get you out of it, in court," said Jinny.

Upstairs Fanny evaded all the thrusts made by his mother, and did not declare her hand. She tidied her hair, washed her hands, and put the tiniest bit of powder on her face, for coolness, there in front of Mrs. Goodall's indignant gaze. It was like a declaration of independence. But the old woman said nothing.

They came down to Sunday tea, with sardines and tinned salmon and tinned peaches, besides tarts and cakes. The chatter was general. It concerned the Nixon family and the scandal.

"Oh, she's a foul-mouthed woman," said Jinny of Mrs. Nixon. "She may well talk about God's holy house, *she* had. It's first time she's set foot in it, ever since she dropped off from being converted. She's a devil and she always was one. Can't you remember how she treated Bob's children, mother, when we lived down in the Buildings? I can remember when I was a little girl she used to bathe them in the yard, in the cold, so that they shouldn't splash the house. She'd half kill them if they made a mark on the floor, and the language she'd use! And one Saturday I can remember Garry, that was Bob's own girl, she ran off when her stepmother was going to bathe her— ran off without a rag of clothes on—can you remember, mother? And she hid in Smedley's closes—it was the time of mowing-grass—and nobody could find her. She hid out there all night, didn't she, mother? Nobody could find her. My word, there was a talk. They found her on Sunday morning——"

"Fred Coutts threatened to break every bone in the woman's body, if she touched the children again," put in the father.

"Anyhow, they frightened her," said Jinny. "But she was nearly as bad with her own two. And anybody can see that she's driven old Bob till he's gone soft."

"Ah, soft as mush," said Jack Goodall. "'E'd never addle a week's wage, nor yet a day's, if th' chaps didn't make it up to him."

"My word, if he didn't bring her a week's wage, she'd pull his head off," said Jinny.

"But a clean woman, and respectable, except for her foul mouth," said Mrs. Goodall. "Keeps to herself like a bull-dog. Never lets anybody come near the house, and neighbours with nobody."

"Wanted it thrashed out of her," said Mr. Goodall, a silent, evasive sort of man.

"Where Bob gets the money for his drink from is a mystery," said Jinny.

"Chaps treats him," said Harry.

"Well, he's got the pair of frightenedest rabbit-eyes you'd wish to see," said Jinny.

"Ay, with a drunken man's murder in them, *I* think," said Mrs. Goodall.

So the talk went on after tea, till it was practically time to start off to chapel again.

"You'll have to be getting ready, Fanny," said Mrs. Goodall.

"I'm not going to-night," said Fanny abruptly. And there was a sudden halt in the family. "I'll stop with *you* to-night, mother," she added.

"Best you had, my gel," said Mrs. Goodall, flattered and assured.

THE LADYBIRD

How many swords had Lady Beveridge in her pierced heart!
Yet there always seemed room for another. Since she had
determined that her heart of pity and kindness should never
die. If it had not been for this determination she herself might
have died of sheer agony, in the years 1916 and 1917, when her
boys were killed, and her brother, and death seemed to be
mowing with wide swaths through her family. But let us
forget.

Lady Beveridge loved humanity, and come what might, she
would continue to love it. Nay, in the human sense, she would
love her enemies. Not the criminals among the enemy, the
men who committed atrocities. But the men who were
enemies through no choice of their own. She would be swept
into no general hate.

Somebody had called her the soul of England. It was not ill
said, though she was half Irish. But of an old, aristocratic,
loyal family famous for its brilliant men. And she, Lady
Beveridge, had for years as much influence on the tone of
English politics as any individual alive. The close friend of the
real leaders in the House of Lords and in the Cabinet, she was
content that the men should act, so long as they breathed from
her as from the rose of life the pure fragrance of truth and
genuine love. She had no misgiving regarding her own spirit.

She, she would never lower her delicate silken flag. For
instance, throughout all the agony of the war she never forgot
the enemy prisoners; she was determined to do her best for
them. During the first years she still had influence. But during
the last years of the war power slipped out of the hands of her
and her sort, and she found she could do nothing any more:
almost nothing. Then it seemed as if the many swords had
gone home into the heart of this little, unyielding Mater
Dolorosa. The new generation jeered at her. She was a shabby,

old-fashioned little aristocrat, and her drawing-room was out of date.

But we anticipate. The years 1916 and 1917 were the years when the old spirit died for ever in England. But Lady Beveridge struggled on. She was being beaten.

It was in the winter of 1917—or in the late autumn. She had been for a fortnight sick, stricken, paralysed by the fearful death of her youngest boy. She felt she *must* give in, and just die. And then she remembered how many others were lying in agony.

So she rose, trembling, frail, to pay a visit to the hospital where lay the enemy sick and wounded, near London. Countess Beveridge was still a privileged woman. Society was beginning to jeer at this little, worn bird of an out-of-date righteousness and æsthetic. But they dared not think ill of her.

She ordered the car and went alone. The Earl, her husband, had taken his gloom to Scotland. So, on a sunny, wan November morning, Lady Beveridge descended at the hospital, Hurst Place. The guard knew her, and saluted as she passed. Ah, she was used to such deep respect! It was strange that she felt it so bitterly, when the respect became shallower. But she did. It was the beginning of the end to her.

The matron went with her into the ward. Alas, the beds were all full, and men were even lying on pallets on the floor. There was a desperate, crowded dreariness and helplessness in the place: as if nobody wanted to make a sound or utter a word. Many of the men were haggard and unshaven, one was delirious, and talking fitfully in the Saxon dialect. It went to Lady Beveridge's heart. She had been educated in Dresden, and had had many dear friendships in the city. Her children also had been educated there. She heard the Saxon dialect with pain.

She was a little, frail, bird-like woman, elegant, but with that touch of the blue-stocking of the 'nineties which was unmistakable. She fluttered delicately from bed to bed, speaking in perfect German, but with a thin, English intonation: and always asking if there was anything she could do. The men were mostly officers and gentlemen. They made little requests which she wrote down in a book. Her long, pale, rather worn face, and her nervous little gestures somehow inspired confidence.

One man lay quite still, with his eyes shut. He had a black beard. His face was rather small and sallow. He might be dead. Lady Beveridge looked at him earnestly, and fear came into her face.

"Why, Count Dionys!" she said, fluttered. "Are you asleep?"

It was Count Johann Dionys Psanek, a Bohemian. She had known him when he was a boy, and only in the spring of 1914 he and his wife had stayed with Lady Beveridge in her country house in Leicestershire.

His black eyes opened: large, black, unseeing eyes, with curved black lashes. He was a small man, small as a boy, and his face too was rather small. But all the lines were fine, as if they had been fired with a keen male energy. Now the yellowish swarthy paste of his flesh seemed dead, and the fine black brows seemed drawn on the face of one dead. The eyes, however, were alive: but only just alive, unseeing and unknowing.

"You know me, Count Dionys? You know me, don't you?" said Lady Beveridge, bending forward over the bed.

There was no reply for some time. Then the black eyes gathered a look of recognition, and there came the ghost of a polite smile.

"Lady Beveridge." The lips formed the words. There was practically no sound.

"I am so glad you can recognize me. And I am so sorry you are hurt. I am so sorry."

The black eyes watched her from that terrible remoteness of death, without changing.

"There is nothing I can do for you? Nothing at all?" she said, always speaking German.

And after a time, and from a distance, came the answer from his eyes, a look of weariness, of refusal, and a wish to be left alone; he was unable to strain himself into consciousness. His eyelids dropped.

"I am so sorry," she said. "If ever there is anything I can do——"

The eyes opened again, looking at her. He seemed at last to hear, and it was as if his eyes made the last weary gesture of a polite bow. Then slowly his eyelids closed again.

Poor Lady Beveridge felt another sword-thrust of sorrow in her heart, as she stood looking down at the motionless face, and at the black fine beard. The black hairs came out of his skin thin and fine, not very close together. A queer, dark aboriginal little face he had, with a fine little nose: not an Aryan, surely. And he was going to die.

He had a bullet through the upper part of his chest, and another bullet had broken one of his ribs. He had been in hospital five days.

Lady Beveridge asked the matron to ring her up if anything happened. Then she drove away, saddened. Instead of going to Beveridge House, she went to her daughter's flat near the park—near Hyde Park. Lady Daphne was poor. She had married a commoner, son of one of the most famous politicians in England, but a man with no money. And Earl Beveridge had wasted most of the large fortune that had come to him, so that the daughter had very little, comparatively.

Lady Beveridge suffered, going in the narrow doorway into the rather ugly flat. Lady Daphne was sitting by the electric fire in the small yellow drawing-room, talking to a visitor. She rose at once, seeing her little mother.

"Why, mother, ought you to be out? I'm sure not."

"Yes, Daphne darling. Of course I ought to be out."

"How are you?" The daughter's voice was slow and sonorous, protective, sad. Lady Daphne was tall, only twenty-five years old. She had been one of the beauties, when the war broke out, and her father had hoped she would make a splendid match. Truly, she had married fame: but without money. Now, sorrow, pain, thwarted passion had done her great damage. Her husband was missing in the East. Her baby had been born dead. Her two darling brothers were dead. And she was ill, always ill.

A tall, beautifully-built girl, she had the fine stature of her father. Her shoulders were still straight. But how thin her white throat! She wore a simple black frock stitched with coloured wool round the top, and held in a loose coloured girdle: otherwise no ornaments. And her face was lovely, fair, with a soft exotic white complexion and delicate pink cheeks. Her hair was soft and heavy, of a lovely pallid gold colour, ash-blonde. Her hair, her complexion were so perfectly cared for as to be almost artificial, like a hot-house flower.

But alas, her beauty was a failure. She was threatened with phthisis, and was far too thin. Her eyes were the saddest part of her. They had slightly reddened rims, nerve-worn, with heavy, veined lids that seemed as if they did not want to keep up. The eyes themselves were large, and of a beautiful green-blue colour. But they were dull, languid, almost glaucous.

Standing as she was, a tall, finely built girl, looking down with affectionate care on her mother, she filled the heart with ashes. The little pathetic mother, so wonderful in her way, was not really to be pitied for all her sorrow. Her life was in her sorrows, and her efforts on behalf of the sorrows of others. But Daphne was not born for grief and philanthropy. With her splendid frame, and her lovely, long, strong legs, she was Artemis or Atalanta rather than Daphne. There was a certain width of brow and even of chin that spoke a strong, reckless nature, and the curious, distraught slant of her eyes told of a wild energy dammed up inside her.

That was what ailed her: her own wild energy. She had it from her father, and from her father's desperate race. The earldom had begun with a riotous, dare-devil border soldier, and this was the blood that flowed on. And alas, what was to be done with it?

Daphne had married an adorable husband: truly an adorable husband. Whereas she needed a dare-devil. But in her *mind* she hated all dare-devils: she had been brought up by her mother to admire only the good.

So, her reckless, anti-philanthropic passion could find no outlet—and *should* find no outlet, she thought. So her own blood turned against her, beat on her own nerves, and destroyed her. It was nothing but frustration and anger which made her ill, and made the doctors fear consumption. There it was, drawn on her rather wide mouth: frustration, anger, bitterness. There it was the same in the roll of her green-blue eyes, a slanting, averted look: the same anger furtively turning back on itself. This anger reddened her eyes and shattered her nerves. And yet, her whole will was fixed in her adoption of her mother's creed, and in condemnation of her handsome, proud, brutal father, who had made so much misery in the family. Yes, her will was fixed in the determination that life should be gentle and good and benevolent. Whereas her blood was reckless, the blood of dare-devils. Her will was the stronger of the two. But her blood had its revenge on her. So it is with strong natures to-day: shattered from the inside.

"You have no news, darling?" asked the mother.

"No. My father-in-law had information that British prisoners had been brought into Hasrun, and that details would be forwarded by the Turks. And there was a rumour from some Arab prisoners that Basil was one of the British brought in wounded."

"When did you hear this?"

"Primrose came in this morning."

"Then we can hope, dear."

"Yes."

Never was anything more dull and bitter than Daphne's affirmative of hope. Hope had become almost a curse to her. She wished there need be no such thing. Ha, the torment of hoping, and the *insult* to one's soul. Like the importunate widow dunning for her deserts. Why could it not all be just clean disaster, and have done with it? This dilly-dallying with despair was worse than despair. She had hoped so much: ah, for her darling brothers she had hoped with such anguish. And the two she loved best were dead. So were most others she had

hoped for, dead. Only this uncertainty about her husband still
rankling.

"You feel better, dear?" said the little, unquenched mother.

"Rather better," came the resentful answer.

"And your night?"

"No better."

There was a pause.

"You are coming to lunch with me, Daphne darling?"

"No, mother dear. I promised to lunch at the Howards'
with Primrose. But I needn't go for a quarter of an hour. Do
sit down."

Both women seated themselves near the electric fire. There
was that bitter pause, neither knowing what to say. Then
Daphne roused herself to look at her mother.

"Are you sure you were fit to go out?" she said. "What took
you out so suddenly?"

"I went to Hurst Place, dear. I had the men on my mind,
after the way the newspapers have been talking."

"Why ever do you read the newspapers!" blurted Daphne,
with a certain burning, acid anger. "Well," she said, more
composed. "And do you feel better now you've been?"

"So many people suffer besides ourselves, darling."

"I know they do. Makes it all the worse. It wouldn't matter
if it were only just us. At least, it would matter, but one could
bear it more easily. To be just one of a crowd all in the same
state."

"And some even worse, dear."

"Oh quite! And the worse it is for all, the worse it is for one."

"Is that so, darling? Try not to see too darkly. I feel if I can
give just a little bit of myself to help the others—you know—
it alleviates me. I feel that what I can give to the men lying
there, Daphne, I give to my own boys. I can only help them
now through helping others. But I can still do that, Daphne,
my girl."

And the mother put her little white hand into the long,
white, cold hand of her daughter. Tears came to Daphne's
eyes, and a fearful stony grimace to her mouth.

"It's so wonderful of you that you can feel like that," she said.

"But you feel the same, my love. I know you do."

"No, I don't. Every one I see suffering these same awful things, it makes me wish more for the end of the world. And I quite see that the world won't end——"

"But it will get better, dear. This time it's like a great sickness—like a terrible pneumonia tearing the breast of the world."

"Do you believe it will get better? I don't."

"It will get better. Of course it will get better. It is perverse to think otherwise, Daphne. Remember what *has* been before, even in Europe. Ah, Daphne, we must take a bigger view."

"Yes, I suppose we must."

The daughter spoke rapidly, from the lips, in a resonant, monotonous tone. The mother spoke from the heart.

"And Daphne, I found an old friend among the men at Hurst Place."

"Who?"

"Little Count Dionys Psanek. You remember him?"

"Quite. What's wrong?"

"Wounded rather badly—through the chest. So ill."

"Did you speak to him?"

"Yes. I recognized him in spite of his beard."

"Beard!"

"Yes—a black beard. I suppose he could not be shaven. It seems strange that he is still alive, poor man."

"Why strange? He isn't old. How old is he?"

"Between thirty and forty. But so ill, so wounded, Daphne. And so small. So small, so sallow—*smòrto*, you know, the Italian word. The way dark people look. There is something so distressing in it."

"Does he look *very* small now—uncanny?" asked the daughter.

"No, not uncanny. Something of the terrible far-awayness of a child that is very ill and can't tell you what hurts it. Poor Count Dionys, Daphne. I didn't know, dear, that his eyes were so black, and his lashes so curved and long. I had never thought of him as beautiful."

"Nor I. Only a little comical. Such a dapper little man."

"Yes. And yet now, Daphne, there is something remote and in a sad way heroic in his dark face. Something primitive."

"What did he say to you?"

"He couldn't speak to me. Only with his lips, just my name."

"So bad as that?"

"Oh yes. They are afraid he will die."

"Poor Count Dionys. I liked him. He was a bit like a monkey, but he had his points. He gave me a thimble on my seventeenth birthday. Such an amusing thimble."

"I remember, dear."

"Unpleasant wife, though. Wonder if he minds dying far away from her. Wonder if she knows."

"I think not. They didn't even know his name properly. Only that he was a Colonel of such and such a regiment."

"Fourth Cavalry," said Daphne. "Poor Count Dionys. Such a lovely name, I always thought: Count Johann Dionys Psanek. Extraordinary dandy he was. And an amazingly good dancer, small, yet electric. Wonder if he minds dying?"

He was so full of life, in his own little animal way. They say small people are always conceited. But he doesn't look conceited now, dear. Something ages old in his face—and, yes, a certain beauty, Daphne."

"You mean long lashes."

"No. So still, so solitary—and ages old, in his race. I suppose he must belong to one of those curious little aboriginal races of Central Europe. I felt quite new beside him."

"How nice of you," said Daphne.

Nevertheless, next day Daphne telephoned to Hurst Place to ask for news of him. He was about the same. She telephoned every day. Then she was told he was a little stronger. The day she received the message that her husband was wounded and a prisoner in Turkey, and that his wounds were healing, she forgot to telephone for news of the little enemy Count. And the following day she telephoned that she was coming to the hospital to see him.

He was awake, more restless, more in physical excitement. They could see the nausea of pain round his nose. His face seemed to Daphne curiously hidden behind the black beard, which nevertheless was thin, each hair coming thin and fine, singly, from the sallow, slightly translucent skin. In the same way his moustache made a thin black line round his mouth. His eyes were wide open, very black, and of no legible expression. He watched the two women coming down the crowded, dreary room, as if he did not see them. His eyes seemed too wide.

It was a cold day, and Daphne was huddled in a black sealskin coat with a skunk collar pulled up to her ears, and a dull gold cap with wings pulled down on her brow. Lady Beveridge wore her sable coat, and had that odd, untidy elegance which was natural to her rather like a ruffled chicken.

Daphne was upset by the hospital. She looked from right to left in spite of herself, and everything gave her a dull feeling of horror: the terror of these sick, wounded enemy men. She loomed tall and obtrusive in her furs by the bed, her little mother at her side.

"I hope you don't mind my coming!" she said in German to the sick man. Her tongue felt rusty, speaking the language.

"Who is it then?" he asked.

"It is my daughter, Lady Daphne. You remembered *me*, Lady Beveridge! This is my daughter, whom you knew in Saxony. She was so sorry to hear you were wounded."

The black eyes rested on the little lady. Then they returned to the looming figure of Daphne. And a certain fear grew on the low sick brow. It was evident the presence loomed and frightened him. He turned his face aside. Daphne noticed how his fine black hair grew uncut over his small, animal ears.

"You don't remember me, Count Dionys?" she said dully.

"Yes," he said. But he kept his face averted.

She stood there feeling confused and miserable, as if she had made a *faux pas* in coming.

E

"Would you rather be left alone?" she said. "I'm sorry."

Her voice was monotonous. She felt suddenly stifled in her closed furs, and threw her coat open, showing her thin white throat and plain black slip dress on her flat breast. He turned again unwillingly to look at her. He looked at her as if she were some strange creature standing near him.

"Good-bye," she said. "Do get better."

She was looking at him with a queer, slanting, downward look of her heavy eyes, as she turned away. She was still a little red round the eyes, with nervous exhaustion.

"You are so tall," he said, still frightened.

"I was always tall," she replied, turning half to him again.

"And I, small," he said.

"I am so glad you are getting better," she said.

"I am not glad," he said.

"Why? I'm sure you are. Just as we are glad because we want you to get better."

"Thank you," he said. "I have wished to die."

"Don't do that, Count Dionys. Do get better," she said, in the rather deep, laconic manner of her girlhood. He looked at her with a farther look of recognition. But his short, rather pointed nose was lifted with the disgust and weariness of pain, his brows were tense. He watched her with that curious flame of suffering which is forced to give a little outside attention, but which speaks only to itself.

"Why did they not let me die?" he said. "I wanted death now."

"No," she said. "You mustn't. You must live. If we *can* live we must."

"I wanted death," he said.

"Ah well," she said, "even death we can't have when we want it, or when we think we want it."

"That is true," he said, watching her with the same wide black eyes. "Please to sit down. You are too tall as you stand."

It was evident he was a little frightened still by her looming, overhanging figure.

"I am sorry I am too tall," she said, taking a chair which a man-nurse had brought her. Lady Beveridge had gone away to speak with the men. Daphne sat down, not knowing what to say further. The pitch-black look in the Count's wide eyes puzzled her.

"Why do you come here? Why does your lady mother come?" he said.

"To see if we can do anything," she answered.

"When I am well, I will thank your ladyship."

"All right," she replied. "When you are well I will let my lord the Count thank me. Please do get well."

"We are enemies," he said.

"Who? You and I and my mother?"

"Are we not? The most difficult thing is to be sure of anything. If they had let me die!"

"That is at least ungrateful, Count Dionys."

"*Lady Daphne*! Yes. *Lady Daphne*! Beautiful, the name is. You are always called Lady Daphne? I remember you were so bright a maiden."

"More or less," she said, answering his question.

"Ach! We should all have new names now. I thought of a name for myself, but I have forgotten it. No longer Johann Dionys. That is shot away. I am Karl or Wilhelm or Ernst or Georg. Those are names I hate. Do you hate them?"

"I don't like them—but I don't hate them. And you mustn't leave off being Count Johann Dionys. If you do I shall have to leave off being Daphne. I like your name so much."

"Lady Daphne! Lady Daphne!" he repeated. "Yes, it rings well, it sounds beautiful to me. I think I talk foolishly. I hear myself talking foolishly to you." He looked at her anxiously.

"Not at all," she said.

"Ach! I have a head on my shoulders that is like a child's windmill, and I can't prevent its making foolish words. Please to go away, not to hear me. I can hear myself."

"Can't I do anything for you?" she asked.

"No, no! No, no! If I could be buried deep, very deep down, where everything is forgotten! But they draw me up, back to the surface. I would not mind if they buried me alive, if it were very deep, and dark, and the earth heavy above."

"Don't say that," she replied rising.

"No, I am saying it when I don't wish to say it. Why am I here? Why am I here? Why have I survived into this? Why can I not stop talking?"

He turned his face aside. The black, fine, elfish hair was so long, and pushed up in tufts from the smooth brown nape of his neck. Daphne looked at him in sorrow. He could not turn his body. He could only move his head. And he lay with his face hard averted, the fine hair of his beard coming up strange from under his chin and from his throat, up to the socket of his ear. He lay quite still, in this position. And she turned away, looking for her mother. She had suddenly realized that the bonds, the connections between him and his life in the world had broken, and he lay there a bit of loose, palpitating humanity, shot away from the body of humanity.

It was ten days before she went to the hospital again. She had wanted never to go again, to forget him, as one tries to forget incurable things. But she could not forget him. He came again and again into her mind. She had to go back. She had heard that he was recovering very slowly.

He looked really better. His eyes were not so wide open, they had lost that black, inky exposure which had given him such an unnatural look, unpleasant. He watched her guardedly. She had taken off her furs, and wore only her dress and a dark, soft feather toque.

"How are you?" she said, keeping her face averted, unwilling to meet his eyes.

"Thank you, I am better. The nights are not so long."

She shuddered, knowing what long nights meant. He saw the worn look in her face, too, the reddened rims of her eyes.

"Are you not well? Have you some trouble?" he asked her.

"No, no," she answered.

She had brought a handful of pinky, daisy-shaped flowers.

"Do you care for flowers?" she asked.

He looked at them. Then he slowly shook his head.

"No," he said. "If I am on horseback, riding through the marshes or through the hills, I like to see them below me. But not here. Not now. Please do not bring flowers into this grave. Even in gardens, I do not like them. When they are upholstery to human life."

"I will take them away again," she said.

"Please do. Please give them to the nurse."

Daphne paused.

"Perhaps," she said, "you wish I would not come to disturb you."

He looked into her face.

"No," he said. "You are like a flower behind a rock, near an icy water. No, you do not live too much. I am afraid I cannot talk sensibly. I wish to hold my mouth shut. If I open it, I talk this absurdity. It escapes from my mouth."

"It is not so very absurd," she said.

But he was silent—looking away from her.

"I want you to tell me if there is really nothing I can do for you," she said.

"Nothing," he answered.

"If I can write any letter for you."

"None," he answered.

"But your wife and your two children. Do they know where you are?"

"I should think not."

"And where are they?"

"I do not know. Probably they are in Hungary."

"Not at your home?"

"My castle was burnt down in a riot. My wife went to Hungary with the children. She has her relatives there. She went away from me. I wished it too. Alas, for her, I wished to be dead. Pardon me the personal tone."

Daphne looked down at him—the queer, obstinate little fellow.

"But you have somebody you wish to tell—somebody you want to hear from?"

"Nobody. Nobody. I wish the bullet had gone through my

heart. I wish to be dead. It is only I have a devil in my body that will not die."

She looked at him as he lay with closed, averted face.

"Surely it is not a devil which keeps you alive," she said. "It is something good."

"No, a devil," he said.

She sat looking at him with long, slow, wondering look.

"Must one hate a devil that makes one live?" she asked.

He turned his eyes to her with a touch of a satiric smile.

"If one lives, no," he said.

She looked away from him the moment he looked at her. For her life she could not have met his dark eyes direct.

She left him, and he lay still. He neither read nor talked, throughout the long winter nights and the short winter days. He only lay for hours with black, open eyes, seeing everything around with a touch of disgust, and heeding nothing.

Daphne went to see him now and then. She never forgot him for long. He seemed to come into her mind suddenly, as if by sorcery.

One day he said to her:

"I see you are married. May I ask you who is your husband?"

She told him. She had had a letter also from Basil. The Count smiled slowly.

"You can look forward," he said, "to a happy reunion, and new, lovely children, Lady Daphne. Is it not so?"

"Yes, of course," she said.

"But you are ill," he said to her.

"Yes—rather ill."

"Of what?"

"Oh!" she answered fretfully, turning her face aside. "They talk about lungs." She hated speaking of it. "Why, how do you know I am ill?" she added quickly.

Again he smiled slowly.

"I see it in your face, and hear it in your voice. One would say the Evil One had cast a spell on you."

"Oh no," she said hastily. "But do I look ill?"

"Yes. You look as if something had struck you across the face, and you could not forget it."

"Nothing has," she said. "Unless it's the war."

"The war!" he repeated.

"Oh well, don't let us talk of it," she said.

Another time he said to her:

"The year has turned—the sun must shine at last, even in England. I am afraid of getting well too soon. I am a prisoner, am I not? But I wish the sun would shine. I wish the sun would shine on my face."

"You won't always be a prisoner. The war will end. And the sun *does* shine even in the winter in England," she said.

"I wish it would shine on my face," he said.

So that when in February there came a blue, bright morning, the morning that suggests yellow crocuses and the smell of a mezereon tree and the smell of damp, warm earth, Daphne hastily got a taxi and drove out to the hospital.

"You have come to put me in the sun," he said the moment he saw her.

"Yes, that's what I came for," she said.

She spoke to the matron, and had his bed carried out where there was a big window that came low. There he was put full in the sun. Turning, he could see the blue sky, and the twinkling tops of purplish, bare trees.

"The world! The world!" he murmured.

He lay with his eyes shut, and the sun on his swarthy, transparent, immobile face. The breath came and went through his nostrils invisibly. Daphne wondered how he could lie so still, how he could look so immobile. It was true as her mother had said: he looked as if he had been cast in the mould when the metal was white hot, all his lines were so clean. So small, he was, and in his way perfect.

Suddenly his dark eyes opened and caught her looking.

"The sun makes even anger open like a flower," he said.

"Whose anger?" she said.

"I don't know. But I can make flowers, looking through my eyelashes. Do you know how?"

"You mean rainbows?"

"Yes, flowers."

And she saw him, with a curious smile on his lips, looking through his almost closed eyelids at the sun.

"The sun is neither English nor German nor Bohemian," he said. "I am a subject of the sun. I belong to the fire-worshippers."

"Do you?" she replied.

"Yes, truly, by tradition." He looked at her smiling. "You stand there like a flower that will melt," he added.

She smiled slowly at him, with a slow, cautious look of her eyes as if she feared something.

"I am much more solid than you imagine," she said.

Still he watched her.

"One day," he said, "before I go, let me wrap your hair round my hands, will you?" He lifted his thin, short dark hands. "Let me wrap your hair round my hands, like a bandage. They hurt me. I don't know what it is. I think it is all the gun explosions. But if you let me wrap your hair round my hands. You know, it is the hermetic gold—but so much of water in it, of the moon. That will soothe my hands. One day, will you?"

"Let us wait till the day comes," she said.

"Yes," he answered, and was still again.

"It troubles me," he said after a while, "that I complain like a child, and ask for things. I feel I have lost my manhood for the time being. The continual explosions of guns and shells! It seems to have driven my soul out of me like a bird frightened away at last. But it will come back, you know. And I am so grateful to you; you are good to me when I am soulless, and you don't take advantage of me. Your soul is quiet and heroic."

"Don't," she said. "Don't talk!"

The expression of shame and anguish and disgust crossed his face.

"It is because I can't help it," he said. "I have lost my soul, and I can't stop talking to you. I can't stop. But I don't talk to any one else. I try not to talk, but I can't prevent it. Do you draw the words out of me?"

Her wide, green-blue eyes seemed like the heart of some curious, full-open flower, some Christmas rose with its petals of snow and flush. Her hair glinted heavy, like water-gold. She stood there passive and indomitable with the wide-eyed persistence of her wintry, blonde nature.

Another day when she came to see him he watched her for a time, then he said:

"Do they all tell you you are lovely, you are beautiful?"

"Not quite all," she replied.

"But your husband?"

"He has said so."

"Is he gentle? Is he tender? Is he a dear lover?"

She turned her face aside, displeased.

"Yes," she replied curtly.

He did not answer. And when she looked again he was lying with his eyes shut, a faint smile seeming to curl round his short, transparent nose. She could faintly see the flesh through his beard, as water through reeds. His black hair was brushed smooth as glass, his black eyebrows glinted like a curve of black glass on the swarthy opalescence of his brow.

Suddenly he spoke, without opening his eyes.

"You have been very kind to me," he said.

"Have I? Nothing to speak of."

He opened his eyes and looked at her.

"Everything finds its mate," he said. "The ermine and the polecat and the buzzard. One thinks so often that only the dove and the nightingale and the stag with his antlers have gentle mates. But the pole-cat and the ice-bears of the north have their mates. And a white she-bear lies with her cubs under a rock as a snake lies hidden, and the male-bear slowly swims back from the sea, like a clot of snow or a shadow of a white cloud passing on the speckled sea. I have seen her too, and I did not shoot her, nor him when he landed with fish in his mouth, wading wet and slow and yellow-white over the black stones."

"You have been in the North Sea?"

"Yes. And with the Eskimo in Siberia, and across the

Tundras. And a white sea-hawk makes a nest on a high stone, and sometimes looks out with her white head over the edge of the rocks. It is not only a world of men, Lady Daphne."

"Not by any means," said she.

"Else it were a sorry place."

"It is bad enough," said she.

"Foxes have their holes. They have even their mates, Lady Daphne, that they bark to and are answered. And an adder finds his female. Psanek means an outlaw; did you know?"

"I did not."

"Outlaws, and brigands, have often the finest woman-mates."

"They do," she said.

"I will be Psanek, Lady Daphne. I will not be Johann Dionys any more. I will be Psanek. The law has shot me through."

"You might be Psanek and Johann and Dionys as well," she said.

"With the sun on my face? Maybe," he said, looking to the sun.

There were some lovely days in the spring of 1918. In March the Count was able to get up. They dressed him in a simple, dark blue uniform. He was not very thin, only swarthy-trans-parent, now his beard was shaven and his hair was cut. His smallness made him noticeable, but he was masculine, perfect in his small stature. All the smiling dapperness that had made him seem like a monkey to Daphne when she was a girl had gone now. His eyes were dark and haughty; he seemed to keep inside his own reserves, speaking to nobody if he could help it, neither to the nurses nor the visitors nor to his fellow-prisoners, fellow-officers. He seemed to put a shadow between himself and them, and from across this shadow he looked with his dark, beautifully fringed eyes, as a proud little beast from the shadow of its lair. Only to Daphne he laughed and chatted.

She sat with him one day in March on the terrace of the hospital, on a morning when white clouds went endlessly and magnificently about a blue sky, and the sunshine felt warm after the blots of shadow.

"When you had a birthday, and you were seventeen, didn't I give you a thimble?" he asked her.

"Yes. I have it still."

"With a gold snake at the bottom, and a Mary-beetle of green stone at the top, to push the needle with."

"Yes."

"Do you ever use it?"

"No. I sew so rarely."

"Would it displease you to sew something for me?"

"You won't admire my stitches. What would you wish me to sew?"

"Sew me a shirt that I can wear. I have never before worn shirts from a shop, with a maker's name inside. It is very distasteful to me."

She looked at him—his haughty little brows.

"Shall I ask my maid to do it?" she said.

"Oh, please no! Oh, please no, do not trouble. No, please, I would not want it unless you sewed it yourself, with the Psanek thimble."

She paused before she answered. Then came her slow: "Why?"

He turned and looked at her with dark, searching eyes.

"I have no reason," he said, rather haughtily.

She left the matter there. For two weeks she did not go to see him. Then suddenly one day she took the bus down Oxford Street and bought some fine white flannel. She decided he must wear flannel.

That afternoon she drove out to Hurst Place. She found him sitting on the terrace, looking across the garden at the red suburb of London smoking fumily in the near distance, interrupted by patches of uncovered ground and a flat, tin-roofed laundry.

"Will you give me measurements for your shirt?" she said.

"The number of the neck-band of this English shirt is fifteen. If you ask the matron she will give you the measurement. It is a little too large, too long in the sleeves, you see," and he shook his shirt cuff over his wrist. "Also too long altogether."

"Mine will probably be unwearable when I've made them," said she.

"Oh no. Let your maid direct you. But please do not let her sew them."

"Will you tell me why you want me to do it?"

"Because I am a prisoner, in other people's clothes, and I have nothing of my own. All the things I touch are distasteful to me. If your maid sews for me, it will still be the same. Only you might give me what I want, something that buttons round my throat and on my wrists."

"And in Germany—or in Austria?"

"My mother sewed for me. And after her, my mother's sister, who was the head of my house."

"Not your wife?"

"Naturally not. She would have been insulted. She was never more than a guest in my house. In my family there are old traditions—but with me they have come to an end. I had best try to revive them."

"Beginning with traditions of shirts?"

"Yes. In our family the shirt should be made and washed by a woman of our own blood: but when we marry, by the wife. So when I married I had sixty shirts, and many other things—sewn by my mother and my aunt, all with my initial, and the ladybird, which is our crest."

"And where did they put the initial?"

"Here!" He put his finger on the back of his neck, on the swarthy, transparent skin. "I fancy I can feel the embroidered ladybird still. On our linen we had no crown: only the ladybird."

She was silent, thinking.

"You will forgive what I ask you?" he said, "since I am a prisoner and can do no other, and since fate has made you so that you understand the world as I understand it. It is not really indelicate, what I ask you. There will be a ladybird on your finger when you sew, and those who wear the ladybird understand."

"I suppose," she mused, "it is as bad to have your bee in your shirt as in your bonnet."

He looked at her with round eyes.

"Don't you know what it is to have a bee in your bonnet?" she said.

"No."

"To have a bee buzzing among your hair! To be out of your wits," she smiled at him.

"So!" he said. "Ah, the Psaneks have had a ladybird in their bonnets for many hundred years."

"Quite, quite mad," she said.

"It may be," he answered. "But with my wife I was quite sane for ten years. Now give me the madness of the ladybird. The world I was sane about has gone raving. The ladybird I was mad with is wise still."

"At least, when I sew the shirts, if I sew them," she said, "I shall have the ladybird at my finger's end."

"You want to laugh at me."

"But surely you know you are funny, with your family insect."

"My family insect? Now you want to be rude to me."

"How many spots must it have?"

"Seven."

"Three on each wing. And what do I do with the odd one?"

"You put that one between its teeth, like the cake for Cerberus."

"I'll remember that."

When she brought the first shirt, she gave it to the matron. Then she found Count Dionys sitting on the terrace. It was a beautiful spring day. Near at hand were tall elm trees, and some rooks cawing.

"What a lovely day!" she said. "Are you liking the world any better?"

"The world?" he said, looking up at her with the same old discontent and disgust on his fine, transparent nose.

"Yes," she replied, a shadow coming over her face.

"Is this the world—all those little red-brick boxes in rows, where couples of little people live, who decree my destiny?"

"You don't like England?"

"Ah, England! Little houses like little boxes, each with its domestic Englishman and his domestic wife, each ruling the world because all are alike, so alike."

"But England isn't all houses."

"Fields then! Little fields with innumerable hedges. Like a net with an irregular mesh, pinned down over this island and everything under the net. Ah, Lady Daphne, forgive me. I am ungrateful. I am so full of bile, of spleen, you say. My only wisdom is to keep my mouth shut."

"Why do you hate everything?" she said, her own face going bitter.

"Not everything. If I were free! If I were outside the law. Ah, Lady Daphne, how does one get outside the law?"

"By going inside oneself," she said. "Not outside."

His face took on a greater expression of disgust.

"No, no. I am a man, I am a man, even if I am little. I am not a spirit, that coils itself inside a shell. In my soul is anger, anger, anger. Give me room for my anger. Give me room for that."

His black eyes looked keenly into hers. She rolled her eyes as if in a half-trance. And in a monotonous, tranced voice she said:

"Much better get over your anger. And *why* are you angry?"

"There is no why. If it were love, you would not ask me, *why do you love?* But it is anger, anger, anger. What else can I call it? And there is no why."

Again he looked at her with his dark, sharp, questioning, tormented eyes.

"Can't you get rid of it?" she said, looking aside.

"If a shell exploded and blew me into a thousand fragments," he said, "it would not destroy the anger that is in me. I know that. No, it will never dissipate. And to die is no release. The anger goes on gnashing and whimpering in death. Lady Daphne, Lady Daphne, we have used up all the love, and this is what is left."

"Perhaps *you* have used up all your love," she replied. "You are not everybody."

"I know it. I speak for me and you."

"Not for me," she said rapidly.

He did not answer, and they remained silent.

At length she turned her eyes slowly to him.

"Why do you say you speak for me?" she said, in an accusing tone.

"Pardon me. I was hasty."

But a faint touch of superciliousness in his tone showed he meant what he had said. She mused, her brow cold and stony.

"And why do you tell *me* about your anger?" she said. "Will that make it better?"

"Even the adder finds his mate. And she has as much poison in her mouth as he."

She gave a sudden little squirt of laughter.

"Awfully poetic thing to say about me," she said.

He smiled, but with the same corrosive quality.

"Ah," he said, "you are not a dove. You are a wild-cat with open eyes, half-dreaming on a bough, in a lonely place, as I have seen her. And I ask myself—What are her memories, then?"

"I wish I were a wild-cat," she said suddenly.

He eyed her shrewdly, and did not answer.

"You want more war?" she said to him bitterly.

"More trenches? More Big Berthas, more shells and poison-gas, more machine-drilled science-manœuvred so-called armies? Never. Never. I would rather work in a factory that makes boots and shoes. And I would rather deliberately starve to death than work in a factory that makes boots and shoes."

"Then what do you want?"

"I want my anger to have room to grow."

"How?"

"I do not know. That is why I sit still here, day after day. I wait."

"For your anger to have room to grow?"

"For that."

"Good-bye, Count Dionys."

"Good-bye, Lady Daphne."

She had determined never to go and see him again. She had no sign from him. Since she had begun the second shirt, she went on with it. And then she hurried to finish it, because she was starting a round of visits that would end in the summer sojourn in Scotland. She intended to post the shirt. But after all, she took it herself.

She found Count Dionys had been removed from Hurst Place to Voynich Hall, where other enemy officers were interned. The being thwarted made her more determined. She took the train next day to go to Voynich Hall.

When he came into the ante-room where he was to receive her, she felt at once the old influence of his silence and his subtle power. His face had still that swarthy-transparent look of one who is unhappy, but his bearing was proud and reserved. He kissed her hand politely, leaving her to speak.

"How are you?" she said. "I didn't know you were here. I am going away for the summer."

"I wish you a pleasant time," he said. They were speaking English.

"I brought the other shirt," she said. "It is finished at last."

"That is a greater honour than I dared expect," he said.

"I'm afraid it may be more honourable than useful. The other didn't fit, did it?"

"Almost," he said. "It fitted the spirit, if not the flesh," he smiled.

"I'd rather it had been the reverse, for once," she said. "Sorry."

"I would not have it one stitch different."

"Can we sit in the garden?"

"I think we may."

They sat on a bench. Other prisoners were playing croquet not far off. But these two were left comparatively alone.

"Do you like it better here?" she said.

"I have nothing to complain of," he said.

"And the anger?"

"It is doing well, I thank you," he smiled.

"You mean getting better?"

"Making strong roots," he said, laughing.

"Ah, so long as it only makes roots!" she said.

"And your ladyship, how is she?"

"My ladyship is rather better," she replied.

"Much better, indeed," he said, looking into her face.

"Do you mean I *look* much better?" she asked quickly.

"Very much. It is your beauty you think of. Well, your beauty is almost itself again."

"Thanks."

"You brood on your beauty as I on my anger. Ah, your ladyship, be wise, and make friends with your anger. That is the way to let your beauty blossom."

"I was not unfriends with you, was I?" she said.

"With me?" His face flickered with a laugh. "Am I your anger? Your vicar in wrath? So then, be friends with the angry me, your ladyship. I ask nothing better."

"What is the use," she said. "being friends with the *angry* you? I would much rather be friends with the happy you."

"That little animal is extinct," he laughed. "And I am glad of it."

"But what remains? Only the angry you? Then it is no use my trying to be friends."

"You remember, dear Lady Daphne, that the adder does not suck his poison all alone, and the pole-cat knows where to find his she-pole-cat. You remember that each one has his own dear mate," he laughed. "Dear, deadly mate."

"And what if I do remember those bits of natural history, Count Dionys?"

"The she-adder is dainty, delicate, and carries her poison lightly. The wild-cat has wonderful green eyes that she closes with memory like a screen. The ice-bear hides like a snake with her cubs, and her snarl is the strangest thing in the world."

"Have you ever heard me snarl?" she asked suddenly.

He only laughed, and looked away.

They were silent. And immediately the strange thrill of

secrecy was between them. Something had gone beyond
sadness into another secret, thrilling communion which she
would never admit.

"What do you do all day here?" she asked.

"Play chess, play this foolish croquet, play billiards, and
read, and wait, and remember."

"What do you wait for?"

"I don't know."

"And what do you remember?"

"Ah, that. Shall I tell you what amuses me? Shall I tell
you a secret?"

"Please don't, if it's anything that matters."

"It matters to nobody but me. Will you hear it?"

"If it does not implicate me in any way."

"It does not. Well, I am a member of a certain old secret
society—no, don't look at me, nothing frightening—only a
society like the freemasons."

"And?"

"And—well, as you know, one is initiated into certain
so-called secrets and rites. My family has always been
initiated. So I am an initiate too. Does it interest you?"

"Why, of course."

"Well. I was always rather thrilled by these secrets. Or
some of them. Some seemed to me far-fetched. The ones that
thrilled me even never had any relation to actual life. When
you knew me in Dresden and Prague, you would not have
thought me a man invested with awful secret knowledge, now
would you?"

"Never."

"No. It was just a little exciting side-show. And I was a
grimacing little society man. But now they become true. It
becomes true."

"The secret knowledge?"

"Yes."

"What, for instance?"

"Take actual fire. It will bore you. Do you want to hear?"

"Go on."

"This is what I was taught. The true fire is invisible. Flame, and the red fire we see burning, has its back to us. It is running away from us. Does that mean anything to you?"

"Yes."

"Well then, the yellowness of sunshine—light itself—that is only the glancing aside of the real original fire. You know that is true. There would be no light if there was no refraction, no bits of dust and stuff to turn the dark fire into visibility. You know that's a fact. And that being so, even the sun is dark. It is only his jacket of dust that makes him visible. You know that too. And the true sunbeams coming towards us flow darkly, a moving darkness of the genuine fire. The sun is dark, the sunshine flowing to us is dark. And light is only the inside out of it all, the lining, and the yellow beams are only the turning away of the sun's directness that was coming to us. Does that interest you at all?"

"Yes," she said dubiously.

"Well, we've got the world inside out. The true living world of fire is dark, throbbing, darker than blood. Our luminous world that we go by is only the reverse of this."

"Yes, I like that," she said.

"Well! Now listen. The same with love. This white love that we have is the same. It is only the reverse, the whited sepulchre of the true love. True love is dark, a throbbing together in darkness, like the wild-cat in the night, when the green screen opens and her eyes are on the darkness."

"No, I don't see that," she said, in a slow, clanging voice.

"You, and your beauty—that is only the inside-out of you. The real you is the wild-cat invisible in the night, with red fire perhaps coming out of its wide, dark eyes. Your beauty is your whited sepulchre."

"You mean cosmetics," she said. "I've got none on to-day—not even powder."

He laughed.

"Very good," he said. "Consider me. I used to think myself small but handsome, and the ladies used to admire me moderately, never very much. A trim little fellow, you know.

Well, that was just the inside-out of me. I am a black tom-cat howling in the night, and it is then that fire comes out of me. This me you look at is my whited sepulchre. What do you say?"

She was looking into his eyes. She could see the darkness swaying in the depths. She perceived the invisible, cat-like fire stirring deep inside them, felt it coming towards her. She turned her face aside. Then he laughed, showing his strong white teeth, that seemed a little too large, rather dreadful.

She rose to go.

"Well," she said. "I shall have the summer in which to think about the world inside-out. Do write if there is anything to say. Write to Thoresway. Good-bye!"

"Ah, your eyes!" he said. "They are like jewels of stone."

Being away from the Count, she put him out of her mind. Only she was sorry for him a prisoner in that sickening Voynich Hall. But she did not write. Nor did he.

As a matter of fact her mind was now much more occupied with her husband. All arrangements were being made to effect his exchange. From month to month she looked for his return. And so she thought of him.

Whatever happened to her, she thought about it, thought and thought a great deal. The consciousness of her mind was like tablets of stone weighing her down. And whoever would make a new entry into her must break these tablets of stone piece by piece. So it was that in her own way she thought often enough of the Count's world inside-out. A curious latency stirred in her consciousness that was not yet an idea.

He said her eyes were like jewels of stone. What a horrid thing to say! What did he want her eyes to be like? He wanted them to dilate and become all black pupil, like a cat's at night. She shrank convulsively from the thought, and tightened her breast.

He said her beauty was her whited sepulchre. Even that, she knew what he meant. The invisibility of her he wanted to love. But ah, her pearl-like beauty was so dear to her, and it was so famous in the world.

He said her white love was like moonshine, harmful, the
reverse of love. He meant Basil, of course. Basil always said
she was the moon. But then Basil loved her for that. The
ecstasy of it! She shivered, thinking of her husband. But it
had also made her nerve-worn, her husband's love. Ah,
nerve-worn.

What then would the Count's love be like? Something so
secret and different. She would not be lovely and a queen to
him. He hated her loveliness. The wild-cat has its mate. The
little wild-cat that he was. Ah!

She caught her breath, determined not to think. When she
thought of Count Dionys she felt the world slipping away from
her. She would sit in front of a mirror, looking at her wonderful
cared-for face that had appeared in so many society magazines.
She loved it so, it made her feel so vain. And she looked at her
blue-green eyes—the eyes of the wild-cat on a bough. Yes, the
lovely blue-green iris drawn tight like a screen. Supposing it
should relax. Supposing it should unfold, and open out the
dark depths, the dark, dilated pupil! Supposing it should?

Never! She always caught herself back. She felt she might
be killed before she could give way to that relaxation that the
Count wanted of her. She could not. She just could not. At
the very thought of it some hypersensitive nerve started with
a great twinge in her breast; she drew back, forced to keep her
guard. Ah no, Monsieur le Comte, you shall never take her
ladyship off her guard.

She disliked the thought of the Count. An impudent little
fellow. An impertinent little fellow! A little madman, really.
A little outsider. No, no. She would think of her husband:
an adorable, tall, well-bred Englishman, so easy and simple,
and with the amused look in his blue eyes. She thought of the
cultured, casual trail of his voice. It set her nerves on fire.
She thought of his strong, easy body—beautiful, white-fleshed,
with the fine springing of warm-brown hair like tiny flames. He
was the Dionysus, full of sap, milk and honey, and northern
golden wine: he, her husband. Not that little unreal Count.
Ah, she dreamed of her husband, of the love-days, and the

honeymoon, the lovely, simple intimacy. Ah, the marvellous revelation of that intimacy, when he left himself to her so generously. Ah, she was his wife for this reason, that he had given himself to her so greatly, so generously. Like an ear of corn he was there for her gathering—her husband, her own, lovely, English husband. Ah, when would he come again, when would he come again!

She had letters from him—and how he loved her. Far away, his life was all hers. All hers, flowing to her as the beam flows from a white star right down to us, to our heart. Her lover, her husband.

He was now expecting to come home soon. It had all been arranged. "I hope you won't be disappointed in me when I do get back," he wrote. "I am afraid I am no longer the plump and well-looking young man I was. I've got a big scar at the side of my mouth, and I'm as thin as a starved rabbit, and my hair's going grey. Doesn't sound attractive, does it? And it isn't attractive. But once I can get out of this infernal place, and once I can be with you again, I shall come in for my second blooming. The very thought of being quietly in the same house with you, quiet and in peace, makes me realize that if I've been through hell, I have known heaven on earth and can hope to know it again. I am a miserable brute to look at now. But I have faith in you. You will forgive my appearance, and that alone will make me feel handsome."

She read this letter many times. She was not afraid of his scar or his looks. She would love him all the more.

Since she had started making shirts—those two for the Count had been an enormous labour, even though her maid had come to her assistance forty times: but since she had started making shirts, she thought she might continue. She had some good suitable silk: her husband liked silk underwear.

But still she used the Count's thimble. It was gold outside and silver inside, and was too heavy. A snake was coiled round the base, and at the top, for pressing the needle, was inlet a semi-translucent apple-green stone, perhaps jade, carved like a scarab, with little dots. It was too heavy. But then she sewed so slowly, And she liked to feel her hand heavy, weighted. And as she sewed she thought about her husband, and she felt herself in love with him. She thought of him, how beautiful he was, and how she would love him now he was thin: she would love him all the more. She would love to trace his bones, as if to trace his living skeleton. The thought made her rest her hands in her lap, and drift into a muse. Then she felt the weight of the thimble on her finger, and took it off, and sat looking at the green stone. The ladybird. The ladybird. And if only her husband would come soon, soon. It was wanting him that made her so ill. Nothing but that. She had wanted him so badly. She wanted now. Ah, if she could go to him now, and find him, wherever he was, and see him and touch him and take all his love.

As she mused, she put the thimble down in front of her, took up a little silver pencil from her work-basket, and on a bit of blue paper that had been the band of a small skein of silk she wrote the lines of the silly little song:

"Wenn ich ein Vöglein wär'
Und auch zwei Flüglein hätt'
Flög' ich zu dir——"

That was all she could get on her bit of pale-blue paper.

"If I were a little bird
And had two little wings
I'd fly to thee——"

Silly enough, in all conscience. But she did not translate it, so it did not seem quite so silly.

At that moment her maid announced Lady Bingham—her husband's sister. Daphne crumpled up the bit of paper in a flurry, and in another minute Primrose, his sister, came in. The newcomer was not a bit like a primrose, being long-faced and clever, smart, but not a bit elegant, in her new clothes.

"Daphne dear, what a domestic scene! I suppose it's rehearsal. Well, you may as well rehearse, he's with Admiral Burns on the *Ariadne*. Father just heard from the Admiralty:

quite fit. He'll be here in a day or two. Splendid, isn't it?
And the war is going to end. At least it seems like it. You'll
be safe of your man now, dear. Thank heaven when it's all
over. What are you sewing?"

"A shirt," said Daphne.

"A shirt! Why, how clever of you. I should never know
which end to begin. Who showed you?"

"Millicent."

"And how did *she* know? She's no business to know how to
sew shirts: nor cushions nor sheets either. Do let me look.
Why, how perfectly marvellous you are!—every bit by hand,
too. Basil isn't worth it, dear, really he isn't. Let him order
his shirts in Oxford Street. Your business is to be beautiful,
not to sew shirts. What a dear little pin-poppet, or rather
needle-woman! I say, a satire on us, that is. But what a
darling, with mother-of-pearl wings to her skirts! And darling
little gold-eyed needles inside her. You screw her head off,
and you find she's full of pins and needles. Woman for you!
Mother says won't you come to lunch to-morrow. And won't
you come to Brassey's to tea with me at this minute. Do,
there's a dear. I've got a taxi."

Daphne bundled her sewing loosely together.

When she tried to do a bit more, two days later, she could
not find her thimble. She asked her maid, whom she could
absolutely trust. The girl had not seen it. She searched
everywhere. She asked her nurse—who was now her housekeeper—and footman. No, nobody had seen it. Daphne even
asked her sister-in-law.

"Thimble, darling? No, I don't remember a thimble. I
remember a dear little needle lady, whom I thought such a
precious satire on us women. I didn't notice a thimble."

Poor Daphne wandered about in a muse. She did not want
to believe it lost. It had been like a talisman to her. She tried
to forget it. Her husband was coming, quite soon, quite soon.
But she could not raise herself to joy. She had lost her thimble.
It was as if Count Dionys accused her in her sleep of something,
she did not quite know what.

And though she did not really want to go to Voynich Hall, yet like a fatality she went, like one doomed. It was already late autumn, and some lovely days. This was the last of the lovely days. She was told that Count Dionys was in the small park, finding chestnuts. She went to look for him. Yes, there he was in his blue uniform stooping over the brilliant yellow leaves of the sweet chestnut tree, that lay around him like a fallen nimbus of glowing yellow, under his feet, as he kicked and rustled, looking for the chestnut burrs. And with his short, brown hands he was pulling out the small chestnuts and putting them in his pockets. But as she approached he peeled a nut to eat it. His teeth were white and powerful.

"You remind me of a squirrel laying in a winter store," said she.

"Ah, Lady Daphne—I was thinking, and did not hear you."

"I thought you were gathering chestnuts—even eating them."

"Also!" he laughed. He had a dark, sudden charm when he laughed, showing his rather large white teeth. She was not quite sure whether she found him a little repulsive.

"Were you *really* thinking?" she said, in her slow, resonant way.

"Very truly."

"And weren't you enjoying the chestnut a bit?"

"Very much. Like sweet milk. Excellent, excellent." He had the fragments of the nut between his teeth, and bit them finely. "Will you take one, too." He held out the little, pointed brown nuts on the palm of his hand.

She looked at them doubtfully.

"Are they as tough as they always were?" she said.

"No, they are fresh and good. Wait, I will peel one for you."

They strayed about through the thin clump of trees.

"You have had a pleasant summer; you are strong?"

"Almost *quite* strong," said she. "Lovely summer, thanks. I suppose it's no good asking you if you have been happy?"

"Happy?" He looked at her direct. His eyes were black, and

seemed to examine her. She always felt he had a little contempt of her. "Oh, yes," he said, smiling. "I have been very
happy."

"So glad."

They drifted a little further, and he picked up an apple-green
chestnut burr out of the yellow-brown leaves, handling it with
sensitive fingers that still suggested paws to her.

"How did you succeed in being happy?" she said.

"How shall I tell you? I felt that the same power which put
up the mountains could pull them down again—no matter how
long it took."

"And was that all?"

"Was it not enough?"

"I should say decidedly too little."

He laughed broadly, showing the strong, negroid teeth.

"You do not know all it means," he said.

"The thought that the mountains were going to be pulled
down?" she said. "It will be so long after my day."

"Ah, you are bored," he said. "But I—I found the God who
pulls things down: especially the things that men have put up.
Do they not say that life is a search after God, Lady Daphne?
I have found my God."

"The god of destruction," she said, blanching.

"Yes—not the devil of destruction, but the god of destruction. The blessed god of destruction. It is strange"—he stood
before her, looking up at her—"but I have found my God.
The god of anger, who throws down the steeples and the
factory chimneys. Ah, Lady Daphne, he is a man's God, a
man's God. I have found my God, Lady Daphne."

"Apparently. And how are you going to serve him?"

A naïve glow transfigured his face.

"Oh, I will help. With my heart I will help while I can do
nothing with my hands. I say to my heart: Beat, hammer,
beat with little strokes. Beat, hammer of God, beat them
down. Beat it all down."

Her brows knitted, her face took on a look of discontent.

"Beat what down?" she asked harshly.

"The world, the world of man. Not the trees—these chestnuts for example"—he looked up at them, at the tufts and loose pinions of yellow—"not these—nor the chattering sorcerers, the squirrels—nor the hawk that comes. Not those."

"You mean beat England?" she said.

"Ah, no. Ah, no. Not England any more than Germany—perhaps not as much. Not Europe any more than Asia."

"Just the end of the world?"

"No, no. No, no. What grudge have I against a world where little chestnuts are so sweet as these! Do you like yours? Will you take another?"

"No, thanks."

"What grudge have I against a world where even the hedges are full of berries, bunches of black berries that hang down, and red berries that thrust up. Never would I hate the world. But the world of man. Lady Daphne"—his voice sank to a whisper—"*I hate it*. Zzz!" he hissed. "Strike, little heart! Strike, strike, hit, smite! Oh, Lady Daphne!"—his eyes dilated with a ring of fire.

"What?" she said, scared.

"I believe in the power of my red, dark heart. God has put the hammer in my breast—the little eternal hammer. Hit—hit—hit! It hits on the world of man. It hits, it hits! And it hears the thin sound of cracking. The thin sound of cracking. Hark!"

He stood still and made her listen. It was late afternoon. The strange laugh of his face made the air seem dark to her. And she could easily have believed that she heard a faint, fine shivering, cracking, through the air, a delicate crackling noise.

"You hear it? Yes? Oh, may I live long! May I live long, so that my hammer may strike and strike, and the cracks go deeper, deeper! Ah, the world of man! Ah, the joy, the passion in every heart-beat! Strike home, strike true, strike sure. Strike to destroy it. Strike! Strike! To destroy the world of man. Ah, God. Ah, God, prisoner of peace. Do I not know you, Lady Daphne? Do I not? Do I not?"

She was silent for some moments, looking away at the twinkling lights of a station beyond.

"Not the white plucked lily of your body. I have gathered no flower for my ostentatious life. But in the cold dark, your lily root, Lady Daphne. Ah, yes, you will know it all your life, that I know where your root lies buried, with its sad, sad quick of life. What does it matter!"

They had walked slowly towards the house. She was silent, Then at last she said, in a peculiar voice:

"And you would never want to kiss me?"

"Ah, no!" he answered sharply.

She held out her hand.

"Good-bye, Count Dionys," she drawled, fashionably. He bowed over her hand, but did not kiss it.

"Good-bye, Lady Daphne."

She went away, with her brow set hard. And henceforth she thought only of her husband, of Basil. She made the Count die out of her. Basil was coming, he was near. He was coming back from the East, from war and death. Ah, he had been through awful fire of experience. He would be something new, something she did not know. He was something new, a stronger lover who had been through terrible fire, and had come out strange and new, like a god. Ah, new and terrible his love would be, pure and intensified by the awful fire of suffering. A new lover—a new bridegroom—a new, supernatural wedding-night. She shivered in anticipation, waiting for her husband. She hardly noticed the wild excitement of the Armistice. She was waiting for something more wonderful to her.

And yet the moment she heard his voice on the telephone, her heart contracted with fear. It was his well-known voice, deliberate, diffident, almost drawling, with the same subtle suggestion of deference and the rather exaggerated Cambridge intonation, up and down. But there was a difference, a new icy note that went through her veins like death.

"Is that you, Daphne? I shall be with you in half an hour. Is that all right for you? Yes, I've just landed, and shall come straight to you? Yes, a taxi. Shall I be too sudden for you, darling? No? Good, oh good! Half an hour, then! I say, Daphne? There won't be anyone else there, will there? Quite alone! Good! I can ring up Dad afterwards. Yes, splendid, splendid. Sure you're all right, my darling? I'm at death's door till I see you. Yes. Good-bye—half an hour. Good-bye."

When Daphne had hung up the receiver she sat down almost in a faint. What was it that so frightened her? His terrible, terrible altered voice, like cold, blue steel. She had no time to think. She rang for her maid.

"Oh, my lady, it isn't bad news?" cried Millicent, when she caught sight of her mistress white as death.

"No, good news. Major Apsley will be here in half an hour. Help me to dress. Ring to Murry's first to send in some roses, red ones, and some lilac-coloured iris—two dozen of each, at once."

Daphne went to her room. She didn't know what to wear, she didn't know how she wanted her hair dressed. She spoke hastily to her maid. She chose a violet coloured dress. She did not know what she was doing. In the middle of dressing the flowers came, and she left off to put them in the bowls. So that when she heard his voice in the hall, she was still standing in front of the mirror reddening her lips and wiping it away again.

"Major Apsley, my lady!" murmured the maid, in excitement.

"Yes, I can hear. Go and tell him I shall be *one* minute."

Daphne's voice had become slow and sonorous, like bronze, as it always did when she was upset. Her face looked almost haggard, and in vain she dabbed with the rouge.

"How does he look?" she asked curtly, when her maid came back.

"A long scar here," said the maid, and she drew her finger from the left-hand corner of her mouth into her cheek, slanting downwards.

"Make him look very different?" asked Daphne.

"Not so *very* different, my lady," said Millicent gently.

"His eyes are the same, I think." The girl also was distressed.

"All right," said Daphne. She looked at herself, a long, last look as she turned away from the mirror. The sight of her own face made her feel almost sick. She had seen so much of herself. And yet even now she was fascinated by the heavy droop of her lilac-veined lids over her slow, strange, large, green-blue eyes. They *were* mysterious-looking. And she gave herself a long, sideways glance, curious and Chinese. How was it possible there was a touch of the Chinese in her face?—she so purely an English blonde, an Aphrodite of the foam, as Basil had called her in poetry. Ah well! She left off her thoughts and went through the hall to the drawing-room.

He was standing nervously in the middle of the room, in his uniform. She hardly glanced at his face—and saw only the scar.

"Hullo, Daphne," he said, in a voice full of the expected emotion. He stepped forward and took her in his arms, and kissed her forehead.

"So glad! So glad it's happened at last," she said, hiding her tears.

"So glad what has happened, darling?" he asked, in his deliberate manner.

"That you're back." Her voice had the bronze resonance, she spoke rather fast.

"Yes, I'm back, Daphne darling—as much of me as there is to bring back."

"Why?" she said. "You've come back whole, surely?" She was frightened.

"Yes, apparently I have. Apparently. But don't let's talk of that. Let's talk of you, darling. How are you? Let me look at you. You are thinner, you are older. But you are more wonderful than ever. Far more wonderful."

"How?" said she.

"I can't exactly say how. You were only a girl. Now you are a woman. I suppose it's all that's happened. But you are wonderful as a woman, Daphne darling—more wonderful than all that's happened. I couldn't have believed you'd be so wonderful. I'd forgotten—or else I'd never known. I say, I'm a lucky chap really. Here I am, alive and well, and I've got you for a wife. It's brought you out like a flower. I say, darling, there is more now of that Venus of the foam—grander. How beautiful you are! But you look like the beauty of all life—as if you were moon-mother of the world—Aphrodite. God is good to me after all, darling. I ought never to utter a single complaint. How lovely you are—how lovely you are, my darling! I'd forgotten you—and I thought I knew you so well. Is it true that you belong to me? Are you really mine?"

They were seated on the yellow sofa. He was holding her hand, and his eyes were going up and down, from her face to her throat and her breast. The sound of his words, and the strong, cold desire in his voice excited her, pleased her, and made her heart freeze. She turned and looked into his light blue eyes. They had no longer the amused light, nor the young look. They burned with a hard, focused light, whitish.

"It's all right. You are mine, aren't you, Daphne darling?" came his cultured, musical voice, that had always the well-bred twang of diffidence.

She looked back into his eyes.

"Yes, I am yours," she said, from the lips.

"Darling! Darling!" he murmured, kissing her hand.

Her heart beat suddenly so terribly, as if her breast would be ruptured, and she rose in one movement and went across the room. She leaned her hand on the mantelpiece and looked down at the electric fire. She could hear the faint, faint noise of it. There was silence for a few moments.

Then she turned and looked at him. He was watching her intently.

His face was gaunt, and there was a curious deathly sub-pallor, though his cheeks were not white. The scar ran livid from the side of his mouth. It was not so very big. But it seemed like a scar in him himself, in his brain as it were. In his eyes was that hard, white, focused light that fascinated her and was terrible to her. He was different. He was like death; like risen death. She felt she dared not touch him.

White death was still upon him. She could tell that he shrank with a kind of agony from contact. "Touch me not, I am not yet ascended unto the Father." Yet for contact he had come. Something, someone seemed to be looking over his shoulder. His own young ghost looking over his shoulder. Oh God! She closed her eyes, seeming to swoon. He remained leaning forward on the sofa, watching her.

"Aren't you well, darling?" he asked. There was a strange, incomprehensible coldness in his very fire. He did not move to come near her.

"Yes, I'm well. It is only that after all it is so sudden. Let me get used to you," she said, turning aside her face from him. She felt utterly like a victim of his white, awful face.

"I suppose I must be a bit of a shock to you," he said. "I hope you won't leave off loving me. It won't be that, will it?"

The strange coldness in his voice! And yet the white, uncanny fire.

"No, I shan't leave off loving you," she admitted, in a low tone, as if almost ashamed. She *dared* not have said otherwise. And the saying it made it true.

"Ah, if you're sure of that," he said. "I'm a pretty unlovely sight to behold, I know, with this wound-scar. But if you can forgive me, darling. Do you think you can?" There was something like compulsion in his tone.

She looked at him, and shivered slightly.

"I love you—more than before," she said hurriedly.

"Even the scar?" came his terrible voice, inquiring.

She glanced again, with that slow, Chinese side-look, and felt she would die.

"Yes," she said, looking away at nothingness. It was an awful moment to her. A little, slightly imbecile smile widened on her face.

He suddenly knelt at her feet, and kissed the toe of her slipper, and kissed the instep, and kissed the ankle in the thin, black stocking.

"I knew," he said in a muffled voice. "I knew you would make good. I knew if I had to kneel, it was before you. I knew you were divine, you were the one—Cybele—Isis. I knew I was your slave. I knew. It has all been just a long initiation. I had to learn how to worship you."

He kissed her feet again and again, without the slightest self-consciousness, or the slightest misgiving. Then he went back to the sofa, and sat there looking at her, saying:

"It isn't love, it is worship. Love between me and you will be a sacrament, Daphne. That's what I had to learn. You are beyond me. A mystery to me. My God, how great it all is. How marvellous!"

She stood with her hand on the mantelpiece, looking down and not answering. She was frightened—almost horrified: but she was thrilled deep down to her soul. She really felt she could glow white and fill the universe like the moon, like Astarte, like Isis, like Venus. The grandeur of her own pale power. The man religiously worshipped her, not merely amorously. She was ready for him—for the sacrament of his supreme worship.

He sat on the sofa with his hands spread on the yellow brocade and pushing downwards behind him, down between the deep upholstery of the back and the seat. He had long, white hands with pale freckles. And his fingers touched something. With his long white fingers he groped and brought it out. It was the lost thimble. And inside it was the bit of screwed-up blue paper.

"I say, is that *your* thimble?" he asked.

She started, and went hurriedly forward for it.

"Where was it?" she said, agitated.

But he did not give it to her. He turned it round and pulled out the bit of blue paper. He saw the faint pencil marks on the screwed-up ball, and unrolled the band of paper, and slowly deciphered the verse.

> "Wenn ich ein Vöglein wär'
> Und auch zwei Flüglein hätt'
> Flög' ich zu dir——"

"How awfully touching that is," he said. "A Vöglein with

F

two little Flüglein! But what a precious darling child you are! Whom did you want to fly to, if you were a Vöglein?" He looked up at her with a curious smile.

"I can't remember," she said, turning aside her head.

"I hope it was to me," he said. "Anyhow I shall consider it was, and shall love you all the more for it. What a darling child! A Vöglein if you please, with two little wings! Why, how beautifully absurd of you, darling!"

He folded the scrap of paper carefully, and put it in his pocket-book, keeping the thimble all the time between his knees.

"Tell me when you lost it, Daphne," he said, examining the bauble.

"About a month ago—or two months."

"About a month ago—or two months. And what were you sewing? Do you mind if I ask? I like to think of you then. I was still in that beastly El Hasrun. What were you sewing, darling, two months ago, when you lost your thimble?"

"A shirt."

"I say, a shirt! Whose shirt?"

"Yours."

"There. Now we've run it to earth. Were you really sewing a shirt for me! Is it finished? Can I put it on at this minute?"

"That one isn't finished, but the first one is."

"I say, darling, let me go and put it on. To think I should have it next my skin! I shall feel you all round me, all over me. I say how marvellous that will be! Won't you come."

"Won't you give me the thimble?" she said.

"Yes, of course. What a noble thimble, too! Who gave it you?"

"Count Dionys Psanek."

"Who was he?"

"A Bohemian Count, in Dresden. He once stayed with us in Thoresway—with a tall wife. Didn't you meet them?"

"I don't think I did. I don't think I did. I don't remember. What was he like?"

"A little man with black hair and a rather low, dark forehead—rather dressy."

"No, I don't remember him at all. So he gave it you. Well, I wonder where he is now? Probably rotted, poor devil."

"No, he's interned in Voynich Hall. Mother and I have been to see him several times. He was awfully badly wounded."

"Poor little beggar! In Voynich Hall! I'll look at him before he goes. Odd thing, to give you a thimble. Odd gift! You were a girl then, though. Do you think he had it made, or do you think he found it in a shop?"

"I think it belonged to the family. The ladybird at the top is part of their crest—and the snake as well, I think."

"A ladybird! Funny thing for a crest. Americans would call it a bug. I must look at him before he goes. And you were sewing a shirt for me! And then you posted me this little letter into the sofa. Well, I'm awfully glad I received it, and that it didn't go astray in the post, like so many things. 'Wenn ich ein Vöglein wär'—you perfect child! But that is the beauty of a woman like you: you are so superb and beyond worship, and then such an exquisite naïve child. Who could help worshipping you and loving you: immortal and mortal together. What, you want the thimble? Here! Wonderful, wonderful white fingers. Ah, darling, you are more goddess than child, you long, limber Isis with sacred hands. White, white, and immortal! Don't tell me your hands could die, darling: your wonderful Proserpine fingers. They are immortal as February and snowdrops. If you lift your hands the spring comes. I *can't* help kneeling before you, darling. I am no more than a sacrifice to you, an offering. I *wish* I could die in giving myself to you, give you all my blood on your altar, for ever."

She looked at him with a long, slow look, as he turned his face to her. His face was white with ecstasy. And she was not afraid. Somewhere, saturnine, she knew it was absurd. But she chose not to know. A certain swoon-sleep was on her. With her slow, green-blue eyes she looked down on his ecstasied face, almost benign. But in her right hand unconsciously she held the thimble fast, she only gave him her left hand. He took her hand and rose to his feet in that curious priestly ecstasy which made him more than a man or a soldier, far, far more than a lover to her.

Nevertheless his home-coming made her begin to be ill again. Afterwards, after his love, she had to bear herself in torment. To her shame and her heaviness, she knew she was not strong enough, or pure enough, to bear this awful out-pouring adoration-lust. It was not her fault she felt weak and fretful afterwards, as if she wanted to cry and be fretful and petulant, wanted someone to save her. She could not turn to Basil, her husband. After his ecstasy of adoration-lust for her, she recoiled from him. Alas, she was not the goddess, the superb person he named her. She was flawed with the fatal humility of her age. She could not harden her heart and burn her soul pure of this humility, this misgiving. She could not finally believe in her own woman-godhead—only in her own female mortality.

That fierce power of being alone, even with your lover, the fierce power of the woman in excelsis—alas, she could not keep it. She could rise to the height for the time, the incandescent, transcendent, moon-fierce womanhood. But alas, she could not stay intensified and resplendent in her white, womanly powers, her female mystery. She relaxed, she lost her glory, and became fretful. Fretful and ill and never to be soothed. And then naturally her man became ashy and somewhat acrid, while she ached with nerves, and could not eat.

Of course she began to dream, about Count Dionys: to yearn wistfully for him. And it was absolutely a fatal thought to her that he was going away. When she thought that—that he was leaving England soon—going away into the dark for ever— then the last spark seemed to die in her. She felt her soul perish, whilst she herself was worn and soulless like a pro-stitute. A prostitute goddess. And her husband, the gaunt, white, intensified priest of her, who never ceased from being before her like a lust.

"To-morrow," she said to him, gathering her last courage and looking at him with a side-look, "I want to go to Voynich Hall."

"What, to see Count Psanek? Oh, good! Yes, very good! I'll come along as well. I should like very much to see him. I suppose he'll be getting sent back before long."

It was a fortnight before Christmas, very dark weather. Her husband was in khaki. She wore her black furs, and a black lace veil over her face, so that she seemed mysterious. But she lifted the veil and looped it behind, so that it made a frame for her face. She looked very lovely like that—her face pure like the most white hellebore flower, touched with winter pink, amid the blackness of her drapery and furs. Only she was rather too much like the picture of a modern beauty: too much the actual thing. She had half an idea that Dionys would hate her for her effective loveliness. He would see it and hate it. The thought was like a bitter balm to her. For herself, she loved her loveliness almost with obsession.

The Count came cautiously forward, glancing from the lovely figure of Lady Daphne to the gaunt well-bred Major at her side. Daphne was so beautiful in her dark furs, the black lace of her veil thrown back over her close-fitting, dull-gold-threaded hat, and her face fair like a winter flower in a cranny of darkness. But on her face, that was smiling with a slow self-satisfaction of beauty and of knowledge that she was dangling the two men, and setting all the imprisoned officers wildly on the alert, the Count could read that acridity of dissatisfaction and of inefficiency. And he looked away to the livid scar on the Major's cheek.

"Count Dionys, I wanted to bring my husband to see you. May I introduce him to you. Major Apsley—Count Dionys Psanek."

The two men shook hands, rather stiffly.

"I can sympathize with you being fastened up in this place," said Basil in his slow, easy fashion. "I hated it, I assure you, out there in the East."

"But your conditions were much worse than mine," smiled the Count.

"Well, perhaps they were. But prison is prison, even if it were heaven itself."

"Lady Apsley has been the one angel of my heaven," smiled the Count.

"I'm afraid I was as inefficient as most angels," said she.

The small smile never left the Count's dark face. It was true as she said, he was low-browed, the black hair growing low on his brow, and his eyebrows making a thick bow above his dark eyes, which had again long black lashes. So that the upper part of his face seemed very dusky-black. His nose was small and somewhat translucent. There was a touch of mockery about him, which was intensified even by his small, energetic stature. He was still carefully dressed in the dark blue uniform, whose shabbiness could not hinder the dark flame of life which seemed to glow through the cloth from his body. He was not thin—but still had a curious swarthy translucency of skin in his low browed face.

"What would you have been more?" he laughed, making equivocal dark eyes at her.

"Oh, of course, a delivering angel—a cinema heroine," she replied, closing her eyes and turning her face aside.

All the while the white-faced, tall Major watched the little man with a fixed, half-smiling scrutiny. The Count seemed not to notice. He turned to the Englishman.

"I am glad that I can congratulate you, Major Apsley, on your safe and happy return to your home."

"Thanks. I hope I may be able to congratulate you in the same way before long."

"Oh yes," said the Count. "Before long I shall be shipped back."

"Have you any news of your family?" interrupted Daphne.

"No news," he replied briefly, with sudden gravity.

"It seems you'll find a fairish mess out in Austria," said Basil.

"Yes, probably. It is what we had to expect," replied the Count.

"Well, I don't know. Sometimes things do turn out for the best. I feel that's as good as true in my case," said the Major.

"Things have turned out for the best?" said the Count, with an intonation of polite inquiry.

"Yes. Just for me personally, I mean—to put it quite selfishly. After all, what we've learned is that a man can only speak for himself. And I feel it's been dreadful, but it's not been lost. It was like an ordeal one had to go through," said Basil.

"You mean the war?"

"The war and everything that went with it."

"And when you've been through the ordeal?" politely inquired the Count.

"Why, you arrive at a higher state of consciousness, and therefore of life. And so, of course, at a higher plane of love. A surprisingly higher plane of love, that you had never suspected the existence of before."

The Count looked from Basil to Daphne, who was posing her head a little self-consciously.

"Then indeed the war has been a valuable thing," he said.

"Exactly!" cried Basil. "I am another man."

"And Lady Daphne?" queried the Count.

"Oh"—her husband faced round to her—"she is *absolutely* another woman—and *much* more wonderful, more marvellous."

The Count smiled and bowed slightly.

"When we knew her ten years ago, we should have said then that it was impossible," said he, "for her to be more wonderful."

"Oh quite!" returned the husband. "It always seems impossible. And the impossible is always happening. As a matter of fact, I think the war has opened another circle of life to us—a wider ring."

"It may be so," said the Count.

"You don't feel it so yourself?" The Major looked with his keen, white attention into the dark, low-browed face of the other man. The Count looked smiling at Daphne.

"I am only a prisoner still, Major, therefore I feel my ring quite small."

"Yes, of course you do. Of course. Well, I do hope you won't be a prisoner much longer. You must be dying to get back into your own country."

"Yes, I shall be glad to be free. Also," he smiled, "I shall miss my prison and my visits from the angels."

Even Daphne could not be sure he was mocking her. It was evident the visit was unpleasant to him. She could see he did not like Basil. Nay more, she could feel that the presence of her tall, gaunt, idealistic husband was hateful to the little swarthy man. But he passed it all off in smiles and polite speeches.

On the other hand, Basil was as if fascinated by the Count. He watched him absorbedly all the time, quite forgetting Daphne. She knew this. She knew that she was quite gone out of her husband's consciousness, like a lamp that has been carried away into another room. There he stood completely in the dark, as far as she was concerned, and all his attention focused on the other man. On his pale, gaunt face was a fixed smile of amused attention.

"But don't you get awfully bored," he said, "between the visits?"

The Count looked up with an affectation of frankness.

"No, I do not," he said. "I can brood, you see, on the things that come to pass."

"I think that's where the harm comes in," replied the Major. "One sits and broods, and is cut off from everything, and one loses one's contact with reality. That's the effect it had on me, being a prisoner."

"Contact with reality—what is that?"

"Well—contact with anybody, really—or anything."

"Why must one have contact?"

"Well, because one must," said Basil.

The Count smiled slowly.

"But I can sit and watch fate flowing, like black water, deep down in my own soul," he said. "I feel that there, in the dark of my own soul, things are happening."

"That may be. But whatever happens, it is only one thing, really. It is a contact between your own soul and the soul of one other being, or of many other beings. Nothing else can happen to man. That's how I figured it out for myself. I may be wrong. But that's how I figured it out, when I was wounded and a prisoner."

The Count's face had gone dark and serious.

"But is this contact an aim in itself?" he asked.

"Well," said the Major—he had taken his degree in philosophy—"it seems to me it is. It results inevitably in some form of activity. But the cause and the origin and the life-impetus of all action, activity, whether constructive or destructive, seems to me to be in the dynamic contact between human beings. You bring to pass a certain dynamic contact between men, and you get war. Another sort of dynamic contact, and you get them all building a cathedral, as they did in the Middle Ages."

"But was not the war, or the cathedral, the real aim, and the emotional contact just the means?" said the Count.

"I don't think so," said the Major, his curious white passion beginning to glow through his face. The three were seated in a little card-room, left alone by courtesy by the other men. Daphne was still draped in her dark, too-becoming drapery. But alas, she sat now ignored by both men. She might just as well have been an ugly little nobody, for all the notice that was taken of her. She sat in the window-seat of the dreary small room with a look of discontent on her exotic, rare face, that was like a delicate white and pink hot-house flower. From time to time she glanced with long, slow looks from man to man: from her husband, whose pallid, intense, white glowing face was pressed forward across the table, to the Count, who sat back in his chair, as if in opposition, and whose dark face seemed clubbed together in a dark, unwilling stare. Her husband was *quite* unaware of anything but his own white identity. But the Count still had a grain of secondary consciousness which hovered round and remained aware of the woman in the window-seat. The whole of his face, and his forward-looking attention was concentrated on Basil. But somewhere at the back of him he kept track of Daphne. She sat uneasy, in discontent, as women always do sit when men are locked together in a combustion of words. At the same time, she followed the argument. It was curious that, while her sympathy at this moment was with the Count, it was her husband whose words she believed to be true. The contact, the emotional contact was the real thing, the so-called "aim" was only a by-product. Even wars and cathedrals, in her mind, were only by-products. The real thing was what the warriors and cathedral-builders had had in common, as a great uniting feeling: the thing they felt for one another, and for their women in particular, of course.

"There are a great many kinds of contact, nevertheless," said Dionys.

"Well, do you know," said the Major, "it seems to me there is really only one supreme contact, the contact of love. Mind you, the love may take on an infinite variety of forms. And in my opinion, no form of love is wrong, so long as it *is* love, and you yourself *honour* what you are doing. Love has an extraordinary variety of forms! And that is all that there is in life, it seems to me. But I grant you, if you deny the *variety* of love you deny love altogether. If you try to specialize love into one set of accepted feelings, you wound the very soul of love. Love *must* be multiform, else it is just tyranny, just death."

"But why call it all *love?*" said the Count.

"Because it seems to me it *is* love: the great power that draws human beings together, no matter what the result of the contact may be. Of course there is hate, but hate is only the recoil of love."

"Do you think the old Egypt was established on love?" asked Dionys.

"Why, of course! And perhaps the most multiform, the most comprehensive love that the world has seen. All that we suffer from now is that our way of love is narrow, exclusive, and therefore not love at all; more like death and tyranny."

The Count slowly shook his head, smiling slowly and as if sadly.

"No," he said. "No. It is no good. You must use another word than love."

"I don't agree at all," said Basil.

"What word then?" blurted Daphne.

The Count looked at her.

"Obedience, submission, faith, belief, responsibility, power," he said slowly, picking out the words slowly, as if searching for what he wanted, and never quite finding it. He looked with his quiet dark eyes into her eyes. It was curious, she disliked his words intensely, but she liked him. On the other hand, she believed absolutely what her husband said, yet her physical sympathy was against him.

"Do you agree, Daphne?" asked Basil.

"Not a bit," she replied, with a heavy look at her husband.

"Nor I," said Basil. "It seems to me, if you love, there is no obedience nor submission, except to the soul of love. If you mean obedience, submission, and all the rest, to the soul of love itself, I quite agree. But if you mean obedience, submission of one person to another, and one man having power over others —I don't agree, and never shall. It seems to me just there where we have gone wrong. Kaiser Wilhelm II wanted power——"

"No, no," said the Count. "He was a mountebank. He had no conception of the sacredness of power."

"He proved himself very dangerous."

"Oh yes. But peace can be even more dangerous still."

"Tell me, then. Do you believe that you, as an aristocrat, should have feudal power over a few hundreds of other men, who happen to be born serfs, or not aristocrats?"

"Not as a hereditary aristocrat, but as a *man* who is by nature an aristocrat," said the Count, "it is my sacred duty to hold the lives of other men in my hands, and to shape the issue. But I can never fulfil my destiny till men will willingly put their lives in my hands."

"You don't expect them to, do you?" smiled Basil.

"At this moment, no."

"Or at any moment!" The Major was sarcastic.

"At a certain moment the men who are really living will come beseeching to put their lives into the hands of the greater men among them, beseeching the greater men to take the sacred responsibility of power."

"Do you think so? Perhaps you mean men will at last begin to choose leaders whom they will *love*," said Basil. "I wish they would."

"No, I mean that they will at last yield themselves before men who are greater than they: become vassals, by choice."

"Vassals!" exclaimed Basil, smiling. "You are still in the feudal ages, Count."

"Vassals. Not to any hereditary aristocrat—Hohenzollern or Hapsburg or Psanek," smiled the Count. "But to the man whose soul is born single, able to be alone, to choose and to command. At last the masses will come to such men and say, 'You are greater than we. Be our lords. Take our life and our death in your hands, and dispose of us according to your will. Because we see a light in your face, and a burning on your mouth.'"

The Major smiled for many moments, really piqued and amused, watching the Count, who did not turn a hair.

"I say, you must be awfully naïve, Count, if you believe the modern masses are ever going to behave like that. I assure you, they never will."

"If they did," said the Count, "would you call it a new reign of love, or something else?"

"Well, of course, it would contain an element of love. There would have to be an element of love in their feeling for their leaders."

"Do you think so? I thought that love assumed an equality in difference. I thought that love gave to every man the right to judge the acts of other men—'This was not an act of love, therefore it was wrong.' Does not democracy, and love, give to every man this right?"

"Certainly," said Basil.

"Ah, but my chosen aristocrat would say to those who chose him: 'If you choose me, you give up forever your right to judge me. If you have truly chosen to follow me, you have thereby rejected all your right to criticize me. You can no longer either approve or disapprove of me. You have performed the sacred act of choice. Henceforth you can only obey."

"They wouldn't be able to help criticizing, for all that," said Daphne, blurting in her say.

He looked at her slowly, and for the first time in her life she was doubtful of what she was saying.

"The day of Judas," he said, "ends with the day of love."

Basil woke up from a sort of trance.

"I think, of course, Count," he said, "that it's an awfully amusing idea. A retrogression slap back to the Dark Ages."

"Not so," said the Count. "Men—the mass of men—were never before free to perform the sacred act of choice. To-day—soon—they may be free."

"Oh, I don't know. Many tribes chose their kings and chiefs."

"Men have never before been quite free to choose: and to know what they are doing."

"You mean they've only made themselves free in order voluntarily to saddle themselves with new lords and masters?"

"I do mean that."

"In short, life is just a vicious circle?"

"Not at all. An ever-widening circle, as you say. Always more wonderful."

"Well, it's all frightfully interesting and amusing—don't you think so, Daphne? By the way, Count, where would women be? Would they be allowed to criticize their husbands?"

"Only before marriage," smiled the Count. "Not after."

"Splendid!" said Basil. "I'm all for that bit of your scheme, Count. I hope you're listening, Daphne."

"Oh, yes. But then I've only married *you*. I've got my right to criticize all the other men," she said, in a dull, angry voice.

"Exactly. Clever of you! So the Count won't get off! Well now, what do you think of the Count's aristocratic scheme for the future, Daphne? Do you approve?"

"Not at all. But then little men have always wanted power," she said, cruelly.

"Oh, big men as well, for that matter," said Basil, conciliatory.

"I have been told before," smiled the Count, "little men are always bossy. I am afraid I have offended Lady Daphne?"

"No," she said. "Not really. I'm amused, really. But I always dislike any suggestion of bullying."

"Indeed, so do I," said he.

"The Count didn't mean bullying, Daphne," said Basil. "Come, there is really an allowable distinction between responsible power and bullying."

"When men put their heads together about it," said she.

She was haughty and angry, as if she were afraid of losing something. The Count smiled mischievously at her.

"You are offended, Lady Daphne? But why? You are safe from any spark of my dangerous and extensive authority."

Basil burst into a roar of laughter.

"It *is* rather funny, you to be talking of power and of not being criticized," he said. "But I should like to hear more: I would like to hear more."

As they drove home, he said to his wife:

"You know I like that little man. He's a quaint little bantam. And he sets one thinking."

Lady Daphne froze to four degrees below zero, under the north-wind of this statement, and not another word was to be thawed out of her.

Curiously enough, it was now Basil who was attracted by the Count and Daphne who was repelled. Not that she was so bound up in her husband. Not at all. She was feeling rather sore against men altogether. But as so often happens, in this life based on the wicked triangle, Basil could only follow his enthusiasm for the Count in his wife's presence. When the two men were alone together, they were awkward, resistant, they could hardly get out a dozen words to one another. When Daphne was there, however, to complete the circuit of the opposing currents, things went like a house on fire.

This, however, was not much consolation to Lady Daphne. Merely to sit as a passive medium between two men who are squibbing philosophical nonsense to one another: no, it was not good enough! She almost hated the Count: low-browed little fellow, belonging to the race of prehistoric slaves. But her grudge against her white-faced, spirtually intense husband was sharp as vinegar. Let down: she was let down between the pair of them.

What next? Well, what followed was entirely Basil's fault. The winter was passing: it was obvious the war was really over, that Germany was finished. The Hohenzollern had fizzled out like a very poor squib, the Hapsburg was popping feebly in obscurity, the Romanov was smudged out without a sputter. So much for imperial royalty. Henceforth democratic peace.

The Count, of course, would be shipped back now like returned goods that had no market any more. There was a world peace ahead. A week or two, and Voynich Hall would be empty.

Basil, however, could not let matters follow their simple course. He was awfully intrigued by the Count. He wanted to entertain him as a guest before he went. And Major Apsley could get anything in reason, at this moment. So he obtained permission for the poor little Count to stay a fortnight at Thoresway, before being shipped back to Austria. Earl Beveridge, whose soul was black as ink since the war, would never have allowed the little alien enemy to enter his house, had it not been for the hatred which had been aroused in him, during the last two years, by the degrading spectacle of the so-called patriots who had been howling their mongrel indecency in the public face. These mongrels had held the Press and the British public in abeyance for almost two years. Their one aim was to degrade and humiliate anything that was proud or dignified remaining in England. It was almost the worst nightmare of all, this coming to the top of a lot of public filth which was determined to suffocate the souls of all dignified men.

Hence, the Earl, who never intended to be swamped by unclean scum, whatever else happened to him, stamped his heels in the ground and stood on his own feet. When Basil said to him, would he allow the Count to have a fortnight's decent peace in Thoresway before all was finished, Lord Beveridge gave a slow consent, scandal or no scandal. Indeed, it was really to defy scandal that he took such a step. For the thought of his dead boys was bitter to him: and the thought of England fallen under the paws of smelly mongrels was bitterer still.

Lord Beveridge was at Thoresway to receive the Count, who arrived escorted by Basil. The English Earl was a big, handsome man, rather heavy, with a dark, sombre face that would have been haughty if haughtiness had not been made so ridiculous. He was a passionate man, with a passionate man's sensitiveness, generosity, and instinctive overbearing. But *his* dark passionate nature, and his violent sensitiveness had been subjected now to fifty-five years' subtle repression, condemnation, repudiation, till he had almost come to believe in his own wrongness. His little, frail wife, all love for humanity, she was the genuine article. Himself, he was labelled selfish, sensual, cruel, etc., etc. So by now he always seemed to be standing aside, in the shadow, letting himself be obliterated by the pallid rabble of the democratic hurry. That was the impression he gave, of a man standing back, half-shamed, half-haughty, semi-hidden in the dark background.

He was a little on the defensive as Basil came in with the Count.

"Ah—how do you do, Count Psanek?" he said, striding largely forward and holding out his hand. Because he was the father of Daphne, the Count felt a certain tenderness for the taciturn Englishman.

"You do me too much honour, my lord, receiving me in your house," said the small Count proudly.

The Earl looked at him slowly, without speaking: seemed to look down on him, in every sense of the word.

"We are still men, Count. We are not beasts altogether."

"You wish to say that my countrymen are so very nearly beasts, Lord Beveridge?" smiled the Count, curling his fine nose.

Again the Earl was slow in replying.

"You have a low opinion of my manners, Count Psanek."

"But perhaps a just appreciation of your meaning, Lord Beveridge," smiled the Count, with the same reckless little look of contempt on his nose.

Lord Beveridge flushed dark, with all his native anger offended.

"I am glad Count Psanek makes my own meaning clear to me," he said.

"I beg your pardon a thousand times, my lord, if I give offence in doing so," replied the Count.

The Earl went black, and felt a fool. He turned his back on the Count. And then he turned round again, offering his cigar-case.

"Will you smoke?" he said. There was kindness in his tone.

"Thank you," said the Count, taking a cigar.

"I daresay," said Lord Beveridge, "that all men are beasts in some way. I am afraid I have fallen into the common habit of speaking by rote, and not what I really mean. Won't you take a seat?"

"It is only as a prisoner that I have learned that I am *not* truly a beast. No, I am myself. I am not a beast," said the Count, seating himself.

The Earl eyed him curiously.

"Well," he said, smiling, "I suppose it is best to come to a decision about it."

"It is necessary, if one is to be safe from vulgarity."

The Earl felt a twinge of accusation. With his agate-brown, hard-looking eyes he watched the black-browed little Count.

"You are probably right," he said.

But he turned his face aside.

They were five people at dinner—Lady Beveridge was there as hostess.

"Ah, Count Dionys," she said with a sigh, "do you really feel that the war is over?"

"Oh, yes," he replied quickly. "*This* war is over. The armies will go home. *Their* cannon will not sound any more. Never again like this."

"Ah, I hope so," she sighed.

"I am sure," he said.

"You think there'll be no more war?" said Daphne.

For some reason she had made herself very fine, in her newest dress of silver and black and pink chenille, with bare shoulders, and her hair fashionably done. The Count in his shabby uniform turned to her. She was nervous, hurried. Her slim white arm was near him, with the bit of silver at the shoulder. Her skin was white like a hot-house flower. Her lips moved hurriedly.

"Such a war as this there will never be again," he said.

"What makes you so sure?" she replied, glancing into his eyes.

"The machine of war has got out of our control. We shall never start it again, till it has fallen to pieces. We shall be afraid."

"Will everybody be afraid?" said she, looking down and pressing back her chin.

"I think so."

"We will hope so," said Lady Beveridge.

"Do you mind if I ask you, Count," said Basil, "what you feel about the way the war has ended? The way it has ended for *you*, I mean."

"You mean that Germany and Austria have lost the war? It was bound to be. We have all lost the war. All Europe."

"I agree there," said Lord Beveridge.

"We've all lost the war?" said Daphne, turning to look at him.

There was pain on his dark, low-browed face. He suffered having the sensitive woman beside him. Her skin had a hot-house delicacy that made his head go round. Her shoulders were broad, rather thin, but the skin was white and so sensitive, so hot-house delicate. It affected him like the perfume of some white, exotic flower. And she seemed to be sending her heart towards him. It was as if she wanted to press her breast to his. From the breast she loved him, and sent out love to him. And it made him unhappy; he wanted to be quiet, and to keep his honour before these hosts.

He looked into her eyes, his own eyes dark with knowledge and pain. She, in her silence and her brief words seemed to be holding them all under her spell. She seemed to have cast a certain muteness on the table, in the midst of which she remained silently master, leaning forward to her plate, and silently mastering them all.

"Don't I think we've all lost the war?" he replied, in answer to her question. "It was a war of suicide. Nobody could win it. It was suicide for all of us."

"Oh, I don't know," she replied. "What about America and Japan?"

"They don't count. They only helped *us* to commit suicide. They did not enter vitally."

There was such a look of pain on his face, and such a sound of pain in his voice, that the other three closed their ears, shut off from attending. Only Daphne was making him speak. It was she who was drawing the soul out of him, trying to read the future in him as the augurs read the future in the quivering entrails of the sacrificed beast. She looked direct into his face, searching his soul.

"You think Europe has committed suicide?" she said.

"Morally."

"Only morally?" came her slow, bronze-like words, so fatal.

"That is enough," he smiled.

"Quite," she said, with a slow droop of her eyelids. Then she turned away her face. But he felt the heart strangling inside his breast. What was she doing now? What was she thinking? She filled him with uncertainty and with uncanny fear.

"At least," said Basil, "those infernal guns are quiet."

"For ever," said Dionys.

"I wish I could believe you, Count," said the Major.

The talk became more general—or more personal. Lady Beveridge asked Dionys about his wife and family. He knew nothing save that they had gone to Hungary in 1916, when his own house was burnt down. His wife might even have gone to Bulgaria with Prince Bogorik. He did not know.

"But your children, Count!" cried Lady Beveridge.

"I do not know. Probably in Hungary, with their grand-mother. I will go when I get back."

"But have you never *written?*—never inquired?"

"I could not write. I shall know soon enough—everything."

"You have no son?"

"No. Two girls."

"Poor things!"

"Yes."

"I say, isn't it an odd thing to have a ladybird on your crest?" asked Basil, to cheer up the conversation.

"Why queer? Charlemagne had bees. And it is a Marienkä-fer—a Mary-beetle. The beetle of Our Lady. I think it is quite a heraldic insect, Major," smiled the Count.

"You're proud of it?" said Daphne, suddenly turning to look at him again, with her slow, pregnant look.

"I am, you know. It has such a long genealogy—our spotted beetle. Much longer than the Psaneks. I think, you know, it is a descendant of the Egyptian scarabæus, which is a very mysterious emblem. So I connect myself with the Pharaohs: just through my ladybird."

"You feel your ladybird has crept through so many ages," she said.

"Imagine it!" he laughed.

"The scarab *is* a piquant insect," said Basil.

"Do you know Fabre?" put in Lord Beveridge. "He suggests that the beetle rolling a little ball of dung before him, in a dry old field, must have suggested to the Egyptians the First Principle that set the globe rolling. And so the scarab became the symbol of the creative principle—or something like that."

"That the earth is a tiny ball of dry dung is good," said Basil.

"Between the claws of a ladybird," added Daphne.

"That is what it is, to go back to one's origin," said Lady Beveridge.

"Perhaps they meant that it was the principle of decomposition which first set the ball rolling," said the Count.

"The ball would have to be *there* first," said Basil.

"Certainly. But it hadn't started to roll. Then the principle of decomposition started it." The Count smiled as if it were a joke.

"I am no Egyptologist," said Lady Beveridge, "so I can't judge."

The Earl and Countess Beveridge left next day. Count Dionys was left with the two young people in the house. It was a beautiful Elizabethan mansion, not very large, but with those magical rooms that are all a twinkle of small-paned windows looking out from the dark panelled interior. The interior was cosy, panelled to the ceiling, and the ceiling moulded and touched with gold. And then the great square bow of the window with its little panes intervening like magic between oneself and the world outside, the crest in stained glass crowning its colour, the broad window-seat cushioned in faded green. Dionys wandered round the house like a little ghost, through the succession of small and large twinkling sitting-rooms and lounge rooms in front, down the long, wide corridor with the wide stairhead at each end, and up the narrow stairs to the bedrooms above, and on to the roof.

It was early spring, and he loved to sit on the leaded, pale-grey roof that had its queer seats and slopes, a little pale world in itself. Then to look down over the garden and the sloping lawn to the ponds massed round with trees, and away to the elms and furrows and hedges of the shires. On the left of the house was the farmstead, with ricks and great-roofed barns and dark-red cattle. Away to the right, beyond the park, was a village among trees, and the spark of a grey church-spire.

He liked to be alone, feeling his soul heavy with its own fate. He would sit for hours watching the elm-trees standing in rows like giants, like warriors across the country. The Earl had told him that the Romans had brought these elms to Britain. And he seemed to see the spirit of the Romans in them still. Sitting there alone in the spring sunshine, in the solitude of the roof, he saw the glamour of this England of hedgerows and elm-trees, and the labourers with slow horses slowly drilling the sod, crossing the brown furrow: and the roofs of the village, with the church-steeple rising beside a big black yew-tree: and the chequer of fields away to the distance.

And the charm of the old manor around him, the garden with its grey stone walls and yew hedges—broad, broad yew hedges —and a peacock pausing to glitter and scream in the busy silence of an English spring, when celandines open their yellow under the hedges, and violets are in the secret, and by the broad paths of the garden polyanthus and crocuses vary the velvet and flame, and bits of yellow wallflower shake raggedly, with a wonderful triumphance, out of the cracks of the wall. There was a fold somewhere near, and he could hear the treble bleat of the growing lambs, and the deeper, contented baa-ing of the ewes.

This was Daphne's home, where she had been born. She loved it with an ache of affection. But now it was hard to forget her dead brothers. She wandered about in the sun, with two old dogs paddling after her. She talked with everybody— gardener, groom, stableman, with the farm-hands. That filled a large part of her life—straying round talking with the work-people. They were, of course, respectful to her—but not at all afraid of her. They knew she was poor, that she could not afford a car, nor anything. So they talked to her very freely: perhaps a little too freely. Yet she let it be. It was her one passion at Thoresway to hear the dependants talk and talk— about everything. The curious feeling of intimacy across a breach fascinated her. Their lives fascinated her: what they thought, what they *felt*. These, what they felt. That fascinated her. There was a gamekeeper she could have loved—an impudent, ruddy-faced laughing, ingratiating fellow; she could have loved him, if she had not been isolated beyond the breach of his birth, her culture, her consciousness. Her *consciousness* seemed to make a great gulf between her and the lower classes, the unconscious classes. She accepted it as her doom. She could never meet in real contact any one but a superconscious, finished being like herself: or like her husband. Her father had some of the unconscious blood-warmth of the lower classes. But he was like a man who is damned. And the Count, of course. The Count had something that was hot and invisible, a dark flame of life that might warm the cold white fire of her own blood. But——

They avoided each other. All three, they avoided one another. Basil, too, went off alone. Or he immersed himself in poetry. Sometimes he and the Count played billiards. Sometimes all three walked in the park. Often Basil and Daphne walked to the village, to post. But truly, they avoided one another, all three. The days slipped by.

At evening they sat together in the small west-room that had books and a piano and comfortable shabby furniture of faded rose-coloured tapestry: a shabby room. Sometimes Basil read aloud: sometimes the Count played the piano. And they talked. And Daphne stitch by stitch went on with a big embroidered bedspread, which she might finish if she lived long enough. But they always went to bed early. They were nearly always avoiding one another.

Dionys had a bedroom in the east bay—a long way from the rooms of the others. He had a habit, when he was quite alone, of singing, or rather crooning to himself the old songs of his childhood. It was only when he felt he was quite alone: when other people seemed to fade out of him, and all the world seemed to dissolve into darkness, and there was nothing but himself, his own soul, alive in the middle of his own small night, isolate for ever. Then, half unconscious, he would croon in a small, high-pitched, squeezed voice, a sort of high dream-voice, the songs of his childhood dialect. It was a curious noise: the sound of a man who is alone in his own blood: almost the sound of a man who is going to be executed.

Daphne heard the sound one night when she was going downstairs again with the corridor lantern, to find a book. She was a bad sleeper, and her nights were a torture to her. She too, like a neurotic, was nailed inside her own fretful self-consciousness. But she had a very keen ear. So she started as she heard the small, bat-like sound of the Count's singing to himself. She stood in the midst of the wide corridor, that was wide as a room, carpeted with a faded lavender-coloured carpet, with a piece of massive dark furniture at intervals by the wall, and an oak arm-chair and sometimes a faded, reddish oriental rug. The big horn lantern which stood at nights at the end of the corridor she held in her hand. The intense "peeping" sound of the Count, like a witchcraft, made her forget everything. She could not understand a word, of course. She could not understand the noise even. After listening for a long time, she went on downstairs. When she came back again he was still, and the light was gone from under his door.

After this, it became almost an obsession to her to listen for him. She waited with fretful impatience for ten o'clock, when she could retire. She waited more fretfully still for the maid to leave her, and for her husband to come and say good night. Basil had the room across the corridor. And then in resentful impatience she waited for the sounds of the house to become still. Then she opened her door to listen.

And far away, as if from far, far away in the unseen, like a ventriloquist sound or a bat's uncanny peeping, came the frail, almost inaudible sound of the Count's singing to himself before he went to bed. It *was* inaudible to any one but herself. But she, by concentration, seemed to hear supernaturally. She had a low arm-chair by the door, and there, wrapped in a huge old black silk shawl, she sat and listened. At first she could not hear. That is, she could hear the sound. But it was only a sound. And then, gradually, gradually she began to follow the thread of it. It was like a thread which she followed out of the world: out of the world. And as she went, slowly, by degrees, far, far away, down the thin thread of his singing, she knew peace—she knew forgetfulness. She could pass beyond the world, away beyond where her soul balanced like a bird on wings, and was perfected.

So it was, in her upper spirit. But underneath was a wild, wild yearning, actually to go, actually to be given. Actually to go, actually to die the death, actually to cross the border and be gone, to be gone. To be gone from this herself, from this Daphne, to be gone from father and mother, brothers and husband, and home and land and world: to be gone. To be gone to the call from the beyond: the call. It was the Count calling. He was calling her. She was sure he was calling her. Out of herself, out of her world, he was calling her.

Two nights she sat just inside her room, by the open door, and listened. Then when he finished she went to sleep, a queer, light, bewitched sleep. In the day she was bewitched. She felt strange and light, as if pressure had been removed from around her. Some pressure had been clamped round her all her life. She had never realized it till now; now it was removed, and her feet felt so light, and her breathing delicate and exquisite. There had always been a pressure against her breathing. Now she breathed delicate and exquisite, so that it was a delight to breathe. Life came in exquisite breaths, quickly, as if it delighted to come to her.

The third night he was silent—though she waited and waited till the small hours of the morning. He was silent, he did not sing. And then she knew the terror and blackness of the feeling that he might never sing any more. She waited like one doomed, throughout the day. And when the night came she trembled. It was her greatest nervous terror, lest her spell should be broken, and she should be thrown back to what she was before.

Night came, and the kind of swoon upon her. Yes, and the call from the night. The call! She rose helplessly and hurried down the corridor. The light was under his door. She sat down in the big oak arm-chair that stood near his door, and huddled herself tight in her black shawl. The corridor was dim with the big, star-studded, yellow lantern-light. Away down she could see the lamplight in her doorway; she had left her door ajar.

But she saw nothing. Only she wrapped herself close in the black shawl, and listened to the sound from the room. It called. Oh, it called her! Why could she not go? Why could she not cross through the closed door.

Then the noise ceased. And then the light went out, under the door of his room. Must she go back? Must she go back? Oh, impossible. As impossible as that the moon should go back on her tracks, once she has risen. Daphne sat on, wrapped in her black shawl. If it must be so, she would sit on through eternity. Return she never could.

And then began the most terrible song of all. It began with a rather dreary, slow, horrible sound, like death. And then suddenly came a real call—fluty, and a kind of whistling and a strange whirr at the changes, most imperative, and utterly inhuman. Daphne rose to her feet. And at the same moment up rose the whistling throb of a summons out of the death moan.

Daphne tapped low and rapidly at the door. "Count! Count!" she whispered. The sound inside ceased. The door suddenly opened. The pale, obscure figure of Dionys.

"Lady Daphne!" he said in astonishment, automatically standing aside.

"You called," she murmured rapidly, and she passed intent into his room.

"No, I did not call," he said gently, his hand on the door still.

"Shut the door," she said abruptly.

He did as he was bid. The room was in complete darkness. There was no moon outside. She could not see him.

"Where can I sit down?" she said abruptly.

"I will take you to the couch," he said, putting out his hand and touching her in the dark. She shuddered.

She found the couch and sat down. It was quite dark.

"What are you singing?" she said rapidly.

"I am so sorry. I did not think any one could hear."

"What was it you were singing?"

"A song of my country."

"Had it any words?"

"Yes, it is a woman who was a swan, and who loved a hunter by the marsh. So she became a woman and married him and had three children. Then in the night one night the king of the swans called to her to come back, or else he would die. So slowly she turned into a swan again, and slowly she opened her wide, wide wings, and left her husband and her children."

There was silence in the dark room. The Count had been really startled, startled out of his mood of the song into the day-mood of human convention. He was distressed and embarrassed by Daphne's presence in his dark room. She, however, sat on and did not make a sound. He, too, sat down in a chair by the window. It was everywhere dark. A wind was blowing in gusts outside. He could see nothing inside his room: only the faint, faint strip of light under the door. But he could feel her presence in the darkness. It was uncanny, to feel her near in the dark, and not to see any sign of her, not to hear any sound.

She had been wounded in her bewitched state by the contact with the every-day human being in him. But now she began to relapse into her spell, as she sat there in the dark. And he, too, in the silence, felt the world sinking away from him once more leaving him once more alone on a darkened earth, with nothing between him and the infinite dark space. Except now her presence. Darkness answering to darkness, and deep answering to deep. An answer, near to him, and invisible.

But he did not know what to do. He sat still and silent as she was still and silent. The darkness inside the room seemed alive like blood. He had no power to move. The distance between them seemed absolute.

Then suddenly, without knowing, he went across in the dark, feeling for the end of the couch. And he sat beside her on the couch. But he did not touch her. Neither did she move. The darkness flowed about them thick like blood, and time seemed dissolved in it. They sat with the small, invisible distance between them, motionless, speechless, thoughtless.

Then suddenly he felt her finger-tips touch his arm, and a flame went over him that left him no more a man. He was something seated in flame, in flame unconscious, seated erect, like an Egyptian King-god in the statues. Her finger-tips slid down him, and she herself slid down in a strange silent rush, and he felt her face against his closed feet and ankles, her hands pressing his ankles. He felt her brow and hair against his ankles, her face against his feet, and there she clung in the dark, as if in space below him. He still sat erect and motionless. Then he bent forward and put his hand on her hair.

"Do you come to me?" he murmured. "Do you come to me?"

The flame that enveloped him seemed to sway him silently.

"Do you really come to me?" he repeated. "But we have nowhere to go."

He felt his bare feet wet with her tears. Two things were struggling in him, the sense of eternal solitude, like space, and the rush of dark flame that would throw him out of his solitude towards her.

He was thinking too. He was thinking of the future. He had no future in the world: of that he was conscious. He had no future in this life. Even if he lived on, it would only be a kind of enduring. But he felt that in the after-life the inheritance was his. He felt the after-life belonged to him.

Future in the world he could not give her. Life in the world he had not to offer her. Better go on alone. Surely better go on alone.

But then the tears on his feet: and her face that would face him as he left her! No, no. The next life was his. He was master of the after-life. Why fear for this life? Why not take the soul she offered him? Now and forever, for the life that would come when they both were dead. Take her into the underworld. Take her into the dark Hades with him, like Francesca and Paolo. And in hell hold her fast, queen of the underworld, himself master of the underworld. Master of the life to come. Father of the soul that would come after.

"Listen," he said to her softly. "Now you are mine. In the dark you are mine. And when you die you are mine. But in the day you are not mine, because I have no power in the day. In the night, in the dark, and in death, you are mine. And that is forever. No matter if I must leave you. I shall come again from time to time. In the dark you are mine. But in the day I cannot claim you. I have no power in the day, and no place. So remember. When the darkness comes, I shall always be in the darkness of you. And as long as I live, from time to time I shall come to find you, when I am able to, when I am not a prisoner. But I shall have to go away soon. So don't forget—

you are the night-wife of the ladybird, while you live and even when you die."

Later, when he took her back to her room, he saw her door still ajar.

"You shouldn't leave a light in your room," he murmured.

In the morning there was a curious remote look about him. He was quieter than ever, and seemed very far away. Daphne slept late. She had a strange feeling as if she had slipped off all her cares. She did not care, she did not grieve, she did not fret any more. All that had left her. She felt she could sleep, sleep, sleep—for ever. Her face, too, was very still, with a delicate look of virginity that she had never had before. She had always been Aphrodite, the self-conscious one. And her eyes, the green-blue, had been like slow, living jewels, resistant. Now, they had unfolded from the hard flower-bud, and had the wonder, and the stillness of a quiet night.

Basil noticed it at once.

"You're different, Daphne," he said. "What are you thinking about?"

"I wasn't thinking," she said, looking at him with candour.

"What were you doing then?"

"What does one do when one doesn't think? Don't make me puzzle it out, Basil."

"Not a bit of it, if you don't want to."

But he was puzzled by her. The sting of his ecstatic love for her seemed to have left him. Yet he did not know what else to do but to make love to her. She went very pale. She submitted to him, bowing her head because she was his wife. But she looked at him with fear, with sorrow, with real suffering. He could feel the heaving of her breast, and knew she was weeping. But there were no tears on her face, she was only death-pale. Her eyes were shut.

"Are you in pain?" he asked her.

"No, no!" She opened her eyes, afraid lest she had disturbed him. She did not want to disturb him.

He was puzzled. His own ecstatic deadly love for her had received a check. He was out of the reckoning.

He watched her when she was with the Count. Then she seemed so meek—so maidenly—so different from what he had known of her. She was so still, like a virgin girl. And it was this quiet, intact quality of virginity in her which puzzled him most, puzzled his emotions and his ideas. He became suddenly ashamed to make love to her. And because he was ashamed, he said to her as he stood in her room that night:

"Daphne, are you in love with the Count?"

He was standing by the dressing-table, uneasy. She was seated in a low chair by the tiny dying wood fire. She looked up at him with wide, slow eyes. Without a word, with wide, soft, dilated eyes she watched him. What was it that made him feel all confused. He turned his face aside, away from her wide, soft eyes.

"Pardon me, dear. I didn't intend to ask such a question. Don't take any notice of it," he said. And he strode away and picked up a book. She lowered her head and gazed abstractedly into the fire, without a sound. Then he looked at her again, at her bright hair that the maid had plaited for the night. Her plait hung down over her soft pinkish wrap. His heart softened to her as he saw her sitting there. She seemed like his sister. The excitement of desire had left him, and now he seemed to see clear and feel true for the first time in his life. She was like a dear, dear sister to him. He felt that she was his blood-sister, nearer to him than he had imagined any woman could be. So near—so dear—and all the sex and the desire gone. He didn't want it—he hadn't wanted it. This new pure feeling was so much more wonderful.

He went to her side.

"Forgive me, darling," he said, "for having questioned you."

She looked up at him with the wide eyes, without a word. His face was good and beautiful. Tears came to her eyes.

"You have the right to question me," she said sadly.

"No," he said. "No, darling. I have no right to question you. Daphne! Daphne, darling! It shall be as *you* wish, between us. Shall it? Shall it be as you wish?"

"You are the husband, Basil," she said sadly.

"Yes, darling. But"—he went on his knees beside her—"perhaps, darling, something has changed in us. I feel as if I ought never to touch you again—as if I never *wanted* to touch you—in that way. I feel it was wrong, darling. Tell me what you think."

"Basil, don't be angry with me."

"It isn't anger; it's pure love, darling—it is."

"Let us not come any nearer to one another than this, Basil—physically—shall we?" she said. "And don't be angry with me, will you?"

"Why," he said. "I think myself the sexual part has been a mistake. I had rather love you—as I love now. I *know* that this is true love. The other was always a bit whipped up. I *know* I love you now, darling: now I'm free from that other. But what if it comes upon me, that other, Daphne?"

"I am always your wife," she said quietly. "I am always your wife. I want always to obey you, Basil: what you wish."

"Give me your hand, dear."

She gave him her hand. But the look in her eyes at the same time warned him and frightened him. He kissed her hand and left her.

It was to the Count she belonged. This had decided itself in her down to the depths of her soul. If she could not marry him and be his wife in the world, it had nevertheless happened to her for ever. She could no more question it. Question had gone out of her.

Strange how different she had become—a strange new quiescence. The last days were slipping past. He would be going away—Dionys: he with the still remote face, the man she belonged to in the dark and in the light, for ever. He would be going away. He said it must be so. And she acquiesced. The grief was deep, deep inside her. He must go away. Their lives could not be one life, in this world's day. Even in her anguish she knew it was so. She knew he was right. He was for her infallible. He spoke the deepest soul in her.

She never *saw* him, as a lover. When she saw him, he was the

little officer, a prisoner, quiet, claiming nothing in all the
world. And when she went to him as his lover, his wife, it was
always dark. She only knew his voice and his contact in
darkness. "My wife in darkness," he said to her. And in this
too she believed him. She would not have contradicted him,
no, not for anything on earth: lest, contradicting him she
should lose the dark treasure of stillness and bliss which she
kept in her breast even when her heart was wrung with the
agony of knowing he must go.

No, she had found this wonderful thing after she had heard
him singing: she had suddenly collapsed away from her old self
into this darkness, this peace, this quiescence that was like a
full dark river flowing eternally in her soul. She had gone to
sleep from the *nuit blanche* of her days. And Basil, wonderful,
had changed almost at once. She feared him, lest he might
change back again. She would always have him to fear. But
deep inside her she only feared for this love of hers for the
Count: this dark, everlasting love that was like a full river
flowing for ever inside her. Ah, let that not be broken.

She was so still inside her. She could sit so still, and feel the
day slowly, richly changing to night. And she wanted nothing,
she was short of nothing. If only Dionys need not go away!
If only he need not go away!

But he said to her, the last morning:

"Don't forget me. Always remember me. I leave my soul in
your hands and your womb. Nothing can ever separate us,
unless we betray one another. If you have to give yourself to
your husband, do so, and obey him. If you are true to me,
innerly, innerly true, he will not hurt us. He is generous, be
generous to him. And never fail to believe in me. Because even
on the other side of death I shall be watching for you. I shall
be king in Hades when I am dead. And you will be at my side.
You will never leave me any more, in the after-death. So don't
be afraid in life. Don't be afraid. If you have to cry tears, cry
them. But in your heart of hearts know that I shall come
again, and that I have taken you for ever. And so, in your
heart of hearts be still, be still, since you are the wife of the

ladybird." He laughed as he left her, with his own beautiful, fearless laugh. But they were strange eyes that looked after him.

He went in the car with Basil back to Voynich Hall.

"I believe Daphne will miss you," said Basil.

The Count did not reply for some moments.

"Well, if she does," he said, "there will be no bitterness in it."

"Are you sure?" smiled Basil.

"Why—if we are sure of anything," smiled the Count.

"She's changed, isn't she?"

"Is she?"

"Yes, she's quite changed since you came, Count."

"She does not seem to me so very different from the girl of seventeen whom I knew."

"No—perhaps not. I didn't know her then. But she's very different from the wife I have known."

"A regrettable difference?"

"Well—no, not as far as she goes. She is much quieter inside herself. You know, Count, something of me died in the war. I feel it will take me an eternity to sit and think about it all."

"I hope you may think it out to your satisfaction, Major."

"Yes, I hope so too. But that is how it has left me—feeling as if I needed eternity now to brood about it all, you know. Without the need to act—or even to love, really. I suppose love is action."

"Intense action," said the Count.

"Quite so. I know really how I feel. I only ask of life to spare me from further effort of action of any sort—even love. And then to fulfil myself, brooding through eternity. Of course I don't mind *work*, mechanical action. That in itself is a form of inaction."

"A man can only be happy following his own inmost need," said the Count.

"Exactly!" said Basil. "I will lay down the law for nobody, not even for myself. And live my day——"

"Then you will be happy in your own way. I find it so

G

difficult to keep from laying the law down for myself," said the Count. "Only the thought of death and the after-life saves me from doing it any more."

"As the thought of eternity helps me," said Basil. "I suppose it amounts to the same thing."

THE FOX

THE two girls were usually known by their surnames, Banford and March. They had taken the farm together, intending to work it all by themselves: that is, they were going to rear chickens, make a living by poultry, and add to this by keeping a cow, and raising one or two young beasts. Unfortunately, things did not turn out well.

Banford was a small, thin, delicate thing with spectacles. She, however, was the principal investor, for March had little or no money. Banford's father, who was a tradesman in Islington, gave his daughter the start, for her health's sake, and because he loved her, and because it did not look as if she would marry. March was more robust. She had learned carpentry and joinery at the evening classes in Islington. She would be the man about the place. They had, moreover, Banford's old grandfather living with them at the start. He had been a farmer. But unfortunately the old man died after he had been at Bailey Farm for a year. Then the two girls were left alone.

They were neither of them young: that is, they were near thirty. But they certainly were not old. They set out quite gallantly with their enterprise. They had numbers of chickens, black Leghorns and white Leghorns, Plymouths and Wyandottes; also some ducks; also two heifers in the fields. One heifer, unfortunately, refused absolutely to stay in the Bailey Farm closes. No matter how March made up the fences, the heifer was out, wild in the woods, or trespassing on the neighbouring pasture, and March and Banford were away, flying after her, with more haste than success. So this heifer they sold in despair. Then, just before the other beast was expecting her first calf, the old man died, and the girls, afraid of the coming event, sold her in a panic, and limited their attentions to fowls and ducks.

In spite of a little chagrin, it was a relief to have no more

cattle on hand. Life was not made merely to be slaved away.
Both girls agreed in this. The fowls were quite enough trouble.
March had set up her carpenter's bench at the end of the open
shed. Here she worked, making coops and doors and other
appurtenances. The fowls were housed in the bigger building,
which had served as barn and cowshed in old days. They had a
beautiful home, and should have been perfectly content.
Indeed, they looked well enough. But the girls were disgusted
at their tendency to strange illnesses, at their exacting way of
life, and at their refusal, obstinate refusal to lay eggs.

March did most of the outdoor work. When she was out and
about, in her puttees and breeches, her belted coat and her
loose cap, she looked almost like some graceful, loose-balanced
young man, for her shoulders were straight, and her movements
easy and confident, even tinged with a little indifference, or
irony. But her face was not a man's face, ever. The wisps of
her crisp dark hair blew about her as she stooped, her eyes were
big and wide and dark, when she looked up again, strange,
startled, shy and sardonic at once. Her mouth, too, was
almost pinched as if in pain and irony. There was something
odd and unexplained about her. She would stand balanced on
one hip, looking at the fowls pattering about in the obnoxious
fine mud of the sloping yard, and calling to her favourite white
hen, which came in answer to her name. But there was an
almost satirical flicker in March's big, dark eyes as she looked
at her three-toed flock pottering about under her gaze, and the
same slight dangerous satire in her voice as she spoke to the
favoured Patty, who pecked at March's boot by way of
friendly demonstration.

Fowls did not flourish at Bailey Farm, in spite of all that
March did for them. When she provided hot food for them in
the morning, according to rule, she noticed that it made them
heavy and dozy for hours. She expected to see them lean
against the pillars of the shed in their languid processes of
digestion. And she knew quite well that they ought to be
busily scratching and foraging about, if they were to come to
any good. So she decided to give them their hot food at night,

and let them sleep on it. Which she did. But it made no difference.

War conditions, again, were very unfavourable to poultry keeping. Food was scarce and bad. And when the Daylight Saving Bill was passed, the fowls obstinately refused to go to bed as usual, about nine o'clock in the summer-time. That was late enough, indeed, for there was no peace till they were shut up and asleep. Now they cheerfully walked around, without so much as glancing at the barn, until ten o'clock or later. Both Banford and March disbelieved in living for work alone. They wanted to read or take a cycle-ride in the evening, or perhaps March wished to paint curvilinear swans on porcelain, with green background, or else make a marvellous fire-screen by processes of elaborate cabinet work. For she was a creature of odd whims and unsatisfied tendencies. But from all these things she was prevented by the stupid fowls.

One evil there was greater than any other. Bailey Farm was a little homestead, with ancient wooden barn and low-gabled farmhouse, lying just one field removed from the edge of the wood. Since the war the fox was a demon. He carried off the hens under the very noses of March and Banford. Banford would start and stare through her big spectacles with all her eyes, as another squawk and flutter took place at her heels. Too late! Another white Leghorn gone. It was disheartening.

They did what they could to remedy it. When it became permitted to shoot foxes, they stood sentinel with their guns, the two of them, at the favoured hours. But it was no good. The fox was too quick for them. So another year passed, and another, and they were living on their losses, as Banford said. They let their farmhouse one summer, and retired to live in a railway-carriage that was deposited as a sort of out-house in a corner of the field. This amused them, and helped their finances. None the less, things looked dark.

Although they were usually the best of friends, because Banford, though nervous and delicate, was a warm, generous soul, and March, though so odd and absent in herself, had a strange magnanimity, yet, in the long solitude, they were apt to become a little irritable with one another, tired of one another. March had four-fifths of the work to do, and though she did not mind, there seemed no relief, and it made her eyes flash curiously sometimes. Then Banford, feeling more nerve-worn than ever, would become despondent, and March would speak sharply to her. They seemed to be losing ground, somehow, losing hope as the months went by. There alone in the fields by the wood, with the wide country stretching hollow and dim to the round hills of the White Horse, in the far distance, they seemed to have to live too much off themselves. There was nothing to keep them up—and no hope.

The fox really exasperated them both. As soon as they had let the fowls out, in the early summer mornings, they had to take their guns and keep guard: and then again, as soon as evening began to mellow, they must go once more. And he was so sly. He slid along in the deep grass; he was difficult as a serpent to see. And he seemed to circumvent the girls deliber-ately. Once or twice March had caught sight of the white tip of his brush, or the ruddy shadow of him in the deep grass, and she had let fire at him. But he made no account of this.

One evening March was standing with her back to the sunset, her gun under her arm, her hair pushed under her cap. She was half watching, half musing. It was her constant state. Her eyes were keen and observant, but her inner mind took no notice of what she saw. She was always lapsing into this odd, rapt state, her mouth rather screwed up. It was a question whether she was there, actually conscious present, or not.

The trees on the wood-edge were a darkish, brownish green in the full light—for it was the end of August. Beyond, the naked, copper-like shafts and limbs of the pine-trees shone in the air. Nearer the rough grass, with its long brownish stalks all agleam, was full of light. The fowls were round about—the ducks were still swimming on the pond under the pine-trees. March looked at it all, saw it all, and did not see it. She heard Banford speaking to the fowls in the distance—and she did not hear. What was she thinking about? Heaven knows. Her consciousness was, as it were, held back.

She lowered her eyes, and suddenly saw the fox. He was looking up at her. His chin was pressed down, and his eyes were looking up. They met her eyes. And he knew her. She was spellbound—she knew he knew her. So he looked into her eyes, and her soul failed her. He knew her, he was not daunted.

She struggled, confusedly she came to herself, and saw him making off, with slow leaps over some fallen boughs, slow, impudent jumps. Then he glanced over his shoulder, and ran smoothly away. She saw his brush held smooth like a feather, she saw his white buttocks twinkle. And he was gone, softly, soft as the wind.

She put her gun to her shoulder, but even then pursed her mouth, knowing it was nonsense to pretend to fire. So she began to walk slowly after him, in the direction he had gone, slowly, pertinaciously. She expected to find him. In her heart she was determined to find him. What she would do when she saw him again she did not consider. But she was determined to find him. So she walked abstractedly about on the edge of the wood, with wide, vivid dark eyes, and a faint flush in her cheeks. She did not think. In strange mindlessness she walked hither and thither.

At last she became aware that Banford was calling her. She made an effort of attention, turned, and gave some sort of screaming call in answer. Then again she was striding off towards the homestead. The red sun was setting, the fowls were retiring towards their roost. She watched them, white creatures, black creatures, gathering to the barn. She watched them spellbound, without seeing them. But her automatic intelligence told her when it was time to shut the door.

She went indoors to supper, which Banford had set on the table. Banford chatted easily. March seemed to listen, in her distant, manly way. She answered a brief word now and then. But all the time she was as if spellbound. And as soon as supper was over, she rose again to go out, without saying why.

She took her gun again and went to look for the fox. For he had lifted his eyes upon her, and his knowing look seemed to have entered her brain. She did not so much think of him: she was possessed by him. She saw his dark, shrewd, unabashed eye looking into her, knowing her. She felt him invisibly master her spirit. She knew the way he lowered his chin as he looked up, she knew his muzzle, the golden brown, and the greyish white. And again, she saw him glance over his shoulder at her, half inviting, half contemptuous, and cunning. So she went, with her great startled eyes glowing, her gun under her arm, along the wood edge. Meanwhile the night fell, and a great moon rose above the pine-trees. And again Banford was calling.

So she went indoors. She was silent and busy. She examined her gun, and cleaned it, musing abstractedly by the lamp-light. Then she went out again, under the great moon, to see if everything was right. When she saw the dark crests of the pine-trees against the blood-red sky, again her heart beat to the fox, the fox. She wanted to follow him, with her gun.

It was some days before she mentioned the affair to Banford. Then suddenly one evening she said:

"The fox was right at my feet on Saturday night."

"Where?" said Banford, her eyes opening behind her spectacles.

"When I stood just above the pond."

"Did you fire?" cried Banford.

"No, I didn't."

"Why not?"

"Why, I was too much surprised, I suppose."

It was the same old, slow, laconic way of speech March always had. Banford stared at her friend for a few moments.

"You saw him?" she cried.

"Oh yes! He was looking up at me, cool as anything."

"I tell you," cried Banford—"the cheek! They're not afraid of us, Nellie."

"Oh no," said March.

"Pity you didn't get a shot at him," said Banford.

"Isn't it a pity! I've been looking for him ever since. But I don't suppose he'll come so near again."

"I don't suppose he will," said Banford.

And she proceeded to forget about it, except that she was more indignant than ever at the impudence of the beggar. March also was not conscious that she thought of the fox. But whenever she fell into her half-musing, when she was half rapt and half intelligently aware of what passed under her vision, then it was the fox which somehow dominated her unconsciousness, possessed the blank half of her musing. And so it was for weeks, and months. No matter whether she had been climbing the trees for the apples, or beating down the last of the damsons, or whether she had been digging out the ditch from the duck-pond, or clearing out the barn, when she had finished, or when she straightened herself, and pushed the wisps of hair away again from her forehead, and pursed up her mouth again in an odd, screwed fashion, much too old for her years, there was sure to come over her mind the old spell of the fox, as it came when he was looking at her. It was as if she could smell him at these times. And it always recurred, at unexpected moments, just as she was going to sleep at night, or just as she was pouring the water into the teapot to make tea—it was the fox, it came over her like a spell.

So the months passed. She still looked for him unconsciously when she went towards the wood. He had become a settled effect in her spirit, a state permanently established, not continuous, but always recurring. She did not know what she felt or thought: only the state came over her, as when he looked at her.

The months passed, the dark evenings came, heavy, dark November, when March went about in high boots, ankle deep in mud, when the night began to fall at four o'clock, and the day never properly dawned. Both girls dreaded these times. They dreaded the almost continuous darkness that enveloped them on their desolate little farm near the wood. Banford was physically afraid. She was afraid of tramps, afraid lest someone should come prowling round. March was not so much afraid as uncomfortable, and disturbed. She felt discomfort and gloom in all her physique.

Usually the two girls had tea in the sitting-room. March

lighted a fire at dusk, and put on the wood she had chopped
and sawed during the day. Then the long evening was in
front, dark, sodden, black outside, lonely and rather oppressive
inside, a little dismal. March was content not to talk, but
Banford could not keep still. Merely listening to the wind in
the pines outside, or the drip of water, was too much for her.

One evening the girls had washed up the tea-things in the
kitchen, and March had put on her house-shoes, and taken up
a roll of crochet-work, which she worked at slowly from time
to time. So she lapsed into silence. Banford stared at the red
fire, which, being of wood, needed constant attention. She
was afraid to begin to read too early, because her eyes would
not bear any strain. So she sat staring at the fire, listening
to the distant sounds, sound of cattle lowing, of a dull, heavy,
moist wind, of the rattle of the evening train on the little
railway not far off. She was almost fascinated by the red
glow of the fire.

Suddenly both girls started, and lifted their heads. They
heard a footstep—distinctly a footstep. Banford recoiled in
fear. March stood listening. Then rapidly she approached the
door that led into the kitchen. At the same time they heard
the footsteps approach the back door. They waited a second.
The back door opened softly. Banford gave a loud cry. A
man's voice said softly:

"Hello!"

March recoiled, and took a gun from a corner.

"What do you want?" she cried, in a sharp voice.

Again the soft, softly vibrating man's voice said:

"Hello! What's wrong?"

"I shall shoot!" cried March. "What do you want?"

"Why, what's wrong? What's wrong?" came the soft,
wondering, rather scared voice: and a young soldier, with his
heavy kit on his back, advanced into the dim light.

"Why," he said, "who lives here then?"

"We live here," said March. "What do you want?"

"Oh!" came the long, melodious, wonder-note from the young
soldier. "Doesn't William Grenfel live here then?"

"No—you know he doesn't."

"Do I? Do I? I don't, you see. He *did* live here, because he was my grandfather, and I lived here myself five years ago. What's become of him then?"

The young man—or youth, for he would not be more than twenty—now advanced and stood in the inner doorway. March, already under the influence of his strange, soft, modulated voice, stared at him spellbound. He had a ruddy, roundish face, with fairish hair, rather long, flattened to his forehead with sweat. His eyes were blue, and very bright and sharp. On his cheeks, on the fresh ruddy skin were fine, fair hairs, like a down, but sharper. It gave him a slightly glistening look. Having his heavy sack on his shoulders, he stooped, thrusting his head forward. His hat was loose in one hand. He stared brightly, very keenly from girl to girl, particularly at March, who stood pale, with great dilated eyes, in her belted coat and puttees, her hair knotted in a big crisp knot behind. She still had the gun in her hand. Behind her, Banford, clinging to the sofa-arm, was shrinking away, with half-averted head.

"I thought my grandfather still lived here? I wonder if he's dead."

"We've been here for three years," said Banford, who was beginning to recover her wits, seeing something boyish in the round head with its rather long sweaty hair.

"Three years! You don't say so! And you don't know who was here before you?"

"I know it was an old man, who lived by himself."

"Ay! Yes, that's him! And what became of him then?"

"He died. I know he died."

"Ay! He's dead then!"

The youth stared at them without changing colour or expression. If he had any expression, beside a slight baffled look of wonder, it was one of sharp curiosity concerning the two girls; sharp, impersonal curiosity, the curiosity of that round young head.

But to March he was the fox. Whether it was the thrusting

forward of his head, or the glisten of fine whitish hairs on the ruddy cheek-bones, or the bright, keen eyes, that can never be said: but the boy was to her the fox, and she could not see him otherwise.

"How is it you didn't know if your grandfather was alive or dead?" asked Banford, recovering her natural sharpness.

"Ay, that's it," replied the softly-breathing youth. "You see I joined up in Canada, and I hadn't heard for three or four years. I ran away to Canada."

"And now have you just come from France?"

"Well—from Salonika really."

There was a pause, nobody knowing quite what to say.

"So you've nowhere to go now?" said Banford rather lamely.

"Oh, I know some people in the village. Anyhow, I can go to the Swan."

"You came on the train, I suppose. Would you like to sit down a bit?"

"Well—I don't mind."

He gave an odd little groan as he swung off his kit. Banford looked at March.

"Put the gun down," she said. "We'll make a cup of tea."

"Ay," said the youth. "We've seen enough of rifles."

He sat down rather tired on the sofa, leaning forward.

March recovered her presence of mind, and went into the kitchen. There she heard the soft young voice musing:

"Well, to think I should come back and find it like this!" He did not seem sad, not at all—only rather interestedly surprised.

"And what a difference in the place, eh?" he continued, looking round the room.

"You see a difference, do you?" said Banford.

"Yes—don't I?"

His eyes were unnaturally clear and bright, though it was the brightness of abundant health.

March was busy in the kitchen preparing another meal. It was about seven o'clock. All the time, while she was active, she was attending to the youth in the sitting-room, not so much listening to what he said as feeling the soft run of his voice. She primmed up her mouth tighter and tighter, puckering it as if it were sewed, in her effort to keep her will uppermost. Yet her large eyes dilated and glowed in spite of her; she lost herself. Rapidly and carelessly she prepared the meal, cutting large chunks of bread and margarine—for there was no butter. She racked her brain to think of something else to put on the tray—she had only bread, margarine, and jam, and the larder was bare. Unable to conjure anything up, she went into the sitting-room with her tray.

She did not want to be noticed. Above all, she did not want him to look at her. But when she came in, and was busy setting the table just behind him, he pulled himself up from his sprawling, and turned and looked over his shoulder. She became pale and wan.

The youth watched her as she bent over the table, looked at her slim, well-shapen legs, at the belted coat dropping around her thighs, at the knot of dark hair, and his curiosity, vivid and widely alert, was again arrested by her.

The lamp was shaded with a dark-green shade, so that the light was thrown downwards and the upper half of the room was dim. His face moved bright under the light, but March loomed shadowy in the distance.

She turned round, but kept her eyes sideways, dropping and lifting her dark lashes. Her mouth unpuckered as she said to Banford:

"Will you pour out?"

Then she went into the kitchen again.

"Have your tea where you are, will you?" said Banford to the youth—"unless you'd rather come to the table."

"Well," said he, "I'm nice and comfortable here, aren't I? I will have it here, if you don't mind."

"There's nothing but bread and jam," she said. And she put his plate on a stool by him. She was very happy now, waiting on him. For she loved company. And now she was no more afraid of him than if he were her own younger brother. He was such a boy.

"Nellie," she called. "I've poured you a cup out."

March appeared in the doorway, took her cup, and sat down in a corner, as far from the light as possible. She was very sensitive in her knees. Having no skirts to cover them, and being forced to sit with them boldly exposed, she suffered. She shrank and shrank, trying not to be seen. And the youth, sprawling low on the couch, glanced up at her, with long, steady, penetrating looks, till she was almost ready to disappear. Yet she held her cup balanced, she drank her tea, screwed up her mouth and held her head averted. Her desire to be invisible was so strong that it quite baffled the youth. He felt he could not see her distinctly. She seemed like a shadow within the shadow. And ever his eyes came back to her, searching, unremitting, with unconscious fixed attention.

Meanwhile he was talking softly and smoothly to Banford, who loved nothing so much as gossip, and who was full of perky interest, like a bird. Also he ate largely and quickly and voraciously, so that March had to cut more chunks of bread and margarine, for the roughness of which Banford apologized.

"Oh well," said March, suddenly speaking, "if there's no butter to put on it, it's no good trying to make dainty pieces."

Again the youth watched her, and he laughed, with a sudden, quick laugh, showing his teeth and wrinkling his nose.

"It isn't, is it," he answered, in his soft, near voice.

It appeared he was Cornish by birth and upbringing. When he was twelve years old he had come to Bailey Farm with his grandfather, with whom he had never agreed very well. So he had run away to Canada, and worked far away in the West. Now he was here—and that was the end of it.

He was very curious about the girls, to find out exactly what they were doing. His questions were those of a farm youth; acute, practical, a little mocking. He was very much amused by their attitude to their losses: for they were amusing on the score of heifers and fowls.

"Oh well," broke in March, "we don't believe in living for nothing but work."

"Don't you?" he answered. And again the quick young

laugh came over his face. He kept his eyes steadily on the obscure woman in the corner.

"But what will you do when you've used up all your capital?" he said.

"Oh, I don't know," answered March laconically. "Hire ourselves out for land-workers, I suppose."

"Yes, but there won't be any demand for women land-workers now the war's over," said the youth.

"Oh, we'll see. We shall hold on a bit longer yet," said March, with a plangent, half-sad, half-ironical indifference.

"There wants a man about the place," said the youth softly.

Banford burst out laughing.

"Take care what you say," she interrupted. "We consider ourselves quite efficient."

"Oh," came March's slow plangent voice, "it isn't a case of efficiency, I'm afraid. If you're going to do farming you must be at it from morning till night, and you might as well be a beast yourself."

"Yes, that's it," said the youth. "You aren't willing to put yourselves into it."

"We aren't," said March, "and we know it."

"We want some of our time for ourselves," said Banford.

The youth threw himself back on the sofa, his face tight with laughter, and laughed silently but thoroughly. The calm scorn of the girls tickled him tremendously.

"Yes," he said, "but why did you begin then?"

"Oh," said March, "we had a better opinion of the nature of fowls then than we have now."

"Of Nature altogether, I'm afraid," said Banford. "Don't talk to me about Nature."

Again the face of the youth tightened with delighted laughter.

"You haven't a very high opinion of fowls and cattle, haven't you?" he said.

"Oh no—quite a low one," said March.

He laughed out.

"Neither fowls nor heifers," said Banford, "nor goats nor the weather."

The youth broke into a sharp yap of laughter, delighted.
The girls began to laugh too, March turning aside her face and
wrinkling her mouth in amusement.

"Oh, well," said Banford, "we don't mind, do we, Nellie?"

"No," said March, "we don't mind."

The youth was very pleased. He had eaten and drunk his
fill. Banford began to question him. His name was Henry
Grenfel—no, he was not called Harry, always Henry. He
continued to answer with courteous simplicity, grave and
charming. March, who was not included, cast long, slow
glances at him from her recess, as he sat there on the sofa, his
hands clasping his knees, his face under the lamp bright and
alert, turned to Banford. She became almost peaceful at last.
He was identified with the fox—and he was here in full
presence. She need not go after him any more. There in the
shadow of her corner she gave herself up to a warm, relaxed
peace, almost like sleep, accepting the spell that was on her.
But she wished to remain hidden. She was only fully at peace
whilst he forgot her, talking to Banford. Hidden in the shadow
of the corner, she need not any more be divided in herself,
trying to keep up two planes of consciousness. She could at
last lapse into the odour of the fox.

For the youth, sitting before the fire in his uniform, sent a
faint but distinct odour into the room, indefinable, but something like a wild creature. March no longer tried to reserve
herself from it. She was still and soft in her corner like a
passive creature in its cave.

At last the talk dwindled. The youth relaxed his clasp of
his knees, pulled himself together a little, and looked round.
Again he became aware of the silent, half-invisible woman in
the corner.

"Well," he said, unwillingly, "I suppose I'd better be going,
or they'll be in bed at the Swan."

"I'm afraid they're in bed anyhow," said Banford. "They've
all got this influenza."

"Have they!" he exclaimed. And he pondered. "Well," he
continued, "I shall find a place somewhere."

"I'd say you could stay here, only——" Banford began.

He turned and watched her, holding his head forward.

"What?" he asked.

"Oh, well," she said, "propriety, I suppose." She was rather confused.

"It wouldn't be improper, would it?" he said, gently surprised.

"Not as far as we're concerned," said Banford.

"And not as far as *I'm* concerned," he said, with grave *naïveté*. "After all, it's my own home, in a way."

Banford smiled at this.

"It's what the village will have to say," she said.

There was a moment's blank pause.

"What do you say, Nellie?" asked Banford.

"I don't mind," said March, in her distinct tone. "The village doesn't matter to me, anyhow."

"No," said the youth, quick and soft. "Why should it? I mean, what should they say?"

"Oh, well," came March's laconic voice, "they'll easily find something to say. But it makes no difference what they say. We can look after ourselves."

"Of course you can," said the youth.

"Well, then, stop if you like," said Banford. "The spare room is quite ready."

His face shone with pleasure.

"If you're quite sure it isn't troubling you too much," he said, with that soft courtesy which distinguished him.

"Oh, it's no trouble," they both said.

He looked, smiled with delight, from one to another.

"It's awfully nice not to have to turn out again, isn't it?" he said gratefully.

"I suppose it is," said Banford.

March disappeared to attend to the room. Banford was as pleased and thoughtful as if she had her own young brother home from France. It gave her just the same kind of gratification to attend on him, to get out the bath for him, and everything. Her natural warmth and kindliness had now an outlet.

And the youth luxuriated in her sisterly attention. But it puzzled him slightly to know that March was silently working for him too. She was so curiously silent and obliterated. It seemed to him he had not really seen her. He felt he should not know her if he met her in the road.

That night March dreamed vividly. She dreamed she heard a singing outside which she could not understand, a singing that roamed round the house, in the fields, and in the darkness. It moved her so that she felt she must weep. She went out, and suddenly she knew it was the fox singing. He was very yellow and bright, like corn. She went nearer to him, but he ran away and ceased singing. He seemed near, and she wanted to touch him. She stretched out her hand, but suddenly he bit her wrist, and at the same instant, as she drew back, the fox, turning round to bound away, whisked his brush across her face, and it seemed his brush was on fire, for it seared and burned her mouth with a great pain. She awoke with the pain of it, and lay trembling as if she were really seared.

In the morning, however, she only remembered it as a distant memory. She arose and was busy preparing the house and attending to the fowls. Banford flew into the village on her bicycle to try and buy food. She was a hospitable soul. But alas, in the year 1918 there was not much food to buy. The youth came downstairs in his shirt-sleeves. He was young and fresh, but he walked with his head thrust forward, so that his shoulders seemed raised and rounded, as if he had a slight curvature of the spine. It must have been only a manner of bearing himself, for he was young and vigorous. He washed himself and went outside, while the women were preparing breakfast.

He saw everything, and examined everything. His curiosity was quick and insatiable. He compared the state of things with that which he remembered before, and cast over in his mind the effect of the changes. He watched the fowls and the ducks, to see their condition; he noticed the flight of wood-pigeons overhead: they were very numerous; he saw the few apples high up, which March had not been able to reach; he remarked that they had borrowed a draw-pump, presumably to empty the big soft-water cistern which was on the north side of the house.

"It's a funny, dilapidated old place," he said to the girls as he sat at breakfast.

His eyes were wise and childish, with thinking about things. He did not say much, but ate largely. March kept her face averted. She, too, in the early morning could not be aware of him, though something about the glint of his khaki reminded her of the brilliance of her dream-fox.

During the day the girls went about their business. In the morning he attended to the guns, shot a rabbit and a wild duck that was flying high towards the wood. That was a great addition to the empty larder. The girls felt that already he had earned his keep. He said nothing about leaving, however. In the afternoon he went to the village. He came back at tea-time. He had the same alert, forward-reaching look on his roundish face. He hung his hat on a peg with a little swinging gesture. He was thinking about something.

"Well," he said to the girls, as he sat at table. "What am I going to do?"

"How do you mean—what are you going to do?" said Banford.

"Where am I going to find a place in the village to stay?" he said.

"I don't know," said Banford. "Where do you think of staying?"

"Well"—he hesitated—"at the Swan they've got this flu, and at the Plough and Harrow they've got the soldiers who are collecting the hay for the army; besides, in the private houses, there's ten men and a corporal altogether billeted in the village, they tell me. I'm not sure where I could get a bed."

He left the matter to them. He was rather calm about it. March sat with her elbows on the table, her two hands supporting her chin, looking at him unconsciously. Suddenly he lifted his clouded blue eyes, and unthinking looked straight into March's eyes. He was startled as well as she. He, too, recoiled a little. March felt the same sly, taunting, knowing spark leap out of his eyes, as he turned his head aside, and fall into her soul, as it had fallen from the dark eyes of the fox. She pursed her mouth as if in pain, as if asleep too.

"Well, I don't know," Banford was saying. She seemed reluctant, as if she were afraid of being imposed upon. She looked at March. But, with her weak, troubled sight, she only saw the usual semi-abstraction on her friend's face. "Why don't you speak, Nellie?" she said.

But March was wide-eyed and silent, and the youth, as if fascinated, was watching her without moving his eyes.

"Go on—answer something," said Banford. And March turned her head slightly aside, as if coming to consciousness, or trying to come to consciousness.

"What do you expect me to say?" she asked automatically.

"Say what you think," said Banford.

"It's all the same to me," said March.

And again there was silence. A pointed light seemed to be on the boy's eyes, penetrating like a needle.

"So it is to me," said Banford. "You can stop on here if you like."

A smile like a cunning little flame came over his face, suddenly and involuntarily. He dropped his head quickly to hide it, and remained with his head dropped, his face hidden.

"You can stop on here if you like. You can please yourself, Henry," Banford concluded.

Still he did not reply, but remained with his head dropped. Then he lifted his face. It was bright with a curious light, as if exultant, and his eyes were strangely clear as he watched March. She turned her face aside, her mouth suffering as if wounded, and her consciousness dim.

Banford became a little puzzled. She watched the steady, pellucid gaze of the youth's eyes as he looked at March, with the invisible smile gleaming on his face. She did not know how he was smiling, for no feature moved. It seemed only in the gleam, almost the glitter of the fine hairs on his cheeks. Then he looked with quite a changed look at Banford.

"I'm sure," he said in his soft, courteous voice, "you're awfully good. You're too good. You don't want to be bothered with me, I'm sure."

"But a bit of bread, Nellie," said Banford uneasily, adding: "It's no bother, if you like to stay. It's like having my own brother here for a few days. He's a boy like you are."

"That's awfully kind of you," the lad repeated. "I should like to stay ever so much, if you're sure I'm not a trouble to you."

"No, of course you're no trouble. I tell you, it's a pleasure to have somebody in the house besides ourselves," said warm-hearted Banford.

"But Miss March?" he said in his soft voice, looking at her.

"Oh, it's quite all right as far as I'm concerned," said March vaguely.

His face beamed, and he almost rubbed his hands with pleasure.

"Well then," he said, "I should love it, if you'd let me pay my board and help with the work."

"You've no need to talk about board," said Banford.

One or two days went by, and the youth stayed on at the farm. Banford was quite charmed by him. He was so soft and courteous in speech, not wanting to say much himself, preferring to hear what she had to say, and to laugh in his quick, half-mocking way. He helped readily with the work—but not too much. He loved to be out alone with the gun in his hands, to watch, to see. For his sharp-eyed, impersonal curiosity was insatiable, and he was most free when he was quite alone, half-hidden, watching.

Particularly he watched March. She was a strange character to him. Her figure, like a graceful young man's, piqued him. Her dark eyes made something rise in his soul, with a curious elate excitement, when he looked into them, an excitement he was afraid to let be seen, it was so keen and secret. And then her odd, shrewd speech made him laugh outright. He felt he must go further, he was inevitably impelled. But he put away the thought of her and went off towards the wood's edge with the gun.

The dusk was falling as he came home, and with the dusk, a fine, late November rain. He saw the fire-light leaping in the window of the sitting-room, a leaping light in the little cluster of the dark buildings. And he thought to himself it would be a good thing to have this place for his own. And then the thought entered him shrewdly: why not marry March? He stood still in the middle of the field for some moments, the dead rabbit hanging still in his hand, arrested by this thought. His mind waited in amazement—it seemed to calculate—and then he smiled curiously to himself in acquiescence. Why not? Why not indeed? It was a good idea. What if it was rather ridiculous? What did it matter? What if she was older than he? It didn't matter. When he thought of her dark, startled, vulnerable eyes he smiled subtly to himself. He was older than she, really. He was master of her.

He scarcely admitted his intention even to himself. He kept it as a secret even from himself. It was all too uncertain as yet. He would have to see how things went. Yes, he would have to see how things went. If he wasn't careful, she would just simply mock at the idea. He knew, sly and subtle as he was, that if he went to her plainly and said: "Miss March, I love you and want you to marry me," her inevitable answer would be: "Get out. I don't want any of that tomfoolery." This was her attitude to men and their "tomfoolery." If he was not careful, she would turn round on him with her savage, sardonic ridicule, and dismiss him from the farm and from her own mind for ever. He would have to go gently. He would have to catch her as you catch a deer or a woodcock when you go out shooting. It's no good walking out into the forest and saying to the deer: "Please fall to my gun." No, it is a slow, subtle, battle. When you really go out to get a deer, you gather yourself together, you coil yourself inside yourself, and you advance secretly, before dawn, into the mountains. It is not so much what you do, when you go out hunting, as how you feel. You have to be subtle and cunning and absolutely fatally ready. It becomes like a fate. Your own fate overtakes and determines the fate of the deer you are hunting. First of all, even before you come in sight of your quarry, there is a strange battle, like mesmerism. Your own soul, as a hunter, has gone out to fasten on the soul of the deer, even before you see any deer. And the soul of the deer fights to escape. Even before the deer has any wind of you, it is so. It is a subtle, profound battle of wills which takes place in the invisible. And it is a battle never finished till your bullet goes home. When you are *really* worked up to the true pitch, and you come at last into range, you don't then aim as you do when you are firing at a bottle. It is your own *will* which carries the bullet into the heart of your quarry. The bullet's flight home is a sheer projection of your own fate into the fate of the deer. It happens like a supreme wish, a supreme act of volition, not as a dodge of cleverness.

He was a huntsman in spirit, not a farmer, and not a soldier stuck in a regiment. And it was as a young hunter that he wanted to bring down March as his quarry, to make her his wife. So he gathered himself subtly together, seemed to withdraw into a kind of invisibility. He was not quite sure how he would go on. And March was suspicious as a hare. So he remained in appearance just the nice, odd stranger-youth, staying for a fortnight on the place.

He had been sawing logs for the fire in the afternoon. Darkness came very early. It was still a cold, raw mist. It was getting almost too dark to see. A pile of short-sawed logs lay beside the trestle. March came to carry them indoors, or into the shed, as he was busy sawing the last log. He was working in his shirt-sleeves, and did not notice her approach; she came unwillingly, as if shy. He saw her stooping to the bright-ended logs, and he stopped sawing. A fire like lightning flew down his legs in the nerves.

"March?" he said, in his quiet, young voice.

She looked up from the logs she was piling.

"Yes!" she said.

He looked down on her in the dusk. He could see her not too distinctly.

"I wanted to ask you something," he said.

"Did you? What was it?" she said. Already the fright was in her voice. But she was too much mistress of herself.

"Why"—his voice seemed to draw out soft and subtle, it penetrated her nerves—"why, what do you think it is?"

She stood up, placed her hands on her hips, and stood looking at him transfixed, without answering. Again he burned with a sudden power.

"Well," he said, and his voice was so soft it seemed rather like a subtle touch, like the merest touch of a cat's paw, a feeling rather than a sound. "Well—I wanted to ask you to marry me."

March felt rather than heard him. She was trying in vain to turn aside her face. A great relaxation seemed to have come over her. She stood silent, her head slightly on one side. He seemed to be bending towards her, invisibly smiling. It seemed to her fine sparks came out of him.

Then very suddenly she said:

"Don't try any of your tomfoolery on me."

A quiver went over his nerves. He had missed. He waited a moment to collect himself again. Then he said, putting all the strange softness into his voice, as if he were imperceptibly stroking her:

"Why, it's not tomfoolery. It's not tomfoolery. I mean it. I mean it. What makes you disbelieve me?"

He sounded hurt. And his voice had such a curious power over her; making her feel loose and relaxed. She struggled somewhere for her own power. She felt for a moment that she was lost—lost—lost. The word seemed to rock in her as if she were dying. Suddenly again she spoke.

"You don't know what you are talking about," she said, in a brief and transient stroke of scorn. "What nonsense! I'm old enough to be your mother."

"Yes, I do know what I'm talking about. Yes, I do," he persisted softly, as if he were producing his voice in her blood. "I know quite well what I'm talking about. You're not old enough to be my mother. That isn't true. And what does it matter even if it was. You can marry me whatever age we are.

What is age to me? And what is age to you! Age is nothing."

A swoon went over her as he concluded. He spoke rapidly—in the rapid Cornish fashion—and his voice seemed to sound in her somewhere where she was helpless against it. "Age is nothing!" The soft, heavy insistence of it made her sway dimly out there in the darkness. She could not answer.

A great exultance leaped like fire over his limbs. He felt he had won.

"I want to marry you, you see. Why shouldn't I?" he proceeded, soft and rapid. He waited for her to answer. In the dusk he saw her almost phosphorescent. Her eyelids were dropped, her face half-averted and unconscious. She seemed to be in his power. But he waited, watchful. He dared not yet touch her.

"Say then," he said, "say then you'll marry me. Say—say!" He was softly insistent.

"What?" she asked, faint, from a distance, like one in pain. His voice was now unthinkably near and soft. He drew very near to her.

"Say yes."

"Oh, I can't," she wailed helplessly, half-articulate, as if semi-conscious, and as if in pain, like one who dies. "How can I?"

"You can," he said softly, laying his hand gently on her shoulder as she stood with her head averted and dropped, dazed. "You can. Yes, you can. What makes you say you can't. You can. You can." And with awful softness he bent forward and just touched her neck with his mouth and his chin.

"Don't!" she cried, with a faint mad cry like hysteria, starting away and facing round on him. "What do you mean?" But she had no breath to speak with. It was as if she was killed.

"I mean what I say," he persisted softly and cruelly. "I want you to marry me. I want you to marry me. You know that, now, don't you? You know that, now? Don't you? Don't you?"

"What?" she said.

"Know," he replied.

"Yes," she said. "I know you say so."

"And you know I mean it, don't you?"

"I know you say so."

"You believe me?" he said.

She was silent for some time. Then she pursed her lips.

"I don't know what I believe," she said.

"Are you out there?" came Banford's voice, calling from the house.

"Yes, we're bringing in the logs," he answered.

"I thought you'd gone lost," said Banford disconsolately. "Hurry up, do, and come and let's have tea. The kettle's boiling."

He stooped at once, to take an armful of little logs and carry them into the kitchen, where they were piled in a corner. March also helped, filling her arms and carrying the logs on her breast as if they were some heavy child. The night had fallen cold.

When the logs were all in, the two cleaned their boots noisily on the scraper outside, then rubbed them on the mat. March shut the door and took off her old felt hat—her farm-girl hat. Her thick, crisp black hair was loose, her face was pale and strained. She pushed back her hair vaguely, and washed her hands. Banford came hurrying into the dimly lighted kitchen, to take from the oven the scones she was keeping hot.

"Whatever have you been doing all this time?" she asked fretfully. "I thought you were never coming in. And it's ages since you stopped sawing. What were you doing out there?"

"Well," said Henry, "we had to stop that hole in the barn, to keep the rats out."

"Why, I could see you standing there in the shed. I could see your shirt-sleeves," challenged Banford.

"Yes, I was just putting the saw away."

They went in to tea. March was quite mute. Her face was pale and strained and vague. The youth, who always had the same ruddy, self-contained look on his face, as though he were keeping himself to himself, had come to tea in his shirt-sleeves as if he were at home. He bent over his plate as he ate his food.

"Aren't you cold?" said Banford spitefully. "In your shirt-sleeves."

He looked up at her, with his chin near his plate, and his eyes very clear, pellucid, and unwavering as he watched her.

"No, I'm not cold," he said with his usual soft courtesy. "It's much warmer in here than it is outside, you see."

"I hope it is," said Banford, feeling nettled by him. He had a strange suave assurance, and a wide-eyed bright look that got on her nerves this evening.

"But perhaps," he said softly and courteously, "you don't like me coming to tea without my coat. I forgot that."

"Oh, I don't mind," said Banford; although she *did*.

"I'll go and get it, shall I?" he said.

March's dark eyes turned slowly down to him.

"No, don't you bother," she said in her queer, twanging tone. "If you feel all right as you are, stop as you are." She spoke with a crude authority.

"Yes," said he, "I *feel* all right, if I'm not rude."

"It's usually considered rude," said Banford. "But we don't mind."

"Go along, 'considered rude,' " ejaculated March. "Who considers it rude?"

"Why you do, Nellie, in anybody else," said Banford, bridling a little behind her spectacles, and feeling her food stick in her throat.

But March had again gone vague and unheeding, chewing her food as if she did not know she was eating at all. And the youth looked from one to another, with bright, watchful eyes.

Banford was offended. For all his suave courtesy and soft voice, the youth seemed to her impudent. She did not like to look at him. She did not like to meet his clear, watchful eyes, she did not like to see the strange glow in his face, his cheeks with their delicate fine hair, and his ruddy skin that

was quite dull and yet which seemed to burn with a curious
heat of life. It made her feel a little ill to look at him: the
quality of his physical presence was too penetrating, too hot.

After tea the evening was very quiet. The youth rarely
went into the village. As a rule he read: he was a great reader,
in his own hours. That is, when he did begin, he read
absorbedly. But he was not very eager to begin. Often he
walked about the fields and along the hedges alone in the dark
at night, prowling with a queer instinct for the night, and
listening to the wild sounds.

To-night, however, he took a Captain Mayne Reid book
from Banford's shelf and sat down with knees wide apart and
immersed himself in his story. His brownish fair hair was
long, and lay on his head like a thick cap, combed sideways.
He was still in his shirt-sleeves, and bending forward under
the lamp-light, with his knees stuck wide apart and the book
in his hand and his whole figure absorbed in the rather strenuous business of reading, he gave Banford's sitting-room the
look of a lumber-camp. She resented this. For on her sitting-
room floor she had a red Turkey rug and dark stain round,
the fire-place had fashionable green tiles, the piano stood open
with the latest dance-music—she played quite well: and on
the walls were March's hand-painted swans and water-lilies.
Moreover, with the logs nicely, tremulously burning in the
grate, the thick curtains drawn, the doors all shut, and the
pine-trees hissing and shuddering in the wind outside, it was
cosy, it was refined and nice. She resented the big, raw, long-
legged youth sticking his khaki knees out and sitting there
with his soldier's shirt-cuffs buttoned on his thick red wrists.
From time to time he turned a page, and from time to time
he gave a sharp look at the fire, settling the logs. Then he
immersed himself again in the intense and isolated business
of reading.

March, on the far side of the table, was spasmodically
crocheting. Her mouth was pursed in an odd way, as when she
had dreamed the fox's brush turned it, her beautiful, crisp
black hair strayed in wisps. But her whole figure was absorbed

in its bearing, as if she herself was miles away. In a sort of semi-dream she seemed to be hearing the fox singing round the house in the wind, singing wildly and sweetly and like a madness. With red but well-shaped hands she slowly crocheted the white cotton, very slowly, awkwardly.

Banford was also trying to read, sitting in her low chair. But between those two she felt fidgety. She kept moving and looking round and listening to the wind, and glancing secretly from one to the other of her companions. March, seated on a straight chair, with her knees in their close breeches crossed, and slowly, laboriously crocheting, was also a trial.

"Oh dear!" said Banford. "My eyes are bad to-night." And she pressed her fingers on her eyes.

The youth looked up at her with his clear, bright look, but did not speak.

"Are they, Jill?" said March absently.

Then the youth began to read again, and Banford perforce returned to her book. But she could not keep still. After a while she looked up at March, and a queer, almost malignant little smile was on her thin face.

"A penny for them, Nell," she said suddenly.

March looked round with big, startled black eyes, and went pale as if with terror. She had been listening to the fox singing so tenderly, so tenderly, as he wandered round the house.

"What?" she said vaguely.

"A penny for them," said Banford sarcastically. "Or two-pence, if they're as deep as all that."

The youth was watching with bright, clear eyes from beneath the lamp.

"Why," came March's vague voice, "what do you want to waste your money for?"

"I thought it would be well spent," said Banford.

"I wasn't thinking of anything except the way the wind was blowing," said March.

"Oh dear," replied Banford, "I could have had as original thoughts as that myself. I'm afraid I *have* wasted my money this time."

"Well, you needn't pay," said March.

The youth suddenly laughed. Both women looked at him: March rather surprised-looking, as if she had hardly known he was there.

"Why, do you ever pay up on these occasions?" he asked.

"Oh yes," said Banford. "We always do.' I've sometimes had to pass a shilling a week to Nellie, in the winter-time. It costs much less in summer.

"What, paying for each other's thoughts?" he laughed.

"Yes, when we've absolutely come to the end of everything else."

He laughed quickly, wrinkling his nose sharply like a puppy and laughing with quick pleasure, his eyes shining.

"It's the first time I ever heard of that," he said.

"I guess you'd hear of it often enough if you stayed a winter on Bailey Farm," said Banford lamentably.

"Do you get so tired, then?" he asked.

"So bored," said Banford.

"Oh!" he said gravely. "But why should you be bored?"

"Who wouldn't be bored?" said Banford.

"I'm sorry to hear that," he said gravely.

"You must be, if you were hoping to have a lively time here," said Banford.

He looked at her long and gravely.

"Well," he said, with his odd, young seriousness, "it's quite lively enough for me."

"I'm glad to hear it," said Banford.

And she returned to her book. In her thin, frail hair were already many threads of grey, though she was not yet thirty. The boy did not look down, but turned his eyes to March, who was sitting with pursed mouth laboriously crocheting, her eyes wide and absent. She had a warm, pale, fine skin, and a delicate nose. Her pursed mouth looked shrewish. But the shrewish look was contradicted by the curious lifted arch of her dark brows, and the wideness of her eyes; a look of startled wonder and vagueness. She was listening again for the fox, who seemed to have wandered farther off into the night.

From under the edge of the lamp-light the boy sat with his face looking up, watching her silently, his eyes round and very clear and intent. Banford, biting her fingers irritably, was glancing at him under her hair. He sat there perfectly still, his ruddy face tilted up from the low level under the light, on the edge of the dimness, and watching with perfect abstract intentness. March suddenly lifted her great, dark eyes from her crocheting, and saw him. She started, giving a little exclamation.

"There he is!" she cried, involuntarily, as if terribly startled.

Banford looked around in amazement, sitting up straight.

"Whatever has got you, Nellie?" she cried.

But March, her face a flushed delicate rose colour, was looking away to the door.

"Nothing! Nothing!" she said crossly. "Can't one speak?"

"Yes, if you speak sensibly," said Banford. "Whatever did you mean?"

"I don't know what I meant," cried March testily.

"Oh, Nellie, I hope you aren't going jumpy and nervy. I feel I can't stand another *thing!* Whoever did you mean? Did you mean Henry?" cried poor, frightened Banford.

"Yes. I suppose so," said March laconically. She would never confess to the fox.

"Oh dear, my nerves are all gone for to-night," wailed Banford.

At nine o'clock March brought in a tray with bread and cheese and tea—Henry had confessed that he liked a cup of tea. Banford drank a glass of milk, and ate a little bread. And soon she said:

"I'm going to bed, Nellie. I'm all nerves to-night. Are you coming?"

"Yes, I'm coming the minute I've taken the tray away," said March.

"Don't be long then," said Banford fretfully. "Good night, Henry. You'll see the fire is safe, if you come up last, won't you?"

"Yes, Miss Banford, I'll see it's safe," he replied in his reassuring way.

March was lighting the candle to go to the kitchen. Banford took her candle and went upstairs. When March came back to the fire, she said to him:

"I suppose we can trust you to put out the fire and everything?" She stood there with her hand on her hip, and one knee loose, her head averted shyly, as if she could not look at him. He had his face lifted, watching her.

"Come and sit down a minute," he said softly.

"No, I'll be going. Jill will be waiting, and she'll get upset if I don't come."

"What made you jump like that this evening?" he asked.

"When did I jump?" she retorted, looking at him.

"Why, just now you did," he said. "When you cried out."

"Oh!" she said. "Then! Why, I thought you were the fox!" And her face screwed into a queer smile, half-ironic.

"The fox! Why the fox?" he asked softly.

"Why, one evening last summer when I was out with the gun I saw the fox in the grass nearly at my feet, looking straight up at me. I don't know—I suppose he made an impression on me." She turned aside her head again, and let one foot stray loose, self-consciously.

"And did you shoot him?" asked the boy.

"No, he gave me such a start, staring straight at me as he did, and then stopping to look back at me over his shoulder with a laugh on his face."

"A laugh on his face!" repeated Henry, also laughing. "He frightened you, did he?"

"No, he didn't frighten me. He made an impression on me, that's all."

"And you thought I was the fox, did you?" he laughed, with the same queer, quick little laugh, like a puppy wrinkling its nose.

"Yes, I did, for the moment," she said. "Perhaps he'd been in my mind without my knowing."

"Perhaps you think I've come to steal your chickens or something," he said, with the same young laugh.

But she only looked at him with a wide, dark, vacant eye.

"It's the first time," he said, "that I've ever been taken for a fox. Won't you sit down for a minute?" His voice was very soft and cajoling.

"No," she said. "Jill will be waiting." But still she did not go, but stood with one foot loose and her face turned aside, just outside the circle of light.

"But won't you answer my question?" he said, lowering his voice still more.

"I don't know what question you mean."

"Yes, you do. Of course you do. I mean the question of you marrying me."

"No, I shan't answer that question," she said flatly.

"Won't you?" The queer, young laugh came on his nose again. "Is it because I'm like the fox? Is that why?" And still he laughed.

She turned and looked at him with a long, slow look.

"I wouldn't let that put you against me," he said. "Let me turn the lamp low, and come and sit down a minute."

He put his red hand under the glow of the lamp, and suddenly made the light very dim. March stood there in the dimness quite shadowy, but unmoving. He rose silently to his feet, on his long legs. And now his voice was extraordinarily soft and suggestive, hardly audible.

"You'll stay a moment," he said. "Just a moment." And he put his hand on her shoulder. She turned her face from him. "I'm sure you don't really think I'm like the fox," he said, with the same softness and with a suggestion of laughter in his tone, a subtle mockery. "Do you now?" And he drew her gently towards him and kissed her neck, softly. She winced and trembled and hung away. But his strong, young arm held her, and he kissed her softly again, still on the neck, for her face was averted.

"Won't you answer my question? Won't you now?" came his soft, lingering voice. He was trying to draw her near to kiss her face. And he kissed her cheek softly, near the ear.

H

At that moment Banford's voice was heard calling fretfully, crossly from upstairs.

"There's Jill!" cried March, starting and drawing erect.

And as she did so, quick as lightning he kissed her on the mouth, with a quick brushing kiss. It seemed to burn through her every fibre. She gave a queer little cry.

"You will, won't you? You will?" he insisted softly.

"Nellie! *Nellie!* Whatever are you so long for?" came Banford's faint cry from the outer darkness.

But he held her fast, and was murmuring with that intolerable softness and insistency:

"You will, won't you? Say yes! Say yes!"

March, who felt as if the fire had gone through her and scathed her, and as if she could do no more, murmured:

"Yes! Yes! Anything you like! Anything you like! Only let me go! Only let me go! Jill's calling."

"You know you've promised," he said insidiously.

"Yes! Yes! I do!" Her voice suddenly rose into a shrill cry. "All right, Jill, I'm coming."

Startled, he let her go, and she went straight upstairs.

In the morning at breakfast, after he had looked round the place and attended to the stock and thought to himself that one could live easily enough here, he said to Banford:

"Do you know what, Miss Banford?"

"Well, what?" said the good-natured, nervy Banford.

He looked at March, who was spreading jam on her bread.

"Shall I tell?" he said to her.

She looked up at him, and a deep pink colour flushed over her face.

"Yes, if you mean Jill," she said. "I hope you won't go talking all over the village, that's all." And she swallowed her dry bread with difficulty.

"Whatever's coming?" said Banford, looking up with wide, tired, slightly reddened eyes. She was a thin, frail little thing, and her hair, which was delicate and thin, was bobbed, so it hung softly by her worn face in its faded brown and grey.

"Why, what do you think?" he said, smiling like one who has a secret.

"How do I know!" said Banford.

"Can't you guess?" he said, making bright eyes, and smiling, pleased with himself.

"I'm sure I can't. What's more, I'm not going to try."

"Nellie and I are going to be married."

Banford put down her knife out of her thin, delicate fingers, as if she would never take it up to eat any more. She stared with blank, reddened eyes.

"You what?" she exclaimed.

"We're going to get married. Aren't we, Nellie?" and he turned to March.

"You say so, anyway," said March laconically. But again she flushed with an agonized flush. She, too, could swallow no more.

Banford looked at her like a bird that has been shot: a poor, little sick bird. She gazed at her with all her wounded soul in her face, at the deep-flushed March.

"Never!" she exclaimed, helpless.

"It's quite right," said the bright and gloating youth.

Banford turned aside her face, as if the sight of the food on the table made her sick. She sat like this for some moments, as if she were sick. Then, with one hand on the edge of the table, she rose to her feet.

"I'll *never* believe it, Nellie," she cried. "It's absolutely impossible!"

Her plaintive, fretful voice had a thread of hot anger and despair.

"Why? Why shouldn't you believe it?" asked the youth, with all his soft, velvety impertinence in his voice.

Banford looked at him from her wide, vague eyes, as if he were some creature in a museum.

"Oh," she said languidly, "because she can never be such a fool. She can't lose her self-respect to such an extent." Her voice was cold and plaintive, drifting.

"In what way will she lose her self-respect?" asked the boy.

Banford looked at him with vague fixity from behind her spectacles.

"If she hasn't lost it already," she said.

He became very red, vermilion, under the slow, vague stare from behind the spectacles.

"I don't see it at all," he said.

"Probably you don't. I shouldn't expect you would," said Banford, with that straying mild tone of remoteness which made her words even more insulting.

He sat stiff in his chair, staring with hot, blue eyes from his scarlet face. An ugly look had come on his brow.

"My word, she doesn't know what she's letting herself in for," said Banford, in her plaintive, drifting, insulting voice.

"What has it got to do with you, anyway?" said the youth, in a temper.

"More than it has to do with you, probably," she replied, plaintive and venomous.

"Oh, has it! I don't see that at all," he jerked out.

"No, you wouldn't," she answered, drifting.

"Anyhow," said March, pushing back her chair and rising uncouthly. "It's no good arguing about it." And she seized the bread and the teapot, and strode away to the kitchen.

Banford let her fingers stray across her brow and along her hair, like one bemused. Then she turned and went away upstairs.

Henry sat stiff and sulky in his chair, with his face and his eyes on fire. March came and went, clearing the table. But Henry sat on, stiff with temper. He took no notice of her. She had regained her composure and her soft, even, creamy complexion. But her mouth was pursed up. She glanced at him each time as she came to take things from the table, glanced from her large, curious eyes, more in curiosity than anything. Such a long, red-faced, sulky boy! That was all he was. He seemed as remote from her as if his red face were a red chimney-pot on a cottage across the fields, and she looked at him just as objectively, as remotely.

At length he got up and stalked out into the fields with the gun.

He came in only at dinner-time, with the devil still in his face, but his manners quite polite. Nobody said anything particular; they sat each one at the sharp corner of a triangle, in obstinate remoteness. In the afternoon he went out again at once with the gun. He came in at nightfall with a rabbit and a pigeon. He stayed in all the evening, but hardly opened his mouth. He was in the devil of a temper, feeling he had been insulted.

Banford's eyes were red, she had evidently been crying. But her manner was more remote and supercilious than ever; the way she turned her head if he spoke at all, as if he were some tramp or inferior intruder of that sort, made his blue eyes go almost black with rage. His face looked sulkier. But he never forgot his polite intonation, if he opened his mouth to speak.

March seemed to flourish in this atmosphere. She seemed to sit between the two antagonists with a little wicked smile on her face, enjoying herself. There was even a sort of complacency in the way she laboriously crocheted this evening.

When he was in bed, the youth could hear the two women talking and arguing in their room. He sat up in bed and strained his ears to hear what they said. But he could hear nothing, it was too far off. Yet he could hear the soft, plaintive drip of Banford's voice, and March's deeper note.

The night was quiet, frosty. Big stars were snapping outside, beyond the ridge-tops of the pine-trees. He listened and listened. In the distance he heard a fox yelping: and the dogs from the farms barking in answer. But it was not that he wanted to hear. It was what the two women were saying.

He got stealthily out of bed, and stood by his door. He could hear no more than before. Very, very carefully he began to lift the door latch. After quite a time he had his door open. Then he stepped stealthily out into the passage. The old oak planks were cold under his feet, and they creaked preposterously. He crept very, very gently up the one step, and along by the wall, till he stood outside their door. And there he held his breath and listened. Banford's voice:

"No, I simply couldn't stand it. I should be dead in a month. Which is just what he would be aiming at, of course.

That would just be his game, to see me in the churchyard. No, Nellie, if you were to do such a thing as to marry him, you could never stop here. I couldn't, I couldn't live in the same house with him. Oh—h! I feel quite sick with the smell of his clothes. And his red face simply turns me over. I can't eat my food when he's at the table. What a fool I was ever to let him stop. One ought *never* to try to do a kind action. It always flies back in your face like a boomerang."

"Well, he's only got two more days," said March.

"Yes, thank heaven. And when he's gone he'll never come in this house again. I feel so bad while he's here. And I know, I know he's only counting what he can get out of you. I *know* that's all it is. He's just a good-for-nothing, who doesn't want to work, and who thinks he'll live on us. But he won't live on me. If you're such a fool, then it's your own look-out. Mrs. Burgess knew him all the time he was here. And the old man could never get him to do any steady work. He was off with the gun on every occasion, just as he is now. Nothing but the gun! Oh, I do hate it. You don't know what you're doing. Nellie, you don't. If you marry him he'll just make a fool of you. He'll go off and leave you stranded. I know he will, if he can't get Bailey Farm out of us—and he's not going to, while I live. While I live he's never going to set foot here. I know what it would be. He'd soon think he was master of both of us, as he thinks he's master of you already."

"But he isn't," said Nellie.

"He thinks he is, anyway. And that's what he wants: to come and be master here. Yes, imagine it! That's what we've got the place together for, is it, to be bossed and bullied by a hateful red-faced boy, a beastly labourer. Oh, we *did* make a mistake when we let him stop. We ought never to have lowered ourselves. And I've had such a fight with all the people here, not to be pulled down to their level. No, he's not coming here. And then you see—if he can't have the place, he'll run off to Canada or somewhere again, as if he'd never known you. And here you'll be, absolutely ruined and made a fool of. I know I shall never have any peace of mind again."

"We'll tell him he can't come here. We'll tell him that," said March.

"Oh, don't you bother; I'm going to tell him that, and other things as well, before he goes. He's not going to have all his own way while I've got the strength left to speak. Oh, Nellie, he'll despise you, he'll despise you, like the awful little beast he is, if you give way to him. I'd no more trust him than I'd trust a cat not to steal. He's deep, he's deep, and he's bossy, and he's selfish through and through, as cold as ice. All he wants is to make use of you. And when you're no more use to him, then I pity you."

"I don't think he's as bad as all that," said March.

"No, because he's been playing up to you. But you'll find out, if you see much more of him. Oh, Nellie, I can't bear to think of it."

"Well, it won't hurt you, Jill, darling."

"Won't it! Won't it! I shall never know a moment's peace again while I live, nor a moment's happiness. No, Nellie——" and Banford began to weep bitterly.

The boy outside could hear the stifled sound of the woman's sobbing, and could hear March's soft, deep, tender voice comforting, with wonderful gentleness and tenderness, the weeping woman.

His eyes were so round and wide that he seemed to see the whole night, and his ears were almost jumping off his head. He was frozen stiff. He crept back to bed, but felt as if the top of his head were coming off. He could not sleep. He could not keep still. He rose, quietly dressed himself, and crept out on to the landing once more. The women were silent. He went softly downstairs and out to the kitchen.

Then he put on his boots and his overcoat, and took the gun. He did not think to go away from the farm. No, he only took the gun. As softly as possible he unfastened the door and went out into the frosty December night. The air was still, the stars bright, the pine-trees seemed to bristle audibly in the sky. He went stealthily away down a fence-side, looking for something to shoot. At the same time he remembered that he ought not to shoot and frighten the women.

So he prowled round the edge of the gorse cover, and through the grove of tall old hollies, to the woodside. There he skirted the fence, peering through the darkness with dilated eyes that seemed to be able to grow black and full of sight in the dark, like a cat's. An owl was slowly and mournfully whooing round a great oak-tree. He stepped stealthily with his gun, listening, listening, watching.

As he stood under the oaks of the wood-edge he heard the dogs from the neighbouring cottage up the hill yelling suddenly and startlingly, and the wakened dogs from the farms around barking answer. And suddenly, it seemed to him England was little and tight, he felt the landscape was constricted even in the dark, and that there were too many dogs in the night, making a noise like a fence of sound, like the network of English hedges netting the view. He felt the fox didn't have a chance. For it must be the fox that had started all this hullabaloo.

Why not watch for him, anyhow! He would, no doubt, be coming sniffing round. The lad walked downhill to where the farmstead with its few pine-trees crouched blackly. In the angle of the long shed in the black dark, he crouched down. He knew the fox would be coming. It seemed to him it would be the last of the foxes in this loudly barking, thick-voiced England, tight with innumerable little houses.

He sat a long time with his eyes fixed unchanging upon the open gateway, where a little light seemed to fall from the stars or from the horizon, who knows. He was sitting on a log in a dark corner with the gun across his knees. The pine-trees snapped. Once a chicken fell off its perch in the barn with a loud crawk and cackle and commotion that startled him, and he stood up, watching with all his eyes, thinking it might be a rat. But he *felt* it was nothing. So he sat down again with the gun on his knees and his hands tucked in to keep them warm, and his eyes fixed unblinking on the pale reach of the open gateway. He felt he could smell the hot, sickly, rich smell of live chickens on the cold air.

And then—a shadow. A sliding shadow in the gateway. He gathered all his vision into a concentrated spark, and saw the shadow of the fox, the fox creeping on his belly through the gate. There he went, on his belly like a snake. The boy smiled to himself and brought the gun to his shoulder. He knew quite well what would happen. He knew the fox would go to where the fowl-door was boarded up, and sniff there. He knew he would lie there for a minute, sniffing the fowls within. And then he would start again prowling under the edge of the old barn, waiting to get in.

The fowl-door was at the top of a slight incline. Soft, soft as a shadow the fox slid up this incline, and crouched with his nose to the boards. And at the same moment there was the awful crash of a gun reverberating between the old buildings, as if all the night had gone smash. But the boy watched keenly. He saw even the white belly of the fox as the beast beat his paws in death. So he went forward.

There was a commotion everywhere. The fowls were scuffling and crawking, the ducks were quark-quarking, the pony had stamped wildly to his feet. But the fox was on his side, struggling in his last tremors. The boy bent over him and smelt his foxy smell.

There was a sound of a window opening upstairs, then March's voice calling:

"Who is it?"

"It's me," said Henry; "I've shot the fox."

"Oh, goodness! You nearly frightened us to death."

"Did I? I'm awfully sorry."

"Whatever made you get up?"

"I heard him about."

"And have you shot him?"

"Yes, he's here," and the boy stood in the yard holding up the warm, dead brute. "You can't see, can you? Wait a minute." And he took his flashlight from his pocket, and flashed it on to the dead animal. He was holding it by the brush. March saw, in the middle of the darkness, just the reddish fleece and the white belly and the white underneath of the pointed chin, and the queer, dangling paws. She did not know what to say.

"He's a beauty," he said. "He will make you a lovely fur."

"You don't catch me wearing a fox fur," she replied.

"Oh!" he said. And he switched off the light.

"Well, I should think you'll come in and go to bed again now," she said.

"Probably I shall. What time is it?"

"What time is it, Jill?" called March's voice. It was a quarter to one.

That night March had another dream. She dreamed that Banford was dead, and that she, March, was sobbing her heart out. Then she had to put Banford into her coffin. And the coffin was the rough wood-box in which the bits of chopped wood were kept in the kitchen, by the fire. This was the coffin, and there was no other, and March was in agony and dazed bewilderment, looking for something to line the box with, something to make it soft with, something to cover up the poor, dead darling. Because she couldn't lay her in there just in her white, thin nightdress, in the horrible wood-box. So she hunted and hunted, and picked up thing after thing, and threw it aside in the agony of dream-frustration. And in her dream-despair all she could find that would do was a fox-skin. She knew that it wasn't right, that this was not what she should have. But it was all she could find. And so she folded the brush of the fox, and laid her darling Jill's head on this, and she brought round the skin of the fox and laid it on the top of the body, so that it seemed to make a whole ruddy, fiery coverlet, and she cried and cried, and woke to find the tears streaming down her face.

The first thing that both she and Banford did in the morning was to go out to see the fox. Henry had hung it up by the heels in the shed, with its poor brush falling backwards. It was a lovely dog-fox in its prime, with a handsome, thick, winter coat: a lovely golden-red colour, with grey as it passed to the belly, and belly all white, and a great full brush with a delicate black and grey and pure white tip.

"Poor brute!" said Banford. "If it wasn't such a thieving wretch, you'd feel sorry for it."

March said nothing, but stood with her foot trailing aside, one hip out; her face was pale and her eyes big and black, watching the dead animal that was suspended upside down. White and soft as snow his belly: white and soft as snow. She passed her hand softly down it. And his wonderful black-glinted brush was full and frictional, wonderful. She passed her hand down this also, and quivered. Time after time, she took the full fur of that thick tail between her fingers, and passed her hand slowly downwards. Wonderful, sharp, thick, splendour of a tail. And he was dead! She pursed her lips, and her eyes went black and vacant. Then she took the head in her hand.

Henry was sauntering up, so Banford walked rather pointedly away. March stood there bemused, with the head of the fox in her hand. She was wondering, wondering, wondering over his long fine muzzle. For some reason it reminded her of a spoon or a spatula. She felt she could not understand it. The beast was a strange beast to her, incomprehensible, out of her range. Wonderful silver whiskers he had, like ice-threads. And pricked ears with hair inside. But that long, long, slender spoon of a nose!—and the marvellous white teeth beneath! It was to thrust forward and bite with, deep, deep into the living prey, to bite and bite the blood.

"He's a beauty, isn't he?" said Henry, standing by.

"Oh yes, he's a fine big fox. I wonder how many chickens he's responsible for," she replied.

"A good many. Do you think he's the same one you saw in the summer?"

"I should think very likely he is," she replied.

He watched her, but he could make nothing of her. Partly she was so shy and virgin, and partly she was so grim, matter-of-fact, shrewish. What she said seemed to him so different from the look of her big, queer, dark eyes.

"Are you going to skin him?" she asked.

"Yes, when I've had breakfast, and got a board to peg him on."

"My word, what a strong smell he's got! Pooo! It'll take some washing off one's hands. I don't know why I was so silly as to handle him." And she looked at her right hand, that had passed down his belly and along his tail, and had even got a tiny streak of blood from one dark place in his fur.

"Have you seen the chickens when they smell him, how frightened they are?" he said.

"Yes, aren't they!"

"You must mind you don't get some of his fleas."

"Oh, fleas!" she replied nonchalant.

Later in the day she saw the fox's skin nailed flat on a board, as if crucified. It gave her an uneasy feeling.

The boy was angry. He went about with his mouth shut, as if he had swallowed part of his chin. But in behaviour he was polite and affable. He did not say anything about his intention. And he left March alone.

That evening they sat in the dining-room. Banford wouldn't have him in her sitting-room any more. There was a very big log on the fire. And everybody was busy. Banford had letters to write. March was sewing a dress, and he was mending some little contrivance.

Banford stopped her letter-writing from time to time to look round and rest her eyes. The boy had his head down, his face hidden over his job.

"Let's see," said Banford. "What train do you go by, Henry?" He looked up straight at her.

"The morning train. In the morning," he said.

"What, the eight-ten or the eleven-twenty?"

"The eleven-twenty, I suppose," he said.

"That is the day after to-morrow?" said Banford.

"Yes, the day after to-morrow."

"Mm!" murmured Banford, and she returned to her writing. But as she was licking her envelope, she asked:

"And what plans have you made for the future, if I may ask?"

"Plans?" he said, his face very bright and angry.

"I mean about you and Nellie, if you are going on with this

business. When do you expect the wedding to come off?" She spoke in a jeering tone.

"Oh, the wedding!" he replied. "I don't know."

"Don't you know anything?" said Banford. "Are you going to clear out on Friday and leave things no more settled than they are?"

"Well, why shouldn't I? We can always write letters."

"Yes, of course you can. But I wanted to know because of this place. If Nellie is going to get married all of a sudden, I shall have to be looking round for a new partner."

"Couldn't she stay on here if she were married?" he said. He knew quite well what was coming.

"Oh," said Banford, "this is no place for a married couple. There's not enough work to keep a man going, for one thing. And there's no money to be made. It's quite useless your thinking of staying on here if you marry. Absolutely!"

"Yes, but I wasn't thinking of staying on here," he said.

"Well, that's what I want to know. And what about Nellie, then? How long is *she* going to be here with me, in that case."

The two antagonists looked at one another.

"That I can't say," he answered.

"Oh, go along," she cried petulantly. "You must have some idea what you are going to do, if you ask a woman to marry you. Unless it's all a hoax."

"Why should it be a hoax? I am going back to Canada."

"And taking her with you?"

"Yes, certainly."

"You hear that, Nellie?" said Banford.

March, who had had her head bent over her sewing, now looked up with a sharp, pink blush on her face, and a queer, sardonic laugh in her eyes and on her twisted mouth.

"That's the first time I've heard that I was going to Canada," she said.

"Well, you have to hear it for the first time, haven't you?" said the boy.

"Yes, I suppose I have," she said nonchalantly. And she went back to her sewing.

"You're quite ready, are you, to go to Canada? Are you, Nellie?" asked Banford.

March looked up again. She let her shoulders go slack, and let her hand that held the needle lie loose in her lap.

"It depends on *how* I'm going," she said. "I don't think I want to go jammed up in the steerage, as a soldier's wife. I'm afraid I'm not used to that way."

The boy watched her with bright eyes.

"Would you rather stay over here while I go first?" he asked.

"I would, if that's the only alternative," she replied.

"That's much the wisest. Don't make it any fixed engagement," said Banford. "Leave yourself free to go or not after he's got back and found you a place, Nellie. Anything else is madness, madness."

"Don't you think," said the youth, "we ought to get married before I go—and then go together, or separate, according to how it happens?"

"I think it's a terrible idea," cried Banford.

But the boy was watching March.

"What do you think?" he asked her.

She let her eyes stray vaguely into space.

"Well, I don't know," she said. "I shall have to think about it."

"Why?" he asked, pertinently.

"Why?" She repeated his question in a mocking way, and looked at him laughing, though her face was pink again. "I should think there's plenty of reasons why."

He watched her in silence. She seemed to have escaped him. She had got into league with Banford against him. There was again the queer sardonic look about her; she would mock stoically at everything he said or which life offered.

"Of course," he said, "I don't want to press you to do anything you don't wish to do."

"I should think not, indeed," cried Banford indignantly.

At bedtime Banford said plaintively to March:

"You take my hot bottle up for me, Nellie, will you."

"Yes, I'll do it," said March, with the kind of willing

unwillingness she so often showed towards her beloved but uncertain Jill.

The two women went upstairs. After a time March called from the top of the stairs: "Good night, Henry. I shan't be coming down. You'll see to the lamp and the fire, won't you?"

The next day Henry went about with the cloud on his brow and his young cub's face shut up tight. He was cogitating all the time. He had wanted March to marry him and go back to Canada with him. And he had been sure she would do it. Why he wanted her he didn't know. But he did want her. He had set his mind on her. And he was convulsed with a youth's fury at being thwarted. To be thwarted, to be thwarted! It made him so furious inside that he did not know what to do with himself. But he kept himself in hand. Because even now things might turn out differently. She might come over to him. Of course she might. It was her business to do so.

Things drew to a tension again towards evening. He and Banford had avoided each other all day. In fact, Banford went in to the little town by the 11.20 train. It was market day. She arrived back on the 4.25. Just as the night was falling Henry saw her little figure in a dark-blue coat and a dark blue tam-o'-shanter hat crossing the first meadow from the station. He stood under one of the wild pear-trees, with the old dead leaves round his feet. And he watched the little blue figure advancing persistently over the rough winter-ragged meadow. She had her arms full of parcels, and advanced slowly, frail thing she was, but with that devilish little certainty which he so detested in her. He stood invisible under the pear-tree, watching her every step. And if looks could have affected her, she would have felt a log of iron on each of her ankles as she made her way forward. "You're a nasty little thing, you are," he was saying softly, across the distance. "You're a nasty little thing. I hope you'll be paid back for all the harm you've done me for nothing. I hope you will—you nasty little thing. I hope you'll have to pay for it. You will, if wishes are anything. You nasty little creature that you are."

She was toiling slowly up the slope. But if she had been

slipping back at every step towards the Bottomless Pit, he
would not have gone to help her with her parcels. Aha, there
went March, striding with her long, land stride in her breeches
and her short tunic! Striding downhill at a great pace, and
even running a few steps now and then, in her great solicitude
and desire to come to the rescue of the little Banford. The boy
watched her with rage in his heart. See her leap a ditch, and
run, run as if a house was on fire, just to get to that creeping,
dark little object down there! So, the Banford just stood still
and waited. And March strode up and took *all* the parcels
except a bunch of yellow chrysanthemums. These the Banford
still carried—yellow chrysanthemums!

"Yes, you look well, don't you," he said softly into the dusk
air. "You look well, pottering up there with a bunch of
flowers, you do. I'd make you eat them for your tea, if you
hug them so tight. And I'd give them you for breakfast again,
I would. I'd give you flowers. Nothing but flowers."

He watched the progress of the two women. He could hear
their voices: March always outspoken and rather scolding in her
tenderness, Banford murmuring rather vaguely. They were
evidently good friends. He could not hear what they said till
they came to the fence of the home meadow, which they must
climb. Then he saw March manfully climbing over the bars
with all her packages in her arms, and on the still air he heard
Banford's fretful:

"Why don't you let me help you with the parcels?" She had
a queer, plaintive hitch in her voice. Then came March's
robust and reckless:

"Oh, I can manage. Don't you bother about me. You've all
you can do to get yourself over."

"Yes, that's all very well," said Banford fretfully. "You say,
Don't you bother about me, and then all the while you feel
injured because nobody thinks of you."

"When do I feel injured?" said March.

"Always. You always feel injured. Now you're feeling
injured because I won't have that boy to come and live on the
farm."

"I'm not feeling injured at all," said March.

"I know you are. When he's gone you'll sulk over it. I know you will."

"Shall I?" said March. "We'll see."

"Yes, we *shall* see, unfortunately. I can't think how you can make yourself so cheap. I can't *imagine* how you can lower yourself like it."

"I haven't lowered myself," said March.

"I don't know what you call it, then. Letting a boy like that come so cheeky and impudent and make a mug of you. I don't know what you think of yourself. How much respect do you think he's going to have for you afterwards? My word, I wouldn't be in your shoes, if you married him."

"Of course you wouldn't. My boots are a good bit too big for you, and not half dainty enough," said March, with rather a miss-fire sarcasm.

"I thought you had too much pride, really I did. A woman's got to hold herself high, especially with a youth like that. Why, he's impudent. Even the way he forced himself on us at the start."

"We asked him to stay," said March.

"Not till he'd almost forced us to. And then he's so cocky and self-assured. My word, he puts my back up. I simply can't imagine how you can let him treat you so cheaply."

"I don't let him treat me cheaply," said March. "Don't you worry yourself, nobody's going to treat me cheaply. And even you aren't, either." She had a tender defiance, and a certain fire in her voice.

"Yes, it's sure to come back to me," said Banford bitterly. "That's always the end of it. I believe you only do it to spite me."

They went now in silence up the steep, grassy slope and over the brow, through the gorse-bushes. On the other side of the hedge the boy followed in the dusk, at some little distance. Now and then, through the huge ancient hedge of hawthorn, risen into trees, he saw the two dark figures creeping up the hill. As he came to the top of the slope he saw the homestead dark in the twilight, with a huge old pear-tree leaning from the near gable, and a little yellow light twinkling in the small side windows of the kitchen. He heard the clink of the latch and saw the kitchen door open into light as the two women went indoors. So, they were at home.

And so!—this was what they thought of him. It was rather in his nature to be a listener, so he was not at all surprised whatever he heard. The things people said about him always missed him personally. He was only rather surprised at the women's way with one another. And he disliked the Banford with an acid dislike. And he felt drawn to the March again. He felt again irresistibly drawn to her. He felt there was a secret bond, a secret thread between him and her, something very exclusive, which shut out everybody else and made him and her possess each other in secret.

He hoped again that she would have him. He hoped with his blood suddenly firing up that she would agree to marry him quite quickly: at Christmas, very likely. Christmas was not far off. He wanted, whatever else happened, to snatch her into a hasty marriage and a consummation with him. Then for the future, they could arrange later. But he hoped it would happen as he wanted it. He hoped that to-night she would stay a little while with him, after Banford had gone upstairs. He hoped he could touch her soft, creamy cheek, her strange, frightened face. He hoped he could look into her dilated, frightened dark eyes, quite near. He hoped he might even put his hand on her bosom and feel her soft breasts under her tunic. His heart beat deep and powerful as he thought of that. He wanted very much to do so. He wanted to make sure of her soft woman's breasts under her tunic. She always kept the brown linen coat buttoned so close up to her throat. It seemed to him like some perilous secret, that her soft woman's breasts must be buttoned up in that uniform. It seemed to him, moreover, that they were so much softer, tenderer, more lovely and lovable, shut up in that tunic, than were the Banford's breasts, under her soft blouses and chiffon dresses. The Banford would have little iron breasts, he said to himself. For all her frailty and fretfulness and delicacy, she would have tiny iron breasts. But March, under her crude, fast, workman's tunic, would have soft, white breasts, white and unseen. So he told himself, and his blood burned.

When he went in to tea, he had a surprise. He appeared at the inner door, his face very ruddy and vivid and his blue eyes shining, dropping his head forward as he came in, in his usual way, and hesitating in the doorway, to watch the inside of the room, keenly and cautiously, before he entered. He was wearing a long-sleeved waistcoat. His face seemed extraordinarily like a piece of the out-of-doors come indoors: as holly-berries do. In his second of pause in the doorway he took in the two women sitting at table, at opposite ends, saw them sharply. And to his amazement March was dressed in a dress of dull, green silk crape. His mouth came open in surprise. If she had suddenly grown a moustache he could not have been more surprised.

"Why," he said, "do you wear a dress, then?"

She looked up, flushing a deep rose colour, and twisting her mouth with a smile, said:

"Of course I do. What else do you expect me to wear, but a dress?"

"A land-girl's uniform, of course," said he.

"Oh," she cried, nonchalant, "that's only for this dirty, mucky work about here."

"Isn't it your proper dress, then?" he said.

"No, not indoors it isn't," she said. But she was blushing all the time as she poured out his tea. He sat down in his chair at table, unable to take his eyes off her. Her dress was a perfectly simple slip of bluey-green crape, with a line of gold stitching round the top and round the sleeves, which came to the elbow. It was cut just plain and round at the top, and showed her white, soft throat. Her arms he knew, strong and firm-muscled, for he had often seen her with her sleeves rolled up. But he looked her up and down, up and down.

Banford, at the other end of the table, said not a word, but piggled with the sardine on her plate. He had forgotten her existence. He just simply stared at March, while he ate his bread and margarine in huge mouthfuls, forgetting even his tea.

"Well, I never knew anything make such a difference!" he murmured, across his mouthfuls.

"Oh goodness!" cried March, blushing still more. "I might be a pink monkey!"

And she rose quickly to her feet and took the teapot to the fire, to the kettle. And as she crouched on the hearth with her green slip about her, the boy stared more wide-eyed than ever. Through the crape her woman's form seemed soft and womanly. And when she stood up and walked he saw her legs move soft within her modernly short skirt. She had on black silk stockings, and small patent shoes with little gold buckles.

No, she was another being. She was something quite different. Seeing her always in the hard-cloth breeches, wide on the hips, buttoned on the knee, strong as armour, and in the brown puttees and thick boots, it had never occurred to him that she had a woman's legs and feet. Now it came upon him. She had a woman's soft, skirted legs, and she was accessible. He blushed to the roots of his hair, shoved his nose in his teacup and drank his tea with a little noise that made Banford simply squirm: and strangely, suddenly he felt a man, no longer a youth. He felt a man, with all a man's grave weight of responsibility. A curious quietness and gravity came over his soul. He felt a man, quiet, with a little of the heaviness of male destiny upon him.

She was soft and accessible in her dress. The thought went home in him like an everlasting responsibility.

"Oh, for goodness' sake, say something, somebody," cried Banford fretfully. "It might be a funeral." The boy looked at her, and she could not bear his face.

"A funeral!" said March, with a twisted smile. "Why, that breaks my dream."

Suddenly she had thought of Banford in the wood-box for a coffin.

"What, have you been dreaming of a wedding?" said Banford sarcastically.

"Must have been," said March.

"Whose wedding?" asked the boy.

"I can't remember," said March.

She was shy and rather awkward that evening in spite of the fact that, wearing a dress, her bearing was much more subdued than in her uniform. She felt unpeeled and rather exposed. She felt almost improper.

They talked desultorily about Henry's departure next morning, and made the trivial arrangement. But of the matter on their minds, none of them spoke. They were rather quiet and friendly this evening; Banford had practically nothing to say. But inside herself she seemed still, perhaps kindly.

At nine o'clock March brought in the tray with the ever-lasting tea and a little cold meat which Banford had managed to procure. It was the last supper, so Banford did not want to be disagreeable. She felt a bit sorry for the boy, and felt she must be as nice as she could.

He wanted her to go to bed. She was usually the first. But she sat on in her chair under the lamp, glancing at her book now and then, and staring into the fire. A deep silence had come into the room. It was broken by March asking, in a rather small tone:

"What time is it, Jill?"

"Five past ten," said Banford, looking at her wrist.

And then not a sound. The boy had looked up from the book he was holding between his knees. His rather wide, cat-shaped face had its obstinate look, his eyes were watchful.

"What about bed?" said March at last.

"I'm ready when you are," said Banford.

"Oh, very well," said March. "I'll fill your bottle."

She was as good as her word. When the hot-water bottle was ready, she lit a candle and went upstairs with it. Banford remained in her chair, listening acutely. March came downstairs again.

"There you are, then," she said. "Are you going up?"

"Yes, in a minute," said Banford. But the minute passed, and she sat on in her chair under the lamp.

Henry, whose eyes were shining like a cat's as he watched from under his brows, and whose face seemed wider, more chubbed and cat-like with unalterable obstinacy, now rose to his feet to try his throw.

"I think I'll go and look if I can see the she-fox," he said. "She may be creeping round. Won't you come as well for a minute, Nellie, and see if we see anything?"

"Me!" cried March, looking up with her startled wondering face.

"Yes. Come on," he said. It was wonderful how soft and warm and coaxing his voice could be, how near. The very sound of it made Banford's blood boil. "Come on for a minute," he said, looking down into her uplifted, unsure face.

And she rose to her feet as if drawn up by his young, ruddy face that was looking down on her.

"I should think you're never going out at this time of night, Nellie!" cried Banford.

"Yes, just for a minute," said the boy, looking round on her, and speaking with an odd, sharp yelp in his voice.

March looked from one to the other, as if confused, vague. Banford rose to her feet for battle.

"Why, it's ridiculous. It's bitter cold. You'll catch your death in that thin frock. And in those slippers. You're not going to do any such thing."

There was a moment's pause. Banford turtled up like a little fighting cock, facing March and the boy.

"Oh, I don't think you need worry yourself," he replied. "A moment under the stars won't do anybody any damage. I'll get the rug off the sofa in the dining-room. You're coming, Nellie."

His voice had so much anger and contempt and fury in it as he spoke to Banford: and as much tenderness and proud authority as he spoke to March, that the latter answered:

"Yes, I'm coming."

And she turned with him to the door.

Banford, standing there in the middle of the room, suddenly burst into a long wail and a spasm of sobs. She covered her face with her poor, thin hands, and her thin shoulders shook in an agony of weeping. March looked back from the door.

"Jill!" she cried in a frantic tone, like someone just coming awake. And she seemed to start towards her darling.

But the boy had March's arm in his grip, and she could not move. She did not know why she could not move. It was as in a dream when the heart strains and the body cannot stir.

"Never mind," said the boy softly. "Let her cry. Let her cry. She will have to cry sooner or later. And the tears will relieve her feelings. They will do her good."

So he drew March slowly through the doorway. But her last look was back to the poor little figure which stood in the middle of the room with covered face and thin shoulders shaken with bitter weeping.

In the dining-room he picked up the rug and said:

"Wrap yourself up in this."

She obeyed—and they reached the kitchen door, he holding her soft and firm by the arm, though she did not know it. When she saw the night outside she started back.

"I must go back to Jill," she said. "I *must!* Oh yes, I must."

Her tone sounded final. The boy let go of her and she turned indoors. But he seized her again and arrested her.

"Wait a minute," he said. "Wait a minute. Even if you go, you're not going yet."

"Leave go! Leave go!" she cried. "My place is at Jill's side. Poor little thing, she's sobbing her heart out."

"Yes," said the boy bitterly. "And your heart too, and mine as well."

"Your heart?" said March. He still gripped her and detained her.

"Isn't it as good as her heart?" he said. "Or do you think it's not?"

"Your heart?" she said again, incredulous.

"Yes, mine! Mine! Do you think I haven't *got* a heart?" And with his hot grasp he took her hand and pressed it under his left breast. "There's my heart," he said, "if you don't believe in it."

It was wonder which made her attend. And then she felt the deep, heavy, powerful stroke of his heart, terrible, like something from beyond. It was like something from beyond, something awful from outside, signalling to her. And the signal paralysed her. It beat upon her very soul, and made her helpless. She forgot Jill. She could not think of Jill any more. She could not think of her. That terrible signalling from outside!

The boy put his arm round her waist.

"Come with me," he said gently. "Come and let us say what we've got to say."

And he drew her outside, closed the door. And she went with him darkly down the garden path. That he should have a beating heart! And that he should have his arm round her, outside the blanket! She was too confused to think who he was or what he was.

He took her to a dark corner of the shed, where there was a tool-box with a lid, long and low.

"We'll sit here a minute," he said.

And obediently she sat down by his side.

"Give me your hand," he said.

She gave him both her hands, and he held them between his own. He was young, and it made him tremble.

"You'll marry me. You'll marry me before I go back, won't you?" he pleaded.

"Why, aren't we both a pair of fools?" she said.

He had put her in the corner, so that she should not look out and see the lighted window of the house, across the dark yard and garden. He tried to keep her all there inside the shed with him.

"In what way a pair of fools?" he said. "If you go back to Canada with me, I've got a job and a good wage waiting for me, and it's a nice place, near the mountains. Why shouldn't you marry me? Why shouldn't we marry? I should like to have you there with me. I should like to feel I'd got somebody there, at the back of me, all my life."

"You'd easily find somebody else who'd suit you better," she said.

"Yes, I might easily find another girl. I know I could. But not one I really wanted. I've never met one I really wanted, for good. You see, I'm thinking of all my life. If I marry, I want to feel it's for all my life. Other girls: well, they're just girls, nice enough to go a walk with now and then. Nice enough for a bit of play. But when I think of my life, then I should be very sorry to have to marry one of them, I should indeed."

"You mean they wouldn't make you a good wife."

"Yes, I mean that. But I don't mean they wouldn't do their duty by me. I mean—I don't know what I mean. Only when I think of my life, and of you, then the two things go together."

"And what if they didn't?" she said, with her odd, sardonic touch.

"Well, I think they would."

They sat for some time silent. He held her hands in his, but he did not make love to her. Since he had realized that she was a woman, and vulnerable, accessible, a certain heaviness had possessed his soul. He did not want to make love to her. He shrank from any such performance, almost with fear. She was a woman, and vulnerable, accessible to him finally, and he held back from that which was ahead, almost with dread. It was a kind of darkness he knew he would enter finally, but of which he did not want as yet even to think. She was the woman, and he was responsible for the strange vulnerability he had suddenly realized in her.

"No," she said at last, "I'm a fool. I know I'm a fool."

"What for?" he asked.

"To go on with this business."

"Do you mean me?" he asked.

"No, I mean myself. I'm making a fool of myself, and a big one."

"Why, because you don't want to marry me, really?"

"Oh, I don't know whether I'm against it, as a matter of fact. That's just it. I don't know."

He looked at her in the darkness, puzzled. He did not in the least know what she meant.

"And don't you know whether you like to sit here with me this minute, or not?" he asked.

"No, I don't really. I don't know whether I wish I was somewhere else, or whether I like being here. I don't know, really."

"Do you wish you were with Miss Banford? Do you wish you'd gone to bed with her?" he asked, as a challenge.

She waited a long time before she answered:

"No," she said at last. "I don't wish that."

"And do you think you would spend all your life with her—when your hair goes white, and you are old?" he said.

"No," she said, without much hesitation. "I don't see Jill and me two old women together."

"And don't you think, when I'm an old man and you're an old woman, we might be together still, as we are now?" he said.

"Well, not as we are now," she replied. "But I could imagine—no, I can't. I can't imagine you an old man. Besides, it's dreadful!"

"What, to be an old man?"

"Yes, of course."

"Not when the time comes," he said. "But it hasn't come. Only it will. And when it does, I should like to think you'd be there as well."

"Sort of old age pensions," she said drily.

Her kind of witless humour always startled him. He never knew what she meant. Probably she didn't quite know herself.

"No," he said, hurt.

"I don't know why you harp on old age," she said. "I'm not ninety."

"Did anybody ever say you were?" he asked, offended.

They were silent for some time, pulling different ways in the silence.

"I don't want you to make fun of me," he said.

"Don't you?" she replied, enigmatic.

"No, because just this minute I'm serious. And when I'm serious, I believe in not making fun of it."

"You mean nobody else must make fun of you," she replied.

"Yes, I mean that. And I mean I don't believe in making fun of it myself. When it comes over me so that I'm serious, then—there it is, I don't want it to be laughed at."

She was silent for some time. Then she said, in a vague, almost pained voice:

"No, I'm not laughing at you."

A hot wave rose in his heart.

"You believe me, do you?" he asked.

"Yes, I believe you," she replied, with a twang of her old tired nonchalance, as if she gave in because she was tired. But he didn't care. His heart was hot and clamorous.

"So you agree to marry me before I go?—perhaps at Christmas?"

"Yes, I agree."

"There!" he exclaimed. "That's settled it."

And he sat silent, unconscious, with all the blood burning in all his veins, like fire in all the branches and twigs of him. He only pressed her two hands to his chest, without knowing. When the curious passion began to die down, he seemed to come awake to the world.

"We'll go in, shall we?" he said: as if he realized it was cold.

She rose without answering.

"Kiss me before we go, now you've said it," he said.

And he kissed her gently on the mouth, with a young, frightened kiss. It made her feel so young, too, and frightened, and wondering: and tired, tired, as if she were going to sleep.

They went indoors. And in the sitting-room, there, crouched by the fire like a queer little witch, was Banford. She looked round with reddened eyes as they entered, but did not rise. He thought she looked frightening, unnatural, crouching there and looking round at them. Evil he thought her look was, and he crossed his fingers.

Banford saw the ruddy, elate face of the youth: he seemed strangely tall and bright and looming. And March had a delicate look on her face; she wanted to hide her face, to screen it, to let it not be seen.

"You've come at last," said Banford uglily.

"Yes, we've come," said he.

"You've been long enough for anything," she said.

"Yes, we have. We've settled it. We shall marry as soon as possible," he replied.

"Oh, you've settled it, have you! Well, I hope you won't live to repent it," said Banford.

"I hope so too," he replied.

"Are you going to bed *now*, Nellie?" said Banford.

"Yes, I'm going now."

"Then for goodness' sake come along."

March looked at the boy. He was glancing with his very bright eyes at her and at Banford. March looked at him wistfully. She wished she could stay with him. She wished she had married him already, and it was all over. For oh, she felt suddenly so safe with him. She felt so strangely safe and peaceful in his presence. If only she could sleep in his shelter, and not with Jill. She felt afraid of Jill. In her dim, tender state, it was agony to have to go with Jill and sleep with her. She wanted the boy to save her. She looked again at him.

And he, watching with bright eyes, divined something of what she felt. It puzzled and distressed him that she must go with Jill.

"I shan't forget what you've promised," he said, looking clear into her eyes, right into her eyes, so that he seemed to occupy all her self with his queer, bright look.

She smiled to him, faintly, gently. She felt safe again—safe with him.

But in spite of all the boy's precautions, he had a set-back. The morning he was leaving the farm he got March to accompany him to the market-town, about six miles away, where they went to the registrar and had their names stuck up as two people who were going to marry. He was to come at Christmas, and the wedding was to take place then. He hoped in the spring to be able to take March back to Canada with him, now the war was really over. Though he was so young, he had saved some money.

"You never have to be without *some* money at the back of you, if you can help it," he said.

So she saw him off in the train that was going West: his camp was on Salisbury Plain. And with big, dark eyes she watched him go, and it seemed as if everything real in life was retreating as the train retreated with his queer, chubby, ruddy face, that seemed so broad across the cheeks, and which never seemed to change its expression, save when a cloud of sulky anger hung on the brow, or the bright eyes fixed themselves in their stare. This was what happened now. He leaned there out of the carriage window as the train drew off, saying good-bye and staring back at her, but his face quite unchanged. There was no emotion on his face. Only his eyes tightened and became fixed and intent in their watching like a cat's when suddenly she sees something and stares. So the boy's eyes stared fixedly as the train drew away, and she was left feeling intensely forlorn. Failing his physical presence, she seemed to have nothing of him. And she had nothing of anything. Only his face was fixed in her mind: the full, ruddy, unchanging cheeks, and the straight snout of a nose, and the two eyes staring above. All she could remember was how he suddenly wrinkled his nose when he laughed, as a puppy does when he is playfully growling. But him, himself, and what he was—she knew nothing, she had nothing of him when he left her.

On the ninth day after he had left her he received this letter.

"DEAR HENRY,
I have been over it all again in my mind, this business of me and you, and it seems to me impossible. When you aren't there I see what a fool I am. When you are there you seem to blind me to things as they actually are. You make me see things all unreal, and I don't know what. Then when I am alone again with Jill I seem to come to my own senses and realize what a fool I am making of myself, and how I am treating you unfairly. Because it must be unfair to you for me to go on with this affair when I can't feel in my heart that I really love you. I know people talk a lot of stuff and nonsense about love, and I don't want to do that. I want to keep to plain facts and act in a sensible way. And that seems to me what I'm not

doing. I don't see on what grounds I am going to marry you. I know I am not head over heels in love with you, as I have fancied myself to be with fellows when I was a young fool of a girl. You are an absolute stranger to me, and it seems to me you will always be one. So on what grounds am I going to marry you? When I think of Jill, she is ten times more real to me. I know her and I'm awfully fond of her, and I hate myself for a beast if I ever hurt her little finger. We have a life together. And even if it can't last for ever, it is a life while it does last. And it might last as long as either of us lives. Who knows how long we've got to live? She is a delicate little thing, perhaps nobody but me knows how delicate. And as for me, I feel I might fall down the well any day. What I don't seem to see at all is you. When I think of what I've been and what I've done with you, I'm afraid I am a few screws loose. I should be sorry to think that softening of the brain is setting in so soon, but that is what it seems like. You are such an absolute stranger, and so different from what I'm used to, and we don't seem to have a thing in common. As for love, the very word seems impossible. I know what love means even in Jill's case, and I know that in this affair with you it's an absolute impossibility. And then going to Canada. I'm sure I must have been clean off my chump when I promised such a thing. It makes me feel fairly frightened of myself. I feel I might do something really silly, that I wasn't responsible for—and end my days in a lunatic asylum. You may think that's all I'm fit for after the way I've gone on, but it isn't a very nice thought for me. Thank goodness Jill is here, and her being here makes me feel sane again, else I don't know what I might do; I might have an accident with the gun one evening. I love Jill, and she makes me feel safe and sane, with her loving anger against me for being such a fool. Well, what I want to say is, won't you let us cry the whole thing off? I can't marry you, and really, I won't do such a thing if it seems to me wrong. It is all a great mistake. I've made a complete fool of myself, and all I can do is to apologize to you and ask you please to forget it, and please to take no further notice of me. Your fox skin is nearly ready, and seems all right. I will post it to you if you will let me know if this address is still right, and if you will accept my apology for the awful and lunatic way I have behaved with you, and then let the matter rest.

Jill sends her kindest regards. Her mother and father are staying with us over Christmas.

Yours very sincerely,
ELLEN MARCH."

The boy read this letter in camp as he was cleaning his kit. He set his teeth, and for a moment went almost pale, yellow round the eyes with fury. He said nothing and saw nothing and felt nothing but a livid rage that was quite unreasoning. Balked! Balked again! Balked! He wanted the woman, he had fixed like doom upon having her. He felt that was his doom, his destiny, and his reward, to have this woman. She was his heaven and hell on earth, and he would have none elsewhere. Sightless with rage and thwarted madness he got through the morning. Save that in his mind he was lurking and scheming towards an issue, he would have committed some insane act. Deep in himself he felt like roaring and howling and gnashing his teeth and breaking things. But he was too intelligent. He knew society was on top of him, and he must scheme. So with his teeth bitten together, and his nose curiously slightly lifted, like some creature that is vicious, and his eyes fixed and staring, he went through the morning's affairs drunk with anger and suppression. In his mind was one thing—Banford. He took no heed of all March's outpouring: none. One thorn rankled, stuck in his mind. Banford. In his mind, in his soul, in his whole being, one thorn rankling to insanity. And he would have to get it out. He would have to get the thorn of Banford out of his life, if he died for it.

With this one fixed idea in his mind, he went to ask for twenty-four hours' leave of absence. He knew it was not due to him. His consciousness was supernaturally keen. He knew where he must go—he must go to the captain. But how could he get at the captain? In that great camp of wooden huts and tents he had no idea where his captain was.

But he went to the officers' canteen. There was his captain standing talking with three other officers. Henry stood in the doorway at attention.

"May I speak to Captain Berryman?" The captain was Cornish like himself.

"What do you want?" called the captain.

"May I speak to you, Captain?"

"What do you want?" replied the captain, not stirring from among his group of fellow-officers.

Henry watched his superior for a minute without speaking.

"You won't refuse me, sir, will you?" he asked gravely.

"It depends what it is."

"Can I have twenty-four hours' leave?"

"No, you've no business to ask."

"I know I haven't. But I must ask you."

"You've had your answer."

"Don't send me away, Captain."

There was something strange about the boy as he stood there so everlasting in the doorway. The Cornish captain felt the strangeness at once, and eyed him shrewdly.

"Why, what's afoot?" he said, curious.

"I'm in trouble about something. I must go to Blewbury," said the boy.

"Blewbury, eh? After the girls?"

"Yes, it is a woman, Captain." And the boy, as he stood there with his head reaching forward a little, went suddenly terribly pale, or yellow, and his lips seemed to give off pain. The captain saw and paled a little also. He turned aside.

"Go on, then," he said. "But for God's sake don't cause any trouble of any sort."

"I won't, Captain, thank you."

He was gone. The captain, upset, took a gin and bitters. Henry managed to hire a bicycle. It was twelve o'clock when he left the camp. He had sixty miles of wet and muddy cross-roads to ride. But he was in the saddle and down the road without a thought of food.

At the farm, March was busy with a work she had had some time in hand. A bunch of Scotch fir-trees stood at the end of the open shed, on a little bank where ran the fence between two of the gorse-shaggy meadows. The furthest of these trees was dead—it had died in the summer, and stood with all its needles brown and sere in the air. It was not a very big tree. And it was absolutely dead. So March determined to have it, although they were not allowed to cut any of the timber. But it would make such splendid firing, in these days of scarce fuel.

She had been giving a few stealthy chops at the trunk for a week or more, every now and then hacking away for five minutes, low down, near the ground, so no one should notice. She had not tried the saw, it was such hard work, alone. Now the tree stood with a great yawning gap in his base, perched as it were on one sinew, and ready to fall. But he did not fall.

It was late in the damp December afternoon, with cold mists creeping out of the woods and up the hollows, and darkness waiting to sink in from above. There was a bit of yellowness where the sun was fading away beyond the low woods of the distance. March took her axe and went to the tree. The small thud-thud of her blows resounded rather ineffectual about the wintry homestead. Banford came out wearing her thick coat, but with no hat on her head, so that her thin, bobbed hair blew on the uneasy wind that sounded in the pines and in the wood.

"What I'm afraid of," said Banford, "is that it will fall on the shed and we sh'll have another job repairing that."

"Oh, I don't think so," said March, straightening herself, and wiping her arm over her hot brow. She was flushed red, her eyes were very wide-open and queer, her upper lip lifted away from her two white, front teeth with a curious, almost rabbit-look.

A little stout man in a black overcoat and a bowler hat came pottering across the yard. He had a pink face and a white beard and smallish pale-blue eyes. He was not very old, but nervy, and he walked with little short steps.

"What do you think, father?" said Banford. "Don't you think it might hit the shed in falling?"

"Shed, no!" said the old man. "Can't hit the shed. Might as well say the fence."

"The fence doesn't matter," said March in her high voice.

"Wrong as usual, am I?" said Banford, wiping her straying hair from her eyes.

The tree stood as it were on one spelch of itself, leaning, and creaking in the wind. It grew on the bank of a little dry ditch between the two meadows. On the top of the bank straggled one fence, running to the bushes uphill. Several trees clustered there in the corner of the field near the shed and near the gate which led into the yard. Towards this gate, horizontal across the weary meadows, came the grassy, rutted approach from the high road. There trailed another rickety fence, long split poles joining the short, thick, wide-apart uprights. The three people stood at the back of the tree, in the corner of the shed meadow, just above the yard gate. The house, with its two gables and its porch, stood tidy in a little grassed garden across the yard. A little, stout, rosy-faced woman in a little red woollen shoulder shawl had come and taken her stand in the porch.

"Isn't it down yet?" she cried, in a high little voice.

"Just thinking about it," called her husband. His tone towards the two girls was always rather mocking and satirical. March did not want to go on with her hitting while he was there. As for him, he wouldn't lift a stick from the ground if he could help it, complaining, like his daughter, of rheumatics in his shoulder. So the three stood there a moment silent in the cold afternoon, in the bottom corner near the yard.

They heard the far-off taps of a gate, and craned to look. Away across, on the green horizontal approach, a figure was just swinging on to a bicycle again, and lurching up and down over the grass, approaching.

"Why, it's one of our boys—it's Jack," said the old man.

"Can't be," said Banford.

March craned her head to look. She alone recognized the khaki figure. She flushed, but said nothing.

"No, it isn't Jack, I don't think," said the old man, staring with little round blue eyes under his white lashes.

In another moment the bicycle lurched into sight, and the rider dropped off at the gate. It was Henry, his face wet and red and spotted with mud. He was altogether a muddy sight.

"Oh!" cried Banford, as if afraid. "Why, it's Henry!"

"What!" muttered the old man. He had a thick, rapid, muttering way of speaking, and was slightly deaf. "What? What? Who is it? Who is it, do you say? That young fellow? That young fellow of Nellie's? Oh! Oh!" And the satiric smile came on his pink face and white eyelashes.

Henry, pushing the wet hair off his steaming brow, had caught sight of them and heard what the old man said. His hot, young face seemed to flame in the cold light.

"Oh, are you all there!" he said, giving his sudden, puppy's little laugh. He was so hot and dazed with cycling he hardly knew where he was. He leaned the bicycle against the fence and climbed over into the corner on to the bank, without going into the yard.

"Well, I must say, we weren't expecting *you*," said Banford laconically.

"No, I suppose not," said he, looking at March.

She stood aside, slack, with one knee drooped and the axe resting its head loosely on the ground. Her eyes were wide and vacant, and her upper lip lifted from her teeth in that helpless, fascinated rabbit-look. The moment she saw his glowing, red face it was all over with her. She was as helpless as if she had been bound. The moment she saw the way his head seemed to reach forward.

"Well, who is it? Who is it, anyway?" asked the smiling, satiric old man in his muttering voice.

"Why, Mr. Grenfel, whom you've heard us tell about, father," said Banford coldly.

"Heard you tell about, I should think so. Heard of nothing else practically," muttered the elderly man, with his queer little jeering smile on his face. "How do you do," he added, suddenly reaching out his hand to Henry.

The boy shook hands just as startled. Then the two men fell apart.

"Cycled over from Salisbury Plain, have you?" asked the old man.

"Yes."

"Hm! Longish ride. How long d'it take you, eh? Some time, eh? Several hours, I suppose."

"About four."

"Eh? Four! Yes, I should have thought so. When are you going back, then?"

"I've got till to-morrow evening."

"Till to-morrow evening, eh? Yes. Hm! Girls weren't expecting you, were they?"

And the old man turned his pale-blue, round little eyes under their white lashes mockingly towards the girls. Henry also looked round. He had become a little awkward. He looked at March, who was still staring away into the distance as if to see where the cattle were. Her hand was on the pommel of the axe, whose head rested loosely on the ground.

"What were you doing there?" he asked in his soft, courteous voice. "Cutting a tree down?"

March seemed not to hear, as if in a trance.

"Yes," said Banford. "We've been at it for over a week."

"Oh! And have you done it all by yourselves then?"

"Nellie's done it all, I've done nothing," said Banford.

"Really! You must have worked quite hard," he said, addressing himself in a curious gentle tone direct to March. She did not answer, but remained half averted, staring away towards the woods above as if in a trance.

"*Nellie!*" cried Banford sharply. "Can't you answer?"

"What—me?" cried March, starting round, and looking from one to the other. "Did anyone speak to me?"

"Dreaming!" muttered the old man, turning aside to smile. "Must be in love, eh, dreaming in the day-time!"

"Did you say anything to me?" said March, looking at the boy as from a strange distance, her eyes wide and doubtful, her face delicately flushed.

"I said you must have worked hard at the tree," he replied courteously.

"Oh that! Bit by bit. I thought it would have come down by now."

"I'm thankful it hasn't come down in the night, to frighten us to death," said Banford.

"Let me just finish it for you, shall I?" said the boy.

March slanted the axe-shaft in his direction.

"Would you like to?" she said.

"Yes, if you wish it," he said.

"Oh, I'm thankful when the thing's down, that's all," she replied, nonchalant.

"Which way is it going to fall?" said Banford. "Will it hit the shed?"

"No, it won't hit the shed," he said. "I should think it will fall there—quite clear. Though it might give a twist and catch the fence."

"Catch the fence!" cried the old man. "What, catch the fence! When it's leaning at the angle? Why, it's further off than the shed. It won't catch the fence."

"No," said Henry, "I don't suppose it will. It has plenty of room to fall quite clear, and I suppose it will fall clear."

"Won't tumble backwards on top of *us*, will it?" asked the old man, sarcastic.

"No, it won't do that," said Henry, taking off his short overcoat and his tunic. "Ducks! Ducks! Go back!"

A line of four brown-speckled ducks led by a brown-and-green drake were stemming away downhill from the upper meadow, coming like boats running on a ruffled sea, cockling their way top speed downwards towards the fence and towards the little group of people, and cackling as excitedly as if they brought news of the Spanish Armada.

"Silly things! Silly things!" cried Banford, going forward to turn them off. But they came eagerly towards her, opening their yellow-green beaks and quacking as if they were so excited to say something.

"There's no food. There's nothing here. You must wait a

bit," said Banford to them. "Go away. Go away. Go round to the yard."

They didn't go, so she climbed the fence to swerve them round under the gate and into the yard. So off they waggled in an excited string once more, wagging their rumps like the stems of little gondolas, ducking under the bar of the gate. Banford stood on the top of the bank, just over the fence, looking down on the other three.

Henry looked up at her, and met her queer, round-pupilled, weak eyes staring behind her spectacles. He was perfectly still. He looked away, up at the weak, leaning tree. And as he looked into the sky, like a huntsman who is watching a flying bird, he thought to himself: "If the tree falls in just such a way, and spins just so much as it falls, then the branch there will strike her exactly as she stands on top of that bank."

He looked at her again. She was wiping the hair from her brow again, with that perpetual gesture. In his heart he had decided her death. A terrible still force seemed in him, and a power that was just his. If he turned even a hair's breadth in the wrong direction, he would lose the power.

"Mind yourself, Miss Banford," he said. And his heart held perfectly still, in the terrible pure will that she should not move.

"Who, me, mind myself?" she cried, her father's jeering tone in her voice. "Why, do you think you might hit me with the axe?"

"No, it's just possible the tree might, though," he answered soberly. But the tone of his voice seemed to her to imply that he was only being falsely solicitous, and trying to make her move because it was his will to move her.

"Absolutely impossible," she said.

He heard her. But he held himself icy still, lest he should lose his power.

"No, it's just possible. You'd better come down this way."

"Oh, all right. Let us see some crack Canadian tree-felling," she retorted.

"Ready, then," he said, taking the axe, looking round to see he was clear.

There was a moment of pure, motionless suspense, when the world seemed to stand still. Then suddenly his form seemed to flash up enormously tall and fearful, he gave two swift, flashing blows, in immediate succession, the tree was severed, turning slowly, spinning strangely in the air and coming down like a sudden darkness on the earth. No one saw what was happening except himself. No one heard the strange little cry which the Banford gave as the dark end of the bough swooped down, down on her. No one saw her crouch a little and receive the blow on the back of the neck. No one saw her flung outwards and laid, a little twitching heap, at the foot of the fence. No one except the boy. And he watched with intense bright eyes, as he would watch a wild goose he had shot. Was it winged, or dead? Dead!

Immediately he gave a loud cry. Immediately March gave a wild shriek that went far, far down the afternoon. And the father started a strange bellowing sound.

The boy leapt the fence and ran to the figure. The back of the neck and head was a mass of blood, of horror. He turned it over. The body was quivering with little convulsions. But she was dead really. He knew it, that it was so. He knew it in his soul and his blood. The inner necessity of his life was fulfilling itself, it was he who was to live. The thorn was drawn out of his bowels. So he put her down gently. She was dead.

He stood up. March was standing there petrified and absolutely motionless. Her face was dead white, her eyes big black pools. The old man was scrambling horribly over the fence.

"I'm afraid it's killed her," said the boy.

The old man was making curious, blubbering noises as he huddled over the fence. "What!" cried March, starting electric.

"Yes, I'm afraid," repeated the boy.

March was coming forward. The boy was over the fence before she reached it.

"What do you say, killed her?" she asked in a sharp voice.

"I'm afraid so," he answered softly.

She went still whiter, fearful. The two stood facing one another. Her black eyes gazed on him with the last look of resistance. And then in a last agonized failure she began to grizzle, to cry in a shivery little fashion of a child that doesn't want to cry, but which is beaten from within, and gives that little first shudder of sobbing which is not yet weeping, dry and fearful.

He had won. She stood there absolutely helpless, shuddering her dry sobs and her mouth trembling rapidly. And then, as in a child, with a little crash came the tears and the blind agony of sightless weeping. She sank down on the grass, and sat there with her hands on her breast and her face lifted in sightless, convulsed weeping. He stood above her, looking down on her, mute, pale, and everlasting seeming. He never moved, but looked down on her. And among all the torture of the scene, the torture of his own heart and bowels, he was glad, he had won.

After a long time he stooped to her and took her hands.

"Don't cry," he said softly. "Don't cry."

She looked up at him with tears running from her eyes, a senseless look of helplessness and submission. So she gazed on him as if sightless, yet looking up to him. She would never leave him again. He had won her. And he knew it and was glad, because he wanted her for his life. His life must have her. And now he had won her. It was what his life must have.

But if he had won her, he had not yet got her. They were married at Christmas as he had planned, and he got again ten days' leave. They went to Cornwall, to his own village, on the sea. He realized that it was awful for her to be at the farm any more.

But though she belonged to him, though she lived in his shadow, as if she could not be away from him, she was not happy. She did not want to leave him: and yet she did not feel free with him. Everything around her seemed to watch her, seemed to press on her. He had won her, he had her with him, she was his wife. And she—she belonged to him, she knew it. But she was not glad. And he was still foiled. He realized that though he was married to her and possessed her in every possible way, apparently, and though she *wanted* him to possess her, she wanted it, she wanted nothing else, now, still he did not quite succeed.

Something was missing. Instead of her soul swaying with new life, it seemed to droop, to bleed, as if it were wounded. She would sit for a long time with her hand in his, looking away at the sea. And in her dark, vacant eyes was a sort of wound, and her face looked a little peaked. If he spoke to her, she would turn to him with a faint new smile, the strange, quivering little smile of a woman who has died in the old way of love, and can't quite rise to the new way. She still felt she ought to *do* something, to strain herself in some direction. And there was nothing to do, and no direction in which to strain herself. And she could not quite accept the submergence which his new love put upon her. If she was in love, she ought to *exert* herself, in some way, loving. She felt the weary need of our day to *exert* herself in love. But she knew that in fact she must no more exert herself in love. He would not have the love which exerted itself towards him. It made his brow go black. No, he wouldn't let her exert her love towards him. No, she had to be passive, to acquiesce, and to be submerged under the surface of love. She had to be like the seaweeds she saw as she peered down from the boat, swaying forever delicately under water, with all their delicate fibrils put tenderly out upon the flood, sensitive, utterly sensitive and receptive within the shadowy sea, and never, never rising and looking forth above water while they lived. Never. Never looking forth from the water until they died, only then washing, corpses, upon the surface. But while they lived, always submerged, always beneath the wave. Beneath the wave they might have powerful roots, stronger than iron; they might be tenacious and dangerous in their soft waving within the flood. Beneath the water they might be stronger, more indestructible than resistant oak trees are on land. But it was always under-water, always under-water. And she, being a woman, must be like that.

And she had been so used to the very opposite. She had had to take all the thought for love and for life, and all the responsibility. Day after day she had been responsible for the coming day, for the coming year; for her dear Jill's health and happiness and well-being. Verily, in her own small way, she had felt herself responsible for the well-being of the world. And this had been her great stimulant, this grand feeling that, in her own small sphere, she was responsible for the well-being of the world.

And she had failed. She knew that, even in her small way, she had failed. She had failed to satisfy her own feeling of responsibility. It was so difficult. It seemed so grand and easy at first. And the more you tried, the more difficult it became. It had seemed so easy to make one beloved creature happy. And the more you tried, the worse the failure. It was terrible. She had been all her life reaching, reaching, and what she reached for seemed so near, until she had stretched to her utmost limit. And then it was always beyond her.

Always beyond her, vaguely, unrealizably beyond her, and she was left with nothingness at last. The life she reached for, the happiness she reached for, the well-being she reached for all slipped back, became unreal, the further she stretched her hand. She wanted some goal, some finality—and there was none. Always this ghastly reaching, reaching, striving for something that might be just beyond. Even to make Jill happy. She was glad Jill was dead. For she had realized that she could never make her happy. Jill would always be fretting herself thinner and thinner, weaker and weaker. Her pains grew worse instead of less. It would be so for ever. She was glad she was dead.

And if Jill had married a man it would have been just the same. The woman striving, striving to make the man happy, striving within her own limits for the well-being of her world. And always achieving failure. Little, foolish successes in money or in ambition. But at the very point where she most wanted success, in the anguished effort to make some one beloved human being happy and perfect, there the failure was almost catastrophic. You wanted to make your beloved happy, and his happiness seemed always achievable. If only you did just this, that, and the other. And you did this, that, and the other, in all good faith, and every time the failure became a little more ghastly. You could love yourself to ribbons, and strive and strain yourself to the bone, and things would go from bad to worse, bad to worse, as far as happiness went. The awful mistake of happiness.

Poor March, in her goodwill and her responsibility, she had strained herself till it seemed to her that the whole of life and everything was only a horrible abyss of nothingness. The more you reached after the fatal flower of happiness, which trembles so blue and lovely in a crevice just beyond your grasp, the more fearfully you become aware of the ghastly and awful gulf of the precipice below you, into which you will inevitably plunge, as into the bottomless pit, if you reach any further. You pluck flower after flower—it is never *the* flower. The flower itself—its calyx is a horrible gulf, it is the bottomless pit.

That is the whole history of the search for happiness, whether it be your own or somebody else's that you want to win. It ends, and it always ends, in the ghastly sense of the bottomless nothingness into which you will inevitably fall if you strain any further.

And women? What goal can any woman conceive, except happiness? Just happiness, for herself and the whole world. That and nothing else. And so, she assumes the responsibility, and sets off towards her goal. She can see it there, at the foot of the rainbow. Or she can see it a little way beyond, in the blue distance. Not far, not far.

But the end of the rainbow is a bottomless gulf down which you can fall forever without arriving, and the blue distance is a void pit which can swallow you and all your efforts into its emptiness, and still be no emptier. You and all your efforts. So, the illusion of attainable happiness!

Poor March, she had set off so wonderfully towards the blue goal. And the further and further she had gone, the more fearful had become the realization of emptiness. An agony, an insanity at last.

She was glad it was over. She was glad to sit on the shore and look westwards over the sea, and know the great strain had ended. She would never strain for love and happiness any more. And Jill was safely dead. Poor Jill, poor Jill. It must be sweet to be dead.

For her own part, death was not her destiny. She would have to leave her destiny to the boy. But then, the boy. He wanted more than that. He wanted her to give herself without defences, to sink and become submerged in him. And she—she wanted to sit still, like a woman on the last mile-stone, and watch. She wanted to see, to know, to understand. She wanted to be alone: with him at her side.

And he! He did not want her to watch any more, to see any more, to understand any more. He wanted to veil her woman's spirit, as Orientals veil the woman's face. He wanted her to commit herself to him, and to put her independent spirit to sleep. He wanted to take away from her all her effort, all that seemed her very *raison d'être*. He wanted to make her submit, yield, blindly pass away out of all her strenuous consciousness. He wanted to take away her consciousness, and make her just his woman. Just his woman.

And she was so tired, so tired, like a child that wants to go to sleep, but which fights against sleep, as if sleep were death. She seemed to stretch her eyes wider in the obstinate effort and tension of keeping awake. She *would* keep awake. She *would* know. She *would* consider and judge and decide. She *would* have the reins of her own life between her own hands. She *would* be an independent woman, to the last. But she was so tired, so tired of everything. And sleep seemed near. And there was such rest in the boy.

Yet there, sitting in a niche of the high, wild cliffs of West Cornwall, looking over the westward sea, she stretched her eyes wider and wider. Away to the West, Canada, America. She *would* know and she *would* see what was ahead. And the boy, sitting beside her, staring down at the gulls, had a cloud between his brows and the strain of discontent in his eyes. He wanted her asleep, at peace in him. He wanted her at peace, asleep in him. And *there* she was, dying with the strain of her own wakefulness. Yet she would not sleep: no, never. Sometimes he thought bitterly that he ought to have left her. He ought never to have killed Banford. He should have left Banford and March to kill one another.

But that was only impatience: and he knew it. He was waiting, waiting to go west. He was aching almost in torment to leave England, to go west, to take March away. To leave this shore! He believed that as they crossed the seas, as they left this England which he so hated, because in some way it seemed to have stung him with poison, she would go to sleep. She would close her eyes at last, and give in to him.

And then he would have her, and he would have his own life at last. He chafed, feeling he hadn't got his own life. He would never have it till she yielded and slept in him. Then he would have all his own life as a young man and a male, and she would have all her own life as a woman and a female. There would be no more of this awful straining. She would not be a man any more, an independent woman with a man's responsibility. Nay, even the responsibility for her own soul she would have to commit to him. He knew it was so, and obstinately held out against her, waiting for the surrender.

"You'll feel better when once we get over the seas to Canada over there," he said to her as they sat among the rocks on the cliff.

She looked away to the sea's horizon, as if it were not real. Then she looked round at him, with the strained, strange look of a child that is struggling against sleep.

"Shall I?" she said.

"Yes," he answered quietly.

And her eyelids dropped with the slow motion, sleep weighing them unconscious. But she pulled them open again to say:

"Yes, I may. I can't tell. I can't tell what it will be like over there."

"If only we could go soon!" he said, with pain in his voice.

TWO BLUE BIRDS

THERE was a woman who loved her husband, but she could not live with him. The husband, on his side, was sincerely attached to his wife, yet he could not live with her. They were both under forty, both handsome and both attractive. They had the most sincere regard for one another, and felt, in some odd way, eternally married to one another. They knew one another more intimately than they knew anybody else, they felt more known to one another than to any other person.

Yet they could not live together. Usually, they kept a thousand miles apart, geographically. But when he sat in the greyness of England, at the back of his mind, with a certain grim fidelity, he was aware of his wife, her strange yearning to be loyal and faithful, having her gallant affairs away in the sun, in the south. And she, as she drank her cocktail on the terrace over the sea, and turned her grey, sardonic eyes on the heavy dark face of her admirer, whom she really liked quite a lot, she was actually preoccupied with the clear-cut features of her handsome young husband, thinking of how he would be asking his secretary to do something for him, asking in that good-natured, confident voice of a man who knows that his request will be only too gladly fulfilled.

The secretary, of course, adored him. She was *very* competent, quite young, and quite good-looking. She adored him. But then all his servants always did, particularly his women-servants. His men-servants were likely to swindle him.

When a man has an adoring secretary, and you are the man's wife, what are you to do? Not that there was anything "wrong"—if you know what I mean!—between them. Nothing you could call adultery, to come down to brass tacks. No, no! They were just the young master and his secretary. He dictated to her, she slaved for him and adored him, and the whole thing went on wheels.

He didn't "adore" her. A man doesn't need to adore his secretary. But he depended on her. "I simply rely on Miss Wrexall." Whereas he could never rely on his wife. The one thing he knew finally about *her* was that she didn't intend to be relied on.

So they remained friends, in the awful unspoken intimacy of the once-married. Usually each year they went away together for a holiday, and, if they had not been man and wife, they would have found a great deal of fun and stimulation in one another. The fact that they were married, had been married for the last dozen years, and couldn't live together for the last three or four, spoilt them for one another. Each had a private feeling of bitterness about the other.

However, they were awfully kind. He was the soul of generosity, and held her in real tender esteem, no matter how many gallant affairs she had. Her gallant affairs were part of her modern necessity. "After all, I've got to *live*. I can't turn into a pillar of salt in five minutes just because you and I can't live together! It takes years for a woman like me to turn into a pillar of salt. At least I hope so!"

"Quite!" he replied. "Quite! By all means put them in pickle, make pickled cucumbers of them, before you crystallize out. That's my advice."

He was like that: so awfully clever and enigmatic. She could more or less fathom the idea of the pickled cucumbers, but the "crystallizing out"—what did that signify?

And did he mean to suggest that he himself had been well pickled and that further immersion was for him unnecessary, would spoil his flavour? Was that what he meant? And herself, was she the brine and the vale of tears?

You never knew how catty a man was being, when he was really clever and enigmatic, withal a bit whimsical. He was adorably whimsical, with a twist of his flexible, vain mouth, that had a long upper lip, so fraught with vanity! But then a handsome, clear-cut, histrionic young man like that, how could he help being vain? The women made him so.

Ah, the women! How nice men would be if there were no other women!

And how nice the women would be if there were no other men! That's the best of a secretary. She may have a husband, but a husband is the mere shred of a man, compared to a boss, a chief, a man who dictates to you and whose words you faithfully write down and then transcribe. Imagine a wife writing down anything her husband said to her! But a secretary! Every *and* and *but* of his she preserves for ever. What are candied violets in comparison!

Now it is all very well having gallant affairs under the southern sun, when you know there is a husband whom you adore dictating to a secretary whom you are too scornful to hate yet whom you rather despise, though you allow she has her good points, away north in the place you ought to regard as home. A gallant affair isn't much good when you've got a bit of grit in your eye. Or something at the back of your mind.

What's to be done? The husband, of course, did not send his wife away.

"You've got your secretary and your work," she said. "There's no room for me."

"There's a bedroom and a sitting-room exclusively for you," he replied. "And a garden and half a motor-car. But please yourself entirely. Do what gives you most pleasure."

"In that case," she said. "I'll just go south for the winter."

"Yes, do!" he said. "You always enjoy it."

"I always do," she replied.

They parted with a certain relentlessness that had a touch of wistful sentiment behind it. Off she went to her gallant affairs, that were like the curate's egg, palatable in parts. And he settled down to work. He said he hated working, but he never did anything else. Ten or eleven hours a day. That's what it is to be your own master!

So the winter wore away, and it was spring, when the swallows homeward fly, or northward, in this case. This winter, one of a series similar, had been rather hard to get

through. The bit of grit in the gallant lady's eye had worked
deeper in the more she blinked. Dark faces might be dark,
and icy cocktails might lend a glow; she blinked her hardest
to blink that bit of grit away, without success. Under the
spicy balls of the mimosa she thought of that husband of hers
in his library, and of that neat, competent but *common* little
secretary of his, for ever taking down what he said!

"How a man can *stand* it! How *she* can stand it, common
little thing as she is, I don't know!" the wife cried to herself.

She meant this dictating business, this ten hours a day inter-
course, *à deux*, with nothing but a pencil between them, and
a flow of words.

What was to be done? Matters, instead of improving, had
grown worse. The little secretary had brought her mother
and sister into the establishment. The mother was a sort of
cook-housekeeper, the sister was a sort of upper maid—she did
the fine laundry, and looked after "his" clothes, and valeted
him beautifully. It was really an excellent arrangement. The
old mother was a splendid plain cook, the sister was all that
could be desired as a valet de chambre, a fine laundress, an
upper parlour-maid, and a table-waiter. And all economical
to a degree. They knew his affairs by heart. His secretary
flew to town when a creditor became dangerous, and she *always*
smoothed over the financial crisis.

"He," of course, had debts, and he was working to pay
them off. And if he had been a fairy prince who could call the
ants to help him, he would not have been more wonderful
than in securing this secretary and her family. They took
hardly any wages. And they seemed to perform the miracle
of loaves and fishes daily.

"She," of course, was the wife who loved her husband, but
helped him into debt, and she still was an expensive item.
Yet when she appeared at her "home," the secretarial family
received her with most elaborate attentions and deference.
The knight returning from the Crusades didn't create a greater
stir. She felt like Queen Elizabeth at Kenilworth, a sovereign
paying a visit to her faithful subjects. But perhaps there

lurked always this hair in her soup! Won't they be glad to be rid of me again!

But they protested No! No! They had been waiting and hoping and praying she would come. They had been pining for her to be there, in charge: the mistress, "his" wife. Ah, "his" wife!

"His" wife! His halo was like a bucket over her head.

The cook-mother was "of the people," so it was the upper-maid daughter who came for orders.

"What will you order for to-morrow's lunch and dinner, Mrs. Gee?"

"Well, what do you usually have?"

"Oh, we want *you* to say."

"No, what do you *usually* have?"

"We don't have anything fixed. Mother goes out and chooses the best she can find, that is nice and fresh. But she thought you would tell her now what to get."

"Oh, I don't know! I'm not very good at that sort of thing. Ask her to go on just the same; I'm quite sure she knows best."

"Perhaps you'd like to suggest a sweet?"

"No, I don't care for sweets—and you know Mr. Gee doesn't. So don't make one for me."

Could anything be more impossible! They had the house spotless and running like a dream; how could an incompetent and extravagant wife dare to interfere, when she saw their amazing and almost inspired economy! But they ran the place on simply nothing!

Simply marvellous people! And the way they strewed palm-branches under her feet!

But that only made her feel ridiculous.

"Don't you think the family manage very well?" he asked her tentatively.

"Awfully well! Almost romantically well!" she replied. "But I suppose you're perfectly happy?"

"I'm perfectly comfortable," he replied.

"I can see you are," she replied. "Amazingly so! I never knew such comfort! Are you sure it isn't bad for you?"

She eyed him stealthily. He looked very well, and extremely handsome, in his histrionic way. He was shockingly well-dressed and valeted. And he had that air of easy *aplomb* and good humour which is so becoming to a man, and which he only acquires when he is cock of his own little walk, made much of by his own hens.

"No!" he said, taking his pipe from his mouth and smiling whimsically round at her. "Do I look as if it were bad for me?"

"No, you don't," she replied promptly: thinking, naturally, as a woman is supposed to think nowadays, of his health and comfort, the foundation, apparently, of all happiness.

Then, of course, away she went on the backwash.

"Perhaps for your work, though, it's not so good as it is for *you*," she said in a rather small voice. She knew he couldn't bear it if she mocked at his work for one moment. And he knew that rather small voice of hers.

"In what way?" he said, bristles rising.

"Oh, I don't know," she answered indifferently. "Perhaps it's not good for a man's work if he is too comfortable."

"I don't know about *that!*" he said, taking a dramatic turn round the library and drawing at his pipe. "Considering I work, actually, by the clock, for twelve hours a day, and for ten hours when it's a short day, I don't think you can say I am deteriorating from easy comfort."

"No, I suppose not," she admitted.

Yet she did think it, nevertheless. His comfortableness didn't consist so much in good food and a soft bed, as in having nobody, absolutely nobody and nothing to contradict him. "I do like to think he's got nothing to aggravate him," the secretary had said to the wife.

"Nothing to aggravate him!" What a position for a man! Fostered by women who would let nothing "aggravate" him. If anything would aggravate his wounded vanity, this would!

So thought the wife. But what was to be done about it? In the silence of midnight she heard his voice in the distance, dictating away, like the voice of God to Samuel, alone and monotonous, and she imagined the little figure of the secretary busily scribbling shorthand. Then in the sunny hours of morning, while he was still in bed—he never rose till noon—from another distance came that sharp insect-noise of the typewriter, like some immense grasshopper chirping and rattling. It was the secretary, poor thing, typing out his notes.

That girl—she was only twenty-eight—really slaved herself to skin and bone. She was small and neat, but she was actually worn out. She did far more work than he did, for she had not only to take down all those words he uttered, she had to type them out, make three copies, while he was still resting.

"What on earth she gets out of it," thought the wife, "I don't know. She's simply worn to the bone, for a very poor salary, and he's never kissed her, and never will, if I know anything about him."

Whether his never kissing her—the secretary, that is—made it worse or better, the wife did not decide. He never kissed anybody. Whether she herself—the wife, that is—wanted to be kissed by him, even that she was not clear about. She rather thought she didn't.

What on earth did she want then? She was his wife. What on earth did she want of him?

She certainly didn't want to take him down in shorthand, and type out again all those words. And she didn't really want him to kiss her; she knew him too well. Yes, she knew him too well. If you know a man too well, you don't want him to kiss you.

What then? What did she want? Why had she such an extraordinary hang-over about him? Just because she was his wife? Why did she rather "enjoy" other men—and she was relentless about enjoyment—without ever taking them seriously? And why must she take him so damn seriously, when she never really "enjoyed" him?

Of course she *had* had good times with him, in the past, before—ah! before a thousand things, all amounting really to nothing. But she enjoyed him no more. She never even

enjoyed being with him. There was a silent, ceaseless tension
between them, that never broke, even when they were a
thousand miles apart.

Awful! That's what you call being married! What's to be
done about it? Ridiculous, to know it all and not do anything
about it!

She came back once more, and there she was, in her own
house, a sort of super-guest, even to him. And the secretarial
family devoting their lives to him.

Devoting their lives to him! But actually! Three women
pouring out their lives for him day and night! And what did
they get in return? Not one kiss! Very little money, because
they knew all about his debts, and had made it their life-
business to get them paid off! No expectations! Twelve hours'
work a day! Comparative isolation, for he saw nobody!

And beyond that? Nothing! Perhaps a sense of uplift and
importance because they saw his name and photograph in the
newspapers sometimes. But would anybody believe that it
was good enough?

Yet they adored it! They seemed to get a deep satisfaction
out of it, like people with a mission. Extraordinary!

Well, if they did, let them. They were, of course, rather
common, "of the people"; there might be a sort of glamour in
it for them.

But it was bad for him. No doubt about it. His work was
getting diffuse and poor in quality—and what wonder! His
whole tone was going down—becoming commoner. Of course
it was bad for him.

Being his wife, she felt she ought to do something to
save him. But how could she? That perfectly devoted,
marvellous secretarial family, how could she make an attack
on them? Yet she'd love to sweep them into oblivion. Of
course they were bad for him: ruining his work, ruining his
reputation as a writer, ruining his life. Ruining him with their
slavish service.

Of course she ought to make an onslaught on them! But how
could she? Such devotion! And what had she herself to offer in

their place? Certainly not slavish devotion to him, nor to his flow of words! Certainly not!

She imagined him stripped once more naked of secretary and secretarial family, and she shuddered. It was like throwing the naked baby in the dust-bin. Couldn't do that!

Yet something must be done. She felt it. She was almost tempted to get into debt for another thousand pounds, and send in the bill, or have it sent in to him, as usual.

But no! Something more drastic!

Something more drastic, or perhaps more gentle. She wavered between the two. And wavering, she first did nothing, came to no decision, dragged vacantly on from day to day, waiting for sufficient energy to take her departure once more.

It was spring! What a fool she had been to come up in spring! And she was forty! What an idiot of a woman to go and be forty!

She went down the garden in the warm afternoon, when birds were whistling loudly from the cover, the sky being low and warm, and she had nothing to do. The garden was full of flowers: he loved them for their theatrical display. Lilac and snowball bushes, and laburnum and red may, tulips and anemones and coloured daisies. Lots of flowers! Borders of forget-me-nots! Bachelor's buttons! What absurd names flowers had! She would have called them blue dots and yellow blobs and white frills. Not so much sentiment, after all!

There is a certain nonsense, something showy and stagey about spring, with its pushing leaves and chorus-girl flowers, unless you have something corresponding inside you. Which she hadn't.

Oh, heaven! Beyond the hedge she heard a voice, a steady rather theatrical voice. Oh, heaven! He was dictating to his secretary in the garden. Good God, was there nowhere to get away from it!

She looked around: there was indeed plenty of escape. But what was the good of escaping? He would go on and on. She went quietly towards the hedge, and listened.

He was dictating a magazine article about the modern novel.

"What the modern novel lacks is architecture." Good God!
Architecture! He might just as well say: What the modern
novel lacks is whalebone, or a teaspoon, or a tooth stopped.

Yet the secretary took it down, took it down, took it down!
No, this could not go on! It was more than flesh and blood
could bear.

She went quietly along the hedge, somewhat wolf-like in
her prowl, a broad, strong woman in an expensive mustard-
coloured silk jersey and cream-coloured pleated skirt. Her
legs were long and shapely, and her shoes were expensive.

With a curious wolf-like stealth she turned the hedge and
looked across at the small, shaded lawn where the daisies grew
impertinently. "He" was reclining in a coloured hammock
under the pink-flowering horse-chestnut tree, dressed in white
serge with a fine yellow-coloured linen shirt. His elegant hand
dropped over the side of the hammock and beat a sort of
vague rhythm to his words. At a little wicker table the little
secretary, in a green knitted frock, bent her dark head over
her note-book, and diligently made those awful shorthand
marks. He was not difficult to take down, as he dictated
slowly, and kept a sort of rhythm, beating time with his
dangling hand.

"In every novel there must be one outstanding character
with which we always sympathize—with *whom* we always
sympathize—even though we recognize its—even when we are
most aware of the human frailties——"

Every man his own hero, thought the wife grimly, forgetting
that every woman is intensely her own heroine.

But what did startle her was a blue bird dashing about near
the feet of the absorbed, shorthand-scribbling little secretary.
At least it was a blue-tit, blue with grey and some yellow.
But to the wife it seemed blue, that juicy spring day, in the
translucent afternoon. The blue bird, fluttering round the
pretty but rather *common* little feet of the little secretary.

The blue bird! The blue bird of happiness! Well, I'm blest,—
thought the wife. Well, I'm blest!

And as she was being blest, appeared another blue bird—that

is, another blue-tit—and began to wrestle with the first blue-tit. A couple of blue birds of happiness, having a fight over it! Well, I'm blest!

She was more or less out of sight of the human preoccupied pair. But "he" was disturbed by the fighting blue birds, whose little feathers began to float loose.

"Get out!" he said to them mildly, waving a dark-yellow handkerchief at them. "Fight your little fight, and settle your private affairs elsewhere, my dear little gentlemen."

The little secretary looked up quickly, for she had already begun to write it down. He smiled at her his twisted whimsical smile.

"No, don't take that down," he said affectionately. "Did you see those two tits laying into one another?"

"No!" said the little secretary, gazing brightly round, her eyes half-blinded with work.

But she saw the queer, powerful, elegant, wolf-like figure of the wife, behind her, and terror came into her eyes.

"I did!" said the wife, stepping forward with those curious, shapely, she-wolf legs of hers, under the very short skirt.

"Aren't they extraordinarily vicious little beasts?" said he.

"Extraordinarily!" she re-echoed, stooping and picking up a little breast-feather. "Extraordinarily! See how the feathers fly!"

And she got the feather on the tip of her finger, and looked at it. Then she looked at the secretary, then she looked at him. She had a queer, were-wolf expression between her brows.

"I think," he began, "these are the loveliest afternoons, when there's no direct sun, but all the sounds and the colours and the scents are sort of dissolved, don't you know, in the air, and the whole thing is steeped, steeped in spring. It's like being on the inside; you know how I mean, like being inside the egg and just ready to chip the shell."

"Quite like that!" she assented, without conviction.

There was a little pause. The secretary said nothing. They were waiting for the wife to depart again.

"I suppose," said the latter, "you're awfully busy, as usual?"

"Just about the same," he said, pursing his mouth deprecatingly.

Again the blank pause, in which he waited for her to go away again.

"I know I'm interrupting you," she said.

"As a matter of fact," he said, "I was just watching those two blue-tits."

"Pair of little demons!" said the wife, blowing away the yellow feather from her finger-tip.

"Absolutely!" he said.

"Well, I'd better go, and let you get on with your work," she said.

"No hurry!" he said, with benevolent nonchalance. "As a matter of fact, I don't think it's a great success, working out of doors."

"What made you try it?" said the wife. "You know you never could do it."

"Miss Wrexall suggested it might make a change. But I don't think it altogether helps, do you, Miss Wrexall?"

"I'm sorry," said the little secretary.

"Why should *you* be sorry?" said the wife, looking down at her as a wolf might look down half-benignly at a little black-and-tan mongrel. "You only suggested it for his good, I'm sure!"

"I thought the air might be good for him," the secretary admitted.

"Why do people like you never think about yourselves?" the wife asked.

The secretary looked her in the eye.

"I suppose we do, in a different way," she said.

"A *very* different way!" said the wife ironically. "Why don't you make *him* think about *you?*" she added, slowly, with a sort of drawl. "On a soft spring afternoon like this, you ought to have him dictating poems to you, about the blue birds of happiness fluttering round your dainty little feet. I know *I* would, if I were his secretary."

There was a dead pause. The wife stood immobile and statuesque, in an attitude characteristic of her, half turning back to the little secretary, half averted. She half turned her back on everything.

The secretary looked at him.

"As a matter of fact," he said, "I was doing an article on the Future of the Novel."

"I know that," said the wife. "That's what's so awful! Why not something lively in the life of the novelist?"

There was a prolonged silence, in which he looked pained, and somewhat remote, statuesque. The little secretary hung her head. The wife sauntered slowly away.

"Just where were we, Miss Wrexall?" came the sound of his voice.

The little secretary started. She was feeling profoundly indignant. Their beautiful relationship, his and hers, to be so insulted!

But soon she was veering downstream on the flow of his words, too busy to have any feelings, except one of elation at being so busy.

Tea-time came; the sister brought out the tea-tray into the garden. And immediately, the wife appeared. She had changed, and was wearing a chicory-blue dress of fine cloth. The little secretary had gathered up her papers and was departing, on rather high heels.

"Don't go, Miss Wrexall," said the wife.

The little secretary stopped short, then hesitated.

"Mother will be expecting me," she said.

"Tell her you're not coming. And ask your sister to bring another cup. I want you to have tea with us."

Miss Wrexall looked at the man, who was reared on one elbow in the hammock, and was looking enigmatical, Hamletish.

He glanced at her quickly, then pursed his mouth in a boyish negligence.

"Yes, stay and have tea with us for once," he said. "I see strawberries, and I know you're the bird for them."

She glanced at him, smiled wanly, and hurried away to tell her mother. She even stayed long enough to slip on a silk dress.

"Why, how smart you are!" said the wife, when the little secretary reappeared on the lawn, in chicory-blue silk.

"Oh, don't look at my dress, compared to yours!" said Miss Wrexall. They were of the same colour, indeed!

"At least you earned yours, which is more than I did mine," said the wife, as she poured tea. "You like it strong?"

She looked with her heavy eyes at the smallish, birdy, blue-clad, overworked young woman, and her eyes seemed to speak many inexplicable dark volumes.

"Oh, as it comes, thank you," said Miss Wrexall, leaning nervously forward.

"It's coming pretty black, if you want to ruin your digestion," said the wife.

"Oh, I'll have some water in it, then."

"Better, I should say."

"How'd the work go—all right?" asked the wife, as they drank tea, and the two women looked at each other's blue dresses.

"Oh!" he said. "As well as you can expect. It was a piece of pure flummery. But it's what they want. Awful rot, wasn't it, Miss Wrexall?"

Miss Wrexall moved uneasily on her chair.

"It interested me," she said, "though not so much as the novel."

"The novel? Which novel?" said the wife. "Is there another new one?"

Miss Wrexall looked at him. Not for words would she give away any of his literary activities.

"Oh, I was just sketching out an idea to Miss Wrexall," he said.

"Tell us about it!" said the wife. "Miss Wrexall, *you* tell us what it's about."

She turned on her chair, and fixed the little secretary.

"I'm afraid"—Miss Wrexall squirmed—"I haven't got it very clearly myself, yet."

"Oh, go along! Tell us what you *have* got then!"

Miss Wrexall sat dumb and very vexed. She felt she was being baited. She looked at the blue pleatings of her skirt.

"I'm afraid I can't," she said.

"Why are you afraid you can't? You're so *very* competent. I'm sure you've got it all at your finger-ends. I expect you write a good deal of Mr. Gee's books for him, really. He gives you the hint, and you fill it all in. Isn't that how you do it?" She spoke ironically, and as if she were teasing a child. And then she glanced down at the fine pleatings of her own blue skirt, very fine and expensive.

"Of course you're not speaking seriously?" said Miss Wrexall, rising on her mettle.

"Of course I am! I've suspected for a long time—at least, for some time—that you write a good deal of Mr. Gee's books for him, from his hints."

It was said in a tone of raillery, but it was cruel.

"I should be terribly flattered," said Miss Wrexall, straightening herself, "if I didn't know you were only trying to make me feel a fool."

"Make you feel a fool? My dear child!—why, nothing could be farther from me! You're twice as clever, and a million times as competent as I am. Why, my dear child, I've the greatest admiration for you! I wouldn't do what you do, not for all the pearls in India. I *couldn't*, anyhow——"

Miss Wrexall closed up and was silent.

"Do you mean to say my books read as if——" he began, rearing up and speaking in a harrowed voice.

"I do!" said the wife. "*Just* as if Miss Wrexall had written them from your hints. I *honestly* thought she did—when you were too busy——"

"How very clever of you!" he said.

"Very!" she cried. "Especially if I was wrong!"

"Which you were," he said.

"How very extraordinary!" she cried. "Well, I am once more mistaken!"

There was a complete pause.

It was broken by Miss Wrexall, who was nervously twisting her fingers.

"You want to spoil what there is between me and him, I can see that," she said bitterly.

"My dear, but what *is* there between you and him?" asked the wife.

"I was *happy* working with him, working for him! I was *happy* working for him!" cried Miss Wrexall, tears of indignant anger and chagrin in her eyes.

"My dear child!" cried the wife, with simulated excitement, "go *on* being happy working with him, go on being happy while you can! If it makes you happy, why then, enjoy it! Of course! Do you think I'd be so cruel as to want to take it away from you?—working with him? *I* can't do shorthand and typewriting and double-entrance book-keeping, or whatever it's called. I tell you, I'm utterly incompetent. I never earn anything. I'm the parasite on the British oak, like the mistletoe. The blue bird doesn't flutter round my feet. Perhaps they're too big and trampling."

She looked down at her expensive shoes.

"If I *did* have a word of criticism to offer," she said, turning to her husband, "it would be to you, Cameron, for taking so much from her and giving her nothing."

"But he gives me everything, everything!" cried Miss Wrexall. "He gives me everything!"

"What do you mean by 'everything'?" said the wife, turning on her sternly.

Miss Wrexall pulled up short. There was a snap in the air, and a change of currents.

"I mean nothing that *you* need begrudge me," said the little secretary rather haughtily. "I've never made myself cheap."

There was a blank pause.

"My God!" said the wife. "You don't call that being cheap? Why, I should say you got nothing out of him at all, you

only give! And if you don't call that making yourself cheap—
My God!"

"You see, we see things different," said the secretary.

"I should say we do!—*thank God!*" rejoined the wife.

"On whose behalf are you thanking God?" he asked
sarcastically.

"Everybody's, I suppose! Yours, because you get everything for nothing, and Miss Wrexall's, because she seems to
like it, and mine because I'm well out of it all."

"You *needn't* be out of it all," cried Miss Wrexall mag-
nanimously, "if you didn't *put* yourself out of it all."

"Thank you, my dear, for your offer," said the wife, rising.
"But I'm afraid no man can expect *two* blue birds of happiness
to flutter round his feet, tearing out their little feathers!"

With which she walked away.

After a tense and desperate interim, Miss Wrexall cried:

"And *really*, need any woman be jealous of *me?*"

"Quite!" he said.

And that was all he did say.

THE CAPTAIN'S DOLL

I

"HANNELE!"

"Ja—a."

"Wo bist du?"

"Hier."

"Wo denn?"

Hannele did not lift her head from her work. She sat in a low chair under a reading-lamp, a basket of coloured silk pieces beside her, and in her hands a doll, or mannikin, which she was dressing. She was doing something to the knee of the mannikin, so that the poor little gentleman flourished head downwards with arms wildly tossed out. And it was not at all seemly, because the doll was a Scotch soldier in tight-fitting tartan trews.

There was a tap at the door, and the same voice, a woman's, calling:

"Hannele?"

"Ja—a!"

"Are you here? Are you alone?" asked the voice, in German.

"Yes—come in."

Hannele did not sound very encouraging. She turned round her doll as the door opened, and straightened his coat. A dark-eyed young woman peeped in through the door, with a roguish coyness. She was dressed fashionably for the street, in a thick cape-wrap, and a little black hat pulled down to her ears.

"Quite, quite alone!" said the newcomer, in a tone of wonder. "Where is he, then?"

"That I don't know," said Hannele.

"And you sit here alone, and wait for him? But no! That I call courage! Aren't you afraid?" Mitchka strolled across to her friend.

"Why shall I be afraid?" said Hannele curtly.

"But no! And what are you doing? Another puppet? He is a good one, though! Ha—ha—ha! *Him!* It is him! No—no—that is too beautiful! No—that is too beautiful, Hannele. It is him—exactly him. Only the trousers."

"He wears those trousers too," said Hannele, standing her doll on her knee. It was a perfect portrait of an officer of a Scottish regiment, slender, delicately made, with a slight, elegant stoop of the shoulders, and close-fitting tartan trousers. The face was beautifully modelled, and a wonderful portrait, dark-skinned, with a little, close-cut, dark moustache, and wide-open dark eyes, and that air of aloofness and perfect diffidence which marks an officer and a gentleman.

Mitchka bent forward, studying the doll. She was a handsome woman with a warm, dark golden skin and clear black eyebrows over her russet-brown eyes.

"No," she whispered to herself, as if awestruck. "That is him. That is him. Only not the trousers. Beautiful, though, the trousers. Has he really such beautiful fine legs?"

Hannele did not answer.

"Exactly him. Just as finished as he is. Just as complete. He is just like that: finished off. Has he seen it?"

"No," said Hannele.

"What will he say, then?" She started. Her quick ear had caught a sound on the stone stairs. A look of fear came to her face. She flew to the door and out of the room, closing the door to behind her.

"Who is it?" her voice was heard calling anxiously down the stairs.

The answer came in German. Mitchka immediately opened the door again and came back to join Hannele.

"Only Martin," she said.

She stood waiting. A man appeared in the doorway—erect, military.

"Ah! Countess Hannele," he said in his quick, precise way, as he stood on the threshold in the distance. "May one come in?"

K

"Yes, come in," said Hannele.

The man entered with a quick, military step, bowed, and kissed the hand of the woman who was sewing the doll. Then, much more intimately, he touched Mitchka's hand with his lips.

Mitchka meanwhile was glancing round the room. It was a very large attic, with the ceiling sloping and then bending in two handsome movements towards the walls. The light from the dark-shaded reading-lamp fell softly on the huge white-washed vaulting of the ceiling, on the various objects round the walls, and made a brilliant pool of colour where Hannele sat in her soft, red dress, with her basket of silks.

She was a fair woman with dark-blond hair and a beautiful fine skin. Her face seemed luminous, a certain quick gleam of life about it as she looked up at the man. He was handsome, clean-shaven, with very blue eyes strained a little too wide. One could see the war in his face.

Mitchka was wandering round the room, looking at everything, and saying: "Beautiful! But beautiful! Such good taste! A man, and such good taste! No, they don't need a woman. No, look here, Martin, the Captain Hepburn has arranged all this room himself. Here you have the man. Do you see? So simple, yet so elegant. He needs no woman."

The room was really beautiful, spacious, pale, soft-lighted. It was heated by a large stove of dark-blue tiles, and had very little furniture save large peasant cupboards or presses of painted wood, and a huge writing table, on which were writing materials and some scientific apparatus and a cactus plant with fine scarlet blossoms. But it was a man's room. Tobacco and pipes were on a little tray, on the pegs in the distance hung military overcoats and belts, and two guns on a bracket. Then there were two telescopes, one mounted on a stand near a window. Various astronomical apparatus lay upon the table.

"And he reads the stars. Only think—he is an astronomer and reads the stars. Queer, queer people, the English!"

"He is Scottish," said Hannele.

"Yes, Scottish," said Mitchka. "But, you know, I am afraid

when I am with him. He is at a closed end. I don't know where I can get to with him. Are you afraid of him, too, Hannele? Ach, like a closed road!"

"Why should I be?"

"Ah, you! Perhaps you don't know when you should be afraid. But if he were to come and find us here? No, no—let us go. Let us go, Martin. Come, let us go. I don't want the Captain Hepburn to come and find me in his room. Oh no!" Mitchka was busily pushing Martin to the door, and he was laughing with the queer, mad laugh in his strained eyes. "Oh no! I don't like. I don't like it," said Mitchka, trying her English now. She spoke a few sentences prettily. "Oh no, Sir Captain, I don't want that you come. I don't like it, to be here when you come. Oh no. Not at all. I go. I go, Hannele. I go, my Hannele. And you will really stay here and wait for him? But when will he come? You don't know? Oh dear, I don't like it, I don't like it. I do not wait in the man's room. No, no—never—*jamais, jamais, voyez vous*. Ach, you poor Hannele! And he has got wife and children in England? Nevair! No, nevair shall I wait for him.

She had bustlingly pushed Martin through the door, and settled her wrap and taken a mincing, elegant pose, ready for the street, and waved her hand and made wide, scared eyes at Hannele, and was gone. The Countess Hannele picked up the doll again and began to sew its shoe. What living she now had she earned making these puppets.

But she was restless. She pressed her arms into her lap, as if holding them bent had wearied her. Then she looked at the little clock on his writing table. It was long after dinner-time—why hadn't he come? She sighed rather exasperated. She was tired of her doll.

Putting aside her basket of silks, she went to one of the windows. Outside the stars seemed white, and very near. Below was the dark agglomeration of the roofs of houses, a fume of light came up from beneath the darkness of roofs, and a faint breakage of noise from the town far below. The room seemed high, remote, in the sky.

She went to the table and looked at his letter-clip with
letters in it, and at his sealing-wax, and his stamp-box, touching things and moving them a little, just for the sake of the
contrast, not really noticing what she touched. Then she took
a pencil, and in stiff gothic characters began to write her
name—Johanna zu Rassentlow—time after time her own
name—and then once, bitterly, curiously, with a curious
sharpening of her nose: Alexander Hepburn.

But she threw the pencil down, having no more interest in
her writing. She wandered to where the large telescope stood
near a further window, and stood for some minutes with her
fingers on the barrel, where it was a little brighter from his
touching it. Then she drifted restlessly back to her chair. She
had picked up her puppet when she heard him on the stairs.
She lifted her face and watched as he entered.

"Hello, you there!" he said quietly, as he closed the door
behind him. She glanced at him swiftly, but did not move
nor answer.

He took off his overcoat, with quick, quiet movements, and
went to hang it up on the pegs. She heard his step, and looked
again. He was like the doll, a tall, slender, well-bred man in
uniform. When he turned, his dark eyes seemed very wide
open. His black hair was growing grey at the temples—the
first touch.

She was sewing her doll. Without saying anything, he
wheeled round the chair from the writing table, so that he sat
with his knees almost touching her. Then he crossed one leg
over the other. He wore fine tartan socks. His ankles seemed
slender and elegant, his brown shoes fitted as if they were part
of him. For some moments he watched her as she sat sewing.
The light fell on her soft, delicate hair, that was full of strands
of gold and of tarnished gold and shadow. She did not look up.

In silence he held out his small, naked-looking brown hand
for the doll. On his forearm were black hairs.

She glanced up at him. Curious how fresh and luminous her
face looked in contrast to his.

"Do you want to see it?" she asked, in natural English.

"Yes," he said.

She broke off her thread of cotton and handed him the puppet. He sat with one leg thrown over the other, holding the doll in one hand, and smiling inscrutably with his dark eyes. His hair, parted perfectly on one side, was jet black and glossy.

"You've got me," he said at last, in his amused, melodious voice.

"What?" she said.

"You've got me," he repeated.

"I don't care," she said.

"What—— You don't care?" His face broke into a smile. He had an odd way of answering, as if he were only half attending, as if he were thinking of something else.

"You are very late, aren't you?" she ventured.

"Yes. I am rather late."

"Why are you?"

"Well, as a matter of fact, I was talking with the Colonel."

"About me?"

"Yes. It was about you."

She went pale as she sat looking up into his face. But it was impossible to tell whether there was distress on his dark brow or not.

"Anything nasty?" she said.

"Well, yes. It was rather nasty. Not about you, I mean. But rather awkward for me."

She watched him. But still he said no more.

"What was it?" she said.

"Oh, well—only what I expected. They seem to know rather too much about you—about you and me, I mean. Not that anybody cares one bit, you know, unofficially. The trouble is, they are apparently going to have to take official notice."

"Why?"

"Oh, well—it appears my wife has been writing letters to the Major-General. He is one of her family acquaintances—known her all his life. And I suppose she's been hearing rumours. In fact, I know she has. She said so in her letter to me."

"And what do you say to her then?"

"Oh, I tell her I'm all right—not to worry."

"You don't expect *that* to stop her worrying, do you?" she asked.

"Oh, I don't know. Why should she worry?" he said.

"I think she might have some reason," said Hannele. "You've not seen her for a year. And if she adores you——"

"Oh, I don't think she adores me. I think she quite likes me."

"Do you think you matter as little as that to her?"

"I don't see why not. Of course she likes to feel *safe* about me."

"But now she doesn't feel safe?"

"No—exactly. Exactly. That's the point. That's where it is. The Colonel advises me to go home on leave."

He sat gazing with curious bright, dark, unseeing eyes at the doll which he held by one arm. It was an extraordinary likeness of himself, true even to the smooth parting of his hair and his peculiar way of fixing his dark eyes.

"For how long?" she asked.

"I don't know. For a month," he replied, first vaguely, then definitely.

"For a month!" She watched him, and seemed to see him fade from her eyes.

"And will you go?" she asked.

"I don't know. I don't know." His head remained bent, he seemed to muse rather vaguely. "I don't know," he repeated. "I can't make up my mind what I shall do."

"Would you like to go?" she asked.

He lifted his brows and looked at her. Her heart always melted in her when he looked straight at her with his black eyes, and that curious, bright unseeing look that was more like second sight than direct human vision. She never knew what he saw when he looked at her.

"No," he said simply. "I don't *want* to go. I don't think I've any desire at all to go to England."

"Why not?" she asked.

"I can't say." Then again he looked at her, and a curious

white light seemed to shine on his eyes, as he smiled slowly with his mouth, and said: "I suppose you ought to know, if anybody does."

A glad, half-frightened look came on her face.

"You mean you don't want to leave me?" she asked, breathless.

"Yes. I suppose that's what I mean."

"But you aren't sure?"

"Yes, I am, I'm quite sure," he said, and the curious smile lingered on his face, and the strange light shone in his eyes.

"That you don't want to leave me?" she stammered, looking aside.

"Yes, I'm quite sure I don't want to leave you," he repeated. He had a curious, very melodious Scottish voice. But it was the incomprehensible smile on his face that convinced and frightened her. It was almost a gargoyle smile, a strange, lurking, changeless-seeming grin.

She was frightened, and turned aside her face. When she looked at him again, his face was like a mask, with strange, deep-graven lines and a glossy dark skin and a fixed look— as if carved half grotesque in some glossy stone. His black hair on his smooth, beautifully-shaped head seemed changeless.

"Are you rather tired?" she asked him.

"Yes, I think I am." He looked at her with black, unseeing eyes, and a mask-like face. Then he glanced aside as if he heard something. Then he rose with his hand on his belt, saying: "I'll take off my belt, and change my coat, if you don't mind."

He walked across the room, unfastening his broad, brown belt. He was in well-fitting, well-cut khaki. He hung up his belt and came back to her wearing an old, light tunic, which he left unbuttoned. He carried his slippers in one hand. When he sat down to unfasten his shoes, she noticed again how black and hairy his forearm was, how naked his brown hand seemed. His hair was black and smooth and perfect on his head, like some close helmet, as he stooped down.

He put on his slippers, carried his shoes aside, and resumed his chair, stretching luxuriously.

"There," he said. "I feel better now." And he looked at her. "Well," he said, "and how are you?"

"Me?" she said. "Do I matter?" She was rather bitter.

"Do you matter?" he repeated, without noticing her bitterness. "Why, what a question! Of course you are of the very highest importance. What? Aren't you?" And smiling his curious smile—it made her for a moment think of the fixed sadness of monkeys, of those Chinese carved soapstone apes. He put his hand under her chin, and gently drew his finger along her cheek. She flushed deeply.

"But I'm not as important as you, am I?" she asked defiantly.

"As important as me! Why, bless you, I'm not important a bit. I'm not important a bit!"—the odd, straying sound of his words mystified her. What did he really mean?

"And I'm even less important than that," she said bitterly.

"Oh no, you're not. Oh no, you're not. You're very important. You're very important indeed, I assure you."

"And your wife?"—the question came rebelliously. "Your wife? Isn't she important?"

"My wife? My wife?" he seemed to let the word stray out of him as if he did not quite know what it meant. "Why, yes, I suppose she is important in her own sphere."

"What sphere?" blurted Hannele, with a laugh.

"Why, her own sphere, of course. Her own house, her own home, and her two children; that's her sphere."

"And you?—where do you come in?"

"At present I don't come in," he said.

"But isn't that just the trouble," said Hannele. "If you have a wife and a home, it's your business to belong to it, isn't it?"

"Yes, I suppose it is, if I want to," he replied.

"And you *do* want to?" she challenged.

"No, I don't," he replied.

"Well, then?" she said.

"Yes, quite," he answered. "I admit it's a dilemma."

"But what will you *do?*" she insisted.

"Why, I don't know. I don't know yet. I haven't made up my mind what I'm going to do."

"Then you'd better begin to make it up," she said.

"Yes, I know that. I know that."

He rose, and began to walk uneasily up and down the room. But the same vacant darkness was on his brow. He had his hands in his pockets. Hannele sat feeling helpless. She couldn't help being in love with the man: with his hands, with his strange, fascinating physique, with his incalculable presence. She loved the way he put his feet down, she loved the way he moved his legs as he walked, she loved the mould of his loins, she loved the way he dropped his head a little, and the strange, dark vacancy of his brow, his not-thinking. But now his restlessness only made her unhappy. Nothing would come of it. Yet she had driven him to it.

He took his hands out of his pockets and returned to her like a piece of iron returning to a magnet. He sat down again in front of her and put his hands out to her, looking into her face.

"Give me your hands," he said softly, with that strange, mindless, soft, suggestive tone which left her powerless to disobey. "Give me your hands, and let me feel that we are together. Words mean so little. They mean nothing. And all that one thinks and plans doesn't amount to anything. Let me feel that we are together, and I don't care about all the rest."

He spoke in his slow, melodious way, and closed her hands in his. She struggled still for voice.

"But you'll *have* to care about it. You'll *have* to make up your mind. You'll just *have* to," she insisted.

"Yes, I suppose I shall. I suppose I shall. But now that we are together, I won't bother. Now that we are together, let us forget it."

"But when we *can't* forget it any more?"

"Well—then I don't know. But—to-night—it seems to me —we might just as well forget it."

The soft, melodious, straying sound of his voice made her feel helpless. She felt that he never answered her. Words of reply seemed to stray out of him, in the need to say *something*. But he himself never spoke. There he was, a continual blank silence in front of her.

She had a battle with herself. When he put his hand again on her cheek, softly, with the most extraordinary soft half-touch, as a kitten's paw sometimes touches one, like a fluff of living air, then, if it had not been for the magic of that almost indiscernible caress of his hand, she would have stiffened herself and drawn away and told him she could have nothing to do with him, while he was so half-hearted and unsatisfactory. She wanted to tell him these things. But when she began he answered invariably in the same soft, straying voice, that seemed to spin gossamer threads all over her, so that she could neither think nor act nor even feel distinctly. Her soul groaned rebelliously in her. And yet, when he put his hand softly under her chin, and lifted her face and smiled down on her with that gargoyle smile of his—she let him kiss her.

"What are you thinking about to-night?" he said. "What are you thinking about?"

"What did your Colonel say to you, exactly?" she replied, trying to harden her eyes.

"Oh, that!" he answered. "Never mind that. That is of no significance whatever."

"But what *is* of any significance?" she insisted. She almost hated him.

"What is of any significance? Well, nothing to me, outside of this room, at this minute. Nothing in time or space matters to me."

"Yes, *this minute!*" she repeated bitterly. "But then there's the future. *I've* got to live in the future."

"The future! The future! The future is used up every day. The future to me is like a big tangle of black thread. Every morning you begin to untangle one loose end—and that's your day. And every evening you break off and throw away what you've untangled, and the heap is so much less: just one thread less, one day less. That's all the future matters to me."

"Then nothing matters to you. And I don't matter to you.

As you say, only an end of waste thread," she resisted him.

"No, there you're wrong. You aren't the future to me."

"What am I then?—the past?"

"No, not any of those things. You're nothing. As far as all that goes, you're nothing."

"Thank you," she said sarcastically. "if I'm nothing."

But the very irrelevancy of the man overcame her. He kissed her with half discernible, dim kisses, and touched her throat. And the meaningless of him fascinated her and left her powerless. She could ascribe no meaning to him, none whatever. And yet his mouth, so strange in kissing, and his hairy forearms, and his slender, beautiful breast with black hair—it was all like a mystery to her, as if one of the men from Mars were loving her. And she was heavy and spellbound, and she loved the spell that bound her. But also she didn't love it.

II

Countess zu Rassentlow had a studio in one of the main streets. She was really a refugee. And nowadays you can be a grand-duke and a pauper, if you are a refugee. But Hannele was not a pauper, because she and her friend Mitchka had the studio where they made these dolls, and beautiful cushions of embroidered coloured wools, and such-like objects of feminine art. The dolls were quite famous, so the two women did not starve.

Hannele did not work much in the studio. She preferred to be alone in her own room, which was another fine attic, not quite so large as the captain's, under the same roof. But often she went to the studio in the afternoon, and if purchasers came, then they were offered a cup of tea.

The Alexander doll was never intended for sale. What made Hannele take it to the studio one afternoon, we do not know. But she did so, and stood it on a little bureau. It was a wonderful little portrait of an officer and gentleman, the physique modelled so that it made you hold your breath.

"And *that*—that is genius!" cried Mitchka. "That is a *chef d'œuvre!* That is my masterpiece, Hannele. That is really marvellous. And beautiful! A beautiful man, what! But no, that is *too* real. I don't understand how you *dare*. I always thought you were *good*, Hannele, so much better-natured than I am. But now you frighten me. I am afraid you are wicked, do you know. It frightens me to think that you are wicked. *Aber nein!* But you won't leave him there?"

"Why not?" said Hannele, satiric.

Mitchka made big dark eyes of wonder, reproach, and fear.

"But you *must* not," she said.

"Why not?"

"No, that you *may* not do. You love the man."

"What then?"

"You can't leave his puppet standing there."

"Why can't I?"

"But you are really wicked. *Du bist wirklich bös.* Only think! —and he is an English officer."

"He isn't sacrosanct even then."

"They will expel you from the town. They will deport you."

"Let them, then."

"But no! What will you do? That would be horrible if we had to go to Berlin or to Munich and begin again. Here everything has happened so well."

"I don't care," said Hannele.

Mitchka looked at her friend and said no more. But she was angry. After some time she turned and uttered her ultimatum.

"When you are not there," she said, "I shall put the puppet away in a drawer. I shall show it to nobody, nobody. And I must tell you, it makes me afraid to see it there. It makes me afraid. And you have no right to get me into trouble, do you see. It is not I who look at the English officers. I don't like them, they are too cold and finished off for me. I shall never bring trouble on *myself* because of the English officers."

"Don't be afraid," said Hannele. "They won't trouble *you*. They know everything we do, well enough. They have their spies everywhere. Nothing will happen to you."

"But if they make you go away—and I am planted here with the studio——"

It was no good, however; Hannele was obstinate.

So, one sunny afternoon there was a ring at the door: a little lady in white, with a wrinkled face that still had its prettiness.

"Good afternoon!"—in rather lardy-dardy middle-class English. "I wonder if I may see your things in your studio."

"Oh yes!" said Mitchka. "Please to come in."

Entered the little lady in her finery and her crumpled prettiness. She would not be very old; perhaps younger than fifty. And it was odd that her face had gone so crumpled, because her figure was very trim, her eyes were bright, and she had pretty teeth when she laughed. She was very fine in her clothes: a dress of thick knitted white silk, a large ermine scarf with the tails only at the ends, and a black hat over which dripped a trail of green feathers of the osprey sort. She wore rather a lot of jewellery, and two bangles tinkled over her white kid gloves as she put up her fingers to touch her hair, whilst she stood complacently and looked round.

"You've got a *charming* studio—*charming*—perfectly delightful! I couldn't imagine anything more delightful."

Mitchka gave a slight ironic bow, and said, in her odd, plangent English:

"Oh yes. We like it very much also."

Hannele, who had dodged behind a screen, now came quickly forth.

"Oh, how do you do!" smiled the elderly lady. "I heard there were two of you. Now which is which, if I may be so bold? This"—and she gave a winsome smile and pointed a white kid finger at Mitchka—"is the——?"

"Annamaria von Prielau-Carolath," said Mitchka, slightly bowing.

"Oh!"—and the white kid finger jerked away. "Then this——"

"Johanna zu Rassentlow," said Hannele, smiling.

"Ah, yes! Countess von Rassentlow! And this is Baroness von—von—but I shall never remember even if you tell me, for I'm awful at names. Anyhow, I shall call one *Countess* and the other *Baroness*. That will do, won't it, for poor me! Now I should like awfully to see your things, if I may. I want to buy a little present to take back to England with me. I suppose I shan't have to pay the world in duty on things like these, shall I?"

"Oh no," said Mitchka. "No duty. Toys, you know, they—there is——" Her English stammered to an end, so she turned to Hannele.

"They don't charge duty on toys, and the embroideries they don't notice," said Hannele.

"Oh well. Then I'm all right," said the visitor. "I hope I can buy something really nice! I see a perfectly lovely jumper over there, perfectly delightful. But a little too gay for me, I'm afraid. I'm not quite so young as I was, alas." She smiled her winsome little smile, showing her pretty teeth, and the old pearls in her ears shook.

"I've heard so much about your dolls. I hear they're perfectly exquisite, quite works of art. May I see some, please."

"Oh yes," came Mitchka's invariable answer, this exclamation being the foundation stone of all her English.

There were never more than three or four dolls in stock. This time there were only two. The famous captain was hidden in his drawer.

"Perfectly beautiful! Perfectly wonderful!" murmured the little lady, in an artistic murmur. "I think they're perfectly delightful. It's wonderful of you, Countess, to make them. It is you who make them, is it not? Or do you both do them together?"

Hannele explained, and the inspection and the rhapsody went on together. But it was evident that the little lady was a cautious buyer. She went over the things very carefully, and thought more than twice. The dolls attracted her—but she thought them expensive, and hung fire.

"I do wish," she said wistfully, "there had been a larger selection of the dolls. I feel, you know, there might have been one which I *just loved*. Of course these are *darlings*—darlings they are: and worth every *penny*, considering the work there is in them. And the art, of course. But I have a feeling, don't you know how it is, that if there had been just one or two more, I should have found one which I *absolutely* couldn't live without. Don't you know how it is? One is so foolish, of course. What does Goethe say—'Dort wo du nicht bist . . .'? My German isn't even a beginning, so you must excuse it. But it means you always feel you would be happy somewhere else, and not just where you are. Isn't that it? Ah well, it's so very often true—so very often. But not always, thank goodness." She smiled an odd little smile to herself, pursed her lips, and resumed: "Well now, that's how I feel about the dolls. If only there had been one or two more. Isn't there a single one?"

She looked winsomely at Hannele.

"Yes," said Hannele, "there is one. But it is ordered. It isn't for sale."

"Oh, do you think I might see it? I'm sure it's lovely. Oh, I'm dying to see it. You know what woman's curiosity is, don't you?"—she laughed her tinkling little laugh. "Well, I'm afraid I'm all woman, unfortunately. One is so much harder if one has a touch of the man in one, don't you think, and more able to bear things. But I'm afraid I'm all woman." She sighed and became silent.

Hannele went quietly to the drawer and took out the captain. She handed him to the little woman. The latter looked frightened. Her eyes became round and childish, her face went yellowish. Her jewels tinkled nervously as she stammered:

"Now *that*—isn't that——" and she laughed a little, hysterical laugh.

She turned round, as if to escape.

"Do you mind if I sit down," she said. "I think the stand-ing——" and she subsided into a chair. She kept her face averted. But she held the puppet fast, her small, white fingers with their heavy jewelled rings clasped round his waist.

"You know," rushed in Mitchka, who was terrified. "You know, that is a life-picture of one of the Englishmen, of a gentleman, you know. A life-picture, you know."

"A portrait," said Hannele brightly.

"Yes," murmured the visitor vaguely. "I'm sure it is. I'm sure it is a very clever portrait indeed."

She fumbled with a chain, and put up a small gold lorgnette before her eyes, as if to screen herself. And from behind the screen of her lorgnette she peered at the image in her hand.

"But," she said, "none of the English officers, or rather Scottish, wear the close-fitting tartan trews any more—except for fancy dress."

Her voice was vague and distant.

"No, they don't now," said Hannele. "But that is the correct dress. I think they are so handsome, don't you?"

"Well. I don't know. It depends"—and the little woman laughed shakily.

"Oh yes," said Hannele. "It needs well-shapen legs."

"Such as the original of your doll must have had—quite," said the lady.

"Oh yes," said Hannele. "I think his legs are very handsome."

"Quite!" said the lady. "Judging from his portrait, as you call it. May I ask the name of the gentleman—if it is not too indiscreet?"

"Captain Hepburn," said Hannele.

"Yes, of course it is. I knew him at once. I've known him for many years."

"Oh, please," broke in Mitchka. "Oh, please, do not tell him you have seen it! Oh, please! Please not to tell any one!"

The visitor looked up with a grey little smile.

"But why not?" she said. "Anyhow, I can't tell him at once, because I hear he is away at present. You don't happen to know when he will be back?"

"I believe to-morrow," said Hannele.

"To-morrow!"

"And please," pleaded Mitchka, who looked lovely in her pleading distress, "please not to tell anybody that you have seen it."

"Must I promise?" smiled the little lady wanly. "Very well,

then, I won't tell him I've seen it. And now I think I must be going. Yes, I'll just take the cushion cover, thank you. Tell me again how much it is, please."

That evening Hannele was restless. He had been away on some duty for three days. He was returning that night—should have been back in time for dinner. But he had not arrived, and his room was locked and dark. Hannele had heard the servant light the stove some hours ago. Now the room was locked and blank as it had been for three days.

Hannele was most uneasy because she seemed to have forgotten him in the three days whilst he had been away. He seemed to have quite disappeared out of her. She could hardly even remember him. He had become so insignificant to her she was dazed.

Now she wanted to see him again, to know if it was really so. She felt that he was coming. She felt that he was already putting out some influence towards her. But what? And was he real? Why had she made his doll? Why had his doll been so important, if he was nothing? Why had she shown it to that funny little woman this afternoon? Why was she herself such a fool, getting herself into tangles in this place where it was so unpleasant to be entangled? Why was she entangled, after all? It was all so unreal. And particularly *he* was unreal: as unreal as a person in a dream, whom one has never heard of in actual life. In actual life, her own German friends were real. Martin was real; German men were real to her. But this other, he was simply not there. He didn't really exist. He was a nullus, in reality. A nullus—and she had somehow got herself complicated with him.

Was it possible? Was it possible she had been so closely entangled with an absolute nothing? Now he was absent she couldn't even *imagine* him. He had gone out of her imagination, and even when she looked at his doll she saw nothing but a barren puppet. And yet for this dead puppet, she had been compromising herself, now, when it was so risky for her to be compromised.

Her own German friends—her own German men—they were

men, they were real beings. But this English officer, he was neither fish, flesh, fowl, nor good red herring, as they say. He was just a hypothetical presence. She felt that if he never came back, she would be just as if she had read a rather peculiar but false story, a *tour de force* which works up one's imagination all falsely.

Nevertheless she was uneasy. She had a lurking suspicion that there might be something else. So she kept uneasily wandering out on to the landing, and listening, to hear if he might be coming.

Yes—there was a sound. Yes, there was his slow step on the stairs, and the slow, straying purr of his voice. And instantly she heard his voice she was afraid again. She knew there *was* something there. And instantly she felt the reality of his presence, she felt the unreality of her own German men-friends. The moment she heard the peculiar, slow melody of his foreign voice everything seemed to go changed in her, and Martin and Otto and Albrecht, her German friends, seemed to go pale and dim as if one could almost see through them, like unsubstantial things.

This was what she had to reckon with, this recoil from one to the other. When he was present, he seemed so terribly real. When he was absent he was completely vague, and her own men of her own race seemed so absolutely the only reality.

But he was talking. Who was he talking to? She heard the steps echo up the hollows of the stone staircase, slowly, as if wearily, and voices slowly, confusedly mingle. The slow, soft trail of his voice—and then the peculiar, quick tones—yes, of a woman. And not one of the maids, because they were speaking English. She listened hard. The quick, and yet slightly hushed, slightly sad-sounding voice of a woman who talks a good deal, as if talking to herself. Hannele's quick ears caught the sound of what she was saying: "Yes, I thought the Baroness a perfectly beautiful creature, perfectly lovely. But so extraordinarily like a Spaniard. Do you remember, Alec, at Malaga? I always thought they fascinated you then, with their mantillas. Perfectly lovely she would look in a mantilla. Only perhaps she is too open-hearted, too impulsive, poor thing. She lacks the Spanish reserve. Poor thing, I feel sorry for her. For them both, indeed. It must be very hard to have to do these things for a living, after you've been accustomed to be made much of for your own sake, and for your aristocratic title. It's very hard for them, poor things. Baroness, Countess, it sounds just a little ridiculous, when you're buying woollen embroideries from them. But I suppose, poor things, they can't help it. Better drop the titles altogether, I think——"

"Well, they do, if people will let them. Only English and American people find it so much easier to say Baroness or Countess than Fräulein von Prielau-Carolath, or whatever it is."

"They could say simply Fräulein, as we do to our governesses —or as we used to, when we *had* German governesses," came the voice of *her*.

"Yes, we *could*," said his voice.

"After all, what is the good, what is the good of titles if you have to sell dolls and woollen embroideries—not so very beautiful, either."

"Oh, quite! Oh, quite! I think titles are perhaps a mistake, anyhow. But they've always had them," came his slow, musical voice, with its sing-song note of hopeless indifference. He sounded rather like a man talking out of his sleep.

Hannele caught sight of the tail of blue-green crane feathers veering round a turn in the stairs away below, and she beat a hasty retreat.

III

There was a little platform out on the roof, where he used sometimes to stand his telescope and observe the stars or the moon: the moon when possible. It was not a very safe platform, just a little ledge of the roof, outside the window at the end of the top corridor: or rather, the top landing, for it was

only the space between the attics. Hannele had the one attic
room at the back, he had the room we have seen, and a littl
bedroom which was really only a lumber-room. Before h
came, Hannele had been alone under the roof. His room
were then lumber-room and laundry-room, where the clothe
were dried. But he had wanted to be high up, because of hi
stars, and this was the place that pleased him.

Hannele heard him quite late in the night, wandering about
She heard him also on the ledge outside. She could not sleep
He disturbed her. The moon was risen, large and bright in the
sky. She heard the bells from the cathedral slowly strike two
two great drops of sound in the livid night. And again, from
outside on the roof, she heard him clear his throat. Then a
cat howled.

She rose, wrapped herself in a dark wrap, and went down the
landing to the window at the end. The sky outside was full o
moonlight. He was squatted like a great cat peering up hi
telescope, sitting on a stool, his knees wide apart. Quite
motionless he sat in that attitude, like some leaden figure or
the roof. The moonlight glistened with a gleam of plumbago
on the great slope of black tiles. She stood still in the window
watching . And he remained fixed and motionless at the end
of the telescope.

She tapped softly on the window-pane. He looked round
like some tom-cat staring round with wide night-eyes. Then
he reached down his hand and pulled the window open.

"Hello," he said quietly. "You not asleep?"

"Aren't *you* tired?" she replied, rather resentful.

"No, I was as wide awake as I could be. *Isn't* the moon
fine to-night! What? Perfectly amazing. Wouldn't you like
to come up and have a look at her?"

"No, thank you," she said hastily, terrified at the thought
He resumed his posture, peering up the telescope.

"Perfectly amazing," he said, murmuring. She waited for
some time, bewitched likewise by the great October moon
and the sky full of resplendent white-green light. It seemed
like another sort of day-time. And there he straddled on the

oof like some cat! It was exactly like day in some other
planet.

At length he turned round to her. His face glistened faintly,
and his eyes were dilated like a cat's at night.

"You know I had a visitor?" he said.

"Yes."

"My wife."

"Your *wife!*"—she looked up really astonished. She had
thought it might be an acquaintance—perhaps his aunt—or
even an elder sister. "But she's years older than you," she
added.

"Eight years," he said. "I'm forty-one."

There was a silence.

"Yes," he mused. "She arrived suddenly, by surprise,
yesterday, and found me away. She's staying in the hotel in
he Vier Jahreszeiten."

There was a pause.

"Aren't you going to stay with her?" asked Hannele.

"Yes, I shall probably join her to-morrow."

There was a still longer pause.

"Why not to-night?" asked Hannele.

"Oh, well—I put it off for to-night. It meant all the bother
of my wife changing her room at the hotel—and it was late—
and I was all mucky after travelling."

"But you'll go to-morrow?"

"Yes, I shall go to-morrow. For a week or so. After that
I'm not sure what will happen."

There was quite a long pause. He remained seated on his
stool on the roof, looking with dilated, blank, black eyes at
nothingness. She stood below in the open window-space,
pondering.

"Do you want to go to her at the hotel?" asked
Hannele.

"Well, I don't, particularly. But I don't mind, really.
We're very good friends. Why, we've been friends for eighteen
years—we've been married seventeen. Oh, she's a nice little
woman. I don't want to hurt her feelings. I wish her no harm,

you know. On the contrary, I wish her all the good in the world."

He had no idea of the blank amazement in which Hannele listened to these stray remarks.

"But——" she stammered. "But doesn't she expect you to make *love* to her?"

"Oh, yes, she expects that. You bet she does: woman-like."

"And you?"—the question had a dangerous ring.

"Why, I don't mind, really, you know, if it's only for a short time. I'm used to her. I've always been fond of her, you know—and so if it gives her any pleasure—why, I like her to get what pleasure out of life she can."

"But *you*—you *yourself!* Don't *you* feel anything?" Hannele's amazement was reaching the point of incredulity. She began to feel that he was making it up. It was all so different from her own point of view. To sit there so quiet and to make such statements in all good faith: no, it was impossible.

"I don't consider I count," he said naïvely.

Hannele looked aside. If that wasn't lying, it was imbecility, or worse. She had for the moment nothing to say. She felt he was a sort of psychic phenomenon like a grasshopper or a tadpole or an ammonite. Not to be regarded from a human point of view. No, he just wasn't normal. And she had been fascinated by him! It was only sheer, amazed curiosity that carried her on to her next question.

"But do you *never* count, then?" she asked, and there was a touch of derision, of laughter in her tone. He took no offence.

"Well—very rarely," he said. "I count very rarely. That's how life appears to me. One matters so *very* little."

She felt quite dizzy with astonishment. And he called himself a man!

"But if you matter so very little, what do you do anything at all for?" she asked.

"Oh, one has to. And then, why not? Why not do things even if oneself hardly matters. Look at the moon. It doesn't matter in the least to the moon whether

I exist or whether I don't. So why should it matter to me?"

After a blank pause of incredulity she said:

"I could die with laughter. It seems to me all so ridiculous—no, I can't believe it."

"Perhaps it is a point of view," he said.

There was a long and pregnant silence: we should not like to say pregnant with what.

"And so I don't mean anything to you at all?" she said.

"I didn't say that," he replied.

"Nothing means anything to you," she challenged.

"I don't say that."

"Whether it's your wife—or me—or the moon—*toute la même chose.*"

"No—no—that's hardly the way to look at it."

She gazed at him in such utter amazement that she felt something would really explode in her if she heard another word. Was this a man?—or what was it!— It was too much for her, that was all.

"Well, good-bye," she said. "I hope you will have a nice time at the Vier Jahreszeiten."

So she left him still sitting on the roof.

"I suppose," she said to herself, "that is love *à l'anglaise.* But it's more than I can swallow."

IV

"Won't you come and have tea with me—do! Come right along now. Don't you find it bitterly cold? Yes—well now—come in with me and we'll have a cup of nice, hot tea, in our little sitting-room. The weather changes so suddenly, and really, one needs a little reinforcement. But perhaps you don't take tea?"

"Oh yes. I got so used to it in England," said Hannele.

"Did you now! Well now, were you long in England?"

"Oh yes——"

The two women had met in the Domplatz. Mrs. Hepburn

was looking extraordinarily like one of Hannele's dolls, in a funny little cape of odd striped skins, and a little dark-green skirt, and a rather fuzzy sort of hat. Hannele looked almost huge beside her.

"But now you will come in and have tea, won't you? Oh, please do. Never mind whether it's *de rigueur* or not. I *always* please myself *what* I do. I'm afraid my husband gets some shocks sometimes—but that we can't help. I won't have anybody laying down the law to me." She laughed her winsome little laugh. "So now come along in, and we'll see if there aren't hot scones as well. I love a hot scone for tea in cold weather. And I hope you do. That is, if there are any. We don't know yet." She tinkled her little laugh. "My husband may or may not be in. But that makes no difference to you and me, does it? There, it's just striking half-past four. In England we always have tea at half-past. My husband *adores* his tea. I don't suppose our man is five minutes off the half-past, ringing the gong for tea, not once in twelve months. My husband doesn't mind at all if dinner is a little late. But he gets quite—well, quite 'ratty' if tea is late." She tinkled a laugh. "Though I shouldn't say that. He is the soul of kindness and patience. I don't think I've ever known him to do an unkind thing—or hardly say an unkind word. But I doubt if he will be in to-day."

He *was* in, however, standing with his feet apart and his hands in his trouser pockets in the little sitting-room upstairs in the hotel. He raised his eyebrows the smallest degree, seeing Hannele enter.

"Ah, Countess Hannele—my wife has brought you along! Very nice, very nice! Let me take your wrap. Oh, yes, certainly . . ."

"Have you rung for tea, dear?" asked Mrs. Hepburn.

"Er—yes. I said as soon as you came in they were to bring it."

"Yes—well. Won't you ring again, dear, and say for *three*."

"Yes—certainly. Certainly."

He rang, and stood about with his hands in his pockets waiting for tea.

"Well now," said Mrs. Hepburn, as she lifted the teapot, and her bangles tinkled, and her huge rings of brilliants twinkled, and her big ear-rings of clustered seed-pearls bobbed against her rather withered cheek, "isn't it charming of Countess zu—Countess zu——"

"Rassentlow," said he. "I believe most people say Countess Hannele. I know we always do among ourselves. We say Countess Hannele's shop."

"Countess Hannele's shop! Now, isn't that perfectly delightful: such a romance in the very sound of it. You take cream?"

"Thank you," said Hannele.

The tea passed in a cloud of chatter, while Mrs. Hepburn manipulated the teapot, and lit the spirit-flame, and blew it out, and peeped into the steam of the teapot, and couldn't see whether there was any more tea or not—and—"At home I *know*—I was going to say to a teaspoonful—how much tea there is in the pot. But this teapot—I don't know what it's made of—it isn't silver, I know that—it is so heavy in itself, that it's deceived me several times already. And my husband is a greedy man, a greedy man—he likes at least three cups—and four if he can get them, or five! Yes, dear, I've plenty of tea to-day. You shall have even five, if you don't mind the last two weak. Do let me fill your cup, Countess Hannele. I think it's a *charming* name."

"There's a play called *Hannele*, isn't there?" said he.

When he had had his five cups, and his wife had got her cigarette perched in the end of a long, slim white holder, and was puffing like a little China-woman from the distance, there was a little lull.

"Alec, dear," said Mrs. Hepburn. "You won't forget to leave that message for me at Mrs. Rackham's. I'm so afraid it will be forgotten."

"No, dear, I won't forget. Er—would you like me to go round now?"

Hannele noticed how often he said "er," when he was beginning to speak to his wife. But they *were* such good friends, the two of them.

"Why if you *would*, dear, I should feel perfectly comfortable. But I don't want you to hurry one bit."

"Oh, I may as well go now."

And he went. Mrs. Hepburn detained her guest.

"He *is* so charming to me," said the little woman. "He's really wonderful. And he always has been the same—invariably. So that if he *did* make a little slip—well, you know, I don't have to take it so seriously."

"No," said Hannele, feeling as if her ears were stretching with astonishment.

"It's the war. It's just the war. It's had a terribly deteriorating effect on the men."

"In what way?" said Hannele.

"Why, morally. Really, there's hardly one man left the same as he was before the war. Terribly degenerated."

"Is that so?" said Hannele.

"It is indeed. Why, isn't it the same with the German men and officers?"

"Yes, I think so," said Hannele.

"And I'm sure so, from what I hear. But of course it is the women who are to blame in the first place. We poor women! We are a guilty race, I am afraid. But I never throw stones. I know what it is myself to have temptations. I have to flirt a little—and when I was younger—well, the men didn't escape me, I assure you. And I was *so* often scorched. But never *quite* singed. My husband never minded. He knew I was *really* safe. Oh yes, I have always been faithful to him. But still— I have been *very* near the flame." And she laughed her winsome little laugh.

Hannele put her fingers to her ears, to make sure they were not falling off.

"Of course during the war it was terrible. I know that in a certain hospital it was quite impossible for a girl to stay on if she kept straight. The matrons and sisters just turned her out.

They wouldn't have her unless she was one of themselves. And you know what that means. Quite like the convent in Balzac's story—you know which I mean, I'm sure." And the laugh tinkled gaily.

"But then, what can you expect, when there aren't enough men to go round! Why, I had a friend in Ireland. She and her husband had been an ideal couple, an *ideal* couple. Real playmates. And you can't say more than that, can you? Well, then, he became a major during the war. And she was so looking forward, poor thing, to the perfectly lovely times they would have together when he came home. She is like me, and is lucky enough to have a little income of her own—not a great fortune—but—well—— Well now, what was I going to say. Oh yes, she was looking forward to the perfectly lovely times they would have when he came home: building on her dreams, poor thing, as we unfortunate women always do. I suppose we shall never be cured of it." A little tinkling laugh. "Well now, not a bit of it. Not a bit of it." Mrs. Hepburn lifted her heavily-jewelled little hand in a motion of protest. It was curious, her hands were pretty and white, and her neck and breast, now she wore a little tea-gown, were also smooth and white and pretty, under the medley of twinkling little chains and coloured jewels. Why should her face have played her this nasty trick of going all crumpled? However, it was so.

"Not one bit of it," reiterated the little lady. "He came home quite changed. She said she could hardly recognize him for the same man. Let me tell you one little incident. Just a trifle, but significant. He was coming home—this was some time after he was free from the army—he was coming home from London, and he told her to meet him at the boat: gave her the time and everything. Well, she went to the boat, poor thing, and he didn't come. She waited, and no word of explanation or anything. So she couldn't make up her mind whether to go next day and meet the boat again. However, she decided she wouldn't. So of course, on that boat he arrived. When he got home, he said to her, 'Why didn't you meet the boat?' 'Well,' she said, 'I went yesterday, and you didn't come.' 'Then why didn't you meet it again to-day?' Imagine it, the sauce! And they had been real playmates. Heart-breaking, isn't it? 'Well,' she said in self-defence, 'why didn't you come yesterday?' 'Oh,' he said, 'I met a woman in town whom I liked, and she asked me to spend the night with her, so I did.' Now what do you think of that? Can you conceive of such a thing?"

"Oh no," said Hannele. "I call that unnecessary brutality."

"Exactly! So terrible to say such a thing to her! The brutality of it! Well, that's how the world is to-day. I'm thankful my husband isn't that sort. I don't say he's perfect. But whatever else he did, he'd never be unkind, and he *couldn't* be brutal. He just couldn't. He'd never tell me a lie—I know *that*. But callous brutality, no thank goodness, he hasn't a spark of it in him. I'm the wicked one, if either of us is wicked." The little laugh tinkled. "Oh! but he's been perfect to me, perfect. Hardly a cross word. Why, on our wedding night, he kneeled down in front of me and promised, with God's help, to make my life happy. And I must say, as far as possible, he's kept his word. It has been his one aim in life, to make my life happy."

The little lady looked away with a bright, musing look, towards the window. She was being a heroine in a romance. Hannele could see her being a heroine, playing the chief part in her own life-romance. It is such a feminine occupation, that no woman takes offence when she is made audience.

"I'm afraid I've more of the woman than the mother in my composition," resumed the little heroine. "I adore my two children. The boy is at Winchester, and my little girl is in a convent in Brittany. Oh, they are perfect darlings, both of them. But the man is first in my mind, I'm afraid. I fear I'm rather old-fashioned. But never mind. I can see the attractions in other men—can't I indeed! There was a perfectly exquisite creature—he was a very clever engineer—but much, much more than *that*. But never mind." The little heroine sniffed as if there were perfume in the air, folded her jewelled hands, and resumed: "However—I know what it is myself to flutter round the flame. You know I'm Irish myself, and we

Irish can't help it. Oh, I wouldn't be English for anything. Just that little touch of imagination, you know . . ." The little laugh tinkled. "And that's what makes me able to sympathize with my husband even when, perhaps, I shouldn't. Why, when he was at home with me, he never gave a thought, not a thought to another woman. I must say, he used to make *me* feel a little guilty sometimes. But there! I don't think he ever thought of another woman as being flesh and blood, after he knew me. I could tell. Pleasant, courteous, charming—but other women were not flesh and blood to him, they were just people, callers—that kind of thing. It used to amaze me, when some perfectly lovely creature came, whom I should have been head over heels in love with in a minute—and he, he was charming, delightful; he could see her points, but she was no more to him than, let me say, a pot of carnations, or a beautiful old piece of punto di Milano. Not flesh and blood. Well, perhaps one can feel too safe. Perhaps one needs a tiny pinch of the salt of jealousy. I believe one does. And I have not had one jealous moment for seventeen years. So that, *really*, when I heard a whisper of something going on here, I felt almost pleased. I felt exonerated for my own little peccadilloes, for one thing. And I felt he was perhaps a little more human. Because, after all, it is nothing but human to fall in love, if you are alone for a long time and in the company of a beautiful woman—and if you're an attractive man yourself."

Hannele sat with her eyes propped open and her ears buttoned back with amazement, expecting the next revelations.

"Why, of course," she said, knowing she was expected to say something.

"Yes, of course," said Mrs. Hepburn, eyeing her sharply. "So I thought I'd better come and see how far things had gone. I had nothing but a hint to go on. I knew no name—nothing. I had just a hint that she was German, and a refugee aristocrat —and that he used to call at the studio." The little lady eyed Hannele sharply, and gave a breathless little laugh, clasping her hands nervously. Hannele sat absolutely blank: really dazed.

"Of course," resumed Mrs. Hepburn, "that was enough. That was quite a sufficient clue. I'm afraid my intentions when I called at the studio were not as pure as they might have been. I'm afraid I wanted to see something more than the dolls. But when you showed me *his* doll, then I knew. Of course there wasn't a shadow of doubt after that. And I saw at once that she loved him, poor thing. She was *so* agitated. And no idea who I was. And you were so unkind to show me the doll. Of course you had no idea who you were showing it to. But for her, poor thing, it was such a trial. I could see how she suffered. And I must say she's very lovely—she's very, very lovely, with her golden skin and her reddish amber eyes and her beautiful, beautiful carriage. And such a naïve, impulsive nature. Gives everything away in a minute. And then her deep voice—'*Oh yes—Oh please!*'—such a child. And such an aristocrat, that lovely turn of her head, and her simple, elegant dress. Oh, she's very charming. And she's just the type I always knew would attract him, if he hadn't got me. I've thought about it many a time—many a time. When a woman is older than a man, she does think these things—especially if he has his attractive points too. And when I've dreamed of the woman he would love if he hadn't got me, it has always been a Spanish type. And the Baroness is extraordinarily Spanish in her appearance. She must have had some noble Spanish ancestor. Don't you think so?"

"Oh yes," said Hannele. "There were such a lot of Spaniards in Austria, too, with the various emperors."

"With Charles V, exactly. Exactly. That's how it must have been. And so she has all the Spanish beauty, and all the German feeling. Of course, for myself, I miss the *reserve*, the haughtiness. But she's very, very lovely, and I'm sure I could never *hate* her. I couldn't even if I tried. And I'm not going to try. But I think she's much too dangerous for my husband to see much of her. Don't you agree, now?"

"Oh, but really," stammered Hannele. "There's nothing in it, really."

"Well," said the little lady, cocking her head shrewdly

aside, "I shouldn't like there to be any *more* in it."

And there was a moment's dead pause. Each woman was reflecting. Hannele wondered if the little lady was just fooling her.

"Anyhow," continued Mrs. Hepburn, "the spark is there, and I don't intend the fire to spread. I am going to be very, very careful, myself, not to fan the flames. The last thing I should think of would be to make my husband scenes. I believe it would be fatal."

"Yes," said Hannele, during the pause.

"I'm going very carefully. You think there isn't much in it —between him and the Baroness?"

"No—no—I'm sure there isn't," cried Hannele, with a full voice of conviction. She was almost indignant, at being slighted so completely herself, in the little lady's suspicions.

"Hm!—mm!" hummed the little woman, sapiently nodding her head slowly up and down. "I'm not so sure! I'm not so sure that it hasn't gone pretty far."

"Oh *no!*" cried Hannele, in real irritation of protest.

"Well," said the other. "In any case, I don't intend it to go any further."

There was dead silence for some time.

"There's more in it than you say. There's more in it than you say," ruminated the little woman. "I know *him,* for one thing. I know he's got a cloud on his brow. And I know it hasn't left his brow for a single minute. And when I told him I had been to the studio, and showed him the cushion-cover, I knew he felt guilty. I am not so easily deceived. We Irish all have a touch of second sight, I believe. Of course I haven't challenged him. I haven't even mentioned the doll. By the way, *who* ordered the doll? Do you mind telling me?"

"No, it wasn't ordered," confessed Hannele.

"Ah—I thought not—I thought not!" said Mrs. Hepburn, lifting her finger. "At least, I knew no outsider had ordered it. Of course I knew." And she smiled to herself.

"So," she continued, "I had too much sense to say anything about it. I don't believe in stripping wounds bare. I believe in gently covering them and letting them heal. But I *did* say I thought her a lovely creature." The little lady looked brightly at Hannele.

"Yes," said Hannele.

"And he was very vague in his manner. 'Yes, not bad,' he said. I thought to myself, Aha, my boy, you don't deceive me with your *not bad*. She's very much more than not bad. I said so, too. I wanted, of course, to let him know I had a suspicion."

"And do you think he knew?"

"Of course he did. Of course he did. 'She's much too dangerous,' I said, 'to be in a town where there are so many strange men: married and unmarried.' And then he turned round to me and gave himself away, oh, so plainly. 'Why?' he said. But such a haughty distant tone. I said to myself, 'It's time, my dear boy, you were removed out of the danger-zone.' But I answered him: 'Surely somebody is bound to fall in love with her.' 'Not at all,' he said, 'she keeps to her own country-men.' 'You don't tell *me*,' I answered him, 'with her pretty broken English! It is a wonder the two of them are allowed to stay in the town.' And then again he rounded on me. 'Good gracious!' he said. 'Would you have them turned out just because they're beautiful to look at, when they have nowhere else to go, and they make their bit of a livelihood here?' I assure you, he hasn't rounded on me in that overbearing way, not once before, in all our married life. So I just said quietly: 'I should like to protect *our own men*.' And he didn't say anything more. But he looked at me under his brows, and went out of the room."

There was a silence. Hannele waited with her hands in her lap, and Mrs. Hepburn mused, with her hands in *her* lap. Her face looked yellow, and *very* wrinkled.

"Well now," she said, breaking again suddenly into life. "What are we to do? I mean what is to be done? You are the Baroness' nearest friend. And I wish her *no* harm, none whatever."

"What can we do?" said Hannele, in the pause.

"I have been urging my husband for some time to get his

discharge from the army," said the little woman. "I know he could have it in three months' time. But like so many more men, he has no income of his own, and he doesn't want to feel dependent. Perfect nonsense! So he says he wants to stay on in the army. I have never known him before go against my real wishes."

"But it *is* better for a man to be independent," said Hannele.

"I know it is. But it is also better for him to be *at home*. And I could get him a post in one of the observatories. He could do something in meteorological work."

Hannele refused to answer any more.

"Of course," said Mrs. Hepburn, "if he *does* stay on here, it would be much better if the Baroness left the town."

"I'm sure she will never leave of her own choice," said Hannele.

"I'm sure she won't either. But she might be made to see that it would be very much *wiser* of her to move of her own free will."

"Why?" said Hannele.

"Why, because she might any time be removed by the British authorities."

"Why should she?" said Hannele.

"I think the women who are a menace to our men should be removed."

"But she is *not* a menace to your men."

"Well, I have my own opinion on that point."

Which was a decided deadlock.

"I'm sure I've kept you an awful long time with my chatter," said Mrs. Hepburn. "But I did want to make everything as simple as possible. As I said before, I can't feel any ill-will against her. Yet I can't let things just go on. Heaven alone knows when they may end. Of course if I can persuade my husband to resign his commission and come back to England— anyhow, we will see. I'm sure I am the last person in the world to bear malice."

The tone in which she said it conveyed a dire threat.

Hannele rose from her chair.

"Oh, and one other thing," said her hostess, taking out a tiny lace handkerchief and touching her nose delicately with it. "Do you think"—dab—dab—"that I might have that *doll*—you know——?"

"That——?"

"Yes, of my husband"—the little lady rubbed her nose with her kerchief.

"The price is three guineas," said Hannele.

"Oh, indeed!"—the tone was very cold. "I thought it was not for sale."

Hannele put on her wrap.

"You'll send it round—will you?—if you will be so kind."

"I must ask my friend, first."

"Yes, of course. But I'm sure she will be so kind as to send it me. It is a little—er—indelicate, don't you think!"

"No," said Hannele. "No more than a painted portrait."

"Don't you?" said her hostess coldly. "Well, even a painted portrait I think I should like in my own possession. This *doll*——"

Hannele waited, but there was no conclusion.

"Anyhow," she said, "the price is three guineas: or the equivalent in marks."

"Very well," said the little lady, "you shall have your three guineas when I get the doll."

v

Hannele went her way pondering. A man never is quite such an abject specimen as his wife makes him look, talking about "my husband." Therefore, if any woman wishes to rescue her husband from the clutches of another female, let her only invite this female to tea and talk quite sincerely about "my husband, you know." Every man has made a ghastly fool of himself with a woman, at some time or other. No woman ever forgets. And most women will give the show away, with real pathos, to another woman. For instance, the picture of Alec at his wife's feet on his wedding night, vowing to devote himself to her lifelong happiness—this picture strayed across Hannele's mind time after time, whenever she thought of her dear captain. With disastrous consequences to the captain. Of course if he had been at her own feet, then Hannele would have thought it almost natural: almost a necessary part of the show of love. But at the feet of that other little woman! And what was that other little woman wearing? Her wedding night! Hannele hoped before heaven it wasn't some awful little nightie of frail flowered silk. Imagine it, that little lady! Perhaps in a chic little boudoir cap of punto di Milano, and this slip of frail flowered silk: and the man, perhaps, in his braces! Oh, merciful heaven, save us from other people's indiscretions. No, let us be sure it was in proper evening dress—twenty years ago—very low cut, with a full skirt gathered behind and trailing a little, and a little feather-erection in her high-dressed hair, and all those jewels: pearls of course: and he in a dinner-jacket and a white waistcoat: probably in an hotel bedroom in Lugano, or Biarritz. And she? Was she standing with one small hand on his shoulder? Or was she seated on the couch in the bedroom? Oh, dreadful thought! And yet, it was almost inevitable, that scene. Hannele had never been married, but she had come quite near enough to the realization of the event to know that such a scene *was* practically inevitable. An indispensable part of any honeymoon. Him on his knees, with his heels up!

And how black and tidy his hair must have been then! And no grey at the temples at all. Such a good-looking bridegroom. Perhaps with a white rose in his button-hole still. And she could see him kneeling there, in his new black trousers, and a wing collar. And she could see his head bowed. And she could hear his plangent, musical voice saying: "With God's help, I will make your life happy. I will live for that and for nothing else." And then the little lady must have had tears in her eyes, and she must have said, rather superbly: "Thank you, dear. I'm perfectly sure of it."

Ach! Ach! Husbands should be left to their own wives: and

wives should be left to their own husbands. And *no* stranger
should ever be made a party to these terrible bits of connubial
staging. Nay, thought Hannele, that scene was really true.
It actually took place. And with the man of that scene I have
been in love! With the devoted husband of that little lady. Oh
God, oh God, how was it possible! Him on his knees, on his
knees, with his heels up!

Am I a perfect fool? she thought to herself. Am I really just
an idiot, gaping with love for him? How *could* I? How could I?
The very way he says "Yes, dear!" to her! The way he does
what she tells him! The way he fidgets about the room with his
hands in his pockets! The way he goes off when she sends him
away because she wants to talk to me. And he knows she wants
to talk to me. And he knows what she *might* have to say to me.
Yet he goes off on his errand without a question, like a servant.
"I will do whatever you wish, darling." He must have said
those words time after time, to the little lady. And fulfilled
them, also. Performed all his pledges and his promises.

Ach! Ach! Hannele wrung her hands to think of *herself*
being mixed up with him. And he had seemed to her so manly.
He seemed to have so much silent male passion in him. And
yet—the little lady! "My husband has *always* been *perfectly
sweet* to me." Think of it! On his knees too. And his "Yes,
dear! Certainly. Certainly." Not that he was afraid of the
little lady. He was just committed to her, as he might have
been committed to gaol, or committed to paradise.

Had she been dreaming, to be in love with him? Oh, she
wished so much she had never been. She *wished* she had never
given herself away. To him!—given herself away to him!—
and so abjectly. Hung upon his words and his emotions, and
looked up to him as if he were Cæsar. So he had seemed to her: like
a mute Cæsar. Like Germanicus. Like—she did not know what.

How had it all happened? What had taken her in? Was it
just his good looks? No, not really. Because they were the
kind of staring good looks she didn't really care for. He must
have had charm. He must have charm. Yes, he *had* charm.
When it worked.

His charm had not worked on her now for some time—never since that evening after his wife's arrival. Since then he had seemed to her—rather awful. Rather awful—stupid—an ass—a limited, rather vulgar person. That was what he seemed to her when his charm wouldn't work. A limited, rather inferior person. And in a world of *Schiebern* and profiteers and vulgar, pretentious persons, this was the worst thing possible. A limited, inferior, slightly pretentious individual! The husband of the little lady! And oh heaven, she was so deeply implicated with him! He had not, however, spoken with her in private since his wife's arrival. Probably he would never speak with her in private again. She hoped to heaven, never again. The awful thing was the past, that which had been between him and her. She shuddered when she thought of it. The husband of the little lady!

But surely there was something to account for it! Charm, just charm. He had a charm. And then, oh heaven, when the charm left off working! It had left off so completely at this moment, in Hannele's case, that her very mouth tasted salt. What *did* it all amount to?

What was his charm, after all? How could it have affected her? She began to think of him again, at his best: his presence, when they were alone high up in that big, lonely attic near the stars. His room! The big white-washed walls, the first scent of tobacco, the silence, the sense of the stars being near, the telescopes, the cactus with fine scarlet flowers: and above all, the strange, remote, insidious silence of his presence, that was so congenial to her also. The curious way he had of turning his head to listen—to listen to what?—as if he heard something in the stars. The strange look like destiny, in his wide-open, almost staring dark eyes. The beautiful lines of his brow, that seemed always to have a certain cloud on it. The slow elegance of his straight, beautiful legs as he walked, and the exquisiteness of his dark, slender chest! Ah, she could feel the charm mounting over her again. She could feel the snake biting her heart. She could feel the arrows of desire rankling.

But then—and she turned from her thoughts back to this

last little tea-party in the Vier Jahreszeiten. She thought of his voice: "Yes, dear. Certainly. Certainly I will." And she thought of the stupid, inferior look on his face. And the something of a servant-like way in which he went out to do his wife's bidding.

And then the charm was gone again, as the glow of sunset goes off a burning city and leaves it a sordid industrial hole. So much for charm!

So much for charm. She had better have stuck to her own sort of men, Martin, for instance, who was a gentleman and a daring soldier, and a queer soul and pleasant to talk to. Only he hadn't any *magic*. Magic? The very word made her writhe. Magic? Swindle. Swindle, that was all it amounted to. Magic!

And yet—let us not be too hasty. If the magic had *really* been there, on those evenings in that great lofty attic. Had it? Yes. Yes, she was bound to admit it. There had been magic. If there had been magic in his presence and in his contact, the husband of the little lady—— But the distaste was in her mouth again.

So she started afresh, trying to keep a tight hold on the tail of that all-too-evanescent magic of his. Dear, it slipped so quickly into disillusion. Nevertheless. If it had existed, it did exist. And if it did exist, it was worth having. You could call it an illusion if you liked. But an illusion which is a real experience is worth having. Perhaps this disillusion was a greater illusion than the illusion itself. Perhaps all this disillusion of the little lady and the husband of the little lady was falser than the illusion and magic of those few evenings. Perhaps the long disillusion of life was falser than the brief moments of real illusion. After all—the delicate darkness of his breast, the mystery that seemed to come with him as he trod slowly across the floor of his room, after changing his tunic—— Nay, nay, if she could keep the illusion of his charm, she would give all disillusion to the devils. Nay, only let her be under the spell of his charm. Only let the spell be upon her. It was all she yearned for. And the thing she had to fight was the vulgarity of disillusion. The vulgarity of the little lady, the vulgarity of the husband of the little lady, the vulgarity of his insincerity, his "Yes, dear. Certainly! Certainly!"—this was what she had to fight. He *was* vulgar and horrible, then. But also, the queer figure that sat alone on the roof watching the stars! The wonderful red flower of the cactus. The mystery that advanced with him as he came across the room after changing his tunic. The glamour and sadness of him, his silence, as he stooped unfastening his boots. And the strange gargoyle smile, fixed, when he caressed her with his hand under the chin! Life is all a choice. And if she chose the glamour, the magic, the charm, the illusion, the spell! Better death than that other, the husband of the little lady. When all was said and done, was he as much the husband of the little lady as he was that queer, delicate-breasted Cæsar of her own knowledge? Which was he?

No, she was *not* going to send her the doll. The little lady should never have the doll.

What a doll she would make herself! Heavens, what a wizened jewel!

VI

Captain Hepburn still called occasionally at the house for his post. The maid always put his letters in a certain place in the hall, so that he should not have to climb the stairs.

Among his letters—that is to say, along with another letter, for his correspondence was very meagre—he one day found an envelope with a crest. Inside this envelope two letters.

"DEAR CAPTAIN HEPBURN,
I had the enclosed letter from Mrs. Hepburn. I don't intend her to have the doll which is your portrait, so I shall not answer this note. Also I don't see why she should try to turn us out of the town. She talked to me after tea that day, and it seems she believes that Mitchka is your lover. I didn't say

anything at all—except that it wasn't true. But she needn't be afraid of me. I don't want you to trouble yourself. But you may as well *know* how things are.

JOHANNA z. R."

The other letter was on his wife's well-known heavy paper, and in her well-known large, "aristocratic" hand.

"MY DEAR COUNTESS,

"I wonder if there has been some mistake, or some mis-understanding. Four days ago you said you would send round that *doll* we spoke of, but I have seen no sign of it yet. I thought of calling at the studio, but did not wish to disturb the Baroness. I should be very much obliged if you could send the doll at once, as I do not feel easy while it is out of my possession. You may rely on having a cheque by return.

"Our old family friend, Major-General Barlow, called on me yesterday, and we had a most interesting conversation on our *Tommies*, and the protection of their morals here. It seems we have full power to send away any person or persons deemed undesirable, with twenty-four hours' notice to leave. But of course all this is done as quietly and with the intention of causing as little scandal as possible.

Please let me have the doll by to-morrow, and perhaps some hint as to your future intentions.

"With very best wishes from one who only seeks to be your friend,

"Yours very sincerely,
"EVANGELINE HEPBURN."

VII

And then a dreadful thing happened: really a very dreadful thing. Hannele read of it in the evening newspaper of the town —the *Abendblatt*. Mitchka came rushing up with the paper at ten o'clock at night, just when Hannele was going to bed.

Mrs. Hepburn had fallen out of her bedroom window, from the third floor of the hotel down on to the pavement below, and was killed. She was dressing for dinner. And apparently she had in the morning washed a certain little camisole, and put it on the window-sill to dry. She must have stood on a chair reaching for it, when she fell out of the window. Her husband, who was in the dressing-room, heard a queer little noise, a sort of choking cry and came into her room to see what it was. And she wasn't there. The window was open, and the chair by the window. He looked round, and thought she had left the room for a moment, so returned to his shaving. He was half shaved when one of the maids rushed in. When he looked out of the window down into the street he fainted, and would have fallen too if the maid had not pulled him in in time.

The very next day the captain came back to his attic. Hannele did not know, until quite late at night when he tapped on her door. She knew his soft tap immediately.

"Won't you come over for a chat?" he said.

She paused for some moments before she answered. And then perhaps surprise made her agree: surprise and curiosity.

"Yes, in a minute," she said, closing her door in his face.

She found him sitting quite still, not even smoking, in his quiet attic. He did not rise, but just glanced round with a faint smile. And she thought his face seemed different, more flexible. But in the half-light she could not tell. She sat at some little distance from him.

"I suppose you've heard," he said.

"Yes."

After a long pause, he resumed:

"Yes. It seems an impossible thing to have happened. Yet it *has* happened."

Hannele's ears were sharp. But strain them as she might she could not catch the meaning of his voice.

"A terrible thing. A *very* terrible thing," she said.

"Yes."

"Do you think she fell quite accidentally?" she said.

"Must have done. The maid was in just a minute before, and

she seemed as happy as possible. I suppose reaching over that broad window-ledge, her brain must suddenly have turned. I can't imagine why she didn't call me. She could never bear even to look out of a high window. Turned her'ill instantly if she saw a space below her. She used to say she couldn't really look at the moon, it made her feel as if she would fall down a dreadful height. She never dared do more than glance at it. She always had the feeling, I suppose, of the awful space beneath her, if she were on the moon."

Hannele was not listening to his words, but to his voice. There was something a little automatic in what he said. But then that is always so when people have had a shock.

"It must have been terrible for you too," she said.

"Ah, yes. At the time it was awful. Awful. I felt the smash right inside me, you know."

"Awful!" she repeated.

"But now," he said, "I feel very strangely happy about it. I feel happy about it. I feel happy for her sake, if you can understand that. I feel she has got out of some great tension. I feel she's free now for the first time in her life. She was a gentle soul, and an original soul, but she was like a fairy who is condemned to live in houses and sit on furniture and all that, don't you know. It was never her nature."

"No?" said Hannele, herself sitting in blank amazement.

"I always felt she was born in the wrong period—or on the wrong planet. Like some sort of delicate creature you take out of a tropical forest the moment it is born, and from the first moment teach it to perform tricks. You know what I mean. All her life she performed the tricks of life, clever little monkey she was at it too. Beat me into fits. But her own poor little soul, a sort of fairy soul, those queer Irish creatures, was cooped up inside her all her life, tombed in. There it was, tombed in, while she went through all the tricks of life that you have to go through if you are born to-day."

"But," stammered Hannele, "what would she have done if she *had* been free?"

"Why, don't you see, there *is* nothing for her to do in the world to-day. Take her language, for instance. She never ought to have been speaking English. I don't know what language she ought to have spoken. Because if you take the Irish language, they only learn it back from English. They think in English, and just put Irish words on top. But English was never her language. It bubbled off her lips, so to speak. And she had no other language. Like a starling that you've made talk from the very beginning, and so it can only shout these talking noises, don't you know. It can't whistle its own whistling to save its life. Couldn't do it. It's lost it. All its own natural mode of expressing itself has collapsed, and it can only be artificial."

There was a long pause.

"Would she have been wonderful, then, if she had been able to talk in some unknown language?" said Hannele jealously.

"I don't say she would have been wonderful. As a matter of fact we think a talking starling is much more wonderful than an ordinary starling. I don't myself, but most people do. And she would have been a sort of starling. And she would have had her own language and her own ways. As it was, poor thing, she was always arranging herself and fluttering and chattering inside a cage. And she never knew she was in the cage, any more than we know we are inside our own skins."

"But," said Hannele, with a touch of mockery, "how do you know you haven't made it all up—just to console yourself?"

"Oh, I've thought it long ago," he said.

"Still," she blurted, "you may have invented it all—as a sort of consolation for—for—for your life."

"Yes, I may," he said. "But I don't think so. It was her eyes. Did you ever notice her eyes? I often used to catch her eyes. And she'd be talking away, all the language bubbling off her lips. And her eyes were so clear and bright and different. Like a child's that is listening to something, and is going to be frightened. She was always listening—and waiting—for something else. I tell you what, she was exactly like that fairy in the Scotch song, who is in love with a mortal, and sits by the high road in terror waiting for him to come, and hearing the plovers and the curlews. Only nowadays motor lorries go along the moor roads, and the poor thing is struck unconscious, and carried into our world in a state of unconsciousness, and when she comes round, she tries to talk our language, and behave as we behave, and she can't remember anything else, so she goes on and on, till she falls with a crash, back to her own world."

Hannele was silent, and so was he.

"You loved her then?" she said at length.

"Yes. But in this way. When I was a boy I caught a bird, a black-cap, and I put it in a cage. And I loved that bird. I don't know why, but I loved it. I simply loved that bird. All the gorse, and the heather, and the rock, and the hot smell of yellow gorse-blossom, and the sky that seemed to have no end to it, when I was a boy, everything that I almost was *mad* with, as boys are, seemed to me to be in that little, fluttering black-cap. And it would peck its seed as if it didn't quite know what else to do; and look round about, and begin to sing. But in quite a few days it turned its head aside and died. Yes, it died. I never had the feeling again that I got from that black-cap when I was a boy—not until I saw her. And then I felt it all again. I felt it all again. And it was the same feeling. I knew, quite soon I knew, that she would die. She would peck her seed and look round in the cage just the same. But she would die in the end. Only it would last much longer. But she would die in the cage, like the black-cap."

"But she loved the cage. She loved her clothes and her jewels. She must have loved her house and her furniture and all that with a perfect frenzy."

"She did. She did. But like a child with playthings. Only they were big, marvellous playthings to her. Oh, yes, she was never away from them. She never forgot her things—her trinkets and her furs and her furniture. She never got away from them for a minute. And everything in her mind was mixed up with them."

"Dreadful!" said Hannele.

"Yes, it was dreadful," he answered.

"Dreadful," repeated Hannele.

"Yes, quite. Quite! And it got worse. And her way of talking got worse. As if it bubbled off her lips. But her eyes never lost their brightness, they never lost that faery look. Only I used to see fear in them. Fear of everything—even all the things she surrounded herself with. Just like my black-cap used to look out of his cage—so bright and sharp, and yet as if he didn't know that it was just the cage that was between him and the outside. He thought it was inside himself the barrier. He thought it was part of his own nature to be shut in. And she thought it was part of her own nature. And so they both died."

"What I can't see," said Hannele, "is what she would have done outside her cage. What other life could she have, except her *bibelots* and her furniture and her talk?"

"Why, none. There *is* no life outside for human beings."

"Then there's nothing," said Hannele.

"That's true. In a great measure, there's nothing."

"Thank you," said Hannele.

There was a long pause.

"And perhaps I was to blame. Perhaps I ought to have made some sort of a move. But I didn't know what to do. For my life, I didn't know what to do, except try to make her happy. She had enough money—and I didn't think it mattered if she shared it with me. I always had a garden—and the astronomy. It's been an immense relief to me watching the moon. It's been wonderful. Instead of looking inside the cage, as I did at my bird, or at her—I look right out—into freedom—into freedom."

"The moon, you mean?" said Hannele.

"Yes, the moon."

"And that's your freedom?"

"That's where I've found the greatest sense of freedom," he said.

"Well, I'm not going to be jealous of the moon," said Hannele at length.

"Why should you. It's not a thing to be jealous of."

In a little while, she bade her good night, and left him.

VIII

The chief thing that the captain knew, at this juncture, was that a hatchet had gone through the ligatures and veins that connected him with the people of his affection, and that he was left with the bleeding ends of all his vital human relationships. Why it should be so he did not know. But then one never can know the whys and the wherefores of one's passional changes.

He only knew that it was so. The emotional flow between him and all the people he knew and cared for was broken, and for the time being he was conscious only of the cleavage. The cleavage that had occurred between him and his fellow-men, the cleft that was now between him and them. It was not the fault of anybody or anything. He could neither reproach himself nor them. What had happened had been preparing for a long time. Now suddenly the cleavage. There had been a long, slow weaning away: and now this sudden silent rupture.

What it amounted to principally was that he did not want even to see Hannele. He did not want to think of her even. But neither did he want to see anybody else, or to think of anybody else. He shrank with a feeling almost of disgust from his friends and acquaintances, and their expressions of sympathy. It affected him with instantaneous disgust, when anybody wanted to share emotions with him. He did not want to share emotions or feelings of any sort. He wanted to be by himself, essentially, even if he was moving about among other people.

So he went to England to settle his own affairs, and out of duty to see his children. He wished his children all the well in the world—everything except any emotional connection with himself. He decided to take his girl away from the convent at once, and to put her into a jolly English school. His boy was all right where he was.

The captain had now an income sufficient to give him his independence, but not sufficient to keep up his wife's house. So he prepared to sell the house and most of the things in it. He decided also to leave the army as soon as he could be free.

And he thought he would wander about for a time, till he came
upon something he wanted.

So the winter passed, without his going back to Germany.
He was free of the army. He drifted along, settling his affairs.
They were of no very great importance. And all the time he
never wrote once to Hannele. He could not get over his
disgust that people insisted on his sharing their emotions. He
could not bear their emotions, neither their activities. Other
people might have all the emotions and feelings and earnest-
nesses and busy activities they liked. Quite nice even that they
had such a multifarious commotion for themselves. But the
moment they approached him to spread their feelings over him
or to entangle him in their activities a helpless disgust came up
in him, and until he could get away he felt sick, even physically.

This was no state of mind for a lover. He could not even
think of Hannele. Anybody else he felt he need not think
about. He was deeply, profoundly thankful that his wife was
dead. It was an end of pity now; because, poor thing, she had
escaped and gone her own way into the void, like a flown bird.

IX

Nevertheless, a man hasn't finished his life at forty. He may,
however, have finished one great phase of his life.

And Alexander Hepburn was not the man to live alone. All
our troubles, says somebody wise, come upon us because we
cannot be alone. And that is all very well. We must all be *able*
to be alone, otherwise we are just victims. But when we *are*
able to be alone, then we realize that the only thing to do is to
start a new relationship with another—or even the same—
human being. That people should all be stuck up apart, like so
many telegraph poles, is nonsense.

So with out dear captain. He had his convulsion into a sort
of telegraph-pole isolation: which was absolutely necessary for
him. But then he began to bud with a new yearning for—for
what? For love?

It was a question he kept nicely putting to himself. And really, the nice young girls of eighteen or twenty attracted him very much: so fresh, so impulsive, and looking up to him as if he were something wonderful. If only he could have married two or three of them, instead of just one!

Love! When a man has no particular ambition, his mind turns back perpetually as a needle towards the pole. That tiresome word Love. It means so many things. It meant the feeling he had had for his wife. He had loved her. But he shuddered at the thought of having to go through such love again. It meant also the feeling he had for the awfully nice young things he met here and there: fresh, impulsive girls ready to give all their hearts away. Oh yes, he could fall in love with half a dozen of them. But he knew he'd better not.

At last he wrote to Hannele: and got no answer. So he wrote to Mitchka and still got no answer. So he wrote for information —and there was none forthcoming, except that the two women had gone to Munich.

For the time being he left it at that. To him, Hannele did not exactly represent rosy love. Rather a hard destiny. He did not adore her. He did not feel one bit of adoration for her. As a matter of fact, not all the beauties and virtues of woman put together with all the gold in the Indies would have tempted him into the business of adoration any more. He had gone on his knees once, vowing with faltering tones to try and make the adored one happy. And now—never again. Never.

The temptation this time was to be adored. One of those fresh young things would have adored him as if he were a god. And there was something *very* alluring about the thought. Very—very alluring. To be a god-almighty in your own house, with a lovely young thing adoring you, and you giving off beams of bright effulgence like a Gloria! Who wouldn't be tempted: at the age of forty? And this was why he dallied.

But in the end he suddenly took the train to Munich. And when he got there he found the town beastly uncomfortable, the Bavarians rude and disagreeable, and no sign of the missing females, not even in the Café Stephanie. He wandered round and round.

And then one day, oh heaven, he saw his doll in a shop window: a little art shop. He stood and stared quite spell-bound.

"Well, if that isn't the devil," he said. "Seeing yourself in a shop-window!"

He was so disgusted that he would not go into the shop.

Then, every day for a week did he walk down that little street and look at himself in the shop window. Yes, there he stood, with one hand in his pocket. And the figure had one hand in its pocket. There he stood, with his cap pulled rather low over his brow. And the figure had its cap pulled low over its brow. But thank goodness, his own cap now was a civilian tweed. But there he stood, his head rather forward, gazing with fixed dark eyes. And himself in little, that wretched figure, stood there with its head rather forward, staring with fixed dark eyes. It was such a real little *man* that it fairly staggered him. The oftener he saw it, the more it staggered him. And the more he hated it. Yet it fascinated him, and he came again to look.

And it was always there. A lonely little individual lounging there with one hand in its pocket, and nothing to do, among the bric-à-brac and the *bibelots*. Poor devil, stuck so incongruously in the world. And yet losing none of his masculinity. A male little devil, for all his forlornness. But such an air of isolation, of not-belonging. Yet taut and male, in his tartan trews. And what a situation to be in—lounging with his back against a little Japanese lacquer cabinet, with a few old pots on his right hand and a tiresome brass ink-tray on his left, while pieces of not-very-nice filet lace hung their length up and down the background. Poor little devil: it was like a deliberate satire.

And then one day it was gone. There was the cabinet and the filet lace and the tiresome ink-stand tray: and the little gentleman wasn't there. The captain at once walked into the shop.

"Have you sold that doll—that unknown soldier?" he added, without knowing quite what he was saying.

The doll was sold.

"Do you know who bought it?"

The girl looked at him very coldly, and did not know.

"I once knew the lady who made it. In fact, the doll was *me*," he said.

The girl now looked at him with sudden interest.

"Don't you think it was like me?" he said.

"Perhaps"—she began to smile.

"It was me. And the lady who made it was a friend of mine. Do you know her name?"

"Yes."

"Gräfin zu Rassentlow," he cried, his eyes shining.

"Oh yes. But her dolls are famous."

"Do you know where she is? Is she in Munich?"

"That I don't know."

"Could you find out?"

"I don't know. I can ask."

"Or the Baroness von Prielau-Carolath."

"The Baroness is dead."

"Dead!"

"She was shot in a riot in Salzburg. They say a lover——"

"How do you know?"

"From the newspapers."

"Dead! Is it possible. Poor Hannele."

There was a pause.

"Well," he said, "if you would enquire about the address—I'll call again."

Then he turned back from the door.

"By the way, do you mind telling me how much you sold the doll for?"

The girl hesitated. She was by no means anxious to give away any of her trade details. But at length she answered reluctantly:

"Five hundred marks."

"So cheap," he said. "Good day. Then I will call again."

X

Then again he got a trace. It was in the chit-chat column of the *Muenchener Neue Zeitung:* under Studio Comments. "Theodor Worpswede's latest picture is a still-life, containing an entertaining group of a doll, two sun-flowers in a glass jar, and a poached egg on toast. The contrast between the three substances is highly diverting and instructive, and this is perhaps one of the most interesting of Worpswede's works. The doll, by the way, is one of the creations of our fertile Countess Hannele. It is the figure of an English, or rather Scottish officer, in the famous tartan trousers which, clinging closely to the legs of the lively Gaul, so shocked the eminent Julius Cæsar and his cohorts. We, of course, are no longer shocked, but full of admiration for the creative genius of our dear Countess. The doll itself is a masterpiece, and has begotten another masterpiece in Theodor Worpswede's Still-life. We have heard, by the way, a rumour of Countess zu Rassentlow's engagement. Apparently the Herr Regierungsrat von Poldi, of th atmost beautiful of summer-resorts, Kaprun, in the Tyrol, is the fortunate man——"

XI

The captain bought the Still-life. This new version of himself along with the poached egg and the sun-flowers was rather frightening. So he packed up for Austria, for Kaprun, with his picture, and had a fight to get the beastly thing out of Germany, and another fight to get it into Austria. Fatigued and furious he arrived in Salzburg, seeing no beauty in anything. Next day he was in Kaprun.

It was an elegant and fashionable watering-place before the war: a lovely little lake in the midst of the Alps, an old Tyrolese town on the water-side, green slopes sheering up opposite, and away beyond, a glacier. It was still crowded and still elegant.

But alas, with a broken, bankrupt, desperate elegance, and almost empty shops.

The captain felt rather dazed. He found himself in an hotel full of Jews of the wrong, rich sort, and wondered what next. The place was beautiful, but the life wasn't.

XII

The Herr Regierungsrat was not at first sight prepossessing. He was approaching fifty, and had gone stout and rather loose, as so many men of his class and race do. Then he wore one of those dreadful full-bottom coats, a kind of poor relation to our full-skirted frock-coat: it would best be described as a family coat. It flapped about him as he walked, and he looked at first glance lower middle-class.

But he wasn't. Of course, being in office in the collapsed Austria he was a republican. But by nature he was a monarchist, nay, an imperialist, as every true Austrian is. And he was a true Austrian. And as such he was much finer and subtler than he looked. As one got used to him, his rather fat face, with its fine nose and slightly bitter, pursed mouth, came to have a resemblance to the busts of some of the late Roman emperors. And as one was with him, one came gradually to realize that out of all his baggy bourgeois appearance came something of a *grande geste*. He could not help it. There was something sweeping and careless about his soul: big, rather assertive, and ill-bred-seeming; but in fact, not ill-bred at all, only a little bitter and a good deal indifferent to his surroundings. He looked at first sight so common and *parvenu*. And then one had to realize that he was a member of a big, old empire, fallen into a sort of epicureanism, and a little bitter. There was no littleness, no meanness, and no real coarseness. But he was a great talker, and relentless towards his audience.

Hannele was attracted to him by his talk. He began as soon as dinner appeared: and he went on, carrying the decanter and the wine-glass with him out on to the balcony of the villa, over-the lake, on and on until midnight. The summer night was still and warm: the lake lay deep and full, and the old town twinkled away across. There was the faintest tang of snow in the air, from the great glacier-peaks that were hidden in the night opposite. Sometimes a boat with a lantern twanged a guitar. The clematis flowers were quite black, like leaves, dangling from the terrace.

It was so beautiful, there in the very heart of the Tyrol. The hotels glittered with lights: electric light was still cheap. There seemed a fullness and a loveliness in the night. And yet for some reason it was all terrible and devastating: the life-spirit seemed to be squirming, bleeding all the time.

And on and on talked the Herr Regierungsrat, with all the witty volubility of the more versatile Austrian. He was really very witty, very human, and with a touch of salty cynicism that reminded one of a real old Roman of the Empire. That subtle stoicism, that unsentimental epicureanism, that kind of reckless hopelessness, of course, fascinated the women. And particularly Hannele. He talked on and on—about his work before the war, when he held an important post and was one of the governing class—then about the war—then about the hopelessness of the present: and in it all there seemed a bigness, a carelessness based on indifference, and hopelessness that laughed at its very self. The real old Austria had always fascinated Hannele. As represented in the witty, bitter-indifferent Herr Regierungsrat it carried her away.

And he, of course, turned instinctively to her, talking in his rapid, ceaseless fashion, with a laugh and a pause to drink and a new start taken. She liked the sound of his Austrian speech: its racy carelessness, its salty indifference to standards of correctness. Oh yes, here was the *grande geste* still lingering.

He turned his large breast towards her, and made a quick gesture with his fat, well-shapen hand, blurted out another subtle, rough-seeming romance, pursed his mouth, and emptied his glass once more. Then he looked at his half-forgotten cigar and started again.

There was something almost boyish and impulsive about

him: the way he turned to her, and the odd way he seemed to open his big breast to her. And again, he seemed almost eternal, sitting there in his chair with knees planted apart. It was as if he would never rise again, but would remain sitting for ever, and talking. He seemed as if he had no legs, save to sit with. As if to stand on his feet and walk would not be natural to him.

Yet he rose at last, and kissed her hand with the grand gesture that France or Germany have never acquired: careless-ness, profound indifference to other people's standards, and then such a sudden stillness, as he bent and kissed her hand. Of course she felt a queen in exile.

And perhaps it is more dangerous to feel yourself a queen in exile than a queen *in situ*. She fell in love with him, with this large, stout, loose widower of fifty, with two children. He had no money except some Austrian money that was worth nothing outside Austria. He could not even go to Germany. There he was, fixed in this hollow in the middle of the Tyrol.

But he had an ambition still, old Roman of the decadence that he was. He had year by year and without making any fuss collected the material for a very minute and thorough history of his own district: the Chiemgau and the Pinzgau. Hannele found that his fund of information on this subject was in-exhaustible, and his intelligence was so delicate, so human, and his scope seemed so wide, that she felt a touch of reverence for him. He wanted to write this history. And she wanted to help him.

For, of course, as things were he would never write it. He was Regierungsrat: that is, he was the petty local governor of his town and immediate district. The Amthaus was a great old building, and there young ladies in high heels flirted among masses of papers with bare-kneed young gentlemen in Tyrolese costume, and occasionally they parted, to take a pleasant, interesting attitude and write a word or two, after which they fluttered together for a little more interesting diversion. It was extraordinary how many finely built, handsome young people of an age fitted for nothing but love-affairs, ran the governmental business of this department. And the Herr Regierungs-rat sailed in and out of the big, old room, his wide coat flying like wings and making the papers flutter, his rather wine-reddened, old-Roman face smiling with its bitter look. And of course it was a witticism he uttered first, even if Hungary was invading the frontier or cholera was in Vienna.

When he was on his legs, he walked nimbly, briskly, and his coat-bottoms always flew. So he waved through the town, greeting somebody at every few strides, and grinning, and yet with a certain haughty reserve. Oh yes, there was a certain salty *hauteur* about him which made the people trust him. And he spoke the vernacular so racily.

Hannele felt she would like to marry him. She would like to be near him. She would like him to write his history. She would like him to make her feel a queen in exile. No one had ever *quite* kissed her hand as he kissed it: with that sudden stillness and strange, chivalric abandon of himself. How he would abandon himself to her!—terribly—wonderfully—perhaps a little horribly. His wife, whom he had married late, had died after seven years of marriage. Hannele could under-stand that too. One or the other must die.

She became engaged. But something made her hesitate before marriage. Being in Austria was like being on a wrecked ship that *must* sink after a certain short length of time. And marrying the Herr Regierungsrat was like marrying the doomed captain of the doomed ship. The sense of fatality was part of the attraction.

And yet she hesitated. The summer weeks passed. The strangers flooded in and crowded the town, and ate up the food like locusts. People no longer counted the paper money, they weighed it by the kilogram. Peasants stored it in a corner of the meal-bin, and mice came and chewed holes in it. Nobody knew where the next lot of food was going to come from: yet it always came. And the lake teemed with bathers. When the captain arrived he looked with amazement on the crowds of strapping, powerful fellows who bathed all day long, magni-ficent blond flesh of men and women. No wonder the old

Romans stood in astonishment before the huge blond limbs of the savage Germans.

Well, the life was like a madness. The hotels charged fifteen-hundred kronen a day: the women, old and young, paraded in the peasant-costume, in flowery cotton dresses with gaudy, expensive silk aprons: the men wore the Tyrolese costume, bare knees and little short jackets. And for the men, the correct thing was to have the leathern hose and the blue linen jacket as old as possible. If you had a hole in your leathern seat, so much the better.

Everything so physical. Such magnificent naked limbs and naked bodies, and in the streets, in the hotels, everywhere, bare, white arms of women and bare, brown, powerful knees and thighs of men. The sense of flesh everywhere, and the endless ache of flesh. Even in the peasants who rowed across the lake, standing and rowing with a slow, heavy, gondolier motion at the once-curved oar, there was the same endless ache of physical yearning.

XIII

It was August when Alexander met Hannele. She was walking under a chintz parasol, wearing a dress of blue cotton with little red roses, and a red silk apron. She had no hat, her arms were bare and soft, and she had white stockings under her short dress. The Herr Regierungsrat was at her side, large, nimble, and laughing with a new witticism.

Alexander, in a light summer suit and Panama hat, was just coming out of the bank, shoving twenty thousand kronen into his pocket. He saw her coming across from the Amtsgericht, with the Herr Regierungsrat at her side, across the space of sunshine. She was laughing, and did not notice him.

She did not notice till he had taken off his hat and was saluting her. Then what she saw was the black, smooth, shining head, and she went pale. His black, smooth, close head—and all the blue Austrian day seemed to shrivel before her eyes.

"How do you do, Countess! I hoped I should meet you."

She heard his slow, sad-clanging, straying voice again, and she pressed her hand with the umbrella stick against her breast. She had forgotten it—forgotten his peculiar, slow voice. And now it seemed like a noise that sounds in the silence of night. Ah, how difficult it was, that suddenly the world could split under her eyes, and show this darkness inside. She wished he had not come.

She presented him to the Herr Regierungsrat, who was stiff and cold. She asked where the captain was staying. And then, not knowing what else to say, she said:

"Won't you come to tea?"

She was staying in a villa across the lake. Yes, he would come to tea.

He went. He hired a boat and a man to row him across. It was not far. There stood the villa, with its brown balconies one above the other, the bright red geraniums and white geraniums twinkling all round, the trees of purple clematis tumbling at one corner. All the green window-doors were open: but nobody about. In the little garden by the water's edge the rose-trees were tall and lank, drawn up by the dark green trees of the background. A white table with chairs and garden seats stood under the shadow of a big willow tree, and a hammock with cushions swung just behind. But no one in sight. There was a little landing bridge on to the garden: and a fairly large boat-house at the garden end.

The captain was not sure that the boat-house belonged to the villa. Voices were shouting and laughing from the water's surface, bathers swimming. A tall, naked youth with a little red cap on his head and a tiny red loin-cloth round his slender young hips was standing on the steps of the boat-house calling to the three women who were swimming near. The dark-haired woman with the white cap swum up to the steps and caught the boy by the ankle. He cried and laughed and remonstrated, and poked her in the breast with his foot.

"Nein, nein, Hardu!" she cried as he tickled her with his toe. "Hardu! Hardu! Hör' auf! Leave off!"—and she fell with a crash back into the water. The youth laughed a loud, deep laugh of a lad whose voice is newly broken.

"Was macht er denn?" cried a voice from the waters. "What is he doing?" It was a dark-skinned girl swimming swiftly, her big dark eyes watching amused from the water-surface.

"Jetzt, Hardu, hör' auf. Nein. Jetzt ruhig! Now leave off! Now be quiet." And the dark-haired woman was climbing out in the sunshine on to the pale, raw-wood steps of the boat-house, the water glistening on her dark-blue, stockinette, soft-moulded back and loins: while the boy, with his foot stretched out, was trying to push her back into the water. She clambered out, however, and sat on the steps in the sun, panting slightly. She was dark and attractive-looking, with a mature beautiful figure, and handsome, strong woman's legs.

In the garden appeared a black-and-white maidservant with a tray.

"Kaffee, gnädige Frau!"

The voice came so distinct over the water.

"Hannele! Hannele! Kaffee!" called the woman on the steps of the bathing-house.

"Tante Hannele! Kaffee!" called the dark-eyed girl, turning round in the water, then swimming for home.

"Kaffee! Kaffee!" roared the youth, in anticipation.

"Ja—a! Ich kom—mm," sang Hannele's voice from the water.

The dark-eyed girl, her hair tied up in a silk bandana, had reached the steps and was climbing out, a slim young fish in her close dark suit. The three stood clustered on the steps, the elder woman with one arm over the naked shoulders of the youth, the other arm over the shoulders of the girl. And all in chorus sang:

"Hannele! Hannele! Hannele! Wir warten auf dich."

The boatman had left off rowing, and the boat was drifting slowly in. The family became quiet, because of the intrusion. The attractive-looking woman turned and picked up her blue bath-robe, of a mid-blue colour that became her. She swung it round her as if it were an opera cloak. The youth stared at the boat.

The captain was watching Hannele. With a white kerchief tied round her silky, brownish hair, she was swimming home. He saw her white shoulders, and her white, wavering legs below in the clear water. Round the boat fishes were suddenly jumping.

The three on the steps beyond stood silent, watching the intruding boat with resentment. The boatman twisted his head round and watched them. The captain, who was facing them, watched Hannele. She swam slowly and easily up, caught the rail of the steps and stooping forward, climbed slowly out of the water. Her legs were large and flashing white and looked rich, the rich, white thighs with the blue veins behind, and the full, rich softness of her sloping loins.

"Ach! Schön! 's war schön! Das Wasser ist gut," her voice was heard, half singing as she took her breath. "It was lovely."

"Heiss," said the woman above. "Zu warm. Too warm."

The youth made way for Hannele, who drew herself erect at the top of the steps, looking round, panting a little, and putting up her hands to the knot of her kerchief on her head. Her legs were magnificent and white.

"Kuck die Leute die da bleiben," said the woman in the blue wrap, in a low voice. "Look at the people stopping there."

"Ja!" said Hannele negligently. Then she looked. She started as if in fear, looked round, as if to run away, looked back again, and met the eyes of the captain, who took off his hat.

She cried, in a loud frightened voice:

"Oh, but—I thought it was *to-morrow!*"

"No—to-day," came the quiet voice of the captain over the water.

"*To-day!* Are you *sure?*" she cried, calling to the boat.

"Quite sure. But we'll make it to-morrow if you like," he said.

"To-day! To-day!" she repeated in bewilderment. "No! Wait a minute." And she ran into the boat-house.

"Was ist es?" asked the dark woman, following her. "What is it?"

"A friend—a visitor—Captain Hepburn," came Hannele's voice.

The boatman now rowed slowly to the landing stage. The dark woman, huddled in her blue wrap as in an opera cloak, walked proudly and unconcernedly across the background of the garden, and up the steps to the first balcony. Hannele, her feet slip-slopping in loose slippers, clutching an old yellow wrap round her, came to the landing stage and shook hands.

"I am so sorry. It is so stupid of me. I was sure it was to-morrow," she said.

"No, it was to-day. But I wish for your sake it had been to-morrow," he replied.

"No. No. It doesn't matter. You won't mind waiting a minute, will you? You mustn't be angry with me for being so stupid."

So she went away, the heel-less slippers flipping up to her naked heels. Then the big-eyed, dusky girl stole into the house: and then the naked youth, who went with sang-froid. He would make a fine, handsome man: and he knew it.

XIV

Hepburn and Hannele were to make a small excursion to the glacier which stood there always in sight, coldly grinning in the sky. The weather had been very hot, but this morning there were loose clouds in the sky. The captain rowed over the lake soon after dawn. Hannele stepped into the little craft, and they pulled back to the town. There was a wind ruffling the water, so that the boat leaped and chuckled. The glacier, in a recess among the folded mountains, looked cold and angry. But morning was very sweet in the sky, and blowing very sweet with a faint scent of the second hay, from the low lands at the head of the lake. Beyond stood naked grey rock like a wall of mountains, pure rock, with faint thin slashes of snow.

Yesterday it had rained on the lake. The sun was going to appear from behind the Breitsteinhorn, the sky with its clouds floating in blue light and yellow radiance was lovely and cheering again. But dark clouds seemed to spout up from the Pinzgau valley. And once across the lake, all was shadow, when the water no longer gave back the sky-morning.

The day was a feast day, a holiday. Already so early three young men from the mountains were bathing near the steps of the Badeanstalt. Handsome, physical fellows, with good limbs rolling and swaying in the early morning water. They seemed to enjoy it too. But to Hepburn it was always as if a dark wing were stretched in the sky, over these mountains, like a doom. And these three young, lusty naked men swimming and rolling in the shadow.

Hepburn's was the first boat stirring. He made fast in the hotel boat-house, and he and Hannele went into the little town. It was deep in shadow, though the light of the sky, curdled with cloud, was bright overhead. But dark and chill and heavy lay the shadow in the black-and-white town, like a sediment.

The shops were all shut, but peasants from the hills were already strolling about, in their holiday dress: the men in their short leather trousers, like football drawers, and bare brown knees, and great boots: their little grey jackets faced with green, and their green hats with the proud chamois-brush behind. They seemed to stray about like lost souls, and the proud chamois-brush behind their hats, this proud, cocky, perking-up tail, like a mountain-buck with his tail up, was belied by the lost-soul look of the men, as they loitered about with their hands shoved in the front pockets of their trousers. Some women also were creeping about: peasant women, in the funny little black hats that had thick gold under the brim and long black streamers of ribbon, broad, black, water-wave ribbon starting from a bow under the brim behind, and streaming right to the bottom of the skirt. These women, in their thick, dark dresses with tight bodices, and massive, heavy, full skirts, and bright or dark aprons, strode about with the heavy stride of the mountain women, the heavy, quick,

forward-leaning motion. They were waiting for the town-day
to begin.

Hepburn had a knapsack on his back, with food for the day.
But bread was wanting. They found the door of the bakery
open, and got a loaf: a long, hot loaf of pure white bread,
beautiful sweet bread. It cost seventy kronen. To Hepburn
it was always a mystery where this exquisite bread came from,
in a lost land.

In the little square where the clock stood were bunches of
people, and a big motor-omnibus, and a motor-car that would
hold about eight people. Hepburn had paid his seven hundred
kronen for the two tickets. Hannele tied up her head in a thin
scarf, and put on her thick coat. She and Hepburn sat in
front by the peaked driver. And at seven o'clock away went
the car, swooping out of the town, past the handsome old
Tyrolese Schloss, or manor, black-and-white, with its little
black spires pricking up, past the station, and under the trees
by the lake-side. The road was not good, but they ran at a
great speed, out past the end of the lake, where the reeds
grew, out into the open valley-mouth, where the mountains
opened in two clefts. It was cold in the car. Hepburn buttoned
himself up to the throat and pulled his hat down on his ears.
Hannele's scarf fluttered. She sat without saying anything,
erect, her face fine and keen, watching ahead. From the deep
Pinzgau valley came the river roaring and raging, a glacier
river of pale, seething ice-water. Over went the car, over the
log bridge, darting towards the great slopes opposite. And
then a sudden immense turn, a swerve under the height of the
mountain-side, and again a darting lurch forward, under the
pear-trees of the high-road, past the big old ruined castle that
so magnificently watched the valley mouth, and the foaming
river; on, rushing under the huge roofs of the balconied peasant
houses of a village, then swinging again to take another valley
mouth, there where a little village clustered all black and white
on a knoll, with a white church that had a black steeple, and
a white castle with black spines, and clustering, ample black-
and-white houses of the Tyrol. There is a grandeur even in

the peasant houses, with their great wide passage halls where the swallows build, and where one could build a whole English cottage.

So the motor-car darted up this new, narrow, wilder, more sinister valley. A herd of almost wild young horses, handsome reddish things, burst around the car, and one great mare with full flanks went crashing up the road ahead, her heels flashing to the car, while her foal whinneyed and screamed from behind. But no, she could not turn from the road. On and on she crashed, forging ahead, the car behind her. And then at last she did swerve aside, among the thin alder trees by the wild river-bed.

"If it isn't a cow, it's a horse," said the driver, who was thin and weaselish and silent, with his ear-flaps over his ears.

But the great mare had shaken herself in a wild swerve, and screaming and whinneying was plunging back to her foal. Hannele had been frightened.

The car rushed on, through water-meadows, along a naked, white bit of mountain road. Ahead was a darkness of mountain front and pine trees. To the right was the stony, furious, lion-like river, tawny-coloured here, and the slope up beyond. But the road for the moment was swinging fairly level through the stunned water-meadows of the savage valley. There were gates to open, and Hepburn jumped down to open them, as if he were the foot-boy. The heavy Jews of the wrong sort, seated behind, of course did not stir.

At a house on a knoll the driver sounded his horn, and out rushed children crying "Papa! Papa!"—then a woman with a basket. A few brief words from the weaselish man, who smiled with warm, manly blue eyes at his children, then the car leaped forward. The whole bearing of the man was so different when he was looking at his own family. He could not even say thank-you when Hepburn opened the gates. He hated and even despised his human cargo of middle-class people. Deep, deep is class-hatred, and it begins to swallow all human feeling in its abyss. So, stiff, silent, thin, capable, and neuter towards his fares, sat the little driver with the flaps over his ears, and his thin nose cold.

The car swept round, suddenly, into the trees: and into the ravine. The river shouted at the bottom of a gulf. Bristling pine-trees stood around. The air was black and cold and forever sunless. The motor-car rushed on, in this blackness, under the rock-walls and the fir-trees.

Then it suddenly stopped. There was a huge motor-omnibus ahead, drab and enormous-looking. Tourists and trippers of last night coming back from the glacier. It stood like a great rock. And the smaller motor-car edged past, tilting into the rock-gutter under the face of stone.

So, after a while of this valley of the shadow of death, lurching in steep loops upwards, the motor-car scrambling wonderfully, struggling past trees and rock upwards, at last they came to the end. It was a huge inn or tourist-hotel of brown wood: and here the road ended in a little wide bay surrounded and overhung by trees. Beyond was a garage and a bridge over a roaring river: and always the overhung darkness of trees and the intolerable steep slopes immediately above.

Hannele left her big coat. The sky looked blue above the gloom. They set out across the hollow-sounding bridge, over the everlasting mad rush of ice-water, to the immediate up-slope of the path, under dark trees. But a little old man in a sort of sentry-box wanted fifty or sixty kronen: apparently for the upkeep of the road, a sort of toll.

The other tourists were coming—some stopping to have a drink first. The second omnibus had not yet arrived. Hannele and Hepburn were the first two, treading slowly up that dark path, under the trees. The grasses hanging on the rock face were still dewy. There were a few wild raspberries, and a tiny tuft of bilberries with black berries here and there, and a few tufts of unripe cranberries. The many hundreds of tourists who passed up and down did not leave much to pick. Some mountain hare-bells, like bells of blue water, hung coldly glistening in their darkness. Sometimes the hairy mountain-bell, pale-blue and bristling, stood alone, curving his head right down, stiff and taut. There was an occasional yig, moist, lolling daisy.

So the two climbed slowly up the steep ledge of a road. This valley was just a mountain cleft, cleft sheer in the hard, living rock, with black trees like hair flourishing in this secret, naked place of the earth. At the bottom of the open wedge forever roared the rampant, insatiable water. The sky from above was like a sharp wedge forcing its way into the earth's cleavage, and that eternal ferocious water was like the steel edge of the wedge, the terrible tip biting it into the rocks' intensity. Who could have thought that the soft sky of light, and the soft foam of water could thrust and penetrate into the dark, strong earth? But so it was. Hannele and Hepburn, toiling up the steep little ledge of a road that hung half-way down the gulf, looked back, time after time, back down upon the brown timbers and shingle roofs of the hotel, that now, away below, looked damp and wedged in like boulders. Then back at the next tourists struggling up. Then down at the water, that rushed like a beast of prey. And then, as they rose higher, they looked up also, at the livid great sides of rock, livid bare rock that sloped from the sky-ridge in a hideous sheer swerve downwards.

In his heart of hearts Hepburn hated it. He hated it, he loathed it, it seemed almost obscene, this livid, naked slide of rock, unthinkably huge and massive, sliding down to this gulf where bushes grew like hair in the darkness, and water roared. Above, there were thin slashes of snow.

So the two climbed slowly on, up the eternal side of that valley, sweating with the exertion. Sometimes the sun, now risen high, shone full on their side of the gulley. Tourists were trickling downhill too: two maidens with bare arms and bare heads and huge boots: men tourists with great knapsacks and edelweiss in their hats: giving Bergheil for a greeting. But the captain said Good-day. He refused this Bergheil business. People swarming touristy on these horrible mountains made him feel almost sick.

He and Hannele also were not in good company together. There was a sort of silent hostility between them. She hated the effort of climbing; but the high air, the cold in the air,

M

the savage cat-howling sound of the water, those awful flanks of livid rock, all this thrilled and excited her to another sort of savageness. And he, dark, rather slender and feline, with something of the physical suavity of a delicate-footed race, he hated beating his way up the rock, he hated the sound of the water, it frightened him, and the high air bit him in his chest, like a viper.

"Wonderful! Wonderful!" she cried, taking great breaths in her splendid chest.

"Yes. And horrible. Detestable," he said.

She turned with a flash, and the high strident sound of the mountain in her voice.

"If you don't like it," she said, rather jeering, "why ever did you come?"

"I had to try," he said.

"And if you don't like it," she said, "why should you try to spoil it for me?"

"I hate it," he answered.

They were climbing more into the height, more into the light, into the open, in the full sun. The valley-cleft was sinking below them. Opposite was only the sheer livid slide of the naked rock, tipping from the pure sky. At a certain angle they could see away beyond, the lake lying far off and small, the wall of those other rocks like a curtain of stone, dim and diminished to the horizon. And the sky with curdling clouds and blue sunshine intermittent.

"Wonderful, wonderful, to be high up," she said, breathing great breaths.

"Yes," he said. "It *is* wonderful. But very detestable. I want to live near the sea-level. I am no mountain-topper."

"Evidently not," she said.

"Bergheil!" cried a youth with bare arms and bare chest, bare head, terrific fanged boots, a knapsack and an alpenstock, and all the bronzed wind and sun of the mountain snow in his skin and his faintly bleached hair. With his great heavy knapsack, his rumpled thick stockings, his ghastly fanged boots, Hepburn found him repulsive.

"Guten Tag," he answered coldly.

"Grüss Gott," said Hannele.

And the young Tannhäuser, the young Siegfried, this young Balder beautiful strode climbing down the rocks, marching and swinging with his alpenstock. And immediately after the youth came a maiden, with hair on the wind and her shirt-breast open, striding in corduroy breeches, rumpled worsted stockings, thick boots, a knapsack, and an alpenstock. She passed without greeting. And our pair stopped in angry silence and watched her dropping down the mountain-side.

xv

Ah, well, everything comes to an end, even the longest up-climb. So, after much sweat and effort and crossness, Hepburn and Hannele emerged on to the rounded bluff where the road wound out of that hideous great valley-cleft, into upper regions. So they emerged more on the level, out of the trees as out of something horrible, on to a naked, great bank of rock and grass.

"Thank the Lord!" said Hannele.

So they trudged on round the bluff, and then in front of them saw what is always, always wonderful, one of those shallow upper valleys, naked, where the first waters are rocked. A flat, shallow, utterly desolate valley, wide as a wide bowl under the sky, with rock slopes and grey stone-slides and precipices all around, and the zigzag of snow-stripes and ice-roots descending, and then rivers, streams and rivers rushing from many points downwards, down out of the ice-roots and the snow-dagger points, waters rushing in newly-liberated frenzy downwards, down in waterfalls and cascades and threads, down into the wide, shallow bed of the valley, strewn with rocks and stones innumerable, and not a tree, not a visible bush.

Only, of course, two hotels or restaurant places. But these no more than low, sprawling, peasant-looking places lost among the stones, with stones on their roofs so that they seemed just a part of the valley bed. There was the valley, dotted with rock and rolled-down stone, and these two house-places, and woven with innumerable new waters, and one hoarse stone-tracked river in the desert, and the thin road-track winding along the desolate flat, past first one house, then the other, over one stream, then another, on to the far rock-face above which the glacier seemed to loll like some awful great tongue put out.

"Ah, it is wonderful!" he said, as if to himself.

And she looked quickly at his face, saw the queer, blank, sphinx-look with which he gazed out beyond himself. His eyes were black and set, and he seemed so motionless, as if he were eternal, facing these upper facts.

She thrilled with triumph. She felt he was overcome.

"It *is* wonderful," she said.

"Wonderful. And for ever wonderful," he said.

"Ah, in *winter* ——" she cried.

His face changed, and he looked at her.

"In winter you couldn't get up here," he said.

They went on. Up the slopes cattle were feeding: came that isolated tong-tong-tong of cowbells, dropping like the slow clink of ice on the arrested air. The sound always woke in him a primeval, almost hopeless melancholy. Always made him feel *navré*. He looked round. There was no tree, no bush, only great grey rocks and pale boulders scattered in place of trees and bushes. But yes, clinging on one side like a dark close beard were the alpenrose shrubs.

"In May," he said, "that side there must be all pink with alpenroses."

"I *must* come. I *must* come!" she cried.

There were tourists dotted along the road: and two tiny low carts drawn by silky, long-eared mules. These carts went right down to meet the motor-cars, and to bring up provisions for the Glacier Hotel: for there was still another big hotel ahead. Hepburn was happy in that upper valley, that first rocking cradle of early water. He liked to see the great fangs and slashes of ice and snow thrust down into the rock, as if the ice had bitten into the flesh of the earth. And from the fang-tips the hoarse water crying its birth-cry, rushing down.

By the turfy road and under the rocks were many flowers: wonderful hare-bells, big and cold and dark, almost black, and seeming like purple-dark ice: then little tufts of tiny pale-blue bells, as if some fairy frog had been blowing spume-bubbles out of the ice: then the bishop's-crozier of the stiff, bigger, hairy mountain-bell: then many stars of pale-lavender gentian, touched with earth-colour: and then monkshood, yellow, primrose yellow monkshood and sudden places full of dark monkshood. That dark-blue, black-blue, terrible colour of the strange rich monkshood made Hepburn look and look and look again. How did the ice come by that lustrous blue-purple intense darkness? And by that royal poison—that laughing-snake gorgeousness of much monkshood?

XVI

By one of the loud streams, under a rock in the sun, with scented minty or thyme flowers near, they sat down to eat some lunch. It was about eleven o'clock. A thin bee went in and out the scented flowers and the eyebright. The water poured with all the lust and greed of unloosed water over the stones. He took a cupful for our Hannele, bright and icy, and she mixed it with the red Hungarian wine.

Down the road strayed the tourists like pilgrims, and at the closed end of the valley they could be seen, quite tiny, climbing the cut-out road that went up like a stair-way. Just by their movement you perceived them. But on the valley-bed they went like rolling stones, little as stones. A very elegant mule came stepping by, following a middle-aged woman in tweeds and a tall, high-browed man in knickerbockers. The mule was drawing a very amusing little cart, a chair, rather like a round office-chair upholstered in red velvet, and mounted on two wheels. The red velvet had gone gold and orange and like fruit-juice, being old: really a lovely colour. And the muleteer, a little shabby creature, waddled beside excitedly.

"Ach," cried Hannele, "that looks almost like before the war: almost as peaceful."

"Except that the chair is too shabby, and that they all feel exceptional," he remarked.

There in that upper valley, there was no sense of peace. The rush of the waters seemed like weapons, and the tourists all seemed in a sort of frenzy, in a frenzy to be happy, or to be thrilled. It was a feeling that desolated the heart.

The two sat in the changing sunshine under their rock, with the mountain flowers scenting the snow-bitter air, and they ate their eggs and sausage and cheese, and drank the bright-red Hungarian wine. It seemed lovely: almost like before the war: almost the same feeling of eternal holiday, as if the world was made for man's everlasting holiday. But not quite. Never again quite the same. The world is not made for man's everlasting holiday.

As Alexander was putting the bread back into his shoulder-sack, he exclaimed:

"Oh, look here!"

She looked, and saw him drawing out a flat package wrapped in paper: evidently a picture.

"A picture!" she cried.

He unwrapped the thing, and handed it to her. It was Theodor Worpswede's Still-leben: not very large, painted on a board.

Hannele looked at it, and went pale.

"It's *good*," she cried, in an equivocal tone.

"Quite good," he said.

"Especially the poached egg," she said.

"Yes, the poached egg is almost living."

"But where did you find it?"

"Oh, I found it in the artist's studio." And he told her how he had traced her.

"How extraordinary!" she cried. "But why did you buy it?"

"I don't quite know."

"Did you *like* it?"

"No, not quite that."

"You could *never* hang it up."

"No, never," he said.

"But do you think it is good as a work of art?"

"I think it is quite clever as a painting. I don't like the spirit of it, of course. I'm too catholic for that."

"No. No," she faltered. "It's rather horrid really. That's why I wonder why you bought it."

"Perhaps to prevent any one else's buying it," he said.

"Do you mind very much then," she asked.

"No, I don't mind very much. I didn't quite like it that you sold the doll," he said.

"I needed the money," she said quietly.

"Oh, quite."

There was a pause for some moments.

"I felt you'd sold *me*," she said, quiet and savage.

"When?"

"When your wife appeared. And when you *disappeared*."

Again there was a pause: his pause this time.

"I did write to you," he said.

"When?"

"Oh—March, I believe."

"Oh, yes. I had that letter." Her tone was just as quiet, and even savager.

So there was a pause that belonged to both of them. Then she rose.

"I want to be going," she said. "We shall never get to the glacier at this rate."

He packed up the picture, slung on his knapsack, and they set off. She stooped now and then to pick the starry, earth-lavender gentians from the road-side. As they passed the second of the valley hotels, they saw the man and wife sitting at a little table outside eating bread and cheese, while the mule-chair with its red velvet waited aside on the grass. They passed a whole grove of black-purple nightshade on the left, and some long, low cattle-huts which, with the stones on their roofs, looked as if they had grown up as stones grow in such places through the grass. In the wild, desert place some black pigs were snouting.

So they wound into the head of the valley, and saw the steep face ahead, and high up, like vapour or foam dripping from the fangs of a beast, waterfalls vapouring down from the deep fangs of ice. And there was one end of the glacier, like a great bluey-white fur just slipping over the slope of the rock.

As the valley closed in again the flowers were very lovely, especially the big, dark, icy bells, like hare-bells, that would sway so easily, but which hung dark and with that terrible motionlessness of upper mountain flowers. And the road turned to get on to the long slant in the cliff-face, where it climbed like a stair. Slowly, slowly the two climbed up. Now again they saw the valley below, behind. The mule-chair was coming, hastening, the lady seated tight facing backwards, as the chair faced, and wrapped in rugs. The tall, fair, middle-aged husband in knickerbockers strode just behind, bare-headed.

Alexander and Hannele climbed slowly, slowly up the slant, under the dripping rock-face where the white and veined flowers of the grass of Parnassus still rose straight and chilly in the shadow, like water which had taken on itself white flower-flesh. Above they saw the slipping edge of the glacier, like a terrible great paw, bluey. And from the skyline dark grey clouds were fuming up, fuming up as if breathed black and icily out from some ice-cauldron.

"It is going to rain," said Alexander.

"Not much," said Hannele shortly.

"I hope not," said he.

And still she would not hurry up that steep slant, but insisted on standing to look. So the dark, ice-black clouds fumed solid, and the rain began to fly on a cold wind. The mule-chair hastened past, the lady sitting comfortably with her back to the mule, a little pheasant-trimming in her tweed hat, while her Tannhäuser husband reached for his dark, cape-frilled mantle.

Alexander had his dust-coat, but Hannele had nothing but a light knitted jersey-coat, such as women wear indoors. Over the hollow crest above came the cold, steel rain. They pushed on up the slope. From behind came another mule, and a little old man hurrying, and a little cart like a hand-barrow, on which were hampers with cabbage and carrots and peas and joints of meat, for the hotel above.

"Wird es viel sein?" asked Alexander of the little gnome. "Will it be much?"

"Was meint der Herr?" replied the other. "What does the gentleman say?"

"Der Regen, wird es lang dauern? Will the rain last long?"

"Nein. Nein. Dies ist kein langer Regen."

So, with his mule which had to stand exactly at that spot to make droppings, the little man resumed his way, and Hannele and Alexander were the last on the slope. The air smelt steel-cold of rain, and of hot mule-droppings. Alexander watched the rain beat on the shoulders and on the blue skirt of Hannele.

"It is a pity you left your big coat down below," he said.

"What good is it saying so now!" she replied, pale at the nose with anger.

"Quite," he said, as his eyes glowed and his brow blackened. "What good suggesting anything at any time, apparently!"

She turned round on him in the rain, as they stood perched nearly at the summit of that slanting cliff-climb, with a glacier-paw hung almost invisible above, and waters gloating aloud in the gulf below.

She faced him, and he faced her.

"What have you ever suggested to me?" she said, her face naked as the rain itself with an ice-bitter fury. "What have you ever suggested to me?"

"When have you ever been open to suggestion?" he said, his face dark and his eyes curiously glowing.

"I? I? Ha! Haven't I waited for you to suggest something? And all you can do is to come here with a picture to reproach me for having sold your doll. Ha! I'm glad I sold it.

A foolish barren effigy it was too, a foolish staring thing. What should I do but sell it. Why should I keep it, do you imagine?"

"Why do you come here with me to-day, then?"

"Why do I come here with you to-day?" she replied. "I come to see the mountains, which are wonderful, and give me strength. And I come to see the glacier. Do you think I come here to see *you*? Why should I? You are always in some hotel or other away below."

"You came to see the glacier and the mountains *with* me," he replied.

"Did I? Then I made a mistake. You can do nothing but find fault even with God's mountains."

A dark flame suddenly went over his face.

"Yes," he said, "I hate them, I hate them. I hate their snow and their affectations."

"*Affectation!*" she laughed. "Oh! Even the mountains are affected for you, are they?"

"Yes," he said. "Their loftiness and their uplift. I hate their uplift. I hate people prancing on mountain-tops and feeling exalted. I'd like to make them all stop up there, on their mountain-tops, and chew ice to fill their stomachs. I wouldn't let them down again, I wouldn't. I hate it all, I tell you; I hate it."

She looked in wonder on his dark, glowing, ineffectual face. It seemed to her like a dark flame burning in the daylight and in the ice-rains: very ineffectual and unnecessary.

"You must be a little mad," she said superbly, "to talk like that about the mountains. They are much bigger than you."

"No," he said. "No! They are not."

"What!" she laughed aloud. "The mountains are not bigger than you? But you are extraordinary."

"They are not bigger than me," he cried. "Any more than you are bigger than me if you stand on a ladder. They are not bigger than me. They are less than me."

"Oh! Oh!" she cried in wonder and ridicule. "The mountains are less than you."

"Yes," he cried, "they are less."

He seemed suddenly to go silent and remote as she watched him. The speech had gone out of his face again, he seemed to be standing a long way off from her, beyond some border-line. And in the midst of her indignant amazement she watched him with wonder and a touch of fascination. To what country did he belong then—to what dark, different atmosphere?

"You must suffer from megalomania," she said. And she said what she felt.

But he only looked at her out of dark, dangerous, haughty eyes.

They went on their way in the rain in silence. He was filled with a passionate silence and imperiousness, a curious, dark, masterful force that supplanted thought in him. And she, who always pondered, went pondering: "Is he mad? What does he mean? Is he a madman? He wants to bully me. He wants to bully me into something. What does he want to bully me into? Does he want me to love him?"

At this final question she rested. She decided that what he wanted was that she should love him. And this thought flattered her vanity and her pride and appeased her wrath against him. She felt quite mollified towards him.

But what a way he went about it! He wanted her to love him. Of this she was sure. He had always wanted her to love him, even from the first. Only he had not made up his *mind* about it. He had not made up his mind. After his wife had died he had gone away to make up his mind. Now he had made it up. He wanted her to love him. And he was offended, mortally offended because she had sold his doll.

So, this was the conclusion to which Hannele came. And it pleased her, and it flattered her. And it made her feel quite warm towards him, as they walked in the rain. The rain, by the way, was abating. The spume over the hollow crest to which they were approaching was thinning considerably. They could again see the glacier-paw hanging out, a little beyond. The rain was going to pass. And they were not far now from the hotel, and the third level of Lammerboden.

He wanted her to love him. She felt again quite glowing and triumphant inside herself, and did not care a bit about the rain on her shoulders. He wanted her to love him. Yes, that was how she had to put it. He didn't want to *love* her. No. He wanted *her* to love *him*.

But then, of course, woman-like, she took his love for granted. So many men had been so very ready to love her. And this one—to her amazement, to her indignation, and rather to her secret satisfaction—just blackly insisted that *she* must love *him*. Very well—she would give him a run for his money. That was it: he blackly insisted that *she* must love *him*. What he felt was not to be considered. *She* must love *him*. And be bullied into it. That was what it amounted to. In his silent, black, overbearing soul, he wanted to compel her, he wanted to have power over her. He wanted to make her love him so that he had power over her. He wanted to bully her, physically, sexually, and from the inside.

And she! Well, she was just as confident that she was not going to be bullied. She would love him: probably she would: most probably she did already. But she was not going to be bullied by him in any way whatsoever. No, he must go down on his knees to her if he wanted her love. And then she would love him. Because she *did* love him. But a dark-eyed little master and bully she would never have.

And this was her triumphant conclusion. Meanwhile the rain had almost ceased, they had almost reached the rim of the upper level, towards which they were climbing, and he was walking in that silent diffidence which made her watch him because she was not sure what he was feeling, what he was thinking, or even what he was. He was a puzzle to her: eternally incomprehensible in his feelings and even his sayings. There seemed to her no logic and no reason in what he felt and said. She could never tell what his next mood would come out of. And this made her uneasy, made her watch him. And at the same time it piqued her attention. He had some of the fascination of the incomprehensible. And his curious inscrutable face—it wasn't really only a meaningless mask, because she had seen it half an hour ago melt with a quite incomprehensible and rather, to her mind, foolish passion. Strange, black, inconsequential passion. Asserting with that curious dark ferocity that he was bigger than the mountains. Madness! Madness! Megalomania.

But because he gave himself away, she forgave him and even liked him. And the strange passion of his, that gave out incomprehensible flashes, *was* rather fascinating to her. She felt just a tiny bit sorry for him. But she wasn't going to be bullied by him. She wasn't going to give in to him and his black passion. No, never. It must be love on equal terms, or nothing. For love on equal terms she was quite ready. She only waited for him to offer it.

XVII

In the hotel was a buzz of tourists. Alexander and Hannele sat in the restaurant drinking hot coffee and milk, and watching the maidens in cotton frocks and aprons and bare arms, and the fair youths with maidenly necks and huge voracious boots, and the many Jews of the wrong sort and the wrong shape. These Jews were all being very Austrian, in Tyrol costume that didn't sit on them, assuming the whole gesture and intonation of aristocratic Austria, so that you might think they *were* Austrian aristocrats, if you weren't properly listening, or if you didn't look twice. Certainly they were lords of the Alps, or at least lords of the Alpine hotels this summer, let prejudice be what it might. Jews of the wrong sort. And yet even they imparted a wholesome breath of sanity, disillusion, unsentimentality to the excited "Bergheil" atmosphere. Their dark-eyed, sardonic presence seemed to say to the maidenly-necked mountain youths: "Don't sprout wings of the spirit too much, my dears."

The rain had ceased. There was a wisp of sunshine from a grey sky. Alexander left the knapsack, and the two went out into the air. Before them lay the last level of the up-climb, the Lammerboden. It was a rather gruesome hollow between the peaks, a last shallow valley about a mile long. At the end the enormous static stream of the glacier poured in from the blunt mountain-top of ice. The ice was dull, sullen-coloured, melted on the surface by the very hot summer: and so it seemed a huge, arrested, sodden flood, ending in a wave-wall of stone-speckled ice upon the valley bed of rocky débris. A gruesome descent of stone and blocks of rock, the little valley bed, with a river raving through. On the left rose the grey rock, but the glacier was there, sending down great paws of ice. It was like some great, deep-furred ice-bear lying spread upon the top heights, and reaching down terrible paws of ice into the valley: like some immense sky-bear fishing in the earth's solid hollows from above. Hepburn it just filled with terror. Hannele too it scared, but it gave her a sense of ecstasy. Some of the immense, furrowed, paws of ice held down between the rock were vivid blue in colour, but of a frightening, poisonous blue, like crystal copper-sulphate. Most of the ice was a sullen, semi-translucent greeny grey.

The two set off to walk through the massy, desolate stone-bed, under rocks and over waters, to the main glacier. The flowers were even more beautiful on this last reach. Particularly the dark harebells were large and almost black and ice-metallic: one could imagine they gave a dull ice-chink. And the grass of Parnassus stood erect, white-veined big cups held terribly naked and open to their ice-air.

From behind the great blunt summit of ice that blocked the distance at the end of the valley, a pale-grey, woolly mist or cloud was fusing up, exhaling huge, like some grey-dead aura into the sky, and covering the top of the glacier. All the way along the valley people were threading, strangely insignificant, among the grey dishevel of stone and rock, like insects. Hannele and Alexander went ahead quickly, along the tiring track.

"Are you glad now that you came?" she said, looking at him triumphant.

"Very glad I came," he said. His eyes were dilated with excitement that was ordeal or mystic battle rather than the

Bergheil ecstasy. The curious vibration of his excitement made the scene strange, rather horrible, to her. She too shuddered. But it still seemed to her to hold the key to all glamour and ecstasy, the great silent, living glacier. It seemed to her like a grand beast.

As they came near they saw the wall of ice: the glacier end, thick crusted and speckled with stone and dirt débris. From underneath, secret in stones, water rushed out. When they came quite near, they saw the great monster was sweating all over, trickles and rivulets of sweat running down his sides of pure, slush-translucent ice. There it was, the glacier, ending abruptly in the wall of ice under which they stood. Near to, the ice was pure, but waterlogged, all the surface rather rotten from the hot summer. It was sullenly translucent, and of a watery, darkish bluey-green colour. But near the earth it became again bright coloured, gleams of green like jade, gleams of blue like thin, pale sapphire, in little caverns above the wet stones where the walls trickled forever.

Alexander wanted to climb on to the glacier. It was his one desire—to stand upon it. So under the pellucid wet wall they toiled among rocks upwards, to where the guide-track mounted the ice. Several other people were before them—mere day-tourists—and all uncertain about venturing any further. For the ice-slope rose steep and slithery, pure, sun-locked, sweating ice. Still, it was like a curved back. One could scramble on to it, and on up to the first level, like the flat on top of some huge paw.

There stood the little cluster of people, facing the uphill of sullen, pure, sodden-looking ice. They were all afraid: naturally. But being human, they all wanted to go beyond their fear. It was strange that the ice looked so pure, like flesh. Not bright, because the surface was soft like a soft, deep epidermis. But pure ice away down to immense depths.

Alexander, after some hesitation, began gingerly to try the ice. He was frightened of it. And he had no stick, and only smooth-soled boots. But he had a great desire to stand on the glacier. So, gingerly and shakily, he began to struggle a few steps up the pure slope. The ice was soft on the surface, he could kick his heel in it and get a little sideways grip. So, staggering and going sideways he got up a few yards, and was on the naked ice-slope.

Immediately the youths and the fat man below began to tackle it too: also two maidens. For some time, however, Alexander gingerly and scramblingly led the way. The slope of ice was steeper, and rounded, so that it was difficult to stand up in any way. Sometimes he slipped, and was clinging with burnt finger-ends to the soft ice-mass. Then he tried throwing his coat down, and getting a foothold on that. Then he went quite quickly by bending down and getting a little grip with his fingers, and going ridiculously as on four legs.

Hannele watched from below, and saw the ridiculous exhibition, and was frightened and amused, but more frightened. And she kept calling, to the grey joy of the Austrians down below:

"Come back. Do come back."

But when he got on to his feet again he only waved his hand at her, half crossly, as she stood away down there in her blue frock. The other fellows with sticks and nail-boots had now taken heart and were scrambling like crabs past our hero, doing better than he.

He had come to a rift in the ice. He sat near the edge and looked down. Clean, pure ice, fused with pale colour, and fused into intense copper-sulphate blue away down in the crack. It was not like crystal, but fused as one fuses a borax bead under a blow-flame. And keenly, wickedly blue in the depths of the crack.

He looked upwards. He had not half mounted the slope. So on he went, upon the huge body of the soft-fleshed ice, slanting his way sometimes on all fours, sometimes using his coat, usually hitting-in with the side of his heel. Hannele down below was crying him to come back. But two other youths were now almost level with him.

So he struggled on till he was more or less over the brim. There he stood and looked at the ice. It came down from above in a great hollow world of ice. A world, a terrible place of hills and valleys and slopes, all motionless, all of ice. Away above the grey mist-cloud was looming bigger. And near at hand were long huge cracks, side by side, like gills in the ice. It would seem as if the ice breathed through these great ridged gills. One could look down into the series of gulfs, fearful depths, and the colour burning that acid, intense blue, intenser as the crack went deeper. And the crests of the open gills ridged and grouped pale blue above the crevices. It seemed as if the ice breathed there.

The wonder, the terror, and the bitterness of it. Never a warm leaf to unfold, never a gesture of life to give off. A world sufficient unto itself in lifelessness, all this ice.

He turned to go down, though the youths were passing beyond him. And seeing the naked translucent ice heaving downwards in a vicious curve, always the same dark translucency underfoot, he was afraid. If he slipped, he would certainly slither the whole way down, and break some of his bones. Even when he sat down, he had to cling with his finger-nails in the ice, because if he had started to slide he would have slid the whole way down on his trouser-seat, precipitously, and have landed heaven knows how.

Hannele was watching from below. And he was frightened, perched seated on the shoulder of ice and not knowing how to get off. Above he saw the great blue gills of ice ridging the air. Down below were two blue cracks—then the last wet level claws of ice upon the stones. And there stood Hannele and the three or four people who had got so far.

However, he found that by striking in his heels sideways with sufficient sharpness he could keep his footing, no matter how steep the slope. So he started to jerk his way zigzag downwards.

As he descended, arrived a guide with a black beard and all the paraphernalia of ropes and pole and bristling boots. He and his gentleman began to strike their way up the ice. With those bristling nails like teeth in one's boots, it was quite easy: and a pole to press on to.

Hannele, who had got sick of waiting, and who was also frightened, had gone scuttling on the return journey. He hurried after her, thankful to be off the ice, but excited and gratified. Looking round, he saw the guide and the man on the ice watching the ice-world and the weather. Then they too turned to come down. The day wasn't safe.

XVIII

Pondering, rather thrilled, they threaded their way through the desert of rock and rushing water back to the hotel. The sun was shining warmly for a moment, and he felt happy, though his finger-ends were bleeding a little from the ice.

"But one day," said Hannele, "I should love to go with a guide right up, high, right into the glacier."

"No," said he. "I've been far enough. I prefer the world where cabbages will grow on the soil. Nothing grows on glaciers."

"They say there are glacier-fleas, which only live on glaciers," she said.

"Well, to me the ice didn't look good to eat, even for a flea."

"You never know," she laughed. "But you're glad you've been, aren't you?"

"Very glad. Now I need never go again."

"But you *did* think it wonderful?"

"Marvellous. And awful, to my mind."

XIX

They ate venison and spinach in the hotel, then set off down again. Both felt happier. She gathered some flowers, and put them in her handkerchief so they should not die. And again they sat by the stream, to drink a little wine.

But the fume of cloud was blowing up again, thick from behind the glacier. Hannele was uneasy. She wanted to get down. So they went fairly quickly. Many other tourists were hurrying downwards also. The rain began—a sharp handful of drops flung from beyond the glacier. So Hannele and he did not stay to rest, but dropped easily down the steep, dark valley towards the motor-car terminus.

There they had tea, rather tired but comfortably so. The big hotel restaurant was hideous, and seemed sordid. So in the gloom of a grey, early twilight they went out again and sat on a seat, watching the tourists and the trippers and the motor-car men. There were three Jews from Vienna: and the girl had a huge white woolly dog, as big as a calf, and white and woolly and silky and amiable as a toy. The men, of course, came patting it and admiring it, just as men always do, in life and in novels. And the girl, holding the leash, posed and leaned backwards in the attitude of heroines on novel-covers. She said the white cool monster was a Siberian steppe-dog. Alexander wondered what the steppes made of such a wuffer. And the three Jews pretended they were elegant Austrians out of popular romances.

"Do you think," said Alexander, "you will marry the Herr Regierungsrat?"

She looked round, making wide eyes.

"It looks like it, doesn't it!" she said.

"Quite," he said.

Hannele watched the woolly white dog. So of course it came wagging its ever-amiable hindquarters towards her. She looked at it still, but did not touch it.

"What makes you ask such a question?" she said.

"I can't say. But even so you haven't really answered. Do you really fully intend to marry the Herr Regierungsrat? Is that your final intention at this moment?"

She looked at him again.

"But before I answer," she said, "oughtn't I to know why you ask?"

"Probably you know already," he said.

"I assure you I don't."

He was silent for some moments. The huge, woolly dog

stood in front of him and breathed enticingly, with its tongue out. He only looked at it blankly.

"Well," he said, "if you were not going to marry the Herr Regierungsrat, I should suggest that you marry me."

She stared away at the auto-garage, a very faint look of amusement, or pleasure, or ridicule on her face: or all three. And a certain shyness.

"But why?" she said.

"Why what?" he returned.

"Why should you suggest that I should marry you?"

"*Why?*" he replied, in his lingering tones. "*Why?* Well, for what purpose does a man usually ask a woman to marry him?"

"For what *purpose!*" she repeated, rather haughtily.

"For what reason, then!" he corrected.

She was silent for some moments. Her face was closed and a little numb-looking, her hands lay very still in her lap. She looked away from him, across the road.

"There is usually only one reason," she replied, in a rather small voice.

"Yes?" he replied curiously. "What would you say that was?"

She hesitated. Then she said, rather stiffly:

"Because he really loved her, I suppose. That seems to me the only excuse for a man asking a woman to marry him."

Followed a dead silence, which she did not intend to break. He knew he would have to answer, and for some reason he didn't want to say what was obviously the thing to say.

"Leaving aside the question of whether you love me or I love you——" he began.

"I certainly *won't* leave it aside," she said.

"And I certainly won't consider it," he said, just as obstinately.

She turned now and looked full at him, with amazement, ridicule, and anger in her face.

"I really think you must be mad," she said.

"I doubt if you do think that," he replied. "It is only a

method of retaliation, that is. I think you understand my point very clearly."

"Your point!" she cried. "Your point! Oh, so you have a point in all this palavering?"

"Quite!" said he.

She was silent with indignation for some time. Then she said angrily:

"I assure you I do *not* see your point. I don't see any point at all. I see only impertinence."

"Very good," he replied. "The point is whether we marry on a basis of love."

"Indeed! Marry! We, marry! I don't think that is by any means the point."

He took his knapsack from under the seat, between his feet. And from the knapsack he took the famous picture.

"When," he said, "we were supposed to be in love with one another, you made that doll of me, didn't you?" And he sat looking at the odious picture.

"I never for one moment deluded myself that you *really* loved me," she said bitterly.

"Take the other point, whether *you* loved *me*, or not," said he.

"How could I love you, when I couldn't believe in your love for me?" she cried.

He put the picture down between his knees again.

"All this about love," he said, "is very confusing, and very complicated."

"Very! In *your* case. Love to me is simple enough," she said.

"Is it? Is it? And was it simple love which made you make that doll of me?"

"Why shouldn't I make a doll of you? Does it do you any harm? And *weren't* you a doll, good heavens! You *were* nothing but a doll. So what hurt does it do you?"

"Yes, it does. It does me the greatest possible damage," he replied.

She turned on him with wide-open eyes of amazement and rage.

"Why? Pray why? Can you tell me why?"

"Not quite, I can't," he replied, taking up the picture and holding it in front of him. She turned her face from it as a cat turns its nose away from a lighted cigarette. "But when I look at it—when I look at this—then I *know* that there's no love between you and me."

"Then why are you talking at me in this shameful way," she flashed at him, tears of anger and mortification rising to her eyes. "You want your little revenge on me, I suppose, because I made that doll of you."

"That may be so, in a small measure," he said.

"That is *all*. That is all and everything," she cried. "And that is all you came back to me for—for this petty revenge. Well, you've had it now. But please don't speak to me any more. I shall see if I can go home in the big omnibus."

She rose and walked away. He saw her hunting for the motor-bus conductor. He saw her penetrate into the yard of the garage. And he saw her emerge again, after a time, and take the path to the river. He sat on in front of the hotel. There was nothing else to do.

The tourists who had arrived in the big bus now began to collect. And soon the huge drab vehicle itself rolled up, and stood big as a house before the hotel door. The passengers began to scramble into their seats. The two men of the white dog were going: but the woman of the white dog, and the dog, were staying behind. Hepburn wondered if Hannele had managed to get herself transferred. He doubted it, because he knew the omnibus was crowded.

Moreover, he had her ticket.

The passengers were packed in. The conductor was collecting the tickets. And at last the great bus rolled away. The bay of the road-end seemed very empty. Even the woman with the white dog had gone. Soon the other car, the Luxus, so-called, must appear. Hepburn sat and waited. The evening was falling chilly, the trees looked gruesome.

At last Hannele sauntered up again, unwilingly.

"I think," she said, "you have my ticket."

"Yes, I have," he replied.

"Will you give it me, please?"

He gave it to her. She lingered a moment. Then she walked away.

There was the sound of a motor-car. With a triumphant purr the Luxus came steering out of the garage yard, and drew up at the hotel door. Hannele came hastening also. She went straight to one of the hinder doors—she and Hepburn had their seats in front, beside the driver. She had her foot on the step of the back seat. And then she was afraid. The little sharp-faced driver—there was no conductor—came round looking at the car. He looked at her with his sharp, metallic eye of a mechanic.

"Are all the people going back who came?" she asked, shrinking.

"Jawohl."

"It is full—this car?"

"Jawohl."

"There's no other place?"

"Nein."

Hannele shrank away. The driver was absolutely laconic.

Six of the passengers were here: four were already seated. Hepburn sat still by the hotel door, Hannele lingered in the road by the car, and the little driver, with a huge woollen muffler round his throat, was running round and in and out looking for the two missing passengers. Of course there were two missing passengers. No, he could not find them. And off he trotted again, silently, like a weasel after two rabbits. And at last, when everybody was getting cross, he unearthed them and brought them scuttling to the car.

Now Hannele took her seat, and Hepburn beside her. The driver snapped up the tickets and climbed in past them. With a vindictive screech the car glided away down the ravine. Another beastly trip was over, another infernal joyful holiday done with.

"I think," said Hepburn, "I may as well finish what I had to say."

"What?" cried Hannele, fluttering in the wind of the rushing car.

"I may as well finish what I had to say," shouted he, his breath blown away.

"Finish then," she screamed, the ends of her scarf flickering behind her.

"When my wife died," he said loudly, "I knew I couldn't love any more."

"Oh—h!" she screamed ironically.

"In fact," he shouted, "I realised that, as far as I was concerned, love was a mistake."

"*What* was a mistake?" she screamed.

"Love," he bawled.

"Love!" she screamed. "A mistake!" Her tone was derisive.

"For me, personally," he said, shouting.

"Oh, only for you personally," she cried, with a pouf of laughter.

The car gave a great swerve, and she fell on the driver. Then she righted herself. It gave another swerve, and she fell on Alexander. She righted herself angrily. And now they ran straight on: and it seemed a little quieter.

"I realized," he said, "that I had always made a mistake, undertaking to love."

"It must have been an undertaking, for *you*," she cried.

"Yes, I'm afraid it was. I never really wanted it. But I thought I did. And that's where I made my mistake."

"Whom have you ever loved—even as an undertaking?" she asked.

"To begin with, my mother: and that was a mistake. Then my sister: and that was a mistake. Then a girl I had known all my life: and that was a mistake. Then my wife: and that was my most terrible mistake. And then I began the mistake of loving you."

"Undertaking to love me, you mean," she said. "But then you never did properly undertake it. You never really *undertook* to love me."

"Not quite, did I?" said he.

And she sat feeling angry that he had never made the undertaking.

"No," he continued. "Not quite. That is why I came back to you. I don't want to love you. I don't want marriage on a basis of love."

"On a basis of what, then?"

"I think you know without my putting it into words," he said.

"Indeed, I assure you I don't. You are much too mysterious," she replied.

Talking in a swiftly-running motor-car is a nerve-racking business. They both had a pause, to rest, and to wait for a quieter stretch of road.

"It isn't very easy to put it into words," he said. "But I tried marriage once on a basis of love, and I must say it was a ghastly affair in the long run. And I believe it would be so, for me, *whatever* woman I had."

"There must be something wrong with you, then," said she.

"As far as love goes. And yet I want marriage. I want marriage. I want a woman to honour and obey me."

"If you are quite reasonable and *very* sparing with your commands," said Hannele. "And very careful how you give your orders."

"In fact, I want a sort of patient Griselda. I want to be honoured and obeyed. I don't want love."

"How Griselda managed to honour that fool of a husband of hers, even if she obeyed him, is more than I can say," said Hannele. "I'd like to know what she *really* thought of him. Just what any woman thinks of a bullying fool of a husband."

"Well," said he, "that's no good to me."

They were silent now until the car stopped at the station. There they descended and walked on under the trees by the lake.

"Sit on a seat," he said, "and let us finish."

Hannele, who was really anxious to hear what he should say, and who, woman-like, was fascinated by a man when he began to give away his own inmost thoughts—no matter how much

she might jeer afterwards—sat down by his side. It was a grey
evening, just falling dark. Lights twinkled across the lake, the
hotel over there threaded its strings of light. Some little boats
came rowing quietly to shore. It was a grey, heavy evening,
with that special sense of dreariness with which a public
holiday usually winds up.

"Honour, and obedience: and the proper physical feelings,"
he said. "To me that is marriage. Nothing else."

"But what are the proper physical feelings but love?" asked
Hannele.

"No," he said. "A woman wants you to adore her, and be in
love with her—and I shan't. I will not do it again, if I live a
monk for the rest of my days. I will neither adore you nor be in
love with you."

"You won't get a chance, thank you. And what do you call
the proper physical feelings, if you are not in love? I think you
want something vile."

"If a woman honours me—absolutely from the bottom of
her nature honours me—and obeys me because of that, I take
it, my desire for her goes very much deeper than if I was in love
with her, or if I adored her."

"It's the same thing. If you love, then everything is there—
all the lot: your honour and obedience and everything. And if
love isn't there, nothing is there," she said.

"That isn't true," he replied. "A woman may love you, she
may adore you, but she'll neither honour you nor obey you.
The most loving and adoring woman to-day could any minute
start and make a doll of her husband—as you made of me."

"Oh, that eternal doll! What makes it stick so in your
mind?"

"I don't know. But there it is. It wasn't malicious. It was
flattering, if you like. But it just sticks in me like a thorn: like
a thorn. And there it is, in the world, in Germany somewhere.
And you can say what you like, but *any* woman, to-day, no
matter *how* much she loves her man—she could start any
minute and make a doll of him. And the doll would be her
hero: and her hero would be no more than her doll. My wife

might have done it. She did do it, in her mind. She had her
doll of me right enough. Why, I heard her talk about me to
other women. And her doll was a great deal sillier than the
one you made. But it's all the same. If a woman loves you,
she'll make a doll out of you. She'll never be satisfied till she's
made your doll. And when she's got your doll, that's all she
wants. And that's what love means. And so, I won't be loved.
And I won't love. I won't have anybody loving me. It is an
insult. I feel I've been insulted for forty years: by love, and the
women who've loved me. I won't be loved. And I won't love.
I'll be honoured and I'll be obeyed: or nothing."

"Then it'll most probably be nothing," said Hannele
sarcastically. "For I assure you, I've nothing but love to
offer."

"Then keep your love," said he.

She laughed shortly.

"And you?" she cried. "You! Even suppose you *were*
honoured and obeyed. I suppose all you've got to do is to sit
there like a sultan and sup it up."

"Oh no, I have many things to do. And woman or no
woman, I'm going to start to do them."

"What, pray?"

"Why, nothing very exciting. I'm going to East Africa to
join a man who's breaking his neck to get his three thousand
acres of land under control. And when I've done a few more
experiments and observations, and got all the necessary facts,
I'm going to do a book on the moon. Woman or no woman,
I'm going to do that."

"And the woman—supposing you got the poor thing?"

"Why, she'll come along with me, and we'll set ourselves up
out there."

"And she'll do all the honouring and obeying and housekeeping incidentally, while you ride about in the day and stare
at the moon in the night."

He did not answer. He was staring away across the lake.

"What will you do for the woman, poor thing, while she's
racking herself to pieces honouring you and obeying you and

doing frightful housekeeping in Africa: because I know it can be *awful:* awful."

"Well," he said slowly, "she'll be my wife, and I shall treat her as such. If the marriage service says love and cherish—well, in that sense I shall do so."

"Oh!" cried Hannele. "What, *love* her? Actually love the poor thing?"

"Not in that sense of the word, no. I shan't adore her or be in love with her. But she'll be my wife, and I shall love and cherish her as such."

"Just because she's your wife. Not because she's herself. Ghastly fate for any miserable woman," said Hannele.

"I don't think so. I think it's her highest fate."

"To be your wife?"

"To be a wife—and to be loved and shielded as a wife—not as a flirting woman."

"To be loved and cherished just because you're his wife! No, thank you. All I can admire is the conceit and impudence of it."

"Very well, then—there it is," he said, rising.

She rose too, and then went on towards where the boat was tied.

As they were rowing in silence over the lake, he said:

"I shall leave to-morrow."

She made no answer. She sat and watched the lights of the villa draw near. And then she said:

"I'll come to Africa with you. But I won't promise to honour and obey you."

"I don't want you otherwise," he said, very quietly.

The boat was drifting to the little landing stage. Hannele's friends were hallooing to her from the balcony.

"Hallo!" she cried. "Ja. Da bin ich. Ja, 's war wunderschön."

Then to him she said:

"You'll come in?"

"No," he said, "I'll row straight back."

From the villa they were running down the steps to meet Hannele.

"But won't you have me even if I love you?" she asked him.

"You must promise the other," he said. "It comes in the marriage service."

"Hat's geregnet? Wie war das Wetter? Warst du auf dem Gletscher?" cried the voices from the garden.

"Nein—kein Regen. Wunderschön! Ja, er war ganz auf dem Gletscher," cried Hannele in reply. And to him, *sotto voce:*

"Don't be a solemn ass. Do come in."

"No," he said, "I don't want to come in."

"Do you want to go away to-morrow? Go if you *do*. But anyway, I won't say it *before* the marriage service. I needn't, need I?"

She stepped from the boat on to the plank.

"Oh," she said, turning round, "give me that picture, please, will you? I want to burn it."

He handed it to her.

"And come to-morrow, will you?" she said.

"Yes, in the morning."

He pulled back quickly into the darkness.

To her father, she was The Princess. To her Boston aunts and uncles she was just *Dollie Urquhart, poor little thing*.

Colin Urquhart was just a bit mad. He was of an old Scottish family, and he claimed royal blood. The blood of Scottish kings flowed in his veins. On this point, his American relatives said, he was just a bit "off." They could not bear any more to be told *which* royal blood of Scotland blued his veins. The whole thing was rather ridiculous, and a sore point. The only fact they remembered was that it was not Stuart.

He was a handsome man, with a wide-open blue eye that seemed sometimes to be looking at nothing, soft black hair brushed rather low on his low, broad brow, and a very attractive body. Add to this a most beautiful speaking voice, usually rather hushed and diffident, but sometimes resonant and powerful like bronze, and you have the sum of his charms. He looked like some old Celtic hero. He looked as if he should have worn a greyish kilt and a sporran, and shown his knees. His voice came direct out of the hushed Ossianic past.

For the rest, he was one of those gentlemen of sufficient but not excessive means who fifty years ago wandered vaguely about, never arriving anywhere, never doing anything, and never definitely being anything, yet well received and familiar in the good society of more than one country.

He did not marry till he was nearly forty, and then it was a wealthy Miss Prescott, from New England. Hannah Prescott at twenty-two was fascinated by the man with the soft black hair not yet touched by grey, and the wide, rather vague, blue eyes. Many women had been fascinated before her. But Colin Urquhart, by his very vagueness, had avoided any decisive connection.

Mrs. Urquhart lived three years in the mist and glamour of her husband's presence. And then it broke her. It was like living with a fascinating spectre. About most things he was completely, even ghostly oblivious. He was always charming, courteous, perfectly gracious in that hushed, musical voice of his. But absent. When all came to all, he just wasn't there. "Not all there," as the vulgar say.

He was the father of the little girl she bore at the end of the first year. But this did not substantiate him the more. His very beauty and his haunting musical quality became dreadful to her after the first few months. The strange echo: he was like a living echo! His very flesh, when you touched it, did not seem quite the flesh of a real man.

Perhaps it was that he was a little bit mad. She thought it definitely the night her baby was born.

"Ah, so my little princess has come at last!" he said, in his throaty, singing Celtic voice, like a glad chant, swaying absorbed.

It was a tiny, frail baby, with wide, amazed blue eyes. They christened it Mary Henrietta. She called the little thing *My Dollie*. He called it always *My Princess*.

It was useless to fly at him. He just opened his wide blue eyes wider, and took a childlike, silent dignity there was no getting past.

Hannah Prescott had never been robust. She had no great desire to live. So when the baby was two years old she suddenly died.

The Prescotts felt a deep but unadmitted resentment against Colin Urquhart. They said he was selfish. Therefore they discontinued Hannah's income, a month after her burial in Florence, after they had urged the father to give the child over to them, and he had courteously, musically, but quite finally refused. He treated the Prescotts as if they were not of his world, not realities to him: just casual phenomena, or gramophones, talking-machines that had to be answered. He answered them. But of their actual existence he was never once aware.

They debated having him certified unsuitable to be guardian of his own child. But that would have created a scandal. So

they did the simplest thing, after all—washed their hands of
him. But they wrote scrupulously to the child, and sent her
modest presents of money at Christmas, and on the anniversary
of the death of her mother.

To The Princess her Boston relatives were for many years
just a nominal reality. She lived with her father, and he
travelled continually, though in a modest way, living on his
moderate income. And never going to America. The child
changed nurses all the time. In Italy it was a contadina; in
India she had an ayah; in Germany she had a yellow-haired
peasant girl.

Father and child were inseparable. He was not a recluse.
Wherever he went he was to be seen paying formal calls, going
out to luncheon or to tea, rarely to dinner. And always with
the child. People called her Princess Urquhart, as if that were
her christened name.

She was a quick, dainty little thing with dark gold hair that
went a soft brown, and wide, slightly prominent blue eyes that
were at once so candid and so knowing. She was always grown
up; she never really grew up. Always strangely wise, and
always childish.

It was her father's fault.

"My little Princess must never take too much notice of
people and the things they say and do," he repeated to her.
"People don't know what they are doing and saying. They
chatter-chatter, and they hurt one another, and they hurt
themselves very often, till they cry. But don't take any
notice, my little Princess. Because it is all nothing. Inside
everybody there is another creature, a demon which doesn't
care at all. You peel away all the things they say and do and
feel, as cook peels away the outside of the onions. And in the
middle of everybody there is a green demon which you can't
peel away. And this green demon never changes, and it doesn't
care at all about all the things that happen to the outside leaves
of the person, all the chatter-chatter, and all the husbands and
wives and children, and troubles and fusses. You peel everything away from people, and there is a green, upright demon in

every man and woman; and this demon is a man's real self, and
a woman's real self. It doesn't really care about anybody, it
belongs to the demons and the primitive fairies, who never
care. But, even so, there are big demons and mean demons,
and splendid demonish fairies, and vulgar ones. But there are
no royal fairy women left. Only you, my little Princess. You
are the last of the royal race of the old people; the last, my
Princess. There are no others. You and I are the last. When I
am dead there will be only you. And that is why, darling, you
will never care for any of the people in the world very much.
Because their demons are all dwindled and vulgar. They are
not royal. Only you are royal, after me. Always remember
that. And always remember, it is a *great secret*. If you tell
people, they will try to kill you, because they will envy you for
being a Princess. It is our great secret, darling. I am a prince,
and you a princess, of the old, old blood. And we keep our
secret between us, all alone. And so, darling, you must treat
all people very politely, because *noblesse oblige*. But you must
never forget that you alone are the last of Princesses, and that
all others are less than you are, less noble, more vulgar. Treat
them politely and gently and kindly, darling. But you are the
Princess, and they are commoners. Never try to think of them
as if they were like you. They are not. You will find, always,
that they are lacking, lacking in the royal touch, which only
you have——"

The Princess learned her lesson early——the first lesson, of
absolute reticence, the impossibility of intimacy with any other
than her father; the second lesson, of naïve, slightly benevolent
politeness. As a small child, something crystallized in her
character, making her clear and finished, and as impervious as
crystal.

"Dear child!" her hostesses said of her. "She is so quaint and
old-fashioned; such a lady, poor little mite!"

She was erect, and very dainty. Always small, nearly tiny in
physique, she seemed like a changeling beside her big, handsome, slightly mad father. She dressed very simply, usually in
blues or delicate greys, with little collars of old Milan point, or

very finely-worked linen. She had exquisite little hands, that made the piano sound like a spinet when she played. She was rather given to wearing cloaks and capes, instead of coats, out of doors, and little eighteenth-century sort of hats. Her complexion was pure apple-blossom.

She looked as if she had stepped out of a picture. But no one, to her dying day, ever knew exactly the strange picture her father had framed her in, and from which she never stepped.

Her grandfather and grandmother and her Aunt Maud demanded twice to see her, once in Rome and once in Paris. Each time they were charmed, piqued, and annoyed. She was so exquisite and such a little virgin. At the same time so knowing and so oddly assured. That odd, assured touch of condescension, and the inward coldness, infuriated her American relations.

Only she really fascinated her grandfather. He was spell-bound; in a way, in love with the little faultless thing. His wife would catch him brooding, musing over his grandchild, long months after the meeting, and craving to see her again. He cherished to the end the fond hope that she might come to live with him and her grandmother.

"Thank you so much, grandfather. You are so very kind. But Papa and I are such an old couple, you see, such a crochety old couple, living in a world of our own."

Her father let her see the world—from the outside. And he let her read. When she was in her teens she read Zola and Maupassant, and with the eyes of Zola and Maupassant she looked on Paris. A little later she read Tolstoi and Dostoevsky. The latter confused her. The others, she seemed to understand with a very shrewd, canny understanding, just as she understood the Decameron stories as she read them in their old Italian, or the Nibelung poems. Strange and *uncanny*, she seemed to understand things in a cold light perfectly, with all the flush of fire absent. She was something like a changeling, not quite human.

This earned her, also, strange antipathies. Cabmen and railway-porters, especially in Paris and Rome, would suddenly treat her with brutal rudeness, when she was alone. They seemed to look on her with sudden violent antipathy. They sensed in her curious impertinence, an easy, sterile impertinence towards the things *they* felt most. She was so assured, and her flower of maidenhood was so scentless. She could look at a lusty, sensual Roman cabman as if he were a sort of grotesque, to make her smile. She knew all about him, in Zola. And the peculiar condescension with which she would give him her order, as if she, frail, beautiful thing, were the only reality, and he, coarse monster, were a sort of Caliban floundering in the mud on the margin of the pool of the perfect lotus, would suddenly enrage the fellow, the real Mediterranean who prided himself on his *beauté male*, and to whom the phallic mystery was still the only mystery. And he would turn a terrible face on her, bully her in a brutal, coarse fashion—hideous. For to him she had only the blasphemous impertinence of her own sterility.

Encounters like these made her tremble, and made her know she must have support from the outside. The power of her spirit did not extend to these low people, and they had all the physical power. She realized an implacability of hatred in their turning on her. But she did not lose her head. She quietly paid out money and turned away.

Those were dangerous moments, though, and she learned to be prepared for them. The Princess she was, and the fairy from the North, and could never understand the volcanic phallic rage with which coarse people could turn on her in a paroxysm of hatred. They never turned on her father like that. And quite early she decided it was the New England mother in her whom they hated. Never for one minute could she see with the old Roman eyes, see herself as sterility, the barren flower taking on airs and an intolerable impertinence. This was what the Roman cabman saw in her. And he longed to crush the barren blossom. Its sexless beauty and its authority put him in a passion of brutal revolt.

When she was nineteen her grandfather died, leaving her a considerable fortune in the safe hands of responsible trustees.

They would deliver her her income, but only on condition that she resided for six months in the year in the United States.

"Why should they make me conditions?" she said to her father. "I refuse to be imprisoned six months in the year in the United States. We will tell them to keep their money."

"Let us be wise, my little Princess, let us be wise. No, we are almost poor, and we are never safe from rudeness. I cannot allow anybody to be rude to me. I hate it, I hate it!" His eyes flamed as he said it. "I could kill any man or woman who is rude to me. But we are in exile in the world. We are powerless. If we were really poor, we should be quite powerless, and then I should die. No, my Princess. Let us take their money, then they will not dare to be rude to us. Let us take it, as we put on clothes, to cover ourselves from their aggressions."

There began a new phase, when the father and daughter spent their summers on the Great Lakes or in California, or in the South-West. The father was something of a poet, the daughter something of a painter. He wrote poems about the lakes or the red-wood trees, and she made dainty drawings. He was physically a strong man, and he loved the out-of-doors. He would go off with her for days, paddling in a canoe and sleeping by a camp-fire. Frail little Princess, she was always undaunted, always undaunted. She would ride with him on horseback over the mountain trails till she was so tired she was nothing but a bodiless consciousness sitting astride her pony. But she never gave in. And at night he folded her in her blankets on a bed of balsam-pine twigs, and she lay and looked at the stars unmurmuring. She was fulfilling her rôle.

People said to her as the years passed, and she was a woman of twenty-five, then a woman of thirty, and always the same virgin dainty Princess, "knowing" in a dispassionate way, like an old woman, and utterly intact:

"Don't you ever think what you will do when your father is no longer with you?"

She looked at her interlocutor with that cold, elfin detachment of hers:

"No, I never think of it," she said.

She had a tiny, but exquisite little house in London, and another small, perfect house in Connecticut, each with a faithful housekeeper. Two homes, if she chose. And she knew many interesting literary and artistic people. What more?

So the years passed imperceptibly. And she had that quality of the sexless fairies, she did not change. At thirty-three she looked twenty-three.

Her father, however, was ageing, and becoming more and more queer. It was now her task to be his guardian in his private madness. He spent the last three years of life in the house in Connecticut. He was very much estranged, sometimes had fits of violence which almost killed the little Princess. Physical violence was horrible to her; it seemed to shatter her heart. But she found a woman a few years younger than herself, well-educated and sensitive, to be a sort of nurse-companion to the mad old man. So the fact of madness was never openly admitted. Miss Cummins, the companion, had a passionate loyalty to the Princess, and a curious affection, tinged with love, for the handsome, white-haired, courteous old man, who was never at all aware of his fits of violence once they had passed.

The Princess was thirty-eight years old when her father died. And quite unchanged. She was still tiny, and like a dignified, scentless flower. Her soft brownish hair, almost the colour of beaver fur, was bobbed, and fluffed softly round her apple-blossom face, that was modelled with an arched nose like a proud old Florentine portrait. In her voice, manner and bearing she was exceedingly still, like a flower that has blossomed in a shadowy place. And from her blue eyes looked out the Princess's eternal laconic challenge, that grew almost sardonic as the years passed. She was the Princess, and sardonically she looked out on a princeless world.

She was relieved when her father died, and at the same time, it was as if everything had evaporated around her. She had lived in a sort of hot-house, in the aura of her father's madness. Suddenly the hot-house had been removed from around her, and she was in the raw, vast, vulgar open air.

Quoi faire? What was she to do? She seemed faced with absolute nothingness. Only she had Miss Cummins, who shared with her the secret, and almost the passion for her father. In fact the Princess felt that her passion for her mad father had in some curious way transferred itself largely to Charlotte Cummins during the last years. And now Miss Cummins was the vessel that held the passion for the dead man. She herself, the Princess, was an empty vessel.

An empty vessel in the enormous warehouse of the world.

Quoi faire? What was she to do? She felt that, since she could not evaporate into nothingness, like alcohol from an unstoppered bottle, she must *do* something. Never before in her life had she felt the incumbency. Never, never had she felt she must *do* anything. That was left to the vulgar.

Now her father was dead, she found herself on the *fringe* of the vulgar crowd, sharing their necessity to *do* something. It was a little humiliating. She felt herself becoming vulgarized. At the same time she found herself looking at men with a shrewder eye: an eye to marriage. Not that she felt any sudden interest in men, or attraction towards them. No. She was still neither interested nor attracted towards men vitally. But *marriage*, that peculiar abstraction, had imposed a sort of spell on her. She thought that *marriage*, in the blank abstract, was the thing she ought to *do*. That *marriage* implied a man she also knew. She knew all the facts. But the man seemed a property of her own mind rather than a thing in himself, another being.

Her father died in the summer, the month after her thirty-eighth birthday. When all was over, the obvious thing to do, of course, was to travel. With Miss Cummins. The two women knew each other intimately, but they were always Miss Urquhart and Miss Cummins to one another, and a certain distance was instinctively maintained. Miss Cummins, from Philadelphia, of scholastic stock, and intelligent but untravelled, four years younger than the Princess, felt herself immensely the junior of her "lady." She had a sort of passionate veneration for the Princess, who seemed to her ageless, timeless.

She could not see the rows of tiny, dainty, exquisite shoes in the Princess's cupboard without feeling a stab at the heart, a stab of tenderness and reverence, almost of awe.

Miss Cummins also was virginal, but with a look of puzzled surprise in her brown eyes. Her skin was pale and clear, her features well modelled, but there was a certain blankness in her expression, where the Princess had an odd touch of Renaissance grandeur. Miss Cummins' voice was also hushed almost to a whisper; it was the inevitable effect of Colin Urquhart's room. But the hushedness had a hoarse quality.

The Princess did not want to go to Europe. Her face seemed turned west. Now her father was gone, she felt she would go west, westwards, as if for ever. Following no doubt, the March of Empire, which is brought up rather short on the Pacific coast, among swarms of wallowing bathers.

No, not the Pacific coast. She would stop short of that. The South-West was less vulgar. She would go to New Mexico.

She and Miss Cummins arrived at the Rancho del Cerro Gordo towards the end of August, when the crowd was beginning to drift back east. The ranch lay by a stream on the desert some four miles from the foot of the mountains, a mile away from the Indian pueblo of San Cristobal. It was a ranch for the rich; the Princess paid thirty dollars a day for herself and Miss Cummins. But then she had a little cottage to herself, among the apple-trees of the orchard, with an excellent cook. She and Miss Cummins, however, took dinner at evening in the large guest-house. For the Princess still entertained the idea of *marriage*.

The guests at the Rancho del Cerro Gordo were of all sorts, except the poor sort. They were practically all rich, and many were romantic. Some were charming, others were vulgar, some were movie people, quite quaint and not unattractive in their vulgarity, and many were Jews. The Princess did not care for Jews, though they were usually the most interesting to *talk* to. So she talked a good deal with the Jews, and painted with the artists, and rode with the young men from college, and had altogether quite a good time. And yet she felt something of a

fish out of water, or a bird in the wrong forest. And *marriage*
remained still completely in the abstract. No connecting it
with any of these young men, even the nice ones.

The Princess looked just twenty-five. The freshness of her
mouth, the hushed, delicate-complexioned virginity of her face
gave her not a day more. Only a certain laconic look in her
eyes was disconcerting. When she was *forced* to write her age,
she put twenty-eight, making the figure *two* rather badly, so
that it just avoided being a three.

Men hinted marriage at her. Especially boys from college
suggested it from a distance. But they all failed before the look
of sardonic ridicule in the Princess's eyes. It always seemed to
her rather preposterous, quite ridiculous, and a tiny bit
impertinent on their part.

The only man that intrigued her at all was one of the guides,
a man called Romero—Domingo Romero. It was he who had
sold the ranch itself to the Wilkiesons, ten years before, for two
thousand dollars. He had gone away, then reappeared at the
old place. For he was the son of the old Romero, the last of the
Spanish family that had owned miles of land around San
Cristobal. But the coming of the white man and the failure of
the vast flocks of sheep, and the fatal inertia which overcomes
all men, at last, on the desert near the mountains, had finished
the Romero family. The last descendants were just Mexican
peasants.

Domingo, the heir, had spent his two thousand dollars, and
was working for white people. He was now about thirty years
old, a tall, silent fellow, with a heavy closed mouth and black
eyes that looked across at one almost sullenly. From behind he
was handsome, with a strong natural body, and the back of his
neck very dark and well-shapen, strong with life. But his dark
face was long and heavy, almost sinister, with that peculiar
heavy meaningless in it, characteristic of the Mexicans of his
own locality. They are strong, they seem healthy. They laugh
and joke with one another. But their physique and their
natures seem static, as if there were nowhere, nowhere at all
for their energies to go, and their faces, degenerating to

misshapen heaviness, seem to have no *raison d'etre*, no radical meaning. Waiting either to die or to be aroused into passion and hope. In some of the black eyes a queer, haunting mystic quality, sombre and a bit gruesome, the skull-and-cross-bones look of the Penitentes. They had found their *raison d'etre* in self-torture and death-worship. Unable to wrest a *positive* significance for themselves from the vast, beautiful, but vindictive landscape they were born into, they turned on their own selves, and worshipped death through self-torture. The mystic gloom of this showed in their eyes.

But as a rule the dark eyes of the Mexicans were heavy and half-alive, sometimes hostile, sometimes kindly, often with the fatal Indian glaze on them, or the fatal Indian glint.

Domingo Romero was *almost* a typical Mexican to look at, with the typical heavy, dark, long face, clean-shaven, with an almost brutally heavy mouth. His eyes were black and Indian-looking. Only, at the centre of their hopelessness was a spark of pride, or self-confidence, or dauntlessness. Just a spark in the midst of the blackness of static despair.

But this spark was the difference between him and the mass of men. It gave a certain alert sensitiveness to his bearing and a certain beauty to his appearance. He wore a low-crowned black hat, instead of the ponderous headgear of the usual Mexican, and his clothes were thinnish and graceful. Silent, aloof, almost imperceptible in the landscape, he was an admirable guide, with a startling quick intelligence that anticipated difficulties about to arise. He could cook, too, crouching over the camp-fire and moving his lean deft brown hands. The only fault he had was that he was not forth-coming, he wasn't chatty and cosy.

"Oh, don't send Romero with us," the Jews would say. "One can't get any response from him."

Tourists come and go, but they rarely *see* anything, inwardly. None of them ever saw the spark at the middle of Romero's eye; they were not alive enough to see it.

The Princess caught it one day, when she had him for a guide. She was fishing for trout in the canyon, Miss Cummins was reading a book, the horses were tied under the trees, Romero was fixing a proper fly on her line. He fixed the fly and handed her the line, looking up at her. And at that moment she caught the spark in his eye. And instantly she knew that he was a gentleman, that his "demon," as her father would have said, was a fine demon. And instantly her manner towards him changed.

He had perched her on a rock over a quiet pool, beyond the cotton-wood trees. It was early September, and the canyon already cool, but the leaves of the cotton-woods were still green. The Princess stood on her rock, a small but perfectly-formed figure, wearing a soft, close grey sweater and neatly-cut grey riding breeches, with tall black boots, her fluffy brown hair straggling from under a little grey felt hat. A woman? Not quite. A changeling of some sort, perched in outline there on the rock, in the bristling wild canyon. She knew perfectly well how to handle a line. Her father had made a fisherman of her.

Romero, in a black shirt and with loose black trousers pushed into wide black riding boots, was fishing a little further down. He had put his hat on a rock behind him; his dark head was bent a little forward, watching the water. He had caught three trout. From time to time he glanced upstream at the Princess, perched there so daintily. He saw she had caught nothing.

Soon he quietly drew in his line and came up to her. His keen eye watched her line, watched her position. Then, quietly, he suggested certain changes to her, putting his sensitive brown hand before her. And he withdrew a little, and stood in silence, leaning against a tree, watching her. He was helping her across the distance. She knew it, and thrilled. And in a moment she had a bite. In two minutes she landed a good trout. She looked round at him quickly, her eyes sparkling, the colour heightened in her cheeks. And as she met his eyes a smile of greeting went over his dark face, very sudden, with an odd sweetness.

She knew he was helping her. And she felt in his presence a

subtle, insidious male *kindliness* she had never known before waiting upon her. Her cheek flushed, and her blue eyes darkened.

After this, she always looked for him, and for that curious dark beam of a man's kindliness which he could give her, as it were, from his chest, from his heart. It was something she had never known before.

A vague unspoken intimacy grew up between them. She liked his voice, his appearance, his presence. His natural language was Spanish; he spoke English like a foreign language, rather slow, with a slight hesitation, but with a sad, plangent sonority lingering over from his Spanish. There was a certain subtle correctness in his appearance; he was always perfectly shaved; his hair was thick and rather long on top, but always carefully groomed behind. And his fine black cashmere shirt, his wide leather belt, his well-cut, wide black trousers going into the embroidered cowboy boots had a certain inextinguishable elegance. He wore no silver rings or buckles. Only his boots were embroidered and decorated at the top with an inlay of white *suède*. He seemed elegant, slender, yet he was very strong.

And at the same time, curiously, he gave her the feeling that death was not far from him. Perhaps he too was half in love with death. However that may be, the sense she had that death was not far from him made him "possible" to her.

Small as she was, she was quite a good horsewoman. They gave her at the ranch a sorrel mare, very lovely in colour, and well-made, with a powerful broad neck and the hollow back that betokens a swift runner. Tansy, she was called. Her only fault was the usual mare's failing, she was inclined to be hysterical.

So that every day the Princess set off with Miss Cummins and Romero, on horseback, riding into the mountains. Once they went camping for several days, with two more friends in the party.

"I think I like it better," the Princess said to Romero, "when we three go alone."

And he gave her one of his quick, transfiguring smiles.

It was curious no white man had ever showed her this capacity for subtle gentleness, this power to *help* her in silence across a distance, if she were fishing without success, or tired of her horse, or if Tansy suddenly got scared. It was as if Romero could send her *from his heart* a dark beam of succour and sustaining. She had never known this before, and it was very thrilling.

Then the smile that suddenly creased his dark face, showing the strong white teeth. It creased his face almost into a savage grotesque. And at the same time there was in it something so warm, such a dark flame of kindliness for her, she was elated into her true Princess self.

Then that vivid, latent spark in his eye, which she had seen, and which she knew he was aware she had seen. It made an inter-recognition between them, silent and delicate. Here he was delicate as a woman in this subtle inter-recognition.

And yet his presence only put to flight in her the *idée fixe* of "marriage." For some reason, in her strange little brain, the idea of *marrying* him could not enter. Not for any definite reason. He was in himself a gentleman, and she had plenty of money for two. There was no actual obstacle. Nor was she conventional.

No, now she came down to it, it was as if their two "dæmons" could marry, were perhaps married. Only their two *selves*, Miss Urquhart and Señor Domingo Romero, were for some reason incompatible. There was a peculiar subtle intimacy of inter-recognition between them. But she did not see in the least how it would lead to marriage. Almost she could more easily marry one of the nice boys from Harvard or Yale.

The time passed, and she let it pass. The end of September came, with aspens going yellow on the mountain heights, and oak-scrub going red. But as yet the cotton-woods in the valley and canyons had not changed.

"When will you go away?" Romero asked her, looking at her fixedly, with a blank black eye.

"By the end of October," she said. "I have promised

to be in Santa Barbara at the beginning of November."

He was hiding the spark in his eye from her. But she saw the peculiar sullen thickening of his heavy mouth.

She had complained to him many times that one never saw any wild animals, except chipmunks and squirrels, and perhaps a skunk and a porcupine. Never a deer, or a bear, or a mountain lion.

"Are there no bigger animals in these mountains?" she asked, dissatisfied.

"Yes," he said. "There are deer—I see their tracks. And I saw the tracks of a bear."

"But why can one never see the animals themselves?" She looked dissatisfied and wistful like a child.

"Why, it's pretty hard for you to see them. They won't let you come close. You have to keep still, in a place where they come. Or else you have to follow their tracks a long way."

"I can't bear to go away till I've seen them: a bear, or a deer——"

The smile came suddenly on his face, indulgent.

"Well, what do you want? Do you want to go up into the mountains to some place, to wait till they come?"

"Yes," she said, looking up at him with a sudden naïve impulse of recklessness.

And immediately his face became sombre again, responsible.

"Well," he said, with slight irony, a touch of mockery of her. "You will have to find a house. It's very cold at night now. You would have to stay all night in a house."

"And there are no houses up there?" she said.

"Yes," he replied. "There is a little shack that belongs to me, that a miner built a long time ago, looking for gold. You can go there and stay one night, and maybe you see something. Maybe! I don't know. Maybe nothing come."

"How much chance is there?"

"Well, I don't know. Last time when I was there I see three deer come down to drink at the water, and I shot two raccoons. But maybe this time we don't see anything."

"Is there water there?" she asked.

"Yes, there is a little round pond, you know, below the spruce trees. And the water from the snow runs into it."

"Is it far away?" she asked.

"Yes, pretty far. You see that ridge there"—and turning to the mountains he lifted his arm in the gesture which is somehow so moving, out in the West, pointing to the distance— "that ridge where there are no trees, only rock"—his black eyes were focussed on the distance, his face impassive, but as if in pain—"you go round that ridge, and along, then you come down through the spruce trees to where that cabin is. My father bought that placer claim from a miner who was broke, but nobody ever found any gold or anything, and nobody ever goes there. Too lonesome!"

The Princess watched the massive, heavy-sitting, beautiful bulk of the Rocky Mountains. It was early in October, and the aspens were already losing their gold leaves; high up, the spruce and pine seemed to be growing darker; the great flat patches of oak-scrub on the heights were red like gore.

"Can I go over there?" she asked, turning to him and meeting the spark in his eye.

His face was heavy with responsibility.

"Yes," he said, "you can go. But there'll be snow over the ridge, and it's awful cold, and awful lonesome."

"I should like to go," she said, persistent.

"All right," he said. "You can go if you want to."

She doubted, though, if the Wilkiesons would let her go; at least alone with Romero and Miss Cummins.

Yet an obstinacy characteristic of her nature, an obstinacy tinged perhaps with madness, had taken hold of her. She wanted to look over the mountains into their secret heart. She wanted to descend to the cabin below the spruce trees, near the tarn of bright green water. She wanted to see the wild animals move about in their wild unconsciousness.

"Let us say to the Wilkiesons that we want to make the trip round the Frijoles canyon," she said.

The trip round the Frijoles canyon was a usual thing. It would not be strenuous, nor cold, nor lonely: they could sleep in the log house that was called an hotel.

Romero looked at her quickly.

"If you want to say that," he replied, "you can tell Mrs. Wilkieson. Only I know she'll be mad with me if I take you up in the mountains to that place. And I've got to go there first with a pack-horse, to take lots of blankets and some bread. Maybe Miss Cummins can't stand it. Maybe not. It's a hard trip."

He was speaking, and thinking, in the heavy, disconnected Mexican fashion.

"Never mind!" The Princess was suddenly very decisive and stiff with authority. "I want to do it. I will arrange with Mrs. Wilkieson. And we'll go on Saturday."

He shook his head slowly.

"I've got to go up on Sunday with a pack-horse and blankets," he said. "Can't do it before."

"Very well!" she said, rather piqued. "Then we'll start on Monday."

She hated being thwarted even the tiniest bit.

He knew that if he started with the pack on Sunday at dawn he would not be back until late at night. But he consented that they should start on Monday morning at seven. The obedient Miss Cummins was told to prepare for the Frijoles trip. On Sunday Romero had his day off. He had not put in an appearance when the Princess retired on Sunday night, but on Monday morning, as she was dressing, she saw him bringing in the three horses from the corral. She was in high spirits.

The night had been cold. There was ice at the edges of the irrigation ditch, and the chipmunks crawled into the sun and lay with wide, dumb, anxious eyes, almost too numb to run.

"We may be away two or three days," said the Princess.

"Very well. We won't begin to be anxious about you before Thursday then," said Mrs. Wilkieson, who was young and capable: from Chicago. "Anyway," she added, "Romero will see you through. He's so trustworthy."

The sun was already on the desert as they set off towards the mountains, making the greasewood and the sage pale as pale-grey sands, luminous the great level around them. To the right glinted the shadows of the adobe pueblo, flat and almost invisible on the plain, earth of its earth. Behind lay the ranch and the tufts of tall, plumy cotton-woods, whose summits were yellowing under the perfect blue sky.

Autumn breaking into colour in the great spaces of the South-West.

But the three trotted gently along the trail, towards the sun that sparkled yellow just above the dark bulk of the ponderous mountains. Side-slopes were already gleaming yellow, flaming with a second light, under the coldish blue of the pale sky. The front slopes were in shadow, with submerged lustre of red oak-scrub and dull-gold aspens, blue-black pines and grey-blue rock. While the canyon was full of a deep blueness.

They rode single file, Romero first, on a black horse. Himself in black, he made a flickering black spot in the delicate pallor of the great landscape, where even pine-trees at a distance take a film of blue paler than their green. Romero rode on in silence past the tufts of furry greasewood. The Princess came next, on her sorrel mare. And Miss Cummins, who was not quite happy on horseback, came last, in the pale dust that the others kicked up. Sometimes her horse sneezed, and she started.

But on they went, at a gentle trot. Romero never looked round. He could hear the sound of the hoofs following, and that was all he wanted.

For the rest, he held ahead. And the Princess, with that black, unheeding figure always travelling away from her, felt strangely helpless, withal elated.

They neared the pale, round foot-hills, dotted with the round dark piñon and cedar shrubs. The horses clinked and clattered among stones. Occasionally a big round greasewood held out fleecy tufts of flowers, pure gold. They wound into blue shadow, then up a steep stony slope, with the world lying pallid away behind and below. Then they dropped into the shadow of the San Cristobal canyon.

The stream was running full and swift. Occasionally the horses snatched at a tuft of grass. The trail narrowed and became rocky; the rocks closed in; it was dark and cool as the horses climbed and climbed upwards, and the tree-trunks crowded in in the shadowy, silent tightness of the canyon. They were among cotton-wood trees that ran straight up and smooth and round to an extraordinary height. Above, the tips were gold, and it was sun. But away below, where the horses struggled up the rocks and wound among the trunks, there was still blue shadow by the sound of waters and an occasional grey festoon of old man's beard, and here and there a pale, dipping crane's-bill flower among the tangle and the debris of the virgin place. And again the chill entered the Princess's heart as she realized what a tangle of decay and despair lay in the virgin forests.

They scrambled downwards, splashed across stream, up rocks and along the trail of the other side. Romero's black horse stopped, looked down quizzically at the fallen trees, then stepped over lightly. The Princess's sorrel followed, carefully. But Miss Cummins's bucksin made a fuss, and had to be got round.

In the same silence, save for the clinking of the horses and the splashing as the trail crossed stream, they worked their way upwards in the tight, tangled shadow of the canyon. Sometimes, crossing stream, the Princess would glance upwards, and then always her heart caught in her breast. For high up, away in heaven, the mountain heights shone yellow, dappled with dark spruce firs, clear almost as speckled daffodils against the pale turquoise blue lying high and serene above the dark-blue shadow where the Princess was. And she would snatch at the blood-red leaves of the oak as her horse crossed a more open slope, not knowing what she felt.

They were getting fairly high, occasionally lifted above the canyon itself, in the low groove below the speckled, gold-sparkling heights which towered beyond. Then again they dipped and crossed stream, the horses stepping gingerly across a tangle of fallen, frail aspen stems, then suddenly floundering in a mass of rocks. The black emerged ahead, his black tail waving. The Princess let her mare find her own footing; then she too emerged from the clatter. She rode on after the black. Then came a great frantic rattle of the buckskin behind. The Princess was aware of Romero's dark face looking round, with a strange, demon-like watchfulness, before she herself looked round, to see the buckskin scrambling rather lamely beyond the rocks, with one of his pale buff knees already red with blood.

"He almost went down!" called Miss Cummins.

But Romero was already out of the saddle and hastening down the path. He made quiet little noises to the buckskin, and began examining the cut knee.

"Is he hurt?" cried Miss Cummins anxiously, and she climbed hastily down.

"Oh, my goodness!" she cried, as she saw the blood running down the slender buff leg of the horse in a thin trickle. "Isn't that *awful?*" She spoke in a stricken voice, and her face was white.

Romero was still carefully feeling the knee of the buckskin. Then he made him walk a few paces. And at last he stood up straight and shook his head.

"Not very bad!" he said. "Nothing broken."

Again he bent and worked at the knee. Then he looked up at the Princess.

"He can go on," he said. "It's not bad."

The Princess looked down at the dark face in silence.

"What, go on right up here?" cried Miss Cummins. "How many hours?"

"About five," said Romero simply.

"Five hours!" cried Miss Cummins. "A horse with a lame knee! And a steep mountain! Why-y!"

"Yes, it's pretty steep up there," said Romero, pushing back his hat and staring fixedly at the bleeding knee. The buckskin stood in a stricken sort of dejection. "But I think he'll make it all right," the man added.

"Oh!" cried Miss Cummins, her eyes bright with sudden passion of unshed tears. "I wouldn't think of it. I wouldn't ride him up there, not for any money."

"Why wouldn't you?" asked Romero.

"It *hurts* him."

Romero bent down again to the horse's knee.

"Maybe it hurts him a little," he said. "But he can make it all right, and his leg won't get stiff."

"What! Ride him five hours up the steep mountains?" cried Miss Cummins. "I couldn't. I just couldn't do it. I'll lead him a little way and see if he can go. But I *couldn't* ride him again. I couldn't. Let me walk."

"But Miss Cummins, dear, if Romero says he'll be all right?" said the Princess.

"I know it hurts him. Oh, I just couldn't bear it."

There was no doing anything with Miss Cummins. The thought of a hurt animal always put her into a sort of hysterics.

They walked forward a little, leading the buckskin. He limped rather badly. Miss Cummins sat on a rock.

"Why, it's agony to see him!" she cried. "It's *cruel!*"

"He won't limp after a bit, if you take no notice of him," said Romero. "Now he plays up, and limps very much, because he wants to make you see."

"I don't think there can be much playing up," said Miss Cummins bitterly. "We can *see* how it must hurt him."

"It don't hurt much," said Romero.

But now Miss Cummins was silent with antipathy.

It was a deadlock. The party remained motionless on the trail, the Princess in the saddle, Miss Cummins seated on a rock, Romero standing black and remote near the drooping buckskin.

"Well!" said the man suddenly at last. "I guess we go back, then."

And he looked up swiftly at his horse, which was cropping at the mountain herbage and treading on the trailing reins.

"No!" cried the Princess. "Oh no!" Her voice rang with a great wail of disappointment and anger. Then she checked herself.

Miss Cummins rose with energy.

"Let me lead the buckskin home," she said, with cold dignity, "and you two go on."

This was received in silence. The Princess was looking down at her with a sardonic, almost cruel gaze.

"We've only come about two hours," said Miss Cummins. "I don't mind a bit leading him home. But I *couldn't* ride him. I *couldn't* have him ridden with that knee."

This again was received in dead silence. Romero remained impassive, almost inert.

"Very well, then," said the Princess. "You lead him home. You'll be quite all right. Nothing can happen to you, possibly. And say to them that we have gone on and shall be home to-morrow—or the day after."

She spoke coldly and distinctly. For she could not bear to be thwarted.

"Better all go back, and come again another day," said Romero—non-committal.

"There will never *be* another day," cried the Princess. "I want to go on."

She looked at him square in the eyes, and met the spark in his eye.

He raised his shoulders slightly.

"If you want it," he said. "I'll go on with you. But Miss Cummins can ride my horse to the end of the canyon, and I lead the buckskin. Then I come back to you."

It was arranged so. Miss Cummins had her saddle put on Romero's black horse, Romero took the buckskin's bridle, and they started back. The Princess rode very slowly on, upwards, alone. She was at first so angry with Miss Cummins that she was blind to everything else. She just let her mare follow her own inclinations.

The peculiar spell of anger carried the Princess on, almost unconscious, for an hour or so. And by this time she was beginning to climb pretty high. Her horse walked steadily all the time. They emerged on a bare slope, and the trail wound through frail aspen-stems. Here a wind swept, and some of the aspens were already bare. Others were fluttering their discs of pure, solid yellow leaves, so *nearly* like petals, while the slope ahead was one soft, glowing fleece of daffodil yellow; fleecy like a golden foxskin, and yellow as daffodils alive in the wind and the high mountain sun.

She paused and looked back. The near great slopes were mottled with gold and the dark hue of spruce, like some unsinged eagle, and the light lay gleaming upon them. Away through the gap of the canyon she could see the pale blue of the egg-like desert, with the crumpled dark crack of the Rio Grande Canyon. And far, far off, the blue mountains like a fence of angels on the horizon.

And she thought of her adventure. She was going on alone with Romero. But then she was very sure of herself, and Romero was not the kind of man to do anything to her against her will. This was her first thought. And she just had a fixed desire to go over the brim of the mountains, to look into the inner chaos of the Rockies. And she wanted to go with Romero, because he had some peculiar kinship with her; there was some peculiar link between the two of them. Miss Cummins anyhow would have been only a discordant note.

She rode on, and emerged at length in the lap of the summit. Beyond her was a great concave of stone and stark, dead-grey trees, where the mountain ended against the sky. But nearer was the dense black, bristling spruce, and at her feet was the lap of the summit, a flat little valley, of sere grass and quiet-standing yellow aspens, the stream trickling like a thread across.

It was a little valley or shell from which the stream was gently poured into the lower rocks and trees of the canyon. Around her was a fairy-like gentleness, the delicate sere grass, the groves of delicate-stemmed aspens dropping their flakes of bright yellow. And the delicate, quick little stream threading through the wild, sere grass.

Here one might expect deer and fawns and wild things, as in a little paradise. Here she was to wait for Romero, and they were to have lunch.

She unfastened her saddle and pulled it to the ground with a crash, letting her horse wander with a long rope. How beautiful Tansy looked, sorrel, among the yellow leaves that lay like a patina on the sere ground. The Princess herself wore a fleecy sweater of a pale, sere buff, like the grass, and riding breeches of a pure orange-tawny colour. She felt quite in the picture.

From her saddle pouches she took the packages of lunch, spread a little cloth, and sat to wait for Romero. Then she made a little fire. Then she ate a devilled egg. Then she ran after Tansy, who was straying across-stream. Then she sat in the sun, in the stillness near the aspens, and waited.

The sky was blue. Her little alp was soft and delicate as fairy-land. But beyond and up jutted the great slopes, dark with the pointed feathers of spruce, bristling with grey dead trees among grey rock, or dappled with dark and gold. The beautiful, but fierce, heavy, cruel mountains, with their moments of tenderness.

She saw Tansy start, and begin to run. Two ghost-like figures on horseback emerged from the black of the spruce across the stream. It was two Indians on horseback, swathed like seated mummies in their pale-grey cotton blankets. Their guns jutted beyond the saddles. They rode straight towards her, to her thread of smoke.

As they came near, they unswathed themselves and greeted her, looking at her curiously from their dark eyes. Their black hair was somewhat untidy, the long rolled plaits on their shoulders were soiled. They looked tired.

They got down from their horses near her little fire—a camp was a camp—swathed their blankets round their hips, pulled the saddles from their ponies and turned them loose, then sat down. One was a young Indian whom she had met before, the other was an older man.

"You all alone?" said the younger man.

"Romero will be here in a minute," she said, glancing back along the trail.

"Ah, Romero! You with him? Where are you going?"

"Round the ridge," she said. "Where are you going?"

"We going down to Pueblo."

"Been out hunting? How long have you been out?"

"Yes. Been out five days." The young Indian gave a little meaningless laugh.

"Got anything?"

"No. We see tracks of two deer—but not got nothing."

The Princess noticed a suspicious-looking bulk under one of the saddles—surely a folded-up deer. But she said nothing.

"You must have been cold," she said.

"Yes, very cold in the night. And hungry. Got nothing to eat since yesterday. Eat it all up." And again he laughed his little meaningless laugh. Under their dark skins, the two men looked peaked and hungry. The Princess rummaged for food among the saddle-bags. There was a lump of bacon—the regular stand-back—and some bread. She gave them this, and they began toasting slices of it on long sticks at the fire. Such was the little camp Romero saw as he rode down the slope: the Princess in her orange breeches, her head tied in a blue-and-brown silk kerchief, sitting opposite the two dark-headed Indians across the camp-fire, while one of the Indians was leaning forward toasting bacon, his two plaits of braid-swathed hair dangling as if wearily.

Romero rode up, his face expressionless. The Indians greeted him in Spanish. He unsaddled his horse, took food from the bags, and sat down at the camp to eat. The Princess went to the stream for water, and to wash her hands.

"Got coffee?" asked the Indians.

"No coffee this outfit," said Romero.

They lingered an hour or more in the warm midday sun. Then Romero saddled the horses. The Indians still squatted by the fire. Romero and the Princess rode away, calling *Adios!* to the Indians, over the stream and into the dense spruce whence the two strange figures had emerged.

When they were alone, Romero turned and looked at her curiously, in a way she could not understand, with such a hard glint in his eyes. And for the first time she wondered if she was rash.

"I hope you don't mind going alone with me," she said.

"If you want it," he replied.

They emerged at the foot of the great bare slope of rocky summit, where dead spruce-trees stood sparse and bristling like bristles on a grey dead hog. Romero said the Mexicans, twenty years back, had fired the mountains, to drive out the whites. This grey concave slope of summit was corpse-like.

The trail was almost invisible. Romero watched for the trees which the Forest Service had blazed. And they climbed the stark corpse slope, among dead spruce, fallen and ash-grey, into the wind. The wind came rushing from the west, up the funnel of the canyon, from the desert. And there was the desert, like a vast mirage tilting slowly upwards towards the west, immense and pallid, away beyond the funnel of the canyon. The Princess could hardly look.

For an hour their horses rushed the slope, hastening with a great working of the haunches upwards, and halting to breathe, scrambling again, and rowing their way up length by length, on the livid, slanting wall. While the wind blew like some vast machine.

After an hour they were working their way on the incline, no longer forcing straight up. All was grey and dead around them; the horses picked their way over the silver-grey corpses of the spruce. But they were near the top, near the ridge.

Even the horses made a rush for the last bit. They had worked round to a scrap of spruce forest near the very top. They hurried in, out of the huge, monstrous, mechanical wind that whistled inhumanly and was palely cold. So, stepping through the dark screen of trees, they emerged over the crest.

In front now was nothing but mountains, ponderous, massive, down-sitting mountains, in a huge and intricate knot, empty of life or soul. Under the bristling black feathers of spruce nearby lay patches of white snow. The lifeless valleys were concaves of rock and spruce, the rounded summits and the hog-backed summits of grey rock crowded one behind the other like some monstrous herd in arrest.

It frightened the Princess, it was *so* inhuman. She had not thought it could be so inhuman, so, as it were, anti-life. And yet now one of her desires was fulfilled. She had seen it, the massive, gruesome, repellent core of the Rockies. She saw it there beneath her eyes, in its gigantic, heavy gruesomeness.

And she wanted to go back. At this moment she wanted to turn back. She had looked down into the intestinal knot of these mountains. She was frightened. She wanted to go back.

But Romero was riding on, on the lee side of the spruce forest, above the concaves of the inner mountains. He turned round to her and pointed at the slope with a dark hand.

"Here a miner has been trying for gold," he said. It was a grey, scratched-out heap near a hole—like a great badger hole. And it looked quite fresh.

"Quite lately?" said the Princess.

"No, long ago—twenty, thirty years." He had reined in his horse and was looking at the mountains. "Look!" he said. "There goes the Forest Service trail—along those ridges, on the top, way over there till it comes to Lucytown, where is the Government road. We go down there—no trail—see behind that mountain—you see the top, no trees, and some grass?"

His arm was lifted, his brown hand pointing, his dark eyes piercing into the distance, as he sat on his black horse twisting round to her. Strange and ominous, only the demon of himself, he seemed to her. She was dazed and a little sick, at that height, and she could not see any more. Only she saw an eagle turning in the air beyond, and the light from the west showed the pattern on him underneath.

"Shall I ever be able to go so far?" asked the Princess faintly, petulantly.

"Oh yes! All easy now. No more hard places."

They worked along the ridge, up and down, keeping on the lee side, the inner side, in the dark shadow. It was cold. Then the trail laddered up again, and they emerged on a narrow ridge-track, with the mountain slipping away enormously on either side. The Princess was afraid. For one moment she looked out, and saw the desert, the desert ridges, more desert, more blue ridges, shining pale and very vast, far below, vastly palely tilting to the western horizon. It was ethereal and terrifying in its gleaming, pale, half-burnished immensity, tilted at the west. She could not bear it. To the left was the ponderous, involved mass of mountains all kneeling heavily.

She closed her eyes and let her consciousness evaporate away. The mare followed the trail. So on and on, in the wind again.

They turned their backs to the wind, facing inwards to the mountains. She thought they had left the trail; it was quite invisible.

"No," he said, lifting his hand and pointing. "Don't you see the blazed trees?"

And making an effort of consciousness, she was able to perceive on a pale-grey dead spruce stem the old marks where an axe had chipped a piece away. But with the height, the cold, the wind, her brain was numb.

They turned again and began to descend; he told her they had left the trail. The horses slithered in the loose stones, picking their way downward. It was afternoon, the sun stood obtrusive and gleaming in the lower heavens—about four o'clock. The horses went steadily, slowly, but obstinately onwards. The air was getting colder. They were in among the lumpish peaks and steep concave valleys. She was barely conscious at all of Romero.

He dismounted and came to help her from her saddle. She tottered, but would not betray her feebleness.

"We must slide down here," he said. "I can lead the horses."

They were on a ridge, and facing a steep bare slope of pallid, tawny mountain grass on which the western sun shone full. It was steep and concave. The Princess felt she might start slipping, and go down like a toboggan into the great hollow.

But she pulled herself together. Her eye blazed up again with excitement and determination. A wind rushed past her; she could hear the shriek of spruce trees far below. Bright spots came on her cheeks as her hair blew across. She looked a wild, fairy-like little thing.

"No," she said. "I will take my horse."

"Then mind she doesn't slip down on top of you," said Romero. And away he went, nimbly dropping down the pale, steep incline, making from rock to rock, down the grass, and following any little slanting groove. His horse hopped and

lithered after him, and sometimes stopped dead, with forefeet
pressed back, refusing to go further. He, below his horse,
looked up and pulled the reins gently, and encouraged the
creature. Then the horse once more dropped his forefeet with a
jerk, and the descent continued.

The Princess set off in blind, reckless pursuit, tottering and
yet nimble. And Romero, looking constantly back to see how
she was faring, saw her fluttering down like some queer little
bird, her orange breeches twinkling like the legs of some duck,
and her head, tied in the blue and buff kerchief, bound round
and round like the head of some blue-topped bird. The sorrel
mare rocked and slipped behind her. But down came the
Princess in a reckless intensity, a tiny, vivid spot on the great
hollow flank of the tawny mountain. So tiny! Tiny as a frail
bird's egg. It made Romero's mind go blank with wonder.

But they had to get down, out of that cold and dragging wind.
The spruce trees stood below, where a tiny stream emerged in
stones. Away plunged Romero, zigzagging down. And away
behind, up the slope, fluttered the tiny, bright-coloured
Princess, holding the end of the long reins, and leading the
lumbering, four-footed, sliding mare.

At last they were down. Romero sat in the sun, below the
wind, beside some squaw-berry bushes. The Princess came
near, the colour flaming in her cheeks, her eyes dark blue,
much darker than the kerchief on her head, and glowing
unnaturally.

"We make it," said Romero.

"Yes," said the Princess, dropping the reins and subsiding on
to the grass, unable to speak, unable to think.

But, thank heaven, they were out of the wind and in the sun.
In a few minutes her consciousness and her control began to
come back. She drank a little water. Romero was attending to
the saddles. Then they set off again, leading the horses still a
little further down the tiny stream-bed. Then they could
mount.

They rode down a bank and into a valley grove dense with
aspens. Winding through the thin, crowding, pale-smooth

stems, the sun shone flickering beyond them, and the disc-like
aspen leaves, waving queer mechanical signals, seemed to be
splashing the gold light before her eyes. She rode on in a
splashing dazzle of gold.

Then they entered shadow and the dark, resinous spruce
trees. The fierce boughs always wanted to sweep her off her
horse. She had to twist and squirm past.

But there was a semblance of an old trail. And all at once
they emerged in the sun on the edge of the spruce-grove, and
there was a little cabin, and the bottom of a small, naked valley
with grey rock and heaps of stones, and a round pool of intense
green water, dark green. The sun was just about to leave it.

Indeed, as she stood, the shadow came over the cabin and
over herself; they were in the lower gloom, a twilight. Above
the heights still blazed.

It was a little hole of a cabin, near the spruce trees, with an
earthen floor and an unhinged door. There was a wooden bed-
bunk, three old sawn-off log-lengths to sit on as stools, and a
sort of fire-place; no room for anything else. The little hole
would hardly contain two people. The roof had gone—but
Romero had laid on thick spruce-boughs.

The strange squalor of the primitive forest pervaded the
place, the squalor of animals and their droppings, the squalor
of the wild. The Princess knew the peculiar repulsiveness of it.
She was tired and faint.

Romero hastily got a handful of twigs, set a little fire going
in the stove grate, and went out to attend to the horses. The
Princess vaguely, mechanically, put sticks on the fire, in a sort
of stupor, watching the blaze, stupefied and fascinated. She
could not make much fire—it would set the whole cabin alight.
And smoke oozed out of the dilapidated mud-and-stone
chimney.

When Romero came in with the saddle-pouches and saddles,
hanging the saddles on the wall, there sat the little Princess on
her stump of wood in front of the dilapidated fire-grate, warming her tiny hands at the blaze, while her orange breeches
glowed almost like another fire. She was in a sort of stupor.

"You have some whisky now, or some tea? Or wait for some soup?" he asked.

She rose and looked at him with bright, dazed eyes, half comprehending; the colour glowing hectic in her cheeks.

"Some tea," she said, "with a little whisky in it. Where's the kettle?"

"Wait," he said. "I'll bring the things."

She took her cloak from the back of her saddle, and followed him into the open. It was a deep cup of shadow. But above the sky was still shining, and the heights of the mountains were blazing with aspen like fire blazing.

Their horses were cropping the grass among the stones. Romero clambered up a heap of grey stones and began lifting away logs and rocks, till he had opened the mouth of one of the miner's little old workings. This was his cache. He brought out bundles of blankets, pans for cooking, a little petrol camp-stove, an axe, the regular camp outfit. He seemed so quick and energetic and full of force. This quick force dismayed the Princess a little.

She took a saucepan and went down the stones to the water. It was very still and mysterious and of a deep green colour, yet pure, transparent as glass. How cold the place was! How mysterious and fearful.

She crouched in her dark cloak by the water, rinsing the saucepan, feeling the cold heavy above her, the shadow like a vast weight upon her, bowing her down. The sun was leaving the mountain tops, departing, leaving her under profound shadow. Soon it would crush her down completely.

Sparks? Or eyes looking at her across the water? She gazed, hypnotized. And with her sharp eyes she made out in the dusk the pale form of a bob-cat crouching by the water's edge, pale as the stones among which it crouched, opposite. And it was watching her with cold, electric eyes of strange intentness, a sort of cold, icy wonder and fearlessness. She saw its *museau* pushed forward, its tufted ears pricking intensely up. It was watching her with cold, animal curiosity, something demonish and conscienceless.

She made a swift movement, spilling her water. And in a flash the creature was gone, leaping like a cat that is escaping; but strange and soft in its motion, with its little bob-tail. Rather fascinating. Yet that cold, intent, demonish watching! She shivered with cold and fear. She knew well enough the dread and repulsiveness of the wild.

Romero carried in the bundles of bedding and the camp outfit. The windowless cabin was already dark inside. He lit a lantern, and then went out again with the axe. She heard him chopping wood as she fed sticks to the fire under her water. When he came in with an armful of oak-scrub faggots, she had just thrown the tea into the water.

"Sit down," she said, "and drink tea."

He poured a little bootleg whisky into the enamel cups, and in the silence the two sat on the log-ends, sipping the hot liquid and coughing occasionally from the smoke.

"We burn these oak sticks," he said. "They don't make hardly any smoke."

Curious and remote he was, saying nothing except what had to be said. And she, for her part, was as remote from him. They seemed far, far apart, worlds apart, now they were so near.

He unwrapped one bundle of bedding, and spread the blankets and the sheepskin in the wooden bunk.

"You lie down and rest," he said, "and I make the supper."

She decided to do so. Wrapping her cloak round her, she lay down in the bunk, turning her face to the wall. She could hear him preparing supper over the little petrol stove. Soon she could smell the soup he was heating; and soon she heard the hissing of fried chicken in a pan.

"You eat your supper now?" he said.

With a jerky, despairing movement, she sat up in the bunk, tossing back her hair. She felt cornered.

"Give it me here," she said.

He handed her first the cupful of soup. She sat among the blankets, eating it slowly. She was hungry. Then he gave her an enamel plate with pieces of fried chicken and currant jelly, butter and bread. It was very good. As they ate the chicken he made the coffee. She said never a word. A certain resentment filled her. She was cornered.

When supper was over he washed the dishes, dried them, and put everything away carefully, else there would have been no room to move in the hole of a cabin. The oak-wood gave out a good bright heat.

He stood for a few moments at a loss. Then he asked her: "You want to go to bed soon?"

"Soon," she said. "Where are you going to sleep?"

"I make my bed here——" he pointed to the floor along the wall. "Too cold out of doors."

"Yes," she said. "I suppose it is."

She sat immobile, her cheeks hot, full of conflicting thoughts. And she watched him while he folded the blankets on the floor, a sheepskin underneath. Then she went out into the night.

The stars were big. Mars sat on the edge of a mountain, for all the world like the blazing eye of a crouching mountain lion. But she herself was deep, deep below in a pit of shadow.. In the intense silence she seemed to hear the spruce forest crackling with electricity and cold. Strange, foreign stars floated on that unmoving water. The night was going to freeze. Over the hills came the far sobbing-singing howling of the coyotes. She wondered how the horses would be.

Shuddering a little, she turned to the cabin. Warm light showed through its chinks. She pushed at the rickety, half-opened door.

"What about the horses?" she said.

"My black, he won't go away. And your mare will stay with him. You want to go to bed now?"

"I think I do."

"All right. I feed the horses some oats."

And he went out into the night.

He did not come back for some time. She was lying wrapped up tight in the bunk.

He blew out the lantern, and sat down on his bedding to

take off his clothes. She lay with her back turned. And soon, in the silence, she was asleep.

She dreamed it was snowing, and the snow was falling on her through the roof, softly, softly, helplessly, and she was going to be buried alive. She was growing colder and colder, the snow was weighing down on her. The snow was going to absorb her.

She awoke with a sudden convulsion, like pain. She was really very cold; perhaps the heavy blankets had numbed her. Her heart seemed unable to beat, she felt she could not move.

With another convulsion she sat up. It was intensely dark. There was not even a spark of fire, the light wood had burned right away. She sat in thick oblivious darkness. Only through a chink she could see a star.

What did she want? Oh, what did she want? She sat in bed and rocked herself woefully. She could hear the steady breathing of the sleeping man. She was shivering with cold; her heart seemed as if it could not beat. She wanted warmth, protection, she wanted to be taken away from herself. And at the same time, perhaps more deeply than anything, she wanted to keep herself intact, intact, untouched, that no one should have any power over her, or rights to her. It was a wild necessity in her that no one, particularly no man, should have any rights or power over her, that no one and nothing should possess her.

Yet that other thing! And she was so cold, so shivering, and her heart could not beat. Oh, would not someone help her heart to beat?

She tried to speak, and could not. Then she cleared her throat.

"Romero," she said strangely, "it is so cold."

Where did her voice come from, and whose voice was it, in the dark?

She heard him at once sit up, and his voice, startled, with a resonance that seemed to vibrate against her, saying:

"You want me to make you warm?"

"Yes."

As soon as he had lifted her in his arms, she wanted to scream to him not to touch her. She stiffened herself. Yet she was dumb.

And he was warm, but with a terrible animal warmth that seemed to annihilate her. He panted like an animal with desire. And she was given over to this thing.

She had never, never wanted to be given over to this. But she had *willed* that it should happen to her. And according to her will, she lay and let it happen. But she never wanted it. She never wanted to be thus assailed and handled, and mauled. She wanted to keep herself to herself.

However, she had willed it to happen, and it had happened. She panted with relief when it was over.

Yet even now she had to lie within the hard, powerful clasp of this other creature, this man. She dreaded to struggle to go away. She dreaded almost too much the icy cold of that other bunk.

"Do you want to go away from me?" asked his strange voice. Oh, if it could only have been a thousand miles away from her! Yet she had willed to have it thus close.

"No," she said.

And she could feel a curious joy and pride surging up again in him: at her expense. Because he had got her. She felt like a victim there. And he was exulting in his power over her, his possession, his pleasure.

When dawn came, he was fast asleep. She sat up suddenly.

"I want a fire," she said.

He opened his brown eyes wide, and smiled with a curious tender luxuriousness.

"I want you to make a fire," she said.

He glanced at the chinks of light. His brown face hardened to the day.

"All right," he said. "I'll make it."

She hid her face while he dressed. She could not bear to look at him. He was so suffused with pride and luxury. She hid her face almost in despair. But feeling the cold blast of air as he opened the door, she wriggled down into the warm

o

place where he had been. How soon the warmth ebbed, when he had gone!

He made a fire and went out, returning after a while with water.

"You stay in bed till the sun comes," he said. "It very cold."

"Hand me my cloak."

She wrapped the cloak fast round her, and sat up among the blankets. The warmth was already spreading from the fire.

"I suppose we will start back as soon as we've had breakfast?"

He was crouching at his camp-stove making scrambled eggs. He looked up suddenly, transfixed, and his brown eyes, so soft and luxuriously widened, looked straight at her.

"You want to?" he said.

"We'd better get back as soon as possible," she said, turning aside from his eyes.

"You want to get away from me?" he asked, repeating the question of the night in a sort of dread.

"I want to get away from here," she said decisively. And it was true. She wanted supremely to get away, back to the world of people.

He rose slowly to his feet, holding the aluminium frying-pan.

"Don't you like last night?" he asked.

"Not really," she said. "Why? Do you?"

He put down the frying-pan and stood staring at the wall. She could see she had given him a cruel blow. But she did not relent. She was getting her own back. She wanted to regain possession of all herself, and in some mysterious way she felt that he possessed some part of her still.

He looked round at her slowly, his face greyish and heavy.

"You Americans," he said, "you always want to do a man down."

"I am not American," she said. "I am British. And I don't want to do any man down. I only want to go back, now."

"And what will you say about me, down there?"

"That you were very kind to me, and very good."

He crouched down again, and went on turning the eggs. He gave her her plate, and her coffee, and sat down to his own food.

But again he seemed not to be able to swallow. He looked up at her.

"You don't like last night?" he asked.

"Not really," she said, though with some difficulty. "I don't care for that kind of thing."

A blank sort of wonder spread over his face, at these words, followed immediately by a black look of anger, and then a stony, sinister despair.

"You don't?" he said, looking her in the eyes.

"Not really," she replied, looking back with steady hostility into his eyes.

Then a dark flame seemed to come from his face.

"I make you," he said, as if to himself.

He rose and reached her clothes, that hung on a peg: the fine linen underwear, the orange breeches, the fleecy jumper, the blue-and-buff kerchief; then he took up her riding boots and her bead moccasins. Crushing everything in his arms, he opened the door. Sitting up, she saw him stride down to the dark-green pool in the frozen shadow of that deep cup of a valley. He tossed the clothing and the boots out on the pool. Ice had formed. And on the pure, dark green mirror, in the slaty shadow, the Princess saw her things lying, the white linen, the orange breeches, the black boots, the blue moccasins, a tangled heap of colour. Romero picked up rocks and heaved them out at the ice, till the surface broke and the fluttering clothing disappeared in the rattling water, while the valley echoed and shouted again with the sound.

She sat in despair among the blankets, hugging tight her pale-blue cloak. Romero strode straight back to the cabin.

"Now you stay here with me," he said.

She was furious. Her blue eyes met his. They were like two demons watching one another. In his face, beyond a sort of unrelieved gloom, was a demonish desire for death.

He saw her looking round the cabin, scheming. He saw her eyes on his rifle. He took the gun and went out with it. Returning, he pulled out her saddle, carried it to the tarn, and threw it in. Then he fetched his own saddle, and did the same.

"Now will you go away?" he said, looking at her with a smile.

She debated within herself whether to coax him and wheedle him. But she knew he was already beyond it. She sat among her blankets in a frozen sort of despair, hard as hard ice with anger.

He did the chores, and disappeared with the gun. She got up in her blue pyjamas, huddled in her cloak, and stood in the doorway. The dark-green pool was motionless again, the stony slopes were pallid and frozen. Shadow still lay, like an after-death, deep in this valley. Always in the distance she saw the horses feeding. If she could catch one! The brilliant yellow sun was half-way down the mountain. It was nine o'clock.

All day she was alone, and she was frightened. What she was frightened of she didn't know. Perhaps the crackling in the dark spruce wood. Perhaps just the savage, heartless wildness of the mountains. But all day she sat in the sun in the doorway of the cabin, watching, watching for hope. And all the time her bowels were cramped with fear.

She saw a dark spot that probably was a bear, roving across the pale grassy slope in the far distance, in the sun.

When, in the afternoon, she saw Romero approaching, with silent suddenness, carrying his gun and a dead deer, the cramp in her bowels relaxed, then became colder. She dreaded him with a cold dread.

"There is deer-meat," he said, throwing the dead doe at her feet.

"You don't want to go away from here," he said. "This is a nice place."

She shrank into the cabin.

"Come into the sun," he said, following her. She looked up at him with hostile, frightened eyes.

"Come into the sun," he repeated, taking her gently by the arm, in a powerful grasp.

She knew it was useless to rebel. Quietly he led her out, and seated himself in the doorway, holding her still by the arm.

"In the sun it is warm," he said. "Look, this is a nice place. You are such a pretty white woman, why do you want to act mean to me? Isn't this a nice place? Come! Come here! It is sure warm here."

He drew her to him, and in spite of her stony resistance, he took her cloak from her, holding her in her thin blue pyjamas.

"You sure are a pretty little white woman, small and pretty," he said. "You sure won't act mean to me—you don't want to, I know you don't."

She, stony and powerless, had to submit to him. The sun shone on her white, delicate skin.

"I sure don't mind hell fire," he said. "After this."

A queer, luxurious good-humour seemed to possess him again. But though outwardly she was powerless, inwardly she resisted him, absolutely and stonily.

When later he was leaving her again, she said to him suddenly:

"You think you can conquer me this way. But you can't. You can never conquer me."

He stood arrested, looking back at her, with many emotions conflicting in his face—wonder, surprise, a touch of horror, and an unconscious pain that crumpled his face till it was like a mask. Then he went out without saying a word, hung the dead deer on a bough, and started to flay it. While he was at this butcher's work, the sun sank and cold night came on again.

"You see," he said to her as he crouched, cooking the supper, "I ain't going to let you go. I reckon you called to me in the night, and I've some right. If you want to fix it up right now with me, and say you want to be with me, we'll fix it up now and go down to the ranch to-morrow and get married or whatever you want. But you've got to say you

want to be with me. Else I shall stay right here, till something
happens."

She waited a while before she answered:

"I don't want to be with anybody against my will. I don't
dislike you; at least, I didn't, till you tried to put your will
over mine. I won't have anybody's will put over me. You
can't succeed. Nobody could. You can never get me under
your will. And you won't have long to try, because soon they
will send someone to look for me."

He pondered this last, and she regretted having said it.
Then, sombre, he bent to the cooking again.

He could not conquer her, however much he violated her.
Because her spirit was hard and flawless as a diamond. But
he could shatter her. This she knew. Much more, and she
would be shattered.

In a sombre, violent excess he tried to expend his desire
for her. And she was racked with agony, and felt each time
she would die. Because, in some peculiar way, he had got hold
of her, some unrealized part of her which she never wished
to realize. Racked with a burning, tearing anguish, she felt
that the thread of her being would break, and she would die.
The burning heat that racked her inwardly.

If only, only she could be alone again, cool and intact! If
only she could recover herself again, cool and intact! Would
she ever, ever, ever be able to bear herself again?

Even now she did not hate him. It was beyond that. Like
some racking, hot doom. Personally he hardly existed.

The next day he would not let her have any fire, because of
attracting attention with the smoke. It was a grey day, and
she was cold. He stayed around, and heated soup on the
petrol stove. She lay motionless in the blankets.

And in the afternoon she pulled the clothes over her head
and broke into tears. She had never really cried in her
life. He dragged the blankets away and looked to see what
was shaking her. She sobbed in helpless hysterics. He
covered her over again and went outside, looking at the
mountains, where clouds were dragging and leaving a little

snow. It was a violent, windy, horrible day, the evil of winter rushing down.

She cried for hours. And after this a great silence came between them. They were two people who had died. He did not touch her any more. In the night she lay and shivered like a dying dog. She felt that her very shivering would rupture something in her body, and she would die.

At last she had to speak.

"Could you make a fire? I am so cold," she said, with chattering teeth.

"Want to come over here?" came his voice.

"I would rather you made me a fire," she said, her teeth knocking together and chopping the words in two.

He got up and kindled a fire. At last the warmth spread, and she could sleep.

The next day was still chilly, with some wind. But the sun shone. He went about in silence, with a dead-looking face. It was now so dreary and so like death she wished he would do anything rather than continue in this negation. If now he asked her to go down with him to the world and marry him, she would do it. What did it matter? Nothing mattered any more.

But he would not ask her. His desire was dead and heavy like ice within him. He kept watch around the house.

On the fourth day as she sat huddled in the doorway in the sun, hugged in a blanket, she saw two horsemen come over the crest of the grassy slope—small figures. She gave a cry. He looked up quickly and saw the figures. The men had dismounted. They were looking for the trail.

"They are looking for me," she said.

"Muy bien," he answered in Spanish.

He went and fetched his gun, and sat with it across his knees.

"Oh!" she said. "Don't shoot?"

He looked across at her.

"Why?" he said. "You like staying with me?"

"No," she said. "But don't shoot."

"I ain't going to Pen," he said.

"You won't have to go to Pen," she said. "Don't shoot!"

"I'm going to shoot," he muttered.

And straightway he kneeled and took very careful aim. The Princess sat on in an agony of helplessness and hopelessness.

The shot rang out. In an instant she saw one of the horses on the pale grassy slope rear and go rolling down. The man had dropped in the grass, and was invisible. The second man clambered on his horse, and on that precipitous place went at a gallop in a long swerve towards the nearest spruce-tree cover. Bang! Bang! went Romero's shots. But each time he missed, and the running horse leaped like a kangaroo towards cover.

It was hidden. Romero now got behind a rock; tense silence, in the brilliant sunshine. The Princess sat on the bunk inside the cabin, crouching, paralysed. For hours, it seemed, Romero knelt behind this rock, in his black shirt, bare-headed, watching. He had a beautiful, alert figure. The Princess wondered why she did not feel sorry for him. But her spirit was hard and cold, her heart could not melt. Though now she would have called him to her, with love.

But no, she did not love him. She would never love any man. Never! It was fixed and sealed in her, almost vindictively.

Suddenly she was so startled she almost fell from the bunk. A shot rang out quite close from behind the cabin. Romero leaped straight into the air, his arms fell outstretched, turning as he leaped. And even while he was in the air, a second shot rang out, and he fell with a crash, squirming, his hands clutching the earth towards the cabin door.

The Princess sat absolutely motionless, transfixed, staring at the prostrate figure. In a few moments the figure of a man in the Forest Service appeared close to the house; a young man in a broad-brimmed Stetson hat, dark flannel shirt, and riding-boots, carrying a gun. He strode over to the prostrate figure.

"Got you, Romero!" he said aloud. And he turned the dead man over. There was already a little pool of blood where Romero's breast had been.

"H'm!" said the Forest Service man. "Guess I got you nearer than I thought."

And he squatted there, staring at the dead man.

The distant calling of his comrade aroused him. He stood up.

"Hullo, Bill!" he shouted. "Yep! Got him! Yep! Done him in, apparently."

The second man rode out of the forest on a grey horse. He had a ruddy, kind face, and round brown eyes, dilated with dismay.

"He's not passed out?" he asked anxiously.

"Looks like it," said the first young man, coolly.

The second dismounted and bent over the body. Then he stood up again, and nodded.

"Yea-a!" he said. "He's done in all right. It's him all right, boy! It's Domingo Romero."

"Yep! I know it!" replied the other.

Then in perplexity he turned and looked into the cabin, where the Princess squatted, staring with big owl eyes from her red blanket.

"Hello!" he said, coming towards the hut. And he took his hat off. Oh, the sense of ridicule she felt! Though he did not mean any.

But she could not speak, no matter what she felt.

"What'd this man start firing for?" he asked.

She fumbled for words, with numb lips.

"He had gone out of his mind!" she said, with solemn, stammering conviction.

"Good Lord! You mean to say he'd gone out of his mind? Whew! That's pretty awful! That explains it then. H'm!"

He accepted the explanation without more ado.

With some difficulty they succeeded in getting the Princess down to the ranch. But she, too, was not a little mad.

"I'm not quite sure where I am," she said to Mrs. Wilkieson, as she lay in bed. "Do you mind explaining?"

Mrs. Wilkieson explained tactfully.

"Oh, yes!" said the Princess. "I remember. And I had an accident in the mountains, didn't I? Didn't we meet a man who'd gone mad, and who shot my horse from under me?"

"Yes, you met a man who had gone out of his mind."

The real affair was hushed up. The Princess departed east in a fortnight's time, in Miss Cummins's care. Apparently she had recovered herself entirely. She was the Princess, and a virgin intact.

But her bobbed hair was grey at the temples, and her eyes were a little mad. She was slightly crazy.

"Since my accident in the mountains, when a man went mad and shot my horse from under me, and my guide had to shoot him dead, I have never felt quite myself."

So she put it.

Later, she married an elderly man, and seemed pleased.

THE WOMAN WHO RODE AWAY

I

SHE had thought that this marriage, of all marriages, would be an adventure. Not that the man himself was exactly magical to her. A little, wiry, twisted fellow, twenty years older than herself, with brown eyes and greying hair, who had come to America a scrap of a wastrel, from Holland, years ago, as a tiny boy, and from the gold-mines of the west had been kicked south into Mexico, and now was more or less rich, owning silver-mines in the wilds of the Sierra Madre: it was obvious that the adventure lay in his circumstances, rather than his person. But he was still a little dynamo of energy, in spite of accidents survived, and what he had accomplished he had accomplished alone. One of those human oddments there is no accounting for.

When she actually *saw* what he had accomplished, her heart quailed. Great green-covered, unbroken mountain-hills, and in the midst of the lifeless isolation, the sharp pinkish mounds of the dried mud from the silver-works. Under the nakedness of the works, the walled-in, one-storey adobe house, with its garden inside, and its deep inner verandah with tropical climbers on the sides. And when you looked up from this shut-in flowered patio, you saw the huge pink cone of the silver-mud refuse, and the machinery of the extracting plant against heaven above. No more.

To be sure, the great wooden doors were often open. And then she could stand outside, in the vast open world. And see great, void, tree-clad hills piling behind one another, from nowhere into nowhere. They were green in autumn time. For the rest, pinkish, stark dry and abstract.

And in his battered Ford car her husband would take her into the dead, thrice-dead little Spanish town forgotten among the mountains. The great, sun-dried dead church, the dead portales, the hopeless covered market-place, where, the first time she went, she saw a dead dog lying between the meat stalls and the vegetable array, stretched out as if for ever, nobody troubling to throw it away. Deadness within deadness.

Everybody feebly talking silver, and showing bits of ore. But silver was at a standstill. The great war came and went. Silver was a dead market. Her husband's mines were closed down. But she and he lived on in the adobe house under the works, among the flowers that were never very flowery to her.

She had two children, a boy and a girl. And her eldest, the boy, was nearly ten years old before she aroused from her stupor of subjected amazement. She was now thirty-three, a large, blue-eyed, dazed woman, beginning to grow stout. Her little, wiry tough, twisted, brown-eyed husband was fifty-three, a man as tough as wire, tenacious as wire, still full of energy, but dimmed by the lapse of silver from the market, and by some curious inaccessibility on his wife's part.

He was a man of principles, and a good husband. In a way, he doted on her. He never quite got over his dazzled admiration of her. But essentially, he was still a bachelor. He had been thrown out on the world, a little bachelor, at the age of ten. When he married he was over forty, and had enough money to marry on. But his capital was all a bachelor's. He was boss of his own works, and marriage was the last and most intimate bit of his own works.

He admired his wife to extinction, he admired her body, all her points. And she was to him always the rather dazzling Californian girl from Berkeley, whom he had first known. Like any sheik, he kept her guarded among those mountains of Chihuahua. He was jealous of her as he was of his silver-mine: and that is saying a lot.

At thirty-three she really was still the girl from Berkeley, in all but physique. Her conscious development had stopped mysteriously with her marriage, completely arrested. Her husband had never become real to her, neither mentally nor physically. In spite of his late sort of passion for her, he never meant anything to her, physically. Only morally he swayed her, downed her, kept her in an invincible slavery.

So the years went by, in the adobe house strung round the sunny patio, with the silver-works overhead. Her husband was never still. When the silver went dead, he ran a ranch lower down, some twenty miles away, and raised pure-bred hogs, splendid creatures. At the same time, he hated pigs. He was a squeamish waif of an idealist, and really hated the physical side of life. He loved work, work, work, and making things. His marriage, his children, were something he was making, part of his business, but with a sentimental income this time.

Gradually her nerves began to go wrong: she must get out. She must get out. So he took her to El Paso for three months. And at least it was the United States.

But he kept his spell over her. The three months ended: back she was, just the same, in her adobe house among those eternal green or pinky-brown hills, void as only the undiscovered is void. She taught her children, she supervised the Mexican boys who were her servants. And sometimes her husband brought visitors, Spaniards or Mexicans or occasionally white men.

He really loved to have white men staying on the place. Yet he had not a moment's peace when they were there. It was as if his wife were some peculiar secret vein of ore in his mines, which no one must be aware of except himself. And she was fascinated by the young gentlemen, mining engineers, who were his guests at times. He, too, was fascinated by a real gentleman. But he was an old-timer miner with a wife, and if a gentleman looked at his wife, he felt as if his mine were being looted, the secrets of it pried out.

It was one of these young gentlemen who put the idea into her mind. They were all standing outside the great wooden doors of the patio, looking at the outer world. The eternal, motionless hills were all green, it was September, after the rains. There was no sign of anything, save the deserted mine, the deserted works, and a bunch of half-deserted miner's dwellings.

"I wonder," said the young man, "what there is behind those great blank hills.

"More hills," said Lederman. "If you go that way, Sonora and the coast. This way is the desert—you came from there—and the other way, hills and mountains."

"Yes, but what *lives* in the hills and the mountains? *Surely* there is something wonderful? It looks *so* like nowhere on earth: like being on the moon."

"There's plenty of game, if you want to shoot. And Indians, if you call *them* wonderful."

"Wild ones?"

"Wild enough."

"But friendly?"

"It depends. Some of them are quite wild, and they don't let anybody near. They kill a missionary at sight. And where a missionary can't get, nobody can."

"But what does the government say?"

"They're so far from everywhere, the government leaves 'em alone. And they're wily; if they think there'll be trouble, they send a delegation to Chihuahua and make a formal submission. The government is glad to leave it at that."

"And do they live quite wild, with their own savage customs and religion?"

"Oh, yes. They use nothing but bows and arrows. I've seen them in town, in the Plaza, with funny sort of hats with flowers round them, and a bow in one hand, quite naked except for a sort of shirt, even in cold weather—striding round with their savage's bare legs."

"But don't you suppose it's wonderful, up there in their secret villages?"

"No. What would there be wonderful about it? Savages are savages, and all savages behave more or less alike rather low-down and dirty, unsanitary, with a few cunning tricks, and struggling to get enough to eat."

"But surely they have old, old religions and mysteries—it *must* be wonderful, surely it must."

"I don't know about mysteries—howling and heathen

practices, more or less indecent. No, I see nothing wonderful in that kind of stuff. And I wonder that you should, when you have lived in London or Paris or New York——"

"Ah, *everybody* lives in London or Paris or New York"—said the young man, as if this were an argument.

And this peculiar vague enthusiasm for unknown Indians found a full echo in the woman's heart. She was overcome by a foolish romanticism more unreal than a girl's. She felt it was her destiny to wander into the secret haunts of these timeless, mysterious, marvellous Indians of the mountains.

She kept her secret. The young man was departing, her husband was going with him down to Torreon, on business: would be away for some days. But before the departure, she made her husband talk about the Indians: about the wandering tribes, resembling the Navajo, who were still wandering free; and the Yaquis of Sonora: and the different groups in the different valleys of Chihuahua State.

There was supposed to be one tribe, the Chilchuis, living in a high valley to the south, who were the sacred tribe of all the Indians. The descendants of Montezuma and the old Aztec or Totonac kings still lived among them, and the old priests still kept up the ancient religion, and offered human sacrifices— so it was said. Some scientists had been to the Chilchui country, and had come back gaunt and exhausted with hunger and bitter privation, bringing various curious, barbaric objects of worship, but having seen nothing extraordinary in the hungry, stark village of savages.

Though Lederman talked in this off-hand way, it was obvious he felt some of the vulgar excitement at the idea of ancient and mysterious savages.

"How far away are they?" she asked.

"Oh—three days on horseback—past Cuchitee and a little lake there is up there."

Her husband and the young man departed. The woman made her crazy plans. Of late, to break the monotony of her life, she had harassed her husband into letting her go riding with him, occasionally, on horseback. She was never allowed to go out alone. The country truly was not safe, lawless and crude.

But she had her own horse, and she dreamed of being free as she had been as a girl, among the hills of California.

Her daughter, nine years old, was now in a tiny convent in the little half-deserted Spanish mining-town five miles away.

"Manuel," said the woman to her house-servant, "I'm going to ride to the convent to see Margarita, and take her a few things. Perhaps I shall stay the night in the convent. You look after Freddy and see everything is all right till I come back."

"Shall I ride with you on the master's horse, or shall Juan?" asked the servant.

"Neither of you. I shall go alone."

The young man looked her in the eyes, in protest. Absolutely impossible that the woman should ride alone!

"I shall go alone," repeated the large, placid-seeming, fair-complexioned woman, with peculiar overbearing emphasis. And the man silently, unhappily yielded.

"Why are you going alone, mother?" asked her son, as she made up parcels of food.

"Am I *never* to be let alone? Not one moment of my life?" she cried, with sudden explosion of energy. And the child, like the servant, shrank into silence.

She set off without a qualm, riding astride on her strong roan horse, and wearing a riding suit of coarse linen, a riding skirt over her linen breeches, a scarlet neck-tie over her white blouse, and a black felt hat on her head. She had food in her saddle-bags, an army canteen with water, and a large, native blanket tied on behind the saddle. Peering into the distance, she set off from her home. Manuel and the little boy stood in the gateway to watch her go. She did not even turn to wave them farewell.

But when she had ridden about a mile, she left the wild road and took a small trail to the right, that led into another valley, over steep places and past great trees, and through another deserted mining-settlement. It was September, the water was running freely in the little stream that had fed the now-abandoned mine. She got down to drink, and let the horse drink too.

She saw natives coming through the trees, away up the slope. They had seen her, and were watching her closely. She watched in turn. The three people, two women and a youth, were making a wide detour, so as not to come too close to her. She did not care. Mounting, she trotted ahead up the silent valley, beyond the silver-works, beyond any trace of mining. There was still a rough trail that led over rocks and loose stones into the valley beyond. This trail she had already ridden, with her husband. Beyond that she knew she must go south.

Curiously she was not afraid, although it was a frightening country, the silent, fatal-seeming mountain-slopes, the occasional distant, suspicious, elusive natives among the trees, the great carrion birds occasionally hovering, like great flies, in the distance, over some carrion or some ranch house or some group of huts.

As she climbed, the trees shrank and the trail ran through a thorny scrub, that was trailed over with blue convolvulus and an occasional pink creeper. Then these flowers lapsed. She was nearing the pine-trees.

She was over the crest, and before her another silent, void, green-clad valley. It was past midday. Her horse turned to a little runlet of water, so she got down to eat her midday meal. She sat in silence looking at the motionless unliving valley, and at the sharp-peaked hills, rising higher to rock and pine-trees, southwards. She rested two hours in the heat of the day, while the horse cropped around her.

Curious that she was neither afraid nor lonely. Indeed, the loneliness was like a drink of cold water to one who is very thirsty. And a strange elation sustained her from within.

She travelled on, and camped at night in a valley beside a stream, deep among the bushes. She had seen cattle and had crossed several trails. There must be a ranch not far off. She heard the strange wailing shriek of a mountain-lion, and the answer of dogs. But she sat by her small camp fire in a secret hollow place and was not really afraid. She was buoyed up always by the curious, bubbling elation within her.

It was very cold before dawn. She lay wrapped in her blanket looking at the stars, listening to her horse shivering, and feeling like a woman who has died and passed beyond. She was not sure that she had not heard, during the night, a great crash at the centre of herself, which was the crash of her own death. Or else it was a crash at the centre of the earth, and meant something big and mysterious.

With the first peep of light she got up, numb with cold, and made a fire. She ate hastily, gave her horse some pieces of oil-seed cake, and set off again. She avoided any meeting—and since she met nobody, it was evident that she in turn was avoided. She came at last in sight of the village of Cuchitee, with its black houses with their reddish roofs, a sombre, dreary little cluster below another silent, long-abandoned mine. And beyond, a long, great mountain-side, rising up green and light to the darker, shaggier green of pine-trees. And beyond the pine-trees stretches of naked rock against the sky, rock slashed already and brindled with white stripes of snow. High up, the new snow had already begun to fall.

And now, as she neared, more or less, her destination, she began to go vague and disheartened. She had passed the little lake among yellowing aspen trees whose white trunks were round and suave like the white round arms of some woman. What a lovely place! In California she would have raved about it. But here she looked and saw that it was lovely, but she didn't care. She was weary and spent with her two nights in the open, and afraid of the coming night. She didn't know where she was going, or what she was going for. Her horse plodded dejectedly on, towards that immense and forbidding mountain-slope, following a stony little trail. And if she had had any will of her own left, she would have turned back, to the village, to be protected and sent home to her husband.

But she had no will of her own. Her horse splashed through a brook, and turned up a valley, under immense yellowing

cotton-wood trees. She must have been near nine thousand
feet above sea-level, and her head was light with the altitude
and with weariness. Beyond the cotton-wood trees she could
see, on each side, the steep sides of mountain-slopes hemming
her in, sharp-plumaged with overlapping aspen, and, higher
up, with sprouting, pointed spruce and pine-tree. Her horse
went on automatically. In this tight valley, on this slight trail,
there was nowhere to go but ahead, climbing.

Suddenly her horse jumped, and three men in dark blankets
were on the trail before her.

"Adios!" came the greeting, in the full, restrained Indian
voice.

"Adios!" she replied, in her assured, American woman's
voice.

"Where are you going?" came the quiet question, in
Spanish.

The men in the dark sarapes had come closer, and were
looking up at her.

"On ahead," she replied coolly, in her hard, Saxon Spanish.

These were just natives to her: dark-faced, strongly-built
men in dark sarapes and straw hats. They would have been
the same as the men who worked for her husband, except,
strangely, for the long black hair that fell over their shoulders.
She noted this long black hair with a certain distaste. These
must be the wild Indians she had come to see.

"Where do you come from?" the same man asked. It was
always the one man who spoke. He was young, with quick,
large, bright black eyes that glanced sideways at her. He had
a soft black moustache on his dark face, and a sparse tuft of
beard, loose hairs on his chin. His long black hair, full of
life, hung unrestrained on his shoulders. Dark as he was, he
did not look as if he had washed lately.

His two companions were the same, but older men, powerful
and silent. One had a thin black line of moustache, but was
beardless. The other had the smooth cheeks and the sparse
dark hairs marking the lines of his chin with the beard
characteristic of the Indians.

"I come from far away," she replied, with half-jocular evasion.

This was received in silence.

"But where do you live?" asked the young man, with that same quiet insistence.

"In the north," she replied airily.

Again there was a moment's silence. The young man conversed quietly, in Indian, with his two companions.

"Where do you want to go, up this way?" he asked suddenly, with challenge and authority, pointing briefly up the trail.

"To the Chilchui Indians," answered the woman laconically.

The young man looked at her. His eyes were quick and black, and inhuman. He saw, in the full evening light, the faint sub-smile of assurance on her rather large, calm, fresh-complexioned face; the weary, bluish lines under her large blue eyes; and in her eyes, as she looked down at him, a half-childish, half-arrogant confidence in her own female power. But in her eyes also, a curious look of trance.

"*Usted es Señora?* You are a lady?" the Indian asked her.

"Yes, I am a lady," she replied complacently.

"With a family?"

"With a husband and two children, boy and girl," she said.

The Indian turned to his companions and translated, in the low, gurgling speech, like hidden water running. They were evidently at a loss.

"Where is your husband?" asked the young man.

"Who knows?" she replied airily. "He has gone away on business for a week."

The black eyes watched her shrewdly. She, for all her weariness, smiled faintly in the pride of her own adventure and the assurance of her own womanhood, and the spell of the madness that was on her.

"And what do *you* want to do?" the Indian asked her.

"I want to visit the Chilchui Indians—to see their houses and to know their gods," she replied.

The young man turned and translated quickly, and there was a silence almost of consternation. The grave elder men

were glancing at her sideways, with strange looks, from under
their decorated hats. And they said something to the young
man, in deep chest voices.

The latter still hesitated. Then he turned to the woman.

"Good!" he said. "Let us go. But we cannot arrive until
to-morrow. We shall have to make a camp to-night."

"Good!" she said. "I can make a camp."

Without more ado, they set off at a good speed up the stony
trail. The young Indian ran alongside her horse's head, the
other two ran behind. One of them had taken a thick stick,
and occasionally he struck her horse a resounding blow on the
haunch, to urge him forward. This made the horse jump, and
threw her back in the saddle, which, tired as she was, made
her angry.

"Don't do that!" she cried, looking round angrily at the
fellow. She met his black, large, bright eyes, and for the first
time her spirit really quailed. The man's eyes were not human
to her, and they did not see her as a beautiful white woman.
He looked at her with a black, bright inhuman look, and saw
no woman in her at all. As if she were some strange, un-
accountable *thing*, incomprehensible to him, but inimical. She
sat in her saddle in wonder, feeling once more as if she had
died. And again he struck her horse, and jerked her badly
in the saddle.

All the passionate anger of the spoilt white woman rose in
her. She pulled her horse to a standstill, and turned with
blazing eyes to the man at her bridle.

"Tell that fellow not to touch my horse again," she cried.

She met the eyes of the young man, and in their bright black
inscrutability she saw a fine spark, as in a snake's eye, of
derision. He spoke to his companion in the rear, in the low
tones of the Indian. The man with the stick listened without
looking. Then, giving a strange low cry to the horse, he struck
it again on the rear, so that it leaped forward spasmodically
up the stony trail, scattering the stones, pitching the weary
woman in her seat.

The anger flew like a madness into her eyes, she went white

at the gills. Fiercely she reined in her horse. But before she could turn, the young Indian had caught the reins under the horse's throat, jerked them forward, and was trotting ahead rapidly, leading the horse.

The woman was powerless. And along with her supreme anger there came a slight thrill of exultation. She knew she was dead.

The sun was setting, a great yellow light flooded the last of the aspens, flared on the trunks of the pine-trees, the pine-needles bristled and stood out with dark lustre, the rocks glowed with unearthly glamour. And through this effulgence the Indian at her horse's head trotted unweariedly on, his dark blanket swinging, his bare legs glowing with a strange transfigured ruddiness in the powerful light, and his straw hat with its half-absurd decorations of flowers and feathers shining showily above his river of long black hair. At times he would utter a low call to the horse, and then the other Indian, behind, would fetch the beast a whack with the stick.

The wonder-light faded off the mountains, the world began to grow dark, a cold air breathed down. In the sky, half a moon was struggling against the glow in the west. Huge shadows came down from steep rocky slopes. Water was rushing. The woman was conscious only of her fatigue, her unspeakable fatigue, and the cold wind from the heights. She was not aware how moonlight replaced daylight. It happened while she travelled unconscious with weariness.

For some hours they travelled by moonlight. Then suddenly they came to a standstill. The men conversed in low tones for a moment.

"We camp here," said the young man.

She waited for him to help her down. He merely stood holding the horse's bridle. She almost fell from the saddle, so fatigued.

They had chosen a place at the foot of rocks that still gave off a little warmth of the sun. One man cut pine-boughs, another erected little screens of pine-boughs against the rock for shelter, and put boughs of balsam pine for beds. The third made a small fire, to heat tortillas. They worked in silence.

The woman drank water. She did not want to eat—only to lie down.

"Where do I sleep?" she asked.

The young man pointed to one of the shelters. She crept in and lay inert. She did not care what happened to her, she was so weary, and so beyond everything. Through the twigs of spruce she could see the three men squatting round the fire on their hams, chewing the tortillas they picked from the ashes with their dark fingers, and drinking water from a gourd. They talked in low, muttering tones, with long intervals of silence. Her saddle and saddle-bags lay not far from the fire, unopened, untouched. The men were not interested in her nor her belongings. There they squatted with their hats on their heads, eating, eating mechanically, like animals, the dark sarape with its fringe falling to the ground before and behind, the powerful dark legs naked and squatting like an animal's, showing the dirty white shirt and the sort of loin-cloth which was the only other garment, underneath. And they showed no more sign of interest in her than if she had been a piece of venison they were bringing home from the hunt, and had hung inside a shelter.

After a while they carefully extinguished the fire, and went inside their own shelter. Watching through the screen of boughs, she had a moment's thrill of fear and anxiety, seeing the dark forms cross and pass silently in the moonlight. Would they attack her now?

But no! They were as if oblivious of her. Her horse was hobbled; she could hear it hopping wearily. All was silent, mountain-silent, cold, deathly. She slept and woke and slept in a semi-conscious numbness of cold and fatigue. A long, long night, icy and eternal, and she aware that she had died.

II

Yet when there was a stirring, and a clink of flint and steel, and the form of a man crouching like a dog over a bone, at a red splutter of fire, and she knew it was morning coming, it seemed to her the night had passed too soon.

When the fire was going, she came out of her shelter with one real desire left: for coffee. The men were warming more tortillas.

"Can we make coffee?" she asked.

The young man looked at her, and she imagined the same faint spark of derision in his eyes. He shook his head.

"We don't take it," he said. "There is no time."

And the elder men, squatting on their haunches, looked up at her in the terrible paling dawn, and there was not even derision in their eyes. Only that intense, yet remote, inhuman glitter which was terrible to her. They were inaccessible. They could not see her as a woman at all. As if she *were* not a woman. As if, perhaps, her whiteness took away all her womanhood, and left her as some giant, female white ant. That was all they could see in her.

Before the sun was up, she was in the saddle again, and they were climbing steeply, in the icy air. The sun came, and soon she was very hot, exposed to the glare in the bare places. It seemed to her they were climbing to the roof of the world. Beyond against heaven were slashes of snow.

During the course of the morning, they came to a place where the horse could go no farther. They rested for a time with a great slant of living rock in front of them, like the glossy breast of some earth-beast. Across this rock, along a wavering crack, they had to go. It seemed to her that for hours she went in torment, on her hands and knees, from crack to crevice, along the slanting face of this pure rock-mountain. An Indian in front and an Indian behind walked slowly erect, shod with sandals of braided leather. But she in her riding-boots dared not stand erect.

Yet what she wondered, all the time, was why she persisted in clinging and crawling along these mile-long sheets of rock. Why she did not hurl herself down, and have done! The world was below her.

When they emerged at last on a stony slope, she looked back, and saw the third Indian coming carrying her saddle and saddle-bags on his back, the whole hung from a band across his forehead. And he had his hat in his hand, as he stepped slowly, with the slow, soft, heavy tread of the Indian, unwavering in the chinks of rock, as if along a scratch in the mountain's iron shield.

The stony slope led downwards. The Indians seemed to grow excited. One ran ahead at a slow trot, disappearing round the curve of stones. And the track curved round and down, till at last in the full blaze of the mid-morning sun, they could see a valley below them, between walls of rock, as in a great wide chasm let in the mountains. A green valley, with a river, and trees, and clusters of low flat sparkling houses. It was all tiny and perfect, three thousand feet below. Even the flat bridge over the stream, and the square with the houses around it, the bigger buildings piled up at opposite ends of the square, the tall cotton-wood trees, the pastures and stretches of yellow-sere maize, the patches of brown sheep or goats in the distance, on the slopes, the railed enclosures by the stream-side. There it was, all small and perfect, looking magical, as any place will look magical, seen from the mountains above. The unusual thing was that the low houses glittered white, whitewashed, looking like crystals of salt, or silver. This frightened her.

They began the long, winding descent at the head of the barranca, following the stream that rushed and fell. At first it was all rocks; then the pine-trees began, and soon, the silver-limbed aspens. The flowers of autumn, big pink daisy-like flowers, and white ones, and many yellow flowers, were in profusion. But she had to sit down and rest, she was so weary. And she saw the bright flowers shadowily, as pale shadows hovering, as one who is dead must see them.

At length came grass and pasture-slopes between mingled aspen and pine-trees. A shepherd, naked in the sun save for his hat and his cotton loin-cloth, was driving his brown sheep away. In a grove of trees they sat and waited, she and the young Indian. The one with the saddle had also gone forward.

They heard a sound of someone coming. It was three men, in fine sarapes of red and orange and yellow and black, and with brilliant feather head-dresses. The oldest had his grey hair braided with fur, and his red and orange-yellow sarape was covered with curious black markings, like a leopard-skin. The other two were not grey-haired, but they were elders too. Their blankets were in stripes, and their head-dresses not so elaborate.

The young Indian addressed the elders in a few quiet words. They listened without answering or looking at him or at the woman, keeping their faces averted and their eyes turned to the ground, only listening. And at length they turned and looked at the woman.

The old chief, or medicine-man, whatever he was, had a deeply wrinkled and lined face of dark bronze, with a few sparse grey hairs round the mouth. Two long braids of grey hair, braided with fur and coloured feathers, hung on his shoulders. And yet, it was only his eyes that mattered. They were black and of extraordinary piercing strength, without a qualm of misgiving in their demonish, dauntless power. He looked into the eyes of the white woman with a long, piercing look, seeking she knew not what. She summoned all her strength to meet his eyes and keep up her guard. But it was no good. He was not looking at her as one human being looks at another. He never even perceived her resistance or her challenge, but looked past them both, into she knew not what.

She could see it was hopeless to expect any human communication with this old being.

He turned and said a few words to the young Indian.

"He asks what do you seek here?" said the young man in Spanish.

"I? Nothing! I only came to see what it was like."

This was again translated, and the old man turned his eyes on her once more. Then he spoke again, in his low muttering tone, to the young Indian.

"He says, why does she leave her house with the white men? Does she want to bring the white man's God to the Chilchui?"

"No," she replied foolhardy. "I came away from the white

man's God myself. I came to look for the God of the Chilchui."

Profound silence followed, when this was translated. Then the old man spoke again, in a small voice almost of weariness.

"Does the white woman seek the gods of the Chilchui because she is weary of her own God?" came the question.

"Yes, she does. She is tired of the white man's God," she replied, thinking that was what they wanted her to say. She would like to serve the gods of the Chilchui.

She was aware of an extraordinary thrill of triumph and exultance passing through the Indians, in the tense silence that followed when this was translated. Then they all looked at her with piercing black eyes, in which a steely covetous intent glittered incomprehensible. She was the more puzzled, as there was nothing sensual or sexual in the look. It had a terrible glittering purity that was beyond her. She was afraid, she would have been paralysed with fear, had not something died within her, leaving her with a cold, watchful wonder only.

The elders talked a little while, then the two went away, leaving her with the young man and the oldest chief. The old man now looked at her with a certain solicitude.

"He says are you tired?" asked the young man.

"Very tired," she said.

"The men will bring you a carriage," said the young Indian.

The carriage, when it came, proved to be a litter consisting of a sort of hammock of dark woollen frieze, slung on to a pole which was borne on the shoulders of two long-haired Indians. The woollen hammock was spread on the ground, she sat down on it, and the two men raised the pole to their shoulders. Swinging rather as if she were in a sack, she was carried out of the grove of trees, following the old chief, whose leopard-spotted blanket moved curiously in the sunlight.

They had emerged in the valley-head. Just in front were the maize fields, with ripe ears of maize. The corn was not very tall, in this high altitude. The well-worn path went between it, and all she could see was the erect form of the old chief, in the flame and black sarape, stepping soft and heavy and swift, his

head forward, looking neither to right nor left. Her bearers
followed, stepping rhythmically, the long blue-black hair
glistening like a river down the naked shoulders of the man in
front.

They passed the maize, and came to a big wall or earthwork
made of earth and adobe bricks. The wooden doors were open.
Passing on, they were in a network of small gardens, full of
flowers and herbs and fruit trees, each garden watered by a
tiny ditch of running water. Among each cluster of trees and
flowers was a small, glittering white house, windowless, and
with closed door. The place was a network of little paths, small
streams, and little bridges among square, flowering gardens.

Following the broadest path—a soft narrow track between
leaves and grass, a path worn smooth by centuries of human
feet, no hoof of horse nor any wheel to disfigure it—they came
to the little river of swift bright water, and crossed on a log
bridge. Everything was silent—there was not a human being
anywhere. The road went on under magnificent cotton-wood
trees. It emerged suddenly outside the central plaza or square
of the village.

This was a long oblong of low white houses with flat roofs,
and two bigger buildings, having as it were little square huts
piled on top of bigger long huts, stood at either end of the
oblong, facing each other rather askew. Every little house was
a dazzling white, save for the great round beam-ends which
projected under the flat eaves, and for the flat roofs. Round
each of the bigger buildings, on the outside of the square, was a
stockyard fence, inside which was garden with trees and
flowers, and various small houses.

Not a soul was in sight. They passed silently between the
houses into the central square. This was quite bare and arid,
the earth trodden smooth by endless generations of passing
feet, passing across from door to door. All the doors of the
windowless houses gave on to this blank square, but all the
doors were closed. The firewood lay near the threshold, a clay
oven was still smoking, but there was no sign of moving life.

The old man walked straight across the square to the big

house at the end, where the two upper storeys as in a house of toy bricks, stood each one smaller than the lower one. A stone staircase, outside, led up to the roof of the first storey.

At the foot of this staircase the litter-bearers stood still, and lowered the woman to the ground.

"You will come up," said the young Indian who spoke Spanish.

She mounted the stone stairs to the earthen roof of the first house, which formed a platform round the wall of the second storey. She followed around this platform to the back of the big house. There they descended again, into the garden at the rear.

So far they had seen no one. But now two men appeared, bareheaded, with long braided hair, and wearing a sort of white shirt gathered into a loin-cloth. These went along with the three newcomers, across the garden where red flowers and yellow flowers were blooming, to a long, low white house. There they entered without knocking.

It was dark inside. There was a low murmur of men's voices. Several men were present, their white shirts showing in the gloom, their dark faces invisible. They were sitting on a great log of smooth old wood, that lay along the far wall. And save for this log, the room seemed empty. But no, in the dark at one end was a couch, a sort of bed, and someone lying there, covered with furs.

The old Indian in the spotted sarape, who had accompanied the woman, now took off his hat and his blanket and his sandals. Laying them aside, he approached the couch, and spoke in a low voice. For some moments there was no answer. Then an old man with the snow-white hair hanging round his darkly-visible face, roused himself like a vision, and leaned on one elbow, looking vaguely at the company, in tense silence.

The grey-haired Indian spoke again, and then the young Indian, taking the woman's hand, led her forward. In her linen riding habit, and black boots and hat, and her pathetic bit of a red tie, she stood there beside the fur-covered bed of the old, old man, who sat reared up, leaning on one elbow, remote as a ghost, his white hair streaming in disorder, his face almost black, yet with a far-off intentness, not of this world, leaning forward to look at her.

His face was so old, it was like dark glass, and the few curling hairs that sprang white from his lips and chin were quite incredible. The long white locks fell unbraided and disorderly on either side of the glassy dark face. And under a faint powder of white eyebrows, the black eyes of the old chief looked at her as if from the far, far dead, seeing something that was never to be seen.

At last he spoke a few deep, hollow words, as if to the dark air.

"He says, do you bring your heart to the god of the Chilchui?" translated the young Indian.

"Tell him yes," she said, automatically.

There was a pause. The old Indian spoke again, as if to the air. One of the men present went out. There was a silence as if of eternity in the dim room that was lighted only through the open door.

The woman looked round. Four old men with grey hair sat on the log by the wall facing the door. Two other men, powerful and impassive, stood near the door. They all had long hair, and wore white shirts gathered into a loin-cloth. Their powerful legs were naked and dark. There was a silence like eternity.

At length the man returned, with white and dark clothing on his arm. The young Indian took them, and holding them in front of the woman, said:

"You must take off your clothes, and put these on."

"If all you men will go out," she said.

"No one will hurt you," he said quietly.

"Not while you men are here," she said.

He looked at the two men by the door. They came quickly forward, and suddenly gripped her arms as she stood, without hurting her, but with great power. Then two of the old men came, and with curious skill slit her boots down with keen knives, and drew them off, and slit her clothing so that it came away from her. In a few moments she stood there white and uncovered. The old man on the bed spoke, and they turned her round for him to see. He spoke again, and the young Indian deftly took the pins and comb from her fair hair, so that it fell over her shoulders in a bunchy tangle.

Then the old man spoke again. The Indian led her to the bedside. The white-haired, glassy-dark old man moistened his finger-tips at his mouth, and most delicately touched her on the breasts and on the body, then on the back. And she winced strangely each time, as the finger-tips drew along her skin, as if Death itself were touching her.

And she wondered, almost sadly, why she did not feel ashamed in her nakedness. She only felt sad and lost. Because nobody felt ashamed. The elder men were all dark and tense with some other deep, gloomy, incomprehensible emotion, which suspended all her agitation, while the young Indian had a strange look of ecstasy on his face. And she, she was only utterly strange and beyond herself, as if her body were not her own.

They gave her the new clothing: a long white cotton shift, that came to her knees: then a tunic of thick blue woollen stuff, embroidered with scarlet and green flowers. It was fastened over one shoulder only, and belted with a braid sash of scarlet and black wool.

When she was thus dressed, they took her away, barefoot, to a little house in the stockaded garden. The young Indian told her she might have what she wanted. She asked for water to wash herself. He brought it in a jar, together with a long wooden bowl. Then he fastened the gate-door of her house, and left her a prisoner. She could see through the bars of the gate-door of her house, the red flowers of the garden, and a humming bird. Then from the roof of the big house she heard the long, heavy sound of a drum, unearthly to her in its summons, and an uplifted voice calling from the house-top in a strange language, with a far-away emotionless intonation, delivering some speech or message. And she listened as if from the dead.

But she was very tired. She lay down on a couch of skins, pulling over her the blanket of dark wool, and she slept, giving up everything.

When she woke it was late afternoon, and the young Indian was entering with a basket-tray containing food, tortillas, and corn-mush with bits of meat, probably mutton, and a drink made of honey, and some fresh plums. He brought her also a long garland of red and yellow flowers with knots of blue buds at the end. He sprinkled the garland with water from a jar, then offered it to her, with a smile. He seemed very gentle and thoughtful, and on his face and in his dark eyes was a curious look of triumph and ecstasy, that frightened her a little. The glitter had gone from the black eyes, with their curving dark lashes, and he would look at her with this strange soft glow of ecstasy that was not quite human, and terribly impersonal, and which made her uneasy.

"Is there anything you want?" he said, in his low, slow, melodious voice, that always seemed withheld, as if he were speaking aside to somebody else, or as if he did not want to let the sound come out to her.

"Am I going to be kept a prisoner here?" she asked.

"No, you can walk in the garden to-morrow," he said softly. Always this curious solicitude.

"Do you like that drink?" he said, offering her a little earthen-ware cup. "It is very refreshing."

She sipped the liquor curiously. It was made with herbs and sweetened with honey, and had a strange, lingering flavour. The young man watched her with gratification.

"It has a peculiar taste," she said.

"It is very refreshing," he replied, his black eyes resting on her always with that look of gratified ecstasy. Then he went away. And presently she began to be sick, and to vomit violently, as if she had no control over herself.

Afterwards she felt a great soothing langour steal over her, her limbs felt strong and loose and full of langour, and she lay on her couch listening to the sounds of the village, watching the yellowing sky, smelling the scent of burning cedar-wood, or pine-wood. So distinctly she heard the yapping of tiny dogs, the shuffle of far-off feet, the murmur of voices, so keenly she detected the smell of smoke, and flowers, and evening falling, so vividly she saw the one bright star infinitely remote, stirring above the sunset, that she felt as if all her senses were diffused on the air, that she could distinguish the sound of evening flowers unfolding, and the actual crystal sound of the heavens, as the vast belts of the world-atmosphere slid past one another, and as if the moisture ascending and the moisture descending in the air resounded like some harp in the cosmos.

She was a prisoner in her house, and in the stockaded garden, but she scarcely minded. And it was days before she realized that she never saw another woman. Only the men, the elderly men of the big house, that she imagined must be some sort of temple, and the men priests of some sort. For they always had the same colours, red, orange, yellow, and black, and the same grave, abstracted demeanour.

Sometimes an old man would come and sit in her room with her, in absolute silence. None spoke any language but Indian, save the one younger man. The older men would smile at her, and sit with her for an hour at a time, sometimes smiling at her when she spoke in Spanish, but never answering save with this slow, benevolent-seeming smile. And they gave off a feeling of almost fatherly solicitude. Yet their dark eyes, brooding over her, had something away in their depths that was awesomely ferocious and relentless. They would cover it with a smile, at once, if they felt her looking. But she had seen it.

Always they treated her with this curious impersonal solicitude, this utterly impersonal gentleness, as an old man treats a child. But underneath it she felt there was something else, something terrible. When her old visitor had gone away, in his silent, insidious, fatherly fashion, a shock of fear would come over her; though of what she knew not.

The young Indian would sit and talk with her freely, as if with great candour. But with him, too, she felt that everything real was unsaid. Perhaps it was unspeakable. His big dark eyes would rest on her almost cherishingly, touched with

P

ecstasy, and his beautiful, slow, languorous voice would trail out its simple, ungrammatical Spanish. He told her he was the grandson of the old, old man, son of the man in the spotted sarape: and they were caciques, kings from the old, old days, before even the Spaniards came. But he himself had been in Mexico City, and also in the United States. He had worked as a labourer, building the roads in Los Angeles. He had travelled as far as Chicago.

"Don't you speak English, then?" she asked.

His eyes rested on her with a curious look of duplicity and conflict, and he mutely shook his head.

"What did you do with your long hair, when you were in the United States?" she asked. "Did you cut it off?"

Again, with the look of torment in his eyes, he shook his head.

"No," he said, in a low, subdued voice, "I wore a hat, and a handkerchief tied round my head."

And he relapsed into silence, as if of tormented memories.

"Are you the only man of your people who has been to the United States?" she asked him.

"Yes. I am the only one who has been away from here for a long time. The others come back soon, in one week. They don't stay away. The old men don't let them."

"And why did you go?"

"The old men want me to go—because I shall be the cacique——"

He talked always with the same *naïveté*, an almost childish candour. But she felt that this was perhaps just the effect of his Spanish. Or perhaps speech altogether was unreal to him. Anyhow, she felt that all the real things were kept back.

He came and sat with her a good deal—sometimes more than she wished—as if he wanted to be near her. She asked him if he was married. He said he was—with two children.

"I should like to see your children," she said.

But he answered only with that smile, a sweet, almost ecstatic smile, above which the dark eyes hardly changed from their enigmatic abstraction.

It was curious, he would sit with her by the hour, without ever making her self-conscious, or sex-conscious. He seemed to have no sex, as he sat there so still and gentle and apparently submissive, with his head bent a little forward, and the river of glistening black hair streaming maidenly over his shoulders.

Yet when she looked again, she saw his shoulders broad and powerful, his eyebrows black and level, the short, curved, obstinate black lashes over his lowered eyes, the small, fur-like line of moustache above his blackish, heavy lips, and the strong chin, and she knew that in some other mysterious way he was darkly and powerfully male. And he, feeling her watching him, would glance up at her swiftly with a dark, lurking look in his eyes, which immediately he veiled with that half-sad smile.

The days and the weeks went by, in a vague kind of contentment. She was uneasy sometimes, feeling she had lost the power over herself. She was not in her own power, she was under the spell of some other control. And at times she had moments of terror and horror. But then these Indians would come and sit with her, casting their insidious spell over her by their very silent presence, their silent, sexless, powerful physical presence. As they sat they seemed to take her will away, leaving her will-less and victim to her own indifference. And the young man would bring her sweetened drink, often the same emetic drink, but sometimes other kinds. And after drinking, the languor filled her heavy limbs, her senses seemed to float in the air, listening, hearing. They had brought her a little female dog, which she called Flora. And once, in the trance of her senses, she felt she *heard* the little dog conceive, in her tiny womb, and begin to be complex, with young. And another day she could hear the vast sound of the earth going round, like some immense arrow-string booming.

But as the days grew shorter and colder, when she was cold, she would get a sudden revival of her will, and a desire to go out, to go away. And she insisted to the young man, she wanted to go out.

So one day, they let her climb to the topmost roof of the big house where she was, and look down the square. It was the day of the big dance, but not everybody was dancing. Women with babies in their arms stood in their doorways, watching. Opposite, at the other end of the square, there was a throng before the other big house, and a small, brilliant group on the terrace-roof of the first storey, in front of wide open doors of the upper storey. Through these wide open doors she could see fire glinting in darkness and priests in headdresses of black and yellow and scarlet feathers, wearing robe-like blankets of black and red and yellow, with long green fringes, were moving about. A big drum was beating slowly and regularly, in the dense, Indian silence. The crowd below waited.

Then a drum started on a high beat, and there came the deep, powerful burst of men singing a heavy, savage music, like a wind roaring in some timeless forest, many mature men singing in one breath, like the wind; and long lines of dancers walked out from under the. big house. Men with naked, golden-bronze bodies and streaming black hair, tufts of red and yellow feathers on their arms, and kilts of white frieze with a bar of heavy red and black and green embroidery round their waists, bending slightly forward and stamping the earth in their absorbed, monotonous stamp of the dance, a fox-fur, hung by the nose from their belt behind, swaying with the sumptuous swaying of a beautiful fox-fur, the tip of the tail writhing above the dancer's heels. And after each man, a woman with a strange elaborate headdress of feathers and sea-shells, and wearing a short black tunic, moving erect, holding up tufts of feathers in each hand, swaying her wrists rhythmically and subtly beating the earth with her bare feet.

So, the long line of the dance unfurling from the big house opposite. And from the big house beneath her, strange scent of incense, strange tense silence, then the answering burst of inhuman male singing, and the long line of the dance unfurling.

It went on all day, the insistence of the drum, the cavernous, roaring, storm-like sound of male singing, the incessant swinging of the fox-skins behind the powerful, gold-bronze, stamping legs of the men, the autumn sun from a perfect blue heaven pouring on the rivers of black hair, men's and women's, the valley all still, the walls of rock beyond the awful huge bulking of the mountain against the pure sky, its snow seething with sheer whiteness.

For hours and hours she watched, spell-bound, and as if drugged. And in all the terrible persistence of the drumming and the primeval, rushing deep singing, and the endless stamping of the dance of fox-tailed men, the tread of heavy, bird-erect women in their black tunics, she seemed at last to feel her own death; her own obliteration. As if she were to be obliterated from the field of life again. In the strange towering symbols on the heads of the changeless, absorbed women she seemed to read once more the *Mene Mene Tekel Upharsin*. Her kind of womanhood, intensely personal and individual, was to be obliterated again, and the great primeval symbols were to tower once more over the fallen individual independence of woman. The sharpness and the quivering nervous conscious-ness of the highly-bred white woman was to be destroyed again, womanhood was to be cast once more into the great stream of impersonal sex and impersonal passion. Strangely as if clairvoyant, she saw the immense sacrifice prepared. And she went back to her little house in a trance of agony.

After this, there was always a certain agony when she heard the drums at evening, and the strange uplifted savage sound of men singing round the drum, like wild creatures howling to the invisible gods of the moon and the vanished sun. Something of the chuckling, sobbing cry of the coyote, something of the exultant bark of the fox, the far-off wild melancholy exultance of the howling wolf, the torment of the puma's scream, and the insistence of the ancient fierce human male, with his lapses of tenderness and his abiding ferocity.

Sometimes she would climb the high roof after nightfall, and listen to the dim cluster of young men round the drum on the bridge just beyond the square, singing by the hour. Sometimes there would be a fire, and in the fire-glow, men in their white shirts or naked save for a loin-cloth would be dancing and stamping like spectres, hour after hour in the dark cold air, within the fire-glow, forever dancing and stamping like turkeys, or dropping squatting by the fire to rest, throwing their blankets round them.

"Why do you all have the same colours?" she asked the young Indian. "Why do you all have red and yellow and black, over your white shirts? And the women have black tunics?"

He looked into her eyes, curiously, and the faint, evasive smile came on to his face. Behind the smile lay a soft, strange malignancy.

"Because our men are the fire and the daytime, and our women are the spaces between the stars at night," he said.

"Aren't the women even stars?" she said.

"No. We say they are the spaces between the stars, that keep the stars apart."

He looked at her oddly, and again the touch of derision came into his eyes.

"White people," he said, "they know nothing. They are like children, always with toys. We know the sun, and we know the moon. And we say, when a white woman sacrifice herself to our gods, then our gods will begin to make the world again, and the white man's gods will fall to pieces."

"How sacrifice herself?" she asked quickly.

And he, as quickly covered, covered himself with a subtle smile.

"She sacrifice her own gods and come to our gods, I mean that," he said, soothingly.

But she was not reassured. An icy pang of fear and certainty was at her heart.

"The sun he is alive at one end of the sky," he continued, "and the moon lives at the other end. And the man all the time have to keep the sun happy in his side of the sky, and the woman have to keep the moon quiet at her side of the sky. All the time she have to work at this. And the sun can't ever go into the house of the moon, and the moon can't ever go into the house of the sun, in the sky. So the woman, she asks the moon to come into her cave, inside her. And the man, he draws the sun down till he has the power of the sun. All the time he do this. Then when the man gets a woman, the sun goes into the cave of the moon, and that is how everything in the world starts."

She listened, watching him closely, as one enemy watches another who is speaking with double meaning.

"Then," she said, "why aren't you Indians masters of the white men?"

"Because," he said, "the Indian got weak, and lost his power with the sun, so the white men stole the sun. But they can't keep him—they don't know how. They got him, but they don't know what to do with him, like a boy who catch a big grizzly bear, and can't kill him, and can't run away from him. The grizzly bear eats the boy that catch him, when he want to run away from him. White men don't know what they are doing with the sun, and white women don't know what they do with the moon. The moon she got angry with white women, like a puma when someone kills her little ones. The moon, she bites white women—here inside," and he pressed his side. "The moon, she is angry in a white woman's cave. The Indian can see it. And soon," he added, "the Indian women get the moon back and keep her quiet in their house. And the Indian men get the sun, and the power over all the world. White men don't know what the sun is. They never know."

He subsided into a curious exultant silence.

"But," she faltered, "why do you hate us so? Why do you hate me?"

He looked up suddenly with a light on his face, and a startling flame of a smile.

"No, we don't hate," he said softly, looking with a curious glitter into her face.

"You do," she said, forlorn and hopeless.

And after a moment's silence, he rose and went away.

III

Winter had now come, in the high valley, with snow that melted in the day's sun, and nights that were bitter cold. She lived on, in a kind of daze, feeling her power ebbing more and more away from her, as if her will were leaving her. She felt always in the same relaxed, confused, victimised state, unless the sweetened herb drink would numb her mind altogether, and release her senses into a sort of heightened, mystic acuteness and a feeling as if she were diffusing out deliciously into the harmony of things. This at length became the only state of consciousness she really recognized: this exquisite sense of bleeding out into the higher beauty and harmony of things. Then she could actually hear the great stars in heaven, which she saw through her door, speaking from their motion and brightness, saying things perfectly to the cosmos, as they trod in perfect ripples, like bells on the floor of heaven, passing one another and grouping in the timeless dance, with the spaces of dark between. And she could hear the snow on a cold, cloudy day twittering and faintly whistling in the sky, like birds that flock and fly away in autumn, suddenly calling farewell to the invisible moon, and slipping out of the plains of the air, releasing peaceful warmth. She herself would call to the arrested snow to fall from the upper air. She would call to the unseen moon to cease to be angry, to make peace again with the unseen sun like a woman who ceases to be angry in her house. And she would smell the sweetness of the moon, relaxing to the sun in the wintry heaven, when the snow fell in a faint, cold-perfumed relaxation, as the peace of the sun mingled again in a sort of unison with the peace of the moon.

She was aware too of the sort of shadow that was on the Indians of the valley, a deep stoical disconsolation, almost religious in its depth.

"We have lost our power over the sun, and we are trying to get him back. But he is wild with us, and shy like a horse that has got away. We have to go through a lot." So the young

Indian said to her, looking into her eyes with a strained meaning. And she, as if bewitched, replied:

"I hope you will get him back."

The smile of triumph flew over his face.

"Do you hope it?" he said.

"I do," she answered fatally.

"Then all right," he said. "We shall get him."

And he went away in exultance.

She felt she was drifting on some consummation, which she had no will to avoid, yet which seemed heavy and finally terrible to her.

It must have been almost December, for the days were short when she was taken again before the aged man, and stripped of her clothing, and touched with the old finger-tips.

The aged cacique looked her in the eyes, with his eyes of lonely, far-off, black intentness, and murmured something to her.

"He wants you to make the sign of peace," the young man translated, showing her the gesture. "Peace and farewell to him."

She was fascinated by the black, glass-like, intent eyes of the old cacique, that watched her without blinking, like a basilisk's, overpowering her. In their depths also she saw a certain fatherly compassion, and pleading. She put her hand before her face, in the required manner, making the sign of peace and farewell. He made the sign of peace back again to her, then sank among his furs. She thought he was going to die, and that he knew it.

There followed a day of ceremonial, when she was brought out before all the people, in a blue blanket with white fringe, and holding blue feathers in her hands. Before an altar of one house she was perfumed with incense and sprinkled with ash. Before the altar of the opposite house she was fumigated again with incense by the gorgeous, terrifying priests in yellow and scarlet and black, their faces painted with scarlet paint. And then they threw water on her. Meanwhile she was faintly aware of the fire on the altar, the heavy, heavy sound of a drum, the heavy sound of men beginning powerfully, deeply, savagely to sing, the swaying of the crowd of faces in the plaza below, and the formation for a sacred dance.

But at this time her commonplace consciousness was numb, she was aware of her immediate surroundings as shadows, almost immaterial. With refined and heightened senses she could hear the sound of the earth winging on its journey, like a shot arrow, the ripple-rustling of the air, and the boom of the great arrow-string. And it seemed to her there were two great influences in the upper air, one golden towards the sun, and one invisible silver; the first travelling like rain ascending to the gold presence sunwards, the second like rain silverily descending the ladders of space towards the hovering, lurking clouds over the snowy mountain-top. Then between them, another presence, waiting to shake himself free of moisture, of heavy white snow that had mysteriously collected about him. And in summer, like a scorched eagle, he would wait to shake himself clear of the weight of heavy sunbeams. And he was coloured like fire. And he was always shaking himself clear, of snow or of heavy heat, like an eagle rustling.

Then there was a still stranger presence, standing watching from the blue distance, always watching. Sometimes running in upon the wind, or shimmering in the heat-waves. The blue wind itself, rushing as it were out of the holes into the sky, rushing out of the sky down upon the earth. The blue wind, the go-between, the invisible ghost that belonged to two worlds, that played upon the ascending and the descending chords of the rains.

More and more her ordinary personal consciousness had left her, she had gone into that other state of passional cosmic consciousness, like one who is drugged. The Indians, with their heavily religious natures, had made her succumb to their vision.

Only one personal question she asked the young Indian: "Why am I the only one that wears blue?"

"It is the colour of the wind. It is the colour of what goes away and is never coming back, but which is always here, waiting like death among us. It is the colour of the dead. And it is the colour that stands away off, looking at us from the distance, that cannot come near to us. When we go near, it goes farther. It can't be near. We are all brown and yellow and black hair, and white teeth and red blood. We are the ones that are here. You with blue eyes, you are the messengers from the far-away, you cannot stay, and now it is time for you to go back."

"Where to?" she asked.

"To the way-off things like the sun and the blue mother of rain, and tell them that we are the people on the world again, and we can bring the sun to the moon again, like a red horse to a blue mare; we are the people. The white women have driven back the moon in the sky, won't let her come to the sun. So the sun is angry. And the Indian must give the moon to the sun."

"How?" she said.

"The white woman got to die and go like a wind to the sun, tell him the Indians will open the gate to him. And the Indian women will open the gate to the moon. The white women don't let the moon come down out of the blue coral. The moon used to come down among the Indian women, like a white goat among the flowers. And the sun want to come down to the Indian men, like an eagle to the pine-trees. The sun, he is shut out behind the white man, and the moon she is shut out behind the white woman, and they can't get away. They are angry, everything in the world gets angrier. The Indian says, he will give the white woman to the sun, so the sun will leap over the white man and come to the Indian again. And the moon will be surprised, she will see the gate open, and she not know which way to go. But the Indian woman will call to the moon, *Come! Come! Come back into my grasslands. The wicked white woman can't harm you any more.* Then the sun will look over the heads of the white men, and see the moon in the pastures of our women, with the Red Men standing around like pine-trees. Then he will leap over the heads of the white men, and come running past to the Indians through the spruce trees. And we, who are red and black and yellow, we who stay, we shall have the sun on our right hand and the moon on our left. So we can bring the rain down out of the blue meadows, and up out of the black; and we can call the wind that tells the corn to grow, when we ask him, and we shall make the clouds to break, and the sheep to have twin lambs. And we shall be full of power, like a spring day. But the white people will be a hard winter, without snow——"

"But," said the white woman, "I don't shut out the moon— how can I?"

"Yes," he said, "you shut the gate, and then laugh, think you have it all your own way."

She could never quite understand the way he looked at her. He was always so curiously gentle, and his smile was so soft. Yet there was such a glitter in his eyes, and an unrelenting sort of hate came out of his words, a strange, profound, impersonal hate. Personally he liked her, she was sure. He was gentle with her, attracted by her in some strange, soft, passionless way. But impersonally he hated her with a mystic hatred. He would smile at her, winningly. Yet if, the next moment, she glanced round at him unawares, she would catch that gleam of pure after-hate in his eyes.

"Have I got to die and be given to the sun?" she asked.

"Sometime," he said, laughing evasively. "Sometime we all die."

They were gentle with her, and very considerate, with her. Strange men, the old priests and the young cacique alike, they watched over her and cared for her like women. In their soft, insidious understanding, there was something womanly. Yet their eyes, with that strange glitter, and their dark, shut mouths that would open to the broad jaw, the small, strong, white teeth, had something very primitively male and cruel.

One wintry day, when snow was falling, they took her to a great dark chamber in the big house. The fire was burning in a corner on a high raised dais under a sort of hood or canopy of adobe-work. She saw in the fire-glow the glowing bodies of the almost naked priests, and strange symbols on the roof and walls of the chamber. There was no door or window in the chamber, they had descended by a ladder from the roof. And the fire of pinewood danced continually, showing walls painted with strange devices, which she could not understand, and a ceiling of poles making a curious pattern of black and red and yellow, and alcoves or niches in which were curious objects she could not discern.

The older priests were going through some ceremony near the fire, in silence, intense Indian silence. She was seated on a low projection of the wall, opposite the fire, two men seated beside her. Presently they gave her a drink from a cup, which she took gladly, because of the semi-trance it would induce.

In the darkness and in the silence she was accurately aware of everything that happened to her: how they took off her clothes, and, standing her before a great, weird device on the wall, coloured blue and white and black, washed her all over with water and the amole infusion; washed even her hair, softly, carefully, and dried it on white cloths, till it was soft and glistening. Then they laid her on a couch under another great indecipherable image of red and black and yellow, and now rubbed all her body with sweet-scented oil, and massaged all her limbs, and her back, and her sides, with a long, strange, hypnotic massage. Their dark hands were incredibly powerful, yet soft with a watery softness she could not understand. And the dark faces, leaning near her white body, she saw were darkened with red pigment, with lines of yellow round the cheeks. And the dark eyes glittered absorbed, as the hands worked upon the soft white body of the woman.

They were so impersonal, absorbed in something that was beyond her. They never saw her as a personal woman: she could tell that. She was some mystic object to them, some vehicle of passions too remote for her to grasp. Herself in a state of trance, she watched their faces bending over her, dark, strangely glistening with the transparent red paint, and lined with bars of yellow. And in this weird, luminous-dark mask of living face, the eyes were fixed with an unchanging steadfast gleam, and the purplish-pigmented lips were closed in a full, sinister, sad grimness. The immense fundamental sadness, the grimness of ultimate decision, the fixity of revenge, and the nascent exultance of those that are going to triumph—these things she could read in their faces, as she lay and was rubbed into a misty glow by their uncanny dark hands. Her limbs, her flesh, her very bones at last seemed to be diffusing into a roseate sort of mist, in which her consciousness hovered like some sungleam in a flushed cloud.

She knew the gleam would fade, the cloud would go grey. But at present she did not believe it. She knew she was a victim; that all this elaborate work upon her was the work of victimising her. But she did not mind. She wanted it.

Later, they put a short blue tunic on her and took her to the upper terrace, and presented her to the people. She saw the plaza below her full of dark faces and of glittering eyes. There was no pity: only the curious hard exultance. The people gave a subdued cry when they saw her, and she shuddered. But she hardly cared.

Next day was the last. She slept in a chamber of the big house. At dawn they put on her a big blue blanket with a fringe, and led her out into the plaza, among the throng of silent, dark-blanketed people. There was pure white snow on the ground, and the dark people in their dark-brown blankets looked like inhabitants of another world.

A large drum was slowly pounding, and an old priest was declaring from a housetop. But it was not till noon that a litter came forth, and the people gave that low, animal cry which was so moving. In the sack-like litter sat the old, old cacique, his white hair braided with black braid and large turquoise stones. His face was like a piece of obsidian. He lifted his hand in token, and the litter stopped in front of her. Fixing her with his old eyes, he spoke to her for a few moments, in his hollow voice. No one translated.

Another litter came, and she was placed in it. Four priests moved ahead, in their scarlet and yellow and black, with plumed head-dresses. Then came the litter of the old cacique. Then the light drums began, and two groups of singers burst simultaneously into song, male and wild. And the golden-red, almost naked men, adorned with ceremonial feathers and kilts, the rivers of black hair down their backs, formed into two files and began to tread the dance. So they threaded out of the snowy plaza, in two long, sumptuous lines of dark red-gold and black and fur, swaying with a faint tinkle of bits of shell and flint, winding over the snow between the two bee-clusters of men who sang around the drum.

Slowly they moved out, and her litter, with its attendance of feathered, lurid, dancing priests, moved after. Everybody danced the tread of the dance-step, even, subtly, the litter-bearers. And out of the plaza they went, past smoking ovens, on the trail to the great cotton-wood trees, that stood like grey-silver lace against the blue sky, bare and exquisite above the snow. The river, diminished, rushed among fangs of ice. The chequer-squares of gardens within fences were all snowy, and the white houses now looked yellowish.

The whole valley glittered intolerably with pure snow, away to the walls of the standing rock. And across the flat cradle of snow bed wound the long thread of the dance, shaking slowly and sumptuously in its orange and black motion. The high drums thudded quickly, and on the crystalline frozen air the swell and roar of the chant of savages was like an obsession.

She sat looking out of her litter with big, transfixed blue eyes, under which were the wan markings of her drugged weariness. She knew she was going to die, among the glisten of this snow, at the hands of this savage, sumptuous people. And as she stared at the blaze of the blue sky above the slashed and ponderous mountain, she thought: "I am dead already. What difference does it make, the transition from the dead I am to the dead I shall be, very soon!" Yet her soul sickened and felt wan.

The strange procession trailed on, in perpetual dance, slowly across the plain of snow, and then entered the slopes between the pine-trees. She saw the copper-dark men dancing the dance-tread, onwards, between the copper-pale tree trunks. And at last she, too, in her swaying litter, entered the pine-trees.

They were travelling on and on, upwards, across the snow under the trees, past the superb shafts of pale, flaked copper, the rustle and shake and tread of the threading dance, penetrating into the forest, into the mountain. They were following a stream-bed: but the stream was dry, like summer, dried up by the frozenness of the head-waters. There were dark, red-bronze willow bushes with wattles like wild hair, and pallid aspen-trees looking cold flesh against the snow. Then jutting dark rocks.

At last she could tell that the dancers were moving forward no more. Nearer and nearer she came upon the drums, as to a lair of mysterious animals. Then through the bushes she emerged into a strange amphitheatre. Facing was a great wall of hollow rock, down the front of which hung a great, dripping, fang-like spoke of ice. The ice came pouring over the rock from the precipice above, and then stood arrested, dripping out of high heaven, almost down to the hollow stones where the stream-pool should be below. But the pool was dry.

On either side the dry pool the lines of dancers had formed, and the dance was continuing without intermission, against a background of bushes.

But what she felt was that fanged inverted pinnacle of ice, hanging from the lip of the dark precipice above. And behind the great rope of ice she saw the leopard-like figures of priests climbing the hollow cliff face, to the cave that like a dark socket bored a cavity, an orifice, half-way up the crag.

Before she could realize, her litter-bearers were staggering in the footholds, climbing the rock. She, too, was behind the ice There it hung, like a curtain that is not spread, but hangs like a great fang. And near above her was the orifice of the cave sinking dark into the rock. She watched it as she swayed upwards.

On the platform of the cave stood the priests, waiting in all their gorgeousness of feathers and fringed robes, watching her ascent. Two of them stooped to help her litter-bearer. And at length she was on the platform of the cave, far in behind the shaft of ice, above the hollow amphitheatre among the bushes below, where men were dancing, and the whole populace of the village was clustered in silence.

The sun was sloping down the afternoon sky, on the left. She knew that this was the shortest day of the year, and the last day of her life. They stood her facing the iridescent column of ice, which fell down marvellously arrested, away in front of her.

Some signal was given, and the dance below stopped. There was now absolute silence. She was given a little to drink, then two priests took off her mantle and her tunic, and in her strange pallor she stood there, between the lurid robes of the priests, beyond the pillar of ice, beyond and above the dark-faced people. The throng below gave the low, wild cry. Then the priest turned her round, so she stood with her back to the open world, her long blond hair to the people below. And they cried again.

She was facing the cave, inwards. A fire was burning and flickering in the depths. Four priests had taken off their robes, and were almost as naked as she was. They were powerful men in the prime of life, and they kept their dark, painted faces lowered.

From the fire came the old, old priest, with an incense-pan. He was naked and in a state of barbaric ecstasy. He fumigated his victim, reciting at the same time in a hollow voice. Behind him came another robeless priest, with two flint knives.

When she was fumigated, they laid her on a large flat stone, the four powerful men holding her by the outstretched arms and legs. Behind stood the aged man, like a skeleton covered with dark glass, holding a knife and transfixedly watching the sun; and behind him again was another naked priest, with a knife.

She felt little sensation, though she knew all that was happening. Turning to the sky, she looked at the yellow sun. It was sinking. The shaft of ice was like a shadow between her and it. And she realized that the yellow rays were filling half the cave, though they had not reached the altar where the fire was, at the far end of the funnel-shaped cavity.

Yes, the rays were creeping round slowly. As they grew ruddier, they penetrated farther. When the red sun was about to sink, he would shine full through the shaft of ice deep into the hollow of the cave, to the innermost.

She understood now that this was what the men were waiting for. Even those that held her down were bent and twisted round, their black eyes watching the sun with a glittering eagerness, and awe, and craving. The black eyes of the aged cacique were fixed like black mirrors on the sun, as if sightless, yet containing some terrible answer to the reddening winter planet. And all the eyes of the priests were fixed and glittering on the sinking orb, in the reddening, icy silence of the winter afternoon.

They were anxious, terribly anxious, and fierce. Their ferocity wanted something, and they were waiting the moment. And their ferocity was ready to leap out into a mystic exultance, of triumph. But still they were anxious.

Only the eyes of that oldest man were not anxious. Black, and fixed, and as if sightless, they watched the sun, seeing beyond the sun. And in their black, empty concentration there was power, power intensely abstract and remote, but deep, deep to the heart of the earth, and the heart of the sun. In absolute motionlessness he watched till the red sun should send his ray through the column of ice. Then the old man would strike, and strike home, accomplish the sacrifice and achieve the power.

The mastery that man must hold, and that passes from race to race.

JIMMY AND THE DESPERATE WOMAN

"He is very fine and strong somewhere, but he does need a level-headed woman to look after him."

That was the *friendly* feminine verdict upon him. It flattered him, it pleased him, it galled him.

Having divorced a very charming and clever wife, who had held this opinion for ten years, and at last had got tired of the level-headed protective game, his gall was uppermost.

"I want to throw Jimmy out on the world, but I know the poor little man will go and fall on some woman's bosom. That's the worst of him. If he could only stand alone for ten minutes. But he can't. At the same time, there *is* something fine about him, something rare."

This had been Clarissa's summing-up as she floated away in the arms of the rich young American. The rich young American got rather angry when Jimmy's name was mentioned. Clarissa was now *his* wife. But she did sometimes talk as if she were still married to Jimmy.

Not in Jimmy's estimation, however. That worm had turned. Gall was uppermost. Gall and wormwood. He knew exactly what Clarissa thought—and said—about him. And the "something fine, something rare, something strong" which he was supposed to have "about him" was utterly out-balanced, in his feelings at least, by the "poor little man" nestled upon "some woman's bosom," which he was supposed to *be*.

"I am *not*," he said to himself, "a poor little man nestled upon some woman's bosom. If I could only find the right sort of woman, she should nestle on mine."

Jimmy was now thirty-five, and this point, to nestle or to be nestled, was the emotional crux and turning-point.

He imagined to himself some really *womanly* woman, to whom he should be *only* "fine and strong," and not for one

461

moment "the poor little man." Why not some simple uneducated girl, some Tess of the D'Urbervilles, some wistful
Gretchen, some humble Ruth gleaning an aftermath? Why
not? Surely the world was full of such!

The trouble was he never met them. He only met
sophisticated women. He really never had a chance of meeting
"real" people. So few of us ever do. Only the people we *don't*
meet are the "real" people, the simple, genuine, direct,
spontaneous, unspoilt souls. Ah, the simple, genuine, unspoilt
people we *don't* meet! What a tragedy it is!

Because, of course, they must be there! Somewhere! Only
we never come across them.

Jimmy was terribly handicapped by his position. It brought
him into contact with so many people. Only never the right
sort. Never the "real" people: the simple, genuine, unspoilt,
etc., etc.

He was editor of a high-class, rather high-brow, rather
successful magazine, and his rather personal, very candid
editorials brought him shoals, swarms, hosts of admiring
acquaintances. Realize that he was handsome, and could be
extraordinarily "nice," when he liked, and was really very
clever, in his own critical way, and you see how many chances
he had of being adored and protected.

In the first place his good looks: the fine, clean lines of his
face, like the face of the laughing faun in one of the faun's
unlaughing, moody moments. The long, clean lines of the
cheeks, the strong chin and the slightly arched, full nose, the
beautiful dark-grey eyes with long lashes, and the thick black
brows. In his mocking moments, when he seemed most
himself, it was a pure Pan face, with thick black eyebrows
cocked up, and grey eyes with a sardonic goaty gleam, and nose
and mouth curling with satire. A good-looking, smooth-
skinned satyr. That was Jimmy at his best. In the opinion of
his men friends.

In his own opinion, he was a sort of Martyred Saint Sebastian,
at whom the wicked world shot arrow after arrow—Mater
Dolorosa nothing to him—and he counted the drops of blood as

they fell: when he could keep count. Sometimes—as for instance when Clarissa said she was really departing with the rich young American, and should she divorce Jimmy, or was Jimmy going to divorce her?—then the arrows assailed him like a flight of starlings, flying straight at him, jabbing at him, and the drops of martyred blood simply spattered down, he couldn't keep count.

So, naturally, he divorced Clarissa.

In the opinion of his men friends, he was, or should be, a consistently grinning faun, satyr, or Pan-person. In his own opinion, he was a Martyred Saint Sebastian with the mind of a Plato. In the opinion of his woman friends, he was a fascinating little man with a profound understanding of life and the capacity really to understand a woman and to make a woman feel a queen; which of course was to make a woman feel her *real* self. . . .

He might, naturally, have made rich and resounding marriages, especially after the divorce. He didn't. The reason was, secretly, his resolve never to make any woman feel a queen any more. It was the turn of the women to make him feel a king.

Some unspoilt, unsophisticated, wild-blooded woman, to whom he would be a sort of Solomon of wisdom, beauty, and wealth. She would need to be in reduced circumstances to appreciate his wealth, which amounted to the noble sum of three thousand pounds and a little week-ending cottage in Hampshire. And to be unsophisticated she would have to be a woman of the people. Absolutely.

At the same time, not just the "obscure vulgar simplican."

He received many letters, many, many, many, enclosing poems, stories articles, or more personal unbosomings. He read them all: like a solemn rook pecking and scratching among the litter.

And one—not one letter, but one correspondent—might be *the* one—Mrs. Emilia Pinnegar, who wrote from a mining village in Yorkshire. She was, of course, unhappily married.

Now Jimmy had always had a mysterious feeling about these

dark and rather dreadful mining villages in the north. He himself had scarcely set foot north of Oxford. He felt that these miners up there must be the real stuff. And Pinnegar was a name, surely! And Emilia!

She wrote a poem, with a brief little note, that, if the editor of the *Commentator* thought the verses of no value, would he simply destroy them. Jimmy, as editor of the *Commentator* thought the verses quite good and admired the brevity of the note. But he wasn't sure about printing the poem. He wrote back, Had Mrs. Pinnegar nothing else to submit?

Then followed a correspondence. And at length, upon request, this from Mrs. Pinnegar:

"You ask me about myself, but what shall I say? I am a woman of thirty-one, with one child, a girl of eight, and I am married to a man who lives in the same house with me, but goes to another woman. I try to write poetry, if it is poetry, because I have no other way of expressing myself at all, and even if it doesn't matter to anybody besides myself, I feel I must and will express myself, if only to save myself from developing cancer or some disease that women have. I was a school-teacher before I was married, and I got my certificates at Rotherham College. If I could, I would teach again, and live alone. But married women teachers can't get jobs any more, they aren't allowed——"

THE COAL-MINER

By His Wife

The donkey-engine's beating noise
And the rattle, rattle of the sorting screens
Come down on me like the beat of his heart,
And mean the same as his breathing means.

The burning big pit-hill with fumes
Fills the air like the presence of that fair-haired man.
And the burning fire burning deeper and deeper
Is his will insisting since time began.

As he breathes the chair goes up and down
In the pit-shaft; he lusts as the wheel-fans spin
The sucking air: he lives in the coal
Underground: and his soul is a strange engine.

That is the manner of man he is.
I married him and I should know.
The mother earth from bowels of coal
Brought him forth for the overhead woe.

This was the poem that the editor of the *Commentator* hesitated about. He reflected, also, that Mrs. Pinnegar didn't sound like one of the nestling, unsophisticated rustic type. It was something else that still attracted him: something desperate in a woman, something tragic.

THE NEXT EVENT

If at evening, when the twilight comes,
   You ask me what the day has been,
I shall not know. The distant drums
   Of some new-comer intervene

Between me and the day that's been.
   Some strange man leading long columns
Of unseen soldiers through the green
   Sad twilight of these smoky slums.

And as the darkness slowly numbs
   My senses, everything I've seen
Or heard the daylight through, becomes
   Rubbish behind an opaque screen.

Instead, the sound of muffled drums
   Inside myself: I have to lean
And listen as my strength succumbs,
   To hear what these oncomings mean.

Perhaps the Death-God striking his thumbs
    On the drums in a deadly rat-ta-ta-plan.
Or a strange man marching slow as he strums
    The tune of a new weird hope in Man.

What does it matter! The day that began
    In coal-dust is ending the same, in crumbs
Of darkness like coal. I live if I can;
    If I can't, then I welcome whatever comes.

This poem sounded so splendidly desperate, the editor of the *Commentator* decided to print it, and, moreover, to see the authoress. He wrote, Would she care to see him, if he happened to be in her neighbourhood? He was going to lecture in Sheffield. She replied, Certainly.

He gave his afternoon lecture, on *Men in Books and Men in Life*. Naturally, men in books came first. Then he caught a train to reach the mining village where the Pinnegars lived.

It was February, with gruesome patches of snow. It was dark when he arrived at Mill Valley, a sort of thick, turgid darkness full of menace, where men speaking in a weird accent went past like ghosts, dragging their heavy feet and emitting the weird scent of the coal-mine underworld. Weird and a bit gruesome it was.

He knew he had to walk uphill to the little market-place. As he went, he looked back and saw the black valleys with bunches of light, like camps of demons it seemed to him. And the demonish smell of sulphur and coal in the air, in the heavy, pregnant, clammy darkness.

They directed him to New London Lane, and down he went down another hill. His skin crept a little. The place felt uncanny and hostile, hard, as if iron and minerals breathed into the black air. Thank goodness he couldn't see much, or be seen. When he had to ask his way the people treated him in a "heave-half-a-brick-at-him" fashion.

After much weary walking and asking, he entered a lane

between trees, in the cold slushy mud of the unfrozen February. The mines, apparently, were on the outskirts of the town, in some mud-sunk country. He could see the red, sore fires of the burning pit-hill through the trees, and he smelt the sulphur. He felt like some modern Ulysses wandering in the realms of Hecate. How much more dismal and horrible, a modern Odyssey among mines and factories, than any Sirens, Scyllas or Charybdises.

So he mused to himself as he waded through icy black mud, in a black lane, under black trees that moaned an accompaniment to the sound of the coal-mine's occasional hissing and chuffing, under a black sky that quenched even the electric sparkle of the colliery. And the place seemed unhabitated like a cold black jungle.

At last he came in sight of a glimmer. Apparently, there were dwellings. Yes, a new little street, with one street-lamp, and the houses all apparently dark. He paused. Absolute desertion. Then three children.

They told him the house, and he stumbled up a dark passage. There was light on the little back-yard. He knocked, in some trepidation. A rather tall woman, looking down at him with a "Who are you?" look, from the step above.

"Mrs. Pinnegar?"

"Oh, is it you, Mr. Frith? Come in."

He stumbled up the step into the glaring light of the kitchen. There stood Mrs. Pinnegar, a tall woman with a face like a mask of passive anger, looking at him coldly. Immediately he felt his own shabbiness and smallness. In utter confusion, he stuck out his hand.

"I had an awful time getting here," he said. "I'm afraid I shall make a frightful mess of your house." He looked down at his boots.

"That's all right," she said. "Have you had your tea?"

"No—but don't you bother about me."

There was a little girl with fair hair in a fringe over her forehead, troubled blue eyes under the fringe, and two dolls. He felt easier.

"Is this your little girl?" he asked. "She's awfully nice. What is her name?"

"Jane."

"How are you, Jane?" he said. But the child only stared at him with the baffled, bewildered, pained eyes of a child who lives with hostile parents.

Mrs. Pinnegar set his tea, bread, and butter, jam, and buns. Then she sat opposite him. She was handsome, dark straight brows and grey eyes with yellow grains in them, and a way of looking straight at you as if she were used to holding her own. Her eyes were the nicest part of her. They had a certain kindliness, mingled, like the yellow grains among the grey, with a relentless, unyielding feminine will. Her nose and mouth were straight, like a Greek mask, and the expression was fixed. She gave him at once the impression of a woman who has made a mistake, who knows it, but who will not change: who cannot now change.

He felt very uneasy. Being a rather small, shambling man, she made him aware of his physical inconspicuousness. And she said not a word, only looked down on him, as he drank his tea, with that changeless look of a woman who is holding her own against Man and Fate. While, from the corner across the kitchen, the little girl with her fair hair and her dolls, watched him also in absolute silence, from her hot blue eyes.

"This seems a pretty awful place," he said to her.

"It is. It's absolutely awful," the woman said.

"You ought to get away from it," he said.

But she received this in dead silence.

It was exceedingly difficult to make any headway. He asked about Mr. Pinnegar. She glanced at the clock.

"He comes up at nine," she said.

"Is he down the mine?"

"Yes. He's on the afternoon shift."

There was never a sound from the little girl.

"Doesn't Jane ever talk?" he asked.

"Not much," said the mother, glancing round.

He talked a little about his lectures, about Sheffield, about

London. But she was not really interested. She sat there rather distant, very laconic, looking at him with those curious unyielding eyes. She looked at him like a woman who has had her revenge, and is left stranded on the reefs where she wrecked her opponent. Still unrelenting, unregretting, unyielding, she seemed rather undecided as to what her revenge had been, and what it had all been about.

"You ought to get away from here," he said to her.

"Where to?" she asked.

"Oh"—he made a vague gesture—"anywhere, so long as it is *quite* away."

She seemed to ponder this, under her portentous brow.

"I don't see what difference it would make," she said. Then glancing round at her child: "I don't see what difference anything would make, except getting out of the world altogether. But there's *her* to consider." And she jerked her head in the direction of the child.

Jimmy felt definitely frightened. He wasn't used to this sort of grimness. At the same time he was excited. This handsome, laconic woman, with her soft brown hair and her unflinching eyes with their gold flecks, seemed to be challenging him to something. There was a touch of challenge in her remaining gold-flecked kindness. Somewhere, she had a heart. But what had happened to it? And why?

What had gone wrong with her? In some way, she must have gone against herself.

"Why don't you come and live with me?" he said, like the little gambler he was.

The queer, conflicting smile was on his face. He had taken up her challenge, like a gambler. The very sense of a gamble, in which he could not lose desperately, excited him. At the same time, he was scared of her, and determined to get beyond his scare.

She sat and watched him, with the faintest touch of a grim smile on her handsome mouth.

"How do you mean, live with you?" she said.

"Oh—I mean what it usually means," he said, with a little puff of self-conscious laughter.

"You're evidently not happy here. You're evidently in the wrong circumstances altogether. You're obviously *not* just an ordinary woman. Well, then, break away. When I say, Come and live with me, I mean just what I say. Come to London and live with me as my wife, if you like, and then if we want to marry, when you get a divorce, why, we can do it."

Jimmy made this speech more to himself than to the woman. That was how he was. He worked out all his things inside himself, as if it were all merely an interior problem of his own. And while he did so, he had an odd way of squinting his left eye and wagging his head loosely, like a man talking absolutely to himself, and turning his eyes inwards.

The woman watched him in a sort of wonder. This was something she was *not* used to. His extraordinary manner, and his extraordinary bald proposition, roused her from her own tense apathy.

"Well!" she said. "That's got to be thought about. What about *her?*"—and again she jerked her head towards the round-eyed child in the corner. Jane sat with a completely expressionless face, her little red mouth fallen a little open. She seemed in a sort of trance: as if she understood like a grown-up person, but, as a child, sat in a trance, unconscious.

The mother wheeled round in her chair and stared at her child. The little girl stared back at her mother, with hot, troubled, almost guilty blue eyes. And neither said a word. Yet they seemed to exchange worlds of meaning.

"Why, of course," said Jimmy, twisting his head again; "she'd come, too."

The woman gave a last look at her child, then turned to him, and started watching *him* with that slow, straight stare.

"It's not"—he began, stuttering—"it's not anything *sudden* and unconsidered on my part. I've been considering it for quite a long time—ever since I had the first poem, and your letter."

He spoke still with his eyes turned inwards, talking to himself. And the woman watched him unflinchingly.

"Before you ever saw me?" she asked, with a queer irony.

"Oh, of course. Of course before I ever saw you. Or else I never *should* have seen you. From the very first, I had a definite feeling——"

He made odd, sharp gestures, like a drunken man, and he spoke like a drunken man, his eyes turned inward, talking to himself. The woman was no more than a ghost moving inside his own consciousness, and he was addressing her there.

The actual woman sat outside looking on in a sort of wonder. This was really something new to her.

"And now you see me, do you want me, really, to come to London?"

She spoke in a dull tone of incredulity. The thing was just a little preposterous to her. But why not? It would have to be something a little preposterous, to get her out of the tomb she was in.

"Of course I do!" he cried, with another scoop of his head and scoop of his hand. "*Now* I do *actually* want you, now I actually see you." He never looked at her. His eyes were still turned in. He was still talking to himself, in a sort of drunkenness with himself.

To her, it was something extraordinary. But it roused her from apathy.

He became aware of the hot blue eyes of the hot-cheeked little girl fixed upon him from the distant corner. And he gave a queer little giggle.

"Why, it's more than I could ever have hoped for," he said, "to have you and Jane to live with me! Why, it will mean *life* to me." He spoke in an odd, strained voice, slightly delirious. And for the first time he looked up at the woman and, apparently, *straight* at her. But, even as he seemed to look straight at her, the curious cast was in his eye, and he was only looking at himself, inside himself, at the shadows inside his own consciousness.

"And when would you like me to come?" she asked, rather coldly.

"Why, as soon as possible. Come back with me to-morrow, if you will. I've got a little house in St. John's Wood, *waiting* for you. Come with me to-morrow. That's the simplest."

She watched him for some time, as he sat with ducked head. He looked like a man who is drunk—drunk with himself. He was going bald at the crown, his rather curly black hair was thin.

"I couldn't come to-morrow, I should need a few days," she said.

She wanted to see his face again. It was as if she could not remember what his face was like, this strange man who had appeared out of nowhere, with such a strange proposition.

He lifted his face, his eyes still cast in that inturned, blind look. He looked now like a Mephistopheles who has gone blind. With his black brows cocked up, Mephistopheles, Mephistopheles blind and begging in the street.

"Why, of course it's wonderful that it's happened like this for me," he said, with odd pouting emphasis, pushing out his lips. "I was finished, absolutely finished. I was finished while Clarissa was with me. But after she'd gone, I was *absolutely* finished. And I thought there was no chance for me in the world again. It seems to me perfectly marvellous that this has happened—that I've come across you——" he lifted his face sightlessly—"and Jane—Jane—why she's *really* too good to be true." He gave a slight hysterical laugh. "She really is."

The woman, and Jane, watched him with some embarrassment.

"I shall have to settle up here, with Mr. Pinnegar," she said, rather coldly musing. "Do you want to see him?"

"Oh, I——" he said, with a deprecating gesture, "I don't *care*. But if you think I'd better—why, certainly——"

"I do think you'd better," she said.

"Very well, then, I *will*. I'll see him whenever you like."

"He comes in soon after nine," she said.

"All right, I'll see him then. Much better. But I suppose I'd better see about finding a place to sleep first. Better not leave it too late."

"I'll come with you and ask for you."

"Oh, you'd better not, really. If you tell me where to go——"

He had taken on a protective tone: he was protecting her against herself and against scandal. It was his manner, his rather Oxfordy manner, more than anything else, that went beyond her. She wasn't used to it.

Jimmy plunged out into the gulfing blackness of the Northern night, feeling how horrible it was, but pressing his hat on his brow in a sense of strong adventure. He was going through with it.

At the baker's shop, where she had suggested he should ask for a bed, they would have none of him. Absolutely they didn't like the looks of him. At the Pub, too, they shook their heads: didn't want to have anything to do with him. But, in a voice more expostulatingly Oxford than ever, he said:

"But look here—you can't ask a man to sleep under one of these hedges. Can't I see the landlady?"

He persuaded the landlady to promise to let him sleep on the big, soft settee in the parlour, where the fire was burning brightly. Then, saying he would be back about ten, he returned through mud and drizzle up New London Lane.

The child was in bed, a saucepan was boiling by the fire. Already the lines had softened a little in the woman's face.

She spread a cloth on the table. Jimmy sat in silence, feeling that she was hardly aware of his presence. She was absorbed, no doubt, in the coming of her husband. The stranger merely sat on the sofa, and waited. He felt himself wound up tight. And once he was really wound up, he could go through with anything.

They heard the nine o'clock whistle at the mine. The woman then took the saucepan from the fire and went into the scullery. Jimmy could smell the smell of potatoes being strained. He sat quite still. There was nothing for him to do or to say. He was wearing his big black-rimmed spectacles, and his face, blank and expressionless in the suspense of waiting, looked like the death-mask of some sceptical philosopher, who could wait through the ages, and who could hardly distinguish life from death at any time.

Came the heavy-shod tread up the house entry, and the man

entered, rather like a blast of wind. The fair moustache stuck out from the blackish, mottled face, and the fierce blue eyes rolled their whites in the coal-blackened sockets.

"This gentleman is Mr. Frith," said Emily Pinnegar.

Jimmy got up, with a bit of an Oxford wriggle, and held out his hand, saying: "How do you do?"

His grey eyes, behind the spectacles, had an uncanny whitish gleam.

"My hand's not fit to shake hands," said the miner. "Take a seat."

"Oh, nobody minds coal-dust," said Jimmy, subsiding on to the sofa. "It's clean dirt."

"They say so," said Pinnegar.

He was a man of medium height, thin, but energetic in build.

Mrs. Pinnegar was running hot water into a pail from the bright brass tap of the stove, which had a boiler to balance the oven. Pinnegar dropped heavily into a wooden arm-chair, and stooped to pull off his ponderous grey pit-boots. He smelled of the strange, stale underground. In silence he pulled on his slippers, then rose, taking his boots into the scullery. His wife followed with the pail of hot water. She returned and spread a coarse roller-towel on the steel fender. The man could be heard washing in the scullery, in the semi-dark. Nobody said anything. Mrs. Pinnegar attended to her husband's dinner.

After a while, Pinnegar came running in, naked to the waist, and squatted plumb in front of the big red fire, on his heels. His head and face and the front part of his body were all wet. His back was grey and unwashed. He seized the towel from the fender and began to rub his face and head with a sort of brutal vigour, while his wife brought a bowl, and with a soapy flannel silently washed his back, right down to the loins, where the trousers were rolled back. The man was entirely oblivious of the stranger—this washing was part of the collier's ritual, and nobody existed for the moment. The woman, washing her husband's back, stooping there as he kneeled with knees

wide apart, squatting on his heels on the rag hearthrug, had
a peculiar look on her strong, handsome face, a look sinister
and derisive. She was deriding something or somebody; but
Jimmy could not make out whom or what.

It was a new experience for him to sit completely and
brutally excluded, from a personal ritual. The collier vigor-
ously rubbed his own fair short hair, till it all stood on end,
then he stared into the red-hot fire, oblivious, while the red
colour burned in his cheeks. Then again he rubbed his breast
and his body with the rough towel, brutally, as if his body
were some machine he was cleaning, while his wife, with a
peculiar slow movement, dried his back with another towel.

She took away the towel and bowl. The man was dry. He
still squatted with his hands on his knees, gazing abstractedly,
blankly into the fire. That, too, seemed part of his daily ritual.
The colour flushed in his cheeks, his fair moustache was rubbed
on end. But his hot blue eyes stared hot and vague into the
red coals, while the red glare of the coal fell on his breast and
naked body.

He was a man of about thirty-five, in his prime, with a pure
smooth skin and no fat on his body. His muscles were not
large, but quick, alive with energy. And as he squatted bathing
abstractedly in the glow of the fire, he seemed like some pure-
moulded engine that sleeps between its motions, with incomprehensible eyes of dark iron-blue.

He looked round, always averting his face from the stranger
on the sofa, shutting him out of consciousness. The wife took
out a bundle from the dresser-cupboard, and handed it to the
outstretched, work-scarred hand of the man on the hearth.
Curious, that big, horny, work-battered clean hand, at the
end of the suave, thin, naked arm.

Pinnegar unrolled his shirt and undervest in front of the
fire, warmed them for a moment in the glow, vaguely,
sleepily, then, pulled them over his head. And then at last
he rose, with his shirt hanging over his trousers, and in the
same abstract, sleepy way, shutting the world out of his
consciousness, he went out again to the scullery, pausing at the

same dresser-cupboard to take out his rolled-up day trousers.

Mrs. Pinnegar took away the towels and set the dinner on the table—rich, oniony stew out of a hissing brown stew-jar, boiled potatoes, and a cup of tea. The man returned from the scullery, in his clean flannelette shirt and black trousers, his fair hair neatly brushed. He planked his wooden arm-chair beside the table, and sat heavily down, to eat.

Then he looked at Jimmy, as one wary, probably hostile man looks at another.

"You're a stranger in these parts, I gather?" he said. There was something slightly formal, even a bit pompous, in his speech.

"An absolute stranger," replied Jimmy, with a slight aside grin.

The man dabbed some mustard on his plate, and glanced at his food to see if he would like it.

"Come from a distance, do you?" he asked, as he began to eat. As he ate, he seemed to become oblivious again of Jimmy, bent his head over his plate, and ate. But probably he was ruminating something all the time, with barbaric wariness.

"From London," said Jimmy, warily.

"London!" said Pinnegar, without looking from his plate.

Mrs. Pinnegar came and sat, in ritualistic silence, in her tall-backed rocking-chair under the light.

"What brings you this way, then?" asked Pinnegar, stirring his tea.

"Oh!" Jimmy writhed a little on the sofa. "I came to see Mrs. Pinnegar."

The miner took a hasty gulp of tea.

"You're acquainted then, are you?" he said, still without looking round. He sat with his side-face to Jimmy.

"Yes, we are *now*," explained Jimmy. "I didn't know Mrs. Pinnegar till this evening. As a matter of fact, she sent me some poems for the *Commentator*—I'm the editor —and I thought they were good, so I wrote and told her so. Then I felt I wanted to come and see her, and she was willing, so I came."

The man reached out, cut himself a piece of bread, and swallowed a large mouthful.

"You thought her poetry was good?" he said, turning at last to Jimmy and looking straight at him, with a stare something like the child's, but aggressive. "Are you going to put it in your magazine?"

"Yes, I think I am," said Jimmy.

"I never read but one of her poems—something about a collier she knew all about, because she'd married him," he said, in his peculiar harsh voice, that had a certain jeering clang in it, and a certain indomitableness.

Jimmy was silent. The other man's harsh fighting-voice made him shrink.

"I could never get on with the *Commentator* myself," said Pinnegar, looking round for his pudding, pushing his meat-plate aside. "Seems to me to go a long way round to get nowhere."

"Well, probably it *does*," said Jimmy, squirming a little. "But so long as the *way* is interesting! I don't see that anything gets anywhere at present—certainly no periodical."

"I don't know," said Pinnegar. "There's some facts in the *Liberator*—and there's some ideas in the *Janus*. I can't see the use myself, of all these feelings folk say they have. They get you nowhere."

"But," said Jimmy, with a slight pouf of laughter, "where do you *want* to get? It's all very well talking about getting somewhere, but where, where in the world to-day do you *want* to get? In general, I mean. If you want a better job in the mine—all right, go ahead and get it. But when you begin to talk about getting somewhere, in *life*—why, you've got to know what you're talking about."

"I'm a man, aren't I?" said the miner, going very still and hard.

"But what do you *mean*, when you say you're a man?" snarled Jimmy, really exasperated. "What do you mean? Yes, you *are* a man. But what about it?"

"Haven't I the right to say I won't be made use of?" said the collier, slow, harsh, and heavy.

"You've got a right to *say* it," retorted Jimmy, with a pouf of laughter. "But it doesn't *mean* anything. We're all made use of, from King George downwards. We have to be. When you eat your pudding you're making use of hundreds of people—including your wife."

"I know it. I know it. It makes no difference, though. I'm not going to be made use of."

Jimmy shrugged his shoulders.

"Oh, all right!" he said. "That's just a phrase, like any other."

The miner sat very still in his chair, his face going hard and remote. He was evidently thinking over something that was stuck like a barb in his consciousness, something he was trying to harden over, as the skin sometimes hardens over a steel splinter in the flesh.

"I'm nothing but made use of," he said, now talking hard and final, to himself, and staring out into space. "Down the pit, I'm made use of, and they give me a wage, such as it is. At the house, I'm made use of, and my wife sets the dinner on the table as if I was a customer in a shop."

"But what do you *expect?*" cried Jimmy, writhing in his chair.

"Me? What do I expect? I expect nothing. But I tell you what——" he turned, and looked straight and hard into Jimmy's eyes—"I'm not going to put up with anything, either."

Jimmy saw the hard finality in the other man's eyes, and squirmed away from it.

"If you *know* what you're not going to put up with——" he said.

"I don't want my wife writing poetry! And sending it to a parcel of men she's never seen. *I* don't want my wife sitting like Queen Boadicea, when I come home, and a face like a stone wall with holes in it. I don't know what's wrong with her. She doesn't know herself. But she does as she likes. Only, mark you, I do the same."

"Of course!" cried Jimmy, though there was no of course about it.

"She's told you I've got another woman?"

"Yes."

"And I'll tell you for why. If I give in to the coal face, and go down the mine every day to eight hours' slavery, more or less, somebody's got to give in to me."

"Then," said Jimmy, after a pause, "if you mean you want your wife to submit to you—well, that's the problem. You have to marry the woman who *will* submit."

It was amazing, this from Jimmy. He sat there and lectured the collier like a Puritan Father, completely forgetting the disintegrating flutter of Clarissa, in his own background.

"I want a wife who'll please me, who'll want to please me," said the collier.

"Why should *you* be pleased, any more than anybody else?" asked the wife coldly.

"My child, my little girl wants to please me—if her mother would let her. But the women hang together. I tell you"— and here he turned to Jimmy, with a blaze in his dark blue eyes—"I want a woman to please me, a woman who's anxious to please me. And if I can't find her in my own home, I'll find her out of it."

"I hope she pleases you," said the wife, rocking slightly.

"Well," said the man, "she does."

"Then why don't you go and live with her altogether?" she said.

He turned and looked at her.

"Why don't I?" he said. "Because I've got my home. I've got my house, I've got my wife, let her be what she may, as a woman to live with. And I've got my child. Why should I break it all up?"

"And what about me?" she asked, coldly and fiercely.

"You? You've got a home. You've got a child. You've got a man who works for you. You've got what you want. You do as you like——"

"Do I?" she asked, with intolerable sarcasm.

"Yes. Apart from the bit of work in the house, you do as

you like. If you want to go, you can go. But while you live in my house, you must respect it. You bring no men here, you see."

"Do *you* respect your home?" she said.

"Yes! I do! If I get another woman—who pleases me—I deprive you of nothing. All I ask of you is to do your duty as a housewife."

"Down to washing your back!" she said, heavily sarcastic; and, Jimmy thought, a trifle vulgar.

"Down to washing my back, since it's got to be washed," he said.

"What about the other woman? Let her do it."

"This is my home."

The wife gave a strange movement, like a mad woman.

Jimmy sat rather pale and frightened. Behind the collier's quietness he felt the concentration of almost cold anger and an unchanging will. In the man's lean face he could see the bones, the fixity of the male bones, and it was as if the human soul, or spirit, had gone into the living skull and skeleton, almost invulnerable.

Jimmy, for some strange reason, felt a wild anger against this bony and logical man. It was the hard-driven coldness, fixity, that he could not bear.

"Look here!" he cried, in a resonant Oxford voice, his eyes glaring and casting inwards behind his spectacles. "You say Mrs. Pinnegar is *free*—free to do as she pleases. In that case, you have no objection if she comes with me right away from here."

The collier looked at the pale, strange face of the editor in wonder. Jimmy kept his face slightly averted, and sightless, seeing nobody. There was a Mephistophelian tilt about the eyebrows, and a Martyred Sebastian straightness about the mouth.

"Does she *want* to?" asked Pinnegar, with devastating incredulity. The wife smiled faintly, grimly. She could see the vanity of her husband in his utter inability to believe that she could prefer the other man to him.

"That," said Jimmy, "you must ask her yourself. But it's what I came here for: to ask her to come and live with me, and bring the child."

"You came without having seen her, to ask her that?" said the husband, in growing wonder.

"Yes," said Jimmy, vehemently, nodding his head with drunken emphasis. "Yes! Without ever having seen her!"

"You've caught a funny fish this time, with your poetry," he said, turning with curious husband-familiarity to his wife. She hated this off-hand husband-familiarity.

"What sort of fish have *you* caught?" she retorted. "And what did you catch *her* with?"

"Bird-lime!" he said, with a faint, quick grin.

Jimmy was sitting in suspense. They all three sat in suspense, for some time.

"And what are you saying to him?" said the collier at length.

Jimmy looked up, and the malevolent half-smile on his face made him look rather handsome again, a mixture of faun and Mephisto. He glanced curiously, invitingly, at the woman who was watching him from afar.

"I say yes!" she replied, in a cool voice.

The husband became very still, sitting erect in his wooden arm-chair and staring into space. It was as if he were fixedly watching something fly away from him, out of his own soul. But he was not going to yield at all, to any emotion.

He could not now believe that this woman should *want* to leave him. Yet she did.

"I'm sure it's all for the best," said Jimmy, in his Puritan Father voice. "You don't mind, really"—he drawled uneasily —"if she brings the child. I give you my word I'll do my very best for it."

The collier looked at him as if he were very far away. Jimmy quailed under the look. He could see that the other man was relentlessly killing the emotion in himself, stripping himself, as it were, of his own flesh, stripping himself to the hard unemotional bone of the human male.

"I give her a blank cheque," said Pinnegar, with numb lips. "She does as she pleases."

"So much for fatherly love, compared with selfishness," she said.

He turned and looked at her with that curious power of remote anger. And immediately she became still, quenched.

"I give you a blank cheque, as far as I'm concerned," he repeated abstractedly.

"It *is* blank indeed!" she said, with her first touch of bitterness.

Jimmy looked at the clock. It was growing late: he might be shut out of the public-house. He rose to go, saying he would return in the morning. He was leaving the next day, at noon, for London.

He plunged into the darkness and mud of that black, night-ridden country. There was a curious elation in his spirits, mingled with fear. But then he always needed an element of fear, really, to elate him. He thought with terror of those two human beings left in that house together. The frightening state of tension! He himself could never bear an extreme tension. He always had to compromise, to become apologetic and pathetic. He would be able to manage Mrs. Pinnegar that way. Emily! He must get used to saying it. Emily! The Emilia was absurd. He had never known an Emily.

He felt really scared, and really elated. He was doing something big. It was not that he was in *love* with the woman. But, my God, he wanted to take her away from that man. And he wanted the adventure of her. Absolutely the adventure of her. He felt really elated, really himself, really manly.

But in the morning he returned rather sheepishly to the collier's house. It was another dark, drizzling day, with black trees, black road, black hedges, blackish brick houses, and the smell and the sound of collieries under a skyless day. Like living in some weird underground.

Unwillingly, he went up that passage-entry again, and knocked at the back door, glancing at the miserable little back garden with its cabbage-stalks and its ugly sanitary arrangements.

The child opened the door to him: with her fair hair, flushed cheeks, and hot, dark-blue eyes.

"Hello, Jane!" he said.

The mother stood tall and square, by the table, watching him with portentous eyes, as he entered. She was handsome, but her skin was not very good: as if the battle had been too much for her health. Jimmy glanced up at her smiling his slow, ingratiating smile, that always brought a glow of success into a woman's spirit. And as he saw her gold-flecked eyes searching in his eyes, without a bit of kindliness, he thought to himself: "My God, however am I going to sleep with that woman!" His will was ready, however, and he would manage it somehow.

And when he glanced at the motionless, bony head and lean figure of the collier seated in the wooden arm-chair by the fire, he was the more ready. He must triumph over that man.

"What train are you going by?" asked Mrs. Pinnegar.

"By the 12.30." He looked up at her as he spoke, with the wide, shining, childlike, almost coy eyes that were his peculiar asset. She looked down at him in a sort of interested wonder. She seemed almost fascinated by his childlike, shining, inviting dark-grey eyes, with their long lashes: such an absolute change from that resentful unyielding that looked out always from the back of her husband's blue eyes. Her husband always seemed like a menace to her, in his thinness, his concentration, his eternal unyielding. And this man looked at one with the wide, shining, fascinating eyes of a young Persian kitten, something at once bold and shy and coy and strangely inviting. She fell at once under their spell.

"You'll have dinner before you go," she said.

"No!" he cried in panic, unwilling indeed to eat before that other man. "No, I ate a fabulous breakfast. I will get a sandwich when I change in Sheffield: *really!*"

She had to go out shopping. She said she would go out to the station with him when she got back. It was just after eleven.

"But look here," he said, addressing also the thin abstracted man who sat unnoticing, with a newspaper, "we've got to get this thing settled. I *want* Mrs. Pinnegar to come and live with me, her and the child. And she's coming! So don't you think, now, it would be better if she came right along with me to-day! Just put a few things in a bag and come along. Why drag the thing out?"

"I tell you," replied the husband, "she has a blank cheque from me to do as she likes."

"All right, then! Won't you do that? Won't you come along with me now?" said Jimmy, looking up at her exposedly, but casting his eyes a bit inwards. Throwing himself with deliberate impulsiveness on her mercy.

"I can't!" she said decisively. "I can't come to-day."

"But why not—really? Why not, while I'm here? You have that blank cheque, you can do as you please——"

"The blank cheque won't get me far," she said rudely: "I can't come to-day, anyhow."

"When can you come, then?" he said, with that queer, petulant pleading. "The sooner the better, surely."

"I can come on Monday," she said abruptly.

"Monday!" He gazed up at her in a kind of panic, through his spectacles. Then he set his teeth again, and nodded his head up and down. "All right, then! To-day is Saturday. Then Monday!"

"If you'll excuse me," she said, "I've got to go out for a few things. I'll walk to the station with you when I get back."

She bundled Jane into a little sky-blue coat and bonnet, put on a heavy black coat and black hat herself, and went out.

Jimmy sat very uneasily opposite the collier, who also wore spectacles to read. Pinnegar put down the newspaper and pulled the spectacles off his nose, saying something about a Labour Government.

"Yes," said Jimmy. "After all, best be logical. If you *are* democratic, the only logical thing is a Labour Government. Though, personally, one Government is as good as another, to me."

"Maybe so!" said the collier. "But *something's* got to come to an end, sooner or later."

"Oh, a great deal!" said Jimmy, and they lapsed into silence.

"Have you been married before?" asked Pinnegar, at length.

"Yes. My wife and I are divorced."

"I suppose you want me to divorce *my* wife?" said the collier.

"Why—yes!—that would be best——"

"It's the same to me," said Pinnegar; "divorce or no divorce. I'll *live* with another woman, but I'll never *marry* another. Enough is as good as a feast. But if she wants a divorce, she can have it."

"It would certainly be best," said Jimmy.

There was a long pause. Jimmy wished the woman would come back.

"I look on you as an instrument," said the miner. "Something had to break. You are the instrument that breaks it."

It was strange to sit in the room with this thin, remote, wilful man. Jimmy was a bit fascinated by him. But, at the same time, he hated him because he could not be in the same room with him without being under his spell. He felt himself dominated. And he hated it.

"My wife," said Pinnegar, looking up at Jimmy with a peculiar, almost humorous, teasing grin, "expects to see me go to the dogs when she leaves me. It is her last hope."

Jimmy ducked his head and was silent, not knowing what to say. The other man sat still in his chair, like a sort of infinitely patient prisoner, looking away out of the window and waiting.

"She thinks," he said again, "that she has some wonderful future awaiting her somewhere, and you're going to open the door."

And again the same amused grin was in his eyes.

And again Jimmy was fascinated by the man. And again he hated the spell of this fascination. For Jimmy wanted to be, in his own mind, the strongest man among men, but particularly among women. And this thin, peculiar man could dominate him. He knew it. The very silent unconsciousness of Pinnegar dominated the room, wherever he was.

Jimmy hated this.

At last Mrs. Pinnegar came back, and Jimmy set off with her. He shook hands with the collier.

"Good-bye!" he said.

"Good-bye!" said Pinnegar, looking down at him with those amused blue eyes, which Jimmy knew he would never be able to get beyond.

And the walk to the station was almost a walk of conspiracy against the man left behind, between the man in spectacles and the tall woman. They arranged the details for Monday. Emily was to come by the nine o'clock train: Jimmy would meet her at Marylebone, and install her in his house in St. John's Wood. Then, with the child, they would begin a new life. Pinnegar would divorce his wife, or she would divorce him: and then, another marriage.

Jimmy got a tremendous kick out of it all on the journey home. He felt he had really done something desperate and adventurous. But he was in too wild a flutter to analyse any results. Only as he drew near London, a sinking feeling came over him. He was desperately tired after it all, almost too tired to keep up.

Nevertheless, he went after dinner and sprang it all on Severn.

"You damn fool!" said Severn, in consternation. "What did you do it for?"

"Well," said Jimmy, writhing. "Because I *wanted* to."

"Good God! The woman sounds like the head of Medusa. You're a hero of some stomach, I must say! Remember Clarissa?"

"Oh," writhed Jimmy. "But this is different."

"Ay, her name's Emma, or something of that sort, isn't it?"

"Emily!" said Jimmy briefly.

"Well, you're a fool, anyway, so you may as well keep on acting in character. I've no doubt, by playing weeping-willow, you'll outlive all the female storms you ever prepare for yourself. I never yet did see a weeping-willow uprooted by a gale, so keep on hanging your harp on it, and you'll be all right. Here's luck! But for a man who was looking for a little Gretchen to adore him, you're a corker!"

Which was all that Severn had to say. But Jimmy went home with his knees shaking. On Sunday morning he wrote an anxious letter. He didn't know how to begin it: *Dear Mrs. Pinnegar* and *Dear Emily* seemed either too late in the day or too early. So he just plunged in, without dear anything.

"I want you to have this before you come. Perhaps we have been precipitate. I only beg you to decide *finally*, for yourself, before you come. Don't come, please, unless you are absolutely sure of yourself. If you are *in the least* unsure, wait a while, wait till you are quite certain, one way or the other.

"For myself, if you don't come, I shall understand. But please send me a telegram. If you do come, I shall welcome both you and the child. Yours ever—J. F."

He paid a man his return fare, and three pounds extra, to go on the Sunday and deliver this letter.

The man came back in the evening. He had delivered the letter. There was no answer.

Awful Sunday night: tense Monday morning!

A telegram: "*Arrive Marylebone* 12.50 *with Jane. Yours ever. Emily.*"

Jimmy set his teeth and went to the station. But when he felt her looking at him, and so met her eyes: and after that saw her coming slowly down the platform, holding the child by the hand, her slow cat's eyes smouldering under her straight brows, smouldering at him: he almost swooned. A sickly grin came over him as he held out his hand. Nevertheless he said:

"I'm *awfully* glad you came."

And as he sat in the taxi, a perverse but intense desire for her came over him, making him almost helpless. He could feel, so strongly, the presence of that other man about her, and this went to his head like neat spirits. That other man!

In some subtle, inexplicable way, he was actually bodily present, the husband. The woman moved in his aura. She was hopelessly married to him.

And this went to Jimmy's head like neat whisky. Which of the two would fall before him with a greater fall—the woman, or the man, her husband?

NONE OF THAT

I MET Luis Colmenares in Venice, not having seen him for years. He is a Mexican exile living on the scanty remains of what was once wealth, and eking out a poor and lonely existence by being a painter. But his art is only a sedative to him. He wanders about like a lost soul, mostly in Paris or in Italy, where he can live cheaply. He is rather short, rather fat, pale, with black eyes, which are always looking the other way, and a spirit the same, always averted.

"Do you know who is in Venice?" he said to me. "Cuesta! He is in the Hôtel Romano. I saw him bathing yesterday on the Lido."

There was a world of gloomy mockery in this last sentence.

"Do you mean Cuesta, the bull-fighter?" I asked.

"Yes. Don't you know, he retired? Do you remember? An American woman left him a lot of money. Did you ever see him?"

"Once," said I.

"Was it before the revolution? Do you remember, he retired and bought a hacienda very cheap from one of Madero's generals, up in Chihuahua? It was after the Carranzista, and I was already in Europe."

"How does he look now?" I said.

"Enormously fat, like a yellow, round, small whale in the sea. You saw him? You know he was rather short and rather fat always. I think his mother was a Mixtec Indian woman. Did you ever know him?"

"No," said I. "Did you?"

"Yes. I knew him in the old days, when I was rich, and thought I should be rich for ever."

He was silent, and I was afraid he had shut up for good. It was unusual for him to be even as communicative as he had been. But it was evident that having seen Cuesta, the toreador

489

whose fame once rang through Spain and through Latin
America, had moved him deeply. He was in a ferment, and
could not quite contain himself.

"But he wasn't interesting, was he?" I said. "Wasn't he
just a—a bull-fighter—a brute?"

Colmenares looked at me out of his own blackness. He didn't
want to talk. Yet he had to.

"He was a brute, yes," he admitted grudgingly. "But not
just a brute. Have you seen him when he was at his best?
Where did you see him? I never liked him in Spain, he was
too vain. But in Mexico he was very good. Have you seen
him play with the bull, and play with death? He was marvellous. Do you remember him, what he looked like?"

"Not very well," said I.

"Short, and broad, and rather fat, with rather a yellow
colour, and a pressed-in nose. But his eyes, they were marvellous, also rather small, and yellow, and when he looked at
you, so strange and cool, you felt your inside melting. Do
you know that feeling? He looked into the last little place of
you, where you keep your courage. Do you understand? And
so you felt yourself melting. Do you know what I mean?"

"More or less, perhaps," said I.

Colmenares' black eyes were fixed on my face, dilated and
gleaming, but not really seeing me at all. He was seeing the
past. Yet a curious force streamed out of his face: one understood him by the telepathy of passion, inverted passion.

"And in the bull-ring, he was marvellous. He would stand
with his back to the bull, and pretend to be adjusting his
stocking, while the bull came charging on him. And with a
little glance over his shoulder, he would make a small movement, and the bull had passed him without getting him. Then
he would smile a little, and walk after it. It is marvellous that
he was not killed hundreds of times, but I saw him bathing
on the Lido to-day, like a fat, yellow, small whale. It is
extraordinary! But I did not see his eyes. . . ."

A queer look of abstracted passion was on Colmenares' fat,
pale, clean-shaven face. Perhaps the toreador had cast a spell

over him, as over so many people in the old and the new world.

"It is strange that I have never seen eyes anywhere else like his. Did I tell you, they were yellow, and not like human eyes at all? They didn't look at you. I don't think they ever looked at anybody. He only looked at the little bit inside your body where you keep your courage. I don't think he could see people, any more than an animal can: I mean see them personally, as I see you and you see me. He was an animal, a marvellous animal. I have often thought, if human beings had not developed minds and speech, they would have become marvellous animals like Cuesta, with those marvellous eyes, much more marvellous than a lion's or a tiger's. Have you noticed a lion or a tiger never sees you personally? It never really looks at you. But also it is afraid to look at the last little bit of you, where your courage lives inside you. But Cuesta was not afraid. He looked straight at it, and it melted."

"And what was he like, in ordinary life?" said I.

"He did not talk, was very silent. He was not clever at all. He was not even clever enough to be a general. And he could be very brutal and disgusting. But usually he was quiet. But he was always *something*. If you were in the room with him, you always noticed him more than anybody, more than women or men, even very clever people. He was stupid, but he made you physically aware of him; like a cat in the room. I tell you, that little bit of you where you keep your courage was enchanted by him; he put over you an enchantment."

"Did he do it on purpose?"

"Well! It is hard to say. But he knew he could do it. To some people, perhaps, he could not do it. But he never saw such people. He only saw people who were in his enchantment. And of course, in the bull-ring, he mesmerized everybody. He could draw the natural magnetism of everybody to him— everybody. And then he was marvellous, he played with death as if it were a kitten, so quick, quick as a star, and calm as a flower, and all the time, laughing at death. It is marvellous he was never killed. But he retired very young. And then suddenly it was he who killed the bull, with one hand, one stroke. He was very strong. And the bull sank down at his feet, heavy with death. The people went mad! And he just glanced at them, with his yellow eyes, in a cool, beautiful contempt, as if he were an animal that wrapped the skin of death round him. Ah, he was wonderful! And to-day I saw him bathing on the Lido, in an American bathing-suit, with a woman. His bathing-suit was just a little more yellow than he is. I have held the towel when he was being rubbed down and massaged, often. He had the body of an Indian, very smooth, with hardly any hair, and creamy-yellow. I always thought it had something childish about it, so soft. But also, it had the same mystery as his eyes, as if you could never touch it, as if, when you touched it, still it was not he. When he had no clothes on, he was naked. But it seemed he would have many, many more nakednesses before you really came to *him*. Do you understand me at all? Or does it seem to you foolish?"

"It interests me," I said. "And women, of course, fell for him by the thousand?"

"By the million! And they were mad because of him. Women went mad, once they felt him. It was not like Rudolf Valentino, sentimental. It was madness, like cats in the night which howl, no longer knowing whether they are on earth or in hell or in paradise. So were the women. He could have had forty beautiful women every night, and different ones each night, from the beginning of the year to the end."

"But he didn't, naturally?"

"Oh, no! At first, I think, he took many women. But later, when I knew him, he took none of those that besieged him. He had two Mexican women whom he lived with, humble women, Indians. And all the others he spat at, and spoke of them with terrible, obscene language. I think he would have liked to whip them, or kill them, for pursuing him."

"Only he must enchant them when he was in the bull-ring," said I.

"Yes. But that was like sharpening his knife on them."

"And when he retired—he had plenty of money—how did he amuse himself?"

"He was rich, he had a big *hacienda*, and many people like slaves to work for him. He raised cattle. I think he was very proud to be *hacendado* and *padròn* of so many people, with a little army of his own. I think he was proud, living like a king. I had not heard of him for years. Now, suddenly, he is in Venice with a Frenchwoman, a Frenchwoman who talks bad Spanish——"

"How old is he?"

"How old? He is about fifty, or a little less."

"So young! And will you speak to him?"

"I don't know. I can't make up my mind. If I speak to him, he will think I want money."

There was a certain note of hatred now in Colmenares' voice.

"Well, why shouldn't he give you money? He is still rich, I suppose?"

"Rich, yes! He must always be rich. He has got American money. An American woman left him half a million dollars. Did you never hear of it?"

"No. Then why shouldn't he give you money? I suppose you often gave him some, in the past?"

"Oh, that—that is *quite* the past. He will never give me anything —or a hundred francs, something like that! Because he is mean. Did you never hear of the American woman who left him half a million dollars, and committed suicide?" ·

"No. When was it?"

"It was a long time ago—about 1914, or 1913. I had already lost all my money. Her name was Ethel Cane. Did you never hear of her?"

"I don't think I did," I said, feeling it remiss not to have heard of the lady.

"Ah! You should have known her. She was extraordinary.

I had known her in Paris, even before I came back to Mexico and knew Cuesta well. She was almost as extraordinary as Cuesta: one of those American women, born rich, but what we should call provincial. She didn't come from New York or Boston, but somewhere else. Omaha or something. She was blonde, with thick, straight, blond hair, and she was one of the very first to wear it short, like a Florentine page-boy. Her skin was white, and her eyes very blue, and she was not thin. At first, there seemed something childish about her—do you know that look, rather round cheeks and clear eyes, so false-innocent? Her eyes especially were warm and naïve and false-innocent, but full of light. Only sometimes they were bloodshot. Oh, she was extraordinary! It was only when I knew her better I noticed how her blond eyebrows gathered together above her nose, in a diabolic manner. She was much too much a personality to be a lady, and she had all that terrible American energy! Ah, energy! She was a dynamo. In Paris she was married to a dapper little pink-faced American who got yellow at the gills, bilious, running after her when she would not have him. He painted pictures and wanted to be modern. She knew all the people, and had all sorts come to her, as if she kept a human menagerie. And she bought old furniture and brocades; she would go mad if she saw someone get a piece of velvet brocade with the misty bloom of years on it, that she coveted. She coveted such things, with lust, and would go into a strange sensual trance, looking at some old worm-eaten chair. And she would go mad if someone else got it, and not she: that nasty old wormy chair of the quattrocento! Things! She was mad about 'things.' But it was only for a time. She always got tired, especially of her own enthusiasms.

"That was when I knew her in Paris. Then I think she divorced that husband, and, when the revolutions in Mexico became quieter, she came to Mexico. I think she was fascinated by the idea of Carranza. If ever she heard of a man who seemed to have a dramatic sort of power in him, she must know that man. It was like her lust for brocade and old chairs and a perfect æsthetic setting. Now it was to know the most dangerous man, especially if he looked like a prophet or a reformer. She was a socialist also, at this time. She no longer was in love with chairs.

"She found me again in Mexico: she knew thousands of people, and whenever one of them might be useful to her, she remembered him. So she remembered me, and it was nothing to her that I was now poor. I know she thought of me as 'that little Luis Something,' but she had a certain use for me, and, found, perhaps, a certain little flavour in me. At least she asked me often to dinner, or to drive with her. She was curious, quite reckless and a dare-devil, yet shy and awkward out of her own *milieu*. It was only in intimacy that she was unscrupulous and dauntless as a devil incarnate. In public, and in strange places, she was very uneasy, like one who has a bad conscience towards society, and is afraid of it. And for that reason she could never go out without a man to stand between her and all the others.

"While she was in Mexico, I was that man. She soon discovered that I was satisfactory. I would perform all the duties of a husband without demanding any of the rights. Which was what she wanted. I think she was looking round for a remarkable and epoch-making husband. But, of course, it would have to be a husband who would be a fitting instrument for her remarkable and epoch-making energy and character. She was extraordinary, but she could only work through individuals, through others. By herself she could accomplish nothing. She lay on a sofa and mused and schemed, with the energy boiling inside her. Only when she had a group, or a few real individuals, or just one man, then she could start something, and make them all dance in a tragi-comedy, like marionettes.

"But in Mexico men do not care for women who will make them dance like puppets. In Mexico, women must run in the dust like the Indian women, with meek little heads. American women are not very popular. Their energy, and their power to make other people do things, are not in request. The men

would rather go to the devil in their own way, than be sent
there by the women, with a little basket in which to bring
home the goods.

"So Ethel found not a cold shoulder, but a number of square,
fat backs turned to her. They didn't want her. The revolu-
tionaries would not take any notice of her at all. They wanted
no woman interfering. General Isidor Garabay danced with
her, and expected her immediately to become his mistress.
But, as she said, she was having *none of that*. She had a
terrible way of saying 'I'm having none of that!'—like hitting
a mirror with a hammer. And as nobody wanted to get into
trouble over her, they were having none of her.

"At first, of course, when the generals saw her white
shoulders and blond hair and innocent face, they thought at
once: 'Here is a *type* for us!' They were not deceived by her
innocent look. But they were deceived by what looked like
her helplessness. The blood would come swelling into her neck
and face, her eyes would go hot, her whole figure would swell
with repellent energy, and she would say something very
American and very crushing, in French, or in American. None
of *that!* Stop *that!*

"She, too, had a lot of power. She could send out of her
body a repelling energy, to compel people to submit to her
will. Men in Europe or the United States nearly always
crumpled up before her. But in Mexico she had come to the
wrong shop. The men were a law to themselves. While she
was winning and rather lovely, with her blue eyes so full of
light and her white skin glistening with energetic health, they
expected her to become at once their mistress. And when they
saw, very quickly, that she was having *none of that*, they turned
on their heels and showed her their fat backs. Because she
was clever, and remarkable, and had wonderful energy and a
wonderful power for making people dance while she pulled the
strings, they didn't care a bit. They, too, wanted *none of that*.
They would, perhaps, have carried her off and shared her as
a mistress, except for the fear of trouble with the American
Government.

"So, soon, she began to be bored, and to think of returning to New York. She said that Mexico was a place without a soul and without a culture, and it had not even brain enough to be mechanically efficient. It was a city and a land of naughty little boys doing obscene little things, and one day it would learn its lesson. I told her that history is the account of a lesson which nobody ever learns, and she told me the world certainly *had* progressed. Only not in Mexico, she supposed. I asked her why she had come, then, to Mexico. And she said she had thought there was something doing, and she would like to be in it. But she found it was only naughty and mostly cowardly little boys letting off guns and doing mediocre obscenities, so she would leave them to it. I told her I supposed it was life. And she replied that since it was not good enough for her, it was not life to her.

"She said all she wanted was to live the life of the imagination and get it acted on. At the time, I thought this ridiculous. I thought she was just trying to find somebody to fall in love with. Later, I saw she was right. She had an imaginary picture of herself as an extraordinary and potent woman who would make a stupendous change in the history of man. Like Catherine of Russia, only cosmopolitan, not merely Russian. And it is true, she *was* an extraordinary woman, with tremendous power of will, and truly amazing energy, even for an American woman. She was like a locomotive-engine stoked up inside and bursting with steam, which it has to let off by rolling a lot of trucks about. But I did not see how this was to cause a change in the tide of mortal affairs. It was only a part of the hubbub of traffic. She sent the trucks bouncing against one another with a clash of buffers, and sometimes she derailed some unfortunate item of the rolling-stock. But I did not see how this was to change the history of mankind. She seemed to have arrived just a little late, as some heroes, and heroines also, to-day, always do.

"I wondered always, why she did not take a lover. She was a woman between thirty and forty, very healthy and full of this extraordinary energy. She saw many men, and was always drawing them out, always on the *qui vive* to start them rolling down some incline. She attracted men, in a certain way. Yet she had no lover.

"I wondered even with regard to myself. We were friends, and a great deal together. Certainly I was under her spell. I came running as soon as I thought she wanted me. I did the things she suggested I should do. Even among my own acquaintances, when I found everybody laughing at me and disliking me for being at the service of an American woman, and I tried to rebel against her, and put her in her place, as the Mexicans say—which means, to them, in bed with no clothes on—still, the moment I saw her, with a look and a word she won me round. She was very clever. She flattered me, of course. She made me feel intelligent. She drew me out. There was her cleverness. She made *me* clever. I told her all about Mexico: all my life: all my ideas of history, philosophy, I sounded awfully clever and original to myself. And she listened with such attention, which I thought was deep interest in what I was saying. But she was waiting for something she could fasten on, so that she could 'start something.' That was her constant craving, to 'start something.' But, of course, I thought she was interested in *me*.

"She would lie on a large couch that was covered with old sarapes—she began to buy them as soon as she came to Mexico—herself wrapped in a wonderful black shawl that glittered all over with brilliant birds and flowers in vivid colour, a very fine specimen of the embroidered shawls our Mexican ladies used to wear at a bull-fight or in an open-air *fiesta:* and there, with her white arms glistening through the long fringe of the shawl, the old Italian jewellery rising on her white, dauntless breast, and her short, thick, blond hair falling like yellow metal, she would draw me out, draw me out. I never talked so much in my life before or since. Always talk! And I believe I talked very well, really, really very clever. But nothing besides talk! Sometimes I stayed till after midnight. And sometimes she would snort with impatience or boredom, rather like a horse, flinging back her head and shaking that heavy blond hair. And I think some part of her wanted me to make love to her.

"But I didn't. I couldn't. I was there, under her influence, in her power. She could draw me out in talk, marvellously. I'm sure I was very clever indeed. But any other part of me was stiff, petrified. I couldn't even touch her. I couldn't even take her hand in mine. It was a physical impossibility. When I was away from her, I could think of her white, healthy body with a voluptuous shiver. I could even run to her apartment, intending to kiss her, and make her my mistress that very night. But the moment I was in her presence, it left me. I could not touch her. I was averse from touching her. Physically, for some reason, I hated her.

"And I felt within myself, it was because she was repelling me and because she was always hating men, hating all active maleness in a man. She only wanted passive maleness, and then this 'talk,' this life of the imagination, as she called it. Inside herself she seethed, and she thought it was because she wanted to be made love to, very much made love to. But it wasn't so. She seethed against all men, with repulsion. She was cruel to the body of a man. But she excited his mind, his spirit. She loved to do that. She loved to have a man hanging round, like a servant. She loved to stimulate him, especially his mind. And she, too, when the man was not there, she thought she wanted him to be her lover. But when he was there, and he wanted to gather for himself that mysterious fruit of her body, she revolted against him with a fearful hate. A man must be *absolutely* her servant, and only that. That was what she meant by the life of the imagination.

"And I was her servant. Everybody jeered at me. But I said to myself, I would make her my mistress. I almost set my teeth to do it. That was when I was away from her. When I came to her, I could not even touch her. When I tried to make myself touch her, something inside me began to shudder. It was impossible. And I knew it was because, with her inner body, she was repelling me, always really repelling me.

"Yet she wanted me too. She was lonely: lonesome, she said. She was lonesome, and she would have liked to get me making love to her external self. She would even, I think, have become my mistress, and allowed me to take her sometimes for a little, miserable, humiliating moment, then quickly have got rid of me again. But I couldn't do it. Her inner body *never* wanted me. And I couldn't just be her prostitute. Because, immediately she would have despised me, and insulted me if I had persisted in trying to get some satisfaction of her. I knew it. She had already had two husbands, and she was a woman who always ached to tell *all*, everything. She had told me too much. I had seen one of her American husbands. I did not choose to see myself in a similar light: or plight.

"No, she wanted to live the life of the imagination. She said, the imagination could master everything; so long, of course, as one was not shot in the head, or had an eye put out. Talking of the Mexican atrocities, and of the famous case of raped nuns, she said it was all nonsense that a woman was broken because she had been raped. She could rise above it. The imagination could rise above *anything*, that was not real organic damage. If one lived the life of the imagination, one could rise above any experience that ever happened to one. One could even commit murder, and rise above that. By using the imagination, and by using cunning, a woman can justify herself in anything, even the meanest and most bad things. A woman uses her imagination on her own behalf, and she becomes more innocent to herself than an innocent child, no matter what bad things she has done."

"Men do that, too," I interrupted. "It's the modern dodge. That's why everybody to-day is innocent. To the imagination all things are pure, if you did them yourself."

Colmenares looked at me with quick, black eyes, to see if I were mocking him. He did not care about me and my interruptions. He was utterly absorbed in his recollections of that woman, who had made him so clever, and who had made him her servant, and from whom he had never had any satisfaction.

"And then what?" I asked him. "Then did she try her hand on Cuesta?"

"Ah!" said Colmenares, rousing, and glancing at me suspiciously again. "Yes! That was what she did. And I was jealous. Though I couldn't bring myself to touch her, yet I was excruciated with jealousy, because she was interested in someone else. She was interested in someone besides myself, and my vanity suffered tortures of jealousy. Why was I such a fool? Why, even now, could I kill that fat, yellow pig Cuesta? A man is always a fool."

"How did she meet the bull-fighter?" I asked. "Did you introduce him to her?"

"She went once to the bull-fight, because every one was talking about Cuesta. She did not care for such things as the bull-ring; she preferred the modern theatre, Duse and Reinhardt, and 'things of the imagination.' But now she was going back to New York, and she had never seen a bull-fight, so she must see one. I got seats in the shade—high up, you know—and went with her.

"At first she was very disgusted, and very contemptuous, and a little bit frightened, you know, because a Mexican crowd in a bull-ring is not very charming. She was afraid of people. But she sat stubborn and sulky, like a sulky child, saying: Can't they do anything more subtle than this, to get a thrill? It's on such a low level!

"But when Cuesta at last began to play with a bull, she began to get excited. He was in pink and silver, very gorgeous, and looking very ridiculous, as usual. Till he began to play; and then there really was something marvellous in him, you know, so quick and so light and so playful—do you know? When he was playing with a bull and playing with death in the ring, he was the most playful thing I have ever seen: more playful than kittens or leopard cubs: and you know how they play; do you? Oh, marvellous! More gay and light than if they had lots of wings all over them, all wings of playing! Well, he was like that, playing with death in the ring, as if he had all kinds of gay little wings to spin him with the quickest, tiniest,

most beautiful little movements, quite unexpected, like a soft
leopard cub. And then at the end, when he killed the bull and
the blood squirted past him, ugh! it was as if all his body
laughed, and still the same soft, surprised laughter like a young
thing, but more cruel than anything you can imagine. He
fascinated me, but I always hated him. I would have liked to
stick him as he stuck the bulls.

"I could see that Ethel was trying not to be caught by his
spell. He had the most curious charm, quick and unexpected
like play, you know, like leopard kittens, or slow sometimes,
like tiny little bears. And yet the perfect cruelty. It was the
joy in cruelty! She hated the blood and messiness and dead
animals. Ethel hated all that. It was not the life of the
imagination. She was very pale, and very silent. She leaned
forward and hardly moved, looking white and obstinate and
subdued. And Cuesta had killed three bulls before she made
any sign of any sort. I did not speak to her. The fourth bull
was a beauty, full of life, curling and prancing like a narcissus-
flower in January. He was a very special bull, brought from
Spain, and not so stupid as the others. He pawed the ground
and blew the breath on the ground, lowering his head. And
Cuesta opened his arms to him with a little smile, but endearing,
lovingly endearing, as a man might open his arms to a little
maiden he really loves, but, really, for her to come to his body,
his warm, open body, to come softly. So he held his arms out
to the bull, with love. And that was what fascinated the
women. They screamed and they fainted, longing to go into
the arms of Cuesta, against his soft, round body, that was more
yearning than a fico. But the bull, of course, rushed past him,
and only got two darts sticking in his shoulder. That was the
love.

"Then Ethel shouted, *Bravo! Bravo!* and I saw that she,
too, had gone mad. Even Cuesta heard her, and he stopped a
moment and looked at her. He saw her leaning forward, with
her short, thick hair hanging like yellow metal, and her face
dead-white, and her eyes glaring to his, like a challenge. They
looked at one another, for a second, and he gave a little bow,

then turned away. But he was changed. He didn't play so unconsciously any more: he seemed to be thinking of something, and forgetting himself. I was afraid he would be killed; but so afraid! He seemed absent-minded, and taking risks too great. When the bull came after him over the gangway barrier, he even put his hand on its head as he vaulted back, and one horn caught his sleeve and tore it just a little. Then he seemed to be absent-mindedly looking at the tear, while the bull was almost touching him again. And the bull was mad. Cuesta was a dead man it seemed, for sure: yet he seemed to wake up and *waked* himself just out of reach. It was like an awful dream, and it seemed to last for hours. I think it must have been a long time, before the bull was killed. He killed him at last, as a man takes his mistress at last because he is almost tired of playing with her. But he liked to kill his own bull.

"Ethel was looking like death, with beads of perspiration on her face. And she called to him: 'That's enough! That's enough now! *Ya es bastante! Basta!*' He looked at her, and heard what she said. They were both alike there, they heard and saw in a flash. And he lifted his face, with the rather squashed nose and the yellow eyes, and he looked at her, and though he was so far away, he seemed quite near. And he was smiling like a small boy. But I could see he was looking at the little place in her body, where she kept her courage. And she was trying to catch his look on her imagination, not on her naked inside body. And they both found it difficult. When he tried to look at her, she set her imagination in front of him, like a mirror they put in front of a wild dog. And when she tried to catch him in her imagination, he seemed to melt away, and was gone. So neither really had caught the other.

"But he played with two more bulls, and killed them, without ever looking at her. And she went away when the people were applauding him, and did not look at him. Neither did she speak to me of him. Neither did she go to any more bull-fights.

"It was Cuesta who spoke to me of her, when I met him at Clavel's house. He said to me, in his very coarse Spanish: And what about your American skirt? I told him, there was nothing to say about her. She was leaving for New York. So he told me to ask her if she would like to come and say good-bye to Cuesta, before she went. I said to him: But why should I mention your name to her? She has never mentioned yours to me. He made an obscene joke to me.

"And it must have been because I was thinking of him that she said that evening: Do you know Cuesta? I told her I did, and she asked me what I thought of him. I told her I thought he was a marvellous beast, but he wasn't really a man. 'But he is a beast with imagination,' she said to me. 'Couldn't one get a response out of him?' I told her I didn't know, but I didn't want to try. I would leave Cuesta to the bull-ring. I would never dream of trying my imagination on him. She said, always ready with an answer: 'But wasn't there a marvellous *thing* in him, something quite exceptional?' I said, maybe! But so has a rattlesnake a marvellous thing in him: two things, one in his mouth, one in his tail. But I didn't want to try to get response out of a rattlesnake. She wasn't satisfied, though. She was tortured. I said to her: 'Anyhow, you are leaving on Thursday.' 'No, I've put it off,' she said. 'Till when?' 'Indefinite,' she said.

"I could tell she was tormented. She had been tormented ever since she had been to the bull-fight, because she couldn't get past Cuesta. She couldn't get past him, as the Americans say. He seemed like a fat, squat, yellow-eyed demon just smiling at her, and dancing ahead of her. 'Why don't you bring him here?' she said at last, though she didn't want to say it. 'But why? What is the good of bringing him here? Would you bring a criminal here, or a yellow scorpion?'—'I would if I wanted to find out about it.'—'But what is there to find out about Cuesta? He is just a sort of beast. He is less than a man.'—'Maybe he's a *schwarze Bestie*,' she said, 'and I'm a *blonde Bestie*. Anyway, bring him.'

"I always did what she wanted me, though I never wanted to myself. So it was now. I went to a place where I knew Cuesta would be, and he asked me: 'How is the blonde skirt?

Has she gone yet?' I said, 'No. Would you like to see her?' He looked at me with his yellow eyes, and that pleasant look which was really hate undreaming. 'Did she tell you to ask me?' he said. 'No,' I said. 'We were talking of you, and she said, bring the fabulous animal along and let us see what he really is.'—'He is the animal for her meat, this one,' he said, in his vulgar way. Then he pretended he wouldn't come. But I knew he would. So I said I would call for him.

"We were going in the evening, after tea, and he was dressed to kill, in a light French suit. We went in his car. But he didn't take flowers or anything. Ethel was nervous and awkward, offering us cocktails and cigarettes, and speaking French, though Cuesta didn't understand any French at all. There was another old American woman there, for chaperon.

"Cuesta just sat on a chair, with his knees apart and his hands between his thighs, like an Indian. Only his hair, which was done up in his little pigtail, and taken back from his forehead, made him look like a woman, or a Chinaman; and his flat nose and little yellow eyes made him look like a Chinese idol, maybe a god or a demon, as you please. He just sat and said nothing, and had that look on his face which wasn't a smile, and wasn't a grimace, it was nothing. But to me it meant rhapsodic hate.

"She asked him in French if he liked his profession, and how long he had been doing it, and if he got a great kick out of it, and was he a pure-blood Indian?—all that kind of thing. I translated to him as short as possible, Ethel flushing with embarrassment. He replied just as short, to me, in his coarse, flat sort of voice, as if he knew it was mere pretence. But he looked at her, straight into her face, with that strange, far-off sort of stare, yet very vivid, taking no notice of her, yet staring right into her: as if all that she was putting forward to him was merely window-dressing, and he was just looking way in, to the marshes and the jungle in her, where she didn't even look herself. It made one feel as if there was a mountain behind her, Popocatepetl, that he was staring at, expecting a mountain-lion to spring down off a tree on the slopes of the mountain, or a snake to lean down from a bough. But the mountain was all she stood for, and the mountain-lion or the snake was her own animal self, that he was watching for, like a hunter.

"We didn't stay long, but when we left she asked him to come in whenever he liked. He wasn't really the person to have calling on one: and he knew it, as she did. But he thanked her, and hoped he would one day be able to receive her at her— meaning his—humble house in the Guadalupe Road, where everything was her own. She said: 'Why, sure, I'll come one day. I should love to.' Which he understood, and bowed himself out like some quick but lurking animal: quick as a scorpion, with silence of venom the same.

"After that he would call fairly often, at about five o'clock, but never alone, always with some other man. And he never said anything, always responded to her questions in the same short way, and always looked at her when he was speaking to the other man. He never once *spoke* to her—always spoke to his interpreter, in his flat, coarse Spanish. And he always looked at *her* when he was speaking to someone else.

"She tried every possible manner in which to touch his imagination: but never with any success. She tried the Indians, the Aztecs, the history of Mexico, politics, Don Porfirio, the bull-ring, love, women, Europe, America—and all in vain. All she got out of him was *Verdad!* He was utterly uninterested. He actually *had* no mental imagination. Talk was just a noise to him. The only spark she roused was when she talked of money. Then the queer half-smile deepened on his face, and he asked his interpreter if the Señora was very rich. To which Ethel replied she didn't really know what he meant by rich: he must be rich himself. At which, he asked the interpreter friend if she had more than a million American dollars. To which she replied that perhaps she had—but she wasn't sure. And he looked at her so strangely, even more like a yellow scorpion about to sting.

"I asked him later, what made him put such a crude question? Did he think of offering to marry her? 'Marry a ——?' he replied, using an obscene expression. But I didn't

NONE OF THAT

know even then what he really intended. Yet I saw he had her on his mind.

"Ethel was gradually getting into a state of tension. It was as if something tortured her. She seemed like a woman who would go insane. I asked her: 'Why, whatever's wrong with you?' 'I'll tell you, Luis,' she said, 'but don't you say anything to anybody, mind. It's Cuesta! I don't know whether I want him or not.'—'You don't know whether he wants *you* or not,' said I.—'I can handle that,' she said, 'if I know about myself: if I know my own mind. But I don't. My mind says he's a nada-nada, a dumb-bell, no brain, no imagination, no anything. But my body says he's marvellous, and he's got something I haven't got, and he's stronger than I am, and he's more an angel or a devil than a man, and I'm too merely human to get him—and all that, till I feel I shall just go crazy, and take an overdose of drugs. What am I to *do* with my body, I tell you? What am I to *do* with it? I've got to master it. I've got to be *more* than that man. I've got to get all round him, and past him. I've *got* to.'—'Then just take the train to New York to-night, and forget him,' I said.—'I can't! That's side-tracking. I *won't* side-track my body. I've got to get the best of it. I've got to.'—'Well,' I said, 'you're a point or two beyond me. If it's a question of getting all round Cuesta, and getting past him, why, take the train, and you'll forget him in a fortnight. Don't fool yourself you're in love with the fellow.'—'I'm afraid he's stronger than I am,' she cried out.—And what then? He's stronger than I am, but that doesn't prevent me sleeping. A jaguar even is stronger than I am, and an anaconda could swallow me whole. I tell you, it's all in a day's march. There's a kind of animal called Cuesta. Well, what of it?'

"She looked at me, and I could tell I made no impression on her. She despised me. She sort of wanted to go off the deep end about something. I said to her: 'God's love, Ethel, cut out the Cuesta caprice! It's not even good acting.' But I might just as well have mewed, for all the notice she took of me.

"It was as if some dormant Popocatepetl inside her had

R

begun to erupt. She didn't love the fellow. Yet she was in a blind kill-me-quick sort of state, neither here nor there, nor hot nor cold, nor desirous nor undesirous, but just simply *insane*. In a certain kind of way, she seemed to want him. And in a very definite kind of way, she seemed *not* to want him. She was in a kind of hysterics, lost her feet altogether. I tried might and main to get away to the United States. She'd have come sane enough, once she was there. But I thought she'd kill me, when she found I'd been trying to interfere. Oh, she was not quite in her mind, that's sure.

" 'If my body is stronger than my imagination, I shall kill myself,' she said.—'Ethel,' I said, 'people who talk of killing themselves always call a doctor if they cut their finger. What's the quarrel between your body and your imagination? Aren't they the same thing?'—'No!' she said. 'If the imagination has the body under control, you can do anything, it doesn't matter what you do, physically. If my body was under the control of my imagination, I could take Cuesta for my lover, and it would be an imaginative act. But if my body acted without my imagination, I—I'd kill myself.—'But what do you mean by your body acting without your imagination?' I said. 'You are not a child. You've been married twice. You know what it means. You even have two children. You must have had at least several lovers. If Cuesta is to be another of your lovers, I think it is deplorable, but I think it only shows you are very much like all the other women who fall in love with him. If you've fallen in love with him, your imagination has nothing to do but to accept the fact and put as many roses on the ass's head as you like.' She looked at me very solemnly, and seemed to think about it. Then she said: 'But my imagination has not fallen in love with him. He wouldn't meet me imaginatively. He's a brute. And once I start, where's it going to end? I'm afraid my body has fallen—not fallen in love with him, but fallen *for* him. It's abject! And if I can't get my body on its feet again, and either forget him or else get him to make it an imaginative act with me—I—I shall kill myself.'—'All right,' said I. 'I don't know what you are talking about, imaginative acts and unimaginative acts. The act is always the same.'—'It isn't!' she cried, furious with me. 'It is either imaginative or else it's *impossible*—to me.' Well, I just spread my hands. What could I say, or do? I simply hated her way of putting it. Imaginative act! Why, I would hate performing an imaginative act with a woman. Damn it, the act is either real, or let it alone. But now I knew why I had never even touched her, or kissed her, not once: because I couldn't stand that imaginative sort of bullying from her. It is death to a man.

"I said to Cuesta: 'Why do you go to Ethel? Why don't you stay away, and make her go back to the United States? Are you in love with her?' He was obscene, as usual. 'Am I in love with a cuttle-fish, that is all arms and eyes, and no legs or tail! That blonde is a cuttlefish. She is an octopus, all arms and eyes and beak, and a lump of jelly.'—'Then why don't you leave her alone?'—'Even cuttlefish is good when it's cooked in sauce,' he said. 'You had much better leave her alone,' I said. —'Leave her alone yourself, my esteemed Señor,' he said to me. And I knew I had better go no further.

"She said to him one evening, when only I was there—and she said it in Spanish, direct to him: 'Why do you never come alone to see me? Why do you always come with another person? Are you afraid?' He looked at her, and his eyes never changed. But he said, in his usual flat, meaningless voice: 'It is because I cannot speak, except Spanish.'—'But we could understand one another,' she said, giving one of her little violent snorts of impatience and embarrassed rage. 'Who knows!' he replied, imperturbably.

"Afterwards, he said to me: 'What does she want? She hates a man as she hates a red-hot iron. A white devil, as sacred as the communion wafer!'—'Then why don't you leave her alone?' I said.—'She is so rich,' he smiled. 'She has all the world in her thousand arms. She is as rich as God. The Archangels are poor beside her, she is so rich and so white-skinned and white-souled.'—'Then all the more, why don't you leave her alone?' But he did not answer me.

"He went alone, however, to see her. But always in the early evening. And he never stayed more than half an hour. His car, well-known everywhere, waited outside: till he came out in his French-grey suit and glistening brown shoes, his hat rather on the back of his head.

"What they said to one another, I don't know. But she became always more distraught and absorbed, as if she were brooding over a single idea. I said to her: 'Why take it so seriously? Dozens of women have slept with Cuesta, and think no more of it. Why take him seriously?'—'I don't,' she said. 'I take myself seriously, that's the point.'—'Let it be the point. Go on taking yourself seriously, and leave him out of the question altogether.'

"But she was tired of my playing the wise uncle, and I was tired of her taking herself seriously. She took herself so seriously, it seemed to me she would deserve what she got, playing the fool with Cuesta. Of course she did not love him at all. She only wanted to see if she could make an impression on him, make him yield to her will. But all the impression she made on him was to make him call her a squid and an octopus and other nice things. And I could see their 'love' did not go forward at all.

" 'Have you made love to her?' I asked him.—'I have not touched the zopilote,' he said. 'I hate her bare white neck.'

"But still he went to see her: always, for a very brief call, before sundown. She asked him to come to dinner, with me. He said he could never come to dinner, nor after dinner, as he was always engaged from eight o'clock in the evening onwards. She looked at him as much as to tell him she knew it was a lie and a subterfuge, but he never turned a hair. He was, she put it, utterly unimaginative: an impervious animal.

" 'You however, come one day to your poor house in the Guadalupe Road,' he said—meaning his house. He had said it, suggestively, several times.

" 'But you are always engaged in the evening,' she said.

" 'Come, then, at night—come at eleven, when I am free,' he said, with supreme animal impudence, looking into her eyes.

" 'Do you receive calls so late?' she said, flushing with anger and embarrassment and obstinacy.

" 'At times,' he said. 'When it is very special.'

"A few days later, when I called to see her as usual, I was told she was ill, and could see no one. The next day, she was still not to be seen. She had had a dangerous nervous collapse. The third day, a friend rang me up to say Ethel was dead.

"The thing was hushed up. But it was known she had poisoned herself. She left a note to me, in which she merely said: 'It is as I told you. Good-bye. But my testament holds good.'

"In her will, she had left half her fortune to Cuesta. The will had been made some ten days before her death—and it was allowed to stand. He took the money——"

Colmenares' voice tailed off into silence.

"Her body had got the better of her imagination, after all," I said.

"It was worse than that," he said.

"How?"

He was a long time before he answered. Then he said:

"She actually went to Cuesta's house that night, way down there beyond the Volador market. She went by appointment. And there in his bedroom he handed her over to half a dozen of his bull-ring gang, with orders not to bruise her. Yet at the inquest there were a few deep, strange bruises and the doctors made reports. Then apparently the visit to Cuesta's house came to light, but no details were ever told. Then there was another revolution, and in the hubbub this affair was dropped. It was too shady, anyhow. Ethel had certainly encouraged Cuesta at her apartment."

"But how do you know he handed her over like that?"

"One of the men told me himself. He was shot afterwards."

THE MAN WHO LOVED ISLANDS

I

THERE was a man who loved islands. He was born on one, but it didn't suit him, as there were too many other people on it, besides himself. He wanted an island all of his own: not necessarily to be alone on it, but to make it a world of his own.

An island, if it is big enough, is no better than a continent. It has to be really quite small, before it *feels* like an island; and this story will show how tiny it has to be, before you can presume to fill it with your own personality.

Now circumstances so worked out, that this lover of islands, by the time he was thirty-five, actually acquired an island of his own. He didn't own it as freehold property, but he had a ninety-nine years' lease of it, which, as far as a man and an island are concerned, is as good as everlasting. Since, if you are like Abraham, and want your offspring to be numberless as the sands of the sea-shore, you don't choose an island to start breeding on. Too soon there would be overpopulation, over-crowding, and slum conditions. Which is a horrid thought, for one who loves an island for its insulation. No, an island is a nest which holds one egg, and one only. This egg is the islander himself.

The island acquired by our potential islander was not in the remote oceans. It was quite near to home, no palm trees nor boom of surf on the reef, nor any of that kind of thing; but a good solid dwelling-house, rather gloomy, above the landing-place, and beyond, a small farmhouse with sheds, and a few outlying fields. Down on the little landing-bay were three cottages in a row, like coastguards' cottages, all neat and white-washed.

What could be more cosy and home-like? It was four miles if you walked all round your island, through the gorse and the blackthorn bushes, above the steep rocks of the sea and down in the little glades where the primroses grew. If you walked straight over the two humps of hills, the length of it, through the rocky fields where the cows lay chewing, and through the rather sparse oats, on into the gorse again, and so to the low cliffs' edge, it took you only twenty minutes. And when you came to the edge, you could see another, bigger island lying beyond. But the sea was between you and it. And as you returned over the turf where the short, downland cowslips nodded, you saw to the east still another island, a tiny one this time, like the calf of the cow. This tiny island also belonged to the islander.

Thus it seems that even islands like to keep each other company.

Our islander loved his island very much. In early spring, the little ways and glades were a snow of blackthorn, a vivid white among the Celtic stillness of close green and grey rock, blackbirds calling out in the whiteness their first long, triumphant calls. After the blackthorn and the nestling primroses came the blue apparition of hyacinths, like elfin lakes and slipping sheets of blue, among the bushes and under the glade of trees. And many birds with nests you could peep into, on the island all your own. Wonderful what a great world it was!

Followed summer, and the cowslips gone, the wild roses faintly fragrant through the haze. There was a field of hay, the foxgloves stood looking down. In a little cove, the sun was on the pale granite where you bathed, and the shadow was in the rocks. Before the mist came stealing, you went home through the ripening oats, the glare of the sea fading from the high air as the fog-horn started to moo on the other island. And then the sea-fog went, it was autumn, the oat-sheaves lying prone, the great moon, another island, rose golden out of the sea, and rising higher, the world of the sea was white.

So autumn ended with rain, and winter came, dark skies and dampness and rain, but rarely frost. The island, your island, cowered dark, holding away from you. You could feel, down in the wet, sombre hollows, the resentful spirit coiled upon itself, like a wet dog coiled in gloom, or a snake that is neither asleep nor awake. Then in the night, when the wind left off blowing in great gusts and volleys, as at sea, you felt that your island was a universe, infinite and old as the darkness; not an island at all, but an infinite dark world where all the souls from all the other bygone nights lived on, and the infinite distance was near.

Strangely, from your little island in space, you were gone forth into the dark, great realms of time, where all the souls that never die veer and swoop on their vast, strange errands. The little earthly island has dwindled, like a jumping-off place, into nothingness, for you have jumped off, you know not how, into the dark wide mystery of time, where the past is vastly alive, and the future is not separated off.

This is the danger of becoming an islander. When, in the city, you wear your white spats and dodge the traffic with the fear of death down your spine, then you are quite safe from the terrors of infinite time. The moment is your little islet in time, it is the spatial universe that careers round you.

But once isolate yourself on a little island in the sea of space, and the moment begins to heave and expand in great circles, the solid earth is gone, and your slippery, naked dark soul finds herself out in the timeless world, where the chariots of the so-called dead dash down the old streets of centuries, and souls crowd on the foot-ways that we, in the moment, call bygone years. The souls of all the dead are alive again, and pulsating actively around you. You are out in the other infinity.

Something of this happened to our islander. Mysterious "feelings" came upon him, that he wasn't used to; strange awarenesses of old, far-gone men, and other influences; men of Gaul, with big moustaches, who had been on his island, and had vanished from the face of it, but not out of the air of night. They were there still, hurtling their big, violent, unseen bodies through the night. And there were priests, with golden knives and mistletoe; then other priests with a crucifix; then pirates with murder on the sea.

Our islander was uneasy. He didn't believe, in the daytime,

in any of this nonsense. But at night it just was so. He had reduced himself to a single point in space, and, a point being that which has neither length nor breadth, he had to step off it into somewhere else. Just as you must step into the sea, if the waters wash your foothold away, so he had, at night, to step off into the other worlds of undying time.

He was uncannily aware, as he lay in the dark, that the blackthorn grove that seemed a bit uncanny even in the realm of space and day, at night was crying with old men of an invisible race, around the altar stone. What was a ruin under the hornbeam trees by day, was a moaning of blood-stained priests with crucifixes, on the ineffable night. What was a cave and a hidden beach between coarse rocks, became in the invisible dark the purple-lipped imprecation of pirates.

To escape any more of this sort of awareness, our islander daily concentrated upon his material island. Why should it not be the Happy Isle at last? Why not the last small isle of the Hesperides, the perfect place, all filled with his own gracious, blossom-like spirit? A minute world of pure perfection, made by man, himself.

He began, as we begin all our attempts to regain Paradise, by spending money. The old, semi-feudal dwelling-house he restored, let in more light, put clear lovely carpets on the floor, clear, flower-petal curtains at the sullen windows, and wines in the cellars of rock. He brought over a buxom housekeeper from the world, and a soft-spoken, much-experienced butler. These two were to be islanders.

In the farmhouse he put a bailiff, with two farm-hands. There were Jersey cows, tinkling a slow bell, among the gorse. There was a call to meals at midday, and the peaceful smoking of chimneys at evening when rest descended.

A jaunty sailing-boat with a motor accessory rode in the shelter in the bay, just below the row of three white cottages. There was also a little yawl, and two row-boats drawn up on the sand. A fishing-net was drying on its supports, a boat-load of new white planks stood criss-cross, a woman was going to the well with a bucket.

In the end cottage lived the skipper of the yacht, and his wife and son. He was a man from the other, large island, at home on this sea. Every fine day he went out fishing, with his son, every fair day there was fresh fish in the island.

In the middle cottage lived an old man and wife, a very faithful couple. The old man was a carpenter, and man of many jobs. He was always working, always the sound of his plane or his saw; lost in his work, he was another kind of islander.

In the third cottage was a mason, a widower with a son and two daughters. With the help of his boy, this man dug ditches and built fences, raised buttresses and erected a new out-building, and hewed stone from the little quarry. One daughter worked at the big house.

It was a quiet, busy little world. When the islander brought you over as his guest, you met first the dark-bearded, thin, smiling skipper, Arnold, then his boy Charles. At the house, the smooth-lipped butler who had lived all over the world valeted you, and created that curious creamy-smooth, dis-arming sense of luxury around you which only a perfect and rather untrustworthy servant can create. He disarmed you and had you at his mercy. The buxom housekeeper smiled and treated you with the subtly respectful familiarity that is only dealt out to the true gentry. And the rosy maid threw a glance at you, as if you were very wonderful, coming from the great outer world. Then you met the smiling but watchful bailiff, who came from Cornwall, and the shy farm-hand from Berkshire, with his clean wife and two little children; then the rather sulky farm-hand from Suffolk. The mason, a Kent man, would talk to you by the yard, if you let him. Only the old carpenter was gruff and elsewhere absorbed.

Well then, it was a little world to itself, and everybody feeling very safe, and being very nice to you, as if you were really something special. But it was the islander's world, not yours. He was the Master. The special smile, the special attention was to the Master. They all knew how well off they were. So the islander was no longer Mr. So-and-so.

To everyone on the island, even to you yourself, he was "the Master."

.Well, it was ideal. The Master was no tyrant. Ah, no! He was a delicate, sensitive, handsome Master, who wanted everything perfect and everybody happy. Himself, of course, to be the fount of this happiness and perfection.

But in his way, he was a poet. He treated his guests royally, his servants liberally. Yet he was shrewd, and very wise. He never came the boss over his people. Yet he kept his eye on everything, like a shrewd, blue-eyed young Hermes. And it was amazing what a lot of knowledge he had at hand. Amazing what he knew about Jersey cows, and cheese-making, ditching and fencing, flowers and gardening, ships and the sailing of ships. He was a fount of knowledge about everything, and this knowledge he imparted to his people in an odd, half-ironical, half-portentous fashion, as if he really belonged to the quaint, half-real world of the gods.

They listened to him with their hats in their hands. He loved white clothes; or creamy white; and cloaks, and broad hats. So, in fine weather, the bailiff would see the elegant tall figure in creamy-white serge coming like some bird over the fallow, to look at the weeding of the turnips. Then there would be a doffing of hats, and a few minutes of whimsical, shrewd, wise talk, to which the bailiff answered admiringly, and the farm-hands listened in silent wonder, leaning on their hoes. The bailiff was almost tender, to the Master.

Or, on a windy morning, he would stand with his cloak blowing in the sticky sea-wind, on the edge of the ditch that was being dug to drain a little swamp, talking in the teeth of the wind to the man below, who looked up at him with steady and inscrutable eyes.

Or at evening in the rain he would be seen hurrying across the yard, the broad hat turned against the rain. And the farm-wife would hurriedly exclaim: "The Master! Get up, John, and clear him a place on the sofa." And then the door opened, and it was a cry of: "Why, of all things, if it isn't the Master! Why, have ye turned out then, of a night like this, to come across to the like of we?" And the bailiff took his cloak, and the farm-wife his hat, the two farm-hands drew their chairs to the back, he sat on the sofa and took a child up near him. He was wonderful with children, talked to them simply wonderful, made you think of Our Saviour Himself, said the woman.

He was always greeted with smiles, and the same peculiar deference, as if he were a higher, but also frailer being. They handled him almost tenderly, and almost with adulation. But when he left, or when they spoke of him, they had often a subtle, mocking smile on their faces. There was no need to be afraid of "the Master." Just let him have his own way. Only the old carpenter was sometimes sincerely rude to him; so he didn't care for the old man.

It is doubtful whether any of them really liked him, man to man, or even woman to man. But then it is doubtful if he really liked any of them, as man to man, or man to woman. He wanted them to be happy, and the little world to be perfect. But anyone who wants the world to be perfect must be careful not to have real likes or dislikes. A general goodwill is all you can afford.

The sad fact is, alas, that general goodwill is always felt as something of an insult, by the mere object of it; and so it breeds a quite special brand of malice. Surely general goodwill is a form of egoism, that it should have such a result!

Our islander, however, had his own resources. He spent long hours in his library, for he was compiling a book of reference to all the flowers mentioned in the Greek and Latin authors. He was not a great classical scholar; the usual public-school equipment. But there are such excellent translations nowadays. And it was so lovely, tracing flower after flower as it blossomed in the ancient world.

So the first year on the island passed by. A great deal had been done. Now the bills flooded in, and the Master, conscientious in all things, began to study them. The study left him pale and breathless. He was not a rich man. He knew he had been making a hole in his capital, to get the island into running order. When he came to look, however, there was

hardly anything left but hole. Thousands and thousands of
pounds had the island swallowed into nothingness.

But surely the bulk of the spending was over! Surely the
island would now begin to be self-supporting, even if it made no
profit! Surely he was safe. He paid a good many of the bills,
and took a little heart. But he had had a shock, and the next
year, the coming year, there must be economy, frugality. He
told his people so, in simple and touching language. And they
said: "Why, surely! Surely!"

So, while the wind blew and the rain lashed outside, he
would sit in his library with the bailiff over a pipe and pot of
beer, discussing farm projects. He lifted his narrow handsome face, and his blue eye became dreamy. "*What* a wind!"
It blew like cannon shots. He thought of his island, lashed with
foam, and inaccessible, and he exulted. . . . No, he must not
lose it. He turned back to the farm projects with the zest of
genius, and his hands flicked white emphasis, while the bailiff
intoned: "Yes, sir! Yes, sir! You're right, Master!"

But the man was hardly listening. He was looking at the
Master's blue lawn shirt and curious pink tie with the fiery red
stone, at the enamel sleeve-links, and at the ring with the
peculiar scarab. The brown searching eyes of the man of the
soil glanced repeatedly over the fine, immaculate figure of the
Master, with a sort of slow, calculating wonder. But if he
happened to catch the Master's bright, exalted glance, his own
eye lit up with a careful cordiality and deference, as he bowed
his head slightly.

Thus between them they decided what crops should be
sown, what fertilizers should be used in different places, which
breed of pigs should be imported, and which line of turkeys.
That is to say, the bailiff, by continually cautiously agreeing
with the Master, kept out of it, and let the young man have his
own way.

The Master knew what he was talking about. He was
brilliant at grasping the gist of a book, and knowing how to
apply his knowledge. On the whole, his ideas were sound. The
bailiff even knew it. But in the man of the soil there was no

answering enthusiasm. The brown eyes smiled their cordial deference, but the thin lips never changed. The Master pursed his own flexible mouth in a boyish versatility, as he cleverly sketched in his ideas to the other man, and the bailiff made eyes of admiration, but in his heart he was not attending, he was only watching the Master as he would have watched a queer, caged animal, quite without sympathy, not implicated.

So, it was settled, and the Master rang for Elvery, the butler, to bring a sandwich. He, the Master, was pleased. The butler saw it, and came back with anchovy and ham sandwiches, and a newly opened bottle of vermouth. There was always a newly opened bottle of something.

It was the same with the mason. The Master and he discussed the drainage of a bit of land, and more pipes were ordered, more special bricks, more this, more that.

Fine weather came at last; there was a little lull in the hard work on the island. The Master went for a short cruise in his yacht. It was not really a yacht, just a little bit of a thing. They sailed along the coast of the mainland, and put in at the ports. At every port some friend turned up, the butler made elegant little meals in the cabin. Then the Master was invited to villas and hotels, his people disembarked him as if he were a prince.

And oh, how expensive it turned out! He had to telegraph to the bank for money. And he went home again, to economize.

The marsh-marigolds were blazing in the little swamp where the ditches were being dug for drainage. He almost regretted, now, the work in hand. The yellow beauties would not blaze again.

Harvest came, and a bumper crop. There must be a harvest-home supper. The long barn was now completely restored and added to. The carpenter had made long tables. Lanterns hung from the beams of the high-pitched roof. All the people of the island were assembled. The bailiff presided. It was a gay scene.

Towards the end of the supper the Master, in a velvet jacket, appeared with his guests. Then the bailiff rose and proposed

"The Master! Long life and health to the Master!" All the people drank the health with great enthusiasm and cheering. The Master replied with a little speech: They were on an island in a little world of their own. It depended on them all to make this world a world of true happiness and content. Each must do his part. He hoped he himself did what he could, for his heart was in his island, and with the people of his island.

The butler responded: As long as the island had such a Master, it could not help but be a little heaven for all the people on it. This was seconded with virile warmth by the bailiff and the mason, the skipper was beside himself. Then there was dancing, the old carpenter was fiddler.

But under all this, things were not well. The very next morning came the farm-boy to say that a cow had fallen over the cliff. The Master went to look. He peered over the not very high declivity, and saw her lying dead, on a green ledge under a bit of late-flowering broom. A beautiful, expensive creature, already looking swollen. But what a fool, to fall so unnecessarily!

It was a question of getting several men to haul her up the bank, and then of skinning and burying her. No one would eat the meat. How repulsive it all was!

This was symbolic of the island. As sure as the spirits rose in the human breast, with a movement of joy, an invisible hand struck malevolently out of the silence. There must not be any joy, nor even any quiet peace. A man broke a leg, another was crippled with rheumatic fever. The pigs had some strange disease. A storm drove the yacht on a rock. The mason hated the butler, and refused to let his daughter serve at the house.

Out of the very air came a stony, heavy malevolence. The island itself seemed malicious. It would go on being hurtful and evil for weeks at a time. Then suddenly again one morning it would be fair, lovely as a morning in Paradise, everything beautiful and flowing. And everybody would begin to feel a great relief, and a hope for happiness.

Then as soon as the Master was opened out in spirit like an open flower, some ugly blow would fall. Somebody would send him an anonymous note, accusing some other person on the island. Somebody else would come hinting things against one of his servants.

"Some folks think they've got an easy job out here, with all the pickings they make!" the mason's daughter screamed at the suave butler, in the Master's hearing. He pretended not to hear.

"My man says this island is surely one of the lean kine of Egypt, it would swallow a sight of money, and you'd never get anything back out of it," confided the farm-hand's wife to one of the Master's visitors.

The people were not contented. They were not islanders. "We feel we're not doing right by the children," said those who had children. "We feel we're not doing right by ourselves," said those who had no children. And the various families fairly came to hate one another.

Yet the island was so lovely. When there was a scent of honeysuckle and the moon brightly flickering down on the sea, then even the grumblers felt a strange nostalgia for it. It set you yearning, with a wild yearning; perhaps for the past, to be far back in the mysterious past of the island, when the blood had a different throb. Strange floods of passion came over you, strange violent lusts and imaginations of cruelty. The blood and the passion and the lust which the island had known. Uncanny dreams, half-dreams, half-evocated yearnings.

The Master himself began to be a little afraid of his island. He felt here strange violent feelings he had never felt before, and lustful desires that he had been quite free from. He knew quite well now that his people didn't love him at all. He knew that their spirits were secretly against him, malicious, jeering, envious, and lurking to down him. He became just as wary and secretive with regard to them.

But it was too much. At the end of the second year, several departures took place. The housekeeper went. The Master always blamed self-important women most. The mason said he wasn't going to be monkeyed about any more, so he took his departure, with his family. The rheumatic farm-hand left.

And then the year's bills came in, the Master made up his accounts. In spite of good crops, the assets were ridiculous, against the spending. The island had again lost, not hundreds but thousands of pounds. It was incredible. But you simply couldn't believe it! Where had it all gone?

The Master spent gloomy nights and days going through accounts in the library. He was thorough. It became evident, now the housekeeper had gone, that she had swindled him. Probably everybody was swindling him. But he hated to think it, so he put the thought away.

He emerged, however, pale and hollow-eyed from his balancing of unbalanceable accounts, looking as if something had kicked him in the stomach. It was pitiable. But the money had gone, and there was an end of it. Another great hole in his capital. How could people be so heartless?

It couldn't go on, that was evident. He would soon be bankrupt. He had to give regretful notice to his butler. He was afraid to find out how much his butler had swindled him. Because the man was such a wonderful butler, after all. And the farm-bailiff had to go. The Master had no regrets in that quarter. The losses on the farm had almost embittered him.

The third year was spent in rigid cutting down of expenses. The island was still mysterious and fascinating. But it was also treacherous and cruel, secretly, fathomlessly malevolent. In spite of all its fair show of white blossom and bluebells, and the lovely dignity of foxgloves bending their rose-red bells, it was your implacable enemy.

With reduced staff, reduced wages, reduced splendour, the third year went by. But it was fighting against hope. The farm still lost a good deal. And once more, there was a hole in that remnant of capital. Another hole in that which was already a mere remnant round the old holes. The island was mysterious in this also: it seemed to pick the very money out of your pocket, as if it were an octopus with invisible arms stealing from you in every direction.

Yet the Master still loved it. But with a touch of rancour now.

He spent, however, the second half of the fourth year intensely working on the mainland, to be rid of it. And it was amazing how difficult he found it, to dispose of an island. He had thought that everybody was pining for such an island as his; but not at all. Nobody would pay any price for it. And he wanted now to get rid of it, as a man who wants a divorce at any cost.

It was not till the middle of the fifth year that he transferred it, at a considerable loss to himself, to an hotel company who were willing to speculate in it. They were to turn it into a handy honeymoon-and-golf island.

There, take that, island which didn't know when it was well off. Now be a honeymoon-and-golf island!

II

THE SECOND ISLAND

The islander had to move. But he was not going to the mainland. Oh, no! He moved to the smaller island, which still belonged to him. And he took with him the faithful old carpenter and wife, the couple he never really cared for; also a widow and daughter, who had kept house for him the last year; also an orphan lad, to help the old man.

The small island was very small; but being a hump of rock in the sea, it was bigger than it looked. There was a little track among the rocks and bushes, winding and scrambling up and down around the islet, so that it took you twenty minutes to do the circuit. It was more than you would have expected.

Still, it was an island. The islander moved himself, with all his books, into the commonplace six-roomed house up to which you had to scramble from the rocky landing-place. There were also two joined-together cottages. The old carpenter lived in one, with his wife and the lad, the widow and daughter lived in the other.

At last all was in order. The Master's books filled two

rooms. It was already autumn, Orion lifting out of the sea. And in the dark nights, the Master could see the lights on his late island, where the hotel company were entertaining guests who would advertise the new resort for honeymoon-golfers.

On his lump of rock, however, the Master was still master. He explored the crannies, the odd handbreadths of grassy level, the steep little cliffs where the last harebells hung, and the seeds of summer were brown above the sea, lonely and untouched. He peered down the old well. He examined the stone pen where the pig had been kept. Himself, he had a goat.

Yes, it was an island. Always, always, underneath among the rocks the Celtic sea sucked and washed and smote its feathery greyness. How many different noises of the sea! Deep explosions, rumblings, strange long sighs and whistling noises; then voices, real voices of people clamouring as if they were in a market, under the waters: and again, the far-off ringing of a bell, surely an actual bell! Then a tremendous trilling noise, very long and alarming, and an undertone of hoarse gasping.

On this island there were no human ghosts, no ghosts of any ancient race. The sea, and the spume and the weather, had washed them all out, washed them out so there was only the sound of the sea itself, its own ghost, myriad-voiced, communing and plotting and shouting all winter long. And only the smell of the sea, with a few bristly bushes of gorse and coarse tufts of heather, among the grey, pellucid rocks, in the grey, more-pellucid air. The coldness, the greyness, even the soft, creeping fog of the sea, and the islet of rock humped up in it all, like the last point in space.

Green star Sirius stood over the sea's rim. The island was a shadow. Out at sea a ship showed small lights. Below, in the rocky cove, the row-boat and the motor-boat were safe. A light shone in the carpenter's kitchen. That was all.

Save, of course, that the lamp was lit in the house, where the widow was preparing supper, her daughter helping. The islander went in to his meal. Here he was no longer the Master, he was an islander again and he had peace. The old carpenter, the widow and daughter were all faithfulness itself. The old man worked while ever there was light to see, because he had a passion for work. The widow and her quiet, rather delicate daughter of thirty-three worked for the Master, because they loved looking after him, and they were infinitely grateful for the haven he provided them. But they didn't call him "the Master." They gave him his name: "Mr. Cathcart, sir!" softly, and reverently. And he spoke back to them also softly, gently, like people far from the world, afraid to make a noise.

The island was no longer a "world." It was a sort of refuge. The islander no longer struggled for anything. He had no need. It was as if he and his few dependents were a small flock of sea-birds alighted on this rock, as they travelled through space, and keeping together without a word. The silent mystery of travelling birds.

He spent most of his day in his study. His book was coming along. The widow's daughter could type out his manuscript for him, she was not uneducated. It was the one strange sound on the island, the typewriter. But soon even its spattering fitted in with the sea's noises, and the wind's.

The months went by. The islander worked away in his study, the people of the island went quietly about their concerns. The goat had a little black kid with yellow eyes. There were mackerel in the sea. The old man went fishing in the row-boat with the lad, when the weather was calm enough; they went off in the motor-boat to the biggest island for the post. And they brought supplies, never a penny wasted. And the days went by, and the nights, without desire, without ennui.

The strange stillness from all desire was a kind of wonder to the islander. He didn't want anything. His soul at last was still in him, his spirit was like a dim-lit cave under water, where strange sea-foliage expands upon the watery atmosphere, and scarcely sways, and a mute fish shadowily slips in and slips away again. All still and soft and uncrying, yet alive as rooted seaweed is alive.

The islander said to himself: "Is this happiness?" He said to himself: "I am turned into a dream. I feel nothing, or I don't know what I feel. Yet it seems to me I am happy."

Only he had to have something upon which his mental activity could work. So he spent long, silent hours in his study, working not very fast, nor very importantly, letting the writing spin softly from him as if it were drowsy gossamer. He no longer fretted whether it were good or not, what he produced. He slowly, softly spun it like gossamer, and if it were to melt away as gossamer in autumn melts, he would not mind. It was only the soft evanescence of gossamy things which now seemed to him permanent. The very mist of eternity was in them. Whereas stone buildings, cathedrals for example, seemed to him to howl with temporary resistance, knowing they must fall at last; the tension of their long endurance seemed to howl forth from them all the time.

Sometimes he went to the mainland and to the city. Then he went elegantly, dressed in the latest style, to his club. He sat in a stall at the theatre, he shopped in Bond Street. He discussed terms for publishing his book. But over his face was that gossamy look of having dropped out of the race of progress, which made the vulgar city people feel they had won it over him, and made him glad to go back to his island.

He didn't mind if he never published his book. The years were blending into a soft mist, from which nothing obtruded. Spring came. There was never a primrose on his island, but he found a winter-aconite. There were two little sprayed bushes of blackthorn, and some wind-flowers. He began to make a list of the flowers of his islet, and that was absorbing. He noted a wild currant bush and watched for the elder flowers on a stunted little tree, then for the first yellow rags of the broom, and wild roses. Bladder campion, orchids, stitchwort, celandine, he was prouder of them than if they had been people on his island. When he came across the golden saxifrage, so inconspicuous in a damp corner, he crouched over it in a trance, he knew not for how long, looking at it. Yet it was nothing to look at. As the widow's daughter found, when he showed it her.

He had said to her, in real triumph:

"I found the golden saxifrage this morning."

The name sounded splendid. She looked at him with fascinated brown eyes, in which was a hollow ache that frightened him a little.

"Did you, sir? Is it a nice flower?"

He pursed his lips and tilted his brows.

"Well—not showy exactly. I'll show it you if you like."

"I should like to see it."

She was so quiet, so wistful. But he sensed in her a persistency which made him uneasy. She said she was so happy: really happy. She followed him quietly, like a shadow, on the rocky track where there was never room for two people to walk side by side. He went first, and could feel her there, immediately behind him, following so submissively, gloating on him from behind.

It was a kind of pity for her which made him become her lover: though he never realized the extent of the power she had gained over him, and how *she* willed it. But the moment he had fallen, a jangling feeling came upon him, that it was all wrong. He felt a nervous dislike of her. He had not wanted it. And it seemed to him, as far as her physical self went, she had not wanted it either. It was just her will. He went away, and climbed at the risk of his neck down to a ledge near the sea. There he sat for hours, gazing all jangled at the sea, and saying miserably to himself: "We didn't want it. We didn't really want it."

It was the automatism of sex that had caught him again. Not that he hated sex. He deemed it, as the Chinese do, one of the great life-mysteries. But it had become mechanical, automatic, and he wanted to escape that. Automatic sex shattered him, and filled him with a sort of death. He thought he had come through, to a new stillness of desirelessness. Perhaps beyond that, there was a new fresh delicacy of desire, an unentered frail communion of two people meeting on untrodden ground.

Be that as it might, this was not it. This was nothing new or fresh. It was automatic, and driven from the will. Even she, in her true self, hadn't wanted it. It was automatic in her.

When he came home, very late, and saw her face white with fear and apprehension of his feeling against her, he pitied her, and spoke to her delicately, reassuringly. But he kept himself remote from her.

She gave no sign. She served him with the same silence, the same hidden hunger to serve him, to be near where he was. He felt her love following him with strange, awful persistency. She claimed nothing. Yet now, when he met her bright, brown, curiously vacant eyes, he saw in them the mute question. The question came direct at him, with a force and a power of will he never realized.

So he succumbed, and asked her again.

"Not," she said, "if it will make you hate me."

"Why should it?" he replied nettled. "Of course not."

"You know I would do anything on earth for you."

It was only afterwards, in his exasperation, he remembered what she had said, and was more exasperated. Why should she pretend to do this *for him?* Why not for herself? But in his exasperation, he drove himself deeper in. In order to achieve some sort of satisfaction, which he never did achieve, he abandoned himself to her. Everybody on the island knew. But he did not care.

Then even what desire he had left him, and he felt only shattered. He felt that only with her will had she wanted him. Now he was shattered and full of self-contempt. His island was smirched and spoiled. He had lost his place in the rare, desireless levels of Time to which he had at last arrived, and he had fallen right back. If only it had been true, delicate desire between them, and a delicate meeting on the third rate place where a man might meet a woman, when they were both true to the frail, sensitive, crocus-flame of desire in them. But it had been no such thing: automatic, an act of will, not of true desire, it left him feeling humiliated.

He went away from the islet, in spite of her mute reproach. And he wandered about the continent, vainly seeking a place where he could stay. He was out of key; he did not fit in the world any more.

There came a letter from Flora—her name was Flora—to say she was afraid she was going to have a child. He sat down as if he were shot, and he remained sitting. But he replied to her: "Why be afraid? If it is so, it is so, and we should rather be pleased than afraid."

At this very moment, it happened there was an auction of islands. He got the maps, and studied them. And at the auction he bought, for very little money, another island. It was just a few acres of rock away in the north, on the outer fringe of the isles. It was low, it rose low out of the great ocean. There was not a building, not even a tree on it. Only northern sea-turf, a pool of rain-water, a bit of sedge, rock, and sea-birds. Nothing else. Under the weeping wet western sky.

He made a trip to visit his new possession. For several days, owing to the seas, he could not approach it. Then, in a light sea-mist, he landed, and saw it hazy, low, stretching apparently a long way. But it was illusion. He walked over the wet, springy turf, and dark-grey sheep tossed away from him, spectral, bleating hoarsely. And he came to the dark pool, with the sedge. Then on in the dampness, to the grey sea sucking angrily among the rocks.

This was indeed an island.

So he went home to Flora. She looked at him with guilty fear, but also with a triumphant brightness in her uncanny eyes. And again he was gentle, he reassured her, even he wanted her again, with that curious desire that was almost like toothache. So he took her to the mainland, and they were married, since she was going to have his child.

They returned to the island. She still brought in his meals, her own along with them. She sat and ate with him. He would have it so. The widowed mother preferred to stay in the kitchen. And Flora slept in the guest-room of his house, mistress of his house.

His desire, whatever it was, died in him with nauseous finality. The child would still be months coming. His island was hateful to him, vulgar, a suburb. He himself had lost all his finer distinction. The weeks passed in a sort of prison, in humiliation. Yet he stuck it out, till the child was born. But he was meditating escape. Flora did not even know.

A nurse appeared, and ate at table with them. The doctor came sometimes, and, if the sea were rough, he too had to stay. He was cheery over his whisky.

They might have been a young couple in Golders Green.

The daughter was born at last. The father looked at the baby, and felt depressed, almost more than he could bear. The millstone was tied round his neck. But he tried not to show what he felt. And Flora did not know. She still smiled with a kind of half-witted triumph in her joy, as she got well again. Then she began again to look at him with those aching, suggestive, somehow impudent eyes. She adored him so.

This he could not stand. He told her that he had to go away for a time. She wept, but she thought she had got him. He told her he had settled the best part of his property on her, and wrote down for her what income it would produce. She hardly listened, only looked at him with those heavy, adoring, impudent eyes. He gave her a cheque-book, with the amount of her credit duly entered. This did arouse her interest. And he told her, if she got tired of the island, she could choose her home wherever she wished.

She followed him with those aching, persistent brown eyes, when he left, and he never even saw her weep.

He went straight north, to prepare his third island.

III

THE THIRD ISLAND

The third island was soon made habitable. With cement and the big pebbles from the shingle beach, two men built him a hut, and roofed it with corrugated iron. A boat brought over a bed and table, and three chairs, with a good cupboard, and a few books. He laid in a supply of coal and paraffin and food— he wanted so little.

The house stood near the flat shingle bay where he landed, and where he pulled up his light boat. On a sunny day in August the men sailed away and left him. The sea was still and pale blue. On the horizon he saw the small mail-steamer slowly passing northwards, as if she were walking. She served the outer isles twice a week. He could row out to her if need be, in calm weather, and he could signal her from a flagstaff behind his cottage.

Half a dozen sheep still remained on the island, as company; and he had a cat to rub against his legs. While the sweet, sunny days of the northern autumn lasted, he would walk among the rocks, and over the springy turf of his small domain, always coming to the ceaseless, restless sea. He looked at every leaf, that might be different from another, and he watched the endless expansion and contraction of the water-tossed sea-weed. He had never a tree, not even a bit of heather to guard. Only the turf, and tiny turf-plants, and the sedge by the pool, the seaweed in the ocean. He was glad. He didn't want trees or bushes. They stood up like people, too assertive. His bare, low-pitched island in the pale blue sea was all he wanted.

He no longer worked at his book. The interest had gone. He liked to sit on the low elevation of his island, and see the sea; nothing but the pale, quiet sea. And to feel his mind turn soft and hazy, like the hazy ocean. Sometimes, like a mirage, he would see the shadow of land rise hovering to northwards. It was a big island beyond. But quite without substance.

He was soon almost startled when he perceived the steamer on the near horizon, and his heart contracted with fear, lest it were going to pause and molest him. Anxiously he watched it go, and not till it was out of sight did he feel truly relieved, himself again. The tension of waiting for human approach was cruel. He did not want to be approached. He did not want to hear voices. He was shocked by the sound of his own voice, if he inadvertently spoke to his cat. He rebuked himself for having broken the great silence. And he was irritated when his cat would look up at him and mew faintly, plaintively.

He frowned at her. And she knew. She was becoming wild, lurking in the rocks, perhaps fishing.

But what he disliked most was when one of the lumps of sheep opened its mouth and baa-ed its hoarse, raucous baa. He watched it, and it looked to him hideous and gross. He came to dislike the sheep very much.

He wanted only to hear the whispering sound of the sea, and the sharp cries of the gulls, cries that came out of another world to him. And best of all, the great silence.

He decided to get rid of the sheep when the boat came. They were accustomed to him now, and stood and stared at him with yellow or colourless eyes, in an insolence that was almost cold ridicule. There was a suggestion of cold indecency about them. He disliked them very much. And when they jumped with staccato jumps off the rocks, and their hoofs made the dry, sharp hit, and the fleece flopped on their square backs, he found them repulsive, degrading.

The fine weather passed, and it rained all day. He lay a great deal on his bed, listening to the water trickling from his roof into the zinc water-butt, looking through the open door at the rain, the dark rocks, the hidden sea. Many gulls were on the island now: many sea-birds of all sorts. It was another world of life. Many of the birds he had never seen before. His old impulse came over him, to send for a book, to know their names. In a flicker of the old passion, to know the name of everything he saw, he even decided to row out to the steamer. The names of these birds! He must know their names, otherwise he had not got them, they were not quite alive to him.

But the desire left him, and he merely watched the birds as they wheeled or walked around him, watched them vaguely, without discrimination. All interest had left him. Only there was one gull, a big, handsome fellow, who would walk back and forth, back and forth in front of the open door of the cabin, as if he had some mission there. He was big, and pearl-grey, and his roundnesses were as smooth and lovely as a pearl. Only the folded wings had shut black pinions, and on the closed black feathers were three very distinct white dots, making a pattern.

The islander wondered very much, why this bit of trimming or the bird out of the far, cold seas. And as the gull walked back and forth, back and forth in front of the cabin, strutting on pale-dusky gold feet, holding up his pale yellow beak, that was curved at the tip, with curious alien importance, the man wondered over him. He was portentous, he had a meaning.

Then the bird came no more. The island, which had been full of sea-birds, the flash of wings, the sound and cut of wings and sharp eerie cries in the air, began to be deserted again. No longer they sat like living eggs on the rocks and turf, moving their heads, but scarcely rising into flight round his feet. No longer they ran across the turf among the sheep, and lifted themselves upon low wings. The host had gone. But some remained, always.

The days shortened, and the world grew eerie. One day the boat came: as if suddenly, swooping down. The islander found it a violation. It was torture to talk to those two men, in their homely clumsy clothes. The air of familiarity around them was very repugnant to him. Himself, he was neatly dressed, his cabin was neat and tidy. He resented any intrusion, the clumsy homeliness, the heavy-footedness of the two fishermen was really repulsive to him.

The letters they had brought he left lying unopened in a little box. In one of them was his money. But he could not bear to open even that one. Any kind of contact was repulsive to him. Even to read his name on an envelope. He hid the letters away.

And the hustle and horror of getting the sheep caught and tied and put in the ship made him loathe with profound repulsion the whole of the animal creation. What repulsive god invented animals and evil-smelling men? To his nostrils, the fishermen and the sheep alike smelled foul; an uncleanness on the fresh earth.

He was still nerve-racked and tortured when the ship at last lifted sail and was drawing away, over the still sea. And sometimes days after, he would start with repulsion, thinking he heard the munching of sheep.

The dark days of winter drew on. Sometimes there was no real day at all. He felt ill, as if he were dissolving, as if dissolution had already set in inside him. Everything was twilight, outside, and in his mind and soul. Once, when he went to the door, he saw black heads of men swimming in his bay. For some moments he swooned unconscious. It was the shock, the horror of unexpected human approach. The horror in the twilight! And not till the shock had undermined him and left him disembodied, did he realize that the black heads were the heads of seals swimming in. A sick relief came over him. But he was barely conscious, after the shock. Later on, he sat and wept with gratitude, because they were not men. But he never realized that he wept. He was too dim. Like some strange, ethereal animal, he no longer realized what he was doing.

Only he still derived his single satisfaction from being alone, absolutely alone, with the space soaking into him. The grey sea alone, and the footing of his sea-washed island. No other contact. Nothing human to bring its horror into contact with him. Only space, damp, twilit, sea-washed space! This was the bread of his soul.

For this reason, he was most glad when there was a storm, or when the sea was high. Then nothing could get at him. Nothing could come through to him from the outer world. True, the terrific violence of the wind made him suffer badly. At the same time, it swept the world utterly out of existence for him. He always liked the sea to be heavily rolling and tearing. Then no boat could get at him. It was like eternal ramparts round his island.

He kept no track of time, and no longer thought of opening a book. The print, the printed letters, so like the depravity of speech, looked obscene. He tore the brass label from his paraffin stove. He obliterated any bit of lettering in his cabin.

His cat had disappeared. He was rather glad. He shivered at her thin, obtrusive call. She had lived in the coal-shed. And each morning he had put her a dish of porridge, the same

as he ate. He washed her saucer with repulsion. He did no
like her writhing about. But he fed her scrupulously. The
one day she did not come for her porridge; she always mewe
for it. She did not come again.

He prowled about his island in the rain, in a big oilskin coat
not knowing what he was looking at, nor what he went out t
see. Time had ceased to pass. He stood for long spaces, gazin;
from a white, sharp face, with those keen, far-off blue eyes o
his, gazing fiercely and almost cruelly at the dark sea under th
dark sky. And if he saw the labouring sail of a fishing-boa
away on the cold waters, a strange malevolent anger passe
over his features.

Sometimes he was ill. He knew he was ill, because h
staggered as he walked, and easily fell down. Then he pause
to think what it was. And he went to his stores and took ou
dried milk and malt, and ate that. Then he forgot again. H
ceased to register his own feelings.

The days were beginning to lengthen. All winter th
weather had been comparatively mild, but with much rain
much rain. He had forgotten the sun. Suddenly, however, th
air was very cold, and he began to shiver. A fear came ove
him. The sky was level and grey, and never a star appeared a
night. It was very cold. More birds began to arrive. Th
island was freezing. With trembling hands he made a fire i
his grate. The cold frightened him.

And now it continued, day after day, a dull, deathly cold
Occasional crumblings of snow were in the air. The days wer
greyly longer, but no change in the cold. Frozen grey daylight
The birds passed away, flying away. Some he saw lying frozen
It was as if all life were drawing away, contracting away from
the north, contracting southwards. "Soon," he said t
himself, "it will all be gone, and in all these regions nothing
will be alive." He felt a cruel satisfaction in the thought.

Then one night there seemed to be a relief; he slept better, di
not tremble half-awake, and writhe so much, half-conscious. H
had become so used to the quaking and writhing of his body, h
hardly noticed it. But when for once it slept deep, he noticed that

He woke in the morning to a curious whiteness. His window was muffled. It had snowed. He got up and opened his door, and shuddered. Ugh! how cold! All white, with a dark leaden sea, and black rocks curiously speckled with white. The foam was no longer pure. It seemed dirty. And the sea ate at the whiteness of the corpse-like land. Crumbles of snow were silting down the dead air.

On the ground the snow was a foot deep, white and smooth and soft, windless. He took a shovel to clear round his house and shed. The pallor of morning darkened. There was a strange rumbling of far-off thunder, in the frozen air, and through the newly-falling snow, a dim flash of lightning. Snow fell steadily down, in the motionless obscurity.

He went out for a few minutes. But it was difficult. He stumbled and fell in the snow, which burned his face. Weak, faint, he toiled home. And when he recovered, took the trouble to make hot milk.

It snowed all the time. In the afternoon again there was a muffled rumbling of thunder, and flashes of lightning blinking reddish through the falling snow. Uneasy, he went to bed and lay staring fixedly at nothingness.

Morning seemed never to come. An eternity long he lay and waited for one alleviating pallor on the night. And at last it seemed the air was paler. His house was a cell faintly illuminated with white light. He realized the snow was walled outside his window. He got up, in the dead cold. When he opened his door, the motionless snow stopped him in a wall as high as his breast. Looking over the top of it, he felt the dead wind slowly driving, saw the snow-powder lift and travel like a funeral train. The blackish sea churned and champed, seeming to bite at the snow, impotent. The sky was grey, but luminous.

He began to work in a frenzy, to get at his boat. If he was to be shut in, it must be by his own choice, not by the mechanical power of the elements. He must get to the sea. He must be able to get at his boat.

But he was weak, and at times the snow overcame him. It fell on him, and he lay buried and lifeless. Yet every time, he struggled alive before it was too late, and fell upon the snow with the energy of fever. Exhausted, he would not give in. He crept indoors and made coffee and bacon. Long since he had cooked so much. Then he went at the snow once more. He must conquer the snow, this new, white brute force which had accumulated against him.

He worked in the awful, dead wind, pushing the snow aside, pressing it with his shovel. It was cold, freezing hard in the wind, even when the sun came out for a while, and showed him his white, lifeless surroundings, the black sea rolling sullen, flecked with dull spume, away to the horizons. Yet the sun had power on his face. It was March.

He reached the boat. He pushed the snow away, then sat down under the lee of the boat, looking at the sea, which nearly swirled to his feet, in the high tide. Curiously natural the pebbles looked, in a world gone all uncanny. The sun shone no more. Snow was falling in hard crumbs, that vanished as if by a miracle as they touched the hard blackness of the sea. Hoarse waves rang in the shingle, rushing up at the snow. The wet rocks were brutally black. And all the time the myriad swooping crumbs of snow, demonish, touched the dark sea and disappeared.

During the night there was a great storm. It seemed to him he could hear the vast mass of snow striking all the world with a ceaseless thud; and over it all, the wind roared in strange hollow volleys, in between which came a jump of blindfold lightning, then the low roll of thunder heavier than the wind. When at last the dawn faintly discoloured the dark, the storm had more or less subsided, but a steady wind drove on. The snow was up to the top of his door.

Sullenly, he worked to dig himself out. And he managed through sheer persistency, to get out. He was in the tail of a great drift, many feet high. When he got through, the frozen snow was not more than two feet deep. But his island was gone. Its shape was all changed, great heaping white hills rose where no hills had been, inaccessible, and they fumed like volcanoes, but with snow powder. He was sickened and overcome.

His boat was in another, smaller drift. But he had not the strength to clear it. He looked at it helplessly. The shovel slipped from his hands, and he sank in the snow, to forget. In the snow itself, the sea resounded.

Something brought him to. He crept to his house. He was almost without feeling. Yet he managed to warm himself, just that part of him which leaned in snow-sleep over the coal fire. Then again, he made hot milk. After which, carefully, he built up the fire.

The wind dropped. Was it night again? In the silence, it seemed he could hear the panther-like dropping of infinite snow. Thunder rumbled nearer, crackled quick after the bleared reddened lightning. He lay in bed in a kind of stupor. The elements! The elements! His mind repeated the word dumbly. You can't win against the elements.

How long it went on, he never knew. Once, like a wraith, he got out, and climbed to the top of a white hill on his unrecognizable island. The sun was hot. "It is summer," he said to himself, "and the times of leaves." He looked stupidly over the whiteness of his foreign island, over the waste of the lifeless sea. He pretended to imagine he saw the wink of a sail. Because he knew too well there would never again be a sail on that stark sea.

As he looked, the sky mysteriously darkened and chilled. From far off came the mutter of the unsatisfied thunder, and he knew it was the signal of the snow rolling over the sea. He turned, and felt its breath on him.

RAWDON'S ROOF

RAWDON was the sort of man who said, privately, to his men friends, over a glass of wine after dinner: "No woman shall sleep again under my roof!"

He said it with pride, rather vaunting, pursing his lips. "Even my housekeeper goes home to sleep.

But the housekeeper was a gentle old thing of about sixty, so it seemed a little fantastic. Moreover the man had a wife, of whom he was secretly rather proud, as a piece of fine property, and with whom he kept up a very witty correspondence, epistolary, and whom he treated with humorous gallantry when they occasionally met for half an hour. Also he had a love affair going on. At least, if it wasn't a love affair, what was it? However!

"No, I've come to the determination that no woman shall ever sleep under my roof again—not even a female cat!"

One looked at the roof, and wondered what it had done amiss. Besides, it wasn't his roof. He only rented the house. What does a man mean, anyhow, when he says "my roof"? *My* roof! The only roof I am conscious of having, myself, is the top of my head. However, he hardly can have meant that no woman should sleep under the elegant dome of his skull. Though there's no telling. You see the top of a sleek head through a window, and you say, "By Jove, what a pretty girl's head!" And after all, when the individual comes out, it's in trousers.

The point, however, is that Rawdon said so emphatically— no, not emphatically, succinctly: "No woman shall ever again sleep under my roof." It was a case of futurity. No doubt he had had his ceilings whitewashed, and their memories put out. Or rather, repainted, for it was a handsome wooden ceiling. Anyhow, if ceilings have eyes, as walls have ears, then Rawdon had given his ceilings a new outlook, with a new coat of paint, and all memory of any woman having slept under them—for after all, in decent circumstances we sleep under ceilings, not under roofs—was wiped out for ever.

"And will you neither sleep under any woman's roof?"

That pulled him up rather short. He was not prepared to sauce his gander as he had sauced his goose. Even I could see the thought flitting through his mind, that some of his pleasantest holidays depended on the charm of his hostess. Even some of the nicest hotels were run by women.

"Ah! Well! That's not quite the same thing, you know. When one leaves one's own house one gives up the keys of circumstance, so to speak. But, as far as possible, I make it a rule not to sleep under a roof that is openly, and obviously, and obtrusively a woman's roof!"

"Quite!" said I with a shudder. "So do I!"

Now I understood his mysterious love affair less than ever. He was never known to speak of this love affair: he did not even write about it to his wife. The lady—for she was a lady—lived only five minutes' walk from Rawdon. She had a husband but he was in diplomatic service or something like that, which kept him occupied in the sufficiently-far distance. Yes, far enough. And, as a husband, he was a complete diplomat. A balance of power. If he was entitled to occupy the wide field of the world, she, the other and contrasting power, might concentrate and consolidate her position at home.

She was a charming woman, too, and even a beautiful woman. She had two charming children, long-legged, stalky, clove-pink-half-opened sort of children. But really charming. And she was a woman with a certain mystery. She never talked. She never said anything about herself. Perhaps she suffered; perhaps she was frightfully happy, and made *that* her cause for silence. Perhaps she was wise enough even to be beautifully silent about her happiness. Certainly she never mentioned her sufferings, or even her trials: and certainly she must have a fair handful of the latter, for Alec Drummond sometimes fled home in the teeth of a gale of debts. He simply got through his own money and through hers, and, third and fatal stride, through other people's as well. Then something had to be done about it. And Janet, dear soul, had to put her hat on and take journeys. But she never said anything of it. At least, she did just hint that Alec didn't *quite* make enough money to meet expenses. But after all, we don't go about with our eyes shut, and Alec Drummond, whatever else he did, didn't hide his prowess under a bushel.

Rawdon and he were quite friendly, but really! None of them ever talked. Drummond didn't talk, he just went off and behaved in his own way. And though Rawdon would chat away till the small hours, *he* never "talked." Not to his nearest male friend did he ever mention Janet save as a very pleasant woman and his neighbour: he admitted he adored her children. They often came to see him.

And one felt about Rawdon, he was making a mystery of something. And that was rather irritating. He went every day to see Janet, and of course we saw him going: going or coming. How can one help but see? But he always went in the morning, at about eleven, and did not stay for lunch: or he went in the afternoon, and came home to dinner. Apparently he was never there in the evening. Poor Janet, she lived like a widow.

Very well, if Rawdon wanted to make it so blatantly obvious that it was only platonic, purely platonic, why wasn't he natural? Why didn't he say simply: "I'm very fond of Janet Drummond, she is my very dear friend?" Why did he sort of curl up at the very mention of her name, and curdle into silence: or else say rather forcedly: "Yes, she is a charming woman. I see a good deal of her, but chiefly for the children's sake. I'm devoted to the children!" Then he would look at one in such a curious way, as if he were hiding something. And after all, what was there to hide? If he was the woman's friend, why not? It could be a charming friendship. And if he were her lover, why, heaven bless me, he ought to have been proud of it, and showed just a glint, just an honest man's glint.

But no, never a glint of pride or pleasure in the relation either way. Instead of that, this rather theatrical reserve. Janet, it is true, was just as reserved. If she could, she avoided mentioning his name. Yet one knew, sure as houses, she felt something. One suspected her of being more in love with Rawdon than ever she had been with Alec. And one felt that there was a hush put upon it all. She had had a hush put upon her. By whom? By both the men? Or by Rawdon only? Or by Drummond? Was it for her husband's sake? Impossible! For her children's? But why! Her children were devoted to Rawdon.

It now had become the custom for them to go to him three times a week, for music. I don't mean he taught them the piano. Rawdon was a very refined musical amateur. He had them sing, in their delicate girlish voices, delicate little songs, and really he succeeded wonderfully with them; he made them so true, which children rarely are, musically, and so pure and effortless, like little flamelets of sound. It really was rather beautiful, and sweet of him. And he taught them *music*, the delicacy of the feel of it. They had a regular teacher for the practice.

Even the little girls, in their young little ways, were in love with Rawdon! So if their mother were in love too, in her ripened womanhood, why not?

Poor Janet! She was so still, and so elusive: the hush upon her! She was rather like a half-opened rose that somebody had tied a string round, so that it couldn't open any more. But why? Why? In her there was a real touch of mystery. One could never *ask* her, because one knew her heart was too keenly involved: or her pride.

Whereas there was, really, no mystery about Rawdon, refined and handsome and subtle as he was. He *had* no mystery: at least, to a man. What *he* wrapped himself up in was a certain amount of mystification.

Who wouldn't be irritated to hear a fellow saying, when for months and months he has been paying a daily visit to a lonely and very attractive woman—nay, lately even a twice-daily visit, even if always before sundown—to hear him say, pursing his lips after a sip of his own very moderate port: "I've taken a vow that no woman shall sleep under my roof again!"

I almost snapped out: "Oh, what the hell! And what about your Janet?" But I remembered in time, it was not *my* affair, and if he wanted to have his mystifications, let him have them.

If he meant he wouldn't have his wife sleep under his roof again, that one could understand. They were really very witty with one another, he and she, but fatally and damnably married.

Yet neither wanted a divorce. And neither put the slightest claim to any control over the other's behaviour. He said: "Women live on the moon, men on the earth." And she said: "I don't mind in the least if he loves Janet Drummond, poor thing. It would be a change for him, from loving himself. And a change for her, if somebody loved her——"

Poor Janet! But he wouldn't have her sleep under his roof, no, not for any money. And apparently he never slept under hers—if she could be said to have one. So what the deuce?

Of course, if they were friends, just friends, all right! But then in that case, why start talking about not having a woman sleep under your roof? Pure mystification!

The cat never came out of the bag. But one evening I distinctly heard it mewing inside its sack, and I even believe I saw a claw through the canvas.

It was in November—everything much as usual—myself pricking my ears to hear if the rain had stopped, and I could go home, because I was just a little bored about "cornemuse" music. I had been having dinner with Rawdon, and listening to him ever since on his favourite topic: not, of course, women, and why they shouldn't sleep under his roof, but fourteenth-century melody and windbag accompaniment.

It was not late—not yet ten o'clock—but I was restless, and wanted to go home. There was no longer any sound of rain. And Rawdon was perhaps going to make a pause in his monologue.

Suddenly there was a tap at the door, and Rawdon's man, Hawken, edged in. Rawdon, who had been a major in some fantastic capacity during the war, had brought Hawken back with him. This fresh-faced man of about thirty-five appeared

in the doorway with an intensely blank and bewildered look
on his face. He was really an extraordinarily good actor.

"A lady, sir!" he said, with a look of utter blankness.

"A what?" snapped Rawdon.

"A lady!"—then with a most discreet drop in his voice:
"Mrs. Drummond, sir!" He looked modestly down at his feet.

Rawdon went deathly white, and his lips quivered.

"Mrs. Drummond! Where?"

Hawken lifted his eyes to his master in a fleeting glance.

"I showed her into the dining-room, there being no fire in
the drawing-room."

Rawdon got to his feet, and took two or three agitated
strides. He could not make up his mind. At last he said, his
lips working with agitation:

"Bring her in here."

Then he turned with a theatrical gesture to me.

"What this is all about, I *don't* know," he said.

"Let me clear out," said I, making for the door.

He caught me by the arm:

"No, for God's sake! For God's sake, stop and see me
through!"

He gripped my arm till it really hurt, and his eyes were
quite wild. I did not know my Olympic Rawdon.

Hastily I backed away to the side of the fire—we were in
Rawdon's room, where the books and piano were—and Mrs.
Drummond appeared in the doorway. She was much paler
than usual, being a rather warm-coloured woman, and she
glanced at me with big reproachful eyes, as much as to say:
You intruder! You interloper! For my part, I could do
nothing but stare. She wore a black wrap, which I knew quite
well, over her black dinner-dress.

"Rawdon!" she said, turning to him, and blotting out my
existence from her consciousness. Hawken softly closed the
door, and I could *feel* him standing on the threshold outside,
listening keen as a hawk.

"Sit down, Janet," said Rawdon, with a grimace of a sour
smile, which he could not get rid of once he had started it,

so that his face looked very odd indeed, like a mask which he was unable either to fit on or take off. He had several conflicting expressions all at once, and they had all stuck.

She let her wrap slip back on her shoulders, and knitted her white fingers against her skirt, pressing down her arms, and gazing at him with a terrible gaze. I began to creep to the door.

Rawdon started after me.

"No, don't go! Don't go! I specially want you not to go," he said in extreme agitation.

I looked at her. She was looking at him with a heavy, sombre kind of stare. Me she absolutely ignored. Not for a second could she forgive me for existing on the earth. I slunk back to my post behind the leather arm-chair, as if hiding.

"Do sit down, Janet," he said to her again. "And have a smoke. What will you drink?"

"No, thanks!" she said, as if it were one word slurred out. "Nothanks."

And she proceeded again to fix him with that heavy, portentous stare.

He offered her a cigarette, his hand trembling as he held out the silver box.

"Nothanks!" she slurred out again, not even looking at the box, but keeping him fixed with that dark and heavy stare.

He turned away, making a great delay lighting a cigarette, with his back to her, to get out of the stream of that stare. He carefully went for an ash-tray, and put it carefully within reach—all the time trying not to be swept away on that stare. And she stood with her fingers locked, her straight, plump, handsome arms pressed downwards against her skirt, and she gazed at him.

He leaned his elbow on the mantelpiece abstractedly for a moment—then he started suddenly, and rang the bell. She turned her eyes from him for a moment, to watch his middle finger pressing the bell-button. Then there was a tension of waiting, an interruption in the previous tension. We waited. Nobody came. Rawdon rang again.

"That's very curious!" he murmured to himself. Hawken was usually so prompt. Hawken, not being a woman, slept under the roof, so there was no excuse for his not answering the bell. The tension in the room had now changed quality, owing to this new suspense. Poor Janet's sombre stare became gradually loosened, so to speak. Attention was divided. Where was Hawken? Rawdon rang the bell a third time, a long peal. And now Janet was no longer the centre of suspense. Where was Hawken? The question loomed large over every other.

"I'll just look in the kitchen," said I, making for the door.

"No, no. I'll go," said Rawdon.

But I was in the passage—and Rawdon was on my heels.

The kitchen was very tidy and cheerful, but empty; only a bottle of beer and two glasses stood on the table. To Rawdon the kitchen was as strange a world as to me—he never entered the servants' quarters. But to me it was curious that the bottle of beer was empty, and both the glasses had been used. I knew Rawdon wouldn't notice.

"That's very curious!" said Rawdon: meaning the absence of his man.

At that moment we heard a step on the servants' stairs, and Rawdon opened the door, to reveal Hawken descending with an armful of sheets and things.

"What are you doing?"

"Why!——" and a pause. "I was airing the clean laundry, like—not to waste the fire last thing."

Hawken descended into the kitchen with a very flushed face and very bright eyes and rather ruffled hair, and proceeded to spread the linen on chairs before the fire.

"I hope I've not done wrong, sir," he said in his most winning manner. "Was you ringing?"

"Three times! Leave that linen, and bring a bottle of the fizz."

"I'm sorry, sir. You can't hear the bell from the front, sir."

It was perfectly true. The house was small, but it had been built for a very nervous author, and the servants' quarters were shut off, padded off from the rest of the house.

Rawdon said no more about the sheets and things, but he looked more peaked than ever.

We went back to the music-room. Janet had gone to the hearth, and stood with her hand on the mantel. She looked round at us, baffled.

"We're having a bottle of fizz," said Rawdon. "Do let me take your wrap."

"And where was Hawken?" she said satirically.

"Oh, busy somewhere upstairs."

"He's a busy young man, that!" she said sardonically. And she sat uncomfortably on the edge of the chair where I had been sitting.

When Hawken came with the tray, she said:

"I'm not going to drink."

Rawdon appealed to me, so I took a glass. She looked inquiringly at the flushed and bright-eyed Hawken, as if she understood something.

The man-servant left the room. We drank our wine, and the awkwardness returned.

"Rawdon!" she said suddenly, as if she were firing a revolver at him. "Alec came home to-night in a bigger mess than ever, and wanted to make love to me to get it off his mind. I can't stand it any more. I'm in love with you, and I simply can't stand Alec getting too near to me. He's dangerous when he's crossed—and when he's worked up. So I just came here. I didn't see what else I could do."

She left off as suddenly as a machine-gun leaves off firing. We were just dazed.

"You are quite right," Rawdon began, in a vague and neutral tone. . . .

"I am, am I not?" she said eagerly.

"I'll tell you what I'll do," he said. "I'll go round to the hotel to-night, and you can stay here."

"Under the kindly protection of Hawken, you mean!" she said, with quiet sarcasm.

"Why!—I could send Mrs. Betts, I suppose," he said.

Mrs. Betts was his housekeeper.

"You couldn't stay and protect me yourself?" she said quietly.

"I! I! Why, I've made a vow—haven't I, Joe?"—he turned to me—"not to have any woman sleep under my roof again."—He got the mixed sour smile on his face.

She looked up at the ceiling for a moment, then lapsed into silence. Then she said:

"Sort of monastery, so to speak!"

And she rose and reached for her wrap, adding:

"I'd better go, then."

"Joe will see you home," he said.

She faced round on me.

"Do you mind *not* seeing me home, Mr. Bradley?" she said, gazing at me.

"Not if you don't want me," said I.

"Hawken will drive you," said Rawdon.

"Oh, no, he won't!" she said. "I'll walk. Good night."

"I'll get my hat," stammered Rawdon, in an agony. "Wait! Wait! The gate will be locked."

"It was open when I came," she said.

He rang for Hawken to unlock the iron doors at the end of the short drive, whilst he himself huddled into a great-coat and scarf, fumbling for a flashlight.

"You won't go till I come back, will you?" he pleaded to me. "I'd be awfully glad if you'd stay the night. The sheets *will* be aired."

I had to promise—and he set off with an umbrella, in the rain, at the same time asking Hawken to take a flashlight and go in front. So that was how they went, in single file along the path over the fields to Mrs. Drummond's house, Hawken in front, with flashlight and umbrella, curving round to light up in front of Mrs. Drummond, who, with umbrella only, walked isolated between two lights, Rawdon shining his flashlight on her from the rear from under his umbrella. I turned indoors.

So that was over! At least, for the moment!

I thought I would go upstairs and see how damp the bed in the guest-chamber was, before I actually stayed the night with

Rawdon. He never had guests—preferred to go away himself.

The guest-chamber was a good room across a passage and round a corner from Rawdon's room—its door just opposite the padded service-door. This latter service-door stood open, and a light shone through. I went into the spare bedroom, switching on the light.

To my surprise, the bed looked as if it had just been left— the sheets tumbled, the pillows pressed. I put in my hands under the bedclothes, and it was warm. Very curious!

As I stood looking round in mild wonder, I heard a voice call softly: "Joe!"

"Yes!" said I instinctively, and, though startled, strode at once out of the room and through the servants' door, towards the voice. Light shone from the open doorway of one of the servants' rooms.

There was a muffled little shriek, and I was standing looking into what was probably Hawken's bedroom, and seeing a soft and pretty white leg and a very pretty feminine posterior very thinly dimmed in a rather short night-dress, just in the act of climbing into a narrow little bed, and, then arrested, the owner of the pretty posterior burying her face in the bed-clothes, to be invisible, like the ostrich in the sand.

I discreetly withdrew, went downstairs and poured myself a glass of wine. And very shortly Rawdon returned looking like Hamlet in the last Act.

He said nothing, neither did I. We sat and merely smoked. Only as he was seeing me upstairs to bed, in the now immaculate bedroom, he said pathetically:

"Why aren't women content to be what a man wants them to be?"

"Why aren't they!" said I wearily.

"I thought I had made everything clear," he said.

"You start at the wrong end," said I.

And as I said it, the picture came into my mind of the pretty feminine butt-end in Hawken's bedroom. Yes, Hawken made better starts, wherever he ended.

When he brought me my cup of tea in the morning, he was

very soft and catlike. I asked him what sort of day it was, and he asked me if I'd had a good night, and was I comfortable.

"Very comfortable!" said I. "But I turned you out, I'm afraid."

"Me, sir?" He turned on me a face of utter bewilderment.

But I looked him in the eye.

"Is your name Joe?" I asked him.

"You're right, sir."

"So is mine," said I. "However, I didn't see her face, so it's all right. I suppose you *were* a bit tight in that little bed!"

"Well, sir!" and he flashed me a smile of amazing impudence, and lowered his tone to utter confidence. "This is the best bed in the house, this is." And he touched it softly.

"You've not tried them all, surely?"

A look of indignant horror on his face!

"No, sir, indeed I haven't."

That day, Rawdon left for London, on his way to Tunis, and Hawken was to follow him. The roof of his house looked just the same.

The Drummonds moved too—went away somewhere, and left a lot of unsatisfied tradespeople behind.

THE ROCKING-HORSE WINNER

There was a woman who was beautiful, who started with all the advantages, yet she had no luck. She married for love, and the love turned to dust. She had bonny children, yet she felt they had been thrust upon her, and she could not love them. They looked at her coldly, as if they were finding fault with her. And hurriedly she felt she must cover up some fault in herself. Yet what it was that she must cover up she never knew. Nevertheless, when her children were present, she always felt the centre of her heart go hard. This troubled her, and in her manner she was all the more gentle and anxious for her children, as if she loved them very much. Only she herself knew that at the centre of her heart was a hard little place that could not feel love, no, not for anybody. Everybody else said of her: "She is such a good mother. She adores her children." Only she herself, and her children themselves, knew it was not so. They read it in each other's eyes.

There were a boy and two little girls. They lived in a pleasant house, with a garden, and they had discreet servants, and felt themselves superior to anyone in the neighbourhood.

Although they lived in style, they felt always an anxiety in the house. There was never enough money. The mother had a small income, and the father had a small income, but not nearly enough for the social position which they had to keep up. The father went in to town to some office. But though he had good prospects, these prospects never materialized. There was always the grinding sense of the shortage of money, though the style was always kept up.

At last the mother said, "I will see if *I* can't make something." But she did not know where to begin. She racked her brains, and tried this thing and the other, but could not find anything successful. The failure made deep lines come into her face. Her children were growing up, they would have to go to school. There must be more money, there must be more money. The father, who was always very handsome and expensive in his tastes, seemed as if he never *would* be able to do anything worth doing. And the mother, who had a great belief in herself, did not succeed any better, and her tastes were just as expensive.

And so the house came to be haunted by the unspoken phrase: *There must be more money! There must be more money!* The children could hear it all the time, though nobody said it aloud. They heard it at Christmas, when the expensive and splendid toys filled the nursery. Behind the shining modern rocking-horse, behind the smart doll's-house, a voice would start whispering: "There *must* be more money! There *must* be more money!" And the children would stop playing, to listen for a moment. They would look into each other's eyes, to see if they had all heard. And each one saw in the eyes of the other two that they too had heard. "There *must* be more money! There *must* be more money!"

It came whispering from the springs of the still-swaying rocking-horse, and even the horse, bending his wooden, champing head, heard it. The big doll, sitting so pink and smirking in her new pram, could hear it quite plainly, and seemed to be smirking all the more self-consciously because of it. The foolish puppy, too, that took the place of the teddy-bear, he was looking so extraordinarily foolish for no other reason but that he heard the secret whisper all over the house: "There *must* be more money!"

Yet nobody ever said it aloud. The whisper was everywhere, and therefore no one spoke it. Just as no one ever says: "We are breathing!" in spite of the fact that breath is coming and going all the time.

"Mother," said the boy Paul one day, "why don't we keep a car of our own? Why do we always use uncle's, or else a taxi?"

"Because we're the poor members of the family," said the mother.

"But why *are* we, mother?"

"Well—I suppose," she said slowly and bitterly, "it's because your father has no luck."

The boy was silent for some time.

"Is luck money, mother?" he asked, rather timidly.

"No, Paul. Not quite. It's what causes you to have money."

"Oh!" said Paul vaguely. "I thought when Uncle Oscar said *filthy lucker*, it meant money."

"*Filthy lucre* does mean money," said the mother. "But it's lucre, not luck."

"Oh!" said the boy. "Then what *is* luck, mother?"

"It's what causes you to have money. If you're lucky you have money. That's why it's better to be born lucky than rich. If you're rich, you may lose your money. But if you're lucky, you will always get more money."

"Oh! Will you? And is father not lucky?"

"Very unlucky, I should say," she said bitterly.

The boy watched her with unsure eyes.

"Why?" he asked.

"I don't know. Nobody ever knows why one person is lucky and another unlucky."

"Don't they? Nobody at all? Does *nobody* know?"

"Perhaps God. But He never tells."

"He ought to, then. And aren't you lucky either, mother?"

"I can't be, if I married an unlucky husband."

"But by yourself, aren't you?"

"I used to think I was, before I married. Now I think I am very unlucky indeed."

"Why?"

"Well—never mind! Perhaps I'm not really," she said.

The child looked at her, to see if she meant it. But he saw, by the lines of her mouth, that she was only trying to hide something from him.

"Well, anyhow," he said stoutly, "I'm a lucky person."

"Why?" said his mother, with a sudden laugh.

He stared at her. He didn't even know why he had said it.

"God told me," he asserted, brazening it out.

"I hope He did, dear!" she said again with a laugh, but rather bitter.

"He did, mother!"

"Excellent!" said the mother, using one of her husband's exclamations.

The boy saw she did not believe him; or rather, that she paid no attention to his assertion. This angered him somewhere, and made him want to compel her attention.

He went off by himself, vaguely, in a childish way, seeking for the clue to "luck." Absorbed, taking no heed of other people, he went about with a sort of stealth, seeking inwardly for luck. He wanted luck, he wanted it, he wanted it. When the two girls were playing dolls in the nursery, he would sit on his big rocking-horse, charging madly into space, with a frenzy that made the little girls peer at him uneasily. Wildly the horse careered, the waving dark hair of the boy tossed, his eyes had a strange glare in them. The little girls dared not speak to him.

When he had ridden to the end of his mad little journey, he climbed down and stood in front of his rocking-horse, staring fixedly into its lowered face. Its red mouth was slightly open, its big eye was wide and glassy-bright.

"Now!" he would silently command the snorting steed. "Now, take me to where there is luck! Now take me!"

And he would slash the horse on the neck with the little whip he had asked Uncle Oscar for. He *knew* the horse could take him to where there was luck, if only he forced it. So he would mount again, and start on his furious ride, hoping at last to get there. He knew he could get there.

"You'll break your horse, Paul!" said the nurse.

"He's always riding like that! I wish he'd leave off!" said his elder sister Joan.

But he only glared down on them in silence. Nurse gave him up. She could make nothing of him. Anyhow he was growing beyond her.

One day his mother and his Uncle Oscar came in when he was on one of his furious rides. He did not speak to them.

"Hallo, you young jockey! Riding a winner?" said his uncle.

"Aren't you growing too big for a rocking-horse? You're not a very little boy any longer, you know," said his mother.

But Paul only gave a blue glare from his big, rather close-set eyes. He would speak to nobody when he was in full tilt. His mother watched him with an anxious expression on her face.

At last he suddenly stopped forcing his horse into the mechanical gallop, and slid down.

"Well, I got there!" he announced fiercely, his blue eyes still flaring, and his sturdy long legs straddling apart.

"Where did you get to?" asked his mother.

"Where I wanted to go," he flared back at her.

"That's right, son!" said Uncle Oscar. "Don't you stop till you get there. What's the horse's name?"

"He doesn't have a name," said the boy.

"Gets on without all right?" asked the uncle.

"Well, he has different names. He was called Sansovino last week."

"Sansovino, eh? Won the Ascot. How did you know his name?"

"He always talks about horse-races with Bassett," said Joan.

The uncle was delighted to find that his small nephew was posted with all the racing news. Bassett, the young gardener, who had been wounded in the left foot in the war and had got his present job through Oscar Cresswell, whose batman he had been, was a perfect blade of the "turf." He lived in the racing events, and the small boy lived with him.

Oscar Cresswell got it all from Bassett.

"Master Paul comes and asks me, so I can't do more than tell him, sir," said Bassett, his face terribly serious, as if he were speaking of religious matters.

"And does he ever put anything on a horse he fancies?"

"Well—I don't want to give him away—he's a young sport, a fine sport, sir. Would you mind asking him himself? He sort of takes a pleasure in it, and perhaps he'd feel I was giving him away, sir, if you don't mind."

Bassett was serious as a church.

The uncle went back to his nephew, and took him off for a ride in the car.

"Say, Paul, old man, do you ever put anything on a horse?" the uncle asked.

The boy watched the handsome man closely.

"Why, do you think I oughtn't to?" he parried.

"Not a bit of it! I thought perhaps you might give me a tip for the Lincoln."

The car sped on into the country, going down to Uncle Oscar's place in Hampshire.

"Honour bright?" said the nephew.

"Honour bright, son!" said the uncle.

"Well, then, Daffodil."

"Daffodil! I doubt it, sonny. What about Mirza?"

"I only know the winner," said the boy. "That's Daffodil."

"Daffodil, eh?"

There was a pause. Daffodil was an obscure horse comparatively.

"Uncle!"

"Yes, son?"

"You won't let it go any further, will you? I promised Bassett."

"Bassett be damned, old man! What's he got to do with it?"

"We're partners. We've been partners from the first. Uncle, he lent me my first five shillings, which I lost. I promised him, honour bright, it was only between me and him; only you gave me that ten-shilling note I started winning with, so I thought you were lucky. You won't let it go any further, will you?"

The boy gazed at his uncle from those big, hot, blue eyes, set rather close together. The uncle stirred and laughed uneasily.

"Right you are, son! I'll keep your tip private. Daffodil, eh? How much are you putting on him?"

"All except twenty pounds," said the boy. "I keep that in reserve."

The uncle thought it a good joke.

"You keep twenty pounds in reserve, do you, you young romancer? What are you betting, then?"

"I'm betting three hundred," said the boy gravely. "But it's between you and me, Uncle Oscar! Honour bright?"

The uncle burst into a roar of laughter.

"It's between you and me all right, you young Nat Gould," he said, laughing. "But where's your three hundred?"

"Bassett keeps it for me. We're partners."

"You are, are you! And what is Bassett putting on Daffodil?"

"He won't go quite as high as I do, I expect. Perhaps he'll go an hundred and fifty."

"What, pennies?" laughed the uncle.

"Pounds," said the child, with a surprised look at his uncle. "Bassett keeps a bigger reserve than I do."

Between wonder and amusement Uncle Oscar was silent. He pursued the matter no further, but he determined to take his nephew with him to the Lincoln races.

"Now, son," he said, "I'm putting twenty on Mirza, and I'll put five for you on any horse you fancy. What's your pick?"

"Daffodil, uncle."

"No, not the fiver on Daffodil!"

"I should if it was my own fiver," said the child.

"Good! Good! Right you are! A fiver for me and a fiver for you on Daffodil."

The child had never been to a race-meeting before, and his eyes were blue fire. He pursed his mouth tight, and watched. A Frenchman just in front had put his money on Lancelot. Wild with excitement, he flayed his arms up and down, yelling "*Lancelot! Lancelot!*" in his French accent.

Daffodil came in first, Lancelot second, Mirza third. The child, flushed and with eyes blazing, was curiously serene. His uncle brought him four five-pound notes, four to one.

"What am I to do with these?" he cried, waving them before the boy's eyes.

"I suppose we'll talk to Bassett," said the boy. "I expect I have fifteen hundred now; and twenty in reserve; and this twenty."

His uncle studied him for some moments.

"Look here, son!" he said. "You're not serious about Bassett and that fifteen hundred, are you?"

"Yes, I am. But it's between you and me, uncle. Honour bright!"

"Honour bright all right, son! But I must talk to Bassett."

"If you'd like to be a partner, uncle, with Bassett and me, we could all be partners. Only, you'd have to promise, honour bright, uncle, not to let it go beyond us three. Bassett and I are lucky, and you must be lucky, because it was your ten shillings I started winning with. . . ."

Uncle Oscar took both Bassett and Paul into Richmond Park for an afternoon, and there they talked.

"It's like this, you see, sir," Bassett said. "Master Paul would get me talking about racing events, spinning yarns, you know, sir. And he was always keen on knowing if I'd made or if I'd lost. It's about a year since, now, that I put five shillings on Blush of Dawn for him: and we lost. Then the luck turned, with that ten shillings he had from you: that we put on Singhalese. And since that time, it's been pretty steady, all things considering. What do you say, Master Paul?"

"We're all right when we're sure," said Paul. "It's when we're not quite sure that we go down."

"Oh, but we're careful then," said Bassett.

"But when are you *sure?*" smiled Uncle Oscar.

"It's Master Paul, sir," said Bassett, in a secret, religious voice. "It's as if he had it from heaven. Like Daffodil, now, for the Lincoln. That was as sure as eggs."

"Did you put anything on Daffodil?" asked Oscar Cresswell.

"Yes, sir. I made my bit."

"And my nephew?"

Bassett was obstinately silent, looking at Paul.

"I made twelve hundred, didn't I, Bassett? I told uncle I was putting three hundred on Daffodil."

"That's right," said Bassett, nodding.

"But where's the money?" asked the uncle.

"I keep it safe locked up, sir. Master Paul he can have it any minute he likes to ask for it."

"What, fifteen hundred pounds?"

"And twenty! And *forty*, that is, with the twenty he made on the course."

"It's amazing!" said the uncle.

"If Master Paul offers you to be partners, sir, I would, if I were you: if you'll excuse me," said Bassett.

Oscar Cresswell thought about it.

"I'll see the money," he said.

They drove home again, and, sure enough, Bassett came round to the garden-house with fifteen hundred pounds in notes. The twenty pounds reserve was left with Joe Glee, in the Turf Commission deposit.

"You see, it's all right, uncle, when I'm *sure!* Then we go strong, for all we're worth. Don't we, Bassett?"

"We do that, Master Paul."

"And when are you sure?" said the uncle, laughing.

"Oh, well, sometimes I'm *absolutely* sure, like about Daffodil," said the boy; "and sometimes I have an idea; and sometimes I haven't even an idea, have I, Bassett? Then we're careful, because we mostly go down."

"You do, do you! And when you're sure, like about Daffodil, what makes you sure, sonny?"

"Oh, well, I don't know," said the boy uneasily. "I'm sure, you know, uncle; that's all."

"It's as if he had it from heaven, sir," Bassett reiterated.

"I should say so!" said the uncle.

But he became a partner. And when the Leger was coming on Paul was "sure" about Lively Spark, which was a quite inconsiderable horse. The boy insisted on putting a thousand on the horse, Bassett went for five hundred, and Oscar Cresswell two hundred. Lively Spark came in first, and the betting had been ten to one against him. Paul had made ten thousand.

"You see," he said, "I was absolutely sure of him."

Even Oscar Cresswell had cleared two thousand.

"Look here, son," he said, "this sort of thing makes me nervous."

"It needn't, uncle! Perhaps I shan't be sure again for a long time."

"But what are you going to do with your money?" asked the uncle.

"Of course," said the boy, "I started it for mother. She said she had no luck, because father is unlucky, so I thought if *I* was lucky, it might stop whispering."

"What might stop whispering?"

"Our house. I *hate* our house for whispering."

"What does it whisper?"

"Why—why"—the boy fidgeted—"why, I don't know. But it's always short of money, you know, uncle."

"I know it, son, I know it."

"You know people send mother writs, don't you, uncle?"

"I'm afraid I do," said the uncle.

"And then the house whispers, like people laughing at you behind your back. It's awful, that is! I thought if I was lucky——"

"You might stop it," added the uncle.

The boy watched him with big blue eyes, that had an uncanny cold fire in them, and he said never a word.

"Well, then!" said the uncle. "What are we doing?"

"I shouldn't like mother to know I was lucky," said the boy.

"Why not, son?"

"She'd stop me."

"I don't think she would."

"Oh!"—and the boy writhed in an odd way—"I *don't* want her to know, uncle."

"All right, son! We'll manage it without her knowing."

They managed it very easily. Paul, at the other's suggestion, handed over five thousand pounds to his uncle, who deposited it with the family lawyer, who was then to inform Paul's mother that a relative had put five thousand pounds into his hands, which sum was to be paid out a thousand pounds at a time, on the mother's birthday, for the next five years.

"So she'll have a birthday present of a thousand pounds for five successive years," said Uncle Oscar. "I hope it won't make it all the harder for her later."

Paul's mother had her birthday in November. The house had been "whispering" worse than ever lately, and, even in spite of his luck, Paul could not bear up against it. He was very anxious to see the effect of the birthday letter, telling his mother about the thousand pounds.

When there were no visitors, Paul now took his meals with his parents, as he was beyond the nursery control. His mother went into town nearly every day. She had discovered that she had an odd knack of sketching furs and dress materials, so she worked secretly in the studio of a friend who was the chief "artist" for the leading drapers. She drew the figures of ladies in furs and ladies in silk and sequins for the newspaper advertisements. This young woman artist earned several thousand pounds a year, but Paul's mother only made several hundreds, and she was again dissatisfied. She so wanted to be first in something, and she did not succeed, even in making sketches for drapery advertisements.

She was down to breakfast on the morning of her birthday. Paul watched her face as she read her letters. He knew the lawyer's letter. As his mother read it, her face hardened and became more expressionless. Then a cold, determined look came on her mouth. She hid the letter under the pile of others, and said not a word about it.

"Didn't you have anything nice in the post for your birthday, mother?" said Paul.

"Quite moderately nice," she said, her voice cold and absent.

She went away to town without saying more.

But in the afternoon Uncle Oscar appeared. He said Paul's mother had had a long interview with the lawyer, asking if the whole five thousand could not be advanced at once, as she was in debt.

"What do you think, uncle?" said the boy.

"I leave it to you, son."

"Oh, let her have it, then! We can get some more with the other," said the boy.

"A bird in the hand is worth two in the bush, laddie!" said Uncle Oscar.

"But I'm sure to *know* for the Grand National; or the Lincolnshire; or else the Derby. I'm sure to know for *one* of them," said Paul.

So Uncle Oscar signed the agreement, and Paul's mother touched the whole five thousand. Then something very curious happened. The voices in the house suddenly went mad, like a chorus of frogs on a spring evening. There were certain new furnishings, and Paul had a tutor. He was *really* going to Eton, his father's school, in the following autumn. There were flowers in the winter, and a blossoming of the luxury Paul's mother had been used to. And yet the voices in the house, behind the sprays of mimosa and almond-blossom, and from under the piles of iridescent cushions, simply trilled and screamed in a sort of ecstasy: "There *must* be more money! Oh-h-h; there *must* be more money. Oh, now, now-w! Now-w-w—there *must* be more money!—more than ever! More than ever!"

It frightened Paul terribly. He studied away at his Latin and Greek with his tutors. But his intense hours were spent with Bassett. The Grand National had gone by: he had not "known," and had lost a hundred pounds. Summer was at hand. He was in agony for the Lincoln. But even for the Lincoln he didn't "know," and he lost fifty pounds. He became wild-eyed and strange, as if something were going to explode in him.

"Let it alone, son! Don't you bother about it!" urged Uncle Oscar. But it was as if the boy couldn't really hear what his uncle was saying.

"I've got to know for the Derby! I've got to know for the Derby!" the child reiterated, his big blue eyes blazing with a sort of madness.

His mother noticed how overwrought he was.

"You'd better go to the seaside. Wouldn't you like to go now to the seaside, instead of waiting? I think you'd better," she said, looking down at him anxiously, her heart curiously heavy because of him.

But the child lifted his uncanny blue eyes.

"I couldn't possibly go before the Derby, mother!" he said. "I couldn't possibly!"

"Why not?" she said, her voice becoming heavy when she was opposed. "Why not? You can still go from the seaside to see the Derby with your Uncle Oscar, if that's what you wish. No need for you to wait here. Besides, I think you care too much about these races. It's a bad sign. My family has been a gambling family, and you won't know till you grow up how much damage it has done. But it has done damage. I shall have to send Bassett away, and ask Uncle Oscar not to talk racing to you, unless you promise to be reasonable about it: go away to the seaside and forget it. You're all nerves!"

"I'll do what you like, mother, so long as you don't send me away till after the Derby," the boy said.

"Send you away from where? Just from this house?"

"Yes," he said, gazing at her.

"Why, you curious child, what makes you care about this house so much, suddenly? I never knew you loved it."

He gazed at her without speaking. He had a secret within a secret, something he had not divulged, even to Bassett or to his Uncle Oscar.

But his mother, after standing undecided and a little bit sullen for some moments, said:

"Very well, then! Don't go to the seaside till after the Derby, if you don't wish it. But promise me you won't let your nerves go to pieces. Promise you won't think so much about horse-racing and *events*, as you call them!"

"Oh, no," said the boy casually. "I won't think much about them, mother. You needn't worry. I wouldn't worry, mother, if I were you."

"If you were me and I were you," said his mother, "I wonder what we *should* do!"

"But you know you needn't worry, mother, don't you?" the boy repeated.

"I should be awfully glad to know it," she said wearily.

"Oh, well, you *can*, you know. I mean, you *ought* to know you needn't worry," he insisted.

"Ought I? Then I'll see about it," she said.

Paul's secret of secrets was his wooden horse, that which had no name. Since he was emancipated from a nurse and a nursery-governess, he had had his rocking-horse removed to his own bedroom at the top of the house.

"Surely, you're too big for a rocking-horse!" his mother had remonstrated.

"Well, you see, mother, till I can have a *real* horse, I like to have *some* sort of animal about," had been his quaint answer.

"Do you feel he keeps you company?" she laughed.

"Oh, yes! He's very good, he always keeps me company, when I'm there," said Paul.

So the horse, rather shabby, stood in an arrested prance in the boy's bedroom.

The Derby was drawing near, and the boy grew more and more tense. He hardly heard what was spoken to him, he was very frail, and his eyes were really uncanny. His mother had sudden strange seizures of uneasiness about him. Sometimes, for half an hour, she would feel a sudden anxiety about him that was almost anguish. She wanted to rush to him at once, and know he was safe.

Two nights before the Derby, she was at a big party in town, when one of her rushes of anxiety about her boy, her first-born, gripped her heart till she could hardly speak. She fought with the feeling, might and main, for she believed in common sense. But it was too strong. She had to leave the dance and go downstairs to telephone to the country. The children's nursery-governess was terribly surprised and startled at being rung up in the night.

"Are the children all right, Miss Wilmot?"

"Oh, yes, they are quite all right."

"Master Paul? Is he all right?"

"He went to bed as right as a trivet. Shall I run up and look at him?"

"No," said Paul's mother reluctantly. "No! Don't trouble. It's all right. Don't sit up. We shall be home fairly soon." She did not want her son's privacy intruded upon.

"Very good," said the governess.

It was about one o'clock when Paul's mother and father drove up to their house. All was still. Paul's mother went to her room and slipped off her white fur cloak. She had told her maid not to wait up for her. She heard her husband downstairs, mixing a whisky and soda.

And then, because of the strange anxiety at her heart, she stole upstairs to her son's room. Noiselessly she went along the upper corridor. Was there a faint noise? What was it?

She stood, with arrested muscles, outside his door, listening. There was a strange, heavy, and yet not loud noise. Her heart stood still. It was a soundless noise, yet rushing and powerful. Something huge, in violent, hushed motion. What was it? What in God's name was it? She ought to know. She felt that she knew the noise. She knew what it was.

Yet she could not place it. She couldn't say what it was. And on and on it went, like a madness.

Softly, frozen with anxiety and fear, she turned the door-handle.

The room was dark. Yet in the space near the window, she heard and saw something plunging to and fro. She gazed in fear and amazement.

Then suddenly she switched on the light, and saw her son, in his green pyjamas, madly surging on the rocking-horse. The blaze of light suddenly lit him up, as he urged the wooden horse, and lit her up, as she stood, blonde, in her dress of pale green and crystal, in the doorway.

"Paul!" she cried. "Whatever are you doing?"

"It's Malabar!" he screamed, in a powerful, strange voice. "It's Malabar!"

His eyes blazed at her for one strange and senseless second, as he ceased urging his wooden horse. Then he fell with a crash to the ground, and she, all her tormented motherhood flooding upon her, rushed to gather him up.

But he was unconscious, and unconscious he remained, with some brain-fever. He talked and tossed, and his mother sat stonily by his side.

"Malabar! It's Malabar! Bassett, Bassett, I *know!* It's Malabar!"

So the child cried, trying to get up and urge the rocking-horse that gave him his inspiration.

"What does he mean by Malabar?" asked the heart-frozen mother.

"I don't know," said the father stonily.

"What does he mean by Malabar?" she asked her brother Oscar.

"It's one of the horses running for the Derby," was the answer.

And, in spite of himself, Oscar Cresswell spoke to Bassett, and himself put a thousand on Malabar: at fourteen to one.

The third day of the illness was critical: they were waiting for a change. The boy, with his rather long, curly hair, was tossing ceaselessly on the pillow. He neither slept nor regained consciousness, and his eyes were like blue stones. His mother sat, feeling her heart had gone, turned actually into a stone.

In the evening, Oscar Cresswell did not come, but Bassett sent a message, saying could he come up for one moment, just one moment? Paul's mother was very angry at the intrusion, but on second thoughts she agreed. The boy was the same. Perhaps Bassett might bring him to consciousness.

The gardener, a shortish fellow with a little brown moustache and sharp little brown eyes, tiptoed into the room, touched his imaginary cap to Paul's mother, and stole to the bedside, staring with glittering, smallish eyes at the tossing, dying child.

"Master Paul!" he whispered. "Master Paul! Malabar came in first all right, a clean win. I did as you told me. You've made over seventy thousand pounds, you have; you've got over eighty thousand. Malabar came in all right, Master Paul."

"Malabar! Malabar! Did I say Malabar, mother? Did I say Malabar? Do you think I'm lucky, mother? I knew Malabar, didn't I? Over eighty thousand pounds! I call that lucky, don't you, mother? Over eighty thousand pounds! I knew, didn't I know I knew? Malabar came in all right. If I ride my horse till I'm sure, then I tell you, Bassett, you can go as high as you like. Did you go for all you were worth, Bassett?"

"I went a thousand on it, Master Paul."

"I never told you, mother, that if I can ride my horse, and *get there*, then I'm absolutely sure—oh, absolutely! Mother, did I ever tell you? I *am* lucky!"

"No, you never did," said the mother.

But the boy died in the night.

And even as he lay dead, his mother heard her brother's voice saying to her: "My God, Hester, you're eighty-odd thousand to the good, and a poor devil of a son to the bad. But, poor devil, poor devil, he's best gone out of a life where he rides his rocking-horse to find a winner."

THE BLUE MOCCASINS

THE fashion in women changes nowadays even faster than women's fashions. At twenty, Lina M'Leod was almost painfully modern. At sixty, almost obsolete!

She started off in life to be really independent. In that remote day, forty years ago, when a woman said she was going to be independent, it meant she was having no nonsense with men. She was kicking over the masculine traces, and living her own life, manless.

To-day, when a girl says she is going to be independent, it means she is going to devote her attentions almost exclusively to men; though not necessarily to "a man."

Miss M'Leod had an income from her mother. Therefore, at the age of twenty, she turned her back on that image of tyranny, her father, and went to Paris to study art. Art having been studied, she turned her attention to the globe of earth. Being terribly independent, she soon made Africa look small: she dallied energetically with vast hinterlands of China: and she knew the Rocky Mountains and the deserts of Arizona, as if she had been married to them. All this, to escape mere man.

It was in New Mexico she purchased the blue moccasins, blue bead moccasins, from an Indian who was her guide and her subordinate. In her independence she made use of men, of course, but merely as servants, subordinates.

When the war broke out she came home. She was then forty-five, and already going grey. Her brother, two years older than herself, but a bachelor, went off to the war; she stayed at home in the small family mansion in the country, and did what she could. She was small and erect and brief in her speech, her face was like pale ivory, her skin like a very delicate parchment, and her eyes were very blue. There was no nonsense about her, though she did paint pictures. She never even touched her delicately parchment face with pigment. She was good enough as she was, honest-to-God, and the country town had a tremendous respect for her.

In her various activities she came pretty often into contact with Percy Barlow, the clerk at the bank. He was only twenty-two when she first set eyes on him, in 1914, and she immediately liked him. He was a stranger in the town, his father being a poor country vicar in Yorkshire. But he was of the confiding sort. He soon confided in Miss M'Leod, for whom he had a towering respect, how he disliked his stepmother, how he feared his father was but as wax in the hands of that downright woman, and how, in consequence, he was homeless. Wrath shone in his pleasant features, but somehow it was an amusing wrath; at least to Miss M'Leod.

He was distinctly a good-looking boy, with stiff dark hair and odd, twinkling grey eyes under thick dark brows, and a rather full mouth and a queer, deep voice that had a caressing touch of hoarseness. It was his voice that somehow got behind Miss M'Leod's reserve. Not that he had the faintest intention of so doing. He looked up to her immensely: "she's miles above me."

When she watched him playing tennis, letting himself go a bit too much, hitting too hard, running too fast, being too nice to his partner, her heart yearned over him. The orphan in him! Why should he go and be shot? She kept him at home as long as possible, working with her at all kinds of war-work. He was so absolutely willing to do everything she wanted: devoted to her.

But at last the time came when he must go. He was now twenty-four, and she forty-seven. He came to say good-bye, in his awkward fashion. She suddenly turned away, leaned her forehead against the wall, and burst into bitter tears. He was frightened out of his wits. Before he knew what was happening he had his arm in front of his face and was sobbing too.

She came to comfort him. "Don't cry, dear, don't! It will all be all right."

At last he wiped his face on his sleeve and looked at her

sheepishly. "It was you crying as did me in," he said. Her blue eyes were brilliant with tears. She suddenly kissed him.

"You are such a dear!" she said wistfully. Then she added, flushing suddenly vivid pink under her transparent parchment skin: "It wouldn't be right for you to marry an old thing like me, would it?"

He looked at her dumbfounded.

"No, I'm too old," she added hastily.

"Don't talk about old! You're not old!" he said hotly.

"At least I'm too old for *that*," she said sadly.

"Not as far as I'm concerned," he said. "You're younger than me, in most ways, I'm hanged if you're not!"

"Are you hanged if I'm not?" she teased wistfully.

"I am," he said. "And if I thought you wanted me, I'd be jolly proud if you married me. I would, I assure you."

"Would you?" she said, still teasing him.

Nevertheless, the next time he was home on leave she married him, very quietly, but very definitely. He was a young lieutenant. They stayed in her family home, Twybit Hall, for the honeymoon. It was her house now, her brother being dead. And they had a strangely happy month. She had made a strange discovery: a man.

He went off to Gallipoli, and became a captain. He came home in 1919, still green with malaria, but otherwise sound. She was in her fiftieth year. And she was almost white-haired; long, thick, white hair, done perfectly, and perfectly creamy, colourless face, with very blue eyes.

He had been true to her, not being very forward with women. But he was a bit startled by her white hair. However, he shut his eyes to it, and loved her. And she, though frightened and somewhat bewildered, was happy. But she was bewildered. It always seemed awkward to her, that he should come wandering into her room in his pyjamas when she was half dressed, and brushing her hair. And he would sit there silent, watching her brush the long swinging river of silver, of her white hair, the bare, ivory-white slender arm working with a strange mechanical motion, sharp and forcible, brushing

T

down the long silvery stream of hair. He would sit as if mesmerized, just gazing. And she would at last glance round sharply, and he would rise, saying some little casual thing to her and smiling to her oddly with his eyes. Then he would go out, his thin cotton pyjamas hitching up over his hips, for he was a rather big-built fellow. And she would feel dazed, as if she did not quite know her own self any more. And the queer, ducking motion of his silently going out of her door impressed her ominously, his curious cat head, his big hips and limbs.

They were alone in the house, save for the servants. He had no work. They lived modestly, for a good deal of her money had been lost during the war. But she still painted pictures. Marriage had only stimulated her to this. She painted canvases of flowers, beautiful flowers that thrilled her soul. And he would sit, pipe in fist, silent, and watch her. He had nothing to do. He just sat and watched her small, neat figure and her concentrated movements, as she painted. Then he knocked out his pipe, and filled it again.

She said that at last she was perfectly happy. And he said that he was perfectly happy. They were always together. He hardly went out, save riding in the lanes. And practically nobody came to the house.

But still, they were very silent with one another. The old chatter had died out. And he did not read much. He just sat still, and smoked, and was silent. It got on her nerves sometimes, and she would think as she had thought in the past, that the highest bliss a human being can experience is perhaps the bliss of being quite alone, quite, quite alone.

His bank firm offered to make him manager of the local branch, and, at her advice, he accepted. Now he went out of the house every morning and came home every evening, which was much more agreeable. The rector begged him to sing again in the church choir: and again she advised him to accept. These were the old grooves in which his bachelor life had run. He felt more like himself.

He was popular: a nice, harmless fellow, everyone said of him. Some of the men secretly pitied him. They made rather

much of him, took him home to luncheon, and let him loose
with their daughters. He was popular among the daughters
too: naturally, for if a girl expressed a wish, he would instinctively say: "What! Would you like it? I'll get it for you."
And if he were not in a position to satisfy the desire, he would
say: "I only wish I could do it for you. I'd do it like a shot."
All of which he meant.

.At the same time, though he got on so well with the maidens
of the town, there was no coming forward about him. He was,
in some way, not wakened up. Good-looking, and big, and
serviceable, he was inwardly remote, without self-confidence,
almost without a self at all.

The rector's daughter took upon herself to wake him up.
She was exactly as old as he was, a smallish, rather sharp-faced
young woman who had lost her husband in the war, and it
had been a grief to her. But she took the stoic attitude of the
young: "You've got to live, so you may as well do it!" She
was a kindly soul, in spite of her sharpness. And she had a very
perky little red-brown pomeranian dog that she had bought in
Florence in the street, but which had turned out a handsome
little fellow. Miss M'Leod looked down a bit on Alice Howells
and her pom, so Mrs. Howells felt no special love for Miss
M'Leod—"Mrs. Barlow, that is!" she would add sharply.
"For it's quite impossible to think of her as anything but
Miss M'Leod!"

Percy was really more at ease at the rectory, where the pom
yapped and Mrs. Howells changed her dress three or four times
a day and looked it, than in the semi-cloisteral atmosphere
of Twybit Hall, where Miss M'Leod wore tweeds and a natural
knitted jumper, her skirts rather long, her hair done up pure
silver, and painted her wonderful flower pictures in the
deepening silence of the daytime. At evening she would go
up to change, after he came home. And though it thrilled her
to have a man coming into her room as he dressed, snapping
his collar-stud, to tell her something trivial as she stood bare-
armed in her silk slip, rapidly coiling up the rope of silver hair
behind her head, still, it worried her. When he was there, he

couldn't keep away from her. And he would watch her, watch her, watch her as if she was the ultimate revelation. Sometimes it made her irritable. She was so absolutely used to her own privacy. What was he looking at? She never watched *him*. Rather she looked the other way. His watching tried her nerves. She was turned fifty. And his great silent body loomed almost dreadful.

He was quite happy playing tennis or croquet with Alice Howells and the rest. Alice was choir-mistress, a bossy little person outwardly, inwardly rather forlorn and affectionate, and not very sure that life hadn't let her down for good. She was now over thirty—and had no one but the pom and her father and the parish—nothing in her really intimate life. But she was very cheerful, busy, even gay, with her choir and school work, her dancing, and flirting, and dressmaking.

She was intrigued by Percy Barlow. "How *can* a man be so nice to *everybody?*" she asked him, a little exasperated. "Well, why not?" he replied, with the odd smile of his eyes. "It's not why he shouldn't, but how he manages to do it! How can you have so much good-nature? I *have* to be catty to some people, but you're nice to *everybody*."

"Oh, am I!" he said ominously.

He was like a man in a dream, or in a cloud. He was quite a good bank-manager, in fact very intelligent. Even in appearance, his great charm was his beautifully-shaped head. He had plenty of brains, really. But in his will, in his body, he was asleep. And sometimes this lethargy, or coma, made him look haggard. And sometimes it made his body seem inert and despicable, meaningless.

Alice Howells longed to ask him about his wife. "*Do* you love her? *Can* you really care for her?" But she daren't. She daren't ask him one word about his wife. Another thing she couldn't do, she couldn't persuade him to dance. Never, not once. But in everything else he was pliable as wax.

Mrs. Barlow—Miss M'Leod—stayed out at Twybit all the time. She did not even come in to church on Sunday. She had shaken off church, among other things. And she watched

Percy depart, and felt just a little humiliated. He was going to sing in the choir! Yes, marriage was also a humiliation to her. She had distinctly married beneath her.

The years had gone by: she was now fifty-seven, Percy was thirty-four. He was still, in many ways, a boy. But in his curious silence, he was ageless. She managed him with perfect ease. If she expressed a wish, he acquiesced at once. So now it was agreed he should not come to her room any more. And he never did. But sometimes she went to him in his room, and was winsome in a pathetic, heart-breaking way.

She twisted him round her little finger, as the saying goes. And yet secretly she was afraid of him. In the early years he had displayed a clumsy but violent sort of passion, from which she had shrunk away. She felt it had nothing to do with her. It was just his indiscriminating desire for Woman, and for his own satisfaction. Whereas she was not just unidentified Woman, to give him his general satisfaction. So she had recoiled, and withdrawn herself. She had put him off. She had regained the absolute privacy of her room.

He was perfectly sweet about it. Yet she was uneasy with him now. She was afraid of him; or rather, not of him, but of a mysterious something in him. She was not a bit afraid of *him*, oh no! And when she went to him now, to be nice to him, in her pathetic winsomeness of an unused woman of fifty-seven, she found him sweet-natured as ever, but really indifferent. He saw her pathos and her winsomeness. In some way, the mystery of her, her thick white hair, her vivid blue eyes, her ladylike refinement still fascinated him. But his bodily desire for her had gone, utterly gone. And secretly, she was rather glad. But as he looked at her, looked at her, as he lay there so silent, she was afraid, as if some finger were pointed at her. Yet she knew, the moment she spoke to him, he would twist his eyes to that good-natured and "kindly" smile of his.

It was in the late, dark months of this year that she missed the blue moccasins. She had hung them on a nail in his room. Not that he ever wore them: they were too small. Nor did she:

they were too big. Moccasins are male footwear, among the Indians, not female. But they were of a lovely turquoise-blue colour, made all of little turquoise beads, with little forked flames of dead-white and dark-green. When, at the beginning of their marriage, he had exclaimed over them, she had said: "Yes! Aren't they a lovely colour! So blue!" And he had replied: "Not as blue as your eyes, even then."

So naturally, she had hung them up on the wall in his room, and there they had stayed. Till, one November day, when there were no flowers, and she was pining to paint a still-life with something blue in it—oh, so blue, like delphiniums!—she had gone to his room for the moccasins. And they were not there. And though she hunted, she could not find them. Nor did the maids know anything of them.

So she asked him: "Percy, do you know where those blue moccasins are, which hung in your room?" There was a moment's dead silence. Then he looked at her with his good-naturedly twinkling eyes, and said: "No, *I* know nothing of them." There was another dead pause. She did not believe him. But being a perfect lady, she only said, as she turned away: "Well then, how curious it is!" And there was another dead pause. Out of which he asked her what she wanted them for, and she told him. Whereon the matter lapsed.

It was November, and Percy was out in the evening fairly often now. He was rehearsing for a "play" which was to be given in the church schoolroom at Christmas. He had asked her about it. "Do you think it's a bit *infra dig.* if I play one of the characters?" She had looked at him mildly, disguising her real feeling. "If you don't feel *personally* humiliated," she said, "then there's nothing else to consider." And he had answered: "Oh, it doesn't upset *me* at all." So she mildly said: "Then do it, by all means." Adding at the back of her mind: If it amuses you, child!—but she thought, a change had indeed come over the world, when the master of Twybit Hall, or even, for that matter, the manager of the dignified Stubbs' Bank, should perform in public on a schoolroom stage in amateur theatricals. And she kept calmly aloof, preferring not to know any details. She had a world of her own.

When he had said to Alice Howells: "You don't think other folk'll mind—clients of the bank and so forth—think it beneath my dignity?" she had cried, looking up into his twinkling eyes: "Oh, you don't have to keep *your* dignity on ice, Percy—any more than I do mine."

The play was to be performed for the first time on Christmas Eve: and after the play, there was the midnight service in church. Percy therefore told his wife not to expect him home till the small hours, at least. So he drove himself off in the car.

As night fell, and rain, Miss M'Leod felt a little forlorn. She was left out of everything. Life was slipping past her. It was Christmas Eve, and she was more alone than she had ever been. Percy only seemed to intensify her aloneness, leaving her in this fashion.

She decided not to be left out. She would go to the play too. It was past six o'clock, and she had worked herself into a highly nervous state. Outside was darkness and rain: inside was silence, forlornness. She went to the telephone and rang up the garage in Shewbury. It was with great difficulty she got them to promise to send a car for her: Mr. Slater would have to fetch her himself in the two-seater runabout: everything else was out.

She dressed nervously, in a dark-green dress with a few modest jewels. Looking at herself in the mirror, she still thought herself slim, young looking and distinguished. She did not see how old-fashioned she was, with her uncompromising erectness, her glistening knob of silver hair sticking out behind, and her long dress.

It was a three-miles drive in the rain, to the small country town. She sat next to old Slater, who was used to driving horses and was nervous and clumsy with a car, without saying a word. He thankfully deposited her at the gate of St. Barnabas' School.

It was almost half-past seven. The schoolroom was packed and buzzing with excitement. "I'm afraid we haven't a seat left, Mrs. Barlow!" said Jackson, one of the church sidesmen, who was standing guard in the school porch, where people were still fighting to get in. He faced her in consternation. She faced him in consternation. "Well, I shall have to stay somewhere, till Mr. Barlow can drive me home," she said. "Couldn't you put me a chair somewhere?"

Worried and flustered, he went worrying and flustering the other people in charge. The schoolroom was simply packed solid. But Mr. Simmons, the leading grocer, gave up his chair in the front row to Mrs. Barlow, whilst he sat in a chair right under the stage, where he couldn't see a thing. But he could see Mrs. Barlow seated between his wife and daughter, speaking a word or two to them occasionally, and that was enough.

The lights went down: *The Shoes of Shagput* was about to begin. The amateur curtains were drawn back, disclosing the little amateur stage with a white amateur back-cloth daubed to represent a Moorish courtyard. In stalked Percy, dressed as a Moor, his face darkened. He looked quite handsome, his pale grey eyes queer and startling in his dark face. But he was afraid of the audience—he spoke away from them, stalking around clumsily. After a certain amount of would-be funny dialogue, in tripped the heroine, Alice Howells, of course. She was an Eastern houri, in white gauze Turkish trousers, silver veil, and—the blue moccasins. The whole stage was white, save for her blue moccasins, Percy's dark-green sash, and a negro boy's red fez.

When Mrs. Barlow saw the blue moccasins, a little bomb of rage exploded in her. This, of all places! The blue moccasins that she had bought in the western deserts! The blue moccasins that were not so blue as her own eyes! *Her* blue moccasins! On the feet of that creature, Mrs. Howells.

Alice Howells was not afraid of the audience. She looked full at them, lifting her silver veil. And of course she saw Mrs. Barlow, sitting there like the Ancient of Days in judgment, in the front row. And a bomb of rage exploded in *her* breast too.

In the play, Alice was the wife of the grey-bearded old Caliph, but she captured the love of the young Ali, otherwise

Percy, and the whole business was the attempt of these two to evade Caliph and negro-eunuchs and ancient crones, and get into each other's arms. The blue shoes were very important: for while the sweet Leila wore them, the gallant Ali was to know there was danger. But when she took them off, he might approach her.

It was all quite childish, and everybody loved it, and Miss M'Leod might have been quite complacent about it all, had not Alice Howells got her monkey up, so to speak. Alice, with a lot of make-up, looked boldly handsome. And suddenly bold she was, bold as the devil. All these years the poor young widow had been "good," slaving in the parish, and only even flirting just to cheer things up, never going very far and knowing she could never get anything out of it, but determined never to mope.

Now the sight of Miss M'Leod sitting there so erect, so coolly "higher plane," and calmly superior, suddenly let loose a devil in Alice Howells. All her limbs went suave and molten, as her young sex, long pent up, flooded even to her finger-tips. Her voice was strange, even to herself, with its long, plaintive notes. She felt all her movements soft and fluid, she felt herself like living liquid. And it was lovely. Underneath it all was the sting of malice against Miss M'Leod, sitting there so erect, with her great knob of white hair.

Alice's business, as the lovely Leila, was to be seductive to the rather heavy Percy. And seductive she was. In two minutes, she had him spell-bound. He saw nothing of the audience. A faint, fascinated grin came on to his face, as he acted up to the young woman in the Turkish trousers. His rather full, hoarse voice changed and became clear, with a new, naked clang in it. When the two sang together, in the simple banal duets of the play, it was with a most fascinating intimacy. And when, at the end of Act One, the lovely Leila kicked off the blue moccasins, saying: "Away, shoes of bondage, shoes of sorrow!" and danced a little dance all alone, barefoot, in her Turkish trousers, in front of her fascinated hero, his smile was so spell-bound that everybody else was spell-bound too.

Miss M'Leod's indignation knew no bounds. When the blue moccasins were kicked across the stage by the brazen Alice, with the words: "Away, shoes of bondage, shoes of sorrow!" the elder woman grew pink with fury, and it was all she could do not to rise and snatch the moccasins from the stage, and bear them away. She sat in speechless indignation during the brief curtain between Act One and Act Two. Her moccasins! Her blue moccasins! Of the sacred blue colour, the turquoise of heaven.

But there they were, in Act Two, on the feet of the bold Alice. It was becoming too much. And the love-scenes between Percy and the young woman were becoming nakedly shameful. Alice grew worse and worse. She was worked up now, caught in her own spell, and unconscious of everything save of him, and the sting of that other woman, who presumed to own him. Own him? Ha-ha! For he was fascinated. The queer smile on his face, the concentrated gleam of his eyes, the queer way he leaned forward from his loins towards her, the new, reckless, throaty twang in his voice—the audience had before their eyes a man spell-bound and lost in passion.

Miss M'Leod sat in shame and torment, as if her chair was red-hot. She too was fast losing her normal consciousness, in the spell of rage. She was outraged. The second Act was working to its climax. The climax came. The lovely Leila kicked off the blue shoes: "Away, shoes of bondage, away!" and flew barefoot to the enraptured Ali, flinging herself into his arms. And if ever a man was gone in sheer desire, it was Percy, as he pressed the woman's lithe form against his body, and seemed unconsciously to envelop her, unaware of everything else. While she, blissful in his spell, but still aware of the audience and of the superior Miss M'Leod, let herself be wrapped closer and closer.

Miss M'Leod rose to her feet and looked towards the door. But the way out was packed with people standing holding their breath as the two on the stage remained wrapped in each other's arms, and the three fiddles and the flute softly woke up. Miss M'Leod could not bear it. She was on her feet, and beside herself. She could not get out. She could not sit down again.

"Percy!" she said, in a low clear voice. "Will you hand me my moccasins?"

He lifted his face like a man startled in a dream, lifted his face from the shoulder of his Leila. His gold-grey eyes were like softly-startled flames. He looked in sheer horrified wonder at the little white-haired woman standing below.

"Eh!" he said, purely dazed.

"Will you please hand me my moccasins!"—and she pointed to where they lay on the stage.

Alice had stepped away from him, and was gazing at the risen viper of the little elderly woman on the tip of the audience. Then she watched him move across the stage, bending forward from the loins in his queer mesmerized way, pick up the blue moccasins, and stoop down to hand them over the edge of the stage to his wife, who reached up for them.

"Thank you!" said Miss M'Leod, seating herself, with the blue moccasins in her lap.

Alice recovered her composure, gave a sign to the little orchestra, and began to sing at once, strong and assured, to sing her part in the duet that closed the Act. She knew she could command public opinion in her favour.

He too recovered at once, the little smile came back on his face, he calmly forgot his wife again as he sang his share in the duet. It was finished. The curtains were pulled to. There was immense cheering. The curtains opened, and Alice and Percy bowed to the audience, smiling both of them their peculiar secret smile, while Miss M'Leod sat with the blue moccasins on her lap.

The curtains were closed, it was the long interval. After a few moments of hesitation, Mrs. Barlow rose with dignity, gathered her wrap over her arm, and with the blue moccasins in her hand, moved towards the door. Way was respectfully made for her.

"I should like to speak to Mr. Barlow," she said to Jackson, who had anxiously ushered her in, and now would anxiously usher her out.

"Yes, Mrs. Barlow."

He led her round to the smaller class-room at the back, that acted as dressing-room. The amateur actors were drinking lemonade, and chattering freely. Mrs. Howells came forward, and Jackson whispered the news to her. She turned to Percy.

"Percy, Mrs. Barlow wants to speak to you. Shall I come with you?"

"Speak to me? Aye, come on with me."

The two followed the anxious Jackson into the other half-lighted class-room, where Mrs. Barlow stood in her wrap, holding the moccasins. She was very pale, and she watched the two butter-muslin Turkish figures enter, as if they could not possibly be real. She ignored Mrs. Howells entirely.

"Percy," she said, "I want you to drive me home."

"Drive you home?" he echoed.

"Yes, please!"

"Why—when?" he said, with vague bluntness.

"Now,—if you don't mind——"

"What—in this get-up?" He looked at himself.

"I could wait while you changed."

There was a pause. He turned and looked at Alice Howells, and Alice Howells looked at him. The two women saw each other out of the corners of their eyes: but it was beneath notice. He turned to his wife, his black face ludicrously blank, his eyebrows cocked.

"Well, you see," he said, "it's rather awkward. I can hardly hold up the third Act while I've taken you home and got back here again, can I?"

"So you intend to play in the third Act?" she asked with cold ferocity.

"Why, I must, mustn't I?" he said blankly.

"Do you *wish* to?" she said, in all her intensity.

"I do, naturally. I want to finish the thing up properly," he replied, in the utter innocence of his head; about his heart he knew nothing.

She turned sharply away.

"Very well!" she said. And she called to Jackson, who was

standing dejectedly by the door: "Mr. Jackson, will you please find some car or conveyance to take me home?"

"Aye! I say, Mr. Jackson," called Percy in his strong, democratic voice, going forward to the man. "Ask Tom Lomas if he'll do me a good turn and get my car out of the rectory garage, to drive Mrs. Barlow home. Aye, ask Tom Lomas! And if not him, ask Mr. Pilkington—Leonard. The key's there. You don't mind, do you? I'm ever so much obliged——"

The three were left awkwardly alone again.

"I expect you've had enough with two acts," said Percy soothingly to his wife. "These things aren't up to your mark. I know it. They're only child's play. But, you see, they please the people. We've got a packed house, haven't we?"

His wife had nothing to answer. He looked so ludicrous, with his dark-brown face and butter-muslin bloomers. And his mind was so ludicrously innocent. His body, however, was not so ridiculously innocent as his mind, as she knew when he turned to the other woman.

"You and I, we're more on the nonsense level, aren't we?" he said, with the new, throaty clang of naked intimacy in his voice. His wife shivered.

"Absolutely on the nonsense level," said Alice, with easy assurance.

She looked into his eyes, then she looked at the blue moccasins in the hand of the other woman. He gave a little start, as if realizing something for himself.

At that moment Tom Lomas looked in, saying heartily: "Right you are, Percy! I'll have my car here in half a tick. I'm more handy with it than yours."

"Thanks, old man! You're a Christian."

"Try to be—especially when you turn Turk! Well——" He disappeared.

"I say, Lina," said Percy in his most amiable democratic way; "would you mind leaving the moccasins for the next act? We s'll be in a bit of a hole without them."

Miss M'Leod faced him and stared at him with the full blast of her forget-me-not blue eyes, from her white face.

"Will you pardon me if I don't?" she said.

"What!" he exclaimed. "Why? Why not? It's nothing but play, to amuse the people. I can't see how it can hurt the *moccasins*. I understand you don't quite like seeing me make a fool of myself. But anyhow, I'm a bit of a born fool. What?"— and his blackened face laughed with a Turkish laugh. "Oh, yes, you have to realize I rather enjoy playing the fool," he resumed. "And, after all, it doesn't really hurt *you*, now does it? Shan't you leave us those moccasins for the last act?"

She looked at him, then at the moccasins in her hand. No, it was useless to yield to so ludicrous a person. The vulgarity of his wheedling, the commonness of the whole performance! It was useless to yield even the moccasins. It would be treachery to herself.

"I'm sorry," she said. "But I'd so much rather they weren't used for this kind of thing. I never intended them to be." She stood with her face averted from the ridiculous couple.

He changed as if she had slapped his face. He sat down on top of the low pupils' desk, and gazed with glazed interest round the class-room. Alice sat beside him, in her white gauze and her bedizened face. They were like two rebuked sparrows on one twig, he with his great, easy, intimate limbs, she so light and alert. And as he sat he sank into an unconscious physical sympathy with her. Miss M'Leod walked towards the door.

"You'll have to think of something as'll do instead," he muttered to Alice in a low voice, meaning the blue moccasins. And leaning down, he drew off one of the grey shoes she had on, caressing her foot with the slip of his hand over its slim bare shape. She hastily put the bare foot behind her other, shod foot.

Tom Lomas poked in his head, his overcoat collar turned up to his ears.

"Car's here," he said.

"Right-o! Tom! I'll chalk it up to thee, lad!" said Percy with heavy breeziness. Then, making a great effort with himself, he rose heavily and went across to the door, to his wife, saying to her, in the same stiff voice of false heartiness:

"You'll be as right as rain with Tom. You won't mind if I don't come out? No! I'd better not show myself to the audience. Well—I'm glad you came, if only for a while. Good-bye then! I'll be home after the service—but I shan't disturb you. Good-bye! Don't get wet now——" And his voice, falsely cheerful, stiff with anger, ended in a clang of indignation.

Alice Howells sat on the infants' bench in silence. She was ignored. And she was unhappy, uneasy, because of the scene.

Percy closed the door after his wife. Then he turned with a looming slowness to Alice, and said in a hoarse whisper: "Think o' that, now!"

She looked up at him anxiously. His face, in its dark pigment, was transfigured with indignant anger. His yellow-grey eyes blazed, and a great rush of anger seemed to be surging up volcanic in him. For a second his eyes rested on her upturned, troubled dark-blue eyes, then glanced away, as if he didn't want to look at her in his anger. Even so, she felt a touch of tenderness in his glance.

"And that's all she's ever cared about—her own things and her own way," he said, in the same hoarse whisper, hoarse with suddenly-released rage. Alice Howells hung her head in silence.

"Not another damned thing, but what's her own, her own— and her own holy way—damned holy-holy-holy, all to herself." His voice shook with hoarse, whispering rage, burst out at last.

Alice Howells looked up at him in distress.

"Oh, don't say it!" she said. "I'm sure she's fond of you."

"*Fond* of me! Fond of *me!*" he blazed, with a grin of trans-cendent irony. "It makes her sick to look at me. I am a hairy brute, I own it. Why, she's never once touched me to be fond of me—never once—though she pretends sometimes. But a man knows——" and he made a grimace of contempt. "He knows when a woman's just stroking him, good doggie!—and when she's really a bit woman-fond of him. That woman's never been real fond of anybody or anything, all her life—she couldn't, for all her show of kindness. She's limited to herself, that woman is; and I've looked up to her as if she was God. More fool me!

If God's not good-natured and good-hearted, then what is He——?"

Alice sat with her head dropped, realizing once more that men aren't really fooled. She was upset, shaken by his rage, and frightened, as if she too were guilty. He had sat down blankly beside her. She glanced up at him.

"Never mind!" she said soothingly. "You'll like her again to-morrow."

He looked down at her with a grin, a grey sort of grin. "Are you going to stroke me good doggie! as well?" he said.

"Why?" she asked, blank.

But he did not answer. Then after a while he resumed: "Wouldn't even leave the moccasins! And she'd hung them up in my room, left them there for years—any man'd consider they were his. And I did want this show to-night to be a success! What are you going to do about it?"

"I've sent over for a pair of pale-blue satin bed-slippers of mine—they'll do just as well," she replied.

"Aye! For all that, it's done me in."

"You'll get over it."

"Happen so! She's curdled my inside, for all that. I don't know how I'm going to be civil to her."

"Perhaps you'd better stay at the rectory to-night," she said softly.

He looked into her eyes. And in that look, he transferred his allegiance.

"*You* don't want to be drawn in, do you?" he asked, with troubled tenderness.

But she only gazed with wide, darkened eyes into his eyes, so she was like an open, dark doorway to him. His heart beat thick, and the faint, breathless smile of passion came into his eyes again.

"You'll have to go on, Mrs. Howells. We can't keep them waiting any longer."

It was Jim Stokes, who was directing the show. They heard the clapping and stamping of the impatient audience.

"Goodness!" cried Alice Howells, darting to the door.

ADOLF

WHEN we were children our father often worked on the night-shift. Once it was spring-time, and he used to arrive home, black and tired, just as we were downstairs in our nightdresses. Then night met morning face to face, and the contact was not always happy. Perhaps it was painful to my father to see us gaily entering upon the day into which he dragged himself soiled and weary. He didn't like going to bed in the spring morning sunshine.

But sometimes he was happy, because of his long walk through the dewy fields in the first daybreak. He loved the open morning, the crystal and the space, after a night down pit. He watched every bird, every stir in the trembling grass, answered the whinnying of the pewits and tweeted to the wrens. If he could, he also would have whinnied and tweeted and whistled in a native language that was not human. He liked non-human things best.

One sunny morning we were all sitting at table when we heard his heavy slurring walk up the entry. We became uneasy. His was always a disturbing presence, trammelling. He passed the window darkly, and we heard him go into the scullery and put down his tin bottle. But directly he came into the kitchen. We felt at once that he had something to communicate. No one spoke. We watched his black face for a second.

"Give me a drink," he said.

My mother hastily poured out his tea. He went to pour it out into his saucer. But instead of drinking he suddenly put something on the table among the teacups. A tiny brown rabbit! A small rabbit, a mere morsel, sitting against the bread as still as if it were a made thing.

"A rabbit! A young one! Who gave it you, father?"

But he laughed enigmatically, with a sliding motion of his

yellow-grey eyes, and went to take off his coat. We pounced on the rabbit.

"Is it alive? Can you feel its heart beat?"

My father came back and sat down heavily in his armchair. He dragged his saucer to him, and blew his tea, pushing out his red lips under his black moustache.

"Where did you get it, father?"

"I picked it up," he said, wiping his naked forearm over his mouth and beard.

"Where?"

"It is a wild one!" came my mother's quick voice.

"Yes, it is."

"Then why did you bring it?" cried my mother.

"Oh, we wanted it," came our cry.

"Yes, I've no doubt you did——" retorted my mother. But she was drowned in our clamour of questions.

On the field path my father had found a dead mother rabbit and three dead little ones—this one alive, but unmoving.

"But what had killed them, daddy?"

"I couldn't say, my child. I s'd think she'd aten something."

"Why did you bring it!" again my mother's voice of condemnation. "You know what it will be."

My father made no answer, but we were loud in protest.

"He must bring it. It's not big enough to live by itself. It would die," we shouted.

"Yes, and it will die now. And then there'll be *another* outcry."

My mother set her face against the tragedy of dead pets. Our hearts sank.

"It won't die, father, will it? Why will it? It won't."

"I s'd think not," said my father.

"You know well enough it will. Haven't we had it all before!" said my mother.

"They dunna always pine," replied my father testily.

But my mother reminded him of other little wild animals he had brought, which had sulked and refused to live, and brought storms of tears and trouble in our house of lunatics.

Trouble fell on us. The little rabbit sat on our lap, un-moving, its eye wide and dark. We brought it milk, warm milk, and held it to its nose. It sat as still as if it was far away, retreated down some deep burrow, hidden, oblivious. We wetted its mouth and whiskers with drops of milk. It gave no sign, did not even shake off the wet white drops. Somebody began to shed a few secret tears.

"What did I say?" cried my mother. "Take it and put it down in the field."

Her command was in vain. We were driven to get dressed for school. There sat the rabbit. It was like a tiny obscure cloud. Watching it, the emotions died out of our breast. Useless to love it, to yearn over it. Its little feelings were all ambushed. They must be circumvented. Love and affection were a trespass upon it. A little wild thing, it became more mute and asphyxiated still in its own arrest, when we approached with love. We must not love it. We must circumvent it, for its own existence.

So I passed the order to my sister and my mother. The rabbit was not to be spoken to, nor even looked at. Wrapping it in a piece of flannel I put it in an obscure corner of the cold parlour, and put a saucer of milk before its nose. My mother was forbidden to enter the parlour whilst we were at school.

"As if I should take any notice of your nonsense," she cried affronted. Yet I doubt if she ventured into the parlour.

At midday, after school, creeping into the front room, there we saw the rabbit still and unmoving in the piece of flannel. Strange grey-brown neutralization of life, still living! It was a sore problem to us.

"Why won't it drink its milk, mother?" we whispered. Our father was asleep.

"It prefers to sulk its life away, silly little thing." A profound problem. Prefers to sulk its life away! We put young dandelion leaves to its nose. The sphinx was not more oblivious. Yet its eye was bright.

At tea-time, however, it had hopped a few inches, out of its flannel, and there it sat again, uncovered, a little solid cloud of muteness, brown, with unmoving whiskers. Only its side palpitated slightly with life.

Darkness came; my father set off to work. The rabbit was still unmoving. Dumb despair was coming over the sisters, a threat of tears before bedtime. Clouds of my mother's anger gathered as she muttered against my father's wantonness.

Once more the rabbit was wrapped in the old pit-singlet. But now it was carried into the scullery and put under the copper fireplace, that it might imagine itself inside a burrow. The saucers were placed about, four or five, here and there on the floor, so that if the little creature *should* chance to hop abroad, it could not fail to come upon some food. After this my mother was allowed to take from the scullery what she wanted and then she was forbidden to open the door.

When morning came and it was light, I went downstairs. Opening the scullery door, I heard a slight scuffle. Then I saw dabbles of milk all over the floor and tiny rabbit-droppings in the saucers. And there the miscreant, the tips of his ears showing behind a pair of boots. I peeped at him. He sat bright-eyed and askance, twitching his nose and looking at me while not looking at me.

He was alive—very much alive. But still we were afraid to trespass much on his confidence.

"Father!" My father was arrested at the door. "Father, the rabbit's alive."

"Back your life it is," said my father.

"Mind how you go in."

By evening, however, the little creature was tame, quite tame. He was christened Adolf. We were enchanted by him. We couldn't really love him, because he was wild and loveless to the end. But he was an unmixed delight.

We decided he was too small to live in a hutch—he must live at large in the house. My mother protested, but in vain. He was so tiny. So we had him upstairs, and he dropped his tiny pills on the bed and we were enchanted.

Adolf made himself instantly at home. He had the run

of the house, and was perfectly happy, with his tunnels and his holes behind the furniture.

We loved him to take meals with us. He would sit on the table humping his back, sipping his milk, shaking his whiskers and his tender ears, hopping off and hobbling back to his saucer, with an air of supreme unconcern. Suddenly he was alert. He hobbled a few tiny paces, and reared himself up inquisitively at the sugar basin. He fluttered his tiny fore-paws, and then reached and laid them on the edge of the basin, whilst he craned his thin neck and peeped in. He trembled his whiskers at the sugar, then did his best to lift down a lump.

"*Do* you think I will have it! Animals in the sugar pot!" cried my mother, with a rap of her hand on the table.

Which so delighted the electric Adolf that he flung his hind-quarters and knocked over a cup.

"It's your own fault, mother. If you left him alone——"

He continued to take tea with us. He rather liked warm tea. And he loves sugar. Having nibbled a lump, he would turn to the butter. There he was shooed off by our parent. He soon learned to treat her shooing with indifference. Still, she hated him to put his nose in the food. And he loved to do it. And one day between them they overturned the cream-jug. Adolf deluged his little chest, bounced back in terror, was seized by his little ears by my mother and bounced down on the hearth-rug. There he shivered in momentary discomfort, and suddenly set off in a wild flight to the parlour.

This last was his happy hunting ground. He had cultivated the bed habit of pensively nibbling certain bits of cloth in the hearth-rug. When chased from this pasture he would retreat under the sofa. There he would twinkle in Buddhist meditation until suddenly, no one knew why, he would go off like an alarm clock. With a sudden bumping scuffle he would whirl out of the room, going through the doorway with his little ears flying. Then we would hear his thunderbolt hurtling in the parlour, but before we could follow, the wild streak of Adolf would flash past us, on an electric wind that swept him round the scullery and carried him back, a little mad thing, flying possessed like a ball round the parlour. After which ebullition he would sit in a corner composed and distant, twitching his whiskers in abstract meditation. And it was in vain we questioned him about his outbursts. He just went off like a gun, and was as calm after it as a gun that smokes placidly.

Alas, he grew up rapidly. It was almost impossible to keep him from the outer door.

One day, as we were playing by the stile, I saw his brown shadow loiter across the road and pass into the field that faced the houses. Instantly a cry of "Adolf!"—a cry he knew full well. And instantly a wind swept him away down the sloping meadow, his tail twinkling and zigzagging through the grass. After him we pelted. It was a strange sight to see him, ears back, his little loins so powerful, flinging the world behind him. We ran ourselves out of breath, but could not catch him. Then somebody headed him off, and he sat with sudden unconcern, twitching his nose under a bunch of nettles.

His wanderings cost him a shock. One Sunday morning my father had just been quarrelling with a pedlar, and we were hearing the aftermath indoors, when there came a sudden unearthly scream from the yard. We flew out. There sat Adolf cowering under a bench, whilst a great black and white cat glowered intently at him, a few yards away. Sight not to be forgotten. Adolf rolling back his eyes and parting his strange muzzle in another scream, the cat stretching forward in a slow elongation.

Ha, how we hated that cat! How we pursued him over the chapel wall and across the neighbours' gardens.

Adolf was still only half grown.

"Cats!" said my mother. "Hideous detestable animals, why do people harbour them?"

But Adolf was becoming too much for her. He dropped too many pills. And suddenly to hear him clumping downstairs when she was alone in the house was startling. And to keep him from the door was impossible. Cats prowled outside. It was worse than having a child to look after.

Yet we would not have him shut up. He became more lusty, more callous than ever. He was a strong kicker, and many a scratch on face and arms did we owe to him. But he brought his own doom on himself. The lace curtains in the parlour—my mother was rather proud of them—fell on the floor very full. One of Adolf's joys was to scuffle wildly through them as though through some foamy undergrowth. He had already torn rents in them.

One day he entangled himself altogether. He kicked, he whirled round in a mad nebulous inferno. He screamed—and brought down the curtain-rod with a smash, right on the best beloved pelargonium, just as my mother rushed in. She extricated him, but she never forgave him. And he never forgave either. A heartless wildness had come over him.

Even we understood that he must go. It was decided, after a long deliberation, that my father should carry him back to the wild-woods. Once again he was stowed into the great pocket of the pit-jacket.

"Best pop him i' th' pot," said my father, who enjoyed raising the wind of indignation.

And so, next day, our father said that Adolf, set down on the edge of the coppice, had hopped away with utmost indifference, neither elated nor moved. We heard it and believed. But many, many were the heart-searchings. How would the other rabbits receive him? Would they smell his tameness, his humanized degradation, and rend him? My mother pooh-poohed the extravagant idea.

However, he was gone, and we were rather relieved. My father kept an eye open for him. He declared that several times passing the coppice in the early morning, he had seen Adolf peeping through the nettle-stalks. He had called him, in an odd, high-voiced, cajoling fashion. But Adolf had not responded. Wildness gains so soon upon its creatures. And they become so contemptuous then of our tame presence. So it seemed to me. I myself would go to the edge of the coppice, and call softly. I myself would imagine bright eyes between the nettle-stalks, flash of a white, scornful tail past the bracken. That insolent white tail, as Adolf turned his flank on us! It reminded me always of a certain rude gesture, and a certain unprintable phrase, which may not even be suggested.

But when naturalists discuss the meaning of the rabbit's white tail, that rude gesture and still ruder phrase always come to my mind. Naturalists say that the rabbit shows his white tail in order to guide his young safely after him, as a nurse-maid's flying strings are the signal to her toddling charges to follow on. How nice and naïve! I only know that my Adolf wasn't naïve. He used to whisk his flank at me, push his white feather in my eye, and say *"Merde!"* It's a rude word—but one which Adolf was always semaphoring at me, flag-wagging it with all the derision of his narrow haunches.

That's a rabbit all over—insolence, and the white flag of spiteful derision. Yes, and he keeps his flag flying to the bitter end, sporting, insolent little devil that he is. See him running for his life. Oh, how his soul is fanned to an ecstasy of fright, a fugitive whirlwind of panic. Gone mad, he throws the world behind him, with astonishing hind legs. He puts back his head and lays his ears on his sides and rolls the white of his eyes in sheer ecstatic agony of speed. He knows the awful approach behind him; bullet or stoat. He knows! He knows, his eyes are turned back almost into his head. It is agony. But it is also ecstasy. Ecstasy! See the insolent white flag bobbing. He whirls on the magic wind of terror. All his pent-up soul rushes into agonized electric emotion of fear. He flings himself on, like a falling star swooping into extinction. White heat of the agony of fear. And at the same time, bob! bob! bob! goes the white tail, *merde! merde! merde!* it says to the pursuer. The rabbit can't help it. In his utmost extremity he still flings the insult at the pursuer. He is the inconquerable fugitive, the indomitable meek. No wonder the stoat becomes vindictive.

And if he escapes, this precious rabbit! Don't you see him sitting there, in his earthly nook, a little ball of silence and rabbit triumph? Don't you see the glint on his black eye?

Don't you see, in his very immobility, how the whole world is *merde* to him? No conceit like the conceit of the meek. And if the avenging angel in the shape of the ghostly ferret steals down on him, there comes a shriek of terror out of that little hump of self-satisfaction sitting motionless in a corner. Falls the fugitive. But even fallen, his white feather floats. Even in death it seems to say: "I am the meek, I am the righteous, I am the rabbit. All you rest, you are evil doers, and you shall be *bien emmerdés!*"

THINGS

They were true idealists, from New England. But that is some time ago: before the war. Several years before the war, they met and married; he a tall, keen-eyed young man from Connecticut, she a smallish, demure, Puritan-looking young woman from Massachusetts. They both had a little money. Not much, however. Even added together, it didn't make three thousand dollars a year. Still—they were free. Free!

Ah! Freedom! To be free to live one's own life! To be twenty-five and twenty-seven, a pair of true idealists with a mutual love of beauty, and an inclination towards "Indian thought"—meaning, alas, Mrs. Besant—and an income a little under three thousand dollars a year! But what is money? All one wishes to do is to live a full and beautiful life. In Europe, of course, right at the fountain-head of tradition. It might possibly be done in America: in New England, for example. But at a forfeiture of a certain amount of "beauty." True beauty takes a long time to mature. The baroque is only half-beautiful, half-matured. No, the real silver bloom, the real golden-sweet bouquet of beauty had its roots in the Renaissance, not in any later or shallower period.

Therefore the two idealists, who were married in New Haven, sailed at once to Paris: Paris of the old days. They had a studio apartment on the Boulevard Montparnasse, and they became real Parisians, in the old, delightful sense, not in the modern, vulgar. It was the shimmer of the pure impressionists, Monet and his followers, the world seen in terms of pure light, light broken and unbroken. How lovely! How lovely the nights, the river, the mornings in the old streets and by the flower-stalls and the book-stalls, the afternoons up on Montmartre or in the Tuileries, the evenings on the boulevards!

They both painted, but not desperately. Art had not taken them by the throat, and they did not take Art by the throat.

They painted: that's all. They knew people—nice people, if possible, though one had to take them mixed. And they were happy.

Yet it seems as if human beings must set their claws in *something*. To be "free," to be "living a full and beautiful life," you must, alas, be attached to something. A "full and beautiful life" means a tight attachment to *something*—at least, it is so for all idealists—or else a certain boredom supervenes; there is a certain waving of loose ends upon the air, like the waving, yearning tendrils of the vine that spread and rotate, seeking something to clutch, something up which to climb towards the necessary sun. Finding nothing, the vine can only trail, half-fulfilled, upon the ground. Such is freedom!—a clutching of the right pole. And human beings are all vines. But especially the idealist. He is a vine, and he needs to clutch and climb. And he despises the man who is a mere *potato*, or turnip, or lump of wood.

Our idealists were frightfully happy, but they were all the time reaching out for something to cotton on to. At first, Paris was enough. They explored Paris *thoroughly*. And they learned French till they almost felt like French people, they could speak it so glibly.

Still, you know, you never talk French with your *soul*. It can't be done. And though it's very thrilling, at first, talking in French to clever Frenchmen—they seem *so* much cleverer than oneself—still, in the long run, it is not satisfying. The endlessly clever *materialism* of the French leaves you cold, in the end, gives a sense of barrenness and incompatibility with true New England depth. So our two idealists felt.

They turned away from France—but ever so gently. France had disappointed them. "We've loved it, and we've got a great deal out of it. But after a while, after a considerable while, several years, in fact, Paris leaves one feeling disappointed. It hasn't quite got what one wants."

"But Paris isn't France."

"No, perhaps not. France is quite different from Paris. And France is lovely—quite lovely. But *to us*, though we love it, it doesn't say a great deal."

So, when the war came, the idealists moved to Italy. And they loved Italy. They found it beautiful, and more poignant than France. It seemed much nearer to the New England conception of beauty: something pure, and full of sympathy, without the *materialism* and the *cynicism* of the French. The two idealists seemed to breathe their own true air in Italy.

And in Italy, much more than in Paris, they felt they could thrill to the teachings of the Buddha. They entered the swelling stream of modern Buddhistic emotion, and they read the books, and they practised meditation, and they deliberately set themselves to eliminate from their own souls greed, pain and sorrow. They did not realize—yet—that Buddha's very eagerness to free himself from pain and sorrow is in itself a sort of greed. No, they dreamed of a perfect world, from which all greed, and nearly all pain, and a great deal of sorrow, were eliminated.

But America entered the war, so the two idealists had to help. They did hospital work. And though their experience made them realize more than ever that greed, pain, and sorrow *should* be eliminated from the world, nevertheless the Buddhism, or the theosophy, didn't emerge very triumphant from the long crisis. Somehow, somewhere, in some part of themselves, they felt that greed, pain, and sorrow would never be eliminated, because most people don't care about eliminating them, and never will care. Our idealists were far too western to think of abandoning all the world to damnation, while they saved their two selves. They were far too unselfish to sit tight under a bho-tree and reach Nirvana in a mere couple.

It was more than that, though. They simply hadn't enough *Sitzfleisch* to squat under a bho-tree and get to Nirvana by contemplating anything, least of all their own navel. If the whole wide world was not going to be saved, they, personally, were not so very keen on being saved just by themselves. No, it would be so lonesome. They were New Englanders, so it must be all or nothing. Greed, pain, and sorrow must either be eliminated from *all the world*, or else, what was the use of eliminating them from oneself? No use at all! One was just a victim.

And so, although they still *loved* "Indian thought," and felt very tender about it: well, to go back to our metaphor, the pole up which the green and anxious vines had clambered so far now proved dry-rotten. It snapped, and the vines came slowly subsiding to earth again. There was no crack and crash. The vines held themselves up by their own foliage, for a while. But they subsided. The beanstalk of "Indian thought" had given way before Jack and Jill had climbed off the tip of it to a further world.

They subsided with a slow rustle back to earth again. But they made no outcry. They were again "disappointed." But they never admitted it. "Indian thought" had let them down. But they never complained. Even to one another, they never said a word. They were disappointed, faintly but deeply disillusioned, and they both knew it. But the knowledge was tacit.

And they still had so much in their lives. They still had Italy—dear Italy. And they still had freedom, the priceless treasure. And they still had so much "beauty." About the fulness of their lives they were not quite so sure. They had one little boy, whom they loved as parents should love their children, but whom they wisely refrained from fastening upon, to build their lives on him. No, no, they must live their own lives! They still had strength of mind to know that.

But they were now no longer so very young. Twenty-five and twenty-seven had become thirty-five and thirty-seven. And though they had had a very wonderful time in Europe, and though they still loved Italy—dear Italy!—yet: they were disappointed. They had got a lot out of it: oh, a very great deal indeed! Still, it hadn't given them quite, not *quite* what they had expected. Europe was lovely, but it was dead. Living in Europe, you were living on the past. And Europeans, with all their superficial charm, were not *really* charming. They were materialistic, they had no *real* soul. They just did not understand the inner urge of the spirit, because the inner urge was dead in them, they were all survivals. There, that was the truth about Europeans: they were survivals, with no more getting ahead in them.

It was another bean-pole, another vine-support crumbled under the green life of the vine. And very bitter it was, this time. For up the old tree-trunk of Europe the green vine had been clambering silently for more than ten years, ten hugely important years, the years of real living. The two idealists had *lived* in Europe, lived on Europe and on European life and European things as vines in an everlasting vine-yard.

They had made their home here: a home such as you could never make in America. Their watchword had been "beauty." They had rented, the last four years, the second floor of an old Palazzo on the Arno, and here they had all their "things." And they derived a profound, profound satisfaction from their apartment: the lofty, silent, ancient rooms with windows on the river, with glistening, dark-red floors, and the beautiful furniture that the idealists had "picked up."

Yes, unknown to themselves, the lives of the idealists had been running with a fierce swiftness horizontally, all the time. They had become tense, fierce hunters of "things" for their home. While their souls were climbing up to the sun of old European culture or old Indian thought, their passions were running horizontally, clutching at "things." Of course they did not buy the things for the things' sake, but for the sake of "beauty." They looked upon their home as a place entirely furnished by loveliness, not by "things" at all. Valerie had some very lovely curtains at the windows of the long *salotto*, looking on the river: curtains of queer ancient material that looked like finely-knitted silk, most beautifully faded down from vermilion and orange, and gold, and black, down to a sheer soft glow. Valerie hardly ever came into the *salotto* without mentally falling on her knees before the curtains. "Chartres!" she said. "To me they are Chartres!" And Melville never turned and looked at his sixteenth-century Venetian bookcase, with its two or three dozen of choice books, without feeling his marrow stir in his bones. The holy of holies!

The child silently, almost sinisterly, avoided any rude contact with these ancient monuments of furniture, as if they had been nests of sleeping cobras, or that "thing" most perilous to the touch, the Ark of the Covenant. His childish awe was silent and cold, but final.

Still, a couple of New England idealists cannot live merely on the bygone glory of their furniture. At least, one couple could not. They got used to the marvellous Bologna cupboard, they got used to the wonderful Venetian bookcase, and the books, and the Siena curtains and bronzes, and the lovely sofas and side-tables and chairs they had "picked up" in Paris. Oh, they had been picking things up since the first day they landed in Europe. And they were still at it. It is the last interest Europe can offer to an outsider: or to an insider either.

When people came, and were thrilled by the Melville interior, then Valerie and Erasmus felt they had not lived in vain: that they still were living. But in the long mornings, when Erasmus was desultorily working at Renaissance Florentine literature and Valerie was attending to the apartment: and in the long hours after lunch; and in the long, usually very cold and oppressive evenings in the ancient palazzo: then the halo died from around the furniture, and the things became things, lumps of matter that just stood there or hung there, *ad infinitum*, and said nothing; and Valerie and Erasmus almost hated them. The glow of beauty, like every other glow, dies down unless it is fed. The idealists still dearly loved their things. But they had got them. And the sad fact is, things that glow vividly while you're getting them, go almost quite cold after a year or two. Unless, of course, people envy them very much, and the museums are pining for them. And the Melvilles' "things," though very good, were not quite so good as that.

So, the glow gradually went out of everything, out of Europe, out of Italy—"the Italians are *dears*"—even out of that marvellous apartment on the Arno. "Why, if I had this

apartment, I'd never, never even want to go out of doors! It's
too lovely and perfect." That was something of course—to
hear that.

And yet Valerie and Erasmus went out of doors: they even
went out to get away from its ancient, cold-floored, stone-
heavy silence and dead dignity. "We're living on the past, you
know, Dick," said Valerie to her husband. She called him Dick.

They were grimly hanging on. They did not like to give in.
They did not like to own up that they were through. For
twelve years, now, they had been "free" people living a "full
and beautiful life." And America for twelve years had been
their anathema, the Sodom and Gomorrah of industrial
materialism.

It wasn't easy to own that you were "through." They hated
to admit that they wanted to go back. But at last, reluctantly,
they decided to go, "for the boy's sake."—"We can't *bear* to
leave Europe. But Peter is an American, so he had better look
at America while he's young." The Melvilles had an entirely
English accent and manner; almost; a little Italian and French
here and there.

They left Europe behind, but they took as much of it along
with them as possible. Several van-loads, as a matter of fact.
All those adorable and irreplaceable "things." And all arrived
in New York, idealists, child, and the huge bulk of Europe they
had lugged along.

Valerie had dreamed of a pleasant apartment, perhaps on
Riverside Drive, where it was not so expensive as east of Fifth
Avenue, and where all their wonderful things would look
marvellous. She and Erasmus house-hunted. But alas! their
income was quite under three thousand dollars a year. They
found—well, everybody knows what they found. Two small
rooms and a kitchenette, and don't let us unpack a *thing!*

The chunk of Europe which they had bitten off went into a
warehouse, at fifty dollars a month. And they sat in two small
rooms and a kitchenette, and wondered why they'd done it.

Erasmus, of course, ought to get a job. This was what was
written on the wall, and what they both pretended not to see.

But it had been the strange, vague threat that the Statue of Liberty had always held over them: "Thou shalt get a job!" Erasmus had the tickets, as they say. A scholastic career was still possible for him. He had taken his exams brilliantly at Yale, and had kept up his "researches," all the time he had been in Europe.

But both he and Valerie shuddered. A scholastic career! The scholastic world! The *American* scholastic world! Shudder upon shudder! Give up their freedom, their full and beautiful life? Never! Never! Erasmus would be forty next birthday.

The "things" remained in warehouse. Valerie went to look at them. It cost her a dollar an hour, and horrid pangs. The "things" poor things, looked a bit shabby and wretched, in that warehouse.

However, New York was not all America. There was the great clean West. So the Melvilles went West, with Peter, but without the things. They tried living the simple life, in the mountains. But doing their own chores became almost a nightmare. "Things" are all very well to look at, but it's awful handling them, even when they're beautiful. To be the slave of hideous things, to keep a stove going, cook meals, wash dishes, carry water and clean floors: pure horror of sordid anti-life!

In the cabin on the mountains, Valerie dreamed of Florence, the lost apartment; and her Bologna cupboard and Louis-Quinze chairs, above all, her "Chartres" curtains, stood in New York and costing fifty dollars a month.

A millionaire friend came to the rescue, offering them a cottage on the Californian coast—California! Where the new soul is to be born in man. With joy the idealists moved a little farther west, catching at new vine-props of hope.

And finding them straws! The millionaire cottage was perfectly equipped. It was perhaps as labour-savingly perfect as is possible: electric heating and cooking, a white-and-pearl-enamelled kitchen, nothing to make dirt except the human being himself. In an hour or so the idealists had got through their chores. They were "free"—free to hear the great Pacific pounding the coast, and to feel a new soul filling their bodies.

Alas! the Pacific pounded the coast with hideous brutality, brute force itself! And the new soul, instead of sweetly stealing into their bodies, seemed only meanly to gnaw the old soul out of their bodies. To feel you are under the fist of the most blind and crunching brute force: to feel that your cherished idealist's soul is being gnawed out of you, and only irritation left in place of it: well, it isn't good enough.

After about nine months, the idealists departed from the Californian west. It had been a great experience, they were glad to have had it. But, in the long run, the West was not the place for them, and they knew it. No, the people who wanted new souls had better get them. They, Valerie and Erasmus Melville, would like to develop the old soul a little further. Anyway, they had not felt any influx of new soul, on the Californian coast. On the contrary.

So, with a slight hole in their material capital, they returned to Massachusetts and paid a visit to Valerie's parents, taking the boy along. The grandparents welcomed the child—poor expatriated boy—and were rather cold to Valerie, but really cold to Erasmus. Valerie's mother definitely said to Valerie, one day, that Erasmus ought to take a job, so that Valerie could live decently. Valerie haughtily reminded her mother of the beautiful apartment on the Arno, and the "wonderful" things in store in New York, and of the "marvellous and satisfying life" she and Erasmus had led. Valerie's mother said that she didn't think her daughter's life looked so very marvellous at present: homeless, with a husband idle at the age of forty, a child to educate, and a dwindling capital: looked the reverse of marvellous to *her*. Let Erasmus take some post in one of the universities.

"What post? What university?" interrupted Valerie.

"That could be found, considering your father's connections and Erasmus's qualifications," replied Valerie's mother. "And you could get all your valuable things out of store, and have a really lovely home, which everybody in America would be proud to visit. As it is, your furniture is eating up your income, and you are living like rats in a hole, with nowhere to go to."

This was very true. Valerie was beginning to pine for a home, with her "things." Of course she could have sold her furniture for a substantial sum. But nothing would have induced her to. Whatever else passed away, religions, cultures, continents, and hopes, Valerie would *never* part from the "things" which she and Erasmus had collected with such passion. To these she was nailed.

But she and Erasmus still would not give up that freedom, that full and beautiful life they had so believed in. Erasmus cursed America. He did not *want* to earn a living. He panted for Europe.

Leaving the boy in charge of Valerie's parents, the two idealists once more set off for Europe. In New York they paid two dollars and looked for a brief, bitter hour at their "things." They sailed "student class"—that is, third. Their income now was less than two thousand dollars, instead of three. And they made straight for Paris—cheap Paris.

They found Europe, this time, a complete failure. "We have returned like dogs to our vomit," said Erasmus; "but the vomit has staled in the meantime." He found he couldn't stand Europe. It irritated every nerve in his body. He hated America too. But America at least was a darn sight better than this miserable, dirt-eating continent; which was by no means cheap any more, either.

Valerie, with her heart on her things—she had really burned to get them out of that warehouse, where they had stood now for three years, eating up two thousand dollars—wrote to her mother she thought Erasmus would come back if he could get some suitable work in America. Erasmus, in a state of frustration bordering on rage and insanity, just went round Italy in a poverty-stricken fashion, his coat-cuffs frayed, hating everything with intensity. And when a post was found for him in Cleveland University, to teach French, Italian, and Spanish literature, his eyes grew more beady, and his long, queer face grew sharper, and more rat-like, with utter baffled fury. He was forty, and the job was upon him.

"I think you'd better accept, dear. You don't care for Europe any longer. As you say, it's dead and finished. They offer us a house on the college lot, and mother says there's room in it for all our things. I think we'd better cable 'Accept'."

He glowered at her like a cornered rat. One almost expected to see rat's whiskers twitching at the sides of the sharp nose.

"Shall I send the cablegram?" she asked.

"Send it!" he blurted.

And she went out and sent it.

He was a changed man, quieter, much less irritable. A load was off him. He was inside the cage.

But when he looked at the furnaces of Cleveland, vast and like the greatest of black forests, with red and white-hot cascades of gushing metal, and tiny gnomes of men, and terrific noises, gigantic, he said to Valerie:

"Say what you like, Valerie, this is the biggest thing the modern world has to show."

And when they were in their up-to-date little house on the college lot of Cleveland University, and that woebegone débris of Europe, Bologna cupboard, Venice book-shelves, Ravenna bishop's chair, Louis-Quinze side-tables, "Chartres" curtains, Siena bronze lamps, all were arrayed, and all looked perfectly out of keeping, and therefore very impressive; and when the idealists had had a bunch of gaping people in, and Erasmus had showed off in his best European manner, but still quite cordial and American; and Valerie had been most ladylike, but for all that, "we prefer America"; then Erasmus said, looking at her with queer sharp eyes of a rat:

"Europe's the mayonnaise all right, but America supplies the good old lobster—what?"

"Every time!" she said, with satisfaction.

And he peered at her. He was in the cage: but it was safe inside. And she, evidently, was her real self at last. She had got the goods. Yet round his nose was a queer, evil, scholastic look, of pure scepticism. But he liked lobster.